THE CELLULOID CLOSET SERIES:

PROFILES OF HOPE

Brennen Tammons

Special consideration to Right-Think for brand design marketing.
https://right-think.com

Do you like the cover design? So do I. It was illustrated by Miha Brumec
https://www.artstation.com/feedington

TITLE: PROFILES OF HOPE (THE CELLULOID CLOSET SERIES #2)
AUTHOR: TAMMONS, BRENNEN
1st EDITION
ISBN: 978-1733776219 (Paperback)

This story is a work of fiction. Any correlation between people, names, places, events, or politics, are simply coincidental. Although, in this and in practically every other story, there are elements of inspiration based on actual events. However, any exact correlations are simply coincidental.

This story is graphic. There is strong vulgar language, criminal activity, drug use, and strong violent content. Due to the extreme subject matter, reader should be advised.

The opinions expressed by characters in this story, may reflect the opinions of the author, or may not. The author wishes to have a neutral stance.

CHAPTERS

To my twin brother, Berton.
To my mother, Brenda.
To my grandmother, Sharon.

To everyone else close to me, I appreciate you as well.

To God Be The Glory

PROLOGUE:

My name is Dr. Gary Swanson, and I'm thirty years old. As a matter of fact, today is my thirtieth birthday, and it might be coincidence that today being my birthday, is also the day this project starts. What project, you may be asking? You're going to have to hold on for a short while, I'll explain everything, don't worry. I am a reasonably averaged heighted man, and I'm slender and thin. But back to explaining more about myself, I will keep this as brief as possible. I like to think of myself as an attractive looking man, and I'm quite happy with the way I look. Always making sure that I keep in shape, and that I'm exercising regularly.

Being honest, there is one qualm I sometimes dislike about myself, and that's the fact I have to wear glasses due to my poor eyesight. As far as hobbies are concerned, I do like to play a variety of sports occasionally. With one in particular that I favor above rest, and I'm very skilled at, which is volleyball. I'm an avid reader, both fiction and nonfiction works; I am always reading internet blogs and magazines as well. Music is something that I enjoy as well, it doesn't matter what kind or style. At this time, I don't have any friends, being that I'm an introvert. Growing up was extremely difficult for me, and I feel that it wasn't until after I went to university, that I was reborn and felt free. I was born and raised in Provo, Utah; whether I wanted to or not, following a strict Mormon family. With religion, I was actually a youth elder for the Mormon church. Due to many harsh situations and details which I will explain a little later, I excommunicated myself from the church, and had to distance myself from my family. I decided to peruse psychology, going to school at the "University of Southern California." Although I do believe in god, and I respect the Mormon faith, I no longer a practice that religion, and I am very content with my life now.

I am a gay man, and it has taken me a great deal of time to accept this part of myself. My family not being supportive of me. My relationship with them is now isn't that good. I don't speak to them at all much, and they don't wish to speak to me. I know it's tough for them to accept their son is gay. My only hope is that someday they will be more accepting. I'm more concerned over my mother; my father has always been a more conservative man, but I always suspected my mother to be more lenient. It was a tough decision, but I sadly had to move on, and remove myself from their agenda. They had no intentions of accepting me, so as I do love them dearly, I have to move on with my life.

Once I graduated from university, receiving my masters in psychology; also receiving my doctorate a few months ago, I would partake in an unrelated field. I was a real estate agent, and as someone who studied something totally different than that, it is rather puzzling. This is a tough job market, and getting my real estate license seemed to be the logical thing to do right now. A guy has to eat right? However, my main goal was to eventually work towards psychology and help others. With that, I have decided to stop doing real estate, and focus more on field research. Thus, why I am now concerned with this current project.

There I go mentioning that project again, just wait a teeny bit more I'll explain, trust me. At the moment, I am single, and I would like to experience love someday. Not that I haven't been in love before, I most certainly have. This again I will explain more a little bit later. Don't mean to toot my own horn, but I am a licensed psychologist and call me an asshole or stuck up, but I worked hard for the position I have. I do get to own and accept the fancy "Dr." title as well, thank you very much. I have been one for now two years. Even though I am relatively new to being a licensed psychologist, all my life I have been studying humans, and observing how they operate and deal with one another. The reason I wanted to become one, is that this is what I feel I was put on this earth to do. It's rather hard to explain and to give you a deep answer on that. All I can say is that this is something I'm passionate about.

I'm now in my bedroom, getting myself ready for today. Like I usually do, I have my lucky tie on. My shoes are shined and polished fine, and I shaved last night, so my face is smooth. Today is the day of the project, so I'm anxious and excited about that. Okay fuck, I know you're tired of me mentioning this damn project, so here it goes. I was going to wait just a little bit longer, but now is the time for me to lay it all down.

I would like to take this time to explain this whole project to you. This is quite complex, but I will try my best to lay it down for you to understand. Due to me being a psychologist, that gives me more leniency to be more experimental with my lifestyle. I'm not the only one, many psychologists have also done similar projects to what I'm doing. We are always trying to find new ways to learn about mental health, and sociology, and human interactions. I can't tell you the amount of documentaries I watched on topics I don't have the strongest knowledge on, to better myself on these situations. Just because I haven't witnessed, or gone through those specific events, it is my job to go into further detail and analyze every corner, and see every side that subject is about. I'm going to cut right to the chase, and tell you what my project is.

My project, or the project I mentioned a million fucking times now, is called, "Profiles of Hope." Basically, over the course of the past few months, I went on the website "Reddit", which my "Reddit" name is "DrGareBear", and I asked on many LGBTQ related pages, if there were any gay or bisexual men over the ages of 21 that live in the Los Angeles area, and would like to take part in a study. With this study, I will only ask for a few hours of their time, and for them to meet me at the "University of Southern California", so I can interview and film them in a private room. I explained that what I film, will be seen by me and me alone, only to be used for my own personal research. I would like to know everything about their personal lives, and how them being gay played a factor, and all the trials and tribulations they had to go through. One main thing, was I didn't want them to hold back, or to filter themselves. If there is something that has left deep mental scars, I want them to tell me all about it. I of course would have to by law have to report any type of illegal abuse activity going on, but generally anything the men mentioned should be fair game, and I don't want them to feel ashamed.

On the post, I attached an application form, and based on the answers from that form, would determine which men would move on further into the process. Shockingly, I only received a little under a hundred inquiries. Of those hundred, several of the men were being rather inane and ignorant, and half of these applications were trolls and people who were trying to waste my time.

Thankfully, I did manage to find five men whom I felt were worthy enough to be involved with this project. A couple weeks ago, I reached out to these men by telephone, and explained everything to them. I was relieved when they seemed very compliant and safe with my intentions and agenda. One interesting thing to consider, out of these five men; four of them had a significant other that didn't originally respond to my application post, who based on what they mentioned about them, I also felt needed to be included. Using my gut feeling, I decided to add these men to the project. Now upping the total men to nine. Nine is lovely number, but ten sounds much better, so I decided to add myself to this project as I believe it's only fair. In addition to me taping the other men, I would also tape myself and explain my own story.

Over the past week Monday through Friday, all of the guys arrived at the location I told them to meet at so they can participate in this project. The men who happened to have a partner they recommended to join this event as well, arrived together. One of the men didn't have someone he wanted to add to the project. Even though most of the men had someone they wanted to add, all nine of them were to participate in the project in private seclusion. The guy who he arrived with, would have to wait outside the room, not hearing what is being discussed or mentioned. With this being my only condition towards the men who did have someone close to them that also wanted to be included. So in essence, whether the man knew another guy that was involved in the project or not, he would not know what exactly that particular guy mentioned when he was inside the room with me. I will say, even though these men were only with me for a little over two hours, that was more than enough time for them to tell me some very harsh shit.

All nine of these guys had a unique story to tell, and each one left me shocked, and I felt such empathy and connection towards these men. I feel that the gay and bisexual male community is so ostracized and artificial at times, that I'm happy that I put together this project to fully gain a better understanding of all of this. The stories these men have will make you laugh, they will make you cry, they will make you feel scared and nervous, but I truly have to say that most importantly, these stories will impact you in a way you've never imagined.

These men lives have changed forever based on these stories, myself included. Mind you, don't forget my story is also involved in the project. I'm sure you're wondering who these men exactly are, and why I decided to personally pick them. Okay, I'll tell you their names, and a brief summary of their personality. I don't want to spoil too much, that would be very foolish of me. At this time, I can only give you a small hint. At a later time when the men tell their own individual stories, you will learn more shocking facts about their lives.

Before I continue, I want to further elaborate on the "Profile of Hope" name I gave this project. As all of the subjects, myself included, are gay or bisexual men, I think it's better fitting if each man including me, is represented by a color. These colors include Red, Blue, Yellow, Green, Orange, Purple, Pink, Brown, Black and White. In total, that makes ten colors, with every man being associated with one. I wanted each color to be random and by chance. Taking ten different single pieces of construction paper, each with one of the ten colors, I cut them into a small size, about the size of a credit card, and stuck all ten small color pieces into a shoebox I decorated by gluing the discarded pieces of construction paper with glue on the outside of it. I placed a lid on top of the box which is also decorated, with a rainbow theme as well, cutting a small circular opening in the center of it. This way, the person cannot tell or pick which color they will pull out the box; I want each color the men will have to be completely random. With me being the first to pick, I stuck my hand inside the box, and pulled out white.

For the duration of this project, I will now be dubbed, "Man of White". I have already explained a little about my life and my current position. I have also explained why I am choosing to go along with this project. But, I will mention a few more details about myself. I did say that I was brought up, and was taught to follow the Mormon religion. However, as far as my culture, I am Greek. My family held hold onto strict values that I also had to obey. My grandparents immigrated to the United States, so they hold onto many traditional values. With politics, I try to keep a neutral stance. I'm neither liberal or conservative, and what I believe varies on a case by case basis. As far as this project is concerned, I don't care what values these other men hold. That isn't the point at all for this; my main objective is not to bring like-minded opinions and views.

I want this whole situation to be diverse as it possibly can. Trying to squash stigmas that gay men are faced with, and proving that we are all different in our own ways. With my story In particular, I was struggling with my own sexuality, being told my religion doesn't support how I truly feel. It was from my dealings with the Mormon church, that I was faced with many depressing and difficult circumstances. My family did not want to accept my sexuality, and have tried many different methods to break me out of being gay.

With my own personal story needing to be told, hoping that other men can learn from the issues I had to deal with. I will also take in as much as I can hearing their stories as well. One thing which I am proud and happy for, is I'm doing what I love. I am a psychologist, and I get to help and solve mental health problems and concerns that the world is faced with. Finding it very fascinating and exciting to get into the minds of individuals, understating why things happen in the way they do. There have been times to where I hit rock bottom and felt like giving up. When you find out about my story, you will see the pain and suffering that I had to witness. It is simply a miracle that I am still here, and I was able to survive all of the foolishness I was forced to be a part of. But, feel that all of it has paid off; I'm doing what I love, and life couldn't be better for me now. I now have a lovely home in the Hollywood Hills, with my salary doing private practice as a psychologist, and my real estate connections, I'm thankful for that.

I have a nice sports car, a brand new Mercedes which I love. I have two dogs; a Pomeranian and a Shiba Inu. I'm also doing well financially, and I'm thankful and blessed for all of that. I don't have any friends, but I'm sure that after this project is over, that will most likely change. Being that I'm turning thirty, I figure this would be an interesting thing to plan out. Putting my story with the rest of the guys stories, is something that I wasn't originally intending doing. However, I think it's only fair that if I'm asking for other men to express themselves and reveal some of their most deepest facts about themselves, that I should do the same and tell my story.

Before I reveal the other nine men in this project, I have a confession to make which I had forgotten to explain. When I orchestrated this project, I told the men that I simply wanted to film them for a few hours in a private room. I explained that the questions I ask them, and the material I film will be strictly confidential. That it would only be used for my own personal research and intentions. I have to now reveal that this is a complete lie. The next phases of the "Profile of Hope" project, will now finally be revealed. A big fear of mine, is that the men are not going to be comfortable with any of this. This is a risk I'm willing to take, and I can only hope that things will move smoothly. The first secret I wish to reveal, is that I told all the men that I interviewed for this project to come to my house this afternoon, as I'm throwing a house party.

I also told them that other men who were interviewed would be attending as well. What I didn't mention, is that during this party, I plan on showing all of the guys the tapes from their sessions with me, on the big screen television that is in my living room. I will also be showing the men the recordings I took of myself, documenting my own story. The reason why I didn't reveal this with them beforehand, is that I knew the guys wouldn't arrive if I told them this information. If this isn't enough, I also plan on revealing to the men during the party, that with their permission, I wish to enter in all of the tapes into a film festival.

In order for me to submit the tapes, all nine men have to agree, and if one guy says that he isn't comfortable with the idea, then I cannot go along with it. All the guys must agree. If I am able to enter the film festival, this would be lovely as I feel the stories these men have gone through, others deserve to see them, and will be touched by them as well. Although, it would be nice if this project were to win the festival, I would be equally as happy to simply to be featured. That would be enough for me to feel satisfied with it. At this time, I would now like to introduce the other nine men who are going to be in this project.

I decided to randomly pick which guys I would schedule to interview in which order. As four of the men had someone close who they brought with them to the sessions, there would only be a total of five sessions. The order which I'm describing the men, is the order I interviewed them. Please note, that before the interview sessions began, I asked the men to do the same as I did, and stick their hand into the rainbow decorated box to pull out a color card. Earlier before all the interviews began, I picked white. Also noting, this is also the order their stories will be presented when the men sit down at my house to watch them, also the same order when I submit the project to the film festival. One final thing to mention before present the other men, is that with the exception of one other man, all of them virtually smoke cigarettes. I don't smoke, and this was something that bothered me at first, but I am not one to judge. So be mindful that these men, with one guy being the exception which isn't the rule, all smoke cigarettes.

In addition, when I invited all the men to my home, I asked if they drank. They all mentioned that they did, so I will be provided libation for them all to enjoy. Making one absolute final remark now, being that I am a licensed psychologist, please take my descriptions of these men lightly. I mean everything well and in the nicest of ways, but

I can't help if I am an asshole with the way I perceive some of those men.

The first man that I interview was Troy Lockwood. He pulled out the yellow card from the box, so he is "Man of Yellow". Troy's "Reddit" name is "TitaniumRangerX", explaining to me that he picked the name, from being a huge fan of "Mighty Morphin Power Rangers". Troy has blond hair, as it's styled in a schoolboy like fashion in a bowl cut. He also has light blue eyes, and a youthful round face. Troy is twenty-eight years old. As with him being the youngest, Troy in my perspective was the sweetest and polite out of all the men. Despite his age, Troy looks like he is twelve years old. This is because as he mentioned to me, he has a growth hormone disorder. He is a healthy person, but because of that, it causes him to look much younger than he actually is. Troy is the smallest of the whole group. Both height and weight wise; Troy is a very short man, and he's also quite slim and skinny. His speaking voice is also very high and cheerful; listening to him speak was cute and his personality brought much joy to me. Troy was born and raised in Nashville, Tennessee, but he now lives in Los Angeles.

Troy decided to add his partner Harry to the project. Whom Harry was actually one of the bullies at his school. It's an interesting situation. Troy works at a retail department store. I can tell that Troy has a delicate personality, and it doesn't take much for him to worry and get upset over things. He has a deep fear of being taking advantage of and bullied, as he has been tossed around his entire life. As you find out about Troy's story, you will come to find out all the emotional and mental issues he has gone through. I was shocked to find out that Troy not only smokes cigarettes, but he likes to drink as well. Maybe it is due to his youthful personality and appearance, that I never would assume that about him.

Troy was raised by his mother, and had no father figure growing up. He currently lives with his partner Harry, who incidentally is the person I tagged along to be involved with this group as well. Harry is an interesting character, and he and Troy make a strange pair, but they care for each other. I'll get to Harry in a minute, but more importantly with Troy. Troy has always felt gay when he was little, and felt different from the other boys when he was at school. He was constantly bullied for not only being a smaller and weaker boy, but being homosexual as well. Growing up in the south, and dealing with bigotry. He didn't have any friends growing up, and kept to himself mostly. He turned to comic book reading, and watching cartoons to help him deal with the depression he was keeping inside. From what Troy has mentioned to me, I was shocked and stunned to listen and take in all of it. This young man has experienced a lot of sadness, and I have extreme empathy for the strength that he has.

Even though he is the polar opposite of Harry, Harry plays important part in Troy's story, and vice versa. Troy loves Harry very much, and you will soon get to know their complicated and complex relationship with one another. Being that Troy was the first that I interviewed, if his story was unique as it was, it only made me want to find out more about Harry, and what he had to say. I am thankful that Troy did mention to me about Harry, as he and three other men weren't originally going to be included with this at all. Troy has been faced with danger many times in his life, and he still manages to stay positive and happy. Having him in this project is a delight, and he's a lovely young man that simply amazes me and makes me feel happy. Troy brings a smile to my heart, and I know life has many great things in store for him in the future.

The next man I interviewed was Harry Bruner. Harry pulled out the orange card from the box, so that makes him "Man of Orange". Harry is twenty-eight years old. Harry's "Reddit" name that he uses is "HarryMachine". I strictly asked him the reasoning behind the online handle, and he refused to give me an answer. He gave me a look which would be one he would customarily give throughout the session when I asked him a question he was uncomfortable with. Harry by looking at his face, is extremely intimidating to look at. Possibly due to his beard. Again, taking whatever I describe about these guys in the nicest of ways, Harry is by far the scariest man looks wise of the bunch. Harry is redheaded, and he is a ginger. His hair however is very unkempt and shaggy. Harry despite not being that old, is already starting to bald, and showing signs of it. His hairline is quite receding, but his shaggy red hair which is styled in a caveman like fashion seems to hide that. Harry has a bushy lumberjack style beard, and has a puffy mustache as well. He is slight pudgy built man, and his arms are quite toned and muscled. Harry, is also quite hairy, pun intended. Ha-Ha. By looking at his arms during the interview sessions, and his chest hair that could easily be seen through his buttoned shirt, he has quite a lot of body hair. Harry is the tallest out of all the men, but not by much, there is another man who is slightly shorter than him.

Harry's parents sadly tragically died when he was young. He grew up with his older brothers; with Harry being the youngest. Harry, like Troy, smokes cigarettes. In addition he likes to drink quite often. With all of the men in consideration, Harry was one of the most defiant and rude, with one other guy matching his same behavior. His husky and rough voice also scared me at times. Harry would always be seen crossing his arms, and his beard and mustache made it hard for me to tell if he was smirking or grinning or anything. I tried my best to make Harry feel comfortable, but he was way too tense during the whole ordeal, and I began to feel sorry for him. I know it's not easy to participate in something like this, and explain delicate and difficult times you have gone through in your life. You would think by how nice and polite Troy was acting, Harry would reciprocate that. You'd be incorrect, as I'd really had to press Harry to get to him explain situations and events. I would ask him certain questions, and he would roll his eyes like I was bothering him. I wasn't forcing him to take part, at any time Harry could have excused himself from this project, and I would have been disappointed, but I would have understood.

I am glad that Harry, perhaps for the sake of Troy, managed to stick through this, as his story like the other guys is important to be highlighted. Harry like Troy was born and raised in Nashville, Tennessee. He unlike Troy, considers himself a natural born redneck, and enjoyed partaking in the country lifestyle. He has many hobbies, which include hunting and fishing. Harry also owns many guns. Harry also seemed to like sports and football quite a lot, and played football in High School. Harry would originally bully and torment Troy in school at first, and it's strange how their relationship changed. Harry was bisexual, and was only tormenting Troy to suppress his own issues. Harry loves Troy very much. Just based on how Harry acts, it doesn't seem that way on face value. At a later time, you will find out more about both their stories. Harry works as a butcher, at the same grocery store, and also works at his older brothers restaurant. He enjoys his job at the supermarket, and likes to help out the customers as well. Harry is quite frankly a gentle giant, and I was glad to include him in this project, being recommended by Troy.

The following man that I interviewed was Aaron Chen. Aaron pulled out the pink card from the box, so that makes him "Man of Pink". He is twenty-eight years old, and he was born and raised in Seattle, Washington. Aaron is a second generation Chinese American. His parents, likewise with my grandparents from Greece, immigrated from China to America. Aaron has short black hair, and brown eyes. He is feminine and flamboyant looking, and so is his personality. He is of slender weight, and of average height. His voice is soothing and pleasing to listen to, as it's high pitched. Aaron out of all the men, in my findings happened to be the most descriptive and detailed. He tries to break down situations in a unique way, and I find that very interesting. I can understand that with him being a gay Asian man, the struggles which he has explained to me are justified. Although it didn't take him long to accept and come out to himself, he was still struggling with his sexuality in his own way. Aaron's "Reddit" name that he uses is "AaronMonster". He is into anime and video games and Pokémon, so he picked his name to relate towards that.

Aaron's family originally were shocked at him coming out, but learned to love and respect him unconditionally. Occasionally he does talk to his parents and his sister, but the relationship with them is distant. Aaron went onto University to study nursing. Even though the journey before that was rough and you'll find out all the details later upon learning his story, Aaron is now a registered nurse, and is happy with his career path. He goes to work to help other people, and feels good with himself that he's able to do all of that. With his hobbies, Aaron likes yoga, and he meditates every morning after he wakes up as part of his ritual. Aaron lives with his husband and partner Steven, who incidentally is the man he recommended to join this study, whom I accepted. I'll get to Steven shortly, but back to Aaron. From what Aaron has told me, the circumstances on how he and Steven met are interesting indeed. When Aaron was in High School, his teacher was Steven, and their initial relationship was convoluted to say the least. I at this time cannot reveal more than what I have already mentioned, but once you hear both of their stories, you will gain a clear understanding of how everything branched out the way it has. One thing I like about Aaron, is how he is able to handle being a double minority as well as he does.

His political stances seem to be neutral like mine, neither leaning left or right. Being an open minded person, despite all the abuse he has had to come across, and many people bashing him over his race, or by the fact he is gay. However, Aaron felt comfortable throughout the session, and there wasn't a single time that I can remember to where anything I asked of him became too much for him to handle. Don't get me wrong, Aaron's story is one that will make you have a million different emotions, and is deep and sad. I give Aaron credit for being able to tell all the events as calm as he was able to. One thing to note about Aaron, is that he does like to smoke cigarettes, and being that virtually most of the other men with a couple exceptions do as well, I was able to dismiss this. The reason I chose for Aaron to be involved, because his personality seemed vibrant, and I saw many things in common with myself in him. Aaron being Chinese, and not only honoring his culture, but being proud as a gay man, really speaks volumes. He admits that he is more feminine, and can be considered a queen, but that is simply who he is. Aaron doesn't wish to paint himself as a victim, and this is one quality that I like about him. Aaron doesn't wish to sulk in self-pity. Judging based on courage alone, I give him props for that.

The next man I interviewed was Aaron's husband and life partner Steven Pankowski. Steven pulled out the red card out of the box, so he is "Man of Red". Steven is thirty-seven years old. With all the men, Steven like Harry, was slightly defiant and sassy. He is a man that's very sarcastic and was one of the men that would joke around quite often. Steven also was the man who used the foulest language, and cursed quite often. Most of the time when he did use vulgar words, they had no validity at all. Steven loves to say the word fuck a lot, which I find shocking as he's a teacher. Again, my job isn't to judge, only to observe and report. Steven is Jewish. He in my perspective feels some type of complex from being Jewish. Steven is also ashamed of his bald head, and says because he was balding like Harry was, he decided to shave all of his hair off. He does happen to have a mustache, and a scruffy beard that's nearly groomed unlike Harry's. Steven like myself, happens to wear glasses, as he has terrible eyesight. Steven has hazel eyes. He is an average weight man, and also of average height. Both of Stevens parents are now deceased.

He is an only child, and like Aaron, has a complicated relationship with his family. Steven was born and raised in Seattle, Washington, but he decided to move to California where he currently lives with Aaron. It was difficult for me to talk to Steven, as the way he has conversations is interesting. I don't know how he deals with Aaron considering that they are a couple and that's none of my business how he deals with him really, but Steven's rudeness at times, I could do without. Steven was uncomfortable through most of the process, and it took me a while to figure out whether he was joking and being sarcastic, or if what he was mentioning was legitimate and if it was genuine or not. Steven's "Reddit" name is "Justaweirdman", which he wouldn't explain to me the reason behind it. It's oddly goes quite well with his personality. Steven is a weird man, and I only say that as a friendly compliment. I do think when he wants to be, he can be a lovely man.

One important thing to mention about Steven, which I don't want to say explains his attitude and agenda, is that Steven is wheelchair bound, as he's paralyzed from the waist down. The exact situations as to why he is, you will find out later upon hearing the story that both he and Aaron tell. Steven began to show much emotion upon retelling the events which caused him to live the rest of his life in a wheelchair. Steven also struggles labelling himself a bisexual, and refuses to join any type of gay community. Steven along with a couple other men during their sessions have said the word "faggot", but Steven has said it a record number of times more than the other men have. The context in the way he expressed himself towards that word also had a more hurtful power and conviction towards it. Steven likes to watch the History channel quite often, and he like myself enjoys reading both fiction and non-fiction. He also recommended me several titles to consider, which I will check out as well. Steven like Aaron, smokes cigarettes and likes to drink alcohol as well, with beer being his drink of choice.

Steven now is a University professor, and despite the fact he's disabled and is confined to a wheelchair, he keeps going. I don't care for Steven's vulgar mouth, and his unfunny sense of humor at times, but he's a harmless man, and his position towards this project is needed. Steven is the most apprehensive out of the men, and unlike Aaron, does consider himself a victim most of the time. His temper and attitude gets the better of him, and if there is something he doesn't want to do, he won't do it. I picked Steven because I feel his personality is special and unique and different, it deserves to be highlighted and showcased. Steven despite being a strange man to perceive, is still nice.

The man I next interviewed was Jerald Williams. Jerald reached into the box and pulled out the brown card, making him "Man of Brown". Jerald is a twenty-eight-year-old, African American man with brown eyes. Jerald is a slender man, who is of average height. Out of all the men, Jerald was defiantly the most theatrical and diva. The way he talked was identical to that of a woman's and so were his emotions. He like with Aaron, is quite feminine and flamboyant with how he carries himself. Jerald has short dreadlock braids, which I love. His hair is nice to see, and I like his sense of style. Jerald after all is a fashion designer, so it's his job to know about trends and what looks good. His "Reddit" name is "JayJazzy", as Jerald's nickname is Jay, and he also likes jazz music as well.

Jerald was born in Los Angeles, and had a tough childhood. He is an only child, and never met his father at all. His mother whom he loved dearly and was raised by, sadly passed away. Upon hearing Jerald's story, you will find out the unfortunate details surrounding his mother's death. Jerald grew up in poverty, and was teased for his passion for fashion and taking up knitting and crocheting.

He and his mother lived off very little, and were struggling to live. I am proud that Jerald was able to overcome all the problems he was faced with. Jerald refuses to be a victim. There have been numerous times to where Jerald has been attacked for his race and sexuality, sometimes for both reasons. Ever since he was little, Jerald has been a flamboyant person, and has taken an interest into sewing. Jerald after the passing of his mother, lived on the street for a while, and then moved into a youth shelter. Jerald luckily was able to graduate High School., Jerald did receive a scholarship to a fashion trade school, which he used to his advantage to better his position, later graduating from the school. He has had a difficult and depressing life, but he knows that it's important for him to stay strong. Something that Jerald feels blessed about, is that he was able to meet his now fiancé Carl, whom he lives with. Jerald loves Carl very much, and considers him his best friend. I should mind you, they actually are total complete opposites, so I find it fascinating indeed that they are so close to one another. Carl is also included with this project as well.

Jerald likes a variety of hobbies, which include breakdancing, doing gymnastics and tumbling, and he of course likes to sew, knit, crochet, and cross-stich. Jerald also enjoys shopping often, and he likes to visit thrift stores, he enjoys vintage clothes, and always tries to make his wardrobe fashionable. He is a friendly man most importantly, and I feel honored to have him included with the project. I know it's difficult trying to fit into society, being a black man who's gay. He's not stereotypically and prototypically the ideal and average black man. Jerald is quite feminine with his personality, so he does have this unique mold and agenda towards society.

Jerald speaks in an urban fashionable tone as well, and I also find that intriguing. His own special speaking voice and style is one that stands out from others. Jerald has a good sense of humor about him, similar to Carl, which I can see is a trait which makes them enjoy each other's company. I didn't choose Jerald because I felt sorry for him, or because I pitied him either. The reason I chose Jerald to join this project because I liked his story, and his personality. He brings something different, like the rest of the men do, and I appreciate his position.

The following man I interviewed was Jerald's fiancé Carl. Carl pulled out the purple card, so he is "Man of Purple". He is a twenty-nine-year-old man, with medium-long straight blond hair that is combed to the back of his head. He has hazel eyes, and he has stubble and a five o clock shadow on his face. Carl is one of the taller guys of the bunch, being only slightly shorter than Harry. As far as his weight, he is slightly pudgy, with a chubby face, completing his semi long hair. I will say, that Carl quite arguably is the wildest and hyper out of all the men. Carl is autistic, but is very high functioning. He has a very grizzly and active speaking voice, which is interesting. But after a while, you learned to get used to his voice.

Carl does not have an off button on him, and once he starts talking, he will not stop until he's ready to stop. He not only speaks fast, but speaks like he is a wild animal in a rapid and fast tone. Carl is autistic and he also has Asperger syndrome, so he doesn't always think before he talks, and says whatever is on his mind. Carl like Jerald, has a nice sense of humor, and was one of the funniest guys I interviewed. The "Reddit" name that he uses is "MetallicaGuy". Carl likes all types of music, but the type of music he favors over everything else, would have to be hard rock and metal music, with Metallica being his favorite band.

Carl grew up in Boston, Massachusetts, but he later moved to Los Angeles, where he now lives with Jerald. The circumstances as to how he and Jerald met will be revealed later, but they both have made an interesting impact towards each other lives. Carl has an older brother Mark who sadly passed away. Ever since he was young, Carl along with his brother Mark have realized their talent for art. After Carl and Mark graduated University, they both became artists. Carl himself has developed his talent for drawing on canvas pieces quite well. Carl enjoys art galleries, and showcasing his art, making money by selling his pieces over the internet and at auctions. He is very serious about his oil painting, and he makes the difficult look easy. However, Carl is holding onto harsh secrets about his life, and his particular story is one that is noteworthy. Carl being a bisexual man has always struggled with personal affection, and never would imagine he would be in a relationship with someone. I tried to press Carl further on what about Jerald he likes, but he simply in a friendly way would divert the discussion away to something else. I do appreciate that Carl is definitely a type of man I've never met before in my life. His personality and attitude is wild and strange, but when it comes to his art, the man is so damn talented. I've seen his work, and I would never think a guy like him could be patient enough to come up with pieces such as that.

Carl along with his brother Mark, also enjoy street art and wall murals, and has done a few pieces on those as well. The fact Jerald is a fashion designer, both of their artistic passions are able to match well with each other. The reason I chose Carl, is I couldn't believe a man like this actually exists. I don't say that to disrespect or demean him, but I appreciate how different he is, and I had to include him based on how happy he makes me feel. He is interesting, and the way he comes across is also memorable.

The next man I interviewed was Jamal Benson. Jamal pulled out the green card from the box, so he is "Man of Green". He is twenty-eight years old. Like with Jerald, Jamal is an African-American gay man.. Jamal is slender as far as his weight, and he has short black hair, and brown eyes. Jamal has a soft high pitched voice, not unlike some of the other men as well. His voice although is direct and loud, I can tell that Jamal doesn't joke around like most of the other guys, and is forthright with his comments. Like Jerald, Jamal grew up in a complex manner. He was abandoned by his parents, and grew up in a home with other orphaned children. This caused Jamal to feel upset, having to grow up without family. However, Jamal was later adopted by a family. Jamal is more serious and dramatic with his personality. He has a slight feminine personality towards himself, and he can get diva at times. I was trying my best to make him feel comfortable, but Jamal was one of the guys who became emotional during the sessions. I explained to him that it's okay for him to feel sad and to cry, and he's allowed to show emotions. Jamal's "Reddit" name is "Urbanunited", without any specific reasoning to why he picked that name in particular to use. Being gay was something Jamal didn't understand originally, and it took him some time to accept that part of his life. Jamal after finishing High School, went to college to study journalism, and later graduated. Jamal has an interesting story, which you will explore more about later. IIis story includes the man who he very recently began to form a close friendship with, and I guess you can say he's his boyfriend now. His name is Ralph, who I also added to this project as well. His attachment to Ralph is interesting, and you need to understand both of their stories more to know the full details.

Jamal for his spare time, likes to keep up with entertainment and media. Whether that's pop culture gossip, or it's politics and other hot topics. Jamal out of all the men, to me seems to be the one who is the most curious. His opinions and the way he spoke told me that he is open to many things, and wants to learn as much as he can. As I talked more with Jamal during his session, I had empathy towards his story, and the problems that he was faced with. Even though he was originally from New York, Jamal along with Ralph are now living in Los Angeles. I gave credit where credit was due to Jamal, due to the amount of times he cried during the sessions. No other man was upset to the level that he was. I know that Jamal was trying his best to contain his emotions and feelings, but sometimes you can't keep that inside, and I assured him that it's alright to cry.

Jamal feels that his life has had so many depressing twists and turns, and I completely understand. Having to live with being black and gay. The strange connection which you will find about later towards Ralph, also altered the way he lives. Putting his virtues and values to the ultimate test. I chose Jamal for this project, because I have faith in him. I know that he's only human, and his particular story was one that I couldn't pass up or push aside. Jamal is an emotional man, and most if not all of the reasons for him feeling emotional are understood, and having his story shown is important.

The following man I interviewed, was the man Jamal recommended to me. His close companion named Ralph Maligrino. Ralph pulled out the black card, so that makes him "Man of Black". Out of all the men, Ralph is the oldest, being that he's forty years old. Ralph is half Cuban, and half Italian American. Ralph has short black hair, and a beard. Ralph has an interesting way of how he talks, it's very professional and direct. It might be because of his age, but Ralph seemed to not joke or fool around like most of the other men have in their sessions. He was polite when I asked him a question, and didn't beat around the bush towards any of our discussions. Ralph's "Reddit" name is "WiseguyLA". I asked him several times for him to explain the meaning behind that name, and I was unfortunately not able to come up with any reasoning's towards it.

Ralph also has a stoic personality, and rarely would be crack a smile. He kept a firm face at me always, once again perhaps having to do with his age, and the level of maturity he has. After noticing how well tailored the suit he wore to the session was, I asked him if he always wears suits. He responded by saying that he does, and he prefers to wear suits above any other type of clothing. Ralph is interesting, and it took me a while to get information that I wanted out of him, but alas I was able to succeed. He revealed to me that he was a member of top secret "mafia" group in University, and found it fascinating that Ralph revealed this to me.

With all the men considered, I know the least about Ralph's personal life, as there wasn't much he wanted to reveal to me. I asked him about his family, he simply told me that he doesn't have a family anymore. I didn't bother him further on that, because the situations surrounding that must be difficult, so I respected his wishes. The most noteworthy thing about Ralph, is that the man is rather wealthy. This was something for whatever reason, Jamal did a good job of concealing, but I was thinking and assuming it anyways based on hints that Jamal mentioned about Ralph. I'm not sure how much of his connections with the "mafia" have to do with his wealth, but I do know that he has a lot of money.

Ralph works as a business tradesmen, dealing with third party good transfers. He also works with financial records and data as well. Anything related to this business, from gold transfers, stock transfers, and imported goods and manufacturing transfers. A startling discovery to mention about Ralph, is that he is legally blind. Once you hear his story, you will know why he is. Jamal is able to help him move around, and helps take care of him. It is strange the relationship he has with Jamal, but this will all be covered later. Ralph is a bisexual man, and has never liked that part of him. Having to live his life being blind, Ralph still makes his money, and continues his career. Not letting barriers such as that get in the way with how he wants to live his life. Ralph even though he can't see well, enjoys golf, and he plays regularly. Ralph likes to watch the news often, and he's into finances and money, and he is involved with world trade. I am happy that Ralph is included in the project, although I know this isn't something he is happy doing; talking about his life caused a great deal of stress for him.

Ralph is from New York, but now lives in a mansion in Los Angeles with Jamal. Ralph is different than the other men, not only for his age, but how reserved and cordial he is as well. Ralph is a conservative man no doubt, and made it clear to me from the beginning. The fact he is bisexual, doesn't stop him from the opinions and values that he holds onto, and he's always going to stand and stick behind. I chose Ralph, because I need an older man's perspective.

The final man I interviewed, was Frank Ealing. There was only one card left in the box, as Frank was the last man I had a session with. I didn't make him reach into the box, I told him the whole color situation which he understood, explaining to him the final color is blue which it is. Frank is "Man of Blue". Frank is twenty-nine years old. He is the most masculine man out of all of the men, and he is a handsome rugged man. He has a bushy mustache and beard combo, which I found manly and cute. Frank had a deep a rough voice, but he was still a sweet natured man. The way he smelled was also nice. He was just a nice man to be around, and was happy to interview him. His "Reddit" name is "Electrowaved", as he's really into electronics, which is why he picked the name. Frank has short dirty blonde hair which he was rubbed a lot of hair gel onto his scalp to have his hair neatly pressed like that. The smell of his cologne was also nice, and yes I mentioned it again, because damn it, he smelled good. Frank was definitely my type, and I'm not going to lie, he was the guy I was the most attracted to. He has lovely blue eyes, that you can get lost in. He wasn't that muscular, but he had a masculine build. Frank was the only guy who didn't have someone close to him be included in the project. I asked Frank if he was single, which sadly to my chagrin, Frank did mention he was taken, and had a partner named Laura. Why I didn't mention this already, but Frank is actually a police officer for the "Los Angeles Police Department." He actually came to the session in his police uniform actually. He had just gotten off work, and didn't have time to change, I found that so nice. Frank was born in San Francisco, and he later moved to Los Angeles.

It is important to note that Frank is different from the other men. He himself wanted me to know this, and upon him telling me, I began to cry, and feel the upmost empathy. Frank let me know not to feel sad, and he put his hand on my lap which made me feel safer with him. Frank is transgender, meaning that he was born female. He lived the first part of his life as a woman, and he went through female puberty, which caused him much confusion. Frank is bisexual. He is attracted to both men and women. I asked Frank more information about his partner, but I respected his wishes when he simply said that she was a woman, and how they met, and that didn't want to be included in this project at all. Frank has gone through many procedures to transition into the gender he feels he truly is.

The fact Frank is transgender, makes me care a lot for him, and I admire all of the strength he has. Knowing more about his story later, you can understand more of the gender dysphoria that he had to deal with. Being transgender, but also wanting to pursue his dream of being a police officer. You can only imagine the stress he had, with being a transgender man and the type of work that he does. I am so happy to have frank with this project. I still can't get over how good he smells. Listening to Frank talk is also lovely, and he's such an amazing man.

His story I have to be honest, is one that is upsetting, and one that I will always remember and really hold close to my heart. Frank enjoys going to the gym quite often, and keeping his body in shape. As a police officer, he has to keep fit, and keep his body healthy. Luckily, Frank manages to find a good support system with his partner, and his friends, whom he has revealed and came out as transgender to. I chose

Frank, because I know the other men are going to be shocked once they find out more about him, and also appreciate him for the man he is, and everything he has to offer.

So now that you have met the other men, the only thing left now is for them to all meet each other, which they will very shortly. The men are now each on their way to my home. I have plenty of snacks and refreshments available, and I have all the session tapes ready for the men to see. I knew that this could either go one of two ways; either the men will be delighted over this project I have planned, or they will all leave and go home. But either way, I can say I tried my best with this, and I'm willing to risk this and give it a shot. I am happy that I did decide to take a chance, as everything which happens next are truly worthwhile to remember.

So with that, it's now time for me to start the next stage of this project. I introduced all the men you are going to get to know better, so it's now it's time for it to begin. I continue to set everything up, as the men have not arrived yet. I'm finding it weird that all ten of us will shortly be in my living room together, and our big project will start at that time. I'm Dr. Gary Swanson, and I want to thank you for taking the time for letting me explain this whole event. The time for explaining is now finished, and I have to now move on. I'll try to stay with you for only a short while longer, but then the rest will be up to guys and the stories they wanted to tell. I shall speak with all of you later, as my doorbell has just rang.

CHAPTER 1:

GUYS FIRST MEET

I opened the door, only to find out it's just the mailman delivering a package for me. False alarm. I was expecting for one of the guys to arrive. I grab the package, and sign the form, setting the box down in my living room. After opening it up, I see that the package is a set of books I had ordered online. I place all the books neatly onto my bookshelf that's on the other side of my living room. Immediately after that, I walk myself to the kitchen. Making sure I have everything set for when the men show up. I have alcohol and beer for them to drink, and other snacks for them to eat such as chicken wings, chips, mozzarella sticks, and a favorite of mine which are deep fried pickles. With this, I can hope they will feel more at home and comfortable.

If I didn't mention already, I'm doing so now; I told the men to bring a change of clothes as I am planning a sleepover for all of them. I'm letting them all spend the night at my place. The men were all compliant and comfortable with that, so that's good. I figure they trust my position and credentials well enough to agree to do it. They feel that me being who I am, I don't mean any harm. Now that everything is all set for the guys, all I can do is now is wait for their arrival. As I'm in the living room, I start to pour myself a glass of wine. I'm starting to feel slightly nervous, and I don't know what is going to happen from now. I feel that maybe I should have been honest and upfront with my agenda to the rest of the guys, rather than waiting until now to reveal this whole project to them. The chance they do not take the news well is a main concern that I'm currently thinking about.

While I'm sipping on my wine, I take a seat down on the sofa. I think about all nine men. How each of them are different from each other, and have a special unique place into this experiment and project that I'm doing. I wonder how they each will react to hearing their stories, and the suffering and issues that they all have gone through. Knowing that this could be a time for them to reflect on their own personal lives as being gay and bisexual men. This community I feel as of late has been very ostracized and separated. So many false narratives are being tagged to gay and bisexual men, and this is the perfect time for me to hold this event. To be honest, I studied psychology for reasons such as this.

There are so many gay and bisexual men that are struggling with their lives, and hold onto beliefs that they are alone in this world. I understand and empathize completely with their plight and sorrows. With this project I have planned, I am certain that it will bring an interesting perspective towards this debate and issue. Anything I can do to squash any social stigmas that I believe aren't being reported and shown in the correct light. I owe it to not only myself, but to any other man who struggles with identical problems. Who knows, depending on the success of how this project goes, I may damn well do it again with a different set of guys. That is thinking way ahead yes, but I will consider all of that.

For now, I remain tense on the sofa, wondering which guys will be the first to arrive. I am assuming that eight of the men will show up in pairs, with the companion they participated in the project with. The only man who will not be arriving with someone else, will be Frank. I pull out my phone, and turn on the internet radio to some nice mellow mood music. Even though I will be showing the guys all of their session tapes, including my own personal tape, I want them to first unwind. Any minute now, they are going to walk in. As time passes on, the more stressed I become. I know it's silly of me to think they won't show up, but I can't help but think about that. It is now 4 P.M. and I am now starting to feel slightly worried. When I called the men inviting them to my home for the party, I asked if Friday at four was a good time. I don't know their work schedules, but all the men said that time was okay. While I have this spare time, I start to get my thoughts in order. I'm going to have to fess up to the men and explain to them what's really going on. They believe this is simply a party and a sleepover as a token of appreciation for them participating in the project. In a way it slightly is, but I have more in store for them.

None of them have any idea that they are here to watch over all the session tapes that they all thought were to never be seen. Hence why most of them discussed what they did on the tapes, under pretenses that they were privately giving those stories and information to me. With that not being enough, I will also reveal to the men that I wish to enter in all their session tapes in this project, towards a film festival later. This news I am already preparing myself for them to not be thrilled and happy about. One thing I want to make clear, is that I interviewed each man for over three hours with breaks, but they are not going to see three hours' worth of videos though.

Through the course of the past week, I've edited all the sessions down to a shorter equal length. I made sure to edit out any details that I felt were redundant, or if they guys revealed something too personal such as someone's name I haven't cleared up towards this project. If there happened to be a tidbit or anecdote the men mentioned that I felt wasn't that noteworthy to be included in final cut of the session, I've edited all that stuff out. Also, I condensed most of the session videos as well, making sure that overlapping events and stories are being told in a proper manner so that things aren't repeating themselves, as they are simply being told by another person.

Especially considering the fact most of these men intertwine as far as events in their lives go, being that many came into the project with someone close in their lives, who play a major part in their specific story as well. I had to make a choice as to which guy would tell that specific event or story. Even though the editing was frustrating, it was necessary for me to do all of that. This will also make it easier for the guys to sit through all the stories, so they aren't feeling too drained out. I know that the men will spend a large amount of time tonight viewing the stories, which is why I offered for them to spend the night. I have plenty of room, so I'm not worried about that. This will take some time for them to view the stories, and it's okay.

I will make sure the guys take breaks as they are watching the stories. If they need to go outside to take cigarettes breaks, that is fine as well. I will ask that guys wait until all the stories are finished, to ask a specific guy a question on his personal session. As they are viewing the stories, I would like for them to remain quiet, and not give any comments until all the sessions videos are finished. I will show the videos in the following order; I will go first, and I will then play all the sessions in the same exact order when I first interviewed the men. This order consists of Troy, Harry, Aaron, Steven, Jerald, Carl, Jamal, Ralph and Frank. If a guy decides he doesn't want the other men watching his story, I will respect his decision and not show it and skip. But, I really want for all nine of the men to allow me to show their personal story. I also want them to approve my other plans and wishes, by submitting the project to the festival.

In order for me to enter the project into the film festival, all nine men have to agree and sign the consent form. As complicated as this whole process may seem, I will try my best to explain it all to them in a way that doesn't overwhelm them. Being that they made it this far, and have trusted me enough to visit my home, I don't see why they wouldn't agree to this. As soon as the last man arrives, I want to get started on showing the session tapes immediately, and admit my plans to all of the guys. Everything should flow smoothly, and I'm confident and certain that it will. These men I have personally observed and I trust each and every one of them. When they arrive, I don't mean to be rude by rushing things along, and being too direct. I will allow them to briefly meet and introduce themselves to each other, but I do have to get down to businesses as quickly as I possibly can. We are going to be here all night watching the session videos, so we don't have any time to waste.

Still anticipating for the men to arrive, I get up from the sofa, and I make the decision to walk outside to my front porch. Turning my head across the horizon and looking at the California view. It is now late afternoon and early evening, and I happen to like this setting. The sun's glow against the sky, is exhibiting a beautiful view. Quite simply amazing, and I love being front and center to this glorious scene. However, I look down the road over the other side of the cul-de-sac where my house is, facing the open road. I keep my head facing that direction, waiting for a car to pull up.

When I don't see any vehicles approaching, I for a short while become upset and anxious. I don't know why none of the men are here yet, and with it now almost being thirty minutes past four. After adjusting my tie, I sit down on my porch wondering if this was all a big mistake. I think as to whether or not I planned this way too quickly, and didn't give the men ample time before inviting them over for a slumber party. Perhaps I am simply over thinking the situation. The men said they would be here, so I must keep faith alive and trust them, which I do. I have no reason to believe these men aren't on my side, and they aren't trustworthy.

As time keeps passing on, I would like for them to all to show up soon though. I look at my empty driveway, as I parked my car on the street earlier. As I'm examining my driveway, I know that will be enough space for all the men to park once they get here. While I'm sitting on my porch, I look down and rub my fingers through my hair. Several more minutes pass, and I'm not going to lie, I'm starting to panic, and I'm now angry and mad.

I walk back inside my home, and I pour myself another glass of wine. After taking a very small sip, I take my wine glass and sit back on my porch. I'm so angry, I feel like throwing this glass on the ground causing it to shatter. These men should have been here by now, and I don't know what is holding them. I tell myself if they are not here in another thirty minutes, I'm going to call each and every one of them to check and see what's exactly going on. While I'm trying to calm myself down, I sit on my porch drinking my wine. I tell myself that I'm not going back inside the house until the first guy arrives. If I have to sit on this stoop until tomorrow morning, I will. Observing the view and taking in the air, listening to the bird's chirp. I sit and drink my wine, waiting for the men to come. I will not do anything else, I will be completely patient at this time. As I take yet another sip of my mine, I begin to close my eyes and meditate to myself. Keeping my mind calm, and not thinking about anything that would cause me to get angry or stress myself out. This whole event I planned out is causing me to feel worked up, and I need to take this rare chance to ease myself away from all the pressure.

Being a psychologist, I am able to use mind tricks to satisfy my own mental gains and issues. Using these same tactics and methods to help other people out as well. The whole point of me doing this project, was to not only gain a better perspective of myself, but to understand fully the lives of nine other gay and bisexual men. Their stories are all different, mine included. With the main focus of this project, wanting to make a difference with how we connect towards each other and are different, yet similar. This is something I've never seen done before really, and I feel committed to approach this project. My career means that much to me to take risks such as this. Even though I've only known these men for a short while, their stories have captivated me to gather all of my energy to them.

As I continue to wait for the men, I sit in silence taking in my own personal thoughts. In my head, I'm having flashbacks and memories of all the stories, and wondering how the men will react to them, and how they will encounter their own personal story. This project will be interesting, not only for each man who was involved with the sessions, but each man finding out about the other guys stories as well. Even if they already witnessed those events, they are being retold by someone other than them in a different perspective. They will meet and be introduced to men who have gone through similar hardships such as themselves, and also connecting and forming a close bond that way with each other too.

While still thinking about this project, I get up from the porch one more time, setting my wine glass on the porch. I decide once again to look down towards the road to see if there are any cars coming towards my direction. Upon further view, I do see a vehicle creeping closer to where I am. I gaze and inspect through the windshield, and I see a familiar face indeed. In the driver's seat, I see Steven; with Aaron sitting in the passenger seat of a minivan. This action was out of my control, but I started to grin and smile. I am shocked to see that Steven is driving, considering that his legs are paralyzed and he's wheelchair bound. His is still able to have his independence despite that, and I have to give credit to the man. Steven continues to drive closer to my driveway, and we both make eye contact. While they are both sitting inside of their vehicle, Steven looks at me and smiles, and so does Aaron. In the span of only a few seconds, I wave and direct my hands for Steven to park right in front of my garage door in my driveway. He pulls up, parks his car, and turns off the ignition. Immediately after that, Aaron gets out of the passenger side and grabs Steven's wheelchair from the rear area of their van. After Aaron gets Steven's wheelchair, Aaron turns his head to me.

"I don't mean to be rude, but don't just stand there, help me get him out please."

I smile for a bit, and then nod my head towards Aaron's remark. I walk over to the driver's side of the van, and help Aaron get Steven outside of the vehicle, and inside his chair. While we are doing this, in an angry and agitated way, Steven starts to express how he currently feels.

"I'm a grown man, and I feel like a little boy right now. I would like to have some of my independence, and to do things on my own. Which is why I choosing to drive. But meh."

Aaron and I, manage to successfully get Steven in his wheelchair, and for a few seconds, we all awkwardly stare at each other. Steven smiles at me, and sticks his hand out.

"Good to see you again. I'm sorry we are a little bit late. I had an important event at the school. A guest speaker came and was having a conference. Traffic is a bitch as well; roads are blocked. I looked it up online, the news says four guys robbed a bank, and the cops are chasing one of the guys right now. I also had to drive back home and pick Aaron up, luckily he took today off. I wasn't that lucky and had to work, but oh well. But we're here now."

I shake Stevens hand, and I also shake Aaron's hand right after. Aaron then talks to me.

"Thank you for inviting us to your home. I know that Steve at times can be a handful, but never mind how crazy we both are. But he's a great guy, and I love him and he loves me."

Aaron kisses Steven on his head, and Steven awkwardly smiles at him. We remain on my driveway for a short while, then Steven laughs and looks right at me; speaking in a sly way.

"We're the first ones to show up aren't we? I can tell by how you're acting, and because I don't see any other cars. I feel special that we came first, do we win a prize for that? Ha-ha."

I smile and nod my head at Steven. At this time, I tell them both to follow me inside. There is no need for us to stay outside. With Aaron's help, we both manage to get Steven's wheelchair over the threshold of my front door area. All three of us then walk inside of my living room. I was so delighted that the first guys have finally arrived, and I don't feel as nervous as I was previously. I still have to admit to the guys my true intentions, but I will have to cross that bridge when I get there of course.

When I see that Aaron is assisting Steven out of his wheelchair, so he can sit down on the sofa, I walk over to give a hand. After Steven is situated, I grab his wheelchair, and put it out of the way on the other side behind the sofa. I walk back over to where the other guys are, and sit down on my recliner. Aaron and Steven sit at the sofa across from me in silence for a short while, and I am unsure of what to exactly do. Aaron pulls out his phone and I don't know exactly what activity on it he's doing, as it's really none of my business. But Steven is looking down towards the ground with a cold look on his face. He then shakes his head, and makes eye contact with me. Steven then asks me a question.

"You said your name was Gary right? Well Gary, we're company and we're guests, and I uh, I don't know exactly why you invited us here, and I'm starting to second guess myself."

Steven takes one of the beers on the table in front the sofa, and cracks it open. Aaron who's continuing to do whatever he's doing on his phone, ignores him. I then start to put myself in Steven's shoes. I can understand and relate to why he feels confused, as this was a spur of the moment thing. The men did not have to agree to show up, but they decided to anyways. Fully understanding that all of this must be puzzling to them. Hell, it's puzzling to myself; I didn't even get to the scary part yet where I mention they are here to look at the session videos, and for me to also reveal I'm entering them all into a film festival, where millions of people possibly will watch and listen to the most delicate moments in their lives. I try my best to make Steven feel safe and secure with me. Using my best persuasive voice and tone, I respond to him.

"This is my way of thanking all of you for participating in my project. You guys can have a few drinks, meet each other, and kick back and have fun. I know you didn't have to agree to do it, and I also know that it took a considerable amount of time from your schedules as well."

Directly after me saying that, I don't receive any type of response, verbally or non-verbally from either man. I know that they understood what I said and were listening; they decided not to respond. Aaron puts his phone away in his tote bag, and rests his head down on Steven's shoulder. My biggest fear is that Steven is contemplating leaving. By looking at his facial expression and his eyes, he's not happy. Aaron also seems to be bored, and he's most likely going to do whatever Steven tells him to, and leave with him. The other men still have not arrived, and things are going roughly. Being that things are kind of tense right now, I go over to my "Amazon Alexa" device, and I ask it to play some smooth jazz music. I figure that would make the room a little happier.

This seems to work, as Steven starts to loosen himself up a little, and the both of us engage in small talk. I joke about him over several things, and we talk about current hot topics, events, and politics. The alcohol I believe is making him more calm I'm sure, so thankful and glad for that. Although Aaron remains quiet sitting next to Steven, occasionally sipping on his glass of wine, he politely and respectfully listens to us both. While Steven continues to ramble on trivial discussions, I decide to reach under the table and pull out a notebook. Steven continually talks, while I scribble down various words on the paper. Steven then takes another swallow from his beer, and gives me a puzzled expression.

"Is that your diary? Are you writing nasty and hurtful things about us? That's not nice."

While I'm still jotting and scribbling down notes, for a short second, I raise my eyes over at Steven and grin at him. As I'm continuing to write, I softly respond to Steven's concern.

"Relax, I'm not that kind of person to write things like that. These notes are mostly for myself and my own thoughts. You can read them if you like, it's nothing bad at all."

Steven takes another sip of his beer, and shoves Aaron, signaling for him to grab my notebook. Without any struggle or hesitation, I hand my notebook over to Aaron, and he then gives it to Steven to look at. Steven then skims and reads my notes and begins to laugh. He gives the notebook to Aaron, who then walks over and hands it right back to me. I jot down a few more words on my notebook, and I then close it, setting it beside the recliner. After adjusting my tie, I look over at Steven who's cleaning his glasses with his shirt. Perhaps this was out of instinct or some natural reaction, I then started to clean my glasses as well. This was so strange seeing him do that same action, it caused me to do it too. The three of us continue to sit in the living room for a couple more minutes.

Me being a psychologist, it's my job to listen and understand people, so it's impossible for me to ignore Steven's rambling and ranting. I take in every word, where I know damn well to other ordinary people, they would simply ignore every word he's saying. I don't work like that, and I have to listen to people. Whatever opinions someone may have, that isn't my job to dictate how they should think. So even though I do listen to people, I usually stay neutral and agree to agree. I don't even agree to disagree, because I feel they should believe what they believe, as everyone is different and they all come from different backgrounds and lifestyles.

During this particular time, I hear my doorbell ring. Steven stops talking, and I directly head over to the door to open it. Standing on the other side, are Jerald and Carl. Carl and I shake hands, but Jerald launches himself onto me and hugs me tightly, which I wasn't expecting at all. We then all head to over to the sofas. Aaron reaches his hand out for Jerald to shake it, but Jerald decides to hug him instead. Interestingly, I notice that Jerald walks up and hugs Steven as well, who Steven seems to be caught off guard from that. Carl however is more formal, and shakes both Aaron and Steven's hand. Carl grabs himself a beer, and takes a seat down on the sofa. Jerald takes a wine glass, and starts pour himself a glass of wine. As he is preparing his drink, in a comical and playful way, he starts to address all of us.

"I'm sorry you guys, I don't shake hands at parties I hug. I'm a touchy feely person. Oh my god, where are my manners? Everyone I'm Jerald, and this is my boyfriend Carl. I guess you guys were also a part of this too. It's nice to meet you both. So the other guys aren't here yet?"

Jerald takes a seat on another sofa where Carl is sitting by himself. Jerald then lays his head on Carl's shoulder. Carl starts to drink his beer, and he turns his head to speak to me.

"Sorry that we're kinda late. There were so many detours. The police have the roads all messed up. It's all because some guys robbed a bank and shit. If that's not aggravating enough, then we couldn't even find your place. Luckily, we were able to get here alright."

Steven shakes his head at Carl, and Steven continues to drink his beer. Because I study how people work; and yes I did brag about that again, and I'm going to continue to brag about it; Aaron, Carl and Jerald from how they were reacting, are totally unaware that Steven is feeling uncomfortable right now. Steven opens his mouth, and is about to say something directed towards the whole group, but he is interrupted when the doorbell rings in the same exact time. I get up and walk over to the door opening it.

Frank is standing on the other side, and my heart begins to beat rapidly. Feeling like it's going to break out of my chest, every time I look and see Frank, I get captivated by his presence. His cologne is also smelling nice, and the scent of his hair pomade is also nice. I have to keep reminding myself that he is taken, and I need to snap out of whatever infatuations I have of him. Frank and I shake hands, and he walks over to the center of the living room, and talks to the other guys.

"How are you guys doing? I'm Frank, it's nice to see you all."

He shakes all the other guy's hands, except for Jerald who decides to give him a hug. Frank then grabs himself a beer, and takes a seat on the empty recliner next to me. While he's taking several sips of his beer, he softly speaks to all of us.

"Sorry for being late, I had paperwork at the station to do. I'm a cop if you guys can't tell from my uniform. The roads are also hectic, but I managed to get here as quick as I could."

We all nod our heads at Frank, acknowledging his situation. The other guys don't feel as ashamed, knowing that they are possibly all tardy for the same exact reasons. Some of the guys engage and initiate in small meaningless banter, and they start to unwind with one another. With the jazz music continuing to play in the background, the current setting is now more calm. I'm still concerned over Steven, as judging from his body language, and the fake smirks and smiles he gives out, I know out of all the men, he's the most uncomfortable and anxious, and I feel that he possibly wishes he could leave. In order to move forward with the project, all ten men have to agree to it, and if Steven decides to opt out, that ruins my plan, and that's something I would not like to happen.

Shortly, the doorbell rings once again, and I walk towards the door. Troy and Harry have now arrived. I was amazed when I noticed that Harry brought a twenty-four pack case of beer, holding it tightly in his hands. My reaction upon seeing that was uncontrollable, and I couldn't help but laugh. I felt bad that my first reaction to seeing them was like that. I didn't ask the guys to "BYOB" or anything, so I don't understand why Harry felt compelled to bring that. But no matter, it's petty for me to complain and whine over something like that. Not that I was necessarily running out of beer, but due to the amount of guests, I assume it wouldn't hurt to have more supply.

I am able to finally compose myself from that, and be welcoming and cordial. Troy and I shake hands, and Troy immediately walks over to the sofa areas to meet the other men. Following that, I signal for Harry who's still carrying the case of beer to follow me to the kitchen. Once in the kitchen, I help Harry put the cans of beer in the refrigerator.

Before we walk back out into the living room. I tap Harry on the shoulder and quietly speak to him.

"I have plenty of drinks; you really didn't have to do all of that. Thank you though."

Harry looks at me, but due to his bushy mustache and his scruffy beard, I have to look at him deeply, to get a full expression from him. It takes me a while to realize that he's grinning at me. Harry taps me on the shoulder while he's still grinning through his beard, and he takes four cans of beer with him, as he walks out of my kitchen into the living room. I shake my head for a second, and join the rest of the men. Harry and Troy sit on the same sofa that Steven and Aaron are sitting on. Troy is being very sociable and expressing himself greatly, but Harry is extremely quiet, and has his arm wrapped around Troy's back on the sofa sipping on his beer.

Harry didn't even bother to introduce himself to the other guys, and I thought that was a little bit rude. I have to understand that's how Harry is, and I'm not going to nitpick over that with him. I look over at Steven and like Harry, he's also not opening up as much as the other guys are. Unlike Harry though, Steven is a little bit more sociable and occasionally would ramble and rant for a bit, but that's merely a façade he's portraying; generally, he still looks tense. With now only the final two guys waiting to arrive, I understand that the time to where I explain everything is happening very soon.

A couple more minutes pass, and the doorbell rings for one final time. I walk over to the door, and just as I suspected, Jamal and Ralph are now here. Jamal is helping guide Ralph who is blind, over to the sofa areas. Instead of immediately greeting them both, I let Jamal get Ralph situated. Ralph doesn't always use a cane, but Jamal is able to assist him. The rest of the men all become quiet, starting at Jamal and Ralph as they both come closer to them. After they take a seat next to the sofa Carl and Jerald are sitting on, Jamal removes Ralph's sunglasses, which Ralph then looks around the room, using his other senses to observe his surroundings. Jamal then looks at the rest of the guys and speaks.

"Sorry for being late. We tried to get here as quick as possible, but traffic is terrible."

I nod my head at him, and walk over to shake Jamal and Ralph's hand, introducing myself in the process. The rest of the men remain quiet at their arrival, and the room is now in complete silence. Just then, without wanting to waste any more time, I figure I now have to explain this whole event to them in greater detail. Although this is a party, we are all here for more important matters and reasons. This is where I have to explain all the details of the project I didn't mention before to them. Now being that the men are all here, it may seem like I'm rushing them along, but I need to act right now, and I have to be strict as well. I can't wait any longer. As I'm starting to get my thoughts in order, I get myself ready to speak to all the men. I stand in the center of the living room, facing the other nine guys, and begin to address all the men promptly.

"I'm sure you guys are all aware as to why you are here. I called you earlier this week and invited you all. All nine of you were involved in my project to where I wanted to bring all different types of gay and bisexual men together, to find out more about their personal lives and stories. But there is something I wasn't sincere with you all about, and I need to be honest."

All of the men instantly have concerned looks on their faces, and I am rushed with feelings of anxiety. It is important for me to carry on, and I can't keep this secret from them any longer. I decide to bide a little more time, and think of a way to calm them down a bit.

"Why don't we all introduce ourselves officially before I get to that. I want you all to say your name, what you do for a living, and your color that you had during the sessions. You guys probably didn't know that I have a color myself. I was white. My name is of course Gary, or you guys can call me Gary, Dr. Gary, or 'Gee', I don't care what you call me. I'm a licensed psychologist for the state of California. So now, why don't you guys introduce yourselves."

The men all remained quiet for nearly a minute, and I began to wonder why they were so hesitant. I figured they knew I was stalling them perhaps. For a minute, I was worried that this tactic wasn't going to work, and the men were going to see right through it. After all, I am still going to have to eventually come clean to all of them. Eventually, things started to work in my favor, and Aaron was the first man to speak. He stood up from his seat, and walked over by where I was standing, and introduced himself.

"Hey guys, my name is Aaron. My color was pink. I'm a registered nurse, and sometimes I work in the 'E.R.', so it can get hectic sometimes. It's great to meet you. That guy over there is my lovely husband Steven. He isn't as cheerful as me, but he's still a great guy. Well, it's lovely to have met all of you, and I'm ready to party and have a good time I guess."

Aaron then walks over to where he was sitting, and whispers something to Steven. Steven looks as if he's embarrassed, and he's looking down to the ground, while Aaron whispers to him. I look at them both confused, but Steven later nods his head. Aaron walks over back to me, and whispers in my ear. He explains that he wants my help to lift Steven up, so he can stand. I agree, and walk over to where Steven is sitting, and I offer my help. Steven with the guidance of myself and Aaron is now standing upright, and he introduces himself to all the guys.

"My name is Steven, as you can see I can't walk. I'd rather not go into full details. I'm confined to my wheelchair, but I'm just like the rest of you. I have no feeling in my legs, but I can stand too. I'm a University Professor. I've already introduced myself to some of you, but my name is Steven, and my color was red. That's all I have to say, and pleasure meeting all of you."

Immediately following that, Troy and Harry stand up, and Troy introduces himself.

"Hello, I'm Troy, and this is my boyfriend Harry. He doesn't like to talk, and he's shy, but he's nice. I work at a department store, and I enjoy my work quite a lot. I see a lot of different guys here at this party, and I can't wait to get to know you all more. My color was yellow I believe, and that's it. I'm now going to let Harry talk now if he wants to."

Troy pinches Harry on the arm, and Harry very quietly and reluctantly speaks to the men.

"I'm Harry, and uh…, well, Troy is my partner. I'm kinda over protective over him. He's the smallest here, so be nice to him, okay guys? I work at a grocery store, and I'm a butcher, and I know all about meat, so ask me. I also work at my brothers restaurant. My color was Orange. So that's all I have to say, it's nice to meet all you guys, and, uh… yeah. Alright then."

Carl and Jerald then stand up to introduce themselves. Jerald speaks to all the men first.

"What's up you guys, my name is Jerald. My color was brown, and I'm fierce, and I'm a diva, and I'm fabulous. This guy right here is my crazy boyfriend Carl. I know I may seem over the top extra, but I'm not. I work as a freelance fashion designer, and I knit and crochet too. I'm happy to meet all of you, and I'm glad to be here, you are all lovely people by the way."

Carl then calmly speaks to the other men.

"Okay, uh…, my name is Carl. I'm not crazy, I don't know why he said that I was. He is the crazy one not me. I'm autistic, but I'm just like everyone else. I don't let that bother me. I like art and drawing a lot, that's my job. I'm an artist, and a damn good one too. My color was purple, and I'm happy to meet all of you, and I'm happy to be here."

Jamal and Ralph then directly stood up after that, and Jamal began to introduce himself.

"Hey everyone, my name is Jamal. I like to write and research different things. I studied journalism. My color was green. This man is Ralph, and he's a good close friend of mine. I know he's older than me, but that doesn't matter. It's nice to meet you all, and I look forward to talking with all of you and getting to know you better. Okay, that's all."

Ralph right after that, started to speak to men by introducing himself.

"My name is Ralph, I'm a businessman, and its pleasure meeting you. I am blind, I wasn't born blind, I don't want to talk about it. I can't see anything with my eyes, but I have other senses. I still try to adapt my life around being blind. I don't have my vision anymore sadly, but I'm still here. Jamal helps me, and I love him. My color was black."

Jamal and Ralph then take a seat back on the sofa, and I look at Frank who's the final man to introduce himself. I start to wonder whether or not Frank will reveal he's transgender to the other men or not. I know like myself, they possibly have no idea he is. Frank gets up from his chair, and stands in front of all the men. He then introduces himself to us all.

"Alright, I guess you saved the best for last. My name is Frank. I'm a patrol officer for the 'LAPD'. My color was coincidentally blue which is nice. There is something I want you all to know, I am transgender. I was born female, but I've lived as a man for the majority of my life. You guys can ask any questions you want. I know this is shocking and I pass well, it's okay. It's nice to meet you all."

Frank walks back to his seat, and I see many shocked looks. I then speak to the men.

"Okay, now that we all have introduced ourselves, and we all know each other. Let me explain a few things. As you all know, you were all involved with my project, which is called 'Profiles of Hope'. You are all gay or bisexual men, that I felt had an interesting story to tell, and I wanted to document all of that, towards my career as a psychologist. However,."

All of the men are attentive towards everything I'm saying. This is it, this is the time to where I have to be truthful with all of them. I have to accept whatever reaction or response they give, and understand that as well. I can no longer keep this information a secret.

"I haven't been entirely truthful with you all. I mentioned in the sessions, that nobody but myself would know about the sessions. I lied. The reason I called all of you to my home, is not only to hold a party, but I now plan on revealing the session tapes for all of you to see."

Some of the reactions from the men are reasonably negative. They don't respond or say anything, but their facial expressions explain enough. All of their actions speak louder than any words they can say, and I completely understand their plight and how they feel. Despite the fact the men are still taking in what I revealed so far, I'm not finished explaining myself to them.

"I edited all the sessions you guys were in, which were quite lengthy. They were a span of over the course of several hours, and I edited it them down so they aren't as long. I want us all to sit here and watch the sessions together, and reflect on them, knowing each other's stories."

The mood the entire room was in was silent. I carried on describing more of the project.

"To make it fair, I decided to reveal my own personal story. All of us in this room have a separate color, including myself. I'm white. In the order I interviewed you all, with me going first, I will show you all the session tapes tonight. Not only that, I plan to submit all your session tapes to a film festival that's coming up should you all agree to this. I want you..."

I couldn't even finish speaking, before Steven threw a tantrum and had an outburst.

"No, no, no. We signed a contract saying that you couldn't do that. Aaron let's go, now! I'm not about to hear any of this sick shit. I don't care what the fuck the rest of you guys do, but I'm not sitting for any of this. Those sessions were supposed to be private, you lied to us."

Aaron gets up from the sofa and walks over to the back of the sofa to get Steven's wheelchair. Aaron then pushes it over to the sofas. The other seven men sitting in the area, are stunned and silent, and not reacting to the current situation. While Aaron is setting up Steven's wheelchair, I notice that Steven is looking down on the ground, beginning to cry. Aaron walks over to the sofa, and starts to comfort Steven. I walk over to them, and softly speak to them both.

"If you guys want to leave you can. I wanted to say that I tried my best to edit all of the sessions accurately, and I left out anything personal if that makes you feel any better. The decision and choice is yours to leave. I thought this would be a good idea, but clearly it's not. I'm sorry if I humiliated you, and if you felt uncomfortable. You guys can go home if you like."

Right at this moment, shockingly, Harry decides to stand up, walk over to Steven who's now crying heavily with a concerned look on his face. I find it fascinating that Harry is walking over to Steven. Harry kneels down on the floor in front of the sofa where Steven is sitting, and takes off Steven's glasses, setting them on the table, and whispers to him.

"I'm embarrassed to be here too man. But I want to hear your story. Troy, that little punk, got me into this mess as well, and I don't like dealing with people. I didn't want to come here, but I did. Hey, what I do is I use a fifteen-minute rule. If after fifteen minutes I still don't feel happy, then I remove myself. So man, not wait fifteen minutes and see what happens?"

I saw Steven wipe tears from his face, looking at Harry angrily. He then spoke to Harry.

"Who the fuck are you? Moses? I said I'm leaving, and that's my decision. I'm not at all comfortable showing what I said in those tapes to a bunch of guys I don't fucking know."

Aaron starts to rub Steven's head, and I noticed he began to side with Harry's plan.

"Steve, let's just stay for a little while longer. Let's see what happens. I know you don't want people finding out about what happened, but think of this way. Our story is special, like every other guy here has a special story as well. Stay for me, please? What do you say?"

Steven shakes his head, and grabs his glasses that were on the table, putting them back on. Aaron then smiles at Steven, rubbing Steven's face, and Steven smiles back at him. At this time, I saw Frank stand up, and walk over to where Steven was sitting, and rests his hand on the back of his shoulder. Frank then tried to comfort Steven. He leans into his ear, and whispers to him.

"I understand how you feel man, but if we can do it, you can. I don't know what you're trying to hide, but if I revealed a very private aspect of me, you can do the same. We all have a story, and don't feel ashamed. I can't imagine what it's like not being able to walk, but I do know that me, and every other man in this room has been through hell. We have to do this."

I hand Steven some tissues so he can wipe his face. Steven then gives his choice.

"Only because the roads are blocked, and it's going to take us forever to get back home, I'll stay. I'm going to regret this I know. I'm deciding to stay and watch the tapes with you all."

Along with myself, Aaron, Harry and Frank all smile at Steven, and they all return back to their seats. I'm glad that Steven did decide to change his mind, and is going ahead with the project. It wouldn't be the same without him, and I want the other guys to be introduced to his story, as it made a great impact on me, I am certain that the other men will have an emotional impact towards it as well. I'm assuming the men are in mutual agreement to continue with the project. To make sure, I personally ask all the men if they are comfortable with preceding. They all confirm that they are, and I carry on with getting every situated and planned accordingly.

"For now, I'm only going to show you the session tapes. After we finishing watching them all, I will then give you guys a consent form, which will grant me position to enter the tapes into the film festival. You do not have to sign it if you don't want to. If you don't sign it, nobody other than the men in this room will see your tape, and it's alright. Does everyone understand?"

The men all nod their heads to agree with me, and I continue to explain more to them.

"As I said, the session tapes have been edited down. There are ten tapes in total, so I'm going to try to get through them all quickly. I ask that you please not get up unless it's an emergency during the tapes. Once each tape is done, you all can take bathroom breaks, or smoke breaks, and then I will start the next tape. I ask that you all please not laugh out loud or heckle or offer any rude commentary while the tapes are playing. Please be respectful."

I grab my laptop, and begin to hook it up to the big screen television set in the living room. I sit down on the recliner, trying to wirelessly feed my computer screen to the television, so all the files are connected. As I'm getting all the video files ready to be shown on the screen, I'm having slight difficulties. Usually I'm quite skilled with computers, and this shouldn't be complicated for me, but I'm having issues currently. While I'm doing this, I start to wonder if there is anything else I forgot to mention to the men, before I start the session tapes. I can't think of anything, so I try to be clever, and ask the men if there is anything that they need right now.

"Uh, if you guys have any question at this time, you can ask them, I'll answer them."

The guys are quiet for a few seconds, but Steven then asks a question directed to me.

"Is it okay if I can go out and have a smoke? I don't know if anybody else smokes and wants to join me. Harry? Did I get your name right? He looks like he's a smoker. Anyways, I need a cigarette, right now. So If it's okay, can I excuse myself outside to smoke."

Even though I don't care for cigarette smoking, it's something that bothers me to an extent. I understand that Steven is under much stress, and I would prefer for him to wait until later to have a cigarette break; as I would like to get all of these session tapes out as quickly as possible. I'm going to allow him to step outside and smoke, if that will make him calm down. That, and also because for some reason, my computer is not agreeing with me right now, so this is the perfect time for them to take an unprecedented break, while I get everything together.

"Steven, of course you can step out to smoke. Anybody else that wants to can, I'm still trying to get this prepared. I'm having slight technical difficulties anyways, so you all can go have a quick break. But only for a few minutes, because I don't have much time left."

Aaron and Harry help Steven into his wheelchair, and virtually he and every other guy with the exception of Frank and myself who don't smoke cigarettes, stay inside the building. As the guys are preparing to leave, I explain to them my backyard is more intimate.

"Hey, you guys can smoke back here, you don't have to you out to my front porch. It's more quiet back here, and nobody will bother you guys. Open that patio door, right out there."

While the other guys are in my backyard taking a cigarette break, as I'm still tinkering with my computer with my vision directed at that. I then smell Frank's cologne as he creeps close by me. I look up at him, and he smiles at me. I smile back at him, and Frank quietly speaks to me.

"It's all going to work out fine, don't you worry. I think you should have planned this a little better, and you should have told us before we came here you were intending to do all that. Steven's reaction is natural, I don't know that man from Adam, but you have to understand him."

I finally manage to get all the files situated, and everything is properly connected to the television set. I rest my laptop down under the television, and I look at Frank, responding to him.

"I know, but if I told them that nobody would have shown up. I had to keep it a secret. Either way, whatever choice I made would have been tough. If I kept it secret, then people are going to be mad at me because I lied. If I told the truth, none of the guys would have shown up, and thought I was a lunatic. So you cannot win with these type of cases. I did what I felt was the right thing I suppose."

Frank smiles at me. I can't help but feel enthralled by his fragrance. I talk to him about it.

"You smell very nice, I don't know what cologne that is, but I love it. What kind is it?"

Frank continues to smile at me, and laughs. He then softly answers my question.

"Oh I can't tell you, it's a secret brand. But yes it does smell manly and I like it."

Frank then kisses me on the forehead, and walks to the counter and grabs a beer. He opens it and takes several gulps of it. I can hear audible sounds of laughter from the other guys in the backyard, smoking their cigarettes. Frank returns to the sofa and pulls out his phone, drinking his beer, while he's watching a YouTube video. I decide to give the men five more minutes on their break, but then I have to carry on as I do not have much time. I sit in silence, still listening to the audible ambient sounds of the rest of the men goofing off outside. As much as I'm happy they are getting along, at this time, I do have to proceed and carry on, being pressed for time. When their break is over, I walk over to the window of my patio area, staring at the men. I watch them for a few seconds, and they do not even notice my figure or presence peering right at them. I then decide to knock on the glass to get their attention. The men who are too involved with bonding which each other, ignore my knocking. Being slightly annoyed and pestered over this, I continue to knock on the glass, this time louder. Jerald notices me, handing Carl the cigarette he was smoking, and opens the door. I then speak to all the men, which I now have their attention.

"Alright guys, I hope you had a nice break, but it's time to head back inside, I said you guys can take a quick break, and that's exactly what I meant. I need for you all to come back."

Once all the men are back inside of the living room, with the short amount of time I have left to explain everything, I try my best to relay the entire situation and format to the guys.

"This is the order I will be showing the session tapes. The same order that I interviewed you all. I will go first, then the rest will follow in this order. Starting with Troy, they Harry, then Aaron, Steven will follow after that, then Jerald, then Carl, followed by Jamal, then Ralph, and Frank will be last. After every tape, I will give you all a small break, but then immediately we will continue. After all the tapes are done, then we will talk about everything after that."

The men are compliant with what I say, and it seems things are set. I continue to speak.

"I know you guys have all brought a change of clothes, as I did invite you guys to sleep over, as I can tell we are going to be here late into the night watching these stories."

I pick up a bottle of wine, and I pour myself a glass. I speak one final time to the men.

"From this point forward, I ask that you all please be respectful. Please understand that we are all gay and bisexual men yes, but we all come from different backgrounds and lifestyles. The stories you are going to witness; I can't promise that you guys won't feel negatively affected by. I ask that you please be respectful and not have any outbursts please. Thank you."

After they all nod their heads in agreement, I take a swallow of my wine. This is it, the project will now officially begin. I will show and tell the men my story first. I would like to take this time to explain that each story will be told in the perspective and point of view of that man. In the same exact perspective as he was during the sessions. I have edited the sessions down, but I made sure I left any important details together. With my own particular story, I will of course be offering my own personal point of view. The other nine stories will again be told in the same perspective as the other men portray it.

After I tell my story, I will then return at a much later time, after all the men have told their own stories. I will be back to explain how all the men felt about hearing their stories, and if the men will agree to enter the film festival or not. As I'm clicking the files on my computer, in which the feed is being directly shown to the television, I start to not only feel anxious but nervous and excited as well. I'm about to tell nine other men whom I don't know, and have only met for a couple weeks, some of the most deepest and darkest events that have happened in my life. If that isn't enough, I'm also going to relive everything they told me as well, yet this time, these men are explaining their lives more openly for others to know about.

By the time this entire night is over, these men myself included, will hold a special place in their memory to take in this whole project and event. Starting with me being "Man of White", Troy being "Man of Yellow, Harry being "Man of Orange", Aaron being "Man of Pink", Steven being "Man of Red", Jerald being "Man of Brown", Carl being "Man of Purple", Jamal being man of "Green", Ralph being "Man of Black", and Frank being "Man of Blue".

All ten of us have a story to tell, and it's now finally time to hear about these stories. Again, with myself included going first with my story, these men will each have their own separate point of view with how they express themselves with their stories. These sessions will be in their own words, and not mine. I simply edited them for time, and to leave all the important details.

I sit on my recliner, and with I have my view towards my laptop, putting the final strings in order for the sessions to play. I click open my own video file, intentionally pausing it, after the first few seconds started to play. While the video clip is paused, I set a playlist for the videos to automatically start once the session has finished. Before I hit play on my video, as I'm first to tell my story, I feel like the world has stopped. I will not make this a habit anymore, and this is something that I will not do for the duration of this project, but I look at the other nine men that are currently sitting in my living room. Wondering what they all think, and what they will think of me as they are watching certain details, and finding out more parts of my life.

When I was by myself in my bedroom, and recorded this session earlier, it never occurred to me that other people would be watching it. Like I'm sure it didn't occur to the other men that other people will be watching their sessions as well. This was something that when I was thinking it all through, it seemed like a fun an interesting idea, but once I'm now within seconds of starting my video session, and as the hours and night progresses, the other men's video sessions will show as well, my attitude has completely changed, and I can't get my mind together that this is happening.

I take several deep breaths, and calm myself down before I hit the play button. Knowing that once I click that button, there is no going back, my session, and the other nine sessions will be played. This is not the time for me to doubt myself, and I have to be strong and continue on as planned. Whatever happens at this point, is what happens. I must understand that this was my idea, and this is something that I have to do. I need to set an example to the other men, and I have to be professional.

My goal to enter these sessions into the film festival remains, as I believe this could be a ground breaking project that could be detrimental on how gay and bisexual men deal with hardships they are faced in their world. As much as I understand that these stories are brutal, and they are very impactful, it is important for people to be aware of them. I interviewed all of these men that are sitting in my living room, but they were more than simply interviews. From the time

I was able to spend with each of them, recording all the material to put together for these sessions, I was involved with their lives, and got to know a special unique part of them. I respect their courage, that they have in their lives. With the success of this project, who knows, I may perhaps decide to do it again with a new group of people. My career as a psychologist has never been put to this level, and I decided to take advantage of that. I study people for a living, and I want to use my studies to develop projects that have never been done before.

While I'm continuing to look at my laptop, I take a sip of my wine, and I set the wine glass down on the table. It is now time, and I click the play button to start to playlist of the session videos, starting with mine. I close my laptop, and close my eyes tightly. I take another swallow of my wine with my eyes still closed. My heart is starting to beat faster and faster, and I don't know if I can't take this pressure. I turn my view towards the television set, and I see my face, as I begin to talk. The project is now on, and has begun.

While I'm taking another sip of my wine, and not even ten seconds into my session, I'm already starting to choke up, and feel that my body is melting, and I cannot move. I then realize that I'm not the only one involved with this project, nine other men are, and they are feeling just as anxious as I am. I sit myself up in my seat as I listen to my session video.

CHAPTER 2:

MAN OF WHITE (PART 1)

My name is Gary Swanson, and I am the "Man of White". My reddit username is, "DrGareBear". I am 30 years young. As far as my appearance, I'm rather slim and thin. I guess you can refer to me as a geek if you want. I do work out and keep active, but I have a stickly figure to myself, and it's something I take with great pride. If I don't love myself, and if I don't appreciate my body, who will?

I come from a very strict Greek family, and also come from a strict Mormon family. We value and treasure the family very much, so my culture is a big deal due to that. Food was also a major part of our family culture. Both my mother and grandmother would make very interesting dishes. We vaguely ate out. The only thing that would come close to "eating out", is sometimes after church on Sunday, we would visit immediate and extended families at their homes, and have a potluck, or help ourselves to whatever they made. I live in Los Angeles, California, by myself in my lovely home. I am a licensed psychologist, and I also dabble with real estate on the side. I keep to myself usually, and I study people. Hell, my job involves studying people, so even when I'm not working, that's what I do. I wear glasses, and I'm a very nerdy guy. I already told you this shit earlier, I know. But I'm going to tell you again. I am the moderator of this whole project. I guess I'm going to be the first to share my story. I should first begin very swiftly with my childhood, my sexuality, my University life, and my religion.

I knew I was gay ever since I was 9 years old. Before then, I didn't even know what gay or straight or whatever was. I didn't really have an attraction to anyone. However it was in fact when I was nine years old, that I came out to myself as gay. Although, not fully understanding or receiving the repercussions of being a homosexual. Despite the fact I was Mormon. Unfortunately, or fortunately, that's more of an added bonus. As even youth who are not Mormon and deal with sexuality issues, have it rough.

I remember the first instance of knowing I was gay, was going to church one Sunday. One of the youth High School pastors, Pastor Marcus, who was seventeen, was such a handsome man. He had such a perfectly buzzed hair cut style, and had a rocker style to him as well. He looked just like Adam Levine. Oh my god, he was that beautiful. Incidentally, he was also the church musician. He played guitar, and had an immaculate singing voice. His voice was so beautiful, that he could tame dragons, gargoyles and dinosaurs. The music he performed although was religious, he still put a contemporary and non-religious secular spin to it.

Sadly at that young of an age, it was tough having an attraction to a much older man, but a positive thing about it, was that I had no idea what relationships and attraction were at that time. But oh yes lord, I remember I would go home and dream about this man all the time. Life is very strange though, and certain things, certain unfortunate things rather, sometimes happen. Pastor Marcus was killed in an automobile collision. He died so young, and it was such a shame. I remember I would look forward to going to Sunday school every week just for him. Hearing his lovely magical voice.

Every time he would strum his guitar, and I would glance at him. That's life I suppose, and life is very much unfair at times I guess. After Pastor Marcus passed, I stopped worrying and concerning myself with romance. I mostly kept to my studies. Both in education and theology. I learned a hard lesson with Pastor Marcus, that you really should cherish life, and cherish the thoughts that you have, because you never know what might happen. I became so reclusive, and didn't want to socialize myself with anyone at all. Becoming very bitter, was a method of me coping with the trauma of losing Pastor Marcus, and understanding that I'm never going to see him again. But life must go on.

I kept closeted in school. I can count the number of times on my left hand, and still have many fingers left over, from the amount of homophobic experiences I have had young. I maybe had one, if that, to where I was called "faggot", buy some ignorant bully at school. But this technically wasn't because of me being perceived as homosexual, but rather the fact that I came to school with my hair combed, my clothes neatly pressed and ironed, and I guess "faggot", was a way of him saying that I'm too proper and strange than the rest of the boys in the school who would come to school not concerned at all about their appearance.

Everything I said before was true, but for the most part, just ignore all of that. I was actually brought up as a Mormon, and a rather strict one at that. My past is very complicated, but I need to explain everything in detail. Even though I did appreciate some of the Mormon values, I am happy that I am no longer associated with that organization. Despite my infatuation with Pastor Marcus, most of my life before I turned 12 is really a blur. I kept to myself usually, and I very seldom got into trouble. This was mainly in part due to my Mormon teachings. I went to a special private school, whereas my peers went to public school. So that had a lot to do with why I did not experience many things that kids that went to inner city schools, got to see and immerse themselves with.

However, I am grateful that I was put into private school. As it made me a more disciplined person. Later in my life when I did study secondary education in University, I was exposed to more cultures, and people, and events that I never was approached with before. Which is what this part of my story is mostly going to consist of. My first semester at Mormon University. A time I would never forget, which is full of multiple emotions and situations. I should forewarn that the school I went to, was a Mormon college, so although it wasn't technically an escape, it was the next big thing. As there were many parties that were happening. I myself have experimented with drugs, and at the college age, it's only natural for us as young adults to behave in this manner. Although we knew when to put on our stone and poker faces. When it came time for class, and dealing with elders and teachers, we immediately code switched into our Mormon teachings.

I really wish I could go more into detail about my experiment phase, but I'll just keep it to the most pertinent parts. I've made lots of friends during this period of my life. All of this nostalgia is really giving me goosebumps. All the happy times, all the fun times, and sadly all of the violating and haunting times as well. These things have to be mentioned, although I really do not want to bring them up again. It's only fair that I do, as the other nine guys each have a level pegged experience to bring up.

So, I'm not going to list every single thing that happened, but I will try to sum everything up, so that it's told in a way that conveys the message I'm trying to put out. On my first day of school, I went into Mormon University, thinking it was going to be similar and identical to when I went to primary school, and High School. Which as I have said previously, I was very strict during this time. This was not the case, as going into University, everything that was in my mind before, didn't matter at all.

The school was about 2 hours and a half away from my home in Salt Lake. It was in a very rural area. Well no, I'm lying. It wasn't that damn rural. There were fast food restaurants, and dive bars, and thrift stores. An outlet mall was about 20 minutes away too. Inside the outlet mall, there was a movie theatre, which mind you, did not play any recent movies. I'm talking about movies that came out decades ago. But you know, it gave us something to do outside of class. Because the school was so far away, and in the boonies pretty much, I decided that I should get my own car to drive to the school. This is good if I wanted to come back home for the holidays, or drive to the few amenities that were in the immediate area of the school. I had bought, a used Honda Civic that I bought from a guy off craigslist. My parents helped pay for half of the car, and I had to use the little money I had saved to cover the rest of the cost.

Now that my transportation is taken care of, I had to pack my things for school. Even though we were required to wear a shirt and tie to class, once school is dismissed, and during the weekends, we have a free dress code. We are allowed to wear whatever we want. At this time, I wasn't up to date with the latest fashions, so most of my wardrobe wasn't up to par. To say I dressed like an old man that was three times my age, is an understatement. I would take use of the clothing stores that were in the area of the school later to update my fashions. For now, I just had to pack the bland and boring clothes I have. Now that my suitcase was packed, and I had a car to get me to campus, I was all set. I did have to make sure I had my bible, and other miscellany things, but I was prepared. For the next several years, I was going to be on my own, and being taught Mormon values in a University setting.

I distinctly remember the butterflies in my stomach the night before I left home. It was so terrible, I couldn't even sleep. I was that excited, I didn't sleep a wink. Going onto University, is a major step for many young people, but I was ready to take on this milestone. Despite being slightly fatigued from lack of sleep, I put all my belongings in my car, and drove off. I was in such a hurry, that I didn't even tell my parents goodbye.

My relationship with my parents is strange anyways, but I still regret not telling them goodbye leaving for my first day. In hindsight, it's a petty thing to fret about. I was most definitely going to see them again, but still. On my way to campus, I remember it started to rain. Rain is supposed to be a sign of a new beginning, well at least to me. If you disagree that's fine, but that's just my own sentiments. The closer I am, the more my stomach rumbles, and the more I feel a nervous, yet excited feeling.

I was feeling nervous, because in the past, and especially during my High School years, I was extremely introverted. I didn't have any friends at all. So part of me was scared that this was going to be a repeat, or a sequel to that. Understanding how harsh and cruel my experience in school was when I was younger, I kept feeling scared that I everything was going to come full circle, and just the thought of that would make me extremely nervous and agitated. However, I was feeling excited, because this could be a way for me to start fresh. I could lie and create a false sense of identity of myself. "Fake it until you make it", is what they say right? Nevertheless, this is going to be my life for the next several years, so whatever I decide to do, I must be sensible about it. Very soon, I will have to engage with the other students and staff at the school, so I'm going to have to make a choice at that particular time.

When I finally reached the campus I was shocked at how large it actually was. It was a 200 acre rural campus, and there were many buildings connected to it. I was suspecting a more smaller campus, however this was not the case at all. There was a campus tour that I could have attended, but I assumed the campus wasn't going to be as large as it was. Therefore, I decided not to attend the tour. I deeply regretted that, as I knew I was for sure going to get lost several times, due to the size of the campus. I notice many other students queuing up at the admissions and attendance line.

Likewise, I walk over to the attendance line. Already, I started to self-doubt myself on my clothes. All the other students are dressed very snappy and trendy, and I'm dressed like I'm attending a funeral. This was something I knew I needed to update myself on; my wardrobe and my fashion if I wanted to attempt to fit in with my peers at campus.

As I'm standing in line, I'm captivated by another man that I see in an adjacent line. This man wasn't conventional looking, no. He didn't have muscles, he wasn't even thin, he was actually kinda obese. He had wavy blond hair, and a doughboy stature to him. I don't know why I liked him. Realistically, he wasn't a prize, but damn all of that. Forgive me lord, but this guy looked like a younger Donald Trump. Ha-ha. I just kept my attention to him. Unlike the other students, he was also dressing out of date, likewise with myself.

He was reading his bible, and keeping his attention solely on that. I remember the first time I looked at him, I knew this guy would have an extreme hold and impact on me. My goodness, it was just like the situation with Pastor Marcus. As I move closer and closer in the line, I just cannot for the life of me, stop staring at this man. I'm not going to lie, it was an instant crush. I'm not good at explaining romantic thoughts, but this guy had my vision locked directly on him, and only him. I had to know what this guy's name was. But then the other side of me was holding myself back. These thoughts were telling me to leave this man alone, and let him go on about his business. You never talked to people in public before Gary, so why do it now?

That's really having a defeatist attitude though. The absolute worst that can happen, is that he tells me to fuck off, and crawl away. To be honest, this was what I was most afraid of. The rejection. I would rather keep to myself, than embarrass myself with the rejection I might receive. However, rejection or not, if I don't act out I will never know what the outcome will be. I don't know if I'm ever going to see this guy again. This just so happens to be a situation and moment to where I'm in his vicinity. It isn't for certain that I will share classes with him, or see him in the halls, so if I am really feeling this way about this guy, I must act now. Continuing to stare at the man, with me approaching the end of the line very closely, I then did something completely out of character. I started to speak towards his direction.

"Hi, my name is Gary Swanson. Have we met before? I have this strange feeling that we have met before. I'm from Salt Lake, so maybe I've seen you around there?"

The man then looked up from his bible, and gave me the most warming smile. He then shook his head, and went back to reading his bible. The 'have we met before' line, I feel is very risky. Sometimes it works, sometimes it doesn't. I knew damn well, and he knew damn well the both of us haven't met before. But I decided to give it a try anyways. Feeling slightly disappointed that my charm didn't seem to work, I began to take my mind elsewhere.

At least I gave it an attempt right? It didn't work out, but I still felt very shitty about the whole thing. The infatuation would not go away though. I still wanted to get to know this man more, but he doesn't seem that interested in me. I should probably learn to take a hint, and go on with my life. But I didn't want to take a hint. I have had it up to here, and I'm tired of being perfect. I'm tired of doing everything right. Although it may have been childish, I decided to continue to bother this man.

"Again, my name is Gary. I don't have many friends, and you seem like a really cool guy. I could have sworn I have met you sometime before. I guess not. But let's be friends."

This time the man closes his bible, and gives me the same smile he gave before. I also feel warm and safe by his smile, just like the first time he did it. He then responded to me, although in a very depressive and lethargic tone..

"Sorry, I don't talk to people. I have severe anxiety, and nobody has ever come up and talked to me before ever in my life. You're the first person to actually speak to me. But I'm sorry, I appreciate your kindness, but you don't want to be friends with me. It's not you, it's me."

Although I was slightly confused and upset, after a few seconds, I then started to feel empathetic towards him. I understand completely why people may have neglected to talk to him. Maybe it was because he's a bigger guy, or he seems weird. I was a more thin geeky guy that people seemed to also ignore. I figured because of that, we could relate to each other. This man however didn't want to be talked to, and even though I did want to get to know him more, I have to respect his boundaries. This time for sure, I went on about my business. With the thoughts of him still running in my mind, I decided to leave him alone. But a few minutes later, I felt someone tapping my shoulder. Before I could turn my head to see who it was, I hear a voice.

"I'm sorry, that was very rude. I didn't mean to say that. I just have really bad anxiety, and, I don't know, just forget that. My name is Connor. I would love to be your friend Gary. Maybe we can room together? It's my way of making up for acting that way towards you."

His full name was Connor Rollings. He was the same age as I was at the time. He was eighteen as well. Connor was actually not from Salt Lake, he was from Provo. He lived with his parents, and he has no siblings. Also growing up in a strict family, Connor was raised very well, and he rarely got into trouble or misbehaved in his youth. Connor sadly does bout with his anxiety, and he has become mute at times as a result of that. At the time, I had no idea that Connor was bisexual, but he was. At that time, I just wanted to be his friend, and take it from there. This was the start of my adventure with Connor. An adventure which is full of many ups and downs. Connor and I did eventually end up as roommates in our dorm. As we were getting our admissions in order, we talked with the staff at the school to see if it was possible for us to room together. They said it was, and I was most pleased. As the both of us were walking to our dorm, I started to speak to him more.

"Connor, if you don't mind me asking, what are you studying?"

Connor as he's looking down at the ground, very nervously responds to me.

"I'm studying architecture, and I'm also going to dabble onto engineering. I am really fascinated by structures and things of that sort. What are you studying Gary?"

As Connor and I both walk to our dorm, I truthfully respond to him.

"I'm studying sociology and psychology. I want to become a psychologist. I feel that's my calling, and it's what I want to do. I people watch a lot, so it makes sense. It wasn't my first choice, but it's the choice I'm sticking with now."

While we were continuing to walk to the dorm, I ended up dropping some folders I was carrying due to feeling nervous. Connor then picks up the things I dropped, and smiles at me. As he's picking the items up, he asks a question.

"Do you want to become an elder? I figured I might as well study for that too. I love spreading the faith onto others, and healing and all the devotion work. What about you?

Connor hands the items to me, and I then start to respond to what he asked of me.

"Well no, I have no intentions of being an elder. In fact, most of the Mormon faith I don't agree with. I mean, I'm happy for my culture and the faith my family represents. However, that's not my life, and it's not necessarily my vision. But as much as I respect being Mormon, I do not at all want to be an elder. It's something I'm fairly certain about. Well, I may change my mind."

Connor surprisingly didn't seem offended by my response. If anything, he was relieved, or happy that I gave an answer he may have not expected out of me.

"If we all did the same thing, this world would be boring right? I respect your decision to not be an elder, and I also appreciate that you question your faith. I don't judge. As long as you treat other people with respect, I couldn't care less about what you do with your life Gary."

We smile at each other, and continue to walk. When we finally reach our dorm, I notice that the dorm room consists of a bunk bed, instead of two smaller beds situated across from each other in the room. As I'm realizing that one of us had to decide who's going to sleep on top, Connor then starts to speak to me.

"Gary, you can you please take the top bunk? It's not because I'm fat, it's just you can have the top bunk. I know you were thinking who's going to sleep where, but that's settled. I'm going to start unpacking my things, you should too. Then we can go grab a bite. Okay?"

I silently nod my head in accordance to Connor. As we both start to unpack our belongings, I still can't believe me and Connor are sharing a room. I have only known this guy for about a half an hour if that, and I can't believe that I'm going to be bunking with him. When we finish unpacking, I then turn to Connor and ask where he wants to eat at.

"There aren't that many restaurants in this area, but where did you want to eat at?"

Connor grabs his car keys, and starts to head towards the exit of the dorm. He then turns to me and in a hushed tone, responds to what I asked him.

"There is a dive bar like 20 minutes or so from here. That's where we are going. I have a car, and you can ride with me."

The both of us head out towards the bar. It was definitely indeed a dive bar. It was more of a sports bar. From what I remember, it had an 'Australian Outback' theme to it. I don't know. It's from what I gathered at least. As far as food, it was mostly finger food. Burgers, chicken fingers, things like that. So it wasn't anything fancy smancy at all. Connor and I were situated at the bar, and made direct eye contact with each other frequently. Connor has no idea that I have a crush on him, nor does he even know I'm gay. If that isn't bad enough, at the time, I didn't know what orientation Connor was either. Making an extremely long story short, Connor and I took this time to get to know each other more. However, I was doing most of the pressing. Connor was not exaggerating at all when he said he struggled with his anxiety, and was anti-social. The guy would be very quick and vapid with his answers. Don't get me wrong, I wasn't concerned by it.

If anything, I was more attracted to Connor due to the lack of his responses. In the heat of the moment, despite all the small talk we were doing, I decided to rest my hand on Connor's leg. It was something that I did which parts of me regrets. I didn't even remember doing it, it sort of happened by instinct. I know it's not right to touch people without them being approving, but I was deep in the moment. However upon doing that, Connor remarkably doesn't seem to be bothered. I remove my hand away from his lap out of guilt.

We then left the bar, and headed back to campus. As we reached out dorm room, it was late in the evening at this time. There was a knock at the door, and Connor goes to answer it. On the other side of the door, was a very beastly bald headed Caucasian man in his late twenties. He looked much older than his age. Maybe because of the stress he protrudes, causes him to look much older? His name was Elder Gordon Stimson. He was the head dean of the male students, and was the dorm advisor for all of the male dorms.

Whenever a student had an issue, they were to report the situation to him. Elder Stimson was extremely strict, and he was a very terrible man. His behavior was always two faced. He proclaimed to be a very holy and faithful man, he wasn't. The man was extremely bigoted, with his indoctrinating style of his teachings. He was an individual I didn't want to be around, and the thought and presence of him, made me very uncomfortable. Elder Stimson then began to walk into our dorm, looking at the both of us disappointed, however in a façade, attempting to come across as friendly and welcoming.

"Gentlemen, how are you? How are you guys enjoying your first day? I'm just going room by room, letting all the guys know a few things. There is absolutely no illegal drug taking. You may drink alcohol, but you may not keep alcohol in your dorm room. Keep all alcohol consumption off school grounds. Another rule, there is absolutely, and I mean, ABSOLUTELY, no sexual contact in the dorm rooms. Whether this is between male and female students, female and female students, or this disgusts me to holy hell to say, between male and male students."

We both continue to listen to Elder Stimson lay the ground rules.

"Any student who breaks the aforementioned rules, will be expelled immediately. Which that would be a shame not only to your parents, your religion, your faith, your journey, but most importantly, you as a person yourself. Okay, good evening Gentlemen. Take care."

As Elder Stimson leaves out of the dorm, I take in everything he said. These must be common reoccurring issues, for him to specifically point these out. I guess the days of students doing ignorant things and getting away with them are numbered and over. I guess it's not enough to assume youth at a Mormon University are going to be trusted to do the right thing.

We now have to have a PSA on the first day, as a reminder that such behaviors are not acceptable at all. Despite everything Elder Stimson said, I don't worry about it at all. I even kinda forget Elder Stimson came into the room, and I instead turn to look at Connor, as I have something important I need to relay with him. I knew this was the time for me to come out to him. Back at the bar, I put my hand on his leg which I sort of regret. Connor for some reason didn't seem to mind I did that though. I do however have to come out to him that I am gay, and that I have feelings for him. If I don't do it now, it will become an issue. Connor sits at his desk reading his bible quietly. I reluctantly walk up to him during this time, and come out to him.

"Connor, there is something that I need for you to know. I'm gay, which if you haven't already figured out. Not only that, I have feelings for you. It's okay if you don't accept these feelings, and I understand if the staff found out about either one, I would be expelled most likely. But I at least want your approval as a friend. Please support me Connor."

Connor puts his bible down, and smiles at me. He then calmly responds.

"Well I had an idea this was the case. It's okay if you have feelings for me Gary. I sort of have feelings for you. I don't mind you being touchy feely, just if you're going to touch me, make sure I'm okay with it first. I should let you know that I'm Bi myself, and I don't care that you're gay. We both have to keep our secrets to ourselves, and they are safe between us."

Connor then gets up from his desk, and signals out for me to hug him. I do, and at this time, I'm happy to have Connor as a friend. Even though the fact both of us are LGBT, these are violations upon the school. So even if me and Connor don't show sexual displays of our feelings, just simply the mere fact of us having same gender attraction is a major violation.

This is something that upset me greatly. I was torn, because I found a close friend in Connor, yet because I was in this conservative Mormon University, there wasn't anything more I was allowed to do, so it was very frustrating and discouraging. When Connor and I finish hugging, Connor goes back to his desk to read his bible. I then begin to get my coursebooks ready for class the following day. Tomorrow would be the first day of class, and I want to be prepared. Also making sure that I get a good night's sleep, as my first class starts early in the morning at 7 A.M. As it's now creeping up at 9 at night, I start to undress into my sleeping clothes. Connor does the same as well. I climb up onto the top bunk, and start to rest my eyes. I can hear Connor get onto the bottom bunk. Connor then begins to laugh.

When Connor continues to laugh to himself for five minutes, my curiosity peaks the better of me. I then glance down to the bottom bunk. Connor is reading a copy of "Advocate" magazine. It's a magazine geared towards LGBT people. Connor is reading a humorous story that the magazine is featuring. Connor looks up at me from the bottom bunk.

"Why don't you come down here and join me. This is funny. Come read this."

I obey what Connor said, and climb down to the bottom bunk. I lay and cuddle in front of him, as the both of us read the magazine. We both then read more sections of the magazine, and also laughing at funny dating classified ad the magazine has as well. Minutes soon pass and I become very fatigued. I lay my head down on the pillow, and Connor begins to stroke my hair, as my eyes are closed laying down. Connor then kisses me on the forehead, and whispers to me.

"Goodnight and sleep tight Gary. See you tomorrow."

I smile and then drift off to sleep. The next morning I wake up on the bottom bunk, and Connor is not there. He already left for class. I stare at the alarm clock, and I'm running terribly late. I have to be at class at in 15 minutes. I still have my pajamas on, and I'm going to have to rush getting dressed, and rush to class as well. If that's not bad enough, I have no prior knowledge of the layout of campus. So the chances of me being tardy are almost surefire. I manage to get dressed and rush to class. As I'm running in the hallways, I bump into another student.

"Hey faggot, watch where you're going!"

I become immediately shocked, and I regress back to my younger self at High School, to when I was called 'faggot' in the past. Although in the past, I was called 'faggot' for being different and strange from everyone else, this time the term was being used more bluntly. The student I bumped into was named Nathan Long. Nathan was a very vindictive ginger haired man. He had pale skin, and spiky hair. His father is a very prestigious pastor, however Nathan is being very disingenuous with his Mormon faith. Relying only on the fact his father is a pastor, to sort of bend his own behavior at times. Nathan then starts to bully me.

"Don't ask me how I know, but I know you're a fag. I saw you and that fat blond hair guy yesterday. I know it all. Here's the deal, you go to the dean and admit the both of you are fags, or I will. Make your choice. I'm not going to tell how you long you have to make this decision, but it's not a long time. So it's your choice to make."

Nathan then begins to laugh to himself. I however give him a very angry look.

"Bullshit. I'm not gay. We're just friends. Go on ahead and tell the dean. I really don't give a fuck. God forgive me for cussing. If anyone is a fag, it's you for being nosy. Now get the fuck out of my face, I'm running late for class."

Nathan extends his arm out in the direction I was going.

"Well I can't keep you. I would hate to make you late for class. But this isn't over you hear me. This is only the beginning. You're going to be seeing a lot more of me buddy."

I roll my eyes at Nathan, and spring towards class. As suspected, I'm late for class, but I manage to make up for what I missed, by asking some of the students once class was over, if I could glance over at their notes. I continue onto my other classes, and when lunch time approaches, I go to the University cafeteria. The food is very bland, but I don't have time to go outside of campus to eat. I then proceed to my other classes. Throughout my first day, I do not end up seeing Connor at all. I find it very strange I was unable to run into him. I should have at least seen him walking in the hallways. Mind you, there are not that many students that are at the campus. Only about 800 or so students. Despite not seeing Connor, I do think about him. I tell myself that I will see him later back at my dorm.

Once all of my classes are over, I head to my dorm. The anticipation of finally getting to be with Connor is possible. All day I couldn't stop putting him in my mind, and I am now going to be able to interact with my friend. As I am walking inside I see Connor at his desk reading his bible. He has what seems like a depressed and worried look on his face. I walk over to Connor and start to hug him from behind. Connor then violently pushes me off him, and shouts at me.

"I'm not a fag, so don't touch me. What happened last night, forget that happened. I'm going to talk to the dean so we can switch rooms. I'm sorry Gary. I can't afford to get expelled. I don't know how the whole campus knows, but they do. I can't live with that. I'm sorry."

I then start to feel strange over this. If this is how Connor truly feels, then I'm going to have to accept this. He no longer wishes to associate and deal with me, so I guess that's the way it has to be. I don't want to lose him, but I can't force Connor to be with me, if he doesn't want to. I then start walking to my desk to put my books away. I then innocently respond to Connor.

"Well, we can still be friends right? Even if you do go to another dorm, that doesn't mean we have to stop interacting with each other. I think you're a nice guy Connor, and I would hate it if I wasn't allowed to ever talk or hang out with you anymore. We can still be friends right?"

Connor while he is reading his bible, then silently responds to me.

"Gary, I won't tell the dean to switch rooms. However, you can't be touching me, and I'm not going to be your boyfriend, or be seen in public with you. I met some new friends today, and they would disown me if they knew me and you were a thing, and we were friends. The school is gossiping already. I think the walls on these dorms are too paper thin, and some of the students saw us at the bar too."

Connor then continues to express himself at me, and I listen.

"I know you have feelings for me, and I like you too Gary, but we have to be really hush hush about it. I don't want to get expelled, and I know you don't want to get expelled either. I know it sucks, but it's what we have to do. I've made my choice on it."

I continue to put my books away at my desk, and I respond to Connor.

"That's okay, and I understand. As long as we can still be friends, I can handle that. Connor, I have a lot of homework to do, so I'll leave you alone. I'm sorry if I hurt you."

Connor doesn't respond to me after that. In fact, for the next three months, other than occasional small talk, me and Connor would rarely talk to each other. I would mostly keep myself in the dorm room, as Connor would hang out with other students at campus, whom I don't get along or see eye to eye with. Connor would also go onto weightlifting and other sports at campus, while I would play 'World of Warcraft' on my computer. Although I'm not going to lie, I still had feelings for Connor. There would be a few times Connor would climb up to the top bunk and kiss me goodnight, but those instances really didn't count. It was still a strained relationship we had together. I was really feeling miserable from not being with Connor. Once Freshman year ended, I've felt I've accomplished nothing, and Connor still hates me. We both also stayed closeted to the other students at school. There were rumors and gossip yes, but nothing went pass that. As we didn't confirm the rumors, none of that really mattered.

In order to deal with these thoughts, sophomore year of school, I started to hang out with very questionable people. I started to experiment with drugs, and started to drink excessively on the weekends and after class. I don't know how I managed to get my schoolwork done, but I was able to. I'm not proud of myself, for this phase of my life, but it is what happened. It was at this time as well, that I remember the exact moment when things came to a screeching halt as far as my relationship with Connor is concerned. It's an event that I will never forget, and it's something that needs to be mentioned. I'm even going to go detail by detail. It happened on a particular Friday in June as we were wrapping up Sophomore year of school. I was meeting up with some of the students to go to a heavy metal concert. Walking in the school courtyard on my way to the concert, I ran into Nathan again. Nathan however was with Connor this time. Connor upon immediately noticing me, gave me a disgusted look. Nathan then began to bully me, with Connor not in the slightest taking my side, or defending me.

"Oh look, it's the faggot. He better not be going to the concert with us."

I snap right back at Nathan, giving him a taste of his own medicine.

"Yes I'm going to the concert Nathan, I was invited. Why the fuck are you always in my business? You are not my father. Leave me the hell alone. You're just jealous of me most likely"

Nathan and Connor then began to walk away from me. Connor still not taking my side or defending me. Nathan however does give off one final attack.

"You're damn right I'm not your father. I would have disowned your faggot ass."

I ignore Nathan, and continue with the clique that invited me to the concert. Upon reaching the concert, I notice Connor and Nathan hanging out with their group on the other side of the venue. I decide to stray away from the group I was with, to go and mingle with Connor and Nathan. I decided that I am not going to be bullied by Nathan anymore, nor take the fact Connor isn't sticking up for me, and telling Nathan to knock it off. As I approach them, Nathan pours a beer on my head, smacks my glasses off my head as well, kicks my stomach, and pushes me to the ground. As I'm laying down in pain, Nathan spits on me, and shouts.

"No fag, you can't hang with us. Go hang out with people that actually like you, because we don't. Now if you decide to stick around and play, it's going to be worse. Now go away."

As I'm still crawling on the floor in pain, I hear Connor come to my rescue.

"Nathan you prick, you didn't have to do that to him. That's it, we're no longer friends. You're such an asshole man. Go pick on someone your own damn size. Lord have mercy."

Connor then starts to carry me behind his back off the ground, and takes me outside the concert venue. Nathan continues to heckle, feeling very angry that Connor decided to come to my defense. Once we are outside, Connor sets me down on a bench in the parking lot, and starts to hug me, softly speaking to me.

"Are you okay? He didn't hurt you that bad did he? Do you need me to take you to the hospital? It's okay. I'm here, and I'm not going anywhere."

We end up staying put in the parking lot of the concert. We can hear the sound of the musicians playing in the background subtly. Connor and I continue to embrace. This is the first time, in a rather long time, to where I'm happy that he's back, and he's my friend again. Connor and I then reach in together and kiss. I felt truly happy with Connor, and wanted time to stop indefinitely. This gentle moment is sadly quickly disturbed. Nathan comes rushing at the both of us with his posse.

"I'm gonna end the both of you fags. I knew it. All the rumors were true. I can't believe you played me for a fool Connor. So the both of you are going to pay right now."

Nathan then pulls out a gun from his jacket, and points it at Connor. I am shocked where I'm standing, and can't react. Connor then charges at Nathan, tussling with him. They both continue to tussle, while myself, and Nathan's gang watch in shock. Not able to react. This instance is quickly ended, with the sound of a gunshot. I can't believe what has just happened. Nathan had fatally shot Connor in his chest. Nathan feeling guilty of his actions not even a minute later starts to feel extremely sad, and ends up shooting himself in the chest, which kills him. Out of instinct, I immediately run away from the scene, along with Nathan's friends. In absolute shock that Connor was killed, and the whole ordeal makes no sense at all. Happening so fast, but accurate. Unaware of what is to happen now, I continue to run. After hours of running, I finally make it to campus. I run towards my dorm room. With every step I'm taking feeling like my shoes are made of concrete.

Once inside my dorm room, I immediately lay on Connor's bunk. I cry for what seems like the entire night. What happened at the concert, still haunts me. It just doesn't make any sense, but what happened already happened, and I have to accept it. I am going to truly miss Connor, and I wish I could bring him back. This isn't going to happen though. Right when the both of us were making amends, he was taken away from me.

Nathan understanding the extreme guilt of what he has done, took his own life. Too cowardly to accept the consequences of what he did. He took another man's life for basically petty reasons. Understanding his father being a prolific pastor, the impact that it would have on him. Nathan took his own life as an easy way out. This whole ordeal was too much for me to take in. I loved Connor very much, and he loved me. Who knew what the possibilities of us would have been. It is all a big question mark sadly now. I will say that due to this event, which is why I did decide to go on and study psychology in the end. As much as I wish I could take back this event from happening, it was vital.

It allows me to relate to people better as a psychologist, as I have been encountered with many issues myself. I understand exactly where people are coming from, as I have been in very similar and identical circumstances myself. As Connor's murder and Nathan's murder suicide is being investigated, I continue to stay in the dorm, grabbing Connor's pillow. I get up over to Connor's desk, and start to grab his bible as well. Feeling the eerie feeling that he's gone forever, and the man whom I loved deeply, is dead. I don't end up sleeping, and the next morning, Elder Stimson walks into the dorm. He has an extreme angry look on his face.

"Gary, can you please come to my office. I just would like to discuss a few things with you, and they are very important. So if you could come with me, I appreciate it."

I obey what Elder Stimson told me to do, and follow him. Upon reaching his office, I notice two police officers present as well. This doesn't make me feel comfortable at all. You can tell by my body language I'm about to buckle under the pressure. I had no idea what was going on at all. Elder Stimson then beings to question me.

"Gary, these officers are just here for our safety and yours. So just pretend they aren't even in the room. Gary, what do you know about what happened at the concert? Be honest."

As I'm looking down on the floor, not wanting to rehash anything that happened then, I started to put the pieces together as to how I'm going to reenact what happened in the most appropriate way. With my vision still down at the floor, I explain the details.

"I was invited to a concert. I had accidentally injured myself at the concert, and Connor decided to escort me out. As we were out, Connor and Nathan began to feud about the fact Connor was associating with me. Nathan does not like me, and Nathan and Connor were close friends. Nathan just snapped, I don't know. He shot Connor, then killed himself."

Elder Stimson then raises his eyebrows at me, as if he's not satisfied with how I gave my side of the situation. Elder Stimson then gets up from his chair and puts his hands on my back. He then moves close to my ear, and silently speaks to me.

"Now Gary, I want you to be completely honest with me. Tell me exactly how everything panned out. You can I both know that isn't what happened. So just be honest please."

I look up from the ground, and give Elder Stimson an agitated look.

"I did tell the fucking truth. That's exactly what happened. I mean, do you want me to explain me and Connor were together and had a homosexual relationship? Well yes, the rumors are true. So if you want to expel me, go on ahead. I already lost Connor, so I don't care."

Elder Stimson then goes back to his seat, and stares at me very disappointed. I knew at this moment that I was going to be kicked out of school. There is a zero tolerance on male students forming a same gender relationship with another student. To me it doesn't make any sense, but rules are rules. I can't believe I was fished out of admitting this, but at this point I didn't care.

Connor died, and nothing in my life really mattered. This was only the beginning of the end of me feeling hopeless and helpless. Elder Stimson then began to take out several forms from his desk, telling me to sign them. I can't believe as a result of this situation, my career at this school is over. I didn't think it was fair, and I wish I was just given a break given what happened hours ago with the shooting. Elder Stimson then speaks to me.

"Gary, you are being expelled, and you know why. Sign these forms, and you are going to have to pack your things and go home. We won't tell your parents, but I suggest that you tell them the truth as well, as they deserve to know it. Whatever your parents do is on them."

I started to feel scared, as my parents were not going to accept me being gay, but it was something that they really needed to know. Even if I knew I was going to be disowned and kicked out, it was something that I had to do anyways. After signing the forms, I was officially excommunicated from the school, and considered a traitor to the Mormon school.

I didn't even have a chance to fucking grieve over Connor's death. As I'm packing my things, I start to look at Connor's belongings. I decided to take Connor's bible. I later spoke with Connor's family, and they said it was okay if I kept it. I know stealing is wrong, but I felt I needed something to remember Connor by. Once I'm finished packing, I walk to my car, heading home. All throughout the trip home, I'm scared and nervous as to how my parents are going to react to the concert situation, Connor's death, and me essentially coming out as a gay. But I didn't really give a damn at this point. If they were going to kick me out, I'd rather they do it, and get it over with, so I didn't have to constantly worry and live a lie to them about it.

Reaching home, I tell my parents the news, and the reaction isn't anything shocking. My father was surprisingly more understanding. He wasn't supportive by any means, but he wasn't as hurt as my mother. My mother was very deeply hurt. Her vision of me was to get married to a woman, and have multiple children, and for me to be a pastor someday. I understand my mother's hurt. However, if she truly loved me, she would have accepted me. I now my family loves me unconditionally, and my relationship with my mother is still strayed, but I know she acted in the way that was most appropriate to how her emotions were. She didn't want her Greek Mormon son to be gay, and it makes sense.

Upon being kicked out of my home, I moved into a one bedroom apartment in Salt Lake. I took a job working at a coffee house part time, while I took some online courses. Still dealing with the consequences of me being expelled from school, and how that wrecked my transcripts. I went into a deep depression during this time. Even though when Connor died, I excommunicated myself from the Mormon culture, I began to question my faith again. I began to really hate myself for being gay. I felt my entire life was a curse, and that had I not been gay, and had I not had feelings for other men, Connor would still be living. I began to feel an extreme wave of guilt over Connor's death. Even though none of it was my fault, I couldn't understand that.

I began to do something very controversial. I started to look online at ex gay therapy, and ex gay therapy programs for Mormon men in particular. I hated how my family disowned me. I hated how I felt out of place. I hated how Connor was taken away for me being gay. I just began to question to myself, that I'm not honoring god well at all. That I'm living a very sinful and wicked lifestyle, that I need to rid myself of. The self-hate became out of control, and I didn't know how to deal with it an appropriate way. At the time, I felt it was my only choice, and I wasn't mentally well back then. I went on ahead with scheduling an interview to speak with a moderator of an ex gay therapy program for

Mormon men. I felt that there was no going back at this point, and I needed to do this to better myself.

I should warn you, that this part of my story I regret. I was a completely different person back then, to even think of doing ex gay therapy, let alone actually agreeing to go along with it. We have come a long way with LGBT rights, and I understand LGBT people that deal with religion are sometimes torn with their thoughts on what they should do. It is indeed tough, but you should understand that if you truly love god, and your religion, regardless of your sexuality and sexual orientation, you are still loved.

This was something I couldn't tell myself at the time. I just couldn't stop blaming myself over Connor's death, feeling that I was directly responsible for it, when I wasn't. I shouldn't blame myself, for simply being myself. After doing research online, at that time, doing the ex-gay therapy seemed like an appropriate way to deal with all the emotions I was feeling. I remember the first day I met with the president of ex gay therapy center. His name was Harold Jenkins.

He was an older man in his thirties with balding hair. He came across as a friendly man, who claims to be ex gay. He used to be a gay man, but isn't anymore. For the next moments of my life, I would look up to this man as a mentor or a father figure. Not realizing that he would brainwash several incorrect things into my mind, making me feel worse. I sit in front of his desk, and he begins to introduce himself to me.

"Hello Gary, I'm Harold Jenkins. I'm the moderator here at this program. You can call me Mr. Jenkins. I'm here to help you, we are all here to help you. You're in good hands."

We end up shaking hands, and I introduce myself to him as well. As I sit in front of his desk very obedient, he begins to inform me on several things about the program.

"So Gary. I received your email, and I understand your situation completely. I'm sorry about the death of your friend. Now getting down to business, you looked up our program online right? So you know what services we provide and what we are able to help you with?"

I jubilantly respond to him, understanding exactly what I signed up for.

"Oh yes, this is something that I really need to do. I have done a lot of research, and I feel what you have to offer will help me. I hope that upon leaving this program, I will no longer be homosexual, and I will have a guilt free, and healthy life as well."

Mr. Jenkins smiles at me, and responds,

"We will help you with whatever you need. Again, you're in good hands, and we are here to help you. It's going to be fine. It's going to be tough at first, but you're going to get through it. We have a 99 percent success rate with the guys that come to us. You'll be fine."

Feeling completely brainwashed from what he's explaining to me, I smile and nod my head at him. I end up signing the contract, which allows for me to join the program. I also regretfully pay a hefty fee in order to be accepted into the group. The therapy consists of a thirty day camp session. Me and about fifty other guys will go out in the woods, and participate in several events and therapy procedures, in order to rid us of our homosexuality. As I hand Mr. Jenkins back the forms I signed, he then speaks to me again.

"Are you sure you want to do this, once you agree to it, there is no going back. You have to agree with whatever we decide to do to help you. We won't hurt you, but we will do what we have to do in order to help you. Again we won't hurt you, but we will have to do certain things."

I agree to go along with the program despite this warning. Mr. Jenkins continues.

"Well the bus for the camp leaves next Friday. Be here at 2 PM, as we leave very sharply and on the dot at that time. Gary, I'll see you next Friday then."

I smile at Mr. Jenkins, and we shake hands once again. As I'm leaving his office, and walking to my car, I then start to wonder if I made the right decision, which I know I didn't. What happened next, would be the most violating, harmful, and psychologically draining events of my life.

CHAPTER 3:

MAN OF WHITE (PART 2)

To be honest, I was beginning to have slight second thoughts of joining the program, but it was much far too late for me to regret going along with it. From the trauma I've experienced previously, at the time, it was simply something that had to be done. Although it wasn't at all a healthy decision to make, it was something that I felt was beneficial for me. The night before I left for the ex-gay camp, I couldn't sleep a wink at all. I was just too nervous to sleep, and knew that this camp was going to be something that was going to test and challenge all the limits that I had. I ended up informing my parents that I had signed up for the camp, and they of course seemed to be supportive of it. Due to my religion, the fact I was taking steps to rid myself of my homosexuality, seemed to calm them down. I was also captivated by the way Mr. Jenkins made the program seem. Even though this man doesn't even know me, he was giving me the impression that he was my saving grace, and that everything was going to be fine from this point on. This was completely incorrect, and going into this program would be a huge mistake.

The morning for me to leave arrives, and I am overjoyed with both nerves and excitement. I wanted to see who the other participants in the program were, and I wanted to know what techniques they would try to use, in order for me to get rid of my gay thoughts. While I am driving to location of where the bus is going to pick us up, most of my nerves begin to disappear, and at this point, I just want to start the program, and receive help towards my issue. I reach the bus, and I end up seeing about twelve or so other guys, standing outside at the bus. I couldn't believe that all of these guys were going through the same situation as me, wanting help with the same problem that I was facing.

Along with the group of guys, I manage to see Mr. Jenkins standing with them as well. For the sake of privacy, as I know this type of program is rather confidential, I will not be giving the names of the other guys in the program. In fact, if need be, I will just be referring to them as initials. This is simply so their privacy is protected, and there aren't any problems related to that at all. I introduce myself to the men, and some of them are friendly, some are not however. What is for certain, is that I will end up having to live with these guys for the next duration of my life, so whether I get along with them or not is irrelevant.

The bus to take us to the camp has not yet arrived, so I use this time to mingle with the other guys that are in the program. I end up finding out that some of them have come from abusive households, and some of them likewise with myself, are also dealing with religious issues related to their homosexuality. Even though we all have different reasons for entering the program, the goal we wish to achieve is the same. We no longer want to live the lifestyle that we had previously, and would like to be cured of that.

One of the most strange cases of the guys that were going to attend this camp, was one guy who gave graphic detail of him being sexually molested at a gay club. Due to that event, he longer wishes to be gay. I really do wish that somehow these men were taught otherwise. That being gay isn't something to be shameful of. Whether or not a specific incident or trauma caused them to hate being gay, it shouldn't be something that they use to dictate anything evil or bad towards their life. Much of the reasons I did decide to study psychology, is due to the events that I saw whilst I was at this program, and trying to tell others that it's okay to be different, and there is nothing to be ashamed or upset about. I know that I can't play savior to everyone, but it would be nice to play savior to them. I simply cannot force someone to do something that they don't want to do. So it's no use trying to play god, or guardian angel. But I will take everything I can from this program.

The bus to the camp finally arrives, and I start to take my headphones out, and listen to some music. I feel this may be my last time to feel calm. Electronics and other things of that sort, are not allowed at the camp. So I'm going to take this final time I have, to use any type of gadgets before they are confiscated once we arrive there. I end up taking a seat in the far back section of the bus.

No particular reason, that is just where I wanted to sit. Most of the other guys going to the program were seated near the entrance of the bus. There are currently twelve other guys, not including myself, so in total that's thirteen that are currently on the bus. We are going to make another stop an hour and a half from our current location, to pick up another twelve or so guys that will be joining us in the camp. As the bus is moving, I took at all the mountains outside the window. The camp is located in a very top secret desolate area of Utah.

Continuing to listen to my music as the bus drives on through, I naturally begin to daydream and recollect myself on my life from when I was at Mormon University. Thinking if none of that shit even happened, I wouldn't have to go to this camp. At the time, I wasn't even seeing the camp as something that I was dreading, it was something I was thinking of as a lifeline, and a last resort in order for me to seek guidance in this particular point in my life.

About a half an hour into the bus ride, Mr. Jenkins starts to wander his way to the back of the bus where I'm situated. He ends up taking a seat right next to me, but doesn't say anything. Although the both of us are quiet, we can almost read each other's minds as to what we are thinking. He is probably wondering I'm sitting by myself in the back of bus, whereas the other guys are mingling with each other and placed altogether in the front of the bus. He's probably confused at this, and probably thinks maybe I'm seated by myself, due to the fact I don't want to associate with the other participants. That isn't necessarily true. I just wanted to sit at the back of this bus, for no particular reason really. I could read Mr. Jenkins mind as well. He could probably sense that I am a special case, compared to the other guys at the camp. Not specifically because I'm keeping to myself and staying quiet, but it's just one of those things you notice and pick up on. A few minutes later, Mr. Jenkins gets up from sitting beside me, and returns to the front of the bus.

Eventually, the bus makes a stop at a location to pick up the remainder of the guys which will be attending the camp. I noticed with this group of men, they seem to be much older. The group that was with me that came on the bus, were younger. I'm sure this is simply coincidence probably. The men in this group, also end up situating themselves at the front of the bus. I remain by myself in the back of the bus, not bothered. We continue onto the camp, as I steadily listen to my music on my headphones. Enjoying my last minutes of freedom that I will have.

I'm pretty much the only guy that is present on the bus, who isn't talking to anyone. I'm simply in my own trance at this time, and I just want to get to the camp already. The only thing that's on my mind is doing this program, in the result that it will help me with my problem. I didn't join this camp to meet friends, or to gain lifelong friendships. I didn't join this program for a vacation either. My intentions for going along with this, are for self-healing from the previous events that I had to witness. Not that I'm saying that was the intention of the other men either, I will say that speaking only for myself, that wasn't my agenda for joining.

The bus ride actually didn't end up being that grueling. It was about a four hour bus ride, but it didn't feel that uncomfortable at all. I just mostly listened to my music, payed attention to the scenery, and kept in my own thoughts. The bus ends up pulling over and stopping at an outside location. I knew in my head that this wasn't the camp entrance. Common sense told me that we were probably going to have to walk to the entrance from here. This is probably as far as the bus was allowed to go. All of us began to exit out of the bus, unsure of where were currently were, or what exactly was going to happen next. My affirmations were confirmed when Mr. Jenkins began to let us all know, that we are going to take a short hike to the camp.

"Okay men, the camp is about an hour walk from here. There is no way for the bus to safely make it to the area the camp entrance is at, so we are just going to walk from this point. If anyone has any questions, please let me know. It seems like a long walk, but it's not. We will be there before you know it, so don't worry. Follow me gentlemen."

All of us began to follow Mr. Jenkins to the entrance of the camp. I just couldn't stop but notice the lovely outdoor scenery. I love the outdoors, and the air was smelling very fresh. I didn't mind taking a walk to the camp, as long as it allowed me to take a look at the trees, and the woods, and just feeling fascinated by it all. During the walk, likewise when I was in the bus, I didn't associate with the other men. However, some of the men were chatting amongst themselves while we were walking to the camp. I just chose not to participate in that. Maybe when we finally reach the camp I will form some bonds with the men I thought. Or perhaps not.

Either way, my goal for being at this camp was simply to help myself, not to make friends. As I look up at the sky, it's slightly cloudy, but the weather is still nice. It's neither that cold or warm, which for being in Utah, that is quite exquisite weather. Mr. Jenkins continued to guide us to the camp, and all of us continue to stay in suspense. The longer we walk, the more I cannot wait to reach camp, and to see what events they have in store for us to do.

While we were all walking to camp, I actually ended up slipping on a crack on the path. The impact of my trip was so bad, it flung my glasses off to another side of the path. Somehow, I manage to crawl my way off the path, and slouch down away from the other guys. I see there is a cut my on leg. I ended up scraping my right kneecap very badly, and blood was seeping out. The other men in the group began to laugh at me. I don't think they were laughing to be rude or disrespectful. I just simply think it was a natural reaction. I didn't enjoy being laughed at, and I didn't enjoy injuring myself either.

Mr. Jenkins doesn't notice that I fell on the ground, so I begin to ponder as to whether or not I should pretend that never happened. Should I just get myself up and be a man about it and continue walking, or should I tell Mr. Jenkins that I hurt my kneecap. After looking at the cut on my leg, even though it doesn't seem like a deep cut, it still was a pretty nasty cut. I end up staying crouched over on the side of the path, slightly in pain, but not in severe pain. I decide to alert Mr. Jenkins of my injury.

"Uh, excuse me sir. I ended up slipping on the path and hurt my knee pretty bad. I'm pretty sure I can keep walking, but I don't know if you had a first aid kit or anything on you. If you don't it's okay, but I wanted to let you know that I injured myself."

Mr. Jenkins then did something which extremely shocked me. This should have been my first red flag upon reaching camp, but I simply ignored the severity of it at the time. Mr. Jenkins began to walk over to where I was slouched over, and takes a look at my leg. He has an angry look on his face, and then begins to give me eye contact. He then laughs to himself. I give him a very confused look in return, as he then starts to whisper under his breath to me.

"That's nothing. You should get used to feeling pain, because you're going to experience a lot of it at this camp. That cut is fine, not get your ass up, and stop whining like a woman."

I just simply remember feeling shocked at Mr. Jenkins for saying that, and I couldn't believe I didn't remove myself from the program at that moment, but I didn't. I simply obeyed what he said, and got myself up. I was just worried that the cut might get infected, but I carried on. Still in slight pain from the cut in my leg, but understanding that the camp moderator had no intentions of helping me. It was like he used some type of dark magic to get me to be obedient towards him, and to not worry about the cut in my leg. Even tough in normal situations, if I'm hurt and ask for help, I should be able to get it. Mr. Jenkins had no concern over my health, and it was at this early situation and event which proved that. I couldn't continue to fret over this, as my main goal was to get to camp. I didn't have time to worry about my leg, as I'm sure the cut will heal, and I need to be strong during this time.

We all end up finally making it to camp. Mr. Jenkins was right, and that it was about an hour walk from where the bus dropped us off at. The outside of the camp looked very meager. There were only four cabins apart of the north side of the camp. So it wasn't a very big location at all. I could see there was a basketball court located on the east side the camp, and what looked like a recreational field situated on the west side of the camp. The south side of the camp featured nothing but the entrance of the camp. As we reach the entrance of the camp, Mr. Jenkins waves his arms in the air, so he has our undivided attention, and begins to speak with us.

"Alright, this is the camp you guys. No the camp doesn't have a name. It's just called camp. I want you to meet some of the counselors here at the camp that will help you."

In this moment, two heavy set bald Caucasian men came out of one of the cabins. These men were the two counselors of the camp. Again due to privacy, I do not want to tell you what their names were. I'll just refer to them as Counselor 1, and Counselor 2 for the sake of me retelling all of this. These men were very strict, and no bullshit. They were the camp counselors, but they were more like the camp drill instructors. If you had a problem or were feeling down during camp, they were not the ones to help you with any issues. They would simply tell you to stop whining and to stop crying.

This is what you signed up for, so you stick through it. After the camp counselors introduced themselves to us, Mr. Jenkins then directed all of us into the biggest cabin located at the camp. This cabin was the cafeteria, and also the auditorium of the camp. Whenever we wanted to get something to eat, we would simply go to the cafeteria. The Camp Counselors I mentioned earlier were also in charge of all of our meals. We were not allowed to bring our own food to the camp. The only thing we were allowed to take inside the camp were our clothes, and hygiene products. Which reminds me, at this time, all of our electronic devices were confiscated by the counselors at this time.

As the counselors began to take my phone, I immediately began to feel an uneasy feeling in my stomach. My phone was very vital to me, and it wasn't going to be easy to go without it for the duration that I was at this camp. After all of the men had their electronics confiscated, and things went from zero to one hundred rather quick. The camp counselors then all blindfolded us, and took us outside of the cabin, to a wooded area. The fear inside my mind was a lot to handle. I didn't sign up for this, and I realized it was too late for me to run away and change my mind. I didn't know what they were doing, and the fact they were blindfolding us was very frightening to deal with. The main thing on my mind, was being brainwashed by Mr. Jenkins preaching's. We go deeper and deeper into the woods, blindfolded. Not knowing our surroundings, or what antics the camp wants to do with us. At this point, I just wanted to go home.

This is only day one mind you, and I'm already starting to lose it under the pressure. Why did I ever sign up for this program? How is any of this supposed to rid us of our homosexual thoughts? None of this made sense to me at all, but I knew all of this had a purpose somehow. After quite a few minutes later, as we are still blindfolded, we are all situated outside on logs in the woods. After all of the men were seated on the logs, one by one, all of our blindfolds were taken off. At this moment once my vision returns, I could see that all of us were seated in a circle, right in front of a campfire pit. In the center of the circle, I also see Mr. Jenkins holding a long wooden stick that had to be at least 4 feet long, with Counselor 1 and Counselor 2 standing right next to him. Mr. Jenkins then began to speak.

"Men, as this is our first day together, I want you all to participate in an introduction exercise. In order for each man to speak, he must hold the 'talking stick'. If he's not holding the 'talking stick', he may not speak. Please keep it brief, and explain why you are here."

Mr. Jenkins then goes into the center of the campfire pit, and lights it. After the fire pit is lit, Mr. Jenkins then holds the stick up the air, and begins to speak once again.

"I shall go first. I am the owner of this camp, and the reason why I am here is simple. I was just like you. A dirty rotten homosexual that did deviant things. I am no longer that. I am a happy man who no longer has those thoughts. I am a married man with several young children."

As Mr. Jenkins continues to talk, I start to feel a slight wave of motivation. Thinking in a false sense that if Mr. Jenkins could be converted, well then I could as well. I then began to feel safe and secure with my decision to attend this camp. Maybe I was making the right decision after all, and all of my previous doubts I should forget about? Mr. Jenkins continues to talk.

"I created this camp to help all of you. I know each and every one of you are dealing with turmoil and stress. Well, once this camp is over, you will be changed men I guarantee. Every single guy leaves out of this camp happy. That will be the same for all of you."

Mr. Jenkins finally finishes what he had to say, and he passes the stick onto Counselor 1. Counselor 1 then explains why he is at the camp. Explaining an almost near identical story that Mr. Jenkins gave. That he is a changed homosexual, and the camp made him a much happier man. He is not living a life which he deemed was painful and wrong. Being a camp counselor allows him to take his teachings and his beliefs, onto the new participants who enter the camp, wanting the same healing that he received. Counselor 2 then ends up grabbing the sick, and his story is slightly different. Counselor 2 was actually in a long term committed relationship with another man. However, he just simply woke up one day and decided to break up with his partner, as he longer wanted to live a gay lifestyle. He claims his life is now healthy, and he no longer lives a sinful life.

After listening to what the two counselors had to say, I was sure of myself that I could have the same result as far as my recovery to my particular situation went. At this time, it was our turn to explain why we came to the camp. Several men started to give their own unique testimonies as to why they are at the camp. However a couple situations in particular really stuck with me, and were very emotional. One of the guys, who I will call "N", who was a very slender blonde haired man, who had to be in his early 20s, and around my age, gave his story.

"Ever since I was a little boy, I was very feminine. I played with barbies, and I would also like very girly things. I never played with the other boys in schools. One night my father came home and said, 'I'm gonna beat the fag out of you', and he did. Long story short, I'm here because I don't want to live that kind of life. I want to live a normal life, and not a bad life."

I began to feel very empathetic for this young man. I can imagine the type of hardships he had to go through growing up. It must have been very tough having to be told by your own parents, that you cannot be yourself. The homophobia must have been too much for him to handle, and he's now feeling the harsh results of that. He wants this camp to erase all of the damage he was caused during his youth, and feeling he's not good enough, and he's disappointing others. Another man took the stick and began to tell his story. He was a very handsome man with a short crew cut hairstyle. He was also very physically fit. I'll call him "D". I could tell by looking at this man that his story was quite special and sentimental. He was at this camp possibly due to political reasons. The man reluctantly started to explain why he decided to attend the camp, and his story around that.

"I was in the army. I loved being in the army, and I loved serving my county. The army however is not a place for an openly gay man to serve in. Although they claim to be accepting and they don't care, maybe for some people that's the case. It wasn't for me. I don't want to be gay anymore, and I just don't want to live like that anymore. I'm done living like that."

I know that being a gay man and serving in the army is something quite complex. The army isn't necessarily a place for an openly gay man to be at times, but I have known gay men who were in the armed services, and experienced no problems at all. However, I am not the one to challenge what this man was faced with. It's not my job to dictate how he felt. Obviously he felt that this camp would solve whatever issues he was having, so it's not my place to challenge anything he may be feeling. More of the guys got up to talk, and yet another special case got up to speak. This man was much older. He had to be in his late 40s or so. I'll call him "L". The older man while standing in the middle of the circle, started to tell his story.

"I am actually a married man. I've been married to my wife for a long time. I have a son who's ten years old, and daughter who's five. I don't want to be gay, and I don't want my kids to have a gay father. This is my only hope. I really want this camp to change me. Thank you."

In the case of the older man, I knew he had a lot of self-hate issues. He didn't want his children to have a gay father, and I can understand how that might cause a lot of issues and harm to him. He just wanted to be normal, and not have to worry about that. It's almost as if he's torn between two lives. He has gay thoughts, but his other side of him wants him to be a nuclear father to his children, and not have any distractions towards that. Judging by this man's age, I knew he has been dealing with this problem for a rather long time. I have extreme pity for him. It was then my time to express myself to the other men. I started to ferment what I was going to tell them. Do I come up with a fib, or do I say the honest reason as to why I came to seek help here? That I was at a Mormon University, which ended up having my best friend tragically killed. I end up taking the stick, preparing to get my thoughts ready on what I'm going to say. I end up composing myself for a few seconds, before I start talking to all of the men.

"Hey guys, my name is Gary. I come from a Greek family which doesn't support me being homosexual. I'm also Mormon. I actually went to a Mormon University, to where me being gay, ended up having one of my friends killed. I feel I need to be in this camp to erase all the trauma from when that happened, and to be able to change my life for the better."

The guys seemed captivated by my story, and seemed to understand why I was present at the camp. When I was finished speaking, although I was slightly ashamed of replaying the evil events from my past, I am glad that I told them the honest truth. I did think about embellishing why I was at the camp so that it wasn't as dreadful, but I'm glad I was genuine about it. Once all of the men finished explaining all of their life stories, Mr. Jenkins then went to the center of the circle, and began to put the fire out. We were all then once again blindfolded. The second time we were blindfolded, it wasn't as unnerving. We were already blindfolded before, so most of the suspense was taken away the second time it was done.

After being blindfolded again, we were all then directed back inside one of the cabins. Upon reaching the cabin, my blindfold was removed, and I could see that I was in a cabin with bunk beds, with twelve other guys. I could tell that this is where we would be sleeping, and that the other guys were probably in the other cabin that had beds inside. I noticed that some of the guys in the cabin were in my group when I got on the bus, and some of them were not Also inside the cabin was Counselor 1. Counselor 1 began to speak to all of us inside the cabin.

"This is where you guys will be sleeping. This is also where all of your belongings will be. Lights out, is at 9 P.M. Sharp. There are no exceptions. When we say lights out, we mean lights out. There is no funny businesses inside these cabins. No drugs, no sex, nothing. Don't ask how we will find out about these things, we just know. So don't even try it."

Once the counselor was finished, we were all instructed to go back to the auditorium cabin, to get our belongings. Once I got all of my things, I returned back to the cabins. For some strange reason, even though this was only the first day, I felt like there wasn't any way I was going to get use the operations here. It seemed like much to take in, but I knew I had to follow every order they asked of me, if I wanted to achieve treatment at this camp.

At this time, I ended up talking to the other guys that were bunking with me in the cabin. One of the guys, the army guy, "D", actually was in the same cabin as me. I began to speak with him more to get a better understanding of his situation. To be completely honest, the man was very handsome, and it was hard to get rid of my urges. Knowing damn well that I am gay, and that this program wasn't going to change that. It didn't matter, as I still had to follow whatever they told me to do. For the rest of the day, all of us went back to the cafeteria to have dinner.

Every day directly after dinner, Mr. Jenkins gives all of the guys a sermon. This sermon is usually an hour long, and it's supposed to go along with our treatment. The sermons he gave were always boring, and I would always try to think of something else to pass up the time while he was rambling on. However, the sermon he gave on the first day was one that I remembered very vividly.

"Good evening gentlemen. I hope you had a great dinner. Every day after dinner, I'm going to speak to all of you just like this. You so all better get used to it. Anyways, I want you all to know, that I know some of you have been having homosexual urges. Do not worry, this is natural and is customary with the treatment process. For now, just ignore all of those."

Mr. Jenkins continued with his sermon. Although I wasn't directly listening to him, most of what he was saying was correct. Many of us were having urges of being attracted to men, and holding them back was most difficult. It was like he could read our minds and knew how each of us were feeling. This is exactly why this sermon held a lot of power, because he was prodding inside all of our emotions, in order to do strange reverse psychology. Mr. Jenkins was reaching the end of his sermon, and I was listening to what he was relaying to everyone.

"Remember, everything we teach you here is to help you. Even if it seems strange or unusual, don't worry about that. We just want to help you, and let you all live the lives you wish you could live. Every guy in this program left happy and are now living happy lives. The same is going to be said for all of you. Listen to us, and we will help you obtain exactly what you need."

Mr. Jenkins then finished his sermon after that. The camp counselors then informed us that we are to report back to our cabins, as lights out will be soon. As we are walking back to the cabins, everything that Mr. Jenkins said, is playing in my mind like a catchy song I can't get out of my head. I was in total immersion with whatever this man said. Although his way of teaching the sermon was rather boring, I still managed to input most of it, and it was like gravy being poured into my brain. I knew whatever he said was the gospel, and I had to obey whatever he wanted me to do.

Even if the activities they had in this program were unorthodox, which they were, I had to still persevere through all of what they asked me regardless of that. I began to crawl into my bunk, and prepare myself for sleep. I made it through the first day, and I could not believe it. I had no idea what they were going to ask of us to do the following day, but I knew it was going to be hell. I knew we were most likely going to feel like hell, both mentally and physically. Getting a good night's rest was very important. Being that were we're going to be woken up extremely early to take part in the therapy methods they had for us. All of the guys in the bunk, myself included, drifted off the sleep rather quickly. It seemed as soon as I feel asleep, it was time to get up. We had to get up every single day 5 am. This was not up for discussion. This was something we had to simply to. After getting up, we were each instructed to do a chore at camp. Which included raking the leaves outside, trimming the bushes of the camp, watering the plants, digging up the weeds, or going inside the kitchen and washing the dishes, and mopping the floors, and cleaning all the cabins. The jobs we were all assigned, alternated each day. The job I had this particular day, was to rake all the leaves.

The morning air was rather cold, and I much regretted not wearing a jacket. I knew the chores we were assigned had to be done, without any complaint. It was hard work, but we had to do it. So I couldn't complain or make a big deal about it at all. We had until 8 A.M. to finish all our chores. By that time, we were to all report for breakfast. 8 A.M. came, and I was done raking all the leaves. I went back to my cabin to rest for only 10 minutes, before I was instructed to head back to the cafeteria cabin for breakfast. I will say that the meals for breakfasts at the camp were always better than the dinner meals. I remember they gave us Belgian waffles, and they were so delicious.

After this, was when most of the torture began. After breakfast at 9 A.M., we were given our first exercise. We were split into different groups, and they displayed pictures of two men kissing to us. Every time we saw a picture of the men kissing, they would take a belt and whip our palms with it. They would do this to each guy for about five minutes. The pictures were on a slideshow for 10 seconds, so we would get whipped by the belt 30 times in five minutes. Once this exercise was done, we were instructed to go outside. They gave each of us a backpack with had about twenty pounds of stones inside. They instructed us to walk up a three mile hill with the backpack full of stones.

On the path, more images of men kissing were on the ground of the path. There were also messages pinned onto the trees along the path that said various homosexual messages. Things such as, "God is going to kill you fag", "You will die if you continue this lifestyle you faggot." Those were just the g rated messages. There were far more extreme messages which I don't want to say or mention again. It was a very terrible experience, and this was only the second day. This was such a torture filled hike. Having to walk up three miles with a heavy backpack full of rocks, I wouldn't wish this on my mortal enemy. Also the psychology of the messages and pictures in effect as well.

I finally managed to finished this exercise, and it was now noon. During this time, we have lunch. Lunch was always just a bland bologna sandwich and an apple. Unlike breakfast and dinner at the camp, the lunches didn't have the same variety. The sandwiches also tasted like absolute shit, and were bland as hell. I was hungry from the torture hike, so I had to eat something. As terrible tasting as the sandwich was, I ended up eating it anyways. During lunch, I chatted with the rest of the men for a short while. We were all simply too brainwashed to complain about the activities they were having us do. So none of the conversation entailed discussing about that.

During this time, my body was extremely tired, and it was only noon. Even though they gave us an hour to eat our lunch, it seemed like that hour went by very fast. At 1 P.M., we had to return to our duties at camp. During this point of time, from 1 P.M. until 3 P.M., we are instructed to do an art project related to our therapy from being at the camp. So I guess in a sense it's pretty much an art therapy assignment. The task we had for today, was to design a paper hat. We had to fold construction paper in half to make the hat, and after that, we must decorate the hat with both positive and negative feelings we have. Once we were finished with our art project, the second half of the activity required us to wear the hat, and recite how the hat made us feel. Individually, we all had to do this. I had a feeling they were going to make us do that, so I wasn't at all surprised when there was a performance aspect of the project.

Most of the guys had very interesting stories behind the hat, and others didn't. I however did manage to create a special theme related to my hat. Most of it was surrounding my time at the Mormon University, and having to deal with Connor's death. The hat also incorporated most of my youth, and the feelings I now feel as an adult, from when I was feeling young. After I had recited what I had to say about my hat, a couple of the other guys also explained their art projects.

3 P.M. soon came, and during this time, we have to do a physical sport, or exercise until 5 P.M. These usually vary, but you can choose to play basketball, baseball, soccer, tennis, volleyball, or you can go inside of the weight room. As far the sport I decided to go with, I chose to just play volleyball by myself. I was there by myself, there was no other guys at the camp with me. I was mainly spiking the ball over the net, on my own. I was just trying to kill time, as it was mandatory for us to do sports during this section of the day. Many of the guys decided to go to the weight room. Although, I'm not much of a weightlifter, so I opted not to do that. I feel this was the part of the day I most enjoyed. We got some free time to exercise. It was the only part of the day that didn't feel forced, or dangerous. I knew this time wasn't going to last forever, so I had to savor every minute of it I had.

I knew that once 5 P.M. came, they were going to make us do something uncomfortable. I already knew. As I'm continuing to play volleyball by myself, I'm starting to have slight second thoughts about this camp. Day two, and I'm still not getting used to the natural order of things at all. Still wanting to quit and go home, these thoughts continue to sprout in the back of my mind. I still don't feel at all cured of my homosexual thoughts.

Not that I am saying this whole situation was a waste of time, but I don't feel I have recovered from what I came here to receive. I did slightly understand that it was still early on, being only the second day. I have to give it still a little more time, before I decide to leave the camp. I heard a loud alarm, letting me know that recreation time is sadly over. Time does fly when you are having fun, and I was very upset that sports time was over. I grabbed the soccer ball, and walked away from the soccer field, towards the other cabins. Preparing myself for the next activity they had planned.

From 5 P.M., we all then had to do our outdoor group therapy session. All of us were blindfolded, and taken to an outside area of the camp. From here, our blindfolds were taken off, and we were instructed to each take part in a therapy session. Either Counselor 1, Counselor 2, or Mr. Jenkins would moderate our group therapy. Each of us had to hold onto the 'talking stick', and we were asked various private questions about our personal and private lives. Questions such as, "Have you ever had sex with a man?", "Have you ever had erotic thoughts about a man?", "When you think of someone attractive, is a man or a woman?". "When was the earliest thought you had of being homosexual?" It was mostly questions related to that arena.

Along with the questions, we had to give a vivid anecdote relating to our answer. Most of the guys were more ambitious than others, and everyone was being honest with what they had to say. As for myself, I mentioned that I was brought up Mormon, and lived a strict life to where I wasn't able to experience with my sexuality young as much as I had hoped to. This whole exercise I felt was done so we could feel guilty or sorry for whatever homosexual feelings that we may have been festering in our minds. It was to tell us that being gay is wrong, and you should feel deep regret for having these things on your agenda.

Once this particular exercise was over, it was getting close to 7 P.M., and dinner time. We all went back to our cabins to freshen up for dinner, still taking in our second day at camp. At dinner, I was happy with the food they served. They gave us roast beef and potatoes. The food was very good, I can't lie about that. Dinner quickly however quickly passed, and after dinner, we must sit through a sermon that Mr. Jenkins gives. As I said previously, his sermons for the most part were devastatingly boring.

We had no choice but to sit and listen, there was no choice. Although it's convoluted to explain, as although his sermons seemed to drag on for quite a bit, most of what he said I did manage to take to heart. Once he was finished with his sermon, it was now time for us to go to bed. Walking back to my cabin, I felt a multitude of emotions. Knowing that the next day, it's Déjà vu all over again. The same schedule and routine and procedure must be done. I struggle to get to sleep, feeling drained from the things I did this entire day. I'm also anxious, due to how early I have to get up. I know as soon as I start to drift to sleep, it will be time for us to get up.

Day three approaches, and I get up just like I did the day before. The only thing different about day three from day two, is the morning chore I had to do. The previous day I was in charge of raking the leaves, today I had to pull the weeds from around entrance of the camp. It was a very uncomfortable task, however I am not allowed to complain. I just have to simply do it. Another thing different from today, was the task we were instructed to do after breakfast. The day before, they made us carry a heavy backpack through the woods, while looking at pictures of men kissing on the ground, and messages on a tree. Today, they each put a burlap sack over over body, going down to our waist.

Then by taking a wooden stick, one of the counselors would say something along the lines of, "Are you attracted to men.", and if we said yes, we would get hit very hard with the stick. If we said no, they would try to guilt trip and mind trick you into saying yes, but altering to question to something open ended such as, "When you picture two men together what is your thought?"

If you took too long to answer the question, or if you said an answer the counselors didn't like, you were hit very hard with the stick. I was tricked myself on two questions, to where I did end up saying I still find men attractive. The whole point of the exercise was to make sure you have zero homosexual thoughts in your head. This was a painful and humiliating ritual, and I didn't see why they had to go through this approach. At the end of it, I still found men attractive, and I didn't feel it helped me much at all. All it did was make my back hurt from being hit with the stick, and hearing other guys get hit with the stick, also made me feel bad and uncomfortable. For the rest of the day, I really wanted to leave and go home. This camp I felt wasn't doing much good for me, and I didn't think I could take much more of this.

I don't know how, but I managed to stay at this camp for another week or so. I think part of the reason being, is that because the camp was so secluded in the middle of nowhere, my options of running away didn't exist. So I felt kinda stuck. I have now been at the camp for 10 days. We went through more events and tasks which were trying to physically and mentally break us. But day 10 of camp, would be my final day. After this, I eventually snapped out of the brainwashing trance that they were able to keep me under, and garner the strength to get the fuck out of this toxic place. The day started out as normal, except after breakfast, Mr. Jenkins blindfolded us all into an outside area of the camp. Once our blindfolds were taken off, I noticed that two of the men were not present at the scene. Mr. Jenkins then began to speak.

"Gentlemen, I have to say I'm most displeased right now. When you all came into the camp, I gave each of you clear cut rules that you had to obey and follow. Two guys broke this rule, and were caught kissing in the woods this morning. I will say that both of them were beaten and punished, and they are no longer allowed back in camp, with no refund."

I just sit in shock hearing this news. I knew it was only a matter of time before some of the guys were caught breaking that cardinal rule. I was also scared as Mr. Jenkins said both of the guys were beaten before being expelled from the camp. This really scared me to a high degree. All of us then started to get triggered, that perhaps everything we were being told in this program was a lie. If this treatment isn't working for two of the guys, what guarantee is it that it is going to work for us as well. We all began to doubt our existence at this camp. Wondering if maybe we should leave and go home as well. Myself, I knew that my homosexual thoughts were still present, and none of the activities I have done for the past 10 days have seemed to work. Mr. Jenkins with a disappointed look on his face, then shouted at all of us.

"Because of this, we are going to have a special ritual today. Something that wasn't planned, but must be done. Whoever refuses to do this ritual, will be rightfully punished, and will retrieve an even worse task to do, that will hurt even more."

At this instance, Counselor 2 then wheeled in a cart, that had a drape covering it. I sat extremely scared and terrified. I was also sweating profusely, and was feeling very hot. The anxiety was far too much for me to handle, and I was turning red. As Counselor 2 began to lift up the drape from the cart, I could see there was some type of torture device, that still to this day, I can't fully explain. It was a rather large box, maybe three feet tall, by three feet wide, which had spikes and knives sticking through the box, and also what looked like electrical wires through the box as well. As I sit glued to my seat looking at this box, I knew that we were in for a world of pain. I just was unsure as to what this actually was. Once of the counselors then takes a long extension cord, and plugs it into the torture box. Soon as this happens, the box starts to omit a rather eerie and unpleasant electric sound, and I continue to be confused as to what this device is. Mr. Jenkins then grabs one of the guys situated in the circle, and brings him in front of the torture device. The man has a very scared look on his face, and is also sweating. He begins to close his eyes, and starts to shake and tremble. Mr. Jenkins then takes the man's right hand, and sticks it on a platform located on top the machine. The man's hand is shaking tremendously, and I can relate to his pain very much. As much as I don't want to watch, I just sit in shock to this. Mr. Jenkins then looks towards all of us, and continues.

"He's going to be unlucky number one. All of you are going to be next, so be prepared. The whole point of this exercise, is like a lie detector. If I think you are telling the truth, nothing will happen. If I know you are lying, you are going to regret that."

The man shakes his head, and Mr. Jenkins begins to ask the man a question.

"Are you still attracted to men?"

The man pauses for what seems like ten seconds, and doesn't answer the question. I think the reason for him not being able to speak, is the fact his hand is on the torture device. The man after a short while, does belt out his answer very softly and quietly. He tells Mr. Jenkins no, however Mr. Jenkins does not believe the man is telling the truth. Because of this, he sets off a button located on the bottom of the device, which lowers his hand into the box. His right hand is severely sliced severing his pinky finger. The wires located in the box, also give him a static electricity shock. The man then pulls his hand up from the device, and begins to faint on the ground the torture machine.

Upon immediately seeing how brutally tortured this man was, I got up from the circle, and immediately ran towards the entrance of the camp. I noticed that three other guys managed to do this as well. However majority of the men stayed at the circle outside. I distinctively remember Counselor 1 running after me. Saying, "You fag, get back here," or something along those lines. The two guys I was running with, caught up to me. I noticed that the two guys running with me, are the army guy "D", the young blonde guy, "N", and the older guy, "L". By the skin of our teeth, we managed to escape the camp onto the open road, without the counselors catching up to us. We were finally free from that hell. We have successfully escaped.

As we reached the road, we just kept walking until we reached a gas service station, which was about a three hour walk from where we ran from camp. A good Samaritan let us use his phone to call the police. The police came to the service station, and after explaining all the horror details we experienced at the camp, the three of us got into his patrol car back to the direction the camp. However, once we reached the camp, nobody was there. Me, "D", "N" and "L", couldn't believe it. We all ended up giving Mr. Jenkins information, and also the address of his office. The office actually is a rented storefront that has no registered name connected to it. There is also no record of Harold Jenkins, being a licensed psychotherapist, and there is also no record of someone in the state of Utah having that name, or anyone in the United States having that name matching Mr. Jenkins profile. Things just became more strange after that. I began to feel guilty for the guys that didn't run, but there was nothing I can do.

Still to this day, I keep in short contact with "D", "N" and "L", who are actually living healthy lives, with "D", not being ashamed of being an open gay man in the military, still wanting to protect his country. "N", deciding to be proud of himself, now with his own partner, and "L" in particular still married to his wife, but being proud of his bisexuality raising his children. As for the other guys in the camp, thankfully they all ended up fine. The guy who was unfortunate enough to be tortured, healed just fine. The rest of the guys managed to escape the camp as well. Mr. Jenkins, whose real name is Ethan Archer, and the camp counselors were later arrested by the authorities for running illegal psychotherapy sessions.

Although he was licensed at one time, he ended up losing his license. Mr. Archer was given a jail sentence, and I hope to never have to see that man again. I also hope that he never inflicts that type of pain on other men either. Since leaving the camp, I had to be happy and accept who I was. For the first time in a long time, I was happy to be gay, and wanted to see what life had in store for me. Going to that camp was a terrible idea, and it was something I wasn't proud of doing at all. I just have to rebuild my life form that, and try not to let that mistake take charge of me. I can't let something like that ruin my dreams, and stop and prevent me from moving forward. I just can't.

At this time, I decided to go seek out my psychology degree. From the experience at the ex-gay camp, I decided that I was going to move to California to pursue all of my dreams. I was able to forget all of the bullshit which happened before. Still trying to life the life that Connor wanted me to live, and be happy with all the decisions and choices that I make in life. Knowing that I'm turning to psychology to help others. Without the help at all from my family, I managed to graduate University. It was a major accomplishment from me. Despite all the hard times I've been through in the past, I was so happy to be reborn and to do the things I really want to do. My mind is clear, and all of my identity issues have gone away.

Which now leads me onto present day. The rest is truly history. I am now doing this "Profiles of Hope" project. I feel this is something that can really change society. I understand that being gay/bisexual men, it can be tough in society. I know that nine other men are going to share their stories, and they are more than likely going to be just as severe as mine was. I know that by sharing my story first, as haunting as it was, I know that there are other men that have gone through similar circumstances.

Studying psychology I feel is the perfect way to make amends towards things which have happened previously, that didn't go the way I wanted them to. Although I am no longer involved with the Mormon religion, I am still happy about my Greek heritage, and I'm also proud of my sexuality. I no longer wish to convert myself, and I'm proud of myself. I'm not here to force anyone to live a certain way. People can act however they please. I do know that by doing this "Profiles of Hope" project, it not only gives a chance for me to share my story, but for me to also be involved in the lives of the other men in the project as well. I know this whole process isn't easy, and it may bring moments of laughter, tears, and just downright uncomfortable feelings, I feel these stories have to be heard. I want to get to know the other guys lives, and I share my troubles, as they share theirs. Everyone has a story to tell, and now that I've told mine, I feel very comfortable and secure of myself. I'm in a very nice place in my life, and I'm ready to move forward. Yes, I'm ready.

From graduating college, I now happily live in Los Angeles, and I'm very satisfied with my life. I have my own home, and I can manage everything by myself now. Although I would like to have a partner someday, I am at this point focusing on this current project that I am doing. I know that the relationships that I form from doing this particular project will have a great impact on my life. I like trying new ideas with my psychology career, pushing limits that others haven't done. I figure I might as well use my psychology degree for good use. Now that my story is complete, and to be honest my story isn't exactly complete.

My whole story is the "Profiles of Hope" project in a whole. With that being said, I will conclude my story. I understand it was very difficult for me to rehash everything. I'm trying not to live life with that much regret, and just be happy that I'm still here to live out all my journeys. The new people that I meet, and the new experiences that I try to involve myself in, are what matters. The positive experiences, not ones which are damaging and not going to bring success to my life. The "Profiles of Hope" project is my time to make that impact, and I am forever thankful for that, and this is going to be something that I know will make a difference.

This is the end of my story, and I hope that you enjoyed it. I know there were moments that were sad, but it's my story. I managed to overcome all of that, and I'm still here. My name is Gary Swanson, I am man of white, and that was my story.

CHAPTER 4:

MAN OF YELLOW (PART 1)

My name is Troy Lockwood, and I am the "Man of Yellow". My reddit username is, "TitaniumRangerX". I am 28 years old. I have blond hair, and I am a slender man. I am quite short as well. I don't know really where to start with my story. Growing up, I knew I was gay, and it's not like I didn't accept myself for being gay, it was just something at times I had to deal with. I also had many crushes young, and that got me into a lot of trouble you could say. I never knew who my father was, and I still don't. He ran away from my mother and I, and my mother was forced to raise me by herself. This caused much trouble for her, and I can understand completely why. Despite the fact I was an only child, it was still difficult growing up without a father. My mother had to work extra hard, because he wasn't supporting me. Not that I'm glad my father walked out, but I wonder as to whether he would accept me being gay anyways. Part of me thinks that he wouldn't, but the other part of me is just not sure. Either way, I still have a loving relationship with my mother, and I adore her very much. So I guess I can now start my story, and my story deals a lot with self-determination, and love and friendship.

Growing up in the south was tough. I'm proud of my southern roots, and I'm proud that the south is my home, but I'm happy to be in California now. It seems to be a place that resonates with me a lot more.

I actually grew up in the outskirts of Tennessee actually. A land and area full of many country boys. Ha-ha. It's pretty much a farm land, and it's very conservative. I myself wasn't really involved with the farm lifestyle. I lived at my house with my mother alone, and we usually hired guys to come over and do all of the manual labor stuff. Those types of things really aren't up my alley. But if you are into outdoorsy stuff, and into hunting, and other country stuff, it's the place to be. I also had an extreme affinity to country music. I actually like all types of music, but country music seems to be my all-time favorite. How can I forget Southern Barbecue. Oh my goodness, extremely tasty. Barbecue chicken and ribs, mashed potatoes, deviled eggs. That's southern food for you. That's my culture, and I'm proud of it.

I have a high voice, which sometimes I'm insecure about. Also my flamboyant personality makes me question myself as well. Most of the time, I feel that I'm not man enough, and I struggle to get accepted most of the time. It took me quite some time to be proud of myself and accept the person that I am. Before then, I went through several rounds of questioning myself, and being confused. I however am very happy with my life now, and I can be confident. Being confident in myself, allows me to be happy universally. The reason I want to tell my story, is that I want to empower and motivate over young gay guys like myself, who have probably had to experience the same things I had to experience. If raising my voice helps another person, I'm glad with that. With this story, I'm going to start when I was very young, and I'm going to end it to current day. From my early childhood, to now meeting the man of my dreams, and my savior. Harry.

I think my whole journey into figuring out myself started when I was eight years old. In my elementary school talent show as a matter of fact. Well actually, let's go slightly before then. When I was a little boy, like four and five years old, I would always dress up in my mother's clothes. I don't know why I found it so fascinating and exciting, but I would just do it. The feeling of being care free, and not worrying about life at such a young age. Knowing that when I became much older, the fact a boy in a dress is a very difficult political matter as well. My mother would find it very cute and attractive when I would dress up her in clothes, and sing Britney Spears songs. As long as I was happy she didn't care. I really wish things would have stayed this way, and everyone would be happy to see me being myself. This was not always the case. I was constantly beat up in elementary school, and it was a lot for me to deal with as well. Perhaps it was due to jealousy, but none of the kids in school liked me. The boys thought I was too gay and feminine to hang out with them.

Because I wasn't a girl, it was also tough for me to be included in the circuits with all the girls. I didn't know where to fit in, and I would always cry due to this fact. So I actually spent time with both genders. I would play Pokémon and sports with the guys. Although I would feel awkward at times because of that. I wasn't a very masculine boy, and I would constantly be teased and picked on. I would also then hang out with the girls and play jump rope, and talk about Barbie Dolls and other feminine non boyish things. However I was still picked on by the boys for hanging with the girls, and because I wasn't a girl, the girls would make it clear that I should understand I'm a boy, and I can't be included in everything that the girls do. But quickly going back to when I was eight years old.

The school had a talent show going on, and I really wanted to participate in it. I knew exactly what number I wanted to perform, and how exactly I was going to perform it. I was going to have an ensemble which included a dress, a fake pearl necklace, a blue sequin scarf, and some bright ruby red high heels. I knew it was going to be fantastic, and I knew I was going to be styling and profiling. Of course, there had to be someone or something to rain on my parade. When I decided to sign up for the talent show, the school staff wanted to know what my talent was going to consist of. I was speaking with the school secretary, Ms. Virginia Milton, and told her that I'm going to dress up, and sing a Madonna song.

"Yes, my name is Troy. I'm in grade two. I am interested in performing in the talent show. My talent will have me wearing a lovely blue dress, and red high heel shoes."

I vividly remember the look on the school secretary's face after I told her that, and she couldn't be more disgusted.

"But you're a boy. Honey, boys do not wear dresses.."

I remember I looked down at the ground, with a great feeling of defeat. When I was young, I was also a "Dennis the Menace" type person. If I wanted something, I was going to get it. I knew the school wasn't going to let me perform in the dress. However, if I lie and tell them my act is going to be something else, I can still do the act the way I want. Before the show, I'll just quickly change into the outfit that the school doesn't want me to wear. I knew this stunt would work out fine, and I couldn't wait to pull it off. So that's exactly what I decided to do. Lie and tell them my act is going to be one thing, when it's going to be another.

"Yeah, you're right. Boys are not supposed to wear dresses. But may I still sing my act in boy clothes. I really want to be in the talent show. Please?"

Ms. Milton then had no choice but to sign me up for the show. I was so happy that I was going to be in the talent show, and even more happier that everyone was going to be in the shock of their lives once they see me in the dress. Once I got home, I told my mother that the school would not let me perform in a dress. My mother was disappointed and was very close to calling the school to file a grievance over her son not being allowed to perform the way he wanted to in the talent show.

However, after informing her that I embellished my way into earning a spot into the talent show, she was very proud of me. Now that my mother was on board, I couldn't wait for the day of the talent show. When the talent show came after school one day, I was backstage wearing a long raincoat. I guess the fact it was raining that day, didn't bring of any suspicion towards myself at all. I had to put on a stone face, but underneath my raincoat, was a lovely blue dress. I was also wearing rain boots, and under my rain boots were the red high heels I was going to wear during my performance. My emotions were very hard to control as I knew the audience, sans my mother, would be so shocked to see my act. When it was finally my turn to go on stage. I quickly grabbed my radio, and I flung my raincoat off backstage. Once landing on stage, I quickly turn the music on and begin performing. The audience reaction consists of half of them erupting in complete laughter, to the other half being offended and storming out of the school auditorium. Taking a quick glance at my mother, I notice that she is very proud of me and smiling. I continue on with my performance for about twenty or so seconds, before I'm dragged off stage by a PTA mother. Even though I was kicked out of the talent show, I was so happy I got to be myself, and I was able to be free, and do as I wanted.

Sadly, due to this event, my mother was called into Ms. Linda Clover, the principal's office. My mother reassured me that everything was going to be fine. Despite the fact we have to report the principal's office, she knows it's over the talent show situation. My mother told me that even if I am expelled or kicked out, I will not get punished or get into trouble. She said that she understands I did what I did to express myself, and because I wanted to prove a point. As my mother and I are sitting outside the principal's office, I see at least ten different parents walk into the office with their children, complaining about my stunt at the talent show.

During this time, I began to feel slightly guilty that I was the once that caused all this trouble. I just wanted to have fun and sing and dance on stage. Who knew that a little boy wearing a dress on stage would cause this much uproar and controversy in the school. My mother and I were finally called into the principal's office. We both sit in front of her desk, and the principal then with an angered look situated on her face, starts to converse with my mother.

"Ma'am, are you aware of what your son did at the talent show yesterday evening?"

My mother quickly snaps back at the principal.

"Oh course I am aware. My son wore a lovely blue satin dress, a nice sparkled sequin scarf, and he also had on some red high heels. All of the items belong to me, so I'm aware that my son was wearing them. I'm also not ashamed at him at all. So why are you?"

The principal didn't seem to expect that response out of my mother, and is left almost near speechless. She does however manage to respond back to my mother to coax her otherwise.

"Well the school told your son that he was not allowed to perform in the dress, and he deliberately disobeyed our orders. If it was simply up to us, we would have allowed him to perform in the dress, however we are a conservative school district, and we have to take precautions."

My mother was starting to get very mad at the principal, and fired along back at her.

"If that is the case, I want to take my son out of this school, and this district. If the school isn't going to support my son doing something as innocent as wearing a dress for a school talent show, I don't want him attending this school in this district. We will just go to a more open minded school that's elsewhere."

My mother and I then stormed out of the principal's office. That was the last day I ever attended that school. I was so happy that my mother stood up for me, and didn't want to stay in a school that didn't value who I was. Immediately following this, I was then transferred to a school that was a bit farther from my house, but the school personnel were much more kind to me.

This school also held a talent show, and I had decided to test this school as well, to see what their reaction would be. They had no problem, none at all for me wearing a dress. When it came time for the performance, there were a few parents who were offended and complained to the school staff about it, but that was rare. I was allowed to perform on stage as myself.

At the tender age of eight, I was freely allowed to express myself and figured that everything would go up from there. It sadly didn't, as growing up into adolescence only cause more issues and drama for me to face. The junior high school I went to, the school wasn't as friendly as the elementary school I was transferred to. They had a very strict dress code, and the rules and conduct of the school were also strict. I feel junior high are very complicated years. You're still kinda stuck in the elementary school mindset, but not old enough quite yet for the High School mentality. Through all the pain, I managed to survive junior high school in one piece, although I hated it very much. I was looking forward very much to step into High School, even though the students are much older, and are now forming their own opinions and values as young adults.

The High School I attended was very open minded. Our dress code was very lax, and we got to wear whatever we wanted to class, within reason. It was also a big school as well, full of diversity and many cliques. Some of the students happened to have been bussed in, so that explains the large amount of diversity in the school, despite it being in the south. My first day of High School was very interesting. I was definitely in an angsty phase at that time. I wore really tight clothes, and I was doing my best to fit into other groups at the school. I managed to befriend quite a few people on my first day. My classes didn't seem to cause any issues or concern for me. I always excelled in academics, and although I didn't always look like it, I was a very smart student. Being that I was gay, I did start to form many crushes, but none of them exceeded past that.

None of the guys at the school were really my type to be honest. Yeah they were very nice to look at, but none for me to infatuate heavily over at this time. My freshman year of High School caused me to research a lot about myself. I knew that as I continue High School, things were only going to become more complex. The older I was getting, the more I was understanding how cruel the world can be for someone like me. As my freshman year of High School was coming to an end, I was then starting to prepare myself for my Sophomore year of High School, which I had a feeling would be even more of challenge. Which it was, but it wasn't that bad. My second year of High School wasn't that eventful, but I did happen to see a few things which interested me. I had enrolled myself into music class, playing the violin, and it brought a lot of peace to my life.

The violin wasn't something I was intending on learning, it just sort of happened. I am glad that I took it up, as learning to play it really helped me. Learning to play classical music was something I had no experience with prior, but taking on the risk was very nice. As my sophomore year was coming to a close, I was now sixteen years old. I was still unsure of what I wanted to do with my life, and still struggling with my identity somewhat. My mother was a great support system, and was always there for me. However due to the fact she worked graveyard shift, I barely got to interact with her as much as I wanted to.

My junior year of High School came and went rather fast. Nothing out of the ordinary happened. I managed to engage myself with a few friends, but I didn't really develop any deep feelings for any of them. There were a couple of school dances I went to, but I didn't really do anything that noteworthy. I focused on playing the violin more, and I did other after school activities. I was just really happy at this school, and it was drama free and judgment free. My junior year was very detailed, and I managed to put all my attention to my schoolwork, and I didn't really let any outside distractions bother me at all. I had very little issues with the other kids bothering me.

Although most of my friends were girls, I was able to befriend some guy friends. The fact I was gay, did make some of the students not want to hang out with me. I was also gossiped about quite frequently. But it wasn't anything that major to where I was mentally feeling down about any of that. I went to school, did all my classwork, went to my violin class after school, and took the bus home.

Then all of a sudden, there were rumors that the school I was currently going to, was going to shut down. If this were true, I would be devastated at this news. I enjoy this school very much, and would hate to have to attend another school. If the rumors an reports are true as well, that means all the students will have to be placed at an even farther school.

I really enjoy how close this school is to my house, and I do not want to go to another school that's far away. I also have to make an effort to get to know the students at this new school, and be the new kid. That's not what I wanted, and I wasn't looking forward to this at all. During the last month of school in my junior year, we were told a decision as to whether or not the school will close will be made shortly. I couldn't stand to be in suspense during this time, hoping that the outcome would be good, and I wouldn't have to move to another school.

Unfortunately, the school was ultimately shut down. I remember I went home and couldn't stop crying after hearing the news. I didn't have a choice; I would have to go to another school. Whether I wanted to or not, it wasn't up for discussion. I just couldn't understand how they can let a school shut down, and force all the students to go to a school that is miles away from their home. Considering the fact that the school was already quite a distance from where I lived as is. However I couldn't complain, as that was the decision the school board made. So for my senior year of High School, I had to go to a school farther away. One positive thing I guess, was this school was even bigger than my previous school, and also quite more diverse. Another thing that's great, is that over 90 percent of the students at this school, are new. I'm not the only new student, so that makes me feel proud. Going into a new school for your senior year seems overwhelming, when you factor in that students that were there before you, have more than likely formed cliques and are mingling with each other prior. So I was happy that majority of the students at the school were going to be new just like myself.

My first day at this school, I will never forget, as it sort of serves as a defining point for my story. As it was this day, was the first day that I met Harry. The school bus picked me up about a few blocks away from my house, and myself with other kids that went to this school in my neighborhood got on the bus. The extremely long bus ride to the school wasn't something I enjoyed, but I had to deal with it. Finally reaching school, I noticed the large number of students there. There had to have been at least 5000 students at this school. I have never been in a school this large, and had featured this many students.

I just could not believe it. As I went to the school courtyard to see what my classes were, I began to people watch, all the different students at the school. Noticing patterns or different things that each of the students are portraying. What clothes they are wearing, what groups on the first day they have attached themselves with. Things such as that. Due to the fact that I didn't have any friends, I was going to try to make sure I could study everyone at the school. Upon the chance I was able to form bonds with people, I know where each of the different groups at school hung out, and how they operated as well.

After getting a list of my classes, I also go to the school office to get my locker combination. My locker of course is located a substantial amount away from where my first class is. So this upset me slightly. On my way to my locker, I happened to have accidently bumped into another student who was much bigger than I was. He was rather tall, and had a clear mustache and stubble beard. Being that he was only seventeen years old, I found this very strange. He also had red hair, which I found interesting as well. When I bumped into this other student, I couldn't be any more embarrassed. All my books fell onto the ground, and I was so anxious over that. I bend down and begin to pick up my books, and I make contact with this other guy. He begins to help me pick up my books, and hands them to me. He at this moment while still starting deeply at me, then whispers something strange close to my face.

"You should really watch where you are going fag. I won't help you next time."

I had no reaction at all, I instead stood silently, as we continued to stare in silence towards each other. After that, he shoves me into the locker very hard and laughs. He then walks away, but I just stand there in silence, not knowing what to think. At this time, I was having a rush of emotions. I was attracted to this bully. I wasn't just attracted, but I was obsessed with him. Throughout the day, I just kept thinking about that ginger bully who disrespected me, and shoved me into a locker. I wanted to know what his name was, and where he came from. What was his story about, and what exactly was he hiding about himself?

I figured that come lunch time, I would have gotten over him, and forgotten all about it. That was incorrect. I just couldn't get this guy out of my head. I knew that during lunch time, I had to make it my agenda to locate this guy. I sadly was unable to. There were far too many students at this school for me to do that. I walked all around the lunch area trying to find this mystery man, and I had no luck at all. Searching in the outside seating lunch area, and going to other areas. He was simply gone.

I knew that I had to just move on, and that I'm never going to see this guy again. Part of me was beginning to feel delusional as well. Why would I want to try and find a guy who called me a fag? What benefit, if any, would that prove? I was letting my crush and infatuation with him, get in the way of me focusing on my classes. So I quickly changed my mind, and moved on from him. However, I finally struck gold. During last period in my history class, due to the fact the class is the closet to my locker, I was the first to enter class. I end up taking a seat at a table near the front of the class. The teacher stood at her desk greeting all the students who came in. After several students walked into the classroom, in came the mystery ginger man. He ends up sitting at the table in the far back of the class. My heart can't stop beating fast, and I feel like I'm going to faint. I'm torn as to what I should do now. Do I sit by him in that table in the back, or do I simply ignore him? I act on my impulse and scared that another student may sit next to him, so I immediately grab my things and direct myself to that table.

Upon reaching the table, I could see him giving me an uncomfortable look. I ignore this and end up sitting beside him. Feeling strange that he already has a mustache and a slight beard being so young. He was also quite stocky as well, and had a football player build. He was also wearing cologne, which I found strange for a guy in High School to wear. More students arrive in the class, and soon the classroom is packed. There is still about three minutes left until class starts. I figure to myself that I at least want to know what his name was. I take quick glances at him, but he remains looking away from me, towards the front of the class. I then decide to finally introduce myself.

"Hi, my name is Troy, what is your name? I saw you earlier, remember?"

I remember he looked right in my direction, and gave me a very strange look. He then grabbed my right wrist, and as he's still looking at me strange, silently whispers.

"Yeah I know you, you're the fag from earlier. Don't talk to me, or I'll beat the fuck out of you. You don't want to mess with a guy like me. You will end up regretting it. Stop."

Now common sense would tell you that I should probably get up and go to another seat, or say to myself that this guy is nothing but a low down dirty bully. However, this caused me to want to explore this man even more. My crush on him still did not go away, and it instead, feelings became more severe. Class soon starts, and the teacher surprisingly does not take attendance. So I am unable to find out what this guy's name is at all. Although I told myself that I would try extra hard to focus solely on my schoolwork, this becomes impossible. I try so damn hard not to look at him while the teacher is giving her lesson, but it was extremely difficult not to. This guy was really causing my emotions to go wild. I didn't even know what his name was, but that didn't matter. This mystery man still went through my mind, and I didn't want him to go away at all.

Class was then over, and he immediately grabbed his things and sprinted out the classroom. Without any hesitation, I then grab my things and follow him out of class. I try to creep and spy behind him without him knowing. I know this was wrong, but I wanted to get to know this man more. I figured following him was the best way to do that. As I continue to creep behind him in the crowded hallways of the school, I sadly end up losing him in the process.

He was once again gone, and I couldn't find him. I immediately fall to the ground of the hallways feeling disappointed in myself. I had to snap out of this, or else I was going to miss my bus, and end up walking 10 miles home. I make it to the bus right before it leaves, still not knowing who the red headed guy is. On the bus ride home, I have just an intense incomplete feeling. I had a crush on this guy, and who could I tell? How could I express myself positively on this? I just didn't know what to do about this situation at all. My only saving hope, was that he's in my last period, and I'll try again tomorrow to make magic happen. Or at least I was going to attempt to.

The following day, throughout the whole day, I just wanted last period to come. I wanted to see the man of mystery again. I would get my wish finally. Last period was finally arrived, and I went to class. The teacher however is not present. Nobody else in fact was in the classroom. It was only myself present. I sat at table in front, knowing that he was going to go to the back table, and I wanted to do my bait and switch. Ha-Ha. Sure enough a few minutes later, the mystery man arrives in the classroom.

He proceeds directly to the back table, and I start to get butterflies in my stomach. Not even a second later, I run to the back table to sit next to him. However, he immediately gets up, grabs his things, and relocates to another table. I start to feel agitated over this, and follow him to the table he moved to. He is getting quite agitated, and grabs me by my shirt collar, whispering to me.

"You want to sit next to me, don't you fag? Well you can't. Go to another table, before I pound you into next week. Go away and leave me alone, I don't want to sit next to you."

I then prepare to gather my things and retreat from him to another table, as he's still grabbing my collar. Just then, the teacher, Ms. Michelle Walters, who was a young Caucasian blonde haired woman walks into the class. The guy then quickly lets go of me, before the teacher directs her vision to the both of us. I remain seated, and we both stay at the table quietly. The teacher then puts her things on the desk, and begins to speak to the both of us.

"Oh good, so the both of you decided that you want to sit at that table. That's great. I was going to assign seats today, but it seems you guys are comfortable there. So from now on, the both of you will be seated at that table. Thank you for your cooperation."

When the teacher finished talking, I remember the mystery man put his hand over his forehead, shaking his head in disbelief. I was however very happy. This was the golden opportunity, and I was going to sit by him for the rest of the school year. We remain sitting quiet together, and more students come into the classroom. Once all the students arrive, the teacher starts to take attendance. Something that she didn't strangely do the previous day. I knew that this was it. I was going to know what his name was. Once I was able to figure out his name, I would be happy just with that. Not even a few short seconds after taking the roll, the teacher called out his name.

"Harry Bruner? Is there a Harry Bruner that is in this class?"

The guy sitting next to me then starts to shake his head, and raises his hand. I finally knew his name. His name was Harry. Which I thought was so fitting due to how hairy he was. His facial hair was extremely prominent. I knew that he was also going to find out what my name was soon enough once the teacher called it. This happened soon after.

"Troy Lockwood? Is Troy Lockwood currently present in class?"

I immediately raise my hand, and I remember seeing in my peripheral vision, that Harry was staring forward, but he smiled to himself after this. Once the class attendance was finished, we quickly got onto our school work. I couldn't stop thinking about Harry though, just like I couldn't really focus on anything other than him yesterday either. I didn't stare at him at all, and he didn't pay any attention to me. Class went by rather fast strangely, and Harry quickly started to gather his things to leave. Like with yesterday as well, I began to follow him outside of class. The crowd of students once again made it hard for me to catch up with him, but this time I managed to keep my direction locked on him. As he continued to walk through the hallways, I noticed that he was heading straight to the football field.

I still keep my direction aimed at him, and follow him towards the field. Harry walks out onto the football field, and sits down on the end of a bench located in the center of the football field, next to ten other guys. I remain spying on him from behind the bleacher section. He cannot see me at all. I start to realize that he is more than likely trying out for the senior football team. I found this very exciting, and I kept on watching him from the area I was at. I began to infatuate over him more, the fact he is a football player. I was so captivated by him after finding out this fact. Several minutes later, names were called out, and Harry went onto the field.

The school football coach threw several footballs to Harry, and he caught each and every one of them. The coach would throw the ball at a farther yard distance after each throw, and Harry would end up catching them all. As I continue to secretly watch, I remain enthralled by what I am seeing. I was so proud that he was this involved in his athletics. Soon, other guys start to do the same football drills that Harry was doing. After they are done, the coach begins to call of out several names. The guys names he was calling out, where the guys that have secured a spot onto the football team. Harry's name was one that was called, and inside I was extremely happy for him.

Maybe I felt biased, but to me he gave the best effort out of all the guys out there. The guys then start to grab their things and leave after this. I once again start follow Harry, as he walks out of the football field. Being that it is afterschool, most of the hallways in the class are empty, and everyone has gone home. However I manage to catch Harry and some of the other guys from the football team walking together. Unfortunately at this time, I end up sneezing very loud. I try to cover my face so that my sneezing isn't causing any attention, but it does not work. I remember Harry and some of the other guys he was with in football practice, end up staring back in my direction. I immediately try to play it off like I wasn't following them, and pretend to glance at my binder notebook. Harry doesn't end up buying this, and walks over to my direction where I am. I knew he didn't believe I was standing there by chance, so I end up looking at him instead. As he walks closer to me, I begin to feel more nervous. I can't move, and I can't react in any way. I end up bracing myself up against a wall in the hallway, standing in complete fear. I don't know how he's going to react. Harry starts to talk to me.

"Were you following me? Why are you following me?"

I can't move or speak at all. I then return to looking at my binder, pretending I'm reading something from it. Harry is not pleased at all, and he creeps up closer to me. This time, he puts his hand on the wall, and forcefully shoves me into the wall. Harry loudly shouts at me.

"ANSWER ME YOU FAG! I said we're you following me? You were following me, weren't you, you little faggot. Why do you want to always be near me? Didn't I tell you to leave me alone? Every time I look around, I see you. I don't want to be bothered by you fag."

Without looking at Harry, I start to grab my things, and walk away from the scene. However, Harry extends his leg out in my direction, causing me to slip and fall on the hard floor of the hallway. My lip starts to bleed very badly, and the guys Harry was with at football tryouts, start to laugh at me. I feel extremely humiliated, and I don't know how to react. My lip continues bleed, as I pick up my books I dropped on the floor. Harry then begins to have a soft spot, and starts to help pick up my books. He hands me my books, and the both of us make eye contact.

For nearly a minute, I could feel the energy we both were putting out to one another. To say Harry was a bully was an understatement.

He really was making my life hell, but I was so hooked by him for some reason. For the first time, Harry then smiled at me. The guys he went to football practice end up leaving the scene, but Harry and I remain in this area. I end up returning a smile to Harry. Harry then starts to wipe the blood off my mouth. As he is doing that, he begins to softly speak to me for the first time.

"You like me, don't you fag? You want me to protect you don't you?"

I don't know why, but I end up nodding my head. I feel this causes Harry to feel justified in the way he was thinking towards me. We both soon start to walk away from this area, to the entrance of the school. I stand walking by Harry, not speaking to him at all. I am in total disbelief that he's finally being nice to me, although in a rather strange way. As Harry and I exit out of the front door of the school, he turns to me and asks me a question.

"Troy, the late bus is only for the guys on the football team. How are you gonna get home? I have a car, I'll drive you home. Follow me."

Oh my gosh, I just couldn't believe that he is giving me a ride home. This is all happening too fast. This seems like a scene out of a movie, and I just cannot believe any of it. We both end up walking to Harry's vehicle. He has a rather new model white Ford pickup truck. I go inside the car, and Harry starts to drive me home. I avoid looking at Harry, thinking that if I make him too uncomfortable, he will probably kick me out of his car. The ride remains silent until Harry turns to look at me, and has a question on his mind.

"So, I made the football team. However, I need to get my grade point average up, or they are going to kick me off the team. Since you like being around me so much fag, I want you to help tutor me after school so I can stay on the team. If that's not okay, I'll just beat you up."

I end up laughing to myself. He has an ultimatum it seems. I knew he had some sort of a weak spot, and I was glad to have found it. He wants academic help. I respond to Harry.

"Alright, I'll help you with your studies. On one condition. I don't want you to bully me at school anymore. I'll help you, but you can't be acting like a bully around me. Deal?"

Harry then pulls his truck over, and has an angered look on his face. He turns the ignition of his truck off, and turns to look at me. He angrily responds back.

"Hell no. I have a rep. Unlike you, I have friends at that school. If I start acting nice to you faggot, they are gonna think we're a couple. I just can't do that. I'm sorry. Now the deal is if you want to hang out with me, you gotta help me with my classwork. Deal?"

I was not satisfied or happy with this. I did not think this was a fair deal at all. So not only do I have to help a guy who bullies me at school with his classwork, he's still gonna continue to bother and badger me regardless. To me that just did not seem fair. But life isn't fair usually. I really liked Harry, and I guess I understood where he was coming from. He's this big strong guy that's on the football team. I'm a wimpy gay guy, and I guess I have to put myself in his shoes. He doesn't want to be targeted for hanging around me, and I have to understand that. I end up agreeing to Harry's deal. After he drops me off at home, he gives me his phone number, and I get his. When I went to bed that night, I thought about Harry quite a bit. This man just wouldn't stop leaving my thoughts alone. It wasn't possible for me to stop thinking of him. The next day at school, I met up with Harry during final period, and everything was normal.

After class ended, we both went to the school library, and I ended up helping him with his studies. Harry was bad at practically every subject. Math, Science, you name it. He was a good athlete, just a terrible book learner. I could tell he was going to be a hard case to crack. It was only the first day of me tutoring him, so I didn't expect that much. However, I wish Harry would have given me a break at least a little. He didn't know it, but my crush on Harry was also getting strong. I was only helping him with his classwork, yet I was treating this as if it were a date or something.

I continue to help Harry, and it's soon time for us both to go home. Harry gives me a ride back to my home, and I say goodbye. This time when I went to bed that night, I knew I had to let Harry know my feelings about him. I didn't want him to know, but I want the feelings I have with Harry to be known. My crush on him gets worse every day, and I don't know how to deal with it. I told myself the next time I meet with Harry afterschool, I will tell him.

The next day at school, I see Harry with his group of friends during lunch period. I end up finding a bench outside the cafeteria. As I'm preparing to sit down, some of Harry's friends pull the bench away, causing me to fall on the ground, and my lunch splatters all over my clothes. I look up and see Harry and his friends laughing at me. I was at first surprised that Harry did not stick up for me, but then understood the deal we had. After I pick my lunch tray up, Harry kicks the tray out of my hand, causing it to fly across the ground. Harry and his friends laugh and walk away. I had no choice but to take the humiliation.

I grab my tray, and just accept the uneasy feeling of being punished. During final period however, Harry's behavior seemed to have changed. We were doing a group and partner assignment. I helped Harry answer all the questions right, and we both got a passing grade for the group assignment. So I think as long as Harry isn't in the presence of his friends, he won't bother me as much, or at all even. After final period, Harry and I proceed to the library. We are going through all the coursebooks and being focused on that. I hate to change the mood, but I have to say what's on my mind to him. Once a half an hour passes, I begin to feel the need to let Harry know how I really feel. I then speak to him directly, and without bullshitting.

"Harry, there is something I need for you to know. I have a crush on you."

As soon as I finished saying that, Harry slams shut his coursebook, and angrily frowns at me. Harry then starts to grab his things, and walks out of the library, while whispering at me.

"You're such a fag. Leave me alone. The deal is off. I want no more help from you."

I was afraid that something like this would end up happening. I thought the relationship that we were forming, was going so well, but I guess not. I didn't mean to upset or harm him, but he clearly did not take the news well. As I am starting to grab my things, I notice that I don't have a ride home. I try to hurry up and grab my belongings, so I can catch up to Harry to ask him for a ride. Even though I doubt he would agree to give me one. I rush out of the library, and Harry is nowhere to be seen. I end up directing myself to the student parking lot, and Harry's truck is not there. I don't have a choice, I have to take the long walk home. During the walk to my house, I just realized how I fucked up a good thing. I lost my friendship with Harry, all because I couldn't keep my feelings to myself. All I had to do was help him with his classwork, instead of forming a crush on him.

All of that made things worse than they needed to be. I thought that Harry is now not only going to continue to bully me, but any hope I had of being friends with him is over. When I finally reach my house, I go into my bedroom. I get on my bed, and just sob immensely. I feel as though I never want to go back to school again, due to the hurt I'm feeling. I quickly managed to make myself feel better, when I remembered that Harry has a football practice tomorrow evening at Friday. I know that Harry said that he didn't want to be tutored by me, but he didn't say anything about me not going to his football practice.

The following day at school, I tried my best to avoid Harry and his group. I ate my lunch far away from the cafeteria, and mostly hid myself in the hallways. I knew I was going to have to see Harry later in the day at class, but I wasn't worried about that.

At final period, I sat together with Harry, and didn't say a word. We were given a pop quiz for today, and I hoped that I tutored Harry enough for him to pass it. It seems like my tutoring may have helped; I glance quickly over at Harry's test, and most of the questions he is getting right. I see no reason as to why he won't pass it. At the end of the class, the teacher hands everyone back their tests. I end up getting an 'A' on the test, and Harry also passes the test by getting an 'A', as well.

When class ends, Harry immediately proceeds to the football field, to get ready for his football game. At this time to not bring suspicion to myself on him, I instead go to the library to study. I decide to stay there until a few minutes before Harry's practice. After a while, I end up going to the football field, to snoop on Harry. I end up hiding under the bleachers, staring at him and his teammates practice. All the guys are in their football uniforms.

I continue to watch Harry, during his practice. Once his practice is over, I begin to grab my things and walk back inside to the school hallways. I was feeling very happy seeing Harry play, although part of me was upset that the friendship I had with him, doesn't exist anymore. I at least wanted to make amends with Harry despite that. I decide to walk back outside to the football field, and Harry is with his teammates, talking to them. I continue to snoop on him without him seeing me, before I decide to actually go up and speak with him. Once Harry is alone, I walk outside to the football field. The both of us make eye contact, and Harry is not pleased. I then speak out him.

"You're really good Harry. I saw you play. I know you don't like it when I spy on you, but I really like how you play. Listen, the reason I came up to you, is that I wanted to say I'm sorry. I didn't want for you to feel..."

Harry then shoves me down to the grown of the football field.

"I thought I told you to leave me alone fag. Didn't I tell you that? Why is that so hard for you to comprehend? I don't want you by me, and I don't want you sneaking up on me."

I nod my head, and start to talk away from Harry. I don't dare for a second turn my head to look at him in the process. I knew Harry was still at the field, but I pretended he wasn't there. I simply kept walking. I knew that I at least tried to make things better between the both of us. Harry just simply wasn't interested, and I had to accept this.

I had to respect whichever way he was feeling. I thought it was maybe better if we weren't friends. If all he's going to do is bully me, that isn't a good relationship to have with someone. There was only one issue. The crush I had on Harry still remains. I was still unable to completely rid of him through my thoughts.

I continue to walk away from the football field, sobbing heavily. Unable to come to the realization that there is nothing else I can do about this situation. I didn't want the my senior year to end up like this. I also didn't want my relationship with Harry to end this way. To also be honest, I didn't want to take the long walk home. I then did something that I think was very courageous. I went back to the football field. Harry was still at the football field, with a basket of footballs. He was practicing his throws. I end up sitting at the bleachers. It wasn't long before Harry noticed that I was sitting at the bleachers, watching him. He shouts over at me.

"I told you to leave me alone. Go away. I don't want to be bothered."

Harry then throws a football in my direction at the bleachers nearly missing me. Even though Harry doesn't want to be bothered, I'm technically not bothering him. I take out my notebook and begin to do my homework. Trying not to pay Harry any attention, although the only reason I'm in this area is to be near him.

He doesn't have to know that though. As I'm continuing to do my homework, Harry continues to throw balls down the field, seeing how far he can throw each one. When Harry realizes that I'm not going anywhere, he once again throws a football at the direction of the bleachers. This time the football knocks my notebook down. Feeling agitated by this, I let Harry know exactly how I feel.

"Hey, why did you do that? I'm trying to do my work. Harry, you told me to leave you alone, and I am. I'm minding my own business doing my homework. What can you say now?"

Harry then does something unpredictable, and walks up to the bleachers with a football in his hand, to sit beside me. He picks up my notebook that feel down on the bleachers, and hands it to me. Harry and I sit next to each other silently for a few seconds. I then begin to return to doing my homework.

Harry then starts to spin a football in his hand, while looking down. As I keep to doing my homework, Harry then starts to stare at the work I'm doing. He picks up my workbook, skimming through all of the pages. Harry stares at the workbook, very confused. Right after that, he curiously starts to talk to me while looking at my workbook.

"What kind of classwork are you doing? That looks like math. I'm not very good at it as you know. I know I said I don't want your help anymore, but I could use it."

As Harry is still looking through the workbook, I keep my eyes away from him, and laugh to myself, as I write down the answers to the problems in my notebook. Harry continues to sit and spin the football in his hands. I start to feel more pressure from Harry sitting beside me. Harry throws the football up in the air, and then talks to me more.

"How are you gonna get home? The bus for the football players already left."

I continue to stare down at my notebook, but I do respond to Harry.

"Oh that's none of your business how I'm going to get home. So don't worry about that."

Harry throws the football up in the air again, and laughs. He then starts to softly bop the football on top of my head, playfully. As he is doing that, Harry speaks to me.

"So you have a crush on me? Well that's too bad. I don't like you. I think you're an annoying faggot that can't leave me alone. That's why you came to see me at practice."

I did not immediately respond to Harry at all. Instead, I closed my notebook, and started to put my things away. I was beginning to feel uncomfortable, and I decided that now was the right time for me to leave. As much as I had liked Harry in my mind, I didn't enjoy the way he was teasing me about it. It was not good for my health, and I needed to leave from this situation. While I'm getting myself up from the bleachers, Harry grabs the back of my shirt.

"You leave when I say you can leave fag. Where do you think you're going?"

Although my face was turned away from Harry, I had a wide smile. On my face. I don't know why I was experiencing a positive vibe towards this. Harry is nothing but a bully, and I don't need his energy in my life. But now he doesn't want me to go. This feels wrong, but it feels right at the same time. I then knew that we both could play this game. Seconds later, I turn my head, and force my lips to Harry's lips, and we both kiss.

Harry immediately is stunned by his reaction, and is speechless. I start to smile at him, and feel that I have won this battle. I had my first kiss with Harry. It was his own damn fault for giving out hints that he is feeling the same way as well. So no I don't fucking feel bad at all for kissing Harry. I felt so happy to have done it, and I don't regret it at all. Harry shoves me down on the bleachers, and looks at me menacingly. I then speak to him.

"Don't lie and say you didn't like it. I won't tell if you won't tell."

Harry then frowns at me, and starts to pick my books up from the bleachers. As he is picking my books up, he softly cries out something.

"Let me take you home. It's getting late."

I end up walking with Harry to his truck, and he drives me to my house. Harry smiles at me, and I walk out of the vehicle. Following this, I kept the kiss I had with Harry a secret. Harry also stopped bullying me. His friends didn't stop, but Harry himself stopped pestering me. We never talked about the kiss, but we were on good terms. Things kinda got complicated when Harry turned eighteen that November. Being that I didn't turn eighteen until April, it means that I legally I couldn't do anything romantic with him, as I was a still a minor, and Harry was now a legal adult. I continued to tutor Harry after school, and I would come and watch his games quite regularly. Time continued to pass, and my relationship with Harry stayed positive.

When I finally turned eighteen, was when my relationship with Harry bounced back into the infatuation I had with him before. Especially since prom is coming up, graduation is coming up, and we might not see each other ever again. The thought of this scared me. I had to ask Harry if he wanted to be my prom date. I wouldn't be comfortable with myself if I didn't. When I was tutoring Harry afterschool one Friday, I knew this was the perfect time to bring this particular situation up. Harry had changed into his football uniform, as he had a game right after I was going to tutor him. Our tutoring session was over, and I started to ask Harry the important question, but I was much too nervous with my feelings to actually go through with it. I couldn't utter out the words, and was just too nervous. I then had to be strong about it.

"Harry, there is something I need to tell you. I wanted to know if.."

Harry then put his hand behind my neck and smiled. He then whispered to me.

"You want me to be your prom date? The answer is of course Troy. I would love to."

I smile back at Harry with joy. Harry then starts to gather his things.

"I have to get to my game, we can study later, so let's go. I'll give you a ride home after the game okay."

I silently nod to Harry, and the both of us walk to the football field. I watch Harry play, and our school ends up winning. Me and Harry meet at the bleachers after the game, and I tell him something important.

"Harry, my mom is out of town with her boyfriend for the weekend. I don't want to be home alone. Is it okay if I sleep over at your place?"

Harry smiles at me, and nods his head. He then drives me to my house, and I end up packing a few things. I get back into his truck, on his way to his house I couldn't believe I was going to sleep over with Harry.

CHAPTER 5:

MAN OF YELLOW (PART 2)

Was I nervous that Harry invited me over to this house? Well I guess I was a bit. I mean, it's not like I would have gotten mad if he said no. I'm not being truthful, of course I would have been mad if Harry refused to let me come over. Anyways, I guess I'm rambling on too much over that. Harry said yes, and I'm happy to sleep over. On the ride to his house, I wanted to know what his bedroom looked like. You can disagree, but I feel that you can tell a lot about a person from the way their bedroom is arranged. As I'm riding in his truck, I am noticing that his house is quite far. Harry lives even farther from the school than I do. It was something interesting to note I guess. Harry happened to live in a more rural and country area than I lived in. I mean this was Tennessee, and it is the country. It's not the like city. For many people, their property is located on a piece of land. So it's not city, it's not suburbs. It's very complicated to really explain. Harry's truck finally reaches up to his house, and I notice how large his house is from the outside. I didn't know Harry had such a big house. I'm not meaning to make things seem more attractive than they are, but his house looked like a mansion.

Right outside the front door of Harry's house, one of Harry's brothers is seen lifting weights outside the porch. Harry in fact has three other brothers. Harry is the youngest. Harry's second to youngest brother, Harvey, who was nineteen when I first met him; he's now twenty-nine, is the one that's lifting weights. As far as appearance, Harvey could pass as Harry's twin. It's so uncanny how the both of them look alike. However, Harry is actually younger by a year. But man, do they look exactly alike. As far as personality, Harvey is the most friendly out of the bunch of Harry's brothers. His personality is similar to Harry, except he is much more friendlier and nicer. In my opinion, he's also a bit more engaging and welcoming than Harry is. Harvey is currently in university studying engineering, but he doesn't live at campus. He lives at home still. As I get out of Harry's truck, Harvey is still lifting his weights. I'm sure that he is aware that me and Harry have pulled up to the house, but he seems to zone himself out and continue on lifting his weights. For whatever reason, Harry doesn't acknowledge Harvey, and proceeds straight to the front door to unlock it. I decide to do something strange regardless of that. I walk over to Harvey to introduce myself.

"Hi, my name is Troy. You must be one of Harry's brothers. What's your name?"

Harvey continues to lift his weights, ignoring me completely. Harry walks over from the front door, and grabs me by my shirt collar. As we are walking towards the vestibule of the house, Harvey is still lifting his weights, not paying us any attention. Once finally in the house, Harry then closes the front door. While still standing in the vestibule, he whispers into my ear.

"That's Harvey. He's doing his weight training session. He does that every day around this time. It's impossible to bother him during this. He's a cool guy though. Don't worry."

I nod my head, and follow Harry as he heads into the kitchen. I could sense something being cooked, or baked. I couldn't quite decipher what it was. I did know that it smelled great, so it must taste delicious. Inside the kitchen, I see a bearded guy just like Harry chopping up vegetables and cooking in the kitchen. This guy was Harry's oldest brother, Louie. Louie was in his late 20s when I first met him, he's now forty years old. Louie has thinning hair, but he like Harry and the rest of the brothers, has red hair. Louie is also the heaviest and biggest out of all the brothers. He seems to have a great liking towards cooking, which is why he is not only a chef by profession, but he cooks most of the meals in the household. Personality wise, Louie is not a very friendly guy at all. He constantly berates and picks on his brothers quite frequently, and he also isn't much of a social talker. Going by the beat of his own drum, he doesn't surround or engage himself towards the opinions of others. Likewise with Harvey, I attempted to introduce myself to Louie. The meal that Louie was cooking, seemed to be some type of Italian dish. Spaghetti pasta with meatballs most likely. Harry ends up grabbing two bottles of Budweiser beer from the refrigerator. I gaze at Louie cooking the meal. As I am walking towards Louie to say hello, Harry immediately drags me away from Louie by tugging on my shirt collar. As we are now exiting out of the kitchen, heading to the backyard, Harry yet again whispers to me.

"That's Louie. Don't ever talk to him. He's loco. But every dish he makes is delicious."

I nod my head to accept what Harry said. We continue onto the backyard, where I see another one of Harry's brothers. He's tossing a football across the backyard. This is Leif. Leif is the second to oldest brother, and he looks like a much younger version of Louie, and kind of an older version of Harry. However Leif isn't as mean as Louie is. Leif also has a beard, just like the rest of the Bruner brothers do. Leif, identical to Harry, is very invested in football, and that's what he's going to university for. Leif is twenty-one years old, and he's in his junior year of University. He wanted to be drafted into the NFL. That sadly never happened. Although he came relatively close to achieving that dream, it just wasn't meant to be. Leif is now in his thirties, and he is a school gym teacher. Although he didn't notice us at first, Leif eventually stopped throwing the football, and walked over to where Harry and I were placed. Unlike with the other brothers, Leif actually approached me, and began to introduce himself. Leif stuck out his hand for me to shake, and happily spoke to me.

"Who are you? Are you one of Harry's friends? I'm his brother Leif. Nice to meet you."

I end up shaking Leif's hand smiling at him. Really enjoying his friendly energy. I then decide to introduce myself to him, while I'm still shaking his hand.

"Yes, I'm Harry's friend Troy. I'm gonna be spending the weekend with you guys."

Leif nods his head to accept what I said, and goes back to throwing the football. I really enjoyed meeting Leif, as he was the most open out of all the brothers. I stand outside the patio entrance of the backyard, however, Harry walks over to where his brother is. Harry and Leif then began to speak in a hush tone, and I was unable to hear exactly what they were saying. I had an idea they were possibly having trivial talk about me, but I wasn't exactly certain. After a short while, Harry and Leif walk over the area I was in, and Leif starts to talk to me.

"Alright, if you need anything just ask okay. You're our guest. So make yourself at home. We don't bite. Well except Louie, but just never mind him. Nice to meet you Troy."

I shake Leif's hand one more time, and Harry and I both proceeded up to his bedroom. As we are walking up the staircase, there was something plaguing my mind rather badly. I noticed that Harry didn't introduce me to his parents, nor did he mention them at all. I didn't think there was anyone left in the house he neglected to introduce me to, so this was something that I was feeling very confused over. So as we were walking up the stairs to Harry's bedroom, I had to ask him a question and concern that I believed he was avoiding to mention.

"Uh Harry, where are your mom and dad at? I mean you introduced your brothers to me and that's very nice. But where is your mother and father? Do they work a lot?"

Harry had a disappointed look on his face, and remained quiet not replying to my question as we were walking up the stairs. It was like he almost didn't hear me ask that question, but he did. He just wish I didn't bring it up, which part of me regretted bringing it up. If it was going to cause this much trouble, I never would have opened my mouth. When we reached his bedroom door, he stopped for what seemed like a minute. Harry was refusing to answer the question about his parents, and he seemed to not want to talk or discuss it. I knew the story behind it must have been extremely hard for him to explain in detail about. Harry then turned and looked at my direction, and I just stood in silence confused. He turned to his bedroom door, proceeding to turn the doorknob. He then returned his vision back to me. Harry then finally decided to open up about my question, and explain why didn't mention his parents.

"They died when I was three in a car crash okay? Me and my brothers were all little. They worked for the peace corps, and they were in South Africa driving a Humvee when it crashed. I don't want to fucking talk about it. Now don't ask me about my parents ever again."

I felt a slight feeling of guilt after Harry explained the whole situation. I couldn't imagine losing both of my parents young, so that must have been a huge burden to deal with. I later found out that Harry's grandparents would supervise and act as a guardian for Harry and his brothers after their parents death. By the time both of his grandparents had passed, Louie was already a legal adult, and the house which belongs to their parents, passed onto them. I don't know much else about the death of Harry's parents. I didn't want to pressure him too much about this. This event I could understand causes great grief, and I'm not the type of person to trouble someone due to things such as that.

Now that we are in Harry's bedroom, I notice how his room is decorated. I see posters of rock bands on the wall, and I also see many sports collectable items as well. I end up sitting at Harry's desk, and he hands me one of the beers he got from the kitchen. Being that neither Harry or I were of drinking age at the time, I guess it was nice for us to sin, if only for a moment, by participating in underage drinking. I mean it is just one beer. Harry does manage to get his beer open, but I struggle trying to get the bottle cap off. Feeling embarrassed, I couldn't believe how weak I was, that I couldn't even open up a beer bottle. Harry takes several sips of his beer, before noticing that I'm struggling to open the bottle. After realizing that I'm having issues, he walks over to his desk where I'm seated, and snatches the bottle out of my hand. Harry manages to open the bottle without any issues within a flash of a second, and hands the bottle back to me. Harry then laughs at me, and goes over to his bed setting the beer bottle on the side table. As I'm sitting at Harry's desk, I began to open up my workbook. I knew I had a lot of homework to do, so I didn't want to waste any time at all neglecting to do it. Even though Harry was laying down on his bed relaxing, I knew he also had homework to do, and offered to help him out.

"Did you need help with your homework? Since we have to do the same assignment, I figured I would tutor you, if there was a section you needed to help on. I don't mind."

Harry then gets up from his bed, walks over to his closet area to pick up a football. He then takes the football back over to this bed, and lays down again. While lying down, Harry takes the football and throws it up in the air, while responding to the question I asked him.

"No I don't. Fuck school. I fucking hate homework. I just want to play football, and become filthy rich doing that. I don't give a fuck what you do, but I don't want to talk about classwork. Fuck graduation too. That's just not my style."

Feeling disappointed that Harry has little concern of his schoolwork, I wondered if I should persuade him into thinking otherwise. I cared about his future, and I understand that football is a major passion for him, I do. However, his schoolwork and his academics are just as important, if not more important. His football career is not guaranteed, but his education is. There was no way I could just let Harry think like that, and allow him to have that mindset and agenda towards his future. I have to make sure he understands this, as I care about him. While I continue on doing the homework assignment, I try to use my powers of persuasion on Harry.

"But Harry, if you don't graduate, that means you're quitter. I know you care about football, but I care about your education Harry. That's more important. If you drop out, that means you're quitter. You don't want to be quitter right? Now get your ass over here, and do these damn problems."

It seemed to have worked, as Harry got out of bed, and sat next to me at his desk. We worked on the homework assignment for about an hour and a half, until Louie knocked on the door informing us that dinner was ready. We decided to temporarily suspend doing our homework, and proceeded down to the dining room to eat dinner. All of Harry's brothers and myself were situated around the table, eating. For the first few minutes of the meal, everyone was quiet, and they didn't even realize that I was present at the table with them. However, it wasn't long until Louie became way too curious for his own purpose. Louie takes a sip of wine, and decided to speak to me.

"Harry doesn't have friends. None of us do. You're the first person that Harry has brought home from school. So what's your story? Don't lie either. I don't like liars."

I take a few bites of food, and feel uncomfortable by the way Louie is talking to me. But I do manage to stay polite and respond to what he said.

"Well, I don't know. What can I say? I'm just Harry's friend, and we just happened to click. I think you have to ask Harry that question, and not me."

Louie takes another swallow of his wine, and continues to pry at me.

"Well are you attracted to him? Are you his bitch or something? I'm not trying to judge, but I like to call a spade a spade. Harry isn't a fag, just so you know."

Harry then gives Louie a look of disgust, and then angrily shouts back at him.

"Lou, shut the fuck up and leave him alone. You don't talk to company like that."

Louie then pours himself yet another glass of wine, and swallows it. I don't lock my vision towards him, and continue to eat. But I know that Louie is staring at me rather deeply. Louie then continues on.

"Well it's unusual for you to bring friends over Harry. That's not you. Nobody even likes you; you always say how the other kids at school avoid you. I know it's not any of my business, but if I didn't know any better I think you guys were boyfriends. I don't give a fuck though."

At this time, Harry immediately launched up like a tiger ready to attack, and threw Louie onto the ground. Me, Harvey and Leif get up from the table to break them up. Even though Harry and Louie were wrestling and fighting each other on the ground rather violently, we managed to get them to knock it off, without any of them causing serious harm to one another. Louie then takes the bottle of wine off the table, and his plate of food, and begins to walk upstairs to his bedroom. Myself, Harry, Harvey and Leif all go back to the table. Harry covers his hands over his face, and looks down at the table feeling upset. He then tries to comfort me.

"He's drunk, so it's okay. He usually is like that. when he has been drinking. Just give him some time to cool off. He doesn't hate you, he's just drunk."

I nod my head, to acknowledge everything that Harry took in. After a couple minutes or so, Harvey and Leif end up excusing themselves away from the table, taking their plates with them. I felt bad about this whole ordeal, feeling responsible that I was the one who ruined their dinner. Harry and I sat at the dining room table together silent. None of us are touching our food, or eating. It is an awkward and strange vibe, and it doesn't seem right. I honestly deeply feel that Harry is keeping something from me, so I start to pester him about it.

"What's wrong? Is everything okay? Was it something I did? You want me to go home? I didn't mean to ruin dinner. I'm sorry Harry. I'll get my things and you can take me home."

Right after saying that, Harry puts his hand over his head, and starts to talk to me.

"Louie is really thinking about selling our house. He wants to move to California before the end of the summer is out. He doesn't like Tennessee, and wants to move out of here. He says with the money we get from this house, we can use that money to move to California. He wants to start his own restaurant, and he's really convinced. So I don't know what to do."

Harry was not very optimistic about moving to California, and agreeing with his brother to sell the house, and moving to another state. He has happy and comfortable in his own home town, and didn't want to make a drastic change like that. It was tough, because something like this isn't any of my business, and I didn't feel comfortable offering advice to a family situation that didn't involve or pertain to me at all. I was also thinking sort of selfishly about it. The fact of the matter is if Harry were to move to California, I wouldn't be able to see him much anymore. I would be on the other side of the country, away from him. The thought of losing a close friend like Harry, was making me feel sad. However, that wasn't a valid excuse to the current situation. This decision isn't mine to make, or persuade. If he and his brothers do decide to end up moving, that's just the way it is, and no amount of crying or complaining is going to change that. Harry and I end up sitting at the table for what seems like an hour. I understand that he's troubled, and he doesn't want to move away, but there is nothing I can do, but be understanding. We manage completing our meal, and we leave from the table, back up to Harry's bedroom.

Once back in his room, we return to doing our homework assignment. I didn't talk about or discuss any of the family affairs that Harry was going through. Understanding that these types of discussions and situations bring him much sadness. While doing the assignment, I start to also think about prom. Harry did accept my prom invitation, and if Harry were to move away, I would take the prom as a way for me to say goodbye to him.

Bringing up the prom at this time didn't seem correct, so I refused to talk about it. I would just discuss prom with Harry sometime later, not now though. Although I didn't want Harry to move, if he had to move, I didn't want to take whatever little time I had left with him for granted. Getting later onto the night, we both finish our homework. Even though it was late, I wasn't feeling tired at all. It was like creeping up at almost midnight, and I wasn't even sleepy. I ended up playing an adventure video game on Harry's computer, and it's rather addicting. I get lost playing the game and spend quite a bit of time playing. Harry although is visibly tired and fatigued. I then look over at him, and he has his head slouched down on the desk, drifting in and out of staying awake.

This continued for a half an hour of Harry resting down at his desk, falling asleep and waking up repeatedly. He finally walks over to the other side of the bedroom, feeling completely exhausted and tired, and changes into his sleepwear, and puts a bunch of blankets on the floor down next to his bed. I seem confused as to why he is doing this. Harry then prepares to lay down on the floor, while talking to me.

"I'm going to sleep on the floor, you can sleep on my bed. I don't have cooties so it's okay. You can sleep on my bed, when you get tired. If you get hungry, you know where the kitchen is, and you can help yourself to whatever you want. I'm gonna go to bed now."

While I'm playing the game on his computer, I nod my head at Harry. Harry does end up falling asleep on the floor, and I continue to play the video game. An hour and a half later, I start to feel tired, and I change into my pajamas. I then fall asleep on Harry's bed. The next morning, I notice that Harry is not in the bedroom. Feeling rejuvenated, I get out of bed and direct myself down to the kitchen. Harry and Louie are arguing very loudly and violently. I notice that Harvey is eating a bowl of cereal in the living room watching a movie. I go and sit next to him. When Harvey notices that I'm seated on the sofa, he starts to converse with me.

"Good morning. You want some cereal? Come on, I'll make you a bowl."

I follow Harvey into the kitchen, where the sound of Harry and Louie arguing in the background is very dominating and overpowering. It is difficult for me to zone out their fighting, but I managed to do it somehow. Harvey proceeds to get me a bowl from the cabinet, and a carton of milk that was in the refrigerator. He then hands me the cereal box, and I start to prepare myself a bowl of cereal. I don't pay any attention at all to Harry and Louie fighting, as I didn't feel it was my place to get into their affair. Whatever they are discussing, most likely and definitely has nothing at all to do with me. I grab my bowl, and I start to head towards the living room with Harvey. Once the both of us are seated, Harvey eats his cereal, and talks to me.

"I'm sorry about that. They obviously don't get along, and they fight like that all the time. I just ignore it, I don't even notice they are doing it sometimes. We are going to be moving soon, and it's something we all have to accept. Louie got a restaurant offer in California."

What Harvey was saying was correct. The main reason for the brothers moving, is for Louie's career. He was trying to open and own his own restaurant in Tennessee, but received an even better offer to open his own restaurant in Los Angeles. Alongside that, Louie also received an offer to sell the house, that he just simply could not refuse. Louie is 100 percent on board with the decision, and he has pretty much finalized that. Leif and Harvey on the other hand are neutral, and sort of slightly agree more with Louie. Harry however, is not at all happy with this decision, and doesn't want to move. Being happy where he currently is in Tennessee, moving to California is not in his agenda or in his wishes. I did know that whatever decision was made, I had no control over this, as this wasn't my situation to get involved in. I was simply Harry's friend. I was nothing more or less. It was interesting being an unofficial member of the family, as I am in the middle of a family dispute. I decide to kindly respond to Harvey anyways.

"Oh wow. That's rather heavy. So you guys are going to move to California? That's far. It's going to be tough to stay goodbye to Harry. I really enjoy having him as a friend."

Although I had no say in whatever matters were taking place, it was still entertaining to witness nevertheless. It was sort of exciting in that regard.

Throughout the rest of the weekend, Harry continued to fight with Louie. I didn't let that destroy my stay as a guest though. I interacted with Harry's other brothers, and we seemed to click just fine. Louie although he was a jerk in a general sense, was an extremely good cook. That Saturday night that I stayed over a guest, he ended up making the best barbecue chicken I ever tasted. They had a huge grill in their backyard, and Louie took full use of it. So despite the fact I didn't care for Louie personally, his cooking was absolutely perfect. I understand completely why he wants to open his own restaurant in California, as his talent clearly shows. I was really enjoying my time at Harry's place, despite the few times where he and Louie would bout and bicker with each other. I just simply removed myself from the both of them when they got into it, and didn't pay them any attention.

The following Sunday seemed rather boring. Some of the brothers were doing yard work, and Louie actually was gone most of the day. He went to church. I interacted with Harry very little in his room, but for most of the day, he was in the backyard playing football with Leif. Louie later came back to the house from church that night, and cooked an amazing dinner. Fried chicken, with mashed potatoes and grilled vegetables. It was so good, and I've never in my life had fried chicken that tasted that good. Once I finished eating, Harry offered to drive me back home. We had school the following day. I end up saying goodbye to all of Harry's brothers, and Harry takes me back home. I had an amazing time, and I will forever remember the first time I met his family, and how crazy it was.

For the following weeks, my interaction with Harry seemed to weaken. I would see him during final period as usual, but we wouldn't engage in any personal matters. I also ended up forming a tutoring group after school with other students, including Harry. So our tutoring sessions which in the past seemed very intimate between just Harry and I, now were not the case. So after school tutoring became strictly academic focused, and had nothing to do with the relationship that Harry and I had. Despite the fact that Harry would give me a ride home from school every day, he simply was starting to become my chauffeur. He was no longer my close friend. I don't mean to relay this in any negative or bad way.

That is just how it simply seemed. I'm sure that the pressure and turmoil of him having to move away might have something to do with it most likely. In addition to that, I still have not brought up prom any further with Harry yet. Prom is only a week to go. With Harry being my official prom date, we have not talked about anything related to that. That is if Harry is even interested in going to prom me with anymore. Based on recent events, he probably doesn't.

Not because he hates me, or wants to avoid me. It is mostly due to because he has the moving issue, and prom is something not on his agenda. What I feel doesn't really matter. I was looking forward to prom, so I could spend my last moments with Harry before he went away. That was thinking very selfishly though. If Harry doesn't want to go anymore because of family issues, I have to simply accept that, and not be angry over his decision. You cannot force someone to do something that they do not wish to do. That includes forcing Harry to go to prom, without fully understanding the family issues that he has to deal with. Everything is not always about me, and it's Harry's decision at the end of the day. This is something I simply need to understand.

I wanted to try to discuss the prom with him regardless, and how we were going to arrange that. One evening as Harry was driving me home after class, I wanted to know his honest opinion about prom. If he said no, then that's something I'm going to just have to accept. I remember sitting in Harry's truck, afraid to bring the topic up, however I mangled to do it.

"So Harry, as you know prom is next Friday. You didn't mention anything about still wanting to attend. I mean, if you don't want to go, you don't have to. But I would like for you to. Please?"

Harry while he's still driving, smiles at what I said. I felt relieved that he wasn't upset or aggravated by me mentioning and bringing up prom. Harry turns his head in my direction, and nods. Now that it is official that prom is still active, I can ease my mind. Although things with Harry were taking a drastic turn. All of the brothers, including Harry, reluctantly decided to agree to the move to California. They were going to move a week after graduation. So that means I only have a very short time with Harry, before he moves to the other side of the country, and I may sadly not ever see him again.

Time refuses to stand still, and that's how life is. The night of the prom arrives, and I put on a very nice ensemble my mother picked out. A nice suit and tie, something that I rarely wear. Being that it's senior prom, I need to dress nicely. Harry eventually arrives at my house, and picks me up. Harry is also wearing a rather dapper suit and tie, and he can pull of wearing a suit well. We end up driving to the senior prom. I was so shocked and surprised that literally no one was there. You would think for a big event like the prom, the gymnasium would be jam packed with students. There were literally like 20 other students, with myself and Harry included. A possible reason for this, is that the school district allowed students if they wish, to go to the prom at another school closer to their home. There were rumors that rival schools had a live DJ and other goodies, so most of the students probably went to prom elsewhere. Our school didn't have those amenities. We had a cheese and cracker sampler plate, and watered down punch. No DJ, or anything. Just a loop of the radio playing the top 40 hits. But I didn't care. Me and Harry got to experience prom, and it was nice. Wait, hold on. I'm leaving an important detail out.

Some of Harry's jerk friends decided to crash the prom. As a prank, one of Harry's friends Sam, who is a chubby bald headed boy who hung around Harry at school frequently, threw the punchbowl over my head while me and Harry were dancing to hip hop music, and I was covered in the nasty sticky watered down punch. Sam began to make fun of me.

"Oops. I'm sorry, did I do that? My mistake. I didn't mean to interrupt your romantic dance together. How rude of me. Ha-Ha"

I was so embarrassed after having the punch doused on me. I didn't know how to react, and after looking at Harry, he was also extremely angered over this. I feel no matter what I do, I'm always being attacked for no reason. Those assholes just had to bother us for no reason. Evil works in strange ways, and I have really had it. Now you know I was very fired up after that. I had to vent out my frustrations to them.

"Fuck you guys. You guys are a bunch of fucking big babies. Grow the hell up."

Harry also refused to hold back, and also angrily shouted out.

"Wow, really? What assholes. Why the fuck you do that to him. We weren't even bothering you. You guys are such pieces of shit."

Harry takes his handkerchief, and starts to wipe some of the punch off my hair, and takes some napkins trying his best to dry me off. He then softly consoles me.

"Never mind them, they are just white trash. Those guys need to grow the fuck up."

I end up smiling at Harry, due to him protecting and comforting me. Because the prom was unsupervised, which I have no idea why that was, none of the teachers came to punish the guys who did that. As soon as Harry realized the prank his friends pulled, they ran out of the gymnasium, and Harry followed them out. Despite the fact I was covered head to toe in the punch, I scattered with them as well. His friends end up at the football field, where they stop running. At this time, Sam, then begin to heckle both me and Harry.

"We thought your boyfriend needed a bath Harry. We we're doing him a favor."

Harry then punches Sam in the face, which then causes some of Harry's other friends to attack Harry. I stand frozen in place, unable to react due to all of these events. As I'm watching Harry and his friends go back and forth from beating each other up, seconds into this, Sam manages to lift me and up, and carries me outside of the football field, shouting as he's doing it.

"Hey Harry, since you're moving away, that gives us more time to play with your little boyfriend. As a matter of fact, we're going to play a little fun game with him right now."

I am completely terrified, and scared of the unknown. Harry yells out to Sam.

"Don't you dare hurt him. Let him go."

I scream out for Harry to help me, and he does. He runs in the direction Sam and I are. Despite the fact Harry's other friends are trying to restrain him from coming after me, he quickly fights them off. Sam directs me over to his truck, and I sit in the passenger seat. He ties my hands and legs together, and I'm physically unable to move or escape once he does that. Sam then opens up his glove compartment, and begins to douse me in lighter fluid. Not able to be completely clear with my thoughts, I just sit silent and bound. I think of crying out to Harry, but it's not like he can hear me anyway. Sam drives away from the school. As I'm riding in Sam's truck, scared as to what he is intending to do with me, he speaks to me.

"We're just going to play a little senior prank on you. We're not gonna hurt you, and you're not gonna die. You're going to wish you were dead though. Ha-Ha."

I really wish I wasn't tied together, or else I would have tried to run myself out of the car. I however cannot move, due to the fact they tied me together. I look in the rear view mirror, and see the rest of the bullies following Sam in their vehicle. However, my glimmer of hope comes, when I see Harry's truck also following us in the rear view mirror. I am praying that he is able to save me from all of this, and I don't end up getting hurt from whatever trick Sam and his gang are intending to play. We remain on the road for about twenty minutes, when Sam finally pulls over to what looks like an abandoned farm house. Being that it is so late at night, it makes the farm house seem like a haunting location. Sam turns off the ignition and opens the passenger side door, carrying me outside the truck. He ends up taking me to the front porch of the abandoned house tying a rope around my neck, and puts the other end of the rope on a hook on a post hanging outside the front porch. After Sam does this, he pours more lighter fluid on me. Within seconds, Harry and the rest of the bullies arrive at the scene. Harry then screams out to Sam.

"Don't you hurt him. Don't do anything to him. Leave him alone now!"

Harry tries to run after me, but Sam takes a baseball bat, striking it at the back of Harry's head, which the impact stuns and knocks Harry out. Now that Harry is immobilized, Sam then starts to light the rope my neck is attached to. Before he does, he starts to shout out.

"You took Harry away from us. You made him soft. He's not a faggot, and you made him one. So we're gonna take Harry away from you. Harry isn't going to want you anymore after we burn you to a crisp. We won't kill you, but we're gonna teach you a lesson you won't forget."

Once Sam finishes talking, he takes a large lighter, and prepares to ignite the rope that's attached to my neck. The end of the rope has to be about twenty feet, so it wasn't very long and the fire would spread to me very quickly. Before the rope is able to be lit, Harry unexpectedly rises up from being knocked out, and pins Sam down on the floor. The two remaining guys in Sam's group try to get Harry off him, but Harry takes the same baseball bat he was knocked with, to strike both of them. Sam recovers from being pinned on the floor, and goes over to the rope to light it.

I honestly don't think Sam was trying to seriously harm me though, I don't know. Maybe he was just trying to scare me. Harry tries to stop Sam from lighting the rope, but he's sadly a second too late. Sam laughs, and teases by flicking the lighter flame, but remarkably, Sam ends up being badly burned by the fire instead, and ends up, igniting himself instead of the rope I was attached to. Harry then takes off his suit jacket to extinguish the flames off Sam. Luckily, Sam survives, thanks to Harry's diligence.

During this time, the remaining guys in Sam group, both get in their vehicles and leave. Once the flames have been snuffed off Sam's body, Harry runs over to where I'm hung and begins to free me. Immediately after this, Harry takes Sam's badly burned body and asks my help to carry him to Harry's truck. He put Sam in the back seat of Harry's truck, and Harry drives him to the hospital. We arrive to the hospital, and Harry and I, carry Sam inside the emergency room. Harry lies to the hospital staff, that we were all doing a senior prank and it went wrong. Although Sam is badly burned, he's not unconscious and could hear Harry lying to the nurses and doctors at the hospital. Sam is immediately wheeled into the operating room. Harry and I sit in the waiting room in shock. Several hours later, one of the doctors later approach us, and explain to us that Sam is going to be fine, and although his burns were bad, luckily the burns were not that life threatening.

Sam friends reach the hospital, and they quickly make amends with Harry and I, and beg us not to inform the police about the situation. Harry already informs them, that he told the hospital staff they were playing a prank which got out of hand. We all agree to go along with this lie. Sam's parents reach the hospital, and we all explain the same story to them. Hours later, Harry and I went to Sam's recovery room. Sam immediately apologized to the both of us.

"I'm sorry. I don't know what got over me. Please forgive me. I won't bother any of you again. I'm in so much pain, and I'm so sorry. Please forgive me."

Sam begged me not to press charges on him. I decided not to, as Sam being burned, I figured taught him a lesson, and I don't think he really wanted to harm me. I wanted to completely forget about the situation. Harry and I end up leaving the hospital, and he proceeds to drive me home. I couldn't believe that the senior prom ended up being destroyed like this. This could have perhaps been the final time that I could be with Harry, and it is a shame it ended on these terms. I end up saying goodnight to Harry, and Harry kisses me on the cheek. As I'm walking to my door, I look back at Harry who seems very sad. Harry then gets out of his truck, and gives me a big hug. I can't stop crying, because I don't want to lose Harry. He's going to be moving away, and I won't be able to talk or see him again. Once I am finished hugging Harry, I walk inside and immediately walk myself to bed. It wasn't hard for me to sleep as I've had an exhausting night, but I still was anxious that Harry was going to go, and our senior prom moment was ruined. It didn't plan out exactly the way I had intended, and was a disaster.

With it now only being a two weeks left of school, with graduation soon approaching around the corner, my days with Harry are numbered. Harry and his brothers are currently packing all their stuff in preparation for them to move. As soon as graduation is over, he and his brothers are moving to California, and there is nothing I can do about it. I will be stuck here in Tennessee, and I don't know if I am going to see Harry again. I spend my last days tutoring Harry, making sure his grades are all set. I also want to explore all his weak points, as if he fails his final exams, he won't be able to graduate. However, I'm confident that Harry will do just fine. I distinctly remember our last tutoring session. It was the day before final exams, and three days before graduation. I was simply overwhelmed with depression that my time with Harry is limited. Trying my best to hold back the tears, I just couldn't. I began sobbing heavily, and Harry was shocked to see me crying. I immediately bury my head in my chest, crying out to him.

"I don't want you to move. I don't know what I'll do. I'm going to miss you so much. You have been such a good friend to me Harry. I'm really going to miss you. Don't go."

Harry starts rubbing my head, as I just refuse to accept that he's going away forever. Being here with him, I feel very safe. Bittersweet, as he's going to be leaving me. I thought I had already gotten past this, but I haven't. No matter what tactic I use, I'm always going back to my depressive state, on the thought of Harry going away. I continue to cry, as Harry is comforting me. Harry then says something which calms me down.

"You know Troy, I was talking with Louie and my brothers. The house we're moving to has plenty of room. We want you to move to

California with us. Only if you want to. I would like for you to move with us, but if you want to stay you can. But I'm inviting you to move with all of us."

I immediately take my head away from Harry's chest, and start jumping for joy around the library. I am completely ecstatic and jubilant. Weight lifted off my shoulders. Almost feeling too excited to speak. I answer Harry which much glee and joy.

"Oh yes, I would love to move with you. Thank you so much. I can't believe we're going to stay together. We're not going to lose each other. I'm so happy. Yes."

Harry smiles at me, and he shaking his head laughing. He then responds to me.

"I figured that would probably make you stop feeling crabby. Now you can come sit down? We still have a lot of studying to do, so we can pass finals."

I end up return to my seat, although still feeling hyper from everything. Harry and I continue on with our studying. It was impossible for me to take the thought of moving with him away from my mind. That was the best news I have ever received in my life. I couldn't believe that I'm going to move to California with Harry. I no longer felt that uncomfortable feeling inside of me, that he was going to leave me forever. Harry and I finish the tutoring session, and he drives me home. After explaining the situation to my mother, she seems supportive and doesn't mind if I move to California. I will miss her much, but I'll still keep in contact with her. Living in Tennessee was nice, and this is my home, and my birthplace. But it's great that I'm going to start my life over in a new place, and in a new state. I'll also be doing it with my best close friend. So I couldn't be happier about it.

After graduation, I was going to start a new life in California with Harry, to where the possibilities are going to be endless. During final exams, I was confident that I was going to pass all of them with flying colors. I did. As far as my college plans, I didn't have any. I wasn't sure as to what I wanted to do, and now moving to California, I am still rather unsure of what my intentions are going to be. One thing I do know for sure, is that I'll have Harry and his brothers for support, and

I have a place to stay. Harry finished his final exams without any issue. All my tutoring paid off. I understand that football is a big deal for Harry, and I don't know if he wants to still pursue that or not. I guess that's a decision for Harry to make on his own.

My High School graduation was very nice. When my name was called to receive my High School diploma, I was happy to finish High School. I survived school, and everything that happened in the past, is what it is. Not only did I graduate High School, but as an added bonus I made a lifelong friend in the process. It was so nice to finally have High School behind me. My senior year was really wild. I can go back to the first day that I met Harry. He was nothing but a bully, and now he's a really close friend of me.

After graduation, I went to Harry's house, and me along with his brothers had a big party to celebrate. I later began to pack all of my things to move to California. It was a big move, but I was prepared for it. Harry and I both had to put our college or University decisions on hold, to solely focus on this move. It seems like a big whirlwind, but we ended up driving from Tennessee to Los Angeles. As myself and Harry and his brothers reached the house we would be staying at, I was happy with it. The only thing I was slightly ticked off at, was I asked where my bedroom was. I didn't have one. Harry lied and said I would have my own bedroom when I didn't. So I ended up sharing a room with Harry. I don't know if this was a trick for me to end up agreeing with the move, or what. No matter, because nearly ten years later, Harry is my boyfriend, and I love this man. Despite everything that we have been through, and all the troubles we had when we first met. It feels like a dream, but I know everything does have a way of working out. I will grow old with him, and he will never get rid of me. Ha-Ha.

Moving to California at first was a big transition. I mean I do like the weather here, but the people are definitely more attractive. It is very much more a place to where attractive people are, and attractive people mingle. Everyone is completely health conscious here as well. I just wanted to see the beach, that was my main thing. The first day we arrived in California, I asked Harry if he and his brothers wanted to go visit the beach, and they all agreed. So we had a beach party, having a wonderful time. Seeing the Pacific Ocean for the first time was very nice. It was a tough adjustment coming from an area in the south such as Tennessee, to Los Angeles, California. It wasn't long before I got used to everything. This was my home now, and I came to quickly accept it. As far as school, I decided to go to community college, but there wasn't anything that interested me. I studied many things, I just wasn't happy.

Why should I study for a degree that I don't want, and I'm not interested in? That is just a complete waste of time to only for myself, but in general. I had to say the same for Harry. He did end up going to city college to play football, but nothing serious ever came of it. He would end up taking odd jobs, and worked as a janitor for a good while, but the football thing never took off. So as much as we hoped moving to California might expand our academic lives, it really didn't. That's okay though, as we're not going to let something like that drag us down. It just wasn't meant o be.

So I guess the rest is history. Louie ended up opening his restaurant after all, and his restaurant is still doing well. Leif did not end up going onto the NFL sadly, but he is a school gym teacher. Harvey ended up being a construction worker, and enjoys that. As for Harry. Harry became a butcher at a grocery store. Kind of strange of he ended up in a similar position that his brother Louie was in, working with food. He also works with Louie as well in the restaurant as a chef. You're going to have to hear Harry's story to find out how that at happened, as it's rather strange. I know I'm forgetting a bunch of stuff, but oh well. This is all that I can remember, and Harry I'm sure will cover all the stuff I neglected to mention. But yeah, Harry enjoys his job though. As for me, I guess I ended up with a boring job. I work at a large department store selling housewares and things like that. I mean it's a job. I go to work, and come home to my man. Me, Harry and his brothers still live in LA, and we are all one big happy family. We like it like that, and there are no complaints.

However, the complete story doesn't end with me. This is just my part. I don't know Harry's side of it, as he's probably going to bring up something else I didn't mention. I am sure of that. I am just happy with this part of my life. The reason I wanted to tell my story, is that even growing up as a boy being flamboyant and fabulous. Being told that I was not allowed to perform in the talent show. Just things like that from an early age, which I could have given up, and said that I'm always going to be last, and nobody is going to care about me. I'm glad I didn't give up. Although when I first met Harry he was a bully, it's strange how our relationship blossomed from that. Now to present day, I sleep with this man every night. I see him come from work every night, and I'm glad to have him with me. This isn't how I envisioned my life at first, but I'm glad that this is how it panned out.

My story is special, and to some people it may be weird. Especially the fact that I kept trying to be in pursuit of Harry's good graces. In the end I'm glad it worked out, and all the naysayers have to kick rocks. They aren't me, and they are not living my life, so who are they to judge as to what I should do? Participating in this project allows me to make my issues known. I'm not perfect, and I'm happy for my imperfections. I'm happy, Harry is happy, and life seems to be good. I don't feel confused about my life, and although I can be a little crazy at times, I still accept myself. I have found the happiness I felt I always deserved, and the love I felt I always needed.

I can only speak for myself. I can't be the ambassador for everyone that has experienced terrible things in the world. My main goal for my story, is to just tell it. How others perceive it is up to their discretion, although I hope that they do take it to their hearts. It wasn't easy for me to admit to all of my faults, but I did. I have nothing else to say really. Well, I feel strange being that I had to reveal certain private aspects of my life towards this project. I'm not really feeling that guilty about it. People are going to judge you regardless of what you decide to do. My name is Troy Lockwood. I am man of yellow, and that was my story.

CHAPTER 6:

MAN OF ORANGE (PART 1)

My name is Harry Bruner, and I am the "Man of Orange." I am 28 years old. My reddit username is "HarryMachine". Even though I was born in Tennessee, I now live in Los Angeles. I'm going to say first and foremost, that I can't believe Troy dragged me into this shit. This isn't my style at all, and I don't like to be involved in sentimental stuff. I feel everything that has happened in my life, isn't for everyone else to know about, or for me to tell them about either. Especially all the events that surround me and Troy. I feel it's because of him, that my life has changed. Even though I don't regret ever meeting him, or coming into contact with him, there are times to where I do get agitated that it's his fault that I'm like this. I didn't use to be an open person at all. I was a very closed book, and I didn't associate or talk to anyone. That was my choice, because I felt that people weren't interested in me, and didn't want to talk to me anyways. My story is going to be mostly about growing up in Tennessee, with three older brothers, and having to deal with my parents death at such a young age.

Me and my brothers all grew up looking much older than we actually were. I think it's mainly because I started to grow a beard when I was in junior high school. I believe I was thirteen, and I already had a lot of stubble. By the time I got into High School, I was already sporting a beard, and I guess it was intimidating to many people. The only advantage is that me and my brothers would sometimes troll the people in the liquor stores so we could buy cigarettes, cigars, and liquor. I know it's wrong, but oh well. It was just something we did, and it was fun. Pretending to be much older than we actually were. Anyways, I guess I should start with my parents death. I didn't get to know them that well, as they passed away when me and brothers were quite young. The only thing I remember about them, is that my mother liked to go out in the garden a lot and plant stuff. The thing I remember about my father, is that he worked as a Truck Driver.

Other than that, I couldn't tell you much about them. I do sometimes feel upset that I was unable to get to know my parents at a higher level, but I learned to accept their deaths. Growing up with my brothers was tedious at times. Our grandparents watched over us, and our older brother Louie sometimes acted like a father figure, even though he wasn't that much older than all of us. When my grandfather died, our grandmother took care of us, and by the time she died, Louie was already past eighteen, so he became our legal guardian, and watched over is.

I was a country boy, so I did a lot of outdoor stuff. I wasn't the type of guy that sat at home and played video games, or was on the computer all day. That wasn't my style at all. I was a more frontier orientated man, and I didn't just want to sit around the house and not do anything. I actually went outside and smelled the fresh air, felt the sun on my skin, went out and actually did shit. The one thing I hate about this generation is that people usually sit at home and do nothing, and they don't value or appreciate going outside.

I believe that's why the world is so messed up now, because everyone is stuck inside. Then they get involved with social media, which I don't, and that leads to an array of issues. I think the solution is simple; go outside and actually get active. Don't be stuck inside all the time. We as humans were not designed to be inside all day, every day. That isn't healthy, and it's not something that I personally could do. So I didn't. I went outside and did anything and everything active that I could. However, my main thing was playing football, that was the one thing which was my strong point. My brother Leif was also interested in football, so I guess my hobby towards football rubbed off to me, from him. Even though I never made it professional or into the NFL, I do believe that I could have very well been at that level. If I practiced long enough, and if I was disciplined enough, it would have happened. It didn't, and that's okay. I can live with doing something else with my life. I work at a supermarket now, and work at my brothers restaurant sometimes as well. It's not it's not a very glamorous lifestyle, such as being a professional athlete. But it's something I'm happy with, and I can go to work happy with myself.

So I had the football thing, and I also had the hunting thing. I didn't get to hunt as much as I wanted to, but I still had fun doing it. Me and my brothers would take any instance we could to go out in the woods and hunt. We would also fish as well. I didn't like fishing, as I found it terribly boring. Not that fishing isn't good, I just didn't care for it, and would rather be doing something else. I think with fishing, there is the fact that you have to be patient while doing it. You have to be patient while hunting as well, but with fishing it's in a whole another category really. So I didn't fish as much as I wanted to, mostly due to fact I just didn't care for it. Yeah when I was little, I didn't have any toys or any fancy electronics. I went outside and did things that were more active. I enjoyed spending time with my brothers as well.

We didn't always get along, but when we did go outside and do active things, we seemed to put our differences aside for the time being. I really wish that I could do outside stuff all the time. I wish I didn't have to interact with people, or worry about things such as bills, or having to worry about other parts of life. But the time I do get to go outside and enjoy myself, that's my peace. If I had my way, I would make it so I could experience these things forever, and every day. I know I making it seem like I'm a perfect guy, and all I do is hunt and play football, and I don't have any flaws.

That isn't true at all, I'm a very flawed person. You'll find out all the mistakes that I've done. I'm far from perfect, and it wasn't easy for me to accept my imperfections at first. Yes in the past they would bother me to a great degree, but I couldn't really care less now. I love the fact I make mistakes, and I don't want to do everything right all the time. I am no longer a perfectionist, and I love it. Everything being the same is boring, and I don't want to be a boring person. I want to be Harry, and Harry can fuck up from time to time. I move on, and live life the best way possible.

When things started to change for me, had to have been my first day of High School. Before then, kids would always avoid me. Maybe because I looked like a strange mountain man, and nobody wanted to bother or mess with me. I already had facial hair by this time, and this made the other people at school very uncomfortable. I would play football in school, and excel in athletics, but my academics could have been a lot better. My grades began to really go down during this time, and I began to feel extremely insecure about it. It didn't help that whenever I would try to involve myself with the other students so they could tutor and help me, nobody would want to volunteer.

They just thought I was the school bully and nobody wanted to bother or mess with me. I guess I gave up during that time, and didn't want to take the hurt or the rejection anymore. Keeping to myself at school was tough. I would always eat lunch by myself, and walking in the hallways the other kids would be scared of me for some reason. To be honest, life at home wasn't easy either. I would get bullied by my brothers usually. They weren't doing it to be mean, heavens no. But I do remember being picked on quite frequently by them for being the youngest. So be default, I was the one they wanted to teach a lesson to, and challenge all the time. I hate to say it, but because of this, I just got fed up. I told myself that I wasn't going to be Mr. Nice Guy anymore. I was going to start to teach everyone at school that was avoiding and ignoring me lesson.

I became the school bully, and at the time I was proud of it. Walking through the hallways, and having everyone fear me in the beginning made me feel bad. However, I gave the other students at school far too many chances. So if they want me to be big and bad, I will. They want me to be the bully so bad, so they got their wish. I would never pick on the girls though. There were already bullies that were female that would pick on the girls. I would just pick on the boys, and mostly the boys that I felt were most vulnerable. So this included, but was not limited to geeks and dweebs and nerds. Oh my, they were just such easy targets, and I loved causing torment to them. I would never cause that much harm to them. Well there would be a few times to where I would take it too far. I didn't break anybody's bones or anything like that. But yeah, unfortunately things had gotten ugly a couple of times. That was the only drawback about being a bully, is that when I had to see other students get hurt.

But I would typically keep it mild, and I wouldn't bother or hurt them that much. Mainly it was just very childish and innocent stuff. For example, I would just knock books out of their hands as they were walking down the hallways. Or I would trip them as they walking as well. Just funny stuff such as that, nothing that would really harm them. But there were only a few minor times to where I took it too far, but that rarely happened. So now that I was the bully, and being feared by typically everyone at the school, I wore that label on my chest. At times, I didn't even realize I was being the bully and causing so much stress to the other students. It just became my identity, and although it wasn't an identity to be proud of, I accepted it.

I hated doing schoolwork, and if I was lucky I wouldn't get a failing grade on assignments. I don't know, I just didn't like school. It wasn't my forte, and it wasn't something I looked forward to. My ambition was to get up early, and to go out and hunt during the day, and play football in the evening. Waking up early every single day, to go to a school full of people that don't even like me, wasn't my most favorite thing in the world to do. I felt I had the right to be mad at going to school. So I would ditch quite frequently. Yeah ditching school is bad, but it's what I did. I would sometimes ditch school days at a time. I would pretend to walk to the school bus, only to go hide in the woods. As I said previously, I didn't like to fish, but I would take my fishing pole and go to lake on days I was skipping school. Doing juvenile things such as taking off days to school are now kinda fun to mention. I know missing out on my education is very bad, but I didn't care. Why should I have to be in school if I hate it?

There is also something about my life that I don't like to mention. It's something that I've tried to keep secret about to my brothers, but they eventually found out about it. It's very private information, that I feel in regular circumstances nobody needs to know about. But being in this current political climate, I feel that people should know about these types of things. I understand that I'm not a very emotional or social person, so maybe this is dismissive to bring up. However, it is an important part my life. When I was young, I knew I was attracted to both guys and girls. I don't know why I had these thoughts, but I did. I knew my options were to keep the thoughts I had about being attracted to guys a secret. As it was only natural for me to come to accept that. My older brother Louie would be very homophobic at times, and make gay jokes. So I just adapted myself to understand that this is something I don't talk about, and that nobody needs to know about.

I was in the closet about these feelings until I reached High School. I didn't want to tell my brothers, as I was scared as to how they were going to treat me about it. The last thing I wanted, was yet another thing that they were going to torment and punish me over. So I kept my mouth completely shut about it. What made it easier was due to how masculine I was. Due to the fact I was so well versed into doing outdoor type activities, nobody would suspect anything. They would be fooled none the wiser about my feelings regarding my sexuality. I must admit that when I was in school, I would pick on a lot of boys that looked flamboyant or gay, and I felt bad about that.

I was picking on them because of how weak they were, when I was just as guilty for that. I was bisexual myself, and instead of being a role model, I was possibly making things worse. Forgiving myself for that isn't easy, but that was then, and this is now. I'm not even close to being that person anymore, and I treat everyone with respect. I'm open with myself, and if someone wants to know if I'm bisexual or not, I don't lie to them about it. Yes I understand it's only a sliver of my life, and it's something I don't need to tell everybody. But it's something that I grew to support myself over, and I don't let it stress me out.

My senior year of high school was when I met Troy. I consider that my rebirth I guess. Like mostly every other student that went to the school I went to in senior year, we were all transferred from another school. At the time, the school board was going through problems, and as a result the students had to be transferred to another school. I remember being slightly pissed off at this, as the school I was at before was just fine. I didn't want to start all over at a brand new school, when I was just trying to get situated in the school I was at before. Yeah I was being treated as a bully, but it was still my home turf, and it was my stomping ground. My older brother Louie did happen to buy me a truck. So I didn't have to take the raggedy ass school bus every single day. I had my own car, and I could go anywhere I wanted to with it. This was also good as I didn't have to deal with the other kids either.

I was in my own little bubble, and it was great. Oh man, I loved that truck oh so much. I would take it out into the woods usually, and just be myself. When I didn't want to deal with the bullshit my brothers gave me, I would ride in my truck, and just get so far away from them. At times, we would get on each other's nerves, so it was great to escape from them at times. With the help of my truck, I didn't have to get a ride from one of my brothers to go out to the lake, or if I wanted to leave the house. I could simply just do all of that on my own, and I appreciated that very much.

Anyways, so I drove myself to school every day, and I didn't have any issues or problems with that. Even though this school was far away from where me and my brothers lived, it was okay. As long as I didn't have to ride the bus, I couldn't care less. I was not prepared to deal with my first day of High School though, as it would change my life forever. The previous reputation I had at the school I was at previously didn't matter. This was a brand new school, and I had to start everything fresh. So I had a choice to make. Do I continue to be the bully I was at the school before? Or do I simply become a brand new person? I wasn't sure as to what agenda I wanted to portray.

Unfortunately, I would attach myself to some bad influences at school. Bullies usually work in cliques and groups. In the case of myself, it wasn't any different. I hung around a group of baddies, and yes I shouldn't have. I was even best friends with main ringleader, Sam. Sam was just as insecure as I was, and he was very troubled as well. His father was the CEO of a major electronics company, and Sam struggled with the fact he wasn't good enough, or up to par with his father. So he turned to being a school bully I suppose as an only resort. I knew I had no business hanging around Sam, but I couldn't help myself. I needed a partner and a main guy to report myself to, and Sam needed the same. So we confided in one another for that. The past school we were at, we basically ran it up the wall. We were feared, and we enjoyed the power very much. We didn't care at all that we were bringing pain to others. Our agenda was simple; to be as vindictive, selfish, ruthless, and disrespectful as possible. Being nice was not even close to being in our vocabulary. That was not our plan at school. I later find out that Sam is going to be attending the same school I will be transferring to. So if I had any thoughts of wanting to disassemble myself from Sam, I had better think again.

Driving to school on the first day, I immediately see Sam, and a few other boys in our clique. My plan of wanting to start over a new guy at school already failed. Me and Sam are going to continue our reindeer games. Same show, different channel pretty much. This is a new school, but we are immediately going to start our old tricks. What's funny, is that not even ten minutes into me arriving at school on our first day, Sam already had a stunt that he wanted to pull. I couldn't believe it at all. His prank was rather simple, he wanted to go to the school bus yard and puncture all the tires to one of the buses. It seemed innocent and petty enough, so my ignorant ass decided to agree to it. Sam would poke a hole all the tires on the left side of the bus, I would do the same on the right side of the bus. Sam continued to give me the plan.

"Hey Harry, take this knife. Just make sure you slash those tires good. These kids are all going to be going home late, and it's gonna be so cool and fun."

I shake my head and grab the knife that Sam hands me. I respond out to him.

"This is so wrong. It's the first day of school, and you want to pull tricks like this? This is so evil and bad. But let's hurry up and do it before we get caught okay. Ha-Ha."

Sam and I both sprint out to the school bus yard. Making sure that we don't cause any attention or focus to ourselves. We manage to somehow go unseen, and immediately start slashing all the tires of the school bus, puncturing them. Right after, we run away from the scene, making sure again we aren't noticed by any other students. I managed to already do a major bad deed at this school, and it's only the first day. Even though I was supposed to feel happy about doing something bad, I didn't. I didn't always enjoy being bad. Most of it was the temporary feeling of being a bad guy, but I would personally feel sick about it afterwards. In turn, it was also difficult to carry on the rest of the day after doing that bad deed. Focusing on my classes was bad, because I knew I messed with one of the school buses. I felt guilty that many kids are going to be inconvenienced once school is out, because the tires on their bus are flat thanks to me and Sam. I will say that I did happen to meet Troy for the first time on this day. It was rather strange coming into contact with him, as I treated him like I normally would with anyone else. I went straight into my bully mode. I was walking in the hallways, and I believe I bumped into him, and said this to him.

"Watch where you are going, you fag."

Those words, as much as they sadden me to reveal that were the first words I exchanged with Troy, were actually the first words I exchanged with him. I just saw this smaller boy in the school, and I didn't even think twice about it. My thing was to humiliate and make fun of him, and I believe I did my job and my part well. Because it was the first day of school, I helped pick his books up, and I wanted to make sure I wasn't going to be his friend in the process.

"I'm not going to help you next time fag. Just watch where you're going."

Troy just looked at me in shock, and he was so scared of me. I later found out that was when he started to crush on me, and I find it kinda sweet looking back. That was over ten years ago on our senior year of High School. I didn't want Troy to feel scared of me, and I didn't take pleasure in making him feel upset or scared of me. However, you must understand that as my role and reputation as the bully of the school, I had to do what I had to do. I could only think of the repercussions that it would have on my reputation at the school. Understanding that I am letting Sam down, and what he is going to think about me. I continue on about my day forgetting about Troy. He was a bug on the bottom of my shoe, and I didn't have time for him. The only thing was that I did find him very cute, but behind my rugged appearance, I couldn't let Troy know that. I thought for sure I wouldn't have to see him again; boy was I wrong.

During last period, I see Troy walk into the classroom. In my head, I was hoping that he wouldn't come over to my table and sit next to me. He did, and I was so nervous to react. I was under a great deal of anxiety to deal with Troy, as I'm a bully. If he was trying to make friends or be nice to me, I'm the wrong person. However Troy was starting to arrange small talk with me. I wanted to punch the shit out of him. But he was being so annoying, and getting on my nerves. I didn't know how to deal with him. Again, he was just like a damn bug on my shoe I wanted to squish. I couldn't take it anymore, so I was being a little disrespectful and rude to Troy so he can take a hint. It managed to work, and Troy kept his distance.

As soon as class was over, I hauled ass out of there. I went to my car, and drove home. That night at home, I kept thinking about that weird kid I bumped into on my first day of school, and how he's in my final class. I'm going to end up seeing this brat every single day. I knew I had to talk to someone close to me about this, as this was a peculiar situation I have never faced or experienced before at all. You know what, I talked the situation over with my brother Leif. Leif and I were in the backyard tossing a football around. We were both catching the ball and throwing it to each other. I talk to Leif.

"Hey Leif, there is this guy at my school, and he's just a little jerk. But I kinda like him, and I don't know. I sort of picked on him a few times today, and I don't know what to do."

Leif ends up throwing the ball at full force towards me, and he responds to me.

"Well, you can't force friendships. If he is such a brat like you explain, then don't bother him. He'll eventually get the hint leave you alone. If you want to be friends with him, then be friendly and cordial with him, and things will play into effect."

I throw the ball back at Leif. I guess what he said was right, and that if Troy was really getting on my nerves, than I just need to distance myself from him and he'll do the same. However, if I wanted things to go farther between me and Troy, I need to stop the bully schtick, and just be a man and talk to him about it. This is of course very easier said than done. I toss the football back to Leif, and I continue my conversation with him.

"Yeah man, that's right. I don't know how to currently handle this, but I will figure it out soon. He's really getting on my nerves either way. Thanks for the advice man."

Leif tosses the football back to me, and instead of throwing it back, I keep it in my hands and think to myself for a few moments. I ultimately at this time decided that I would leave Troy alone. He doesn't deserve to get mixed up in a guy like me, and I don't want to cause him any problems. Troy deserves someone that is more up his level, and not a slacker such as myself. I'm not very interested in school, and I'm a manipulative bully. Troy is more school orientated, and I'm not even close to being on his level. Once my mind was made up that I wasn't going to deal with Troy anymore, I was able to sleep better about it. I knew that Troy was going to be in my class the next day, but I wasn't going to make it a secret that me and him don't belong. The next day at school. Troy once again sat next to me. Considering the guy that I am, I didn't want to play around with Troy anymore. I grabbed his collar, and laid it to him straight.

"Go sit somewhere else fag, leave me alone. I don't want to be bothered by you."

In that moment the teacher walked into the class. Without trying to draw attention to myself, and because I didn't want to get into trouble for assaulting another student, I quickly let Troy go, and stay in my seat. The teacher then says me and Troy have to sit together for the remainder of the semester. Oh god, I guess Troy won this time, and he got his wish. So now that the both of us have to sit together, my plan of getting Troy out of my life was becoming difficult to achieve. Feeling overwhelmed, I had to ignore Troy, and not associate with him.

I was pleased when class was over, and immediately ran out of the classroom. I had football tryouts, so I was looking forward to that. As you know football is my therapy, and I use that to calm myself down.

Not having any idea that Troy was spying and following me the whole time, I go to my tryouts. I of course make the team. Upon finding out that Troy was following me, at first I was upset, but I don't know. I had that really soft and cute feeling in my heart. I decided not to beat up Troy. I instead allowed him to help me with my studies. As he wanted to be around me so much, I'm going to make him pay for it.

Troy was actually a good tutor, and he helped me with my academic problems. Being thankful for that, it made me hate Troy less. I was happy with the state of the relationship that we had at this point. Things started to get really bad when Troy revealed he had a crush on me. I wasn't expecting this at all, and nobody has ever had romantic feelings for me. Suffice to say, I didn't deal with in the best way. I was just being tutored by Troy one evening, and he expressed himself completely to me.

"Harry, I don't know how to say this, but I have a crush on you."

My hear immediately sank, and all the muscles in my body clenched up. My eyes widened, and I started to turn red due to the embarrassment and I didn't know how to act. I was also feeling tense about the whole situation, as a small part of me also shared the same feelings towards Troy. I didn't want him to know this though. I'm the tough guy, and I'm also the bully at the school. Tough guys and bullies do not let another guy at school say he has a relationship with him. I'm also kinda forgetting that we are both guys. We are going to school in the deep south, and I don't want to deal with all the gossiping and all the hardships of that. It's bad enough people in school like to talk about the most mild of things, but you can imagine with this. Our school wasn't that bigoted, but people still would talk a lot of crap sometimes. I was struggling with my own identity and my own sexuality, so I didn't know how to react. Troy was getting far too comfortable with me, and I couldn't let him do that. Not only for him, but for myself as well. I just wanted to play football, and do my own thing. Not play these types of games with Troy. I had to let Troy know I don't want to play this game with him.

"Stay away from me fag. Don't ever talk to me ever again."

I walk out of the library, vowing to never speak to Troy. What I did wasn't nice, but it had to be done. Troy can't be with me, and I can't be with Troy. It's not healthy for either of us. After that, the only guilt I felt, was not explaining that to Troy at a nicer level. I was very forceful and slightly disrespectful to him, but I have never been encountered in this type of situation before, so I acted in the best way I knew how. Troy if he knew what was good for him, wouldn't mess with me anymore of that. I wouldn't have to deal with his antics, and it's done. This would only be the beginning it seems. I began to develop a soft spot for Troy. I decided to talk this issue over with my older brother Harvey as it was beginning to bother me. Harvey was in the backyard lifting weights, as he normally does. I end up helping him spot, as he's lifting his weights. As Harvey is continuing with his lifting session, I ask him a question.

"Harvey, there is this guy at my school, and he's playing some type of strange game on me. I don't know how to handle it, and I wanted to ask for your advice or help."

As Harvey is going on lifting the weights, he responds out to me.

"Alright, did you beat him up or something? That's all you ever do to the other guys at school, is punch or kick them. So you feel guilty for beating up on this guy right?"

I continue to help Harvey with his weightlifting. I really wish the situation were as simple as that. It's not. I also had a crush on Troy as well, likewise as he had a crush on me. My brother Harvey was usually accepting of these things, so I kept it completely real with him.

"No Harvey, there is this guy at school who has a crush on me. I also have a crush on him. I thought you would understand, so I need your help. But I can't make it public, or else I'm going to be humiliated by my group. You know how it is. Please help."

Harvey ends up lifting the weight, and finishes his session. He then gets up from the bench-press, and stands over near me. Harvey then silently creeps close to me, and responds.

"Well if you really like this guy, let him know. Well I know you Harry, that's not gonna happen. Just give him signs that you like him. I can't help you if you're worried about what your other bully friends are going to think of this. I think you should let those friends go."

I smile at Harvey, and completely agree with him. Dealing with the fact that Troy has a crush on me wasn't easy to accept. But I was lying to myself just as badly. My infatuation with Troy was there as well. But I'm the bully, I just couldn't do it, and didn't want to do it. Us playing games with each other couldn't continue, as it's not helping the situation between the both of us at all. I began to accept Troy's crush on me. I remember the day me and Troy started over. We had our first kiss, and it's something I don't remember that well. I was just glad that there were no other students that saw us do it. The both of us were at the bleachers at the football field, and it was a completely secret kiss. Once the kiss happened, it was almost like the kiss of death. I was gonna be with Troy forever, and Troy was going to be with me forever.

Things changed as well when I invited Troy to my house for the weekend one time. I was only intending on driving Troy home, when he informed me his mother was out of town for the weekend. He said he was going to be home alone, and he didn't want to be stuck bored alone, so I agreed to let him stay at my place for the weekend. I was a little nervous about this, as I know how wild my brothers can be. But at this time, the friendship and bond that I had formed with Troy seemed to have improved. I understand that my brothers will end up accepting Troy and they wouldn't have problems with that.

After introducing Troy to my brothers, I felt slightly more comfortable with Troy. If Troy and I were going to be spending more time together, he had to be introduced to my family, and be supportive of that. The first time Troy was in my bedroom, I was unsure of how to react. All we did was study, and it was completely innocent. Of course, my older brother Louie had to run his fucking mouth. At this time, I had already come out to Harvey and Leif that I find Troy attractive, and they didn't even care about it. However, this was still a big secret I kept hidden from Louie. I know how homophobic Louie is and I didn't want him to know.

Being how Louie at times can be a bigot, he started to assume that me and Troy were a couple, and it was tough to keep it under wraps at that point. My brothers bring friends to the house all the time, and Louie never says anything about that, but he's always picking on me about it. The last thing I wanted to do was cause a scene with Louie in front of Troy. But Louie kept on bullying Troy, trying to belittle him. Louie had been drinking that entire day, and when Louie gets drunk, he gets very disrespectful as well. I know him being drunk wasn't an excuse, but I was understanding that because he was intoxicated, was why he was going on like that. Louie has no filter when he's been drinking. I did have to let Louie know that he's not going to disrespect my guest. He is just getting on my absolute nerves and I couldn't handle it anymore. I got into Louie's face about it.

"Louie, shut the fuck up and leave him alone okay?"

I figured this would make Louie stop, and he would quit. He didn't, and kept this charade up. Again, due to the fact he was drunk, it was no use getting him to stop. As he continued to bully Troy, I had no choice but to get up and prove a point. I immediately launched at Louie, and Harvey, Leif and Troy had to break us up.

I knew Troy was embarrassed over this, and I didn't want this to be his first impression of me and my brothers. This was not the way how I intended for this to happen, but my temper was out of control. I told Louie many times to leave Troy alone, and he didn't. So I did what I needed to do. Most of Louie's frustrations was due to the my defiance on the fact me and my brothers didn't have a choice in leaving for California. This was our childhood house, and I didn't want to move. Tennessee was my home, and I couldn't imagine myself leaving for California then. I had nothing against California, but it's hard to explain. I'm a country boy and this was my home.

If Louie wants to move, he can. But why should the rest of us automatically have to? Louie received a restaurant offer in California, and the money we would get for selling our house, we could get a place when we move. Louie says that myself, Leif and Harvey have to move, and we have no say in the matter. It just simply isn't fair, and I don't like how Louie has to dictate what we do all the time. I also didn't want Troy to be mixed up in all this drama. He is simply here as a guest, and he doesn't deserve to be involved in our family drama. The next morning, I remember I got into a heated fight with Louie over this.

"Louie, I had a guest over, and you don't act that way around guests. I don't know what's up with you. Troy is my friend, and you have to accept that. I'm sorry."

Louie wasn't listening to reason, and whatever I was saying he didn't wish to understand. I don't know what he had against Troy, but he saw him as a deterrent. Louie had a mug of Coffee, that was he was pouring whisky into. I didn't like how Louie drunk so early in the morning, and it aggravated me. So Louie was of course drunk during this whole conversation. Louie takes a sip of his coffee and whisky combination, and responds to me.

"I don't care about your little faggot friend. I don't. He's not family. You're my brother, and you have to listen to me. He's no good, and I want you to stop talking to him."

During this time, I notice that Troy walks into the kitchen with Harvey. I had to make sure that Troy didn't catch that me and Louie were talking about him. Even though Troy didn't eavesdrop, I still wanted to play it safe, and not insult him while he was in the same vicinity of myself and Louie. I had to think very quickly as to how I was going to play it off. So I switched the argument to something else.

'Why do we have to move to California? You want to move there to open your restaurant. This is home for me, Leif and Harvey, so why do we have to get involved?"

Troy and Harvey remain in the kitchen, and Louie continues on with his rambling.

"Because whatever I say goes. We already took a vote, and you're the only one who doesn't want to move Harry. So we're moving and there is nothing you can do about it. I'm sorry. No amount of bitching you do is going to change it. So just accept it."

Troy and Harvey leave the kitchen, and I remain arguing with Louie. I guess I am going to have to come into acceptance that we are moving. My main worry was about how Troy was going to feel. I know that he's going to miss me deeply, and I'm going to also have periods to where I'm going to miss him as well. As the thought of moving to California still lingers, senior prom is also around the corner. Troy asked me to prom, and I agreed. I had no intentions of going to prom, but since I'm going to be moving away from Troy soon, I feel it's only fair that I spend time with him until then. Although Louie hated Troy, I was thinking that a good solution to this, would be to ask Louie if Troy could come live with us in California. Part of me already knew the answer was going to be an extreme no. I reluctantly decided to give it a shot as well. One evening when Louie came home from work, he was sitting in the living room watching a football game. Louie is also sipping a beer in the process, so as usual, he's been drinking. I walk up to the sofa and sit by my brother.

"Louie, you know I never ask anything from you. I don't even think I've ever even asked you for a favor before. But, I have a favor I need now. I wanted to ask you a favor please."

Louie takes a sip of his beer while watching the football game on the television. With his vision still directed at the television, he grumbles out a response at me.

"What the hell do you want Harry? We're moving and its final. So if it's anything about you coaxing me for us to not move, try again. We're moving, and there is nothing you can do."

There was a bowl of tortilla chips, on the coffee table in front of the sofa I end up eating a couple of the chips, before I respond to Louie.

"No Louie, it has nothing to do with that. You remember Troy right? Well, I wanted to ask if it was okay for you, if Troy moved with us. He can stay in my room, it's okay. He won't' cause any trouble at all. I think it would be a great idea for both of us. Please say yes."

Louie takes another sip of his beer, and responds to me quietly.

"Oh you mean that faggot? Absolutely not. I don't even know him, and he's not family. I don't like him, and my answer is no. Leave me alone Harry, my answer is no."

I don't know what erupted over me, but I was at my boiling point with Louie. No matter what I do, he always has to make sure he makes my life total hell. I took the bowl of chips that were on the coffee table, and also threw a cup of salsa at Louie, right in his face.

"Well Troy is coming with us, and you're going to be okay with that. I haven't asked you for a single thing in my fucking life Louie. The one time I ask you for a favor, and you say no. Troy is coming with us, and whether you like it or not, that's how it's gonna be."

Louie starts to brush off the chips and salsa I threw at him, and responds to me.

"Okay, your little friend can come along. You win. But don't ever talk to me ever again in your life. You're no longer considered my brother. Leif and Harvey are my brothers, you aren't. You're a disgrace, and you have been totally disowned by me Harry. Get out my sight."

I walk away from the sofa, happy that I won the battle between myself and Louie. Now I just had to find the right time to explain to Troy that he can come with us. Because I'm evil like that, I wanted Troy to be in suspense for a little, before I explained the news to him. I said that I would let him know after senior prom. When senior prom came up, I wasn't surprised that nobody in the school showed up. There were other schools in the area that were having more features at their prom. Our prom was going to be boring and old fashioned, which is why nobody showed up. I wasn't complaining that much about it, as it gave Troy and I more private time together.

At the prom, I danced and had fun with him, and we were enjoying ourselves. This was until Sam and some of the other bad boys in my bully group decided to crash the prom. Everything good was going to suddenly stop, and I was not expecting it. For no reason at all as a prank, they end up pouring the punchbowl right over Troy. He's immediately soaked with all the punch, and I know that he was upset over that. It was at this moment, that I knew these guys weren't positive role models for me. They picked on Troy for no reason, on our senior prom of all times. They just couldn't pick on people their own size, and they had to rain on someone else's parade just so they could feel better about themselves. I was very angry about the whole thing.

"You guys are such fucking jerks for doing that. You all need to grow up."

I didn't like how Troy was made a fool of by those guys. Going from bad to worse, we end up moving outside of the prom and away from the gymnasium. I knew that they were going to pull another trick on him, and I wasn't going to let them. Sam ends up dragging Troy to his truck, and they drive to another location. My main goal was to save Troy, and to not allow them to cause any more harm than they already have to him. They finally reach an abandoned farm house, and being there caused me to feel immense horror. Whatever Sam and and his friends wanted to do to Troy, wasn't going to be good or positive. I had to play savior rather quick, or else Troy could end up being hurt badly. I unfortunately was knocked in the head by a baseball bat, and was left unconscious temporarily. I was just in fear of Troy's safety, and I had to do something, I just didn't know how I could do it. Sam began to tie Troy up with a rope, and hung him outside on the porch of the house. Sam then began to tease flickering a lighter over the rope Troy was attached to, which was soaked in lighter fluid. Sam ends up somehow burning himself from playing the lighter.

He is burned badly, and I take my jacket off to help put out the fire. Sam's friends run away from the scene, and I decide that although Sam is my enemy, and he tried to hurt Troy, I have to let that go and help him out. I put Sam in my truck, and myself along with Troy drive him to the hospital. After telling the hospital staff that it was just a senior prank gone wrong, they don't suspect anything else. I reached the hospital just in time, and Sam is going to make a full recovery just fine.

This whole night was rather wild, and it is something that I will always remember. I was going to be moving to California soon, and this would be the last most eventful thing that happened back in my hometown of Tennessee. Trying to save my friend Troy, and saving my old friend turned enemy Sam. I was changing as a person, and I was coming to realize this.

Troy was still under the impression that I was moving away. Graduation was coming soon, and I had to let Troy know that I want him to move to California with us. Troy was helping me with my final exams afterschool one day, and I thought this was the perfect time for me to bring this up. I could tell how depressed Troy was. I didn't want him to know I could sense his feelings. During our tutoring session, I could just feel all his thoughts. He didn't want me to leave, and I didn't want him to leave either. I was his protector, that he didn't want to see leave. Troy was under pretenses that after graduation was over, I was going to move to California, and we won't ever contact each other again. That isn't true at all, and not what I had in plan. Troy all of a sudden starts to cry heavily in my chest, explaining his sadness.

"I don't want to you leave Harry. I'm going to miss you so much, and I don't want you to move. I don't want you to ever leave me Harry."

This is it, this is the time for me to lay down the news. As Troy continues to cry and lay his head in my chest crying, I finally reveal something which may change his mood.

"Well Troy, I was talking it over with my brothers, and we want you to come with us."

Soon as I finish saying that, Troy couldn't be any happier. He was going to move to California with me, and he longer feels anxious about me moving away. For the rest of the tutoring session, the weight has been lifted off Troy, and we continue on. Thanks to Troy's tutoring, I manage to pass all of my final exams, and I'm able to graduate. In the last football game I play in senior year of High School, our team ends up winning. So that was also nice as well. I feel I'm totally ready to move to California. Being that Troy is going to travel with me, it makes things even better. I don't have to move away, feeling worried or concerned over Troy, and missing his company and friendship. In the same way, Troy doesn't have to worry that I'm going to be gone forever, or miss me either. High School graduation came and went rather fast. Completing High School was a major milestone for me.

Never did I think being the school bully, that I would find a lifelong friend, and that I would complete High School without any issues. Now as far as college, I didn't know what my intentions were over that. I didn't like High School, so I'm pretty sure I wasn't going to like going to University either. Unlike my brothers, I didn't really have a passion that I wanted to do. Louie was into cooking and being a chef, and Leif and Harvey were really into athletics and had their own agendas that they wanted to do. However as for me, I had no idea. I just knew that I liked to play football, and I know not every guy makes it big as a football player. It's quite rare they become successful, but it's still something that I was ambitious about and something that I wanted to do.

While I was packing to move to California, Louie knocked on my door.

"Hey Harry, is it okay if I chat with you for a few minutes?"

I continue to put all my belongings in boxes, and I don't even think of holding any types of grudges against Louie. I know I'm not his most favorite person in the world, but he's still my brother. I know at the end of the day, we love each other. Even though I'm really concentrated on packing all of my things away, I still respond to Louie's question.

"Yeah, what's up man? I have time to talk. What's going on?"

Louie then starts to help me pack, by putting some of my belonging in the boxes. As he's doing that, Louie discusses whatever is on his mind with me.

"Harry, I wanted to say that I'm sorry. I know this move isn't something you're looking forward to, and I'm sorry that I kinda pressured you into it. Can you please forgive me?"

As much as Louie gets on my nerves and I fucking hate him at times, he is still my brother. I know no matter what I do, he's always going to be there for me, and support me. I know as much as he might not agree with every little thing I do, he still loves me as his brother. I continue to pack my things, and I respond to Louie.

"Yes Lou, you're my brother. Of course I forgive you. All is forgiven. I understand we might not always get along, but we're still bros. Do you mind if I give you a hug?"

Louie continues to help me pack, and laughs. He then walks over to me with his arms extended. I think this is the first time me and Louie ever hugged. I know that's very sad to explain and mention, but it's true. We just did not get along with each other, and this I believe is the first time we ever showed positive affection towards each other. I continue to hug Louie for about a minute. Just taking this rare occurrence very dearly. As we continue to hug, Louie starts to whisper something in my ear very softly and quietly.

"I love you Harry. I support whatever you do. Things are going to be different. Between all of us. We are all brothers, and we have to stick together and support one another. I love you Harry, don't' you forget that, and we're gonna start over from now on."

Louie and I finish hugging, and Louie kisses me on the cheek, and walks out of my bedroom. I couldn't be more satisfied that I rectified everything between me and Louie. We don't mortally hate each other anymore, and I'm happy to have my older brother Louie back. I'm going to go to California fresh, with the help of my brothers, and the help of my close friend Troy.

I finish packing all of my things, and I'm all set to leave. I didn't know what was going to happen next to me, but I didn't care. I had no idea what I wanted to do with my future, and I didn't care about that at all. As long as I had the love from my brothers, which I did, that's all that matters. If I had the love from the people close to me, everything else, I had no worries over, and it was easy. Leaving out of Tennessee, I no longer felt bad. During this time, I wanted to move to California to see where life took me. As long as I had the love from Troy as well, which Troy also loved me, that's all I cared about.

When I moved to California, things were rocky at first. When I told Troy that we were going to share a bedroom, he was shocked at the news at first, but didn't seem to mind it as time went on. There were also very little drama and fights between us. Having five guys live under one roof was hectic at first, but we managed to create a system, so that everyone was happy. I was going to school, and Troy was going to school, but nobody was really happy. Louie was happy, as he had his restaurant to turn to. He was very successful at that I should add. Leif and Harvey were also doing their own thing, and weren't having any problems towards that.

But with me and Troy, we were having difficulties assimilating as soon as we got to California. We both went to school, but I wasn't that happy about it. I still didn't' know what I wanted to study, and because of that I struggled. Troy was identical to that as well. I ended up taking very odd jobs, and worked as a janitor. As time continued to pass, I got a job working as a butcher in the meat department at a grocery store. A job that Louie helped me get. If you would have told me that I would work as a butcher in future, I would have told you hell no.

Remarkably, I really enjoy going to work. In fact, I'm excited every single day I report to work. I get to help customers with whatever meat they want to purchase. Even the vegan customers I began to like, as I also work with vegan meat as well. Working in a grocery store allows me to meet new people every day, and I'm happy to offer customer service with whatever issues that they want served. I also sometimes work with Louie in his restaurant in addition to that. Troy got a retail job, and he doesn't have any complaints about that.

Most recently, all of us decided to take a camping trip. Although we didn't live in Tennessee anymore, we still had a country spirit, and wanted to do something fun. Me and my brothers are all ginger mountain men at heart, so we want to live on the wild side at times. This camping trip would be very eventful. It would be one of the most thrilling parts of my life, and it's something that for me and my brothers, would always stick with us. I should explain that despite the camping trip being wild, it made me a better person overall.

CHAPTER 7:

MAN OF ORANGE (PART 2)

So this part of the story is going to be about the infamous camping trip that myself, my brothers, and Troy decided to go on. The camping trip happened last summer, and it is something that I will remember always. What we thought was going to be an ordinary camping trip, turned out to be something more extravagant than that. It was something that tested all of our strengths, and made us believe that we can accomplish any challenge that we have to face. All we were planning on doing was taking a camping trip, but it ended up being a life altering adventure. The days approaching the trip, we all began to get our supplies in order. Our usual plan was to hike, fish, do all the regular and assumed stuff. So it was just a time for us to kick back and be in our regular element. This was also our first time camping in California, and we wanted to take advantage of the outdoor scenery of California. My only fear was that we were going to be without the use of electronics and social media. Something that in today's age, people are really fussy when they are left without. That only added to the fun of it, being that we had to go back to how people lived in the past. Without the use of cell phones, computers and the internet. The only thing that we could turn to fun, is doing wilderness stuff.

We would only bring a short amount of snacks and food. Louie decided that it would be more exciting if we fished and hunted for our own food. If we didn't catch anything for the night, then we will be going to bed with empty bellies. Ha-Ha. As far as sleeping arrangements, we were only going to bring one tent. I know it's close quarters, but again, we are camping outdoors. This isn't "Motel 6". So we all have to fit into one tent when we go to bed. It's okay, because we were only going to be in the tent to sleep. It's not like we had to spend all day in the tent. During the day, we would do our activities, then at night, we would go back to the tent and sleep. So having five guys fit into a tent at night is cramped yes, but it's really not that bad when you think about in a whole. Louie was the most giddy about the trip, as he couldn't stop talking about it. The night before the trip, Louie created a checklist to make sure everything was all set. Which it was, but Louie was just being super paranoid to make sure that we didn't forget anything.

Even though camping and going outdoors isn't Troy's forte, he was being a good sport about it. I mean, Troy loved hanging out with me and my brothers, so that was the part he enjoyed and liked. Troy didn't know how to fish; hunting grossed him out; and he complains about bugs, the heat, and other stuff when he has to go outside. But as long as me or one of my brothers was there to help him out, he managed to ignore all the complaints that he had. The relationship that I had between Troy had greatly improved at this point. I was used to all of his habits and ticks, and he also began to understand all of my quirks and issues as well.

We made a perfect team, and I couldn't be pleased more about that. His relationship with my brothers was basically identical. Louie no longer had any issues with Troy, and began to accept the fact that he's an honorary member of our family now. Louie also stopped pestering me about my sexuality as well. Louie himself was not a saint when it came to his sexuality. He finds both women and men attractive, and this is something Louie himself has to deal with. I don't get into my brothers sexual personal life, and Louie has learned not to badger or bother me about mine. I guess all of my brothers to a certain degree, are open minded with our sexualities. Come to think of it, Leif and Harvey also admitted they were Bi to me as well. It's okay. So it's something we all learned to accept about one another. It's now a golden rule that we don't talk about any personal stuff. If we happen to bring home a partner or whatever, then we cross that bridge when we approach it.

The night before the trip, I end up going to the garage to talk to Louie. He is packing all our of stuff into his large SUV. We are all going to go to the campsite in Louie's SUV. Louie is making very sure he has everything for the trip managed. Double checking his list, not wanting to leave anything behind. Even though I could tell he seems very attentive to getting everything prepared for our trip, I was scared of bothering him. I continued to watch Louie, and started to have a conversation with him.

"So Lou, is there anything that you need me to do for you? Do you want me to go to the store and pick anything up that we don't have?"

Louie continues to put everything in the back of the SUV, and also continues to look at his list. He takes a quick glance at me, and goes back to his task. He then turns to me, and hands me an empty tackle box. I examine the tackle box, as Louie responds to me.

"Yeah Harry, I want you to go to the fishing shop, and get some bait that doesn't suck. We aren't going to catch fucking anything with bad bait. Appreciate it, thank you."

I nod my head towards Louie, and I go back in the house to get my car keys. As I'm doing that, I ask Troy and Harvey if they would like to go the store with me. They both say yes, and we set out to the fishing store. The three of us get into my car, with Harvey sitting in the passenger seat, and with Troy sitting in the back seat. The fishing store was almost an hour drive from where our house was. So I could understand why Louie didn't want to go himself. He wanted us to do it, so the task was taken away from him. I didn't mind, as I was helping my brother out. He was right as well, if the bait we were using wasn't good enough, we would not be able to catch any fish. If we didn't catch anything, we wouldn't be eating. So having the right bait might seem like it's something trivial, but it wasn't. It was a good thing that I knew what type of bait to get, because if I got the wrong bait, Louie would most definitely get mad at me over that. As I get closer to the fishing store, Harvey starts to speak to me.

"Harry, I'm having a weird feeling about this trip. I don't know. I thought about it, and I'm not going to go. The rest of you can go if you want, but I'm gonna stay home."

Concerned as to why Harvey no longer wants to go on the trip, I start to think to myself the reasons why he doesn't want to participate. Maybe he was feeling ill, or sick. Either way, I wanted to know the official reason as to why he changed his mind on going.

"What's wrong Harv? Why don't you want to go? Are you feeling okay? You know Louie would be very pissed if you didn't come with us. What's up man?"

I look over at Harvey, and he's looking down at the floor. Whatever was on his mind, I could tell was troubling him very terribly. Harvey then whispers out to me.

"No, I'm not sick. I'm fine. It's just I have a really bad feeling about this trip, and I rather not go. But then again, it's probably just me being precautious for no reason. I don't know."

Even though I didn't like to see Harvey nervous and upset, he didn't have a reason to be alarmed, so maybe it was just him acting crazy for no reason. I take my hand and run it through Harvey's hair to calm him down. I continue to drive to the fishing shop, talking to Harvey.

"It's going to be fine, okay? You've gone on camping trips with us before. This time isn't going to be any different. We're going to have fun, and kick it. Nothing to worry about."

Harvey smiles back at me, but I can tell internally he wasn't secure. I was hoping that my talk with him would make him feel better about it. I tried my best, but it wasn't good enough it seemed. I didn't know what was bothering Harvey, and Harvey himself didn't know what was wrong. He just had a gut feeling that the trip was going to go wrong, and thus he didn't want to come with us. In hindsight, maybe I should have just told Harvey if that he didn't want to attend the trip with us, he didn't have to. Just because Louie wanted us all there, doesn't mean that Harvey has to go if he doesn't wish to. That's selfish thinking, and someone's physical or mental health always comes first. But at the time, I ignored it, and told Harvey to ignore it as well. I make it to the fishing shop, and I got the bait that I know Louie would prefer. We then all head back to the house. On the ride back home, Harvey seemed even more apprehensive than he did before. I just couldn't see my brother in this condition, so I press him.

"Harvey are you sure that you're okay? Do you have the flu, or are you feeling sick? You have to be honest with me. Once we get to the campsite, it's going to be extremely difficult to take care of you. So it's better if you're not feeling right, to tell me now."

Harvey responds back to me, speaking under his voice.

"I told you that I was fine Harry. I'm being Honest. I will feel better by tomorrow. It's okay. I don't want to ruin the trip for everyone with my complaining. I'll be fine Harry."

I didn't want to bother Harvey any longer, so I left him alone for the rest of the ride. When I did reach the house, I wanted to talk to Louie about this to see what he had to say about it. Harvey was starting to scare me quite a bit, and I didn't want to go on the trip with him feeling like that. I proceed to the garage, where Louie is still gathering everything for the trip. I walk up to Louie, even though he clearly doesn't want to be bothered.

"Lou, can I speak to you for a bit. It's very important."

Louie then seems bothered, and drops the current task that he's doing, and walks close to me. Louie then with an angry look on his face, shouts at me.

"Harry what the fuck? What is it now? I can already tell you're going to tell me something that's going to upset me. I don't want to hear it, but what is it?"

Louie was right, and that I was going to bring up something which may change the mood. I was second guessing to myself as if I should bring it up, or fib about something else. But I then I thought about the way Harvey was acting in my car. It just didn't seem right, and I rarely see Harvey in that particular mood. So it had to be something very serious that was bothering him. I then decide to be truthful with Louie.

"Well Lou, I think Harvey may be sick or something. When we were riding to the fishing shop, he just didn't seem right. He said nothing was wrong, and said he was okay, but I know he's sick. I was thinking we should maybe not let Harvey go. I'm just really worried about him."

Louie did not take what I said well, and began to throw several things around the garage. Louie had a terrible temper, and it's things like this which really upset and trigger him. While Louie is picking up all the things he threw, he then responded to me angrily.

"I don't have time for this Harry. Harvey is fine, everyone is fine. I don't want to hear that right now. If Harvey said he's fine, he's fine. Everyone is going on this trip, and nothing is going to happen. If something is wrong with him, then he should use his words and say so."

Even though Louie was having a harsh approach about it, he was absolutely right. Harvey is an adult, and if he isn't feeling okay, he should be honest about it. Even though I was going to regret it, I had to let the Harvey situation go. I was just praying that whatever his issue was, that he was neglecting to mention to us, wouldn't play a big factor on this trip. That night when I went to bed, I wasn't able to sleep. I was just concerned about Harvey, and this whole trip that I was so excited and happy for, is ruined because of that. I was also scared to go against Louie's wishes. This whole trip was something he was anticipating for a long time, and I didn't want to let something like this ruin it. We went on about things regularly the next morning. All of us met in the garage, on our way to the camp site. I noticed that Harvey still looked upset. Thinking that maybe the next day he would have a change of pace. Harvey still looked very troubled. For one final time I go up to him, so I'm not worried or concerned about him.

"Harvey, if you don't want to come with us, you don't have to. This is your last chance man. If you're not feeling well, you can stay home. Fuck what Louie thinks."

I smile at Harvey, and Harvey also returns a smile to me. He then responds.

"Actually Harry I'm feeling much better. It's okay. I'll be fine."

At this point, I can't do anything else. Harvey said that he was okay, so I have to accept that. Even though his body language is saying something completely different, that doesn't matter. All of us get into Louie's SUV, and we all head directly to the camp site. During this time, I started to feel comfortable. Harvey wasn't on my mind anymore, and I couldn't let the way Harvey was feeling disturb my trip. As we were riding to the camp site, everything for the moment seemed to be fine. That was until we encountered a major problem.

We were about halfway to the campsite, until our car stalled. I couldn't believe it. We were stranded in the middle of the road, and our car stopped. Louie immediately didn't hesitate to display his anger. He slammed his fists on the steering wheel, and his whole body began to tremble. Louie was sweating heavily, and he couldn't handle his anger. He ran outside of the car, slamming the door behind him. As he opened up the hood of the car, the rest of us sat in the car confused. Louie began to examine the inside of the car. Leif who was sitting in the passenger seat got out to see if he could help Louie. Leif walked to the hood of the car standing next to Louie, speaking to him.

"Hey bro, is something wrong? Is it the oil, the battery? What's wrong?"

Louie immediately shoved Leif away, and shouted back at him.

"I don't need your fucking help. I know what the problem is. Get your ass back in the car and shut the fuck up. If I need your help, I'll ask for it. Get back in the car."

Leif shakes his head, and gets himself back in the car. The rest of us took this as a sign to not bother Louie either. This didn't make sense at all. If we were having car trouble, you would think Louie would want for us to help him sort the situation out. He however didn't want us involved with this for whatever reason. Remarkably, within five minutes or so, Louie closed the hood of the car, and got back inside the car. He started the ignition, and the engine started without any problems. The rest of us remained silent, as Louie continues down the road to the campsite. Louie's behavior was beginning to scare us all, and the trip hasn't even technically started yet. Louie would get into these moods quite frequently, and it concerned me and my brothers deeply.

Without any of us saying a word for the duration of the car ride, we finally reach the campsite. However, we were approached with yet another setback. As we reach the entrance of the campsite, we see the entrance has been gated and barricaded. There was a large sign that said, "For your safety, campsite is closed. We apologize for the inconvenience." This was not good. Our whole camping trip is over pretty much. We came all this way for nothing. All the excitement we all had for this trip, means nothing now.

The campsite is closed, and our only option is to go back home. Well, that seemed to be the logical option. I just couldn't imagine how Louie would react to this. This whole trip was something he really wanted to do. I knew he was going to hit the roof over this. Sure enough, he did. After reading the sign, Louie ran out of the car, and proceeded to the back of the SUV. He began to throw all of our supplies out of the car. His face was red, and I've never seen Louie this angry in my life. Myself, Leif, Harvey and Troy were all scared to get out of the car and stop him. Eventually, Leif did get out of the car to restrain Louie. Louie managed to calm down. Louie then takes out his pack of cigarettes, and begins to sit down on a bench, and smokes a cigarette.

Leif ends up sitting next to him, continuing to calm him down. I look and see that all of our supplies for the trip were all thrown across the entrance of the campsite. This was very awkward, and I remain in the car with Harvey and Troy. The three of us then join Louie and Leif outside. Louie takes puffs of his cigarette, and starts to whisper out to us.

"I'm not going back home. Fuck that. That sign is there most likely because there have been thunderstorms in this area recently. It's okay. I've camped any times, and we'll be okay. I'm sorry for losing my cool you guys. We'll just crawl under the fence, it's okay."

I don't know why we obeyed Louie, but we did. We should have just all went home, however we decided to egg Louie on. All of us began picking up all of supplies that Louie threw. We then managed to squeeze under the locked and chained gated entrance of the camp site.

I don't know why the camp site was closed. It may or may not be because of the recent thunderstorms that have happened. Either way, we were not allowed access to the campsite. So if we are caught, we might get into trouble. But I guess that added to the fun I suppose. We were all trespassing, and we wanted to be bad boys. Louie wanted to do this trip, and the only thing that could stop him from doing the trip, was death. So many clues were telling us to go back home, but we ignored them all. I really wish that we had listened.

We were only concerned about having fun on the trip, and our personal safety wasn't on our minds. As we are walking through the entrance trail to our campsite, I can see the hate on Louie's face. He keeps his vision forward, and it seems he has transformed into an evil monster. This is not the Louie I know, and I'm starting to feel very worried about him. Within fifteen minutes or so, Leif finds a spot which seemed like it would be perfect for us to set our tent up at. Harvey, Troy and I, begin to set our supplies down, as it's assumed we will set up camp here. Louie however turns his head behind us looking puzzled. He then starts to yell at all of us, very angrily.

"What the hell? I didn't say this was where we were going to set up camp was it? No I didn't. I want you all to follow me, and when I say it's time for us to stop, then we stop."

I shake my head, and I can't believe the way Louie is acting. He's being a jerk, and there is nothing I can do. We are in a complete desolate area in the woods, so it's not like I can run away from him. All of us are tired from carrying the supplies, and we found what we thought was a nice shaded spot to camp, but Louie was not pleased. We obey him and continue to walk through the woods, until Louie tells us when to stop walking. This is now becoming annoying, as we continue to walk for another hour or so, and Louie still hasn't found a spot he's happy with yet. I'm this close from going up to Louie and knocking him out. He's doing this to torment us I believe.

What else could the reason be? During this time, I look behind me, and I notice that Harvey is not walking with us. I don't know why it didn't dawn on me to check to see if our entire group was with us. I have no idea as to when Harvey separated from us. It could have been five minutes ago, or it could have been longer than that. I assumed Harvey was walking with us the entire time, but he's not here. As soon as I notice this, I alert Louie.

"Lou, Harvey isn't with us. I have to go back to see where he is."

Louie continues to walk forward, and completely ignores me. This has gone far enough. I can't let Louie continue to behave this way, and I have to put my foot down.

"Lou, me, Leif and Troy are walking back to see where Harvey is. I don't give a fuck what you do, but if you care and love your brother, you would walk with us to find him."

Louie shakes his head, and is clearly frustrated. He then yells to us.

"Fuck, is it that damn hard for us all to stick together? I guess so. Let's see where that fucker went to. All he had to do was walk with us. Damn."

Louie and the rest of us then walk back to see if we can locate Harvey. After about twenty minutes or so, we see Harvey on the side of the trail, laying on his back. Harvey's eyes are closed, and he's also perspiring. His clothes are soaked with sweat, and his mouth is wide open. He doesn't seem to be well at all. Louie then starts to throw his backpack on the ground. Instead of feeling concern for his brother, he seems as though Harvey is a hindrance. Louie folds his arms out of anger, and sits on the side of trail, not paying attention to Harvey lying down on the ground. Me, Leif and Troy immediately walk over to him. With the exception of Louie, we are all concerned over Harvey. Leif then lift's Harvey's body up from the ground, and starts to examine him very closely. After noticing that Harvey is not being receptive, Leif starts to become scared over this, and is more concerned over his health.

"Harvey, can you hear me? If you can hear me, lift your hand up."

Harvey lifts his right hand up, meaning that he is still conscious, and can hear Leif. Leif then starts to take Harvey's shirt off, and takes his shoes and socks off as well. Leif then takes a bottle of water from his backpack, and douses Harry with it. Leif continues to talk to Harvey.

"Harvey, can you speak? Can you say anything? What's my name Harvey?"

Harvey then starts to cough, and starts to regurgitate. Louie then immediately runs over to Harvey, and begins to scream and yell at Harvey.

"I don't know what's wrong with you, but you better snap out of it quick. I'm not calling 911, so you better stop being a princess about it, and be a man. We've already lost two hours of time, and it's going to become dark soon. Be a man, and get the fuck up! Now!"

Leif after realizing that Harry isn't being empathetic towards Harvey, starts to wrestle with Louie, pushing and pinning him against a tree. We decide not to break them up, as Louie kinda deserved this. He was being a complete asshole this entire trip, and we were happy that Leif was putting some sense into him. While Leif is pinning Louie, he silently speaks to him.

"Man, your brother is very ill. We have to get him to a hospital now. I can't fucking believe you Louie. You're little brother I think is having heat stroke, and you don't care."

Louie then starts to slightly have a change of heart. Although he is still upset that we are at a standstill with our camping trip. Louie starts to slightly feel sympathetic, and walks to the area where Harvey is crouched down on the ground. He then kneels down to Harvey, and kisses him on the forehead. Harvey still has his eyes closed, and is not in a well state. Louie then whispers to him.

"You okay little bro? You want to go home?"

Harvey then for the first time, opens up his eyes, and looks directly at Louie. Harvey very weakly responds to Louie, with his voice sounding very rough.

"Yes I'm fine. I just didn't drink enough water. I'm fine. I'm sorry for scaring everyone. I'll be fine. Just give me like five minutes, and we can continue."

Louie then snaps back into his previous form, and no longer feels compassionate towards Harvey. Louie quickly starts to put Harvey's shoes back on, and also puts his shirt back on. As he is doing this, Louie under his breath speaks with Harvey.

"Well good, because we weren't going back home anyways. We didn't come all this way, only to go home. Be a man Harvey, and get yourself together. Shit. Don't scare us like that."

Leif seems extremely unsure, and walks over to where Louie and Harvey are, and starts to comfort Harvey. He then angrily looks at Louie, shouting at him.

"I don't know. I think we should get Harvey to a hospital now. He doesn't seem right, and I don't want his condition to get worse if we keep him out here in the woods."

Harvey then starts to finally get up off the ground, and he composes himself. Harvey then while standing completely up, leans towards Leif, and whispers.

"I'm okay, let's just get to camp, and I'm not feeling better by then, I'll let you guys know. I'll be fine. I just got slightly dehydrated. It's fine. We can continue now."

Leif still seems unsure, but allows Harvey to go in his own way. We all don't know how to react. But since Harvey claims to be fine, we decide to press on. We end up making time despite that, and manage to continue to walk through the woods. Sundown is approaching rather fast, and our plan was to find camp before dark. Every few minutes or so, I would look back at Harvey, and he seems to have recovered quite well. Even though earlier he seemed to have not been in a very well state, everything looks okay now. Continuing to walk through the woods, I was starting to feel tired myself. Finally, Louie manages to find a camp site that he's satisfied with. After four hours of walking through the woods, we finally approach the camp site we will be settling at. Louie starts to take his backpack off, and talks to us.

"This spot is great. Nobody will bother us here. It's right by the lake, and the ground is quite level. We are not going to find a better spot, so this is where we're gonna set camp."

I couldn't be more relieved, as we didn't have to walk anymore. I take my backpack off, and start to unpack all the supplies. Myself and Leif immediately start to set up the tent. I look around, and see that Louie is teaching Troy how to light a fire. Continuing to look around the campsite, I see that Harvey is situated about twenty feet away from us.

He is slouched on the ground, and deep asleep. He is not unconscious, he is simply sleeping. Once Louie notices that Harvey is slacking off, and not contributing to setting up camp like the rest of us, he then pours a great amount of water over Harry, and screams at him in the process.

"Get up. This isn't nap time. Start doing something constructive. Stop faking sick as well. We already lost so much time over your shit. Be a man, and start doing something."

Harvey despite being soaked with the water, stays on the ground ignoring Louie. Feeling extremely angered, and unable to control his temper, Louie drags Harry on the ground to the campsite. Once Leif notices Louie doing this, he goes over to Louie and punches him in the face. Louie and Leif then begin to wrestle, and I walk over to Harvey to comfort him. Louie and Leif eventually stop fighting, and Leif then screams out at Louie.

"Leave him alone, he's not well. Just let him rest Lou. Shit. He's sick."

Louie then shakes his head, and walks over to the camp fire. Louie then begins to grab his fishing pole and his tackle box. Louie could understand that we were wearing thin with him. I could also understand that Louie wanted this camping trip to go perfect, but that doesn't excuse the way he's acting at all. I began to fear him, and my brothers did as well. Harvey's health was also on my mind. It didn't help that we were in the woods, so it's not like we can take Harvey to the hospital quickly. My biggest hope was that Harvey's condition was temporary, and he was simply tired. If it was something more serious, then we would be in serious trouble. Louie understood that he needed time to himself cool off, and we weren't going to support his behavior. Louie then walked away from the camp, directing himself towards the lake, whispering to all of us.

"I'm going to go catch us dinner. Hurry up and set that fucking tent up. I don't know what the fuck is wrong with Harvey, but he's being a big baby. I swear. See y'all later."

As Louie walks away, we seem to be temporary at ease due to his presence being gone. Leif, Troy and myself try to put the tent together.

Harvey continues to lay on the ground, lethargic. We struggle slightly getting the tent up, but we finally manage to pitch it up. As soon as the tent is set, Leif carries Harvey inside the tent. For affirmation, me and Troy go inside the tent as well. I notice that Harvey is very red, and he's sweating. This doesn't seem good, and I'm unsure as to what to do. I didn't like to see my brother like this. Harvey then starts to slowly open his eyes, and tears start rolling down his face. Harvey then cries out to us.

"Do you guys have any food? I'm really hungry for some reason. If you don't have any food, that's okay. But I'm just really hungry."

Leif then goes through his backpack, and tries to find something for Harvey to eat. He manages to find a bag of saltine crackers. As he's opening them up, he whispers to Harvey.

"Louie went to go fish us something for dinner, so you're going to have to wait until he comes back if you want real food. But I have some crackers you can have. Here."

Leif starts to feed Harvey the crackers. It was difficult me to see Harvey struggle to eat the crackers, and I wish I knew what was wrong with him. This wasn't just simple heat stroke. Something more deeper than that was wrong with him. Harvey eats the crackers, but still complains of hunger. Leif then ends up feeding Harvey the entire pack of crackers. I couldn't stand to see Harvey like this, so I left out of the tent. I didn't envision for our camping trip to be like this. Louie is being a complete asshole, Harvey s deathly ill. I didn't want to be here anymore, and I just wanted to go home. I end up sitting outside the tent, looking down at the ground. Just thinking to myself for several minutes. Why am I just letting all of this happen? If there something that I can do to fix all of this? All of my thoughts were blocked, and I didn't know what to do. I couldn't do anything to help it seemed. During this time, I started to feel a little better when Troy walked to the area I was sitting in. He began to put his head on my shoulder, and started to offer me the safety I needed.

"Harvey is going to be okay. Don't worry. Things always work out. We are still going to make this camping trip fun. Worrying isn't going to help anybody. Cheer up."

What Troy said was exactly right. Feeling upset and worried isn't going to solve or accomplish anything. The whole point of this trip, was that so we all could kick back, and escape from the city life. The trip was turning into the complete opposite, and nothing was going right. We had planned to be on this trip for the entire weekend, so we had two more days of this. I didn't even know if we would even survive the first day. Things were not going well so far, and it didn't look great for any of us. The only thing we had for entertainment was each other, and enjoying the outdoors.

There was no escape, as we were in the wilderness. We weren't even allowed to be in the campsite first of all, as it was closed to the public. We just ignored the signs, and kept on going. We were breaking so many rules, and this camping trip we planned accordingly, was becoming a nightmare and a wreck. After a few minutes of sitting with Troy lamenting everything, Leif then yells to us.

"Do any of you guys want a beer. I know Louie is going to be mad we're drinking without him, but I really need a drink."

Troy and I agree to having a drink with Leif. We all start drinking our beers at the campsite. Leif takes a swallow of his beer, and talks to myself and Troy.

"Harvey is going to be just fine. You know Harvey has asthma right? It's probably making him feel this way. He should have just stayed home, but he'll be fine tomorrow."

I nod my head, and take another sip of my beer. I knew that Harvey had asthma, but I didn't know it impacted him this much. We have gone on several camping trips in the past, and this is the first time that Harvey has gotten ill. So I was surprised to see him acting that way. Leif, Troy and I, continue to sit by the camp fire for a couple of hours. With sundown only being about an hour away, the day has pretty much been spent. Leif would intermittently go into the tent to check on Harvey's condition. Harvey seems to be getting better, although he is still extremely tired and exhausted. Leif, Troy and I end up staying at the camp site, chit chatting with each other.

Leif then eventually takes out a deck of playing cards, and the three of us start to play Spades to pass the time. We play the card game, losing track of time quite a bit. Although playing cards isn't an outdoor activity, there was nothing left for us to do. We didn't want to leave the camp site as Louie wasn't there, and Harvey was ill. As it has been quite some time since Louie has returned from fishing, I start to then worry about Louie. I knew that Leif could probably care less about it, but I was still worried. I couldn't pay attention to the card game that much really, without thinking about Louie. My biggest fear was that he may have fallen off a cliff, or slipped and hurt himself. I know that it's never wise to go out in the woods alone.

Even though Louie was acting like a jerk, none of us should allowed him to go out by himself. Despite the fact Louie is quite experienced with hiking and fishing, at least one of us should have went with him to be safe. More minutes pass, and sundown will come in about an half an hour or so. Louie still has not returned. The rest of the guys don't care about Louie, but I do. At the end of the day, he's still my brother. Although Louie is full of himself and an asshole, he's still my brother. I love him very much, like I love all my brothers. I take another swallow of my beer, and I simply cannot pay attention to the card game at all anymore. I knew something has gone wrong. I slam my cards down, then decide to explain to Leif, I'm worried about Louie.

"You know, Lou's been gone a long time. I'm getting scared, and Lou just said he was going fishing. Lou doesn't really fish for this long. The lake is about a two mile walk from here right? Something has happened with him. I'm gonna go to the lake just to be sure."

As I'm getting up, Leif grabs my shirt, signaling me to return to my seat.

"Fuck Lou. He's fine. Sit down Harry, you can't leave in a the middle of a game. We're not done yet. Stop worrying about him. Louie needs time to cool off. Sit down."

I get up again, this time being stern with Leif.

"Not for nearly five hours he doesn't. It shouldn't have taken Lou more than two hours if that to get enough fish for us to eat. I'm just going to check on him, and tell him to come back to camp. I think he's cooled off enough now. I'll be back in a jiffy. Just let me check on him please?"

Leif nods his head in acceptance, and continues the card game with Troy. I then start to walk towards the lake. Throughout my walk, I'm just praying that Louie is safe and sound. I was sure that he was sitting by the lake with his pole, silently. When I reached the lake, and saw no trace of Louie at all, my heart sank. It was like an anvil dropped on my entire chest. Where the fuck is he?

As dusk was about to approach in ten minutes, I knew if Louie was still not at camp come nightfall, this wasn't a good sign. I then began to get down on my knees, and prayed to god that my brother was safe. Louie wasn't my best friend, but he was my brother and I loved him. I began to bargain with god. That if you can just make sure that Louie is safe, I won't do anything bad for the rest of my life. I won't lie, cheat or steal. I just want my brother to be fine. I end up staying at the lake for a few minutes, listening to the calm water, and feeling the breeze from the lake on my skin, as the sun is starting to set. Where the hell is Louie?

I start to walk away from the lake, quickly walking in the surrounding area of the lake, attempting to find my brother. It seems my prayers from god may have been answered. As I'm walking to a bluff about a half a mile away from the lake facing north, I hear a voice cry and scream out from an obscured area close to the bluff.

"Harry! Harry! Please help me! The pain is killing me! Please help!"

That's Louie's voice. I immediately spring into action. I can't see Louie, but that's him crying out for me, and he saw me walking across the bluff path. Louie continues to cry and scream out for me, but I can't see where he is at.

"Harry please hurry! I'm bleeding, and I'm in so much pain!."

Due to the way Louie was shouting, I know that something serious must have happened. He felt into the crest, maybe because of how angry he was. He wasn't paying attention to where he was walking and slipped. I had to locate Louie fast, in order for me to see offer help and assistance to him. By the sound of his voice, I know Louie is down below somewhere. I then decide to very carefully tread down into the crest to locate my brother. I then finally see Louie's face, and that's the same face me and all my brothers share. I knew that I had to help him, as he's my brother. Louie's face is very pale, and from looking at him, he's in much pain. I continue to crawl deeper into the crest, to the area that Louie is in. Louie then cries out to me some more.

"Oh my god, Harry! Please help me! I'm trapped! I can't move! I'm scared!"

I manage to make it to the spot Louie is trapped in, as Louie steadily cries out in pain. I look through where he's located, and it seems Louie's left arm is trapped under a large piece of the cliff. I try my best to move Louie away, but due to his large body weight, this seems impossible. I start to panic, and I know there is only one way, and one way only for Louie to get out of this predicament. His arm is going to have be amputated. As soon as I realize this, I begin to cry, as I don't know how I'm going to let Louie know about this news. I then feel that there is no need for me to keep this information from him. The longer he stays in this spot, the more blood he's going to lose, and he risks dying. I then explain the truth to Louie.

"Lou, your arm is stuck. You're not going to get out, unless they cut your arm off. I'm sorry. I'm going to try to get you some help. Just stay right here for a few minutes."

Louie doesn't take this well, and continues to cry towards me.

"No, I can't lose my arm. I'm a chef. I need my arms. My career is basically over now. You might as well leave me here to die. They aren't taking my arm. Fuck that."

I start to rub Louie's head, and I try my best to console him.

"Lou, you're gonna die if you stay here. I'm going to get you some help. Don't worry."

I start to hike back up to the path, as Louie continues to cry, urging for me not to leave his sight. I understand this is tough for him, but I need to act fast to save him.

"I'll be back in a few minutes Lou. Hold on, I'm going to get you some help right now."

I sprint back to the camp site as fast I could. Knowing that Louie is very close to death, and I can't waste time to get him help. When I reach back to camp with the other guys, I let them know that Louie needs help badly, and we need to act right now to help him. Troy decides to stay at camp with Harvey who is still feeling groggy. Myself and Leif then return back to the area that Louie is at. This time, the sun is setting, and it's slightly dark. I end up locating the area Louie is at again, and Leif and I crawl down to the crest where Louie is stuck. Leif then starts to angrily berate Louie, for getting himself trapped inside the crest.

"Man, how did you get yourself into this position? Weren't you watching where you were going. You might be stuck forever now. I hope you're happy. We have no cell phone reception or anything, so this isn't good. What the fuck are we gonna do?"

Louie's screams are getting louder and louder, and Leif isn't helping the situation. Louie has to be freed, and he has to be freed immediately. I ask Leif to stay with Louie, as I try to see if I can go to an area closer to the highway where I can receive phone reception. Leif remains in the area Louie is at, and I start to run through the woods, to the highway. I run for what seems like an hour, and I still haven't located the highway. I finally reach the highway, yet I still don't have reception to call 911. I decide to pray once again. I kneel down on the ground, and ask that a guardian angel comes.

Louie is going to die if he's not free from that cliff in probably the next few hours or so. I was hoping for some type of miracle to rain down, or anything. After praying to god, I continue to walk through the woods along the highway, hoping for some type of salvation. My prayers were answered yet again, when I by chance happen to reach a park ranger station by the highway. I go to the park rangers cabin, and knock on the door. Nobody comes to the door, and I slam my head against the door hard. This was my chance to save my brother, and I don't know what to do. Seconds later, the park rangers vehicle pulls up to the cabin. The park ranger is a skinny Caucasian bald man with a five o clock shadow on his face. I wave my hands out to the park ranger, and he immediately turns his vehicle off, and starts to run towards me. The park ranger then out of concern shouts to me, pointing his flashlight in my face.

"What the hell are you doing here? The camp site is closed. I'm calling the police as you're trespassing. Give me your name now."

I'm blinded temporarily by the flashlight of the park ranger, but I manage to state myself.

"Sir, my name is Harry Bruner. I know we aren't allowed in the camp site, but we kinda sneaked in. We're sorry. But my brother is trapped in the northern facing trail sir. His arm is caught under the ridge, and I'm scared he's going to lose blood and die. I need your help please."

The park ranger then has a look of shock of horror, and immediately drags me by the wrist to his vehicle. As he's doing that, he starts to converse with me sharply.

"Oh man you're so lucky. I was on my way home for the night. I left my wallet on my desk. Otherwise I wouldn't have pulled up. We'll get him some help right now."

As I'm sitting in the park rangers vehicle, I felt so lucky that I happened by chance to run into the park ranger. Had I not, Louie probably would have died for sure. I was forever thankful for the streak of luck I got from the park ranger coming to the rescue. The park ranger then pulls out his walkie talkie, and begins to shout into it.

"This is Fishman. I need rescue patrol now. This is an extreme emergency. Look for the flares in the northern trail line. I need rescue patrol out fast and immediately."

Within a few minutes, the park ranger and I reach the area where Louie is immobilized at. Along with the park ranger, I crawl down into the crest where Louie is stuck. Being that it's now darkness, it makes it harder to see where Louie is trapped. However we are able to spot him. Leif is still comforting Louie, and Louie is also still conscious. The park ranger then speaks with Louie.

"Sir, what is your name? My name is Luke Fishman, and I'm a park ranger and we're going to get you some help. You're gonna be just fine. Can you tell me your name, and how you got stuck?

Louie at this point is weak, and is finding it difficult to speak. He croaks out his answer to the park ranger, while still in immense pain from being stuck.

"My name is Louie Bruner, and I was trying to go to the lake to fish. I wasn't paying attention and I slipped about thirty feet into this crest this afternoon. I've been stuck ever since."

The park ranger flashes his light on Louie's left arm, which is completely smashed and stuck by the ridges of the crest. The park ranger then gets on his walkie talkie, shouting.

"Yes this is Fishman. I need some help out here right now. Please. I have a guy who's stuck, and we don't have a lot of time. I need rescue patrol right now. Shit!"

Louie then starts to close his eyes, and slowly drifts out of consciousness. At this time, I tell Leif to go back to camp, and to explain to Troy and Harvey what happened, and to stay at camp. I let him know that I was going to stay at the scene with Louie and the park ranger. As Leif is walking away, Louie opens his eyes. Though slightly losing consciousness Louie then starts to cry out to me.

"Harry, I just wanted you and for the rest of the guys to know that I love all of you. I'm sorry for the way I behaved. I should have listened to Harvey and stayed home. I'm sorry for all the trouble I put all you guys through. This is all my fault, and I'm paying for it. I'm sorry."

I then start to rub the back of Louie's head. I start to cry myself from seeing my brother like this. As we are still waiting for the rescue patrol to come, I silently talk to Louie.

"It's not your fault Louie. I know you wanted to go on this trip for a long time. Don't feel bad okay. Harvey doesn't hate you, and none of us hate you. You're gonna be fine man."

I begin to laugh, not because the situation is humorous, but because I just start thinking about how disastrous this day became. I am also happy that Louie is starting to understand how bad he was today. Did Louie deserve to be stuck in a cliff? No he didn't, but he's still my brother, and I'm happy that he's realizing his mistakes so he can move on. Rescue medical patrol reaches the scene fifteen minutes later, and run down to the area where Louie is stuck. They immediately hook Louie up to several medical machines, and give him oxygen. Although Louie is still stuck under the cliff. I know that the only way they are going to free him, is by severing his arm off. This is something that was not only tough for Louie, but for me as well. I didn't want to see them take my brothers arm off, but that's the only way he's going to be free. This is confirmed when a member of rescue medical team also comes to this realization.

"This rock isn't going to move. We're going to have to amputate his arm. Even then, we have to get him to hospital quick enough, or he's going to die from the shock. Let's go."

I am then instructed by several of the medical patrol to walk away from the scene. I immediately follow their orders, and I walk up away from the crest, onto the path up above. I look down at the medical patrol trying to free my brother. Ten minutes later, they manage to free Louie, taking away his arm sadly in the process. During this time, they were awaiting for the medical helicopter to arrive, and it does. Not even a minute after freeing Louie, they airlift him to the nearest hospital. Everything was happening in a quick flash. I ride in the park rangers vehicle back to our campsite, while Louie is being airlifted to the hospital.

Myself, Leif, Harvey, and Troy all get into the park rangers vehicle, back to the entrance of the camp where Louie parked his SUV. The rest of the guys remain in the park rangers vehicle, and I end up following them to the hospital, driving in Louie's SUV. We all make it to the hospital, and I rush through the emergency room, trying to find the room where Louie is in. A security guard restrains me, and tells me I'm not allowed inside. I explain that I'm Louie's brother, and the security guard allows me to continue. I walk to Louie's hospital room, and he's laying down on his hospital bed. Although Louie is knocked out from the medicine the hospital gave him, I go inside his room.

I end up giving a kiss to Louie on his forehead, and I stroke his hair. I still have my brother, and he's going to be fine. I end up staying in the room for several hours, as Leif, Harvey and Troy all come into the room later to see Louie. The next morning at around 10 am, nearly twelve hours later, Louie finally awakens. I was up that entire time starting at him. I get up from my chair to stand next to him bedside. Louie then starts to open his eyes and stares at me, speaking very softly to me.

"I love you Harry. You saved my life, and I'll always respect you for that. I'm going to be different from now on. Thank you again Harry for saving me."

I end up giving another kiss to Louie. The following day, Louie was released from the hospital, and we drove him home. After losing his arm, Louie was still Louie, but he was an nicer Louie. Harvey and Leif, and Troy and I all helped take care of his restaurant while he was recovering. Eventually, Louie was well enough to start cooking again. Despite the heavy learning curve from only having one arm, Louie actually mastered his cooking skills to a higher level than they were before. He continued on being a chef. He didn't let this stop him, and I respect my brother for that.

The camping trip not only changed Louie, but it changed all of us as a matter fact. Harvey experienced an extreme asthma attack and heatstroke, with Louie being stuck by himself on a cliff. If it wasn't for my concern, and acting fast, Louie most likely would have been dead. It was a wild adventure, but as I said previously, it's a camping trip I will always remember.

So, that's the end of my story. It was a wild ride, and the ride has concluded. Everything is fine now, and I continue my job working at the supermarket. I'm supervisor now in charge of the deli and meat department, and a new leaf has turned. Louie continues running his restaurant. I help Louie out at the restaurant as well, being a chef. Louie still bosses us around, however the bossing around is due to love. We all still live together. I still love Troy, even though he gets on my nerves. I don't know how he deals with me and my brothers, but he does. Harvey manages his asthma better. He actually forgot to refill his inhaler before the trip, which is what he was keeping secret from us. But Harvey is doing quite well, and his health is good. Leif is being Leif, and he's still a gym teacher.

I have nothing else to mention, I revealed what I had to reveal. There is nothing left to add to the recipe, and I explained all my secrets. With that, I just ask that you take my story, and understand the importance of it. As long as a moral was learned by telling my story, I don't feel that uncomfortable explaining it all over again. My name is Harry Bruner, and I'm man of orange, and that was my story.

CHAPTER 8:

MAN OF PINK (PART 1)

My name is Aaron Chen, and I am the "Man of Pink". My reddit username is, "AaronMonster". I am 28 years old, but I feel like due to most of the strange events in my life, I feel that I'm much older than that. Even though I was born in Seattle, Washington, my parents were born in Beijing, China. So that would make me second generation Chinese American. I'm not one to really pry on politics, but being Asian American comes with several battles. I should first of all explain how the Chinese culture works in China, and how that conflicts with the way people live here in the United States and North America. In China, you grow up, with the exception as to if you become or marry a politician, or you end up being a concert pianist, or a pop star, or you end up joining an elite gang or something, you do whatever your parents want you to do. This is done without complaint or argument. If your parents want you to become a doctor, that's going to be your career study as an adult, whether you wanted to be a doctor or not. If your parents wanted you to become a car manufacturer, that's what you're doing. You pretty much get the idea, and to be honest, as much as this system seems flawed, it works.

In addition, children are to always obey their parents, and to live just as a successful, if not live a better life, than your parents and ancestors did. If you go against this, you bring dishonor to your family and your culture as well. With all the added pressure of growing up by itself, adding the 'Tiger Parent' culture is difficult. I guess where I may have lucked out, is that I was not born in China. I was born an American, and that makes me an American. Yes I'm Asian, yes I'm Chinese, and I speak fluent Chinese, but I am an American damn it. So being that America is a free county, I'm allowed to live my life the way I want to, without my parents pressuring me to do something that I don't even want to do. I still respect my parents yes, but this is not China, and if I want to do something on my own validity, I have the right to.

Here comes the uncomfortable part, so fasten your seatbelt. As far as LGBT rights in China, they could be better. The Chinese culture considers this at the top of one of the most taboo things. Being homosexual is something that in Chinese culture, and in Asian culture in general, that is still being worked on. I grew up knowing that I was gay, and it wasn't hard or difficult to come out to myself. The hard part was coming out to other people, and coming out as a gay Asian man.

I could accept myself without any issue. I knew being a little boy and watching "Mighty Morphin Power Rangers", and finding Tommy and Billy, and Rocky and Jason attractive. That was something that clicked into my mind rather easily. I liked guys, and that's the way it was. Doing research later in my life, I later came to put a name behind my attraction. Gay, and it was something that despite how open minded America was, was still a delicate topic as well. LGBT rights here in the United States are fair, but we sometimes still get treated less than.

I usually try to outweigh the positives to the negatives. Being that I was a nerdy skinny Asian boy, people just assumed I was an ordinary Asian kid. There are so many misconceptions. Unless he's like a successful macho businessman, or a sumo wrestler, or can do martial arts; Asian men are always painted in the media as being a certain way, and not as strong or assertive.

I think it's bullshit, but I look at a lot of pop music from China and Japan, and I hate to say the stereotypes seem to live up to be true. Here in the western world, you did have Michael Jackson, Prince, David Bowie, Boy George. But that was back in the 80s and stuff. I'm going to leave this alone, but it's something I wanted to mention anyways. I feel people are people, and we all deserve to be treated with respect. We are all different, and we all come in difference shapes and sizes; so respect everyone. Treat people the same way that you want to be treated yourself.

Up until I was thirteen, I was the perfect golden child. I do have an older sister, Amelia. Me and my sister never did anything bad. I'm not trying to paint myself pretty. I am dead fucking serious. We didn't even blink or breathe the wrong way. I think the most devilish thing I have done growing up, had to be stealing a cookie from the cafeteria in the first grade. I swear that had to be the most sinful thing I have done. I'm not saying this to be proud of myself. In fact, at times I did envy others that did more wild and strange things. As I lived an obedient life in my childhood, I don't have any funny stories to tell really.

My studies were the only thing that took up my time. My sister and I would go to school, and then immediately after school, we would go see our tutor. The tutor who was a Chinese man, would not only teach us Chinese, but also teach us advanced math and other topics. It was definitely unnecessary in my opinion, but I guess it was done to keep my sister and I out of mischief I suppose. My grades were always perfect, so I guess I can't be mad or complain that much. I didn't struggle academically, so I want to thank my parents for this. Although I wish I didn't have to go to school, then after school, go through more school. On days when we didn't have after school tutoring, I would go to my piano lessons, or my sister would go to her cello lessons.

I hated learning the piano. So you are probably asking yourself, why did I practice playing if I hated it? Because I didn't have a fucking choice, that's why. I also seemed to naturally be a piano player, because I was playing at concert level by the time I was nine. I even went to many piano recitals, much to my parents chagrin. So I played the piano to please them, and because I was so gifted and talented at the piano, I was damned if I stopped or quit. So I kept on playing, and I actually still play to this day from time to time. There is a piano in my house now, and I play it once a week at least. So I know it's complicated to explain, Ha Ha. But yeah I hate playing the piano, but it's become my main hobby. It's tough to explain I know. You're not me, so let's just leave it there.

Everything really changed for me, and I think most other people growing up, when I went into High School. For elementary and Junior High School, I kept to myself, and did my own studies. I was the only Asian kid in school before High School. It was all white kids. No diversity at all, except for me. So that was tough. Seattle was supposed to be a diverse area, but not when it came to when I went to school. So it was difficult growing up not seeing diversity in school. I became the token Asian kid at the school, and that's what I was known for.

I didn't have any friends. I would talk a little with the other boys in between classes, but they weren't my friends. I was slightly into Pokémon when I was young for a short stint, and I would use that as a crux to talk to them. But again, because I was different and was Asian, they didn't want to deal with me most of the time. So as a result, I didn't deal with them either. But High School was when that all changed. High School was when my identity crisis started to kick in, and all the angst and depression began. My Freshman year of High School really taught me many lessons. The world can sometimes be cruel, and the fact I'm an Asian gay man, makes it open season for all of the evil spirits and energy to attack me.

The first day of High School, I will never forget. The kids looked much older, and there were many subgroups formed in the school. Diversity seemed to finally be present. There were other Asian, and black, and middle eastern, and Hispanic and Latino students either. However the catch was, that it was extremely segregatted. I very rarely saw students from a different race mingle with each other, unless it was an exception. For example, even though most of the goths were white, I did see Asian and black goths hang out with them.

Also, the football, basketball, baseball and all the other sports teams were racially diverse. But I don't really want to count the sports or athletic teams. Beside all of that, everyone stuck to their own culture in the school, and when classes were over afterschool. I didn't make any friends in High School because of this. This angered me greatly, and I hated being alone. I would try to position myself with the other Asian kids at the school, but they were dealing with a lot of cultural issues. For example, I was the only Asian that was Chinese. Most of the Asians were Japanese or Korean, and you would think that is a dismissive thing, but it's actually not. I would ask them if I could come over after school and meet their families, and I would also invite them to my house, and the answer would always be no. I didn't dare pick at them over this, because I'm sure the reasons were valid. I don't know if they thought I was a bad influence or I don't know. So the people that I would think I would have the most support for, I didn't. So this was extremely hard to deal with.

When I tried to get to know students period, regardless of their race or culture, it was mostly a flaky attitude. Because I wasn't a jock, because I wasn't a rich kid, because I wasn't a goth or a punker, or a skater, or any other type of clique the school had, they didn't want to include me in their groups. I gave up, because I just ran out of energy. So I said to myself that I'll just focus all my attention towards my schoolwork, and not trying to make friends. Once I graduate from High School, I'm never going to see them again anyways.

I began to feel very depressed during this time in my life. I also felt jealous of my sister Amelia who for reasons I don't want to get into, went to another school than I did. Her High School was much better, and the students were nicer. The students at my school were just unbelievably cruel for no reason. She was making lots of friends, and she was also on the school orchestra, and her grades were so well, that she was offered a University scholarship by the time she finished Freshman year.

However I was having an opposite reverse effect. I was not involved with any clubs at school, I had no friends, and was actually bullied quite a few times. I neglected to mention this, but I remember being pushed around by some of the bullies at school several times. My grades worst of all were beginning to subside. My parents during this time were never at home, and they stopped forcing my sister and I to go to music lessons, and tutoring afterschool. My mother who worked for an advertising company, and my father who was a primary care physician, worked long hours. My sister also had many activities she did after school. Once school was let out, I would be home alone many times. I began to feel angered, and I would simply go to the pier afterschool. I would get a sandwich from the deli, and take my mp3 player and just go to the pier. I did this everyday afterschool. I would sometimes write in my journal as well. Just writing down the life I wish I had, and all the things I wish I could do.

I hated how boring my life was. I hated how everyone seemed to be doing everything they wanted to do, however I was stuck in a place I didn't want to be. I began to hate myself for being Asian, and I began to hate myself for being gay as well. Why did I have no friends? Why did I not have any passion for my life? Why was I going to the pier every day afterschool to sulk about my problems? I began to feel very bitter about my life and I didn't know what to do about it. This charade continued into my senior year of High School.

Even though my grades were going down slightly, they were good enough so I wasn't expelled out of school, or had to repeat any years. I began to meditate quite often. I was researching online about meditation, and I figured that it would help me with my life ambitions. Due to the meditation, at the start of my senior year of High School, I finally found my passion in life. I wanted to studying nursing. It's a very rewarding career, and I'm guaranteed job placement wherever I am. I'm also helping other people, which is great, and nursing was what I wanted to do. I started to then research about nursing, and self-teaching myself different medical terms.

Even though I would have to go through nursing school later if I wanted to be a licensed nurse, there is no time like the present for me to educate myself on these things. I wanted to discuss this with the career placement counselor at my school. Ms. Zoe Lawrence. Ms. Lawrence was openly Lesbian, and she also had a butch appearance. She had dyed Green short hair, and had piercings on her face. It was unusual to see a member of the school staff with this appearance. She was the coordinator of the schools LGBT alliance. Which for issues related to my own, I didn't really attend any of their meetings before this. But Ms. Lawrence was very nice with all of us. I wanted to speak to her, to see if I can have my classes changed last minute at the start of my senior school year, to coincide with my nursing. An hour before the first day of school began, I went to her office, and sat beside her desk. Ms. Lawrence was surprised to see me.

"Aaron, how are you? Is there something that I can help you with this morning?"

I loved Ms. Lawrence's energy, and she was the only staff member at the school I liked. Everyone else that worked in the school office were stuck up and strict, and they hated younger people. But not Ms. Lawrence. I end up explaining to her why I'm in her office.

"I'm doing fine, thank you. Yes I came to see you, because I was looking at my class schedule, and none of the classes are going to prepare me for my career. I want to be nurse, and would like classes that are going to prepare me for that. If you could help me out please."

Ms. Lawrence goes through her computer, and she politely but bluntly responds.

"Oh Aaron, this is rather last minute. Cutting it kinda close You should have talked to me last year, and we probably could have worked something out. I don't know if I'm going to be able to help you, but due to how great of a student you are, I'm going to try my best."

I try to urge and plead with her the best I can, and put on my powers of persuasion.

"Please, I'm sure there is something you can do. I'm not begging you, but please."

Ms. Lawrence continues to operate on her computer, and gives me an answer.

"Okay Aaron, you're in luck. I managed to pull some strings, and I rearranged your entire schedule. The classes you have now, are going to be more focused on your career path. I put you into advanced physics with Ms. Mullins, and I also put you into Biology with Mr. Pankowski."

Ms. Lawrence hands me my new revised schedule, and I glance at it. I'm happy with my new classes, and I end up thanking Ms. Lawrence for helping me out with this.

"Thank you so much, I appreciate it. I'd better head to my first class now."

I end up shaking Ms. Lawrence's hand, and I end up leaving her office.

"It's not any problem at all Aaron, best of luck to you. Come see me anytime."

After leaving Ms. Lawrence's office, I start heading to my first class, which is advanced physics with Ms. Claudia Mullins. Ms. Mullins was very nice, and I had no issues in the class. I could definitely get used to having her for first period every day, and the interaction that the both of us shared was good. The amount of homework she gave us wasn't that bad either, and if we had any questions, she would also answer them. I couldn't say the same for the rest of my teachers. They were all very strict to me, and ran a tight ship. I feel that teachers are either really nice, or they are really mean.

It's very rare you'll find a teacher that's in between. They are either one way, or they are the other. At lunch, as suspected, all the students sat according to their clique or group. Because I wasn't a member of any of these groups, I ended up sitting by myself in the back of the cafeteria. This was very depressing, as I was alone eating. I had gotten used to it at this point, and it was cool. Once I finished eating my lunch, I went to the courtyard outside of the school, and sat by a nice shaded tree. I just started to read. I had no friends, so there was nobody for me to mingle with during lunch period. I was feeling the sun of my face, enjoying the fall weather, and getting myself used to the first day of school. I knew that after lunch, I would have one final period.

It was biology class with Mr. Pankowski. It's so weird, saying his last name. But I kinda want to be fruitful for a bit. His name is Steven, but at this time he was Mr. Pankowski, and he's still Mr. Pankowski to me. The bell for final period rings, and I end up walking to Mr. Pankowski's class for the first time. Not realizing my life will never be the same after this.

As I reached Mr. Pankowski's class, I notice that I'm the first one in the class, and the whole entire room is empty. For no apparent reason, I end up taking a seat right in front of his desk in the front row. I then begin to take my notebook out. A few moments later, more of the students begin to enter the classroom. Once the classroom is full with many students, Mr. Pankowski enters the room sipping a paper cup of coffee. Mr. Steven Pankowski, I remember the first time I met him. He was Twenty Seven at the time, but he looked a lot older. He was bald, and rather slender. He wore glasses, and he had a geeky frame to him. The outfit he wore on the first day of school was a white shirt, with a blue tie, and black pressed pants.

The very first time I laid my eyes on him, I had a feeling that I could not understand. Whether I wanted to admit it or not, I had a crush on him. As Mr. Pankowski set his briefcase and his coffee cup down on his desk, he began to write his name on the whiteboard behind him. All the other students in the class are caterwauling, but I'm not. I'm silent and attentive, keeping all my attention on him only. After Mr. Pankowski writes his name on the board, he then shouts out to the class.

"ALL OF YOU SHUT THE HELL UP! THAT'S ENOUGH OF THAT!"

The classroom immediately becomes silent, and all the students stop their chit chatting. Mr. Pankowski examines all the students in the class, and notices that a couple girls in the back of the classroom are whispering to each other. Mr. Pankowski then exposes them aloud.

"Uh ladies, if you think I'm going to let the both of talk while I'm trying to teach , think again. Now I want this entire classroom quiet, and I want it quiet now."

Some of the students then begin to snicker and laugh at what Mr. Pankowski said. Mr. Pankowski then reaches in his desk, and takes out a stack of papers. He then separates the stack into several other multiple giant stacks, giving each stack to the student sitting at the first desk at each row, with each student taking one packet, and passing it to the student behind them. Being that I'm situated at one of the desks in front, I knew that he was going to hand me a stack.

When he does in fact do so. This is the first time I make eye contact with him. I remember I stared into his eyes for a good three seconds, and he winced slightly at me. Or maybe that was just wishful thinking, I don't know. Either way, that was the first time I made eye contact with him. After Mr. Pankowski hands out the stacks of papers, he moves to the front of the class, and begins to speak.

"As you can see on the board, my name is Mr. Pankowski. This is biology class. Even though this is final period, don't feel I'm going to let you guys off easy because of that. I'm not your friend, and I will not hesitate to give all of you a failing grade."

Mr. Pankowski continues to lecture the class, and I skim through the paper he handed out. It is actually a class syllabus, and it goes through what we are going to learn during the semester. As I continue to skim through the paper he handed out, Mr. Pankowski continues.

"I have a zero tolerance on tardiness. I give you one warning, and if you are tardy again, I will fail you from my class. Which if I fail you form the class, you will have to do extra credit work to make up for that. Even with the extra credit, you will still fail. So be on time every day."

Mr. Pankowski seemed very strict, and he was starting to intimidate not only me, but the other students that were in the class. This was just the first day of school, and out of all of my teachers, he was giving me the most amount of hell. Remember, I also was forming an strange attraction to him. I have to add this, as it's relevant to how I'm currently feeling. Mr. Pankowski continues to give us an outline as to how his class operates. Out of instinct, I take out my notebook, and begin writing tidbits as to what Mr. Pankowski is discussing and talking about. Not even two minutes or so of me writing what he's saying, Mr. Pankowski throws my notebook off my desk, and also throws the pen I was writing with, clear across the room. He then gets to an uncomfortable level to my face, and whispers under his breath to me.

"Did I tell you to take notes?"

I sit silently not saying anything for about ten seconds. I didn't know if it was an rhetorical question or not, or if I was supposed to answer it. I was also slightly scared of how close he was into my personal space. I felt threatened and nervous. Even if I tried to open my lips to speak, I couldn't. So I stayed silent this entire time. Mr. Pankowski seemed angry at me for not responding to him, and decided to shout at me very violently.

"DID I TELL YOU TO TAKE NOTES? I DIDN'T, RIGHT? PAY ATTENTION! Go get your things from off the floor, and go back to your seat. Don't take any notes, unless I tell you so. If you do that again, you're getting detention. Do you understand me?"

I get up from my seat, and grab my notebook that the teacher threw, and I also end up grabbing my pen that was also on the ground. I return to my seat, feeling humiliated. The rest of the students were laughing at me, and I hated being made a fool of. Mr. Pankowski continued on with his lesson, and this was only the beginning of the strange relationship I had with him. But I did have a slight crush on him. After class was over, I had so many emotions in my head. I was going to have to be with this man for the rest of my school year. My last period was going to be with him.

Whether I enjoyed his company or not, I was forced to be in his class. Instead of going straight home, I went to one of the back staircases of the school, and just cried sitting on the top step. Mr. Pankowski had that effect on me. He was such a mean teacher, but I began to have a strange lust over him. Being that I was only seventeen years old, it would be disaster if I didn't keep my thoughts of him to myself.

I started to cry and sob deeply. The ultimate sin, I was committing. The infamous crush on the teacher sin. I would have never in a million years thought that it would happen to me, but it has. Throughout my entire school career, I never found teachers attractive. Actually, I despised most teachers, and wanted nothing to do with them. Not with Mr. Pankowksi. He was different. I just had to realize that I'm never going to be with him, and I have to start thinking realistically about it.

That night at home, I was in my room, and was thinking about my day at school. Being in Mr. Pankowski's class, and how much of a strain it has on my mental health. Understanding how strict of a teacher he is, and that I have never had a feeling such as this with a teacher ever before. Part of me wanting to skip going to his class the next day. I could just not imagine me being strong enough to sit through his class another day. The following day at school, I thought that I would feel better about it. That's incorrect, I felt even worse about it. Once again,

I was the first one to arrive in Mr. Pankowski's class, and a few of the other students were there. When I walked into the classroom, some of them were laughing and snickering under their breaths. I knew something was up, but I didn't know exactly what it was. I thought maybe I had a 'kick me' sign on my back, or there was something in my hair. Whatever it was, I knew it was some type of inside joke or something I wasn't aware of. I start to sit down at my desk in the front of the class, just like I did the day before. As I'm taking out my notebook, one of the students that was sitting in the back of class, walks over to my desk, and taps me on the shoulder. I turn to look at the student, and they begin to whisper out to me.

"We put super glue on his chair. Don't ruin the secret. When he comes in, just act natural. Don't spoil it. This is going to be so fun, to get back at him."

I end up shaking my head. Even though I found Mr. Pankowski strict, I would never dare imagine playing a prank on him like that. Something like this is only going to make the situation worse, and possibly have him hate us even more. I felt like I was torn as to what I should do. Should I tell Mr. Pankwoski that there is super glue on his seat, or should I just go along with the prank like the other kids are? I mean, he did humiliate me the day before, so I guess this would be the perfect payback for him. Minutes later, the rest of the class enters the classroom, and the whole class is in on the stunt, and everyone seems to be on board. Mr. Pankowski soon arrives inside the classroom, and sets his briefcase and coffee mug down on his desk.

Some of the class erupts in small snickering, but we are all keeping up the charade. Mr. Pankowksi then starts to write down several problems on the board. At this time, I wanted to basically do a good deed, or attempt to. I didn't feel that Mr. Pankowski deserved the prank the class was going to pull on him.

Despite that the rest of the class would hate me and possibly beat me up after class, I was going to snitch about the prank. When the teacher is finished writing what he had to write on the board, I raise my hand. Mr. Pankowski notices my hand is raised, and gives me an agitated and irritated look. He then shouts out to me.

"Put your hand down. Unless I ask you all if you have any questions, I don't want your hand raised while I'm teaching. Put your hand down. You're already on thin ice from yesterday you know that right? Put your hand down, and be quiet."

I couldn't believe it. Here I was trying to do something good. The hell was I thinking? Well you know what, Mr. Pankowksi just blew it. He didn't have to be a complete jerk about it. I couldn't wait to see him sit down on that chair. I was also feeling sadistic about this too. I was going to help him out, and warn him about the prank. But since he yet again humiliated me in front of the whole class, I hope he gets whatever is coming to him. I am going to laugh so hard when he sits down. I couldn't believe his attitude, and I had no intentions of helping him anymore. Mr. Pankowksi continues on talking, as the rest of the class waits for him to sit down on the chair.

"I'm going to give all of you guys a test today. I know it's only the second day, but the packet I gave yesterday, I didn't tell you at the time, but I wanted you all to study everything in it. I really hope you guys studied, if not, expect an big giant 'F'."

The entire classes groaned in disapproval. I thought it was very cruel that Mr. Pankowski tricked us like that. The packet he handed out yesterday, we all assumed was a syllabus. We didn't know that this was a secret code for us to study for a test later. I didn't think that was fair at all, and I don't think any of us payed attention to that section of the packet. So I was pretty sure the entire class was going to fail this test. The other part of me was happy that as soon as Mr. Pankowski sat down on his chair, he was going to be in a big surprise.

So the surprise pop quiz didn't seem that bad after all. Mr. Pankowski then handed out the quiz paper to the entire class. Once looking at the paper, all of the questions seemed foreign, and I knew damn well I was going to fail this test very horribly. This didn't matter, as not one of us in the classroom were fretting about the test. Our main attention was on Mr. Pankowski sitting down.

We were just anticipating for when this was going to happen. We knew that once he passed all the tests out the class, he would sit down, and be stuck to his chair. We would then have the last laugh, and would have taught the teacher a lesson. Not understanding that it's cruel to play pranks and tricks on the teacher. We didn't seem to care about that though. Our main concern was to get back at the way he treated us. He was a mean teacher, and we felt he deserved it. The time finally came, and Mr. Pankowski started to direct himself to his desk. The class tried not draw suspicion by staring at him, and we all had our attention towards the test he gave. Mr. Pankowski then sat down on the chair behind his desk, and half the class couldn't contain themselves, and were laughing extremely loud. This caused Mr. Pankowski to be confused, and shouted out to everyone.

"Why is everyone laughing? Everyone be quiet and do your test."

When the class continued to laugh, Mr. Pankowski attempted to get off his chair. When he struggled to get up, the entire class with the exception of myself, began to laugh hysterically. I didn't laugh though. For some reason, as much as I was hoping to laugh along with the rest of the class and find the prank funny, I simply didn't. I saw the look of embarrassment on Mr. Pankowski's face as he was stuck to his chair. I saw him struggle to get up, and he couldn't.

I was also surprised that the students also put super glue on the arm rests of the chair. So his arms were also stuck to the chair. I felt extremely bad for him, and started to feel guilty. However, I did try my best to warn him of the prank, but he simply did not want to listen to me.

For the next twenty minutes or so, the laughter the class was giving, seemed to slowly fade. Mr. Pankowski just stayed in his seat, looking down at the ground. I found it puzzling as to why Mr. Pankowski kept silent. I think maybe he felt too embarrassed to say or do anything. Class was going to be over eventually, so I wondered if he was going to go through the whole class, not reacting to anything. Just feeling defeated by the prank we all pulled. I then wanted to redeem myself for not warning Mr. Pankowski for the prank I pulled earlier. I ended up getting out my seat, and walked over to Mr. Pankowski's desk. I remember the look he gave me as I was walking to his desk, was one of confusion.

After I made eye contact walking up to him, Mr. Pankowski returned to looking down on the ground. I stood right next to his chair, and then began to try my best to remove him from the chair. I simply couldn't do it, as the super glue was attached to him rather well. I then understood how embarrassing this must be for him.

Teachers are people too, and even though he was a strict and mean teacher, he was still a person. He didn't really deserve this at all, and the least I could do was offer my help and support to him. After a few minutes of struggling to get him off, I noticed Mr. Pankowski kept his vision down. His body language displaying defeat. I then cry out to the rest of the class.

"You guys, he's really stuck. Someone help me. Please."

The rest of the class ignore me, and not a single person in the class walks up to help me. As I continue to attempt to get Mr. Pankowski off the chair, he whispers out to me.

"What's your name? Why are you helping me? Just go back to your desk."

I then respond to Mr. Pankowski very quietly.

"My name is Aaron Chen sir. I'm helping you because I was raised to help out other people if they are in need. I know you're just my teacher, but you're still a human."

Mr. Pankowski then smiles at me. This was the first time I felt a good presence from him. I knew from this point on, my social interactions with Mr. Pankowski would change. Just with that simple smile, it let me know that I'm on good terms with him. Anything that happened before, and all the times he humiliated me in front of the class are gone. That was in the past, and we are officially starting over. I end up staring at him for several more seconds. I then once again attempt to get him off the chair unsuccessfully. Mr. Pankowski then whispers out to me again.

"Aaron, just go back to your seat. When the bell rings, just leave with the rest of the class. I'll be fine. Please go back to your seat."

I disobeyed the teacher, and did not go back to my seat. I didn't want to see Mr. Pankowski unable to move and being stuck on the chair. The rest of the class didn't care about him, but I did. I didn't want to have him stuck to the chair. I knew that he felt very embarrassed over this, but I still wanted to help him regardless of that. I looked him straight in the eyes, and quietly responded to him.

"No. I'm going to get some help. I'll be right back."

Mr. Pankowski looked down on the ground and shook his head. Congruently during this time, the bell for school to be dismissed rang. Virtually the entire class ran out of the room, and proceeded home. I instead went to the school nurses office. I ran to Ms. Pauline Watson, the school nurses office. She was an older African-American woman. The school nurse was nice, but she was very direct. As soon as I made it to the nurses office, I scream out for her help.

"Ms. Watson, Mr. Pankowski is stuck to his chair. The other students in the class played an evil prank on him, and he's really stuck. I can't get him off the chair."

The school nurse alerts the school principal, and the both of us run back to Mr. Pankowski's classroom. When we arrive, Mr. Pankowski is shocked that I had brought the school nurse with me. As soon as we walk into the classroom, Mr. Pankowski yells at the both of us.

"No, I don't need your help. I'll be fine. Go away please, leave me alone."

The school nurse then responds to him in a direct way.

"Okay, so you want to be stuck there all night? Because that's what is going to happen. Now you need to stop being modest, and allow us to help you."

The school nurse then asked me to go to her office to grab a few supplies. I end up doing just that, and I return back to the classroom. The school principal at this time. Mr. Greg Brickstone, also was present in the classroom. The school nurse asked me to grab some special gel that would evaporate the glue that was stuck on the chair, and she also asked me to bring her a pot of boiling hot water. After about ten minutes, the glue that was on the chair was able to become loose enough for Mr. Pankowksi to lift his arms up. When he did so, he let out a scream, and his arms were badly bruised and sore once he lifted them up off the chair. As for the rest of his body being stuck to the chair, we pretty much did the same routine. Luckily, only his pants were stuck by the glue However due to how strong the glue was, it was difficult to separate his pants away from the chair. Thankfully, Mr. Pankowski was finally free, however, he would have to pay the price by having a big rip on the back of his pants. Because we wanted to value his respect and dignity, this was when we all left the classroom. The school principal Mr. Brickstone ended up giving Mr. Pankowski a pair of his gym sweatpants so he can wear, as his pants were now ripped.

I was very pleased that Mr. Pankowksi was free from the chair, and I was happy to have helped him. Even though the rest of the class didn't care and left him there, I wanted to make sure he received help, and he did. As far as the crush if you want to call it that, that was gone. I mean a small part of me did find him charming, but I have to let that go. I'm investing too much time on this man, and I need to focus on other things. I did a good thing by getting him off the chair, and I have to go onto something else now. He's simply my teacher, and I can't put all my eggs in one basket.

But on the other hand, I felt that I wasn't completely being honest between myself and Mr. Pankowski. Something was missing, and there were many puzzle pieces that had to be put together. I didn't know where the pieces were, but I knew that they were missing from the puzzle. I wouldn't feel right unless I resolved this, and I wasn't done with Mr. Pankowski just quite yet. Once I left the classroom, I started walking outside the school, and stood at the bus stop, on my way home. As I was waiting for the bus, several minutes later I notice a car pull up to the curb. After looking through the windshield, I notice that it's Mr. Pankowski driving the car. He rolls his window down, and begins to speak to me.

"Hey Aaron, I'll give you a ride home. I won't take no for an answer. Get in."

I couldn't move, and I just stood there. The feelings I had of Mr. Pankowski then came back, and I couldn't believe it. I didn't want to feel this way. He's simply my teacher. Just tell him "no" Aaron. You're going to catch the bus home, and you'll see him tomorrow. Students don't develop crushes on their teachers, and they sure as hell don't accept a ride home from them. So I made my mind up, I was going to tell him that's okay, and leave it be.

"Oh, no thank you Mr. Pankowski. I'm just going to take the bus."

I said the wrong thing. I meant to say my parents are picking me up. If I used that fib instead, then maybe he would have drove away. Being that I said I'm waiting for the bus, he's going to continue to find a way for me to get a ride from him. What have I done. I've painted myself into a corner, and I have to accept whatever is going to happen next. I could sense that Mr. Pankowski wasn't going to leave without me getting into the car. So he continued.

"Well if you let me give you a ride, you'll get home earlier. I'm not going to let one of my students who helped me wait for the bus. I'll give you a ride home. Get in."

Mr. Pankowski opens up the passenger side door, and I'm left without any choice. I reluctantly get into his car and sit down. Everything that I was taught in the past from my parents on not accepting rides from strangers, didn't matter. I don't even know this teacher that well. It has only been two days, and I accepted a ride from him. As I get into his car, I just pay attention forward. I don't dare look at Mr. Pankowski. I'm simply too anxious and nervous. Students do not accept rides from teachers, so it's kinda awkward. Not to mention I was still crushing on him mind you. Mr. Pankowski drives away from the school and asks me a question.

"So what part of town do you live in Aaron? You don't have to tell me your address. I'll just drop you off at the corner of your house. I understand if you don't feel comfortable."

I continue to stare out of the car window, and I feel I have nothing to be scared or worried about. He is just a teacher, and it's not like he's a monster or something.

"No it's okay. I'll give you my actual address. I don't live that far from here. I'm about another ten minutes or so away. I'll tell you where to turn and stuff. It's okay."

Mr. Pankowski then heads straight to my house. I end up remaining silent to him, and I don't say a word. What is there to say? I mean, he is a teacher, and I didn't feel comfortable talking about anything personal with him. I just wasn't going to do that. He eventually makes it to my house, and he pulls up to my driveway. Before I get out of the car, I start to gather all of my things. Mr. Pankowski then whispers out to me as I'm leaving out the car.

"Hey Aaron. If it's alright with you, I want to pick you up early tomorrow morning. There are some papers I want you to copy and scan for all my classes. I'm not going to give you extra credit or anything as that's not fair to the other students, but I could really use the help."

I didn't know what to say. I felt painted into a corner yet again. If I say no, he's probably going to get angry at me, and be mad at me. Even though he is giving me the option to say no, if I do end up refusing, he's going to be angry. I don't really want to get too attached to him. Going to class early, and doing special tasks for him seems out of my comfort zone.

I don't know why he wants me to do all of that, and I don't want to become his servant. I just want a teacher and student relationship with him, and I want to keep it strictly to that. By arriving at class early, I don't want to get the wrong idea or agenda put out. But if I say yes, I'm doing him a favor, and I will have the feeling that I'm helping a teacher out.

I did like Mr. Pankowski. I didn't like him at first, but I now I enjoy him as a teacher. But that's the thing, I like him only as a teacher. Not as a friend, or anything beyond or above that. I still feel that by me going to school early and helping him out with tasks, is not something I'm comfortable with. I could tell this was going to be a hard decision to make, and I was making sure the pros and cons of everything was well understood. I then finally made my mind up as to what I wanted to. I outlined all of my choices, and I feel the choice I'm making, is the most sensible one.

"Yeah, that's fine. It's no problem, I'll help you out with that tomorrow."

Mr. Pankowski smiles at me, and I smile back at him. He then backs out of my driveway, and carries on. I continue to look out in the road as his car leaves out of my neighborhood. I walk inside my house, and nobody is home as usual. Being home alone, I just go straight to my room, and lay down on my bed. This has been a grueling day, and I took this time to rest my thoughts. This whole ordeal with Mr. Pankowski was really throwing me for a loop.

It wasn't over yet, as I now have to wake up even early tomorrow morning, and pretty much play teacher's pet. The next morning, I get dressed, and wait outside my house for Mr. Pankowski to pick me up. In the back of my mind, I'm just hoping that none of the other students catch any ideas. I know that I'm going to be going to school earlier than everyone else, but people at the school still gossip. It was something that I didn't fathom about really before, but now I am. Mr. Pankowski finally reaches my house, and I end up getting in his car. I don't end up saying a single word to him, and I stay silent. As we get closer to the school, Mr. Pankowski then starts to speak to me.

"Are you hungry? I'm starving, and I was going to go McDonalds to get something to eat and some coffee. It's my treat."

Okay, now things are really getting slightly creepy. First I'm accepting rides from a teacher, and now I'm accepting a teacher offer me breakfast. I don't know what the hell is going on, and it's like I'm in some weird alternate timeline. Maybe I was thinking too much ahead of it. It's just a teacher offering to buy me some breakfast. There is nothing complicated about that at all. I respond by either saying yes or no. It's not a big deal, and I'm making it seem like it's more detailed than that. After coming to this realization, I then respond back to Mr. Pankowksi, letting him know that I appreciate the kindness he's exhibiting.

"Yeah, I don't mind. Thank you for offering."

We both make it to the McDonalds drive thru, and we order our food. We immediately then head straight for the school. Once reaching school, Mr. Pankowski and I both go to his classroom, and we eat our breakfast. Following that, I end up completing the tasks he wanted me to do. I copy and scan and print several papers out. I manage to do this quick enough, so I can make it to my first period. Once finished, I go on about the rest of my day as planned, knowing that my last period will be with Mr. Pankowski. I was wondering how he was going to address the class after the prank we pulled on him. Final period approached, and I sat in Mr. Pankowksi's class, in the front row like I customarily do. Several more of the students then began to rush into the classroom. Eventually, Mr. Pankowski arrived to this class, and he has a wide smile on his face. Despite the fact we played a nasty prank on him the day before, he doesn't seem that angry. Myself and the rest of the class seem shocked at his behavior, and we don't know what to expect from him. Mr. Pankowski then starts to write problems down on the board. The second he finishes writing on the board, he then turns to the entire class, and smiles at all of us. He then responds.

"I want to apologize to all of you. I'm sorry if I came across as a mean teacher. I don't care who pulled the prank. I mean I would like for whoever did it to fess up, but it's okay. Today is a new day, and I want to start fresh. Things are going to be different, and I'm here for you."

The entire class then began to empathize with Mr. Pankowski, and the guy who pulled the stunt, came clean about it. Mr. Pankowski decided to only give the guy detention for one afternoon, which was a rather light punishment. Mr. Pankowski then went on with his lesson, and he was a changed man. He became an entirely new teacher, and the rest of the class was appreciative of that. The class was soon over, and we all left class feeling good. This was the first time we all were happy to have Mr. Pankowski as a teacher. As I was gathering my things to leave, Mr. Pankowski approached me.

"Aaron, you don't have to help me before school tomorrow. It's fine. I just was swamped today because I was stuck to a damn chair yesterday, and couldn't do those tasks. You're a nice person, and I'm happy to have you as a student. I'm sorry for the way I treated you before."

Mr. Pankowski stuck his and out for me to shake, and I shake his hand. I then softly respond to him, continuing to gather my things.

"Thank you Mr. Pankowski. I raised my hand to tell you about the prank, but you shouted at me anyways. All is forgiven. I have to get home now sir, I have chores and homework to do."

As I start to walk outside the classroom, Mr. Pankowski whispers out to me.

"Aaron, you can call me Steven once school is over."

Mr. Pankowksi then winks at me, and he starts to grab his briefcase off the desk. I however in my mind was not ready to prepare myself to call him Steven. Although that's his name when he's not teaching, I'm still on school grounds, and so at this time I stick to calling him Mr. Pankowski. I proceed outside to the hallway, walking away from the classroom. Mr. Pankowski catches up to me, and once again whispers to me.

"Do you want me to give you a ride home? You said you had chores and homework to do. If I give you a ride, you'd get home earlier and…"

I decide to let Mr. Pankowski give me a ride home, but this will be the last time I will let him do this, I can't allow him to keep on doing this.

"You can give me a ride home. But after this, no more. I'm a student, and you're the teacher. Please understand. I appreciate your kindness Mr. Pankowski, but understand."

Mr. Pankowski nods his head, and I end up getting into his car again. He drops me off at home, and I go on about my business. I continue to think about him deeply, and it becomes a harder infatuation to deal with. As I continued on with my school year, Mr. Pankowski simply became a teacher to me.

The previous close bond we had meant nothing. I didn't accept rides from him, I didn't stay after class. I was just a normal student. He wouldn't treat me any different than the rest of the students. My grades were good because I excelled at academics. So all of my passing grades were because I studied and payed attention.

My eighteenth birthday came. I was now a legal adult, and was stepping into adulthood. Only one issue was still at play. My crush on Mr. Pankowski came back. As I was becoming more interested in my nursing career, I ended up volunteering at several local hospitals, and I was doing well in school. But why was I so upset? It was now May, and I was close to final exams, and graduation. I was still extremely upset.

I was upset, because my affection for Mr. Pankowski was getting out of control. I was in love with him, and I wanted to have him. I couldn't be with him, because he's a teacher. He will most likely get fired and in trouble by the school, but I didn't care. As long as I was a legal adult, he shouldn't get into any trouble. One day during lunch break, I just had enough. I didn't give a fuck anymore. Whatever happened from here, is whatever happened.

I took my lunch to Mr. Pankowski's class, and he was sitting at his desk, eating his lunch. I feel this was it, I have to let him know how I feel. I've been well behaved my entire life, and this is the time for me to be honest with myself. I sit down in the front row of the class, right in front of his desk. As he's noticing me sit, he speaks to me.

"Oh hey Aaron. I don't care if you eat lunch with me. You seem upset. What's wrong?"

I just couldn't do it. I couldn't tell him the truth at this time. I simply shake my head, and continue to eat my lunch. I love this man so much, and I want him. Part of me knows that Mr. Pankowski likes me as well. All the thoughts of the interactions we had on the first day. I had a crush on my teacher, and wasn't ashamed of it. I didn't give a fuck what anyone else thought. Once lunch was over, the rest of the class started to come into the classroom. I chickened out during lunch hour, so I have to tell him after class.

It seemed it took the final bell forever to ring. When class was dismissed, the rest of the students exited out of the classroom. Mr. Pankowski then began to grab his things, preparing to leave. I end up walking to the classroom doors, making sure they were shut. This was the time, I had to let him know. Mr. Pankowski then spoke to me.

"Aaron, is everything okay? Is there something you wanted to talk about?"

In my head, I felt that I could do this the easy way, or the hard way. I decided to go with the hard way, and not beat around the fucking bush. I walk up to Mr. Pankowski's desk, and quickly lean in to kiss him on the lips. He immediately reacts to this strangely, and quickly grabs his briefcase, and starts to head to the classroom door. He then stops before opening the door, and turns to look at me, speaking to me softly.

"Do you want a ride home Aaron?"

I smile at him and nod my head. He feels the same way, and I feel so blessed. This concludes this part of my story, as it gets more strange from here. But it is my story. So stick with me please.

CHAPTER 9:

MAN OF PINK (PART 2)

As I continue the story, it becomes more of an issue. The bond that I have with Mr. Pankowski, or Steven. I still seem to call him Mr. Pankowski, when I'm trying to recollect this story. I know his name is Steven, but a part of me still gets a thrill from calling him Mr. Pankowski. I sometimes in my head think of him as Steven. At other times I think of him as Mr. Pankowski. It depends on how I'm feeling. He doesn't seem to mind, so it's fine. Oh well, if that's an issue with you, then sue me I guess. Ha-Ha. Anyways, after I kissed him, which I must say the kiss was rather magical, things started to mushroom even further. I was still trying to understand that I kissed my teacher. I did something really taboo, and I can't take what I did back. I don't even really feel any shame for what I did. The feelings that I had for him were real, and I couldn't help myself any longer. After I kissed him, he seemed to not feel bothered by the kiss. It's assumed that we are going to have to keep the kiss a secret. If the school found out that I was having a relationship with him, he would be fired. Due to the fact I was eighteen when I kissed him and I am a legal adult, legally what we did wasn't wrong. I kissed him, and I would be just as guilty about the whole ordeal. I don't think it's fair to blame Mr. Pankowski himself.

You could argue that he would take advantage of me due to my age, but I disagree. He was in his late 20s, and I was eighteen, so I don't see it like that. He is not that type of person, I know him. I mean, he was my god damn teacher. I pretty sure I can sense as to whether or not he's trying to use me, or take advantage of my youth. This is not the case at all. Some of the guilt I was feeling, was trying to keep our relationship a secret from the rest of the school. That was slightly difficult, as High School is the number one place for people to gossip. However, I don't think anyone was suspecting anything, so I'm sure I would be okay.

This kiss would really be the least of my worries. The last few weeks of my senior year of High School, would continue to showcase many wild events. After our kiss after class, Mr. Pankowski drove me home, and I stayed silent during the entire ride. I still was smiling to myself in the side that I kissed my teacher. It wasn't a dream, and it actually happened. Being that I was brave enough to actually do it. Ordinarily, I would have just kept my feelings to myself, and not worried about it. Common sense would have told me that he's my teacher, and showing any affection to him is off limits. There are just certain things that you don't do in life, and that's one of them.

I get out of his car, not paying any attention to him as I'm walking to my front door. Although he took the kiss rather well, he has to process this event as well. I know the next time I see him at school, it's going to be weird. I'm going sit in the front row of his class during last period, like I always do. Only this time, I have a deep dark secret that the rest of the class, and the entire school doesn't know about. I'm in love with my teacher, and I kissed him.

A part of me was nervous about returning to school, and how I was going to deal with this. Another part of me simply didn't care. All I had to do was keep my mouth shut about it, and nothing would happen. I kissed him, and it's all over now. By continuing to pick through the whole situation, I'm not going to make it an easier to deal with. I have to understand I did what I did, and I have to accept all the consequences from that now. My plan was simple, I'm going to continue to be the same Aaron I was before I kissed him. I'm not going to get my hopes up or down. If my relationship with Mr. Pankowski continues, then I'll be happy. If it doesn't, then I have to accept that. Either way, I still had one more month of school left, and I had to worry about that first and foremost. That's exactly what I did. For the following days, it's not like Mr. Pankowski was being angry towards me, but we would keep the kiss a secret. Never did he once give me a grade I didn't deserve, or any extra credit. Let's get that shit straight right from the get go. The way he treated me, was the same he treated the rest of the students. So I know people are going to assume that because I kissed him, he now all of a sudden was going to start giving me special treatment.

Hell no, and it wasn't like that. I just continued on like regularly with my classes, and didn't care about the infatuation or lust I had for my teacher. Prom and graduation was coming up as well. Mr. Pankowski was going to be one of the chaperones at the school prom, so that was interesting.

I remember distinctively one class I had with Mr. Pankowski. The prom was happening later that day incidentally. We all came into the class, and Mr. Pankowksi was sitting at his desk with his head looking down to the ground. He had a very somber look on his face. I knew that something was up, and that he was going to tell the class some devastating news. As soon as class started, Mr. Pankowski got all of our attention, and the class was extremely quiet. He then informed us on some sad news.

"Class, this is really hard for me to say. But this will be my last year teaching at this school. It was a tough decision, but I'm going to go be a university professor. It's not that I don't like teaching you all, it's just time for me to move on. I want to thank you for the time we had."

My heart literally sank into several levels into my chest. I didn't want to believe what he said was true. Mr. Pankowski was going to retire from being a school teacher. My last year of High School, was going to be his last year as a High School Teacher. He received a job offer to be a professor in California. I guess it was a decision that was difficult to make, but was wise to make. Despite that we treated him very poorly in the past, we were all sad to see Mr. Pankowski move on to be a college professor. He has been teaching at this school for the past few years, and he wants to move onto something else in his life. I also started to feel scared, as if he was going to go away to teach in California, I didn't know if my contact with him would exist anymore. It was a honor knowing that we were going to be his last class, and that held something special I suppose. The prom was going to happen later that night, and I was excited over that. Still depressed over the news that Mr. Pankowski was moving away from the school after this semester, I adapted my mood to be more optimistic towards the school prom.

After class, I went home and changed into a very nice outfit. I want to look nice for prom, so I picked out something formal of course. I knew that Mr. Pankowski was going to be there, but I still had to keep the kiss we had a secret. Even though he is going to be retiring as a High School teacher after the school year, he is still employed at the school, and I have to not let this information get out. The results could be bad if people found out. I lied to my parents that I had a ride to the prom, when the truth was that I didn't. My parents were working, and my sister was at her own prom. So we are all doing our own thing. Which reminds me, I was also keeping the kiss I had with Mr. Pankowski a secret from my family. I didn't dare bring this up to them, as that I knew I would possibly be disowned and removed from my family.

They didn't even know that I was gay, and would most definitely take that news harshly. So you can imagine if I told them that I had feelings for my teacher, and I ended up kissing him. I didn't want to think of how they would react. I just knew that it wouldn't be good. So I was keeping so many secrets, and not that I was proud of keeping the secrets, it made more sense if the secrets didn't get out. I didn't see the sense of being honest about all the forbidden things I have been doing lately. People pictured me as perfect Aaron, and the Aaron that wouldn't do activities like that. My secrets are my own, and they aren't anyone else's business to get involved in. It was safer that way to be dishonest about all the bad things I've done. I was scared of the judgment, and I had good reason to be. It's my life, and the choices that I make are mine, and only mine to deal with.

I didn't have a prom date, but I didn't care. You don't need to have a prom date to attend prom, but I guess it would be nice to have one. I was simply going to go for the food and for the experience. The number of friends I had at the school was zero, so I knew I would be a wall flower at the prom, standing by myself. But again, that's fine. I been by myself for most of my school life, and I don't mind being an introvert. As I'm riding the bus on the way to the school prom, I feel too anxious to think. So many emotions are inside of me, and this isn't going to be like any ordinary prom. This prom is going to consist of me attending a prom that a teacher I'm infatuated with is also attending. The bus stops outside of the school, and I make my way to the gymnasium. There are several students at the prom, and they are all dressed very fancy.

Senior prom is a big deal for them, so I can understand why they take it seriously. I didn't see the thrill in it. I didn't have a date, or another student at the school that I was interested in. The person I was interested in was a teacher standing by the snack and beverage table. I look around the gymnasium and notice Mr. Pankowksi wearing a rather nice suit and tie, passing out food and drinks to the other students.

I end up walking over to him, to get myself something to drink. Every step I was taking to him felt heavy, and I was using a lot of my strength to walk over to him. I finally make it to the table, and we both make eye contact for several seconds. Even though this was only a few seconds in reality, it felt that it was much longer. As if I was staring at him for five minutes. Mr. Pankowski then smiles and laughs at me, and proceeds to hand me a drink of fruit punch.

"Hey Aaron. You having a good time? Here you are, enjoy."

I end up taking the cup of fruit punch, and simply smile back at Mr. Pankowski. I don't respond to him, or make any other gestures other than a smile. There are other students in line at the snack table, so I end up walking away from him. As I take my drink, I end up sitting at the bleachers. Loud electronic music is playing, and all of the school seniors are having fun and dancing with their friends, or if they had a significant other at the school, they were dancing with them as well. I started to feel very depressed, that I was alone and had nobody to dance with. You would think that being in this environment it would be a fun event. Everyone is partying and enjoying themselves. Celebrating the end of their high school year. It was not the case with me. I was sitting by myself on the side, just watching everyone else have fun. The truth was, I wanted to dance with Mr. Pankowski, and I couldn't. He's a teacher, and I'm not supposed to be having those types of interactions at all with a teacher. It's just not socially allowed. After ten minutes of me sitting on the side of the gymnasium watching all the events happen, I had to remove myself from the scene. I decided to run inside of the locker room, and figured I would hide in there until prom was over. I immediately go to the back of the locker room, crying heavily.

This was not supposed to happen at all. This was supposed to be prom; a very happy and pleasant time for me. It was turning into complete misery. I was not happy, and I was not having a great time at all. I knew coming to prom was a bad idea, and I should have just listened to my conscious that was telling me not to go.

This was a complete was of time, and I no longer want to deal with the pain of being here. I remain in the locker room for several minutes crying to myself. The locker room mind you is completely dark and cold. There are lights in the locker room, but the setting is rather dim. This was a perfect place for you to hide, and to let out all of your feelings. All of a sudden, I could hear someone walking into the area I was in. I keep my vision facing down, and I don't know who is walking. Just then, I feel an arm start to rub my back. This can't be who I think it is, but it must be. I then hear a voice whisper to me.

"Aaron, what are you doing in here? Why aren't you outside having fun?"

I know that's Mr. Pankowski's voice. I don't know how to react. I don't want to go back out. I'm not comfortable, it's not my thing. Everyone else is enjoying themselves, and I'm just going to not only ruin their mood, but mine as well. I had to tell Mr. Pankowski the truth. I was hiding in here, because I didn't want to be with anyone else.

"I just don't want to, that's why. I'm just really upset right now."

Mr. Pankowski then starts to wipe the tears from my face. It doesn't make any sense to not be myself with him. I already kissed him before, so it's not like I am trying to stay safe with him. It's too late for that, and he already knows what I'm capable of. I continue to cry, and then I cannot take keeping up with the bullshit act, and I be completely honest with him.

"I want to be here with you. I don't want to go outside with everyone else. I only want to be with you. I can't have you, and that's why I'm upset."

Mr. Pankowski then starts to lean closer to me, and hugs me very closely. I knew that he understood all the pain that I was going through, and wanted to be there for me in this particular time. I didn't ask to feel this way about him, and he knew that I was struggling with this. We continued our embrace for several minutes. It was just the two of us, and we were in our own trance and own private world. Mr. Pankowski then whispered back to me.

"We can stay here as long as you want Aaron, it's fine. I'm here."

This is exactly what I wanted, to experience this moment. I didn't want anything else in the world, but to be cuddling with him. Knowing that there are hundreds of students in the gymnasium dancing and having a good time. Unaware that me and Mr. Pankowski are here by ourselves being very affectionate. If I could just be here for the rest of my life, I would appreciate that so much. I don't want to do anything, or go anywhere else. The music from the gymnasium is blaring loud, and you can still hear in the locker room. I get totally caught up where I am currently, and I lean in closer to Mr. Pankowski's face to give him a kiss. We kiss for several minutes, and I couldn't be any happier. Prom was turning out to be perfect, and I loved it. Mr. Pankowski then pulls my wrist, and whispers to me again.

"I have to go back outside Aaron. I don't want you staying in this cold locker room though. We can talk later, just go back to the dance and just have fun please."

I nod my head at him, and we both end up leaving out of the locker room, back to the gymnasium where the prom is. I decide to simply pretend to have a good time, even though I honestly wasn't seeing the excitement of prom. I would dance by myself to the music, and I would glance over at Mr. Pankowski at the snack table.

Eventually, prom started to end. Many of the students began to go home, and the gymnasium was starting to become more and more empty. Mr. Pankowski and some of the other staff at the school stayed in the gymnasium cleaning everything up. During this time, I decide to help Mr. Pankowksi help tidy everything up. I start by picking up trash the other students left on the floor, putting everything in a trash bag. Mr. Pankowksi notices me help clean, and starts to speak to me.

"You don't have to do that Aaron, that's fine. We'll take care of it."

I kind took this a secret code for him telling me to go home. It's not like he could display affection to me in front of the other teachers. Of course not; that would blow the cover that we had. But I didn't want to leave, and I didn't want to go home. I wanted to stay where I was. But I did decide to just go home. Going home, although prom wasn't exactly the way I intended it to happen, I still managed to have a great time regardless. I got to kiss Mr. Pankowski for the second time so I can't really be upset or mad over that. Prom was over, and it's time to move onto other things. Final exams are the main focus now. I was doing much studying during this time, and Mr. Pankowski was preparing us so we could pass our exams without any issues. Finals week was very difficult for all of us.

Although finals were stressful, I managed to deal with them very easily. I passed them all without any issues, and I was going to graduate. My college plans were still not set, and I knew I wanted to study nursing. I have been applying to many schools, and none of the schools in the Seattle area have accepted me. Although, I have received many offers from schools that are located out of state. I am considering going to school away from home, even though that wasn't exactly my first choice at all.

It took me quite some time, but I learned to accept that Mr. Pankowski wants to move on with his life. The fling I had with him, was spur of the moment. I don't want to distract him from his teaching career, and I know that with the both of us associating with each other, it could lead to him facing repercussions over his career. Mr. Pankowski will always be a special person to me. Whether I end up dealing with him in the future or not. I have learned a lot from him. Not only as a teacher, but as a person I began to look up to greatly. Even if it was a forbidden affair. I didn't care, and I can't take back time. The experiences we went through I don't regret, but I would take what I encountered with me for the future.

However, I was still feeling overwhelmed that I didn't gain any closure with Mr. Pankowski. I wanted to have an official goodbye with him. I didn't even have his phone number, and I would still like to have some sort of contact with hm, even though he's moving away to teach in another state. I didn't have much time to do this, as graduation is only days away. Because time was very limited, I knew I had to act as fast as I could. Still keeping the relationship we had a secret from the school, I wanted to find thc time to say goodbye, and so that we could set things straight. At the time, it seemed clear that Mr. Pankowksi wanted to move on from me and focus on other aspects of his life, and I had to understand this. Not everything is about me, and people have their own plans in their life that they want to take care of. I just was struggling to find the right time.

It was a Friday, and actually a fateful Friday. It was a week before graduation. Finals were over, but we still had regularly scheduled class. I went on about my day like it was normal. However, this day would be different. Very different, in fact so different, it changes everything. This particular day would alter everything between myself and Mr. Pankowski. This would be the day that would sadly cause his entire life to make a drastic turn. On this particular day, a school shooting would happen. I have to be direct, as there is no other way to describe it. We weren't expecting it, and it was just an normal day, but it happened. The number one worst thing that could happen to a school, happened.

Everything seemed normal throughout the whole day, however one student had brought a gun to school, and his agenda was to cause havoc between us all. We weren't expecting it, because it was the end of the school year, and graduation was near. Being concerned or on alert about a school shooting, didn't even cross our minds at all. The fact was clear though, was that a shooting at the school was soon going to happen. The shooting that would make my life different, Mr. Pankowski's life different, and everyone who was present at the school that day, their lives would be forever different.

I walked into Mr. Pankowski's class like I normally do. He was sitting at his desk, minding his own business. A couple other students were in the class, but none of us were aware that disaster was soon going approaching. Why should we have been? It was just a normal ordinary day like it was usually at the school. As we continue on about our day as normal, I did have a small feeling that something wasn't right. It was just one of those feelings you have when you know that something bad is going to happen soon. The feeling wasn't strong enough for me to do anything about it though, so it just went ignored.

The bell for class rang, and Mr. Pankowski went on about his teaching. Within about five minutes of class, we just hear many gunshots. The gunshots were so loud and close, we knew that they were coming from the same building we were currently in. All of us immediately go into panic, and are unsure as to what to do. Several more gunshots begin to fire, and we all continue to panic in shock. Not even ten seconds later, the gunman himself entered into Mr. Pankowski's classroom. Myself and the rest of the students end up hiding under our desks on the floor.

Mr. Pankowski however is standing at his desk right by the classroom door. He is shot several times in the back, and falls to the ground by his desk. The gunman assumes he has killed him, and then runs into a another classroom and fires more shots. The rest of us, remain on the floor for several minutes. Once we all believe the gunman isn't near us, we all get up from the floor. I walk over to Mr. Pankowski's desk, and notices that he was shot, and is bleeding profusely.

I didn't know how to react at first, but I knew that Mr. Pankowski was hurt. I didn't know if he was alive or dead, but he did need help. Some of the students in class start to call 911 on their phones, and the police have already been alerted about the shooting. I then start to worry about the condition that Mr. Pankowski is in. I was not sure if he is going to survive being shot, and I couldn't take seeing him like that at all. His eyes were closed, and he was not responding at all. He was barely breathing, and I knew he was very close to death. I couldn't imagine Mr. Pankowski being killed in this school shooting, but that was how things were looking then. At this point, I have to wait until paramedics arrive to come help him. I was able to take a little from what I researched about nursing, in order to help him. I ended up taking Mr. Pankowski's suit jacket, and pressing it around the bullet wounds. I studied this exact technique before, and I was sure it was going to work until help was able to arrive.

He was losing a lot of blood, and I was doing the best I could to help him at this time. Everything was happening too fast, and the shooting made the whole school go under immense pressure. Minutes pass, and we are still stuck inside of the classroom. The paramedics haven't arrived quite yet. I just hope that we are all rescued from all of this soon, and we will no longer be in fear. We are pleased when we hear members of the police SWAT team rushing through the hallways in the building we are currently in. We are all instructed to leave out of the classroom, but I remain down by Mr. Pankowski's desk, tending to his wounds. As I remain in the classroom, of the police officers shouts out to me.

"We need you to leave out the room now! It's not safe!"

I do not want to leave him in the classroom by himself, but I didn't have a choice as I was instructed by them to exit out of the classroom. I explain back to the swat officers, that my teacher is hurt.

"He's been shot very bad, and he needs to go to the hospital. Please help him."

After I tell the officers the condition he's in, I'm forced to walk out of the classroom. I then feel scared as to if that is the last time I'm ever going to see him. I knew the impact of how badly he was shot, but I didn't know what his chances of survival where. The rest of the students and I, stand outside of the school. We remain standing for several minutes. Not aware of what is going to happen next. The entire school in suspense and fear of the shooting. I continue to worry about Mr. Pankowski, and his health. Eventually, I notice that paramedics are carrying several people in stretchers outside of the school. Some are of students, and some are of teachers and other school staff. I saw at least fifteen or so people shot. I then see Mr. Pankowski's body being carried out through the main front hallway in the school. I didn't even think twice but to run up to him. I knew I wasn't supposed to go up and see him, but I did anyways. As I'm doing this, I notice that many of the paramedics are trying to restrain me from going near him. I was simply defiant and had no intentions of obeying their orders. When I rush past all the paramedics, I then see Mr. Pankowski's body laying down on the stretcher, being wheeled away. My emotions are extremely out of control, and I just freeze where I am standing. I am them immediately halted by several police officers who then let me know that I'm not allowed to proceed.

"Young man, we can't let you in here. There is an active shooter in the building"

In this same time, I hear a voice start to speak. It's Mr. Pankowski.

"It's fine, it's okay. I don't mind him being here. It's alright."

The officers at that point back away from me, and I walk alongside the paramedics, as they are carrying Mr. Pankowksi's body away. This is a very chaotic scene, and a normal day, has turned into the worst disaster. I am happy that Mr. Pankowksi is still alive, despite the amount of times he was hit by the shooter. I know that there were other people in the shooting that may have not been so fortunate, and were probably killed in shooting. In any case, this whole event is very saddening for everyone involved. I continue to walk along Mr. Pankowski, as the paramedics are now directing him to an ambulance. As he's being lifted into the ambulance, several paramedics, huddle over him, and scream and shout to me.

"We can't let you be in this area, you have to leave now."

Mr. Pankowksi then once again reassures all the paramedics that it's fine for me to be with him, and although he's very weak and hurt, he cries out to them.

"He can stay with me, let him please."

The paramedics then reluctantly back away from me. Mr. Pankowski is lifted into the ambulance, and then within seconds, I follow him inside of it. The paramedics then quickly rush him to the hospital, as I'm sitting in the ambulance right by his side. This whole time, I just want this terrible nightmare to end, and I am in complete disbelief that this happened. It's so difficult for me to explain everything again, and it happened in such a complete rush. One second, all of us were in class like it was any other normal day. The next second, a shooter enters the school, and everyone is in terror over that. The ambulance reaches the hospital, and Mr. Pankowksi is taken out of the ambulance and brought inside the hospital.

At this point, I end up waiting in the emergency room, as I see other people that were shot in the shooting being brought into the hospital. I take a seat, and shake my head. I am so confused as what is happening, and I do not like it. At this point, I can only sit and wait in the emergency room. In the meantime, I notice that the television set that is in the hospital emergency room is broadcasting a special report. I listen in, as the female news anchor starts to report the story.

"We have breaking news. There was a mass shooting at a High School this afternoon. There are five deaths being reported, and over thirty people injured. The shooter was later accosted and killed by police. The shooter was identified as eighteen year old student that attended the school. We will keep you updated with further details, with this special report."

I sit and pay attention to the news broadcast of the shooting, and I just cannot believe what I am hearing at all. Five people were killed in the shooting, and that was extremely devastating to hear. School is supposed to be a safe place, and it's horrible that something such as this had to happen today. I was trying my best to ignore all the news coverage of the shooting, as it was only making me feel more anxious about everything. I don't want to give his name, but I did not know the school shooter personally. I don't know what would come over him to do such a horrible thing, but I didn't want to put all my attention on the shooter. My main focus was on praying for the families of all the students that were killed in the shooting. I was also hoping that all the victims that were injured the shooting recover well. As I'm waiting in the emergency room, I take this time to call my parents to let them now that I'm safe. I speak to my mother first, and then a little while later, I'm able to speak to my father. They are happy that I was not hurt during the shooting, and tell me they are on their way to the hospital to see me, and will get there as fast as they can. I have been waiting for now four hours, and I have not heard any news related to the shooting.

The longer I wait, the more nervous that I become about everything. The fact I haven't heard any information on how Mr. Pankowski is doing upsets me greatly. Finally after six hours of not hearing anything, I see that several doctors are coming into the emergency room, and are talking to the relatives of all the victims that were injured in the shooting. I'm not eavesdropping into what they are talking about, as that isn't any of my business. I then at this time go up to the nurses station, and ask them a question.

"Yes, I was wondering if you could give me any information on Steven Pankowski. He was one of the people that was injured in the shooting earlier."

The nurse then goes on the computer for a short while. After that, I remember the look the nurse gave me after she gazed on the computer, was very disappointing. I didn't know why she returned an expression such as that, but I knew that this couldn't be good. She then got up from her seat, and started to converse with the other nurses at the station. The nurse then returned back to her desk a minute later, and then asked me a question.

"May I ask how are you related to the patient please?"

I then stop for a second, and realize that if I'm simply say that I'm a student, I would not get any information about him. I had to be more direct than that. I then very quickly responded to her.

"Well, I'm his boyfriend. Can you please tell me how he is doing?"

The nurse then gives me a skeptical look, and once again walks away from her desk. She then starts to gossip with the other nurses at the station once again. When she returns back to me at her desk, she then very angrily gives me a response.

"You're going to have to speak with the doctor. The doctor will tell you everything that you need to know. So just wait over there, and wait for the doctor to speak with you."

I end up thanking the nurse, and I return to sitting down in the emergency room. So here I am once again playing the waiting game. All I wanted to do was get some information on him, and the staff at the hospital are refusing to give it to me. So I wait for about nearly an hour more, and a doctor finally walks up and speaks to me.

"Yes, I was informed that you are a companion to one of the patients. If you could please step aside and speak to me, there are some things I wanted to discuss with you."

I follow the doctor away to another area. We end up walking out of the emergency waiting room, and he directs me into the hallway of the recovery rooms. The doctor then very quietly leans close to me, and starts to give me devastating news.

"He is in stable condition. However, due to the impact of the way he was shot, he is unfortunately paralyzed from the waist down. He has no feelings in his legs. The damage is permanent, and I'm really sorry to give you this news."

Immediately upon hearing this, I start to cry. This was not something I wanted to hear, and I didn't know how to react to what the doctor told me. I was happy that Mr. Pankowski is alive, although I'm not happy that he was paralyzed due to the shooting. For right now, all I want to do is see him. Hearing that he's badly paralyzed wasn't easy to take in, but I just want to be able to see and talk to him. I calm myself down, and speak with the doctor.

"May I see him please? I would really like to see him."

The doctor then nods his head, and I start to follow him. After a short while, I end up reaching his room, and the doctor and I both walk in. I then see Mr. Pankowski, and he is hooked up to several machines, and his eyes are closed. I approach his bed, and I begin to start massaging his head. His eyes are closed, and I'm not entirely sure that he can tell that it is me by his bedside, but I'm sure that he is aware. Seeing him in the hospital bed, was not easy to deal with. I was trying to not cry, but I couldn't hold back the tears at all. The doctor then starts to look at the machines he is hooked up to, and writes down on his clipboard.

"His vitals are just fine. His blood pressure is good. Heart rate is fine. It seems like he is going to recover quite well."

I continue to massage Mr. Pankowski's head, when he starts to speak for the first time.

"Except I'm not going to be able to walk again. You didn't mention that."

I look over at the doctor, and he has a look of disappoint on his face. The doctor continues to write things down on his clipboard, and responds to Mr. Pankowski.

"I'm going to leave the both of you alone now. If you need any help, just alert one of the nurses, and I'll come by. I'll give you both some privacy now."

The doctor then leaves out of the room, and shuts the door behind him. I remain standing by Mr. Pankowski's bed. Mr. Pankowski then opens his eyes, and looks directly at me. We stare at each other for a minute, and are pleased to see each other. Mr. Pankowski then starts to quietly speak to me.

"I knew that was you Aaron. I'm so happy to see you. I can't believe that I'm never going to walk again. I don't want to live like this. What am I going to do?"

I try my best to comfort Mr. Pankowski during this time. I can't imagine what it would be like to be told that you are paralyzed in the legs, and aren't going to walk again. However, I wanted to make sure that he knew I was here for him, and I was going to offer all of my support. Mr. Pankowski then starts to cry, and continues to speak.

"I don't have any family Aaron. Both of my parents died, and I don't have any siblings. I have some extended family, but they don't live near here. All I have is you, and I really need your help to get me through this. Promise me that you'll help me Aaron?"

It's not that I didn't want to make any promises that I couldn't keep, I just didn't know how to respond. I felt sad that Mr. Pankowski didn't have any family support, and I know that when he is stuck with a situation such as this in his life, it helps to have people that care about you. At this time, I let out a very generic answer out to him.

"If you need my help, I'm here for you. Whatever you need to me to do, I'll do it."

Just then, one of the staff members from the hospital cafeteria walks into the room. She then sets down a tray of food. She then walks out. I raise Mr. Pankowski up in his bed, and I bring the tray of food closer to him. He then angrily shouts back at me.

"Ugh, get this shit away from me. I want some real food. I mean I'll eat the fruit, but I don't want any of the rest of this mess. Aaron, go and get me a burger and fries please."

This was already the first request he was asking of me. I began to feel slightly bitter and angry, and I was scared that I was going to become his personal caretaker now. I was only a concerned student, and I didn't sign up for this. I then remembered that a promise is a promise. I owe it to myself to help him out, and I have to do what he wants. The man can't walk anymore for Christ sake. However, I don't know if he's allowed to eat that type of food. I wanted to clear it up with the hospital staff first. I calmly respond back to him.

"I'll get you whatever you want, but let me talk to the doctor first, to see if you can eat that type of stuff. If they say it's okay, I'll hurry up and go get it."

Mr. Pankowski then grabs me by my wrist, and angrily responds to me.

"No, don't tell them shit. Just go and get me a burger and fries. Thank you."

I nod my head, and I walk out of the hospital room. I then leave out of the hospital, and I go to a hamburger stand that's about a five minute walk away from the hospital. I order the food, and walk directly back to the hospital. I reach Mr. Pankowski's room, and I give him the food that he asked for. He immediately starts to eat the food. After feeding him, his mood seemed to change drastically. He wasn't as irritable as he was before and was calming down. I end up eating with him, and it's almost as if we aren't in a hospital, and a school shooting didn't happen earlier. We are trying to erase all of that. The doctor when walks back into the room, aghast. The doctor then starts to angrily reprimand me.

"He's not supposed to be eating that. He's on a strict diet. He is still trying to recover, and there are certain foods we want him to eat. We can't have him eating that stuff yet."

I then start to feel very guilty for going against the doctor's orders. I was only trying to make someone close to me feel comfortable. Now that I have the doctor angry at me, this wasn't good. While he's eating his food, Mr. Pankowski shouts back at the doctor.

"It's not his fault. I told him to bring me this. Don't get mad at him, get mad at me. Leave him alone, it's not his fault at all. I'm not eating that nasty hospital food."

The doctor shakes his head, and looks at the machines that Mr. Pankowski is hooked up to once again, and writes down on his clipboard. The doctor then walks out of the room. Mr. Pankowski then continues to eat, and speaks to me.

"Aaron, I want you to come stay with me in California. I want you to take care of me. I have a lot of recovering to do if I want to go back teaching, and I really need your help. Please."

I don't up end responding immediately to him, as this was too much information to take in. I just needed some more time to adjust. Despite the fact I nodded my head, that didn't necessarily mean I was saying yes to him, and that I agreed to move with him to California. It also didn't mean that I was submitting to being his caretaker. I did care for Mr. Pankowski, but I just wasn't sure I was prepared for something like this. Mr. Pankowski a short while later then started to go to sleep, and I took a seat next to his bed. I then realized my parents are probably worried about me, and it has been a while since I had last spoke with him. I walk outside the to the emergency room waiting area, to call my parents. However, I see my mother and my sister already there. I immediately go up and hug them. They are so very happy to see I'm safe. They inform me that my father is on the way, and he will be there soon. I then explain to them that one of my teachers was shot during the shooting, and he is paralyzed. All three of us go to Mr. Pankowski's room, and we remain there. It was difficult for me to explain, but I also explained to my mother and sister, that he wants for me to move to California with him.

Shockingly, they were very receptive and understanding to this, and they didn't seem to have any issues related to that. My father arrived about an hour later, and I explained everything to him as well. Although my family do not know that I had a relationship with Mr. Pankowski, they were all acceptive towards me moving to California with him, to help him recover.

I spent the night at the hospital with Mr. Pankowski, as the rest of my family went home. The following day, several police investigators entered the room. I began to feel slightly scared, as police have a habit of intimidating me, and I feel uncomfortable around them usually. Still being in slight shock of the event, it was difficult trying to explain the details that we had. However, both myself and Mr. Pankowksi answered all the questions that the police wanted to know, and they promptly left the room. A short while after that, members of the news media press came into the room and wanted to speak with us. We declined to give any interviews, but we did give a brief relay of our accounts of what happened. Then, the doctor came into the room. I was informed that Mr. Pankowski was going to recover just fine, and he should be allowed to go home the next day.

Then several social workers of the hospital began to walk into the room. They asked me several questions, and some of the questions I was confused to answer. In the end, I was chosen to be Mr. Pankowsi's caretaker. The fact I was a student of his, and also had a romantic relationship somewhat with him wasn't brought up. They also educated me that he will have to be confined to a wheelchair for the rest of his life. He won't be able to walk again, and he will need help with several aspects of his life. I wasn't sure if I was truly up to take on the job. I was only eighteen years old, and I feel this was a huge responsibility to me.

At the time, I agreed to take on the challenge regardless. Knowing that my life now has a different meaning, and I have to make sure this man lives a prosperous life, despite the fact he will never walk again, and he will have to go about his life in a wheelchair.

On the day Mr. Pankowski was released from the hospital, the nurses then presented him with his first wheelchair. The wheelchair that he will use for his daily life wasn't available for him to use yet. This however would be temporary chair. Mr. Pankowski was very reluctant to get on the chair, and started to become very defiant. I was trying my best to calm him, and to accept that this is going to be his life now. After much convincing, me and the other nurses helped him sit in his chair for the first time. I didn't want to cry, but after seeing him stuck on that wheelchair, I just couldn't compose myself at all. I begin crying, and I start to kiss Mr. Pankowski on his forehead. When he notices that I have started crying, he starts to rub my face. As he is doing that, he calmly speaks to me.

"I know it's tough, but if I can handle it, so can you. Everything is going to be okay. Now, start pushing me. Get me the hell out of here."

Mr. Pankowski then starts to laugh, and I start to laugh to myself as well. I start to push Mr. Pankowski's wheelchair for the first time. Knowing that I will probably have to push him a million more times in my life. As me and the rest of the nurses help carry him to the taxi, on the way to Mr. Pankowski's apartment not far from the hospital. I was given a lot of paperwork on the medication he has to take, and also exercises I have to do with him. I was also given information on how to bathe him, and how to get him on and off the wheelchair. I'm not going to have any help with this. I have to learn how to do all of this myself. This is only the first day, so I had much to get used to.

The first few days of me taking care of him was hard. We had several fights and arguments, and there were times to where I had to walk away and leave him alone, as he was feeling crabby and didn't want to bothered. My main goal was for me to take him to graduation on Friday, and the shooting vigil that was happening later on the same day, without any fussing or problems. I don't know how I managed to do it, but I was able to get him dressed and comfortable enough to attend. It was a slight struggle trying to get Mr. Pankowski out of the wheelchair into his car. I was able to do it, and drove the both us to the event. I happened to get my High School diploma and made it through graduation, and Mr. Pankowski was extremely proud of me. We also took part in the vigil that happened directly after. All the students and staff that were killed in the shooting. Sadly Principal Brickstone was one of the staff members that were killed.

Everyone was honored, and we all paid respect for this unfortunate event that happened. As I was driving the both of us back to his apartment, Mr. Pankowksi informed me that we were going to move to California that Monday. The fact he was paralyzed in his legs wasn't going to stop him. I give him so much credit for that. I helped him pack all of his things, and get him prepared to move. I also started to pack my things. It was all happening so fast, but it was happening for a good reason. I was going to start attending nursing school in California, and Mr. Pankowski was also going to be starting to teach fall semester as a University professor.

Once we arrived in California, myself and Mr. Pankowski ended up staying in this apartment home in west Los Angeles. It was lovely, and it was perfect for us to get used to. In the beginning, I would stay in my room, and he would stay in his. I would continue to help him, and we would occasionally have fights and times to where we would run into issues, but we found a way to get through it. I would go to school, and he would teach. But when we were at home, I became his caretaker, and would use him as training for my nursing career.

As years passed, and I continued to take care of him, and nearly graduating from Nursing School, I began to sleep with him more, and we no longer slept in separate bedrooms. We were in love with each other, and we knew that we were going to be inseparable partners. Although he still doesn't like his life in a wheelchair at times, he began to accept that this is his life now.

I finally managed to graduate Nursing school, and I'm a proud registered nurse now. I have very flexible hours, and I even work emergency room at times. I can not only help the man I love and my partner, but I can help other people as well. That is what I truly loved about being a nurse. Being Mr. Pankowski's caretaker was something that I looked forward to being. We love each other, and we can overcome any issues or obstacles that we have. I knew our relationship was extremely strong. He loved me so much that he proposed to me in the rain after we had a terrible fight one time. The proposal later turned into Mr. Pankowski and I getting married. So Mr. Pankowski, who I can now call Steven, is now my husband and I love him very deeply, and he's the man I want to spend my life with.

There are times to where he gets on my nerves, and I get on his nerves. We still fight and run into issues. I still am learning everything I can to take care of him, and understanding that it is difficult to have a relationship with someone that is disabled.

There are days to where I even forget that he is even in a wheelchair, and I love him anyways. Now that we are married, and together, we started coming out to people about our relationship that we kept secret. My family at first were mad at me, but only for a week or so. The media also very briefly made a stint about it. It wasn't headline news or anything, but some news outlets were talking about how one of the teachers that survived the shooting, is now married to one of his students.

I don't feel any guilt. I was eighteen when me and Steven first kissed, so there is nothing they can do about that. I can't be punished for my thoughts or my emotions. Even though I was a minor when I first developed a crush on him, it was simply a crush. Nothing happened until I was a legal adult, so everyone else can save it. I don't want to hear it. Me and Steven live a relatively private life, and it works for us. I'm now in my late 20s, and I don't have any regrets in my life. Life isn't perfect for me, and I would never imagine that this would be the life me and Steven would have, but it's okay, and things work out just fine between us.

This story was not easy for me to explain at all. I understand that my teacher crush, later turned into becoming a caretaker for my teacher, to later becoming the teacher I had a crush on, being my husband. But I love that man, and he loves me. I don't like people trying to see it as something else that it's not. I'm comfortable with myself, and other people should be happy for me. Living my life as a gay Asian male, and I try to avoid all the oppression that I get faced with. I want people to be empowered by my story, and to understand that this isn't what I predicted at all for my life, but it's the way my life is now. My name is Aaron Chen, I am man of pink, and that was my story.

CHAPTER 10:

MAN OF RED (PART 1)

My name is Steven Pankowski. I am man of red, I am 37 years old, and this is my story. My Reddit name is "Justaweirdman". I was born and raised in Seattle, Washington, and I now happen to reside in Los Angeles, California. My culture is Jewish, and being Jewish means a lot to my identity. As Jewish people hold a lot of values with their lives, and my religion and my culture is something that I keep close. I am paralyzed in the waist down, after the result of a school shooting. I am lucky to still be alive. It's a shame that I had to have a devastating life changing event, doing something I loved. Simply doing my job as a teacher, I gave up most of my freedom, by having to be confined to a wheelchair. It took me some time to accept and get used to, but it's now my life. I'm thankful that I have Aaron in my life, and he has been a big help towards how my life is now. I will talk more about how my life adjusted to that later. Right now, I want to focus on a key part of my childhood, and a hobby which took charge of my life. Growing up, I was very serious with my faith, and went to synagogue quite often.

I wasn't orthodox Jewish, but some of my family members were. Because of that, when I was around my orthodox family members, I had to play by certain rules. If I didn't follow these rules, I would get punished by my family, and they would attack me for it. My childhood was okay, and I lived a pretty normal life as a child. My religion was a main factor, but if I don't make a big deal of my religion, my childhood was still fine. I made some friends, and I didn't really participate in sports that often. Athletics were not my strength, but I really excelled in Chess. I don't know, but whenever I played Chess, I became a different man.

I would be ten years old, and I would challenge anybody that lived in downtown Seattle at the park playing chess. Sometimes on days after school, and many times during the weekends, I would take my chessboard and start to challenge. Very rarely would I ever lose a match. I was that good with myself, and I felt like I was unbeatable when I came to Chess. Because there is not one direct way to play Chess, there are over a million move combinations you can do. Sometimes I would make a mistake and end up losing a game. These things happen of course, and there was nothing I could do to avoid this. But usually, I would always win every Chess match I would do. I didn't go to the park and play to lose. I came to win, and I would always win. As far as my parents, whom my father died when I was fifteen years old of an illness. The only thing I remember about my father, was that he was bald, wore glasses, and he had a huge beard. Sorta like how I look like now, Ha-Ha.

My mother sadly passed away of breast cancer when I was in University trying to get my teaching credentials. I miss my mother very dearly, and I was close with her. My parents however wanted me to become a famous Chess player, and there were times that I hated that they would force me to go to Chess matches, even if I was tired and didn't feel like going. Now, I'm happy that they did that, as if I was talented in Chess, which I was. I needed to put my money where my mouth was. When I was twelve, I participated in my first ever chess tournament. It was overwhelming at first, and a Chess tournament is ultimately different that playing Chess with a bunch of random people in the park.

My nerves caught up to me, and the first tournament that I was in, I was beaten so badly. What was sad, the winning move that the guy made I was playing against, I should have seen coming a hundred miles away. I choked under the pressure, and that was the first time that I wanted to really quit Chess. I never wanted to pick up another Chess piece again, and I told myself that I was never going to waste any more of my time with this game ever again. But with strong conviction by my parents, they wouldn't let me give up that easy at all. The following week, I was entered back into another Chess competition. This time, I refused to let my nerves get in the way. All I had to do was calm down, and focus. I would play people in the park all the time, so although this was a bigger scale, I had to envision myself playing like I was at the park. I just needed to focus and calm myself down so I can win.

Keeping my mind clear seemed to have worked this time. I was able to beat my competitor with ease, and I won my first ever tournament game. This was only the start of it though. If I wanted to really excel at being a Chess grand champion, I had to continue to win games. I kept my winning streak, and I won several more tournaments. One after the other and I couldn't be stopped. I was now fourteen years old, and was ready for the Grand World Finals in New York City. Having never been to New York, it was nice to take in the experience. The setting was kind of similar to how it was in Seattle. I know that New York and Seattle are two different places, but the scenery seems to be quite similar.

Anyways, I didn't come to New York for a vacation or to sight see. I am here because I have a job to do. I want to become Chess World Champion. I have proven myself to make it to this stage, and I was totally ready. I would be competing with people from all over the world, and from all different playing styles. Coming from just a kid that played Chess in the park after school and on weekends. To now someone that was going to compete in the world championships.

There was just one problem. The nerves that I experienced in my first ever Chess tournament game, were starting to come back. I was trying so much to tell my nerves to go away, but it was tough. If I didn't control my nerves, I was going to lose for sure. I didn't want to embarrass my parents, and above all, I didn't want to embarrass myself. Coming all this way, only to lose, would be devastating. I know you could say that it's just a game, but it's so much more than that. It's the pride of power of winning, and having the title of World Chess

Champion. My face and my name would be in history books, and I would make National News for being champion. So I had a lot that was at stake, so I couldn't dare wreck this magic moment. The World Championships are played in a course of three days. On the first day, you had the quarterfinals. In which the competition would be dwindled down from over fifty finals, down to twenty five. Day two would be semifinals. In semifinals, the twenty five contestants would then be taken down to nine finalists.

There would be a quick wildcard round, in which one lucky person would be added to the other nine, making ten finalists who would go onto the finals. Then finally on day three, would be the finals. On the day of the finals, part 1 would consists of all ten finals playing their matches. Five players would move on, and another player would be wildcard, being added to make it six. Out of the six players, they would now compete in part two of the finals.

Then the third and final part of World Championships would commence. Out of the three remaining players, the one player that performed the best, would automatically go onto the final game, where the other two would play to see who would play in the final game. Then the remaining two players would face off, and the winner would be World Chess Champion.

I was one of the youngest competitors in the game. That did intimidate me somewhat, but age doesn't mean anything. This is all about Chess. Chess doesn't care how young or old you are, what you look like, where you came from, or what you wore. None of that mattered. That is what I liked about Chess. It was a game of logic and strategy. Only the smartest players win, and you not only have to plan your own moves in advance, but you have to pay attention to what your opponent does as well. So Chess was a lovely game in that aspect. I was now going to play in the quarterfinals. I ended up going through that very easily.

My opponent wasn't that difficult to face against, and I knew I was going to win, so it wasn't much of an obstacle to climb over. I wasn't getting too full of myself, as I still had more rounds to go through, but

I was feeling confident that I had this in the bag. As I had beaten my opponent, I can now go onto the semifinals. When I was playing in the semifinals, my competitor was playing a lot of tricks, and I was not expecting them to be that skilled. I was getting a run for my money, and I should not have underestimated them at all. I think I got extremely lucky, because I managed to still win over my partner, even though they were making moves I wasn't that familiar with.

Going onto the finals, I should have been excited and happy for myself. I wasn't, and I was getting those jitters and nerves yet again. I need to control myself, or I'm going to blow it. All I could think about was winning, and I didn't have any room for error. All I wanted to do was win, and to be World Chess Champion. Nothing could stand in my way, and I wasn't going to let anyone take that dream and ambition away from me. I went into the finals, and my attitude was getting the best of me. I didn't know what I was doing. I sadly choked, and my chances of recovery were not good.

What in the hell happened? I couldn't believe that I was having this poor of a performance. The longer that the game went on for, I knew that I wasn't going to win anymore. Finally, it was all over. My opponent pinned me against a corner, and I wasn't left with any other options, but to retire from the game. I lost the game, and I ended up finishing in third place. I wasn't going to be World Chess Champion, and I came this close to winning. I ended up letting the pressure and all of that attack me, and I lost. My main problem, was that I kept thinking about winning and becoming champion, instead of just focusing and playing. Had I done that, I probably most likely would have won, and became Chess Champion. I could sense how my parents were feeling about this. I knew they were disappointed in me.

I wasn't that far at all from winning, and I wasn't able to achieve total victory. As I was walking off the stage, I didn't want to see anybody. I was far too ashamed at this point. My parents although weren't disappointed in me as much as I thought they would be. The would have liked for me to have won, but they were happy that I got as far as I did. Once I saw that my parents were happy, I shifted my mood, so that I wasn't that mad at myself for not being Chess Champion. After this, I didn't want to play Chess anymore. I lost interest, and I was still letting myself down for not winning the championship. Every single time I would try to move pieces on a Chess board, I just was unable to, and I couldn't do it. So I told myself that I would never play a game of Chess again in my life.

To make things worse, my father started to become very ill at this time. The doctors were not sure if he was going to recover from his illness, and the thought of my father dying when I was so young; I didn't want to think about it. My mother and I would pray for him quite often, even though the doctors persisted that his condition was going to get worse. Unfortunately, my father did end up passing away from complications of his illness. Being told that your father is gone at only fifteen years old, was something difficult for me to accept. I loved my father, and having to deal with his death at a young age was depressing. After my father passed away, I became a more introverted person. My hair was starting to thin before I graduated High School. The other kids in school would pick at me over that.

I became a very nerdy and goofy guy, and the combination of the fact I wore glasses, and I was balding, made me not want to associate or deal with other people. I would go to school, and come home. I wouldn't hang out with any friends, I wouldn't do anything fun. I no longer played Chess. My life at this stage was turning into me wallowing in my own pity. My main goal, was to get myself out of this state of misery, and to do something with my life. I tried to become Chess champion, and that failed. But that doesn't mean that the world stops turning, and that I stop living my life. I decided that I wanted to become a teacher. It was something that I didn't think of overnight, but it was something that I had a big interest to do. I wanted to help others, and to be an educator.

Once I graduated High School, I started to take classes and prepare myself so that I can be a teacher. When I was in University, my life changed, and my social life also started to become different. University was a very special time in my life, and this is where things, if only for a slight moment changed.

My first two semesters of University, nothing that monumental happened. But in my Junior year of University, I happened to meet a special friend. I was walking to class one day, and standing around Student Union. I came across this guy that was very tall, and he had long blonde hair, and he was just as goofy and nerdy as I was. When I was younger, I would have friends, but when I was in University, there wasn't anyone at all that I was close with.

I knew I had to work on my social skills, and that I had to introduce myself to new people. I knew I had to make friends with this guy. Although I have an attraction to both men and women, there wasn't anything romantic involved at all. He wasn't even my type romantically. But I still looked at him as a cool person to be around. I had time to spare anyways. He was standing by himself reading a book, so I didn't want to bother him. However, I went up and spoke to him anyways.

"Hey, I'm Steven. You look like a cool guy, and someone that is up my alley. Would you mind if we went out for a drink sometime?"

The man looked up at me from his book, and started to speak to me.

"That sounds great, sure. My name is Elliott Graves. Very nice to meet you sir."

I end up shaking Elliott's hand, and we became an unstoppable duo right then. Me and Elliott had so much in common. Not only were we freaky looking geeks on the outside, but we also liked the same music, television shows and movies, but our connection seemed to match quite perfectly. We just enjoyed being around one another, and we knew we made a good pair. It was because of Elliott, that I started to play Chess again. He wasn't any good at Chess, but from my friendship with him, he urged me to continue Chess, so I did. Elliott was actually a guitar player, and he also was a vocalist as well. His main dream was to be in a rock band, and to be the next Jim Morrison. That was his whole vision. I didn't know that much about being a musician, or playing instruments. But Elliott and his band would play for me quite a bit, and I began to feel enthralled by their music.

If they released an album, I would definitely buy it. As I was continuing my University career, I picked up Chess again and although

I wasn't at pro level like I was when I was younger, I still played from time to time. Like I still play now sometimes. Elliott however was going to be in a Battle of The Bands competition, and he wanted me to come see him perform. The winner of the competition, would automatically receive a recording contract with a major record label, that I'm not going to name. What I didn't know at the time, was to deal with the nerves Elliott was facing before the band competition, he would turn to drug use. He was actually using pretty hardcore drugs, and I wish I knew about this. I would have tried my best to get him to stop. But I had no idea.

Not that I'm condoning his drug use, but I could understand slightly why he felt the need to do that to himself. I don't want to say that his band mates were a bad influence, but they didn't' seem to help with his drug abuse. Sex, Drugs and Rock and Roll as they all say, and I can't believe that Elliott got wrapped up into all that mess. I do remember the last time I came into contact with Elliott, he was acting extremely strange. I remember I was in my dorm room studying, and Elliott for no apparent reason started to bang on my door very loudly. As I let Elliott into the dorm room, he starts acting very hyper and unusual.

"Hey Steven, how you been man? Me and some of my buds are going to go party for a bit. Did you want to come with us?"

By the way Elliott was reacting, I wanted nothing to do with that. I had a suspicion that he was under the influence and high on drugs at that time, but I didn't want to assume anything. I also thought that maybe he was simply drunk. Had I known at this time, Elliot was abusing drugs very heavily, I would have definitely done something, and got him help. There was no way I was going to tag along with him while he was in that condition, so I had to unfortunately tell him no.

"I'm sorry Elliott, but I have a lot of studying to do, so as much as I would love to come, I sadly cannot. But take care of yourself man. I'll see you later."

Elliott just had a look of sadness on his face, and he didn't respond to me at all. He just gave me a wide frown, and ran out of my dorm room. Slamming the door behind him. This would be the final time that I would ever talk to Elliott. With this being the last memory I have conversating with him, I feel certain waves of guilt because of this. I wish that I could have been able to do something to save him. But I just didn't know the extent of how bad his current state was. He was my best friend, and I didn't like how to handle this situation at all.

The Battle of the Bands Competition happened a few days later. I saw all the bands perform, and it was very stiff competition. I knew that Elliott's band was good, but I was unsure if they were at the level that the rest of the participants were. Elliott's band finally approached the stage, and I saw them perform one of their original songs. I have to be honest and say that Elliott didn't look that well on stage. He seemed like he was very tired, and was out of it. I was worried about him slightly. It was then time to announce the winners of the competition. Elliott's band got second place, and they did not end up winning. I saw how disappointed Elliott looked once he found out his band did not win the competition. The band that ended up winning, I don't want to say was better, but they were good. Like I said before, it was a stiff competition.

I knew that Elliott really wanted to win, and the prize for winning was a guaranteed record deal. I can feel that he believes that all his dreams of being a rock star are over. I wanted Elliott to realize that this wasn't the end, and he can still go for his dreams. His band didn't win the competition, but that doesn't mean that he's a bad musician at all.

The following day however, I received news that Elliott passed away of a drug overdose. I refused to believe any of this at first, but it actually happened. I don't know what happened with Elliott, and I was under much guilt that I should have been there with him as a true friend. I wasn't, and Elliott is now gone. I lost my father, and I now lost my best friend. I was beginning to think that life was just unfair for me, and I was destined to be approached with nothing but badness and sadness for the duration of my life. I graduated University, not only for myself but for Elliott as well. We were supposed to be lifelong friends, and our journey together was cut short. I knew I had to continue on with my life, and do the best that I could do.

My adventure into becoming an educator started off as me being a substitute teacher. It was complete hell, and none of the students ever liked me. There must be some unwritten code, that substitute teachers are always going to be treated like hell. I would be cussed at, spit on, had food thrown at me. I've been called every insulting name in the book. I've had students break my glasses, throw water on my clothes. But the one prank I hated the most, was whenever students would super glue me to my chair. I hated it, because it seems like it would happen quite frequently. The first time that it happened, I was subbing a third grade glass.

The class seemed innocent enough, and I perceived them to be friendly. This was not the case, as one of the students put super glue on my chair. I guess they feel like they wanted to teach the substitute teacher a lesson, so they did. Substitute teaching was very stressful for me, and I didn't enjoy it. However, it was my only way into getting my teaching credentials. I had to have experience if I wanted to be a teacher, and being a sub was pretty much the only way. When I finally got enough credits to go onto being a legitimate teacher, I could not be any happier.

I was no longer going to waste my time being a substitute teacher, and dealing with all the bullshit that surrounds that. But little did I know that being a regular teacher wasn't going to be any easier than being a substitute teacher. There were even some days that I preferred to go back to being a sub.

I was twenty four years old, when I first became a regular teacher. I was teaching Junior High science, and it was something I liked at first. But dealing with Junior High students became to be a job I didn't think I was cut out for. The disrespect continued, and all the pranks continued as well. The students at this age are leaving Elementary School, and Junior High School is a stepping stone into going to High School. Don't get me wrong, some of the students were a delight and a joy to be around.

But being a Junior High Teacher came with many issues and problems that I wasn't prepared to deal with at all. I ended up only teaching Junior High Students for a single semester. Once that semester was over, I later went onto teaching High School students. High School students were very interesting to say the least. High School students were also the most cruelest I had to deal with. Being that I had to teach High School seniors, they were mature, and felt that they could treat me however they wanted. I hated being the mean teacher, but I had to put my foot down and not be taken advantage of by them. If you allow the students to take advantage of you, they will not appreciate or respect you as a teacher.

So I had to be strict. I could tell my students were starting to resent me as a teacher, but I was scared that if I were too nice to the students, they would treat me any which way they wanted. I continued to teach High School for several years, and I remember my third year of teaching High School, would be rather different than previously. This would be the year that I would meet Aaron, and at the end of this school year, I would never be the man I used to be again.

At the start of this school year, I acted the same way as I did before. I was not a very nice teacher, and I made sure the students were aware that I ran a tight ship. I wasn't going to take anything from my students. My job was to simply be their teacher. I wasn't here to be their friend. My job was to be their teacher, and to teach. The class I had for final period, I knew was going to be a challenge for me. I start to write my name on the board like I usually do. I then start to speak to the entire class.

"My name is Mr. Pankowski, and I'm going to be your biology Teacher."

It was during this time, that I noticed a student was writing in his notebook as I was trying to teach. This upset me greatly at first. I didn't like it when students were not paying attention when I was giving a lesson. The student writing in his notebook was Aaron. I saw great potential in him, and knew he was going to be something special and different. But I still didn't like it when students were writing when I was trying to give a lesson. As much as inside I felt cruel and bad for doing what I did to Aaron, I was in my strict teacher mode at the time. I walk up to Aaron's desk, and throw his notebook across the room. I then violently snap at him.

"Why are you taking notes? Did I tell you to write any of this down? I didn't. So unless I tell you to take notes, I don't want to taking down notes."

Aaron walks up and picks his notebook of the floor that I threw. Again, I hated being this type of teacher, but I was stuck in my usual mood of being direct. But Aaron was special, and as I went home that night after teaching, the way I felt bad for the way I treated him. I was starting to feel very remorseful, and I knew that I had to change my attitude with my students. What happened next in that class, would be an embarrassing and humiliating situation. It turns one of the students decided to play the infamous super glue prank on me. I can't believe that I keep falling for this one. It gets done to me quite a bit, and I steadily fall for it. When I arrived to class, the students acting very strange. I knew that something was up.

I didn't know it was the super glue prank, but I could tell they were up to something bad. Part of me feels like I deserved it from the way I was treating them. They knew I was a strict teacher, and by playing a prank, they were going to send a message that they had more power over me. When I finally sat in the seat, by the way the class laughed, I once again fell victim to this prank. However this time, the students put glue on the sides of the chair where my arms rested. So now my arms are also stuck to this chair. I can't look at the rest of the class, and I feel so humiliated.

Aaron then comes up to me, and attempts to get me off the chair. I tell him that I do not need his help, and that he can go back to his seat. Aaron refuses and continues to try and help me. When the final bell rings, I continue stuck to my seat, and I can't move. Aaron gets help for me, and I'm thankful that he decided to help me. Never once has a student ever tried to help me off a chair after playing that prank. I knew that Aaron was going to be different.

I then knew that Aaron deserved a reward for the way he was treating me. I was going to give him a ride home from school, as that was the least I could do. I reluctantly give Aaron a ride, and I can tell he felt weird having his teacher bring him home. I wasn't quite done yet with Aaron, and wanted to test his virtuosity a bit more. So I gave him a request as I was dropping him off at home.

"Hey Aaron, I would like for you to come help me before school tomorrow with a few things. You don't have to, but I would like it if you helped me."

I knew that Aaron was going to say yes, but I wanted to test him regardless. He did end up agreeing to my request. The next morning I picked up Aaron from home, and decided to treat him out to breakfast as well. I never had a connection with a student like this before, but I was happy to have Aaron with me. He was a nice young man, and I just saw the potential he had. Had I knew that he had a crush on me, I definitely would have backed away. How was I supposed to know this though? That didn't even cross my mind at all. I was simply helping out a student, and I don't want to think anything more or anything less related to that.

Aaron without any hassle, helps me out with the tasks that I wanted him to do. I don't want to trouble him anymore. I leave Aaron alone at this time, but still remember how great of a young man he is. I also change my behavior towards my students. I become a more friendlier teacher, and my class appreciates me because of that. As time continued to go on, I wanted to make sure my students were happy and that they enjoyed having a great time in my class. They did, and they no longer played any pranks on me, and my students also liked my company. They looked forward to being in Mr. Pankowski's class, and this nice teacher feeling, was much better than the evil teacher feeling.

Things became strange, the day Aaron decided to kiss me. It's not like I forgot about Aaron. He always sat in the front row of my class, and he was a perfect student. I had no idea on how to react when Aaron expressed his feelings for me. I remember he came into my classroom during lunch period one time. I didn't have any issues if Aaron wanted to eat lunch with me. I now know that he was originally planning confessing his love and affection for me during this time. I am glad he didn't though. He actually waited until school was over. After class, he closed all the doors to the classroom. I was getting ready to leave, and Aaron just went straight up to me and kissed me. At this particular time, Aaron was eighteen. So there wasn't anything I could do. There is no rule in school district that says teachers cannot form a relationship with a student that is of legal age. Being that Aaron was eighteen, and I had no issue with the kiss. Although I wasn't expecting the kiss, and it was strange for Aaron to do that, I didn't mind that he kissed me. I knew that he liked being around me, and if I could make him happy, I would. I didn't want to make Aaron any promises that I probably was not going to keep, but I let him kiss me. It was the least I could do for everything that Aaron has helped me with. Feeling nervous and unsure of how to react, my only response to him after the kiss is if he wants a ride home.

"Do you want me to give you a ride home?"

Aaron agrees to let me drop him off at home, and it was at this time that I knew we couldn't let anyone know of our relationship. If news got out, I would not only lose my job, but Aaron would also be scrutinized. I also didn't want to be accused of manipulating Aaron into forming a relationship with me. Being that I was in my late 20s at the time and still young myself, people are still going to twist the situation around that I was trying to force Aaron to be in a relationship with me. That wasn't the case, as we were both receptive to it.

Aaron kissed me, I didn't kiss him. I figured Aaron would get the hint that it's best that we didn't stay together. So I distanced myself from Aaron. I didn't give him any grades he didn't deserve. I didn't treat Aaron like a teacher's pet. I didn't do any of that. I knew this would make the situation worse, if I did decide to react that way to him. Aaron was deeply infatuated with me, and I wish I could have eased his mind, but I couldn't. I was his teacher, and I wasn't someone for him to crush over, or form a relationship with. The kiss happened, and I wanted to leave it behind me. I wanted to pretend that it never happened, but it did.

I had intentions of this being my final year of teaching High School. I wanted to proceed onto teaching University students. I was going to move out of the Seattle area, and I was going to move to Los Angeles to teach. It was something that I had to advance myself towards, and I decision that was the right thing for me to do. Very slightly in the back of my mind, I knew that this was going to be news that Aaron was not going to take well at all. Aaron wasn't the main thing on my mind, but he would be deeply upset if I had to move away. But again, I was only his teacher, and my relationship with Aaron wasn't that vital. I told the news to each of my classes, and I could tell that Aaron was not taking this news well. Not that I didn't care about his feelings, and not that Aaron didn't have a right to be upset over this, this was my decision to make towards my career, and Aaron had to accept this.

With the remainder of the school year comprising of Senior prom, finals week and graduation, I continue teaching High School students for my final year. As prom as near, I was asked by the school to be a chaperone. I didn't even attend my own damn prom, and the school wants me to be a chaperone at the prom. I quickly agree to the job, even though I was not looking forward to it. I also wondered if Aaron was going to go. He didn't seem like the type of student that would normally attend prom, but I started taking bets with myself as to whether he was going to show up. In the end, I told myself that the chances of Aaron appearing at prom aren't likely.

While at prom, I felt very awkward there, and I'm being a terrible chaperone. A lot of the students are dancing very close to one another, and I'm not really watching the students. My job was to hand out beverages and snacks to the students, and that's what my main focus is on. I continue to gaze around the gym, and I don't see any trace of Aaron. I had a feeling that he wouldn't be here, so this didn't shock me all that much. Later onto the night, I stand corrected, as I do see Aaron arrive at the prom. He doesn't look very happy though, and isn't enjoying himself. Aaron then walks over the drink and snack table. Aaron still looks unhappy with himself, although I wish I knew what I could do to make him feel better.

Aaron grabs his snacks, and walks over to the bleacher area. I know something is troubling him, and I knew exactly what it was. He was upset that I was going away, and he's also upset that I'm not with him. It didn't take a rocket scientist to figure this out. But again, I'm his teacher, and he's the student, so what was I to do in a situation like this? Without Aaron being aware, I continue to watch how uncomfortable he is at the prom. The prom is supposed to be a very special time in a High School student's life, and Aaron is not having a great time at all. I had to do something to make him feel better, and I had to do it now. My time with him is short, so I can't allow him to feel upset. If showing love to Aaron is wrong, then I refuse to be right. Just then I notice that Aaron walks into the locker room, and this was my time to act.

As I'm walking through the dark locker room, I see that Aaron is sitting by himself crying with his head down. I quickly go over to comfort Aaron during this time.

"Why are you sitting in here Aaron, why aren't you outside with everyone else?"

One thing led to another, and me and Aaron end up embracing each other. Aaron and I then kiss for the second time. It's very official at this point that the relationship that Aaron and myself had, wasn't going anywhere. This was going to be more complex than I thought, and I was unsure of how to deal with these feelings. Aaron and I remain in the locker room for quite some time. I knew that if anyone were to know about the union we had, we would be in so much trouble. In certain ways, I was happy that we were having this secret relationship.

The teacher student relationship rather, just how taboo it was. Really, I wanted to make sure that Aaron had a great time at prom, and I believe I made his wish come true. Although I wish we would have stayed together longer, I had to go back to the prom to chaperone. Aaron and I walk out of the locker room, and I return to the snack and drink table. The night of the prom taught me quite a bit about love. Love is very strange, and you cannot control it. I had no agenda or any intentions of falling in love with one of my students, but it happened.

Now that it happened, there was no way out of this. I had to accept whatever came next with Aaron, and deal with the results. Aaron was going to graduate, and I was going to end up moving to California to teach there. We all had our own agendas. At some point, we would go our separate ways, and I would have to face all the facts related to that.

For now, that was thinking a little bit too much ahead, and I was more concerned about the present. Although it was the end of the school year, it wasn't the end of the year quite yet, and there were still many things that would happen.

Finals week for my students was simple for them. I wanted to teach them all that I could, so they could pass their finals no problem. Of course, all of my students ended up completing their finals without any hassle. Now that finals were over, and all my students were going to pass, my job was pretty much over. Or so I thought. My final year of teaching High School was still not complete, and a major event would put my entire life in shambles. It was the day of the shooting. A day I would rather forget, and a day I don't like to discuss that much about really. Forgetting doesn't really help, and it doesn't erase what happened. The shooting was a major event in my life, and it caused me to live my life from a different approach.

The day of the shooting seemed normal enough. It was the Friday before graduation. Graduation would take place exactly next Friday. As finals were all over, I was mostly giving my students ungraded work, and my classes weren't that serious. Not even a few minutes into me teaching, we hear very loud gunshots coming from the building that my classroom was currently in. The minute we heard the impact of all the gunshots, everyone panicked. Unless you've been in that particular situation, you are unsure of what to do. I see that my students immediately duck down on the floor.

As I'm behind my desk facing the door of the classroom, within quick instance, the gunman shot me several times in my lower back. It happened within two seconds, but felt much longer than that. It was an extreme blur and a flash, and it's difficult for me to explain everything again. Getting shot was a very painful experience. Having the bullets impact me, and the pain was very unbearable. I knew that I wasn't dead, and I was still alive. I was still fighting for my life, and I had to handle the pain.

I had so many questions in my head. Why was I shot? Why did the shooter decide to do what he did? All the disbelief and confusion that I was experiencing didn't make me feel any better. After a short while,

Aaron walks to my desk and starts to put pressure on my bullet wounds. Aaron was there for me when nobody else was, and I felt so appreciative of him. I knew that Aaron was a kind spirit, and it was beginning to show. Although I was still involved in an active shooting, I started to calm myself little by little. Aaron was here, and he was going to try his best to get me through this. Like I said before, most of it was a blur, but I was still feeling the pain from the bullet wounds, and feeling like I was approaching death. Police officers then swarm into the school, and paramedics also rush into the school.

I'm taken by ambulance to the hospital, and all I can see is white. I'm starting to fade in and out of consciousness and I'm becoming very tired. Through it all, I can hear that Aaron is arguing with the paramedics, not wanting to leave me. I then respond out to them.

"It's okay, he can stay with me. It's fine."

I didn't want Aaron to leave me. I wanted his energy, and I wanted to know he was going to support me, and continue to stay by my side. Aaron did. He was with my through this whole ordeal, and I love him for that. Aaron refused to leave me. He stayed with me. As I'm being wheeled closer and closer to the ambulance, I begin to feel more scared. I then for the first time, am unable to move any lower part of my body. I was able to shuffle and move my arms and my upper body just fine, however my lower body was unresponsive.

During this exact time, I knew that I was paralyzed, but didn't want to accept the truth. Arguing with myself that this isn't the case, knowing damn well that it is. I'm being lifted into the ambulance, and Aaron once again fights with them, so he can ride in the ambulance with me. Even though it was extremely hard for me to speak, I whisper out to the paramedics.

"It's fine, he can stay. I want him to stay with me."

Aaron then rode with me to the hospital. Others that were injured in the shooting are also being taken to the hospital as well during this time, and this whole chaotic scene is terrible. I was one of the people that was shot, and I was shot very badly. There were also people that sadly were killed in the shooting, and I pray for them, and I pray for their families. I was paralyzed as a result of the shooting, but I did happen to make it out alive. I should be appreciative of that. Nobody saw this shooting coming, and we didn't deserve this. Our school was pretty low profile, and this event causing turmoil to our school was bad. I'm taken to the hospital and wheeled immediately into the operating room.

I am knocked out during this time, but the doctors begin removing the bullets from my body, and start to treat all of my wounds. Part of me was happy that my life was spared during the shooting, but the other part of me didn't want to accept or deal with the fact I was paralyzed. I'm taken to the recovery room, and I still am not able to move the lower part of my body. The doctor comes into the recovery room, and tells me news that I was already suspecting.

"Mr. Pankowski, we are sorry, but due to where the bullets hit you in your spine, you are paralyzed from the waist down. You are extremely fortunate to be alive though. We are going to continue to watch you, and everything is going to be fine. We'll take care of you."

Upon hearing this news, I hit the roof. I was not happy one bit to hear this. I knew that they were going to tell me this, but I was hoping that they wouldn't. I was never going to walk again, and I had to just accept this. But I did throw a tantrum in the recovery room.

"What? No! Why? I can't live my life like that. No! What the fuck? I'm going to be paralyzed for the rest of my life? What the fuck? No!"

I continued my tantrum in the recovery room for about fifteen minutes before several nurses started to calm me down. I had asked the hospital staff for some medication to calm me down, and they gave me some. That seemed to help. I then realized that I don't have any friends or family. If I'm going to be paralyzed, and will never walk, and will have to be stuck to a wheelchair, I'm going to need all the help and assistance I can get.

Then Aaron popped up in my mind. I knew I had Aaron, and he would be there for me. I continue to stay in the recovery room, hoping that I will see Aaron soon. I knew he would come and see me. Several hours later, Aaron did come into my room. Despite the fact I was very tired and low in energy, I was delighted to see Aaron by my bedside. I was hungry at this point, and the food that the hospital gave me, I had no intentions of eating. It looked disgusting, and it probably tasted terrible. The hospital wanted to have me on a strict diet, but I didn't want to follow it. I ask Aaron a request.

"Aaron, can you go and get me a burger and fries. I don't want to eat any of this hospital food. It's nasty. Go and get me a burger and fries."

Aaron was reluctant to process my request at first, in fear that the doctors wouldn't want me eating that, but Aaron later went and did what I asked him to do. He went and got me some food, and I was very happy. Of course when I was caught eating that food, the doctors yelled and screamed at Aaron. This wasn't Aaron's fault at all. I told him to go and get me the food, so the doctors should be mad at me. The doctor was mad that I didn't follow his orders and was eating food out of my diet. I didn't give a fuck. I was hungry, and I wasn't going to eat any of the food that they were going to force down me. I got to meet Aaron's family during this time. They were very nice, and they were all in my room showing me support. It was nice that I had all of these people that cared for me, while I was in this condition.

Aaron stayed with me the entire night. My night in the hospital was tough, as I was trying to recover myself. The next day, the police asked myself and Aaron several questions. I didn't know the student personally who did the shooting, but he was a High School senior named Norman Pankerson. I don't know what issues Norman was going through, or if he was bullied at the school. I didn't want to focus my attention on the shooter. I cared about the victims, and the other people that were killed as a result of the shooting. Aaron and I told the authorities everything we knew, so they could do their investigation. Several news media outlets swarmed into my recovery room, but Aaron and I both refused to do any interviews with them. We are not in a state to talk to them, and I'm still trying to recover.

Aaron agreed to be my caretaker once I left the hospital, and signed the paperwork to do so. I also offered for Aaron to come move with me to California. I was in a wheelchair, but my life isn't over. I still have dreams and plans I want to do. I told myself that I was going to move to California to be a University teacher, and that's still my plan. In order for me to be reliant with my life, I need for Aaron to be there for me. This was also great, as he could go to school in California as well. He can live with me, and help me day to day. It felt like a perfect plan, and it was going to be perfect. Yes it was happening very fast, but I needed to recover fast.

If Aaron was up to the job to be my caretaker, I was going to accept it. Nobody else was standing in line to help me. The following day was my final day in the hospital. This was the day they would present me with my first wheelchair. I did not want to sit down on it at all. I was crying and hollering and screaming.

"You can't make me sit on that. I'm not going to be seen in a wheelchair. Hell no!"

But after much persuading with Aaron, he worked his magic on me. Aaron and the nurses carried me off the bed onto the wheelchair. It was just a strange feeling sitting in the chair for the first time. This was a feeling I was going to have to adapt myself to indefinitely. I would have to make this wheelchair my best friend. Wherever I go, the chair is going to go with me. Aaron then proceeds to push me out of the hospital. Once outside the hospital, I sense reality for the first time. I'm going to be seen as the guy in the wheelchair for the rest of my life. As soon as I got home, The first step was to recover well enough so I could attend graduation, and the memorial vigil the school was having directly following that. In order to do that, Aaron would have to learn how to dress me, and how to transport me out of the house, and into my car.

Aaron was studying to be a nurse, so I knew this would be practice for him. We had many fights and there were times to where I had to tell Aaron to back away from me. However, we finally found a solid system together. Aaron found ways and techniques to get me dressed, to wash me, and to get me on and off the wheelchair. I was more than ready to go to graduation. The day of graduation, I was dressed in a very nice suit, and I began to feel slightly independent of myself. By going to this event, I wasn't going to be the Steven I was before, but I would still feel proud of myself. Aaron and I make it to graduation, and seeing Aaron graduate brought joy to my eyes. I began to cry, and it was nice to see all of this. I was also presented an award from the school. I was honored.

After graduation, was the memorial vigil for those that were killed during the shooting. Principal Brickstone, who was a very nice man, was killed during the shooting. After the vigil, I left feeling bittersweet. It was nice that our school still stood strong. Despite the shooting, we were still united together, and respected everyone involved. The shooting caused me to be paralyzed, but I pray for those that were killed, and I in a sense feel lucky that I'm still here. This was my last year teaching at this school, and it was quite a way to leave.

I'm now off to teach University in Los Angeles, and I have Aaron with me. I'm going to try to rebuild my life, and adapt my life differently. I'm not able to walk anymore, and having to go everywhere with a wheelchair. Aaron and I prepare to move, and I begin to say goodbye to Seattle. I have a brand new life waiting for me in California, and I can't wait for all the new adventures that are going to happen to me. Aaron and I arrive in California, and we end up staying in a nice apartment in Los Angeles. Despite my wheelchair, the place is big enough for me to move around without any problems.

Aaron helps me unpack, and we begin to live our new life in California. Aaron will mostly be in school, and I will be teaching. Aaron will pick me up every day, wheel me into the car, and take care of me at night, and when I wake up. For the remainder of the day I can be independent of myself. There are things I need help with during the day, and Aaron will not always be with me to help towards. I have learned to take care myself when Aaron is not there. There are things however that I will definitely need Aaron's help for, and I am thankful for him. I know he has to give up parts of his life to help me, but I know he loves me regardless.

Our relationship is rather controversial, and Aaron's parents were shocked by it at first. The later came to accept it though. Our relationship very briefly caused controversy in the media, but nobody really cared at the end of the day. Aaron was a legal adult when he kissed me, and there was no persuasion at all. I didn't take advantage of him, and Aaron didn't take advantage me. We formed a special teacher and student bond, and the rest happened to be history. I don't regret meeting Aaron, and Aaron doesn't regret dealing with me. We need each other.

The next step was proposing to Aaron and getting married to him. Which wasn't easy. There was a time to where me and Aaron had a huge fight and almost separated from each other. We are also robbed at gunpoint. We've been through a lot, and my story isn't quite done.

CHAPTER 11:

MAN OF RED (PART 2)

Now that I was living with Aaron, my next objective was to adapt myself to the way my life is going to be from this point forward. It's not that I wasn't happy that I had Aaron as my caretaker, I just wanted to do things by myself sometimes. The fact I had to use a wheelchair to get around, really damaged my independence greatly. I just wanted to be able to do things on my own from time to time, and not have to rely on someone else if I wanted to do it. Every single day when I would wake up, I would need Aaron's help to get dressed. Again, not that I was bothered by having Aaron help me, I miss the days to when I could get dressed on my own. After that, Aaron would have to get me off my bed, and set me in my chair. This had to do be done every single day. Something that bothered me greatly, was that I had to wake up even earlier, so that I could be ready for work on time. Before I was paralyzed, it wouldn't take me that long to get dressed. Now that I cannot walk anymore, it takes three times as long for me to be prepared for the day. So therefore, I have to wake up earlier. Even though most of the complaining would be done on my accord, Aaron typically would help me without any fight or fuss. If Aaron were to get angry with me, it was because I was acting ignorant, and I was refusing his help.

Once I was situated in my chair, Aaron would either cook me breakfast. I couldn't reach the stove or anything, so that sucked. The most I could do is probably help him prepare the meal, or mix something. If Aaron was busy, the microwave that was in the kitchen was at an appropriate enough level so that I could reach it, but if I wanted to cook the proper way on the stove, I couldn't do that without Aaron's help. Something I took totally for granted before I became immobilized, such as making an omelet on the stove, I could no longer do. Depending on how the day was going, Aaron and I would go to a restaurant to eat.

Which brings me to the next issue. I always would feel embarrassed having Aaron push me in public. I still do from time to time. Which is why we very seldom rarely go out. I'm working on this, but I just simply cannot deal with the stares, and people seeing the both of us like that. I get into very envious mood changes, to where I just wish I could be like everyone else, and walk on my own again. But the times where we would go out to eat, we enjoyed ourselves.

The only concern was having to find a restaurant that didn't treat me badly due to my disability. Having to find somewhere that was handicapped accessible. I can only think of one particular incident to where a restaurant was not handicap friendly, so Aaron and I went elsewhere. But that's just one instance as I remember.

But going back to my daily routine. I didn't have a set schedule every single day. Well I guess you can say that I had a mental schedule. Working with Aaron, we just figured out a system that could work between us. After breakfast, I would then be dropped off at work by Aaron. The University that I taught at, was very wheelchair friendly. The location that Aaron would drop me off, was very close by the lecture hall that I taught in. I only had two classes a day. I had a morning class from nine thirty to noon. Then I would have a lunch break at noon until one. Then I had a second class that would happen in the afternoon from one to three thirty.

I would teach advanced chemistry to University freshmen, and this was comfortable for me. There were not that many students in my classes. Each of my courses only had about fifteen or so students, so it was very easy for me to handle these classes. I only had one event to where I had an issue with a student taking a problem with the fact I was in a wheelchair. The remedy for that was simple, I would tell the school staff about the issue, and they were able to take care of it. But my students generally acted like I was never in a wheelchair, and that felt good.

During lunch break, sometimes, no actually usually, I would go without eating. This was generally my own preference. I didn't like most of the food the school would serve. In order for me to go to where some of the food options on campus where, it would take me more time, and I knew I had a second course to teach at one o clock. So typically, I would go without eating lunch, and I was never irritated over that. However, once I alerted Aaron that I was skipping lunch meals, he was slighted perturbed. He would then pack lunches for me, and would force me to eat them. He would hide a sandwich or a salad in my briefcase, and I would eat it. But other than that, I would go without eating and I was fine with that.

The rest of my day would have me teaching my second course, which was always identical to my morning course, except it took place in the afternoon. After my second course that I taught, I would then go meet Aaron at the same location that he dropped me off at. Aaron worked as a registered nurse, but his hours actually were pretty stable. Maybe once a month if that, Aaron would be late to pick me up due to unprecedented rounds he had to do. He would always text me if he had to stay after hours, and it was okay to deal with.

The longest I had to wait for Aaron was two hours, and that was quite stressful. So I had to stay at the University and kill time until then. I would just grade papers, or read or look at a video on my phone. Aaron would eventually arrive to pick me up though. I know that he wasn't always in control of his hours, so I had no grounds to get angry at him because of this. Following that, we would go home, and have dinner. Occasionally we would both go eat out for dinner as well. Aaron would cook dinner usually, and if I was able to, I would help him with the meal. Once dinner was concluded, I would then prepare the lesson plans for the course I was going to teach the next day. If there was any spare time left, Aaron and I would watch television, or a movie or something. Then he would then start to help me prepare for bed.

That was generally how my schedule went usually. Some exceptions would be that on the weekends, our schedule would shift slightly. We would mostly go to the grocery store or to the shopping mall on the weekends, or we would go to the movies. This was very depending on my mood. If I didn't feel like leaving the house, I wouldn't. You can ask Aaron, I'm very fussy.

If I'm not in the mood to do something, I'm not going to do it. Being confined to wheelchair really limits my options as to what I can do. I usually go to work, and I come home. Being in public stresses me out usually, and unless it's a very rare special occasion, I avoid public crowds. Aaron also is understanding of this, and I understand that he has a life as well. I don't think it's fair that he has to be trapped to me all the time. Even though he's not comfortable with it, I tell him that if he wants time by himself, and if he wants to do something without having to worry about me, that's fine. I wouldn't get offended or feel neglected.

My main concern, was that Aaron himself was losing his independence. Every day, he had to take care of me first, then he could take care of his own needs. I always came first, and that's what I appreciated about Aaron. He was never selfish around me. I was the one that was stubborn and would refuse to work with him at times. I would raise my voice at him occasionally, and I would argue with him. We would separate for several minutes, sometimes even hours. But we would always reunite and make up soon following that.

Aaron's sister was about to get married soon, and he really wanted for me to attend the wedding with him. I know that going to a big event, was really going to make my social anxiety go wild. Something that really worried me at first, was that Aaron said that he wanted to go with his sister and her friends to wedding planning events. This is something I'm not comfortable being around, so I told Aaron that he has my permission to go without me. After much pleading and insisting, Aaron was content with this. My main goal was to just stay at home. Aaron was only going to be gone for a few hours, and I could manage things on my own the best way I could. Aaron said that if I really needed his help, I could just call him, and he would immediately be there.

So now that Aaron was gone for the day, I was left at home by myself. It was difficult at first to adjust to Aaron being gone for the day, but I had to deal with it. I remember I started to get hungry, so I went to the refrigerator to see if I can make myself something. I couldn't use the stove, but I was hoping that there was something I could pop in the microwave, or something I didn't have to heat up to snack on. There is nothing for me to eat, and I started to get angry.

My only options are to starve myself until Aaron got back, or I can do something that I know if Aaron found out I did it, he would be very upset. I would have to go out and get something to eat myself. I thought about it for ten minutes or so, then I told myself that I'm going to start to be more independent. I was already dressed, so all I had to do was find a way to leave the house. I was not comfortable driving quite yet, but in the future I would get my car adapted so I can use it without the use of my legs.

For now, I was not able to drive. I then went on my phone to see if I can find an uber or a taxi service that allows people with wheelchairs to use it. It took me a while to find a driver to come and get me, but I found someone. It took forever to the driver to arrive to my house, but he did eventually show up. The driver was not at all helpful to me, and the only accommodating thing he did, was have a vehicle that a wheelchair could fit inside of. I get inside the drivers car, and he takes me to the shopping center.

During this time, I'm really missing Aaron not being here. I would turn to him to calm me down. I become anxious over people seeing me in my chair in public, and I didn't like feeling anxious. After I arrive at the shopping center, I get out of the drivers car, and start to push myself to the grocery store. I couldn't believe this was the first time I was shopping by myself. Although my road to independence was a long one, this was a good start. The stares that I got were not easy to handle at first, but I had to ignore all of that. These people do not know me, and it's only natural for them to stare. Not everyone is staring to make fun of a goofy bald guy with glasses in a wheelchair. As I was going through the store, I remember that I don't have Aaron to help reach or get something that's high up on the shelf. Damn, so I knew I had to ask one of the foolish people that worked in the store to help me with that. I end up finding a very handsome, young and tall supermarket worker with blonde hair stocking the shelves. I ask him for help.

"Yes, I'm trying to reach that jar of Mayonnaise, I would get it myself, but as you can see I cannot. If you could grab it for me, I appreciate it. Thanks."

The man grabs the item I wanted off the shelf, and hands it to me. He smiles at me, and then begins to speak to me.

"Sir, if there is anything else you need just ask me. If you need help checking your items out, just come and get me, and I'll help you very quickly."

I smile back at the young supermarket worker, and I give him a friendly response.

"Well yes, there are a few more things I couldn't reach either, and I would appreciate if you could help me get those things as well. Thank you."

The supermarket worker assists me with anything I need help with in the store. Even though I wasn't being completely independent as I was getting help from someone else that worked in the store, to me it was the next best thing and close enough. I went to the supermarket all by myself, and this was a huge accomplishment.

Yeah I've had people stare at me, and I had to ignore my anxiety, but it was still nice to do this task on my own. I left the market with all of my items, and waited for my ride to return to pick me up to go home. When I arrived home, I started to put the things I purchased from the grocery store in the living room. At this same exact time, Aaron walked into the house with his sister, and some of his friends. He had a look of confusion on his face, and began to shout out to me.

"Steven, did you go to the grocery store? How did you get there? If you needed something form the store, you could have texted me, and I would have brought it."

I didn't know what to say at first. I wasn't mad at Aaron, but I was disappointed that he wasn't proud that I went out and did a task on my own. Wy wasn't he more supportive of me? He was attacking and punishing me for something that I thought he would be glad about. I end up responding to Aaron by reassuring him that everything is fine.

"Well I was hungry, and I didn't know how much longer you were going to be away. It's fine. I called up a driver, and he took me to the store just fine. I'm okay. Everything is okay."

I could tell that Aaron was still concerned over my safety, and wasn't comfortable that I left the house all by myself. He continues to chastise my decision to leave the house.

"What if you got hurt? I care about you, and anything could have happened to you because I wasn't there. In the future, just let me know if you're going to leave. That way I'll know, and if you do need help, I'll come and get you."

Me and Aaron were starting to have an argument. All I did was go to the grocery store. I wasn't even out of the house for an hour, and he's making a huge deal, out of something so little and insignificant. Why should I be forced to stay in the house all the time? I didn't want to fight with him in front of his sister, and his friends, but I get very hot headed sometimes. I start to move myself towards the kitchen area, and I then angrily snap back at Aaron for him not understanding my side of it.

"Aaron, I'm not going to fight with you. I was hungry, so I went to the store and got something to eat. I managed to do everything fine, and I'm okay. Please be supportive of me."

We continued to fight for several more minutes. I couldn't comprehend why Aaron just couldn't accept the fact that sometimes I want my independence. Here I was thinking that I could possibly do what I did again in the future. I'm scared now, because every single time I want to leave on my own, Aaron is going to be uncomfortable that I'm doing something without him. I start to question our relationship as well. I love Aaron, and I know he loves me, but for a while in this instance, I wanted for us to separate from each other. If something as simple as me going to the store by myself caused him this much worry,

I was concerned about the bigger scale of things. After our fight, I end up being cordial to Aaron's sister and the rest of his friends, and apologize for causing a scene in front of them. After they leave, Aaron refuses to speak to me for the rest of the day. He is still angry at the fact I went to the store earlier, and this is his way of punishing me I guess. I was supposed to be ashamed for doing things on my own, and wanting my own independence.

Later on in the day, Aaron helped me get ready for bed, but he was still mad at me, and refusing to speak to me. I was fine with this, as maybe we both needed time to cool off over this. I didn't feel I did anything wrong, and Aaron understands that I didn't do anything wrong either. He wasn't being overprotective of me, he just knows that if something bad were to happen to me, Aaron couldn't live with himself and be in extreme guilt. He is my caretaker after all, and he is supposed to watch over me. But I should be allowed to be independent for a while, and be on my own if I choose to in certain situations.

As the days went on, I began to reconcile with Aaron slightly. I was still haunted from the scolding I got from him, that I didn't do anything, or go anywhere without Aaron being aware, and him watching over me. I would go to work, and come home. Rinse and repeat, and that's how things were. We didn't fight, but our relationship was starting to become strained. With his sister's wedding coming up, I began to wonder if I should even show up. If I'm not feeling in a good mood to attend, I'm not going to. I know that his sister's wedding is something special to him. But if I don't want to go, that's my decision, and Aaron can't force me to do something I don't wish to do.

The wedding was still a week away, so I had to make my mind up in that short frame of time. I was really starting to hate the fact I couldn't walk. I felt like an infant, not being able to do anything that he wanted to do, or go anywhere that he wanted to go. This wheelchair I had to use, felt like a baby pram, and Aaron was starting to baby me. I had no control over doing something on my own, unless it involved me going to the University to teach my courses. Aaron would then pick me up and take me home. During the weekends, Aaron would go out with his friends, and have fun and plan the wedding with his sister. I was stuck at home watching "Seinfeld." I started to feel traumatic on thinking about leaving the house, knowing that Aaron would throw a fit, if I left on my own. To avoid that, I just stayed at home. Even though I really wanted to leave and go outside, and to have my independence. I got tired of this routine, even though it seemed to work for us at first, inside I was unhappy with it. I was also still feeling uneasy about the day I decided to go the market all by myself. Aaron was supposed to be proud of me for that, not attack me.

I figured I would do a test, and by doing this test, I will see whether or not Aaron truly loves me. If he actually loves me, he wouldn't be mad at me. If he doesn't care about me, and only cares about babying me and being overprotective of me, then he doesn't love me. Aaron thinks that over the course of the next week, I'm going to teach my classes like normal. This isn't true, as all my classes have been cancelled for the following week.

As an experiment, I decided to substitute a high school class for a week. I know this is quite random, but I want to do this. Aaron will drop me off at the University, but actually, I'm going to end up catching a ride to a High School nearby and teach there. I will then call Aaron and tell him to pick me up at the school. If he freaks out and gets mad about this, then I'm going to question our relationship, and take it from there. But if Aaron sees no issue with this and values my independence, then I know he actually loves me.

The day to start the test was here. I woke up, and Aaron helped me get ready for the day like he generally does. We also continue our morning routine regularly. Little does he know, that what he thinks my day will consist of, won't Aaron drops me off at the University, and Aaron proceeds off to work. After a few minutes of Aaron dropping me off, I call up a driver to give me a ride to the High School. I arrive at the school and I start to teach. Even though it's only for a week, and it's only being a substitute teacher, it's interesting going back to teaching High School. I see all the students in the class, and I start to introduce myself.

"Hello, my name is Mr. Pankowski. I'm going to be your substitute science teacher for the week. If you have any questions, just ask me. I'm a pretty nice guy."

I start teaching the class, and I totally forget I'm defying Aaron right now. He thinks I'm teaching courses at the University. When I'm actually about ten miles away at a High School, teaching High School seniors. Just like how I used to do in the past. The students also didn't seem to mind the fact I was in a wheelchair. They didn't make fun of me, or play any pranks on me. Maybe the times have changed form when I was teaching, and students don't act like that anymore? As I continue out through the day, I notice that in my last class, there is a student that I'm concerned about.

The student is a young Indian boy, and he seems to be quite introverted. He seems depressed and upset as well, and I know something is troubling him. It's not that he reminded me of Aaron, but it was an identical experience. I knew that he was possibly feeling troubled about his identity and could have been bullied at the school as well. The problem was, I was unsure if I should interact with him or not. One side of me didn't want to get involved with him, and I didn't want to play social worker. But that simply isn't how I'm structured. I wanted to speak with this student. After class is over, I wanted to speak to this student more, to see if there was anything that I could help him with. When the bell rings, several of the students start to exit out of the classroom, but this student remains at this desk. During this time, I go over and speak to him very calmly and softly.

"Is everything okay? Did you want to talk about it? You can tell me what's wrong. I'm just a substitute teacher and I won't be here long. I know something is up. What is it?"

The student then looks up at me, and starts to cry. I am puzzled as to what's upsetting him, but it must be something that is giving him much grief.

"Well, I'm gay, and I can't come out to my parents. They will get mad and disown me. Also the kids at the school bully me, and I don't want to come to school anymore."

Without even thinking twice about it, I reach over to the student and give him a hug. That's all he needed, was someone to tell him that things are going to be okay. I can understand completely how he is feeling, and how isolated and alone it must be to have nobody relate to you. I continue to hug the student, and also continue my conversation with him.

"I understand. It's okay. I know exactly what you're going through. It's okay to feel sad about it. Can I ask what your name is?"

The student then starts to feel safe around me, and tells me what his name is.

"My name is Benjamin, but I also go by Benji. You can call me Benji."

I smile back at Benji, and try to calm him down more.

"Okay Benji, I won't judge you. I'm only here for a week, so I'm going to give you my number, and you can talk to me anytime. My name is Steven. I won't tell your parents about you being gay. Whatever you say with me is going to be secret and safe. Okay?"

Benji continues to smile at me, and I'm happy I saved this student from the sadness he was feeling. I was losing track of time, and noticed that I didn't tell Aaron where I was. I wasn't planning on having a conversation with Benji which lasted as long as it did. I forgot to text Aaron to let him know I'm at the High School. I continue to stay with Benji, as I take out my phone to let Aaron know I'm at the school. Aaron doesn't respond to the text, so I fear that he's most likely disappointed and angry that I'm not where I'm supposed to be.

Twenty minutes later, as I'm still conversing with Benji, Aaron then walks into the classroom. Aaron doesn't immediately walk into the classroom, but he instead politely eavesdrops on our conversation from behind the door. When Aaron does finally walk into the room, he isn't angry or upset, and is actually happy. I then turn to Benji, and start to introduce Aaron to him.

"Benji, this is my partner Aaron. The both of us are like you, so it's okay. I hope this motivates you. Life is going to get better, and you can talk to us anytime."

Aaron then starts to become friendly with Benji, and I couldn't be happier to experience this scene. I opened up with a student that went through the same issues, that Aaron and I go through. Having to be bullied for being gay, no student should have to go through that. We give Benji our information, so that if he ever feels down, he can talk to us, and we would be happy to help him. We actually ended up forming a great bond with Benji as time went on in the future. The relationship Benji had with his parents wasn't easy, but Aaron and I helped him out, and let him sleep over at our house from time to time. I can say that we helped Benji get enrolled in University, and he's doing fine. He knows that we would help him with anything he needs.

As we remain in the classroom, I offer Benji a ride home, which he accepts. We end up dropping Benji off at home, and say goodbye to him. As Aaron and I are heading home, Aaron doesn't bring up the fact that I went out on my own again. He doesn't argue with me or fight with me about it. Aaron passed the test, and he allowed me to be independent. I explained my experiment and test with Aaron, and he took it quite well.

Aaron then for the first time began to understand that I do want to be on my own sometimes. I deserve to be independent, and not rely on him always. It's not that I'll never need Aaron in my life. I will, as there are some things I will not be able to do on my own. But for the things I am able to do on my own, like go shopping, or if I want to do something else without him, I should be able to.

I knew that I was ready for Aaron's sister's wedding. Aaron passed the test, and proved to me that our communication and our interactions with each other is strong. Getting ready for the wedding was stressful, as this is a wedding for Christ sake. I don't want to show up looking any type of fucking way. I have to look proper, as this is a special day for his sister. Aaron helped me get my tuxedo for the wedding on, and I was all set. I didn't feel embarrassed to be seen in the wheelchair at the wedding, but I knew being there in a wheelchair would be slightly overwhelming for me. The drive to the wedding was quite long, as the venue was pretty much in a remote location in California. I mean it was nice, it was just far. That was my only complaint about it. It was an outdoor wedding, and the weather was nice and sunny. Aaron and I arrive at the wedding rather early, which is fine.

The only thing that made me feel uncomfortable, is that Aaron inadvertently left me on my own as soon as we got to the wedding. I'm in a wheelchair, so it's not like I can walk around to find him. I remain in my wheelchair at the wedding venue in the hot sun, unable to move. I notice that there is a Hors d'oeuvre table across on the other side of the area. I'm feeling very hungry, but I can't walk over to that table. I would have to roll my wheelchair through the aisle, and hope I don't bump into anything. I sit for several moments on my own, unsure of what to do. I then realize that it's silly for me to sit and starve myself, so I begin to push myself over to the refreshment table. While I'm doing this, Aaron approaches me at this time, and starts to push me over to the table.

"I'm so sorry Steven. I should have asked if you wanted a drink or something."

Ugh. Yes Aaron, you are sorry. I don't know why he left me there by myself and walked away for nearly an eternity, not asking if I wanted anything. I then end up getting a snack to eat, and Aaron pushes me back to the seating area again. Without warning or alerting me first, Aaron once again walks away from me, and leaves me by myself. This time I'm angry at him. The first time he did it I was mad, but it's okay. He wasn't focusing, and left me alone. This time, there is no excuse and I'm starting to feel fed up. A half an hour later, Aaron returns to where I'm sitting, and I don't hesitate to express my frustrations with him.

"Aaron, don't leave me again like that. I don't know anybody here, and this is a wedding. I can't be roaming around in my chair. From this point forward, whenever you get up, you take me with you. Do you understand me?"

Aaron takes off his sunglasses, and starts to yell back at me quietly to not make a scene.

"I don't get it Steven. You ask me to give you freedom and independence, I do. Then when I leave you on your own, you get in my face about it. I don't fucking get it."

I don't respond to Aaron, and I keep my vision forward. This was not the time to have an argument with him. I'm here to see his sister get married. This is a lovely wedding venue, and I bet a lot of money was used to make this event happen. I didn't want to spoil the mood at all, so I took what Aaron said, not agreeing with it. Yes I wanted my independence, but there are times to where I need Aaron's or someone else's help. In this particular event for example, because I don't know any of the other people involved, and due to how formal and polite a wedding is, I didn't want to be somewhere I'm not supposed to be, or disturb anybody while I'm going through everyone in my chair.

The last thing I wanted to do was embarrass Aaron's sister and make an incorrect impression. I wanted Aaron to just understand this. The wedding finally started. His sister was marrying a very tall bald Caucasian man Winston. Once the ceremony was finished, Aaron yet again left me alone in the seating area. This was the third time he has done it, and I've had enough. I end up wheeling myself over to a secluded area of the venue, as I wait for the reception to the start. I didn't see any trace of Aaron and wanted to see how long it would be before he noticed I was sitting by myself away from everyone. Some of Aaron's family members would walk over to me, wanting to know why that strange goofy bald guy is sitting by himself in a wheelchair.

I would be cordial with them, and introduce myself. Explaining that I am a close friend of Aaron's. Nearly an hour passes, and I still see no sign of Aaron. Ironically, I was thinking of maybe having my own wedding soon with a certain someone I don't want to name. Ha-Ha. But after this, and the way he's treating me, I'm beginning to have several second thoughts of that.

I finally see Aaron approach the common area of the wedding where the rest of the guests are. I scream out his name, and he is shocked to see me sitting by myself.

"Oh my god. Steven. I'm so sorry. I had to go with my sister. She wanted me to be with her, while she and her husband were taking pictures. Please forgive me Steven."

I did forgive Aaron, but I wasn't going to forget the way he just left me there for that long. I didn't like the way he was treating me, and I was losing my patience with Aaron. During the reception, the food was extremely nice. Much planning went into this wedding; even down to the meals that were served during the reception were nice. I sit and eat with Aaron outside, looking at the evening sky. The wedding venue is located in the mountains, so it's a nice view. As I'm eating, I can't stop thinking about how hectic my experience at this wedding was.

I wish that Aaron made a greater effort to make me feel comfortable at the wedding, instead of treating me the way that he did. I am unable to walk, and I feel cramped sometimes when I'm in situations out of my comfort zone. I have so many thoughts concerning Aaron, and I keep them to myself at this time. He's having a moment with his family, and I need to keep my own personal issues with Aaron out of it. There will be a time and a place to where I can address them, and now is not the right time.

We continue eating, and again, the food was very nice. Soon after, we start to eat some of the wedding cake, which was also nice. However, for the first time in the night, I really begin to feel bitter about being the chair. When several people go to the dance floor, I can't help but feel jealous. I can't dance with them, I can't even walk, let alone dance. The music is blasting and blaring loud, and all I can do is look. Aaron asks me if he can go and dance with some of his family members, and I let him. Unable to hold back the tears, I just start to cry.

Something as simple as dancing at a wedding, I cannot do. Soon after, Aaron notices that I'm sitting by myself at the table sad. He quickly understands my sadness, and realizes that it's because I can't go on the dance floor with everyone else. He along with a couple of Aaron's female friends, asks if I want to go and smoke a cigarette with them. I agree.

As we are in a back secluded area smoking cigarettes. I then cry out to Aaron.

"I'm sorry. I just can't look at them have fun like that. It's okay. I'm happy that they are enjoying themselves. I can't experience any of that though. I had to remove myself. I'm sorry."

Aaron then walks over in front of me, and begins to hug me greatly. As Aaron is hugging me, I love the affection that he's giving me greatly. He later starts to kiss me. Our embrace is very nice and warm. I then immediately forget about not being able to dance with the rest of the wedding guests. I don't care about that anymore. I'm with Aaron, and I love him so much. Whenever I feel down, I know I can count on him to change whichever mood that I'm in.

The wedding wasn't bad at all. We got off to a rough start, but the night ended in on a very happy note. I continue to stay in this area with Aaron, accepting that I'm in this wheelchair. I'm going to be in this chair for the rest of my life. I can magically wish I can walk again, but the truth is, that I'm never going to. I need to accept that there are certain things I'm not going to be able to do again. Dancing is one of them. Aaron's female friends then begin to excuse themselves from the area, and I Aaron and I remain embracing each other. Aaron then whispers to me.

"Steven, just because you can't dance anymore, doesn't make you a bad person. Be thankful for the things that you can do. For example, be here with me."

Aaron was right, and I had to understand that yes there are things I most likely would have taken for granted before I lost the use of my legs, but I have to move forward from that. My life still remains, and I do need to appreciate even the little things that I can do. I love Aaron, and I never would think I would be strong enough to go to a wedding with him. I managed to accomplish that, so this was something to be proud of by itself.

I stay with Aaron for nearly an hour, kissing and hugging him. Even though we have separated ourselves from the rest of the wedding guests, we enjoy each other's company very greatly. I now start to wonder about the future of the relationship I have with Aaron.

Wondering to myself, if me and Aaron would have an identical experience such as this. What if me and Aaron were to get married? I haven't even proposed to Aaron yet, and I'm already thinking about marrying him. There is no doubt in my mind that I want Aaron to be the one that I spend my life with. Getting married would be the ultimate sign that Aaron and I are meant for each other, and we should be together. Now is not the right time to propose to Aaron. This is his sister's moment, so I will respect that.

Aaron doesn't even suspect that I even want to propose or get married to him, so this will most likely come as a surprise to him. I suspect that he's going to take me proposing to him rather well, but I cannot be so sure of myself. He has every right to say no, and he may say no. I don't think he will, but it's possible that he might. The both of us leave this area, and had back to the general area of the wedding reception. Once the event is over, Aaron starts to say goodbye to some of his family members, and we ourselves begin to leave out of the wedding. During the ride home, I couldn't keep track of my thoughts.

I had learned a lot during the day, and the relationship I had with Aaron took a new turn. I know Aaron and I struggle with communication, but I was willing to never mind the times we fight. Being involved with the wedding, I was positive that there wasn't anyone else in the world I wanted to be with, but Aaron. I wanted him to be my other half, and I couldn't picture anything else but that.

About a week or so later, I remember it was a Friday evening during the spring. It was raining cats and dogs, all day. I have never seen it rain this bad in Los Angeles. It's not even supposed to rain that bad here, but on this particular day, it was terribly storming. I woke up this particular day, feeling uncomfortable. I knew I had classes to teach, but I didn't want to get up at all. I was simply too tired and weak. I was definitely having one of those off days. I said to myself that I was going to cancel classes and not show up, but I couldn't do my students like that. I had to use whatever strength I had to get up anyways. I remain in bed, running late, and Aaron starts to shout at me.

"Steven, you need to get up now. You're going to be late. Come on, we don't have any time to waste. Get up now, before I drag you out of bed."

Aaron was right, I had to get up to go to work. Whether I felt like going or not. I have an obligation to go to work, and teach my students. It was really difficult for me get up. I wanted to keep my head on the pillow and rest all day. I felt so comfortable staying in bed. Still lying down, I silently mumble out to Aaron, as he's walking to the closet to pick my clothes for the day out.

"Give me like ten more minutes please? I'm just so tired, I don't know why. I really don't want to get up. Can I have ten more minutes, then I promise I'll get up."

Aaron is not pleased, and props my clothes down on the other side of the bed. Aaron then starts to physically sit me up off the bed, grumbling at me in the process.

"No you cannot Steven. We are both running late, so please get up and work with me. If I end up missing work on the account of your bullshit, I'm going to lose it. Get the hell up.!"

I do not know how I managed to get through it, but Aaron got me ready for the day without any further problems. We luckily managed to make up time so we both wouldn't be late for work. When I arrived at the University, I was still so tired. I had no idea how I was going to teach my students on the account of how fatigued I was. I still left all my personal issues aside. As soon as class starts, I have a commitment to my students to be a good instructor. So even though I was very tired, and I was feeling very exhausted, and every part of my body was aching, I still taught my class. None of my students suspected anything, and it was like it was an ordinary day.

During lunch break, I did take a small nap, but I was also alert for my evening class as well. I had to leave whichever way I was feeling before class behind. I woke up not feeling myself today, but that didn't matter. I didn't know why I was so tired, but I was. At the end of my second class, I look out the window of my classroom, and could see that it's still storming. There is also thunder and lightning as well. This rainstorm is like no other it seems. As I start to pack my briefcase up to go home, I notice a small box in my briefcase that I forgot was there. Inside the box, was an engagement ring I wanted to give to Aaron. I bought the ring several weeks ago, waiting for the right time to propose. It just hasn't happened yet. I wanted to put the ring in a place I know Aaron wouldn't check or find it, so I chose my briefcase. Despite the heavy rain, I wait outside the University for Aaron to pick me up. I stand in an area outside the entrance of the building covered by a shelter, so I don't get wet from the rain. When I see Aaron arrive, he takes out an umbrella and puts it over me.

Aaron situates me in the car, and we start to drive home. However, something told me that if I didn't propose to Aaron now, the time to do it will never come. I told myself I would wait until we got home, and would propose to him, but I wanted to do it now. When Aaron reaches a stoplight, I calmly speak to him..

"Aaron, can you pull the car over. There is something I need to tell you."

Aaron seems aggravated at this, and fires back at me.

"Steven, it's pouring rain. Why do you want me to pull over? Whatever you have to tell me can wait until we get home? I'm not pulling the car over."

This was not the answer I wanted Aaron to give me. When the light turns green, I violently grab the steering wheel, and yell out at Aaron.

"I said pull this fucking car over now!"

Aaron then starts to pull the car over next to a warehouse industrial area, full of several docks near the Los Angeles Harbor. Aaron is very upset with me. I then ask Aaron to take me outside, and put me in my chair. He is confused at this at first, but ends up complying with my demand.

"Steven it's pouring rain outside, what the fuck is wrong with you?"

Aaron then gets out of the car, and moves over to the passenger side of the car. He opens the door, and begins to put me in my chair. The rain continues to pour, and me and Aaron are soaking wet due to the rain. After I'm situated in my chair, Aaron then screams out to me.

"So if you catch cold Steven, don't come crying to me. I don't know the hell is wrong with you. What is this about? You know what Steven, I can't with you. Goodbye."

Aaron then starts to run away from me, and leaves me by myself in the rain. Aaron then sits over by the dock area with his head down upset. I remain several feet away from him, with the rain pouring down on me. I then begin to push myself over to the area Aaron is in. I take the small box out of my pocket, and grasp it into my hands. Aaron is still looking down at the ground, sitting on the dock, looking confused. As I creep closer to him, Aaron looks at me.

"Steven, what the fuck are you doing? We are out here in the rain. I don't know what the purpose of this is. You're starting to scare me. What is going on?"

I then immediately begin to plop myself out of my chair. I am lying face down on the ground in the rain, completely soaked. My glasses end up flying off my face. I then begin to laugh to myself. Aaron gets up shocked and confused, and before I allow him to help me up. I then start to open the small box that was in my hand. I take the ring out of the box, lifting it up so Aaron can see it..

"Aaron, will you marry me?"

Aaron then puts his hands over his mouth, and begins to laugh.

"Yes Steven Pankowski. I will marry you."

Aaron then falls down on the grown with me, and kisses me directly on the lips. We both wrestle in the ground, completely soaked in rain. I was so happy that Aaron accepted my proposal. This was the beginning of the rest of my life with Aaron. This isn't exactly how I planned our proposal to go, but it was still lovely. We didn't care that we were all wet and grungy from being in the rain. Aaron notices that my glasses are on the ground, and the lenses are badly cracked. He shows me my glasses, and we both laugh once we see how damaged they are. I didn't give a fuck about my glasses. I can go get them repaired at the eye doctor tomorrow. I had the man I loved dearly in my life, and I know that Aaron felt secure with me. I may not be able to walk, but I'm still a man, and I'm still a human. The both of us remain on the floor, while it's raining very heavily on the both of us. We don't want to do anything else but remain close to each other. I am now engaged to Aaron, and he's mine, and I know that I'm his. We don't want to be bothered. We want to remain close. However, because we both didn't want to catch pneumonia, we unfortunately had to get out of the rain. About five minutes later, Aaron helps me get back into my chair, and we get into the car and go home.

As far as wedding plans, if you imagined a big fancy wedding, and this big extravagant thing. Too bad, as that's not what he had. Aaron and I got married actually quite privately. We went down to the courthouse and got our marriage license. Aaron is now my husband, and it's legally binding. We didn't have to have a big fancy wedding, if that wasn't something that either of us wanted to do. But we still wanted to celebrate our marriage. Even though we didn't have anything major or big, we still wanted to celebrate.

Aaron and I invited everyone close to us, and we had a barbecue at the park, and we had such a great time. Aarons family was very supportive of the two of us getting married. No it wasn't anything too extravagant, but it was our little celebration, and it was something that was comfortable for us. Now that Aaron and I are married, we knew that were here for each other, and we were complete. We may not always agree all the time, and we still fight from time to time. Our love keeps us together through that. There was one more noteworthy event that happened between Aaron and I that want to explain.

It actually happened very recently, and although it was a violating experience, I still want to discuss it. What's funny is the event totally changed the way the night was going beforehand. What turned out to be an exciting and fun night, turned out to be a terrifying and traumatic event. Let me explain it to you vividly. It was during the week, and it was like any normal evening at first. I was getting picked up by Aaron from teaching, and we were going to go home like we usually do. However this evening was different, as Aaron wanted to take me out to eat. It was going to be something he wanted to surprise me with.

Aaron decided to treat me out to a special dinner at a very nice Chinese restaurant. The night was going so well. The restaurant was lovely, and the food was good. It felt so nice that I was having a night alone with Aaron, and it was a romantic evening. Until everything changed directly after that. As we were leaving out of the restaurant on our way home, we were heading directly to our car which was parked a mile away from where the restaurant was located at. Aaron was pushing me. We were about halfway to our car, when he hear a voice yell out to us.

"Give me your wallets, and your phones. I'll be on my way. Just do it!"

Aaron and I were getting robbed, and it was extremely horrific. I couldn't believe that someone was sick enough to rob a guy that's in a wheelchair. Aaron immediately gives the robber his wallet and his phone. The robber was wielding a gun and pointing it at us. The robber then walks right in front of me, and points the gun at me, shouting.

"I don't care that you're in wheelchair. Give me your wallet and your phone now!"

I start to get my wallet out of my back pocket, but I stop. Even though in actuality this was only a few seconds, in my head it was more like several minutes. I couldn't believe that I was going to let this robber steal from us and take property that wasn't his. I had no respect for this man, that he would stoop so low and rob a guy in a wheelchair. Like my life is already wrecked, so why do you have to add unnecessary shit such as this to it. I look at the robber, and see that he's a medium height Caucasian man with a five o clock shadow. He was wearing a hoodie covering his head, but I could tell his hair was buzzed. I refuse to give him my wallet, and I instead look him dead in the eyes for several seconds. He points his gun at me and shouts.

"Give me your wallet and your phone, or I will shoot the both of you!"

I continue to stare at the robber for several more seconds, then whisper out to him.

"I feel so sorry for you. Your life is that bad you have to rob from a guy in a wheelchair? Pathetic. If you had any real guts, you would leave us alone. You don't want to fuck with a guy like me. This is your final warning. So, make your choice."

I then grab a large swiss army knife from my back pocket, making sure the robber sees it. I had the knife for my own protection. In normal circumstances, I would suggest in hindsight if you were to get robbed, you just do what the robber said, and not instigate things further. But the fact I was in a wheelchair, I felt extreme hurt. The robber strangely immediately drops Aaron's wallet and phone down on the ground, and starts to run. Aaron who is terrified, starts to hug me tightly. He then smacks me on the head very hard. He returns to hugging me, and starts to cry out in fear to me.

"Steven, you are so crazy. Why the hell did you that? You could have gotten us killed."

I then kiss Aaron on the lips, as he's hugging me. I then whisper back to him.

"Yeah I could have. I'm sorry. I shouldn't have done that. That guy was a fucking jerk for trying to rob a guy in a wheelchair though. Let's go home."

Aaron then pushes me to our car. Our night of happiness, turned completely the other way due to the event. I knew that Aaron wasn't proud of me for acting violent, just how like the robber was. I knew that he may as well could have shot the both of us. I would never do that again, being that the guy had a gun. I felt guilty that I perhaps made the wrong choice, but I refused to be taken advantage of because I'm in wheelchair. That guy picked us because we were easy targets. The things the robber wanted could be replaced. Your life cannot be. I wanted to however prove a point not only to Aaron, but to myself, that I wasn't going to be taken advantage of. No more. I am in a wheelchair, but I am not to be fooled, and I'm not to be played with. Before we made it home, Aaron and I went to the police station to make a report. Although everything still was fuzzy, and we are in shock from a guy trying to mug us, we tried out best to give an accurate description to the police.

I still deal with problems related to being paralyzed from the waist down. This is how my life is going to be, and it's okay. I have Aaron, and it allows me to continue on with my life, with the wheelchair only being a slight issue. I can no longer walk, and I just adapt my life to make up for that. My love for Aaron is very strong, and this man is going to help me for the rest of my life. My story is coming to a close. This wasn't easy to explain during certain moments, but it's my story. I live my life confined to a wheelchair, and that's how it's going to be. Every day I wake up missing when I was able to walk, and being like everyone else. But that doesn't help or solve anything. I have to accept myself, and be proud of myself.

The Steven Pankwoski that used to walk around on his legs, and wasn't paralyzed doesn't exist anymore. The Steven Pankowski that exists now, is the one that's in the present. I am handicapped, but I am just like everyone else. I have Aaron, and I have my life. It's my destiny, and it's my journey. My name is Steven Pankowski, I am man of red, and that was my story.

CHAPTER 12:

MAN OF BROWN (PART 1)

My name is Jerald Williams. I am 28 years old. I am man of brown, and this I my story. My Reddit name is "JayJazzy". I am a gay African American man. As far as my appearance, I'm a short guy, and I didn't always appreciate being short, but that's the way it was I guess. My role model growing up was Rupaul, and I sort of modeled myself after him. I always carried myself in a fancy way, and my personality was very musical as well. Being black, I knew that my blackness was going to be a factor in my life, but it didn't define me all that much. Black was more of an outside appearance. Looks can be deceiving, and that wasn't my whole personality. Black people are generalized quite often, and this bothers me sometimes. I can't tell you how long it took me to be happy admitting that. For most of my life, I hated being black and gay, and thought of it as the ultimate curse that you can have. It wasn't something that I was particularly proud to life as. I felt strange and weird because of that, and my identity had to suffer because of that. I was unsure of where to locate myself, and so my social interactions struggled.

I was born and raised in Los Angeles, California and I was actually born in south Los Angeles. There were rough and tough times, but it was where I was raised. It wasn't a place for a feminine black boy in my opinion. I was trying my best to be urban enough, but I wasn't. A lot of the black boys around my age growing up were interested in basketball or other athletic things and masculine things. Well, not me. As I can remember when I was young, I wanted to be a fashion designer. I really liked dressy things, and I loved accessories as well. I told myself that when I got older that I was going to become a fashion designer. I knew that was my ultimate calling, and I didn't have an issue with that.

The main issue was, that I knew being a black boy living in inner city Los Angeles, I had a long way to go to achieve that dream. It wasn't impossible no, but I still had a long way to go if I wanted to make this dream a reality. There were a lot of bad influences around me as well. The gang and violence culture was a challenge at times for me to ignore. In the particular neighborhood I grew up in, there were some strange and difficult times. I had to witness a lot of things I don't want to talk about, but that was street life I suppose. My main agenda was that when I got older, was I didn't want to adapt to this hood mentality.

That wasn't who I was, and that wasn't what my goal in life was. I wanted to escape all of that. In order to avoid that, I had to involve myself completely in my studies, and not be distracted by the ignorance. I knew by falling for all of that, it would be quitting and giving in. Being a young boy, I know it can be harsh to think that things could change, but they can. Luckily for me they did, but I had to jump through many hoops at first for life to change for me. I try not to let excuses get to me, and I don't like to play the blame game, but I grew up without a solid family unit. I didn't have the nuclear family that everyone else had; growing up with two parents, and having a bunch of siblings to look up to or be around. I barely had extended family members that you would go and visit during holidays, and cousins to play with as well. I didn't have any of that.

I didn't even have a home at on time. Yes, I was a homeless child, and it saddens me to mention this, but it's true. I'll get back to that later, but right now let's take it from the very start. I'm particular and specific like that, so I'll begin there. I spent the early years of my life with my mother, and she raised me by herself. Never knew who my father was, or who anybody in my father's side of the family were. I don't even know his name. Hell, I don't even really know what the man looked like. Well, that's not completely true. The only memory I have of him, is I had to have maybe been two years old. My mother had already separated from him at this point, but this was at a family function, or some shit like that. I just remember him being very tall, and he had long hair. He was wearing a beige suit, had a fedora hat on, and was wearing sunglasses indoors.

My father was also a musician, and he could play the hell out of a guitar. So now that I'm starting to remember more about him, he was like Jimi Hendrix in a sense I guess. To be honest, he looked like pimp almost. I know this is a strange memory to have of him, but it's the only memory I have. Oh how I hated not having a relationship with my father. Being a boy especially, not having that father and son bond. Oh well, sour grapes. My father chose not to involve himself in my life, so that's the way it was I guess. So me doing wishful thinking doesn't help. Memories of playing catch with him, or him teaching me how to fish. Whatever. But my mother Juanita was my pride and joy. She was such a beautiful woman and I miss her so much.

I don't really know how my mother and my father met, and I really don't care. It's not really any of my business either way. However, my mother gave birth to me when she was only sixteen. So being a teenage mother, I know caused a lot of stress for her. She was only young herself, and already having to raise a child. My mother was a very special woman, and she reminded me of Chaka Khan quite a bit. She had nice hair, and her face was so beautiful. I know that most of my resilience, came from my mother. The way she dressed was also elaborate. The outfits that she would wear would always be over the top and beautiful. My mother became a great inspiration for me to go on to study fashion, because of how she carried herself. The only thing which hindered her, was that my mother had a tendency to surround herself with the wrong type of crowd.

I think had she not done that, she would still be here, and things would have turned out differently for her. Her passion was music, and being a vocalist. She enjoyed singing quite a bit, and wanted to be at the level to where she was like Aretha Franklin or Whitney Houston. I think she had the possibility to do this, but she surrounded herself with the wrong type of people, and that's probably why she couldn't obtain that. My mother worked as a cocktail waitress, and she would also perform as a singer as well. She was usually always gone, as the jobs she worked, happened during the night. I would get to see her when I came home from school, but she would have to leave off to the nightclub immediately after that.

I would be home by myself during this time. The times I did get to see my mother, I tried to cherish the time as much as I could, because I knew I wouldn't see her until a long time after that. Because my mother didn't have a solid job, sometimes we would go without food. She told me herself that if she had a good night, and people were tipping her well, we would eat. If it was a rough night and she didn't receive any tips, we wouldn't eat. She didn't say this to be mean or cruel, but that's how it was. My mother also refused to go on welfare or county aid, so it's not like we had food stamps, or WIC or any of that shit. Nope. Going without food was kind of the least of my worries. The most scary part was that the electricity in our house would cut off, and we would have to live in the dark. That was harsh to deal with really.

I would come home from school, do my homework, and because we couldn't afford the light bill, I would just sit in a dark house. I got used to this, but it still wasn't a pleasant experience. I didn't have a Nintendo, or a game boy, or any brothers or cousins to play with either. So what did I do to entertain myself? Simple, I learned to knit, I learned to crochet, and I learned to sew in that order really. I knew I was weird and strange being a gay black boy back then, because I just naturally took up those hobbies. I was at the library afterschool one day, and I came across this book titled, "How to Knit".

I don't know what possessed me to start reading that book, but I did. After reading the book, I went to the dollar store and purchased yarn and knitting needles. I then began to knit, and I became skilled at it very fast, Other boys around my age were playing basketball and doing stuff like that. Well I sat at home and knitted. I would knit hats, then I would knit sweaters, and then I would knit blankets.

Everything that I had made, I would show to my mother, and she would be proud of me. She didn't find it strange or unusual, but I don't know, I guess she couldn't understand why I took that up. Not that I got tired of knitting, it's just I wanted to do something else. I went back to the library, and I checked out a book titled, "How to crochet." It's sort of similar to knitting, but not quite the same. I actually found crocheting to be easier than knitting.

With crochet, I would mostly make afghan quilts. Like I said it was very close to knitting, but the approach was different. It would take me a month or so to make a five foot long quilt. After I was done making the quilt, I would donate them to the homeless shelters or children's hospitals, and I would just start a new one. By the time I was twelve years old, I have now taken up sewing. The way I got into sewing was quite interesting. My home economics teacher Ms. Carol Higgins, asked if there was anyone in the class that was interested in sewing. I raised my hand, as I had seen sewing machines before, and I knew what sewing was, but at the time I actually did not know how to sew.

During class, Ms. Higgins said that I could practice on the sewing machine. So every home economics class, I would teach myself how to sew. I would start very basic, and just sewing meaningless fabrics and things like that. However after a couple weeks, I naturally became good at sewing, and it wasn't an issue for me anymore. Home economics was the class I had for final period. At the end of class one day, I had sewn a pillow, and Ms. Higgins was very pleased with me. She then approached me, and began to speak with me.

"Jerald, I have never had a student be prolific with a sewing machine such as you. You were so quick to learn too. Do you have a sewing machine at home?"

I respond very truthfully and honestly with Ms. Higgins.

"Oh no ma'am, I do not. I don't have any toys at home, or video games, so I learned how to do tactile and dexterity things. I can also knit and crochet. So I wanted to learn how to sew."

Ms. Higgins then starts to unplug the sewing machine that's in the class. She approaches me and hands me the sewing machine. I am confused. Ms. Higgins then responds to me.

"Jerald, you can take this sewing machine home. You can keep it, it's yours. The only thing is, I want you to present me with a project you made on that machine every month. You are a very creative young man, and I feel you deserve this."

I couldn't be more thankful. I finally had my own sewing machine. I could now sew at home, and the amount of projects I could do were endless. I was very thankful for Ms. Higgins presenting me with my own sewing machine. I end up thanking her for the gift.

"Oh yes, thank you so much. I will show you everything I make on it. I promise. Thank you again, you have no idea how much I appreciate this."

I truly was happy that Ms. Higgins gave me the machine. Once obtaining the machine, I would then start to design clothes. It was a natural gift I had, and I couldn't be stopped. I didn't want to be stopped either. This was something I was really passionate about, and I wasn't going to be disturbed. The only issue was that I could only operate the machine if we had electricity. Which there would be some months where we didn't have power in the house. In this case, I would take my sewing machine to the youth center and do my projects there.

The kids would then tease me for being weird. Here I was a young gay black boy sewing. The kids would take my fabric that I bought with my own money, and rip my fabric. Some of the kids would also fuck with my sewing machine on purpose just to torment me. Mind you I was twelve years old, and having to deal with this. Here I was trying to do something constructive and productive with my life, and these kids had nothing better to do than to bother me. Most of it probably was due to jealousy, or simply because I was different.

I wish that they weren't cruel about it, but they were. You would think they would be happy that I was doing something artistic, but they weren't. It was strange for them, and that was their way of handling it. Things got really bad one day, when some of the kids decided to break my sewing machine. I was working on kinda of a retro patterned dress that I was going to gift to my mother. When one of the kids shouted to me.

"Hey faggot, why are you using a sewing machine? Why are you acting so weird? Why can't you be like us? Fuck your stupid ass sewing machine."

They said something along these lines, and I was trying to ignore them the best way I could. If I could sew at home I would. But we didn't have electricity at home, and the youth center was the only place I could have power to use my machine. The staff at the youth center didn't give a damn. I think they even condoned this. The youth center was mostly for kids to play sports, and to kick around after school. Some of the kids even would deal drugs and do other ignorant stuff they weren't supposed to do. I was just trying to do what I was compassionate about, which was to sew projects on the machine.

This angered my peers for some reason, and the thought of me being happy doing my own thing, upset them. It had to have been over jealousy, and I'm glad they were jealous of me. I would be jealous of myself as well. Ha-Ha. Anyways, the kids continued to torment me, and I then began to fight back with them.

"Why don't you guys mind your own damn business? I'm not bothering y'all. Why don't you guys go do something else, instead of trying to bother and disrupt me? Knock it off."

I shouldn't have done that, because now it became a battle and a war. We would swing back and forth insults, and it was terrible. It became violent and I had to protect myself. The boys started to punch me, and I was trying to hit them back. While I was in the middle of tussling with the other boys, another boy unplugged my sewing machine and lifted it up in the air. The boy then started to scream out.

"I'm going break this damn machine. We don't want you here anymore. This is our club, and this isn't a place for you to be on your faggoty sewing machine."

Ms. Higgins gifted me that sewing machine, and if they were to break it, I would be so devastated. I also spent a lot of time using that machine, and so it was very sentimental. I couldn't allow them to do that, and I didn't know what to do, or how to act. I knew I couldn't' afford another machine, so I would also have to give up sewing, until I saved up to buy another machine. I tried my best to beg them not to break the machine.

"My teacher gave me that, please don't break it! That machine is very special. I won't come back to the center if y'all don't want me here, but don't break that machine. Please."

This wasn't good enough, as the boy slammed the machine down on the ground, damaging it very badly. With the machine broken on the floor, one of the staff members of the youth center who was watching us fight the whole time, and did nothing to stop it, walks out. The boys that were messing with me then run out of the center. I just look at my machine totally wrecked on the ground. It's completely broken and I can't work on it anymore. I couldn't be more upset and angry, and I felt very depressed over it. The staff member at the youth center apologized for the other kids bullying me, and breaking my machine.

But as he didn't know the names of the kids who were pestering me, there was nothing that he could do. The youth center rules state that they are not responsible for lost, stolen, or broken property. So despite the fact the machine breaking at the center wasn't my fault at all, the youth center was not going to replace the machine for me, or pay for the damages. I didn't know how I was going to explain this to Ms. Higgins. She gifted that machine for me, and I knew she would be angry over this news. Sadly, things started to become even more devastating for me. That Monday I when I went to home economics class, I noticed we had a new teacher. Ms. Higgins was not there. Our new home economics teacher gave us some very upsetting news.

"I will be your new home economics teacher. Your last teacher Ms. Higgins sadly passed away from cancer over the weekend. It was something she kept secret, but she was dealing with that illness for a long time. I'm sorry to give you this news."

I was completely shocked. Not only did the machine that Ms. Higgins give me ended up getting destroyed by the kids at the youth center, but Ms. Higgins also passed away. I really liked her as a teacher, and it seems that one bad thing is happening after another. I didn't have a sewing machine, and a teacher I had a respect for, is gone. At this point, I was trying to see how I was going to get another sewing machine. I couldn't afford one, so I knew it was going to become difficult for me to get another one. So I had to make the decision to give up sewing. I couldn't come up with the money to buy another machine, so I had to quit sewing. In the process, I also stopped knitting and crocheting. I no longer had interest in these things, and I was allowing my own pity to get the better of me. I was choosing to do this to myself, and I didn't care anymore. My main goal was to get out of the inner city, and to not be involved with any of this ignorance. It seemed impossible for me to escape from this at the time.

Things continued to get worse, as my mother was fired from her job. She didn't how to deal with this, so she turned to abusing drugs. Then was the beginning of the end, once my mother was addicted to drugs. She would be away for several weeks, and I would never see her. Her attitude changed, and she was around a group of people she had no business being with. I started to fear for her safety, and there was nothing I could do to help her. I began to feel extremely worried, when we were given an eviction notice from the landlord.

The eviction notice came on my thirteenth birthday, and that was a good birthday present to receive. A paper saying that if we didn't pay the rent in two weeks, that we would be kicked out. I knew that we couldn't afford this rent, and we would be promptly thrown out in the street. My mother continued to stay away from the home, and her drug problems continued. When my mother came home found out about the notice, she was really deep into her drug abuse. This was the last time I ever saw my mother. I remember the last conversation we had.

"Jerald, I can't take care of you anymore. You're going to stay with your aunt and your cousins. I'm sorry, but I want you to have the best life, and I can't take care of you. I love you, and I know you're going to grow up and be wonderful. I love you Jerald."

My mother then told me pack all of my things. I didn't even know I had an aunt or cousins. The truth was, that I didn't. My "aunt", was actually one of my mother's friends. My "cousins", were actually different street children that my "aunt", took in and watched over. Going to my "aunt's" house was tough. I was around nineteen other kids. I am not exaggerating that at all. Yes there were nineteen other kids in this small house. We were all kids that were abandoned by our parents for several reasons. Whether they were dealing with drug problems, or they were in jail, or they simply didn't want us.

This was not a place that I wanted to be. The other children in the home did not like me one bit. I was different, and because I was gay and feminine, they thought they could attack me for no reason. I wasn't going to take their bullshit, so I was angry and rude to them as well. My "aunt" who acted as guardian for all of us, was never there. She would smoke and drink and hang out in the street, and all of us in the house were left unsupervised. I'm talking a house full of kids without an adult watching, is bad. The youngest kid in the house was about six, and the oldest one was seventeen. This didn't make any damn sense, and I had no business being in this environment.

Some of the kids in the house were also gang members, and they would deal drugs in the house. They would also stock guns and other stuff. I don't like to talk about this really, but it's true. By god's grace, I just ignored all of this. I would mostly do my homework and read. I wouldn't get involved. They would see how feminine I was, and I guess maybe that saved me from joining their clique. My mother also never stayed in contact with me. I just assumed she was doing okay. I never heard any news from her, and she said she would come and see me at the house from time to time, but she never did.

I wanted to get the hell out of this house. By the time I was fifteen, I had now lived in this house for two years. My mother still hasn't contacted me by this time, and I was very concerned. The "aunt" that runs the house just approached me one day, and in a very disrespectful way gave me news that I did not want to hear.

"Oh Jerald, your mother passed away last week. The police said she had a drug overdose. I don't know if they are having a funeral. I'm sorry."

I immediately began to cry, as my mother meant so much to me. The way I was told the news I didn't feel was good either. I replied back to my "aunt", still in shock at the news.

"My mother died? So what do I do now? My mother can't be dead. She is the only family I have. What am I supposed to do now?"

My "aunt" couldn't care less, and rudely responds back to me.

"I don't know, I was just walking through the streets, and they told me she died of an overdose, and that's all I know. I'm sorry, what do you want me to do?"

Directly following that, I ran out of the house. I didn't want to stay there anymore, and I couldn't grieve with my mother's death in that way. I knew I had to find out more information related to her death, but I didn't know how I was going to obtain this. I decide to walk to the county building, in an effort to get as much news as I could surrounding her death. As soon as I made it to the county building, I noticed how crowded it was. I also didn't know where I was supposed to go. After speaking with the appropriate people, I later found out my mother did in fact pass away of a drug overdose, and she actually passed away several days ago. I did not admit the fact I was her son, as I was scared they would put me in foster care, which was what I was scared of.

They informed me that my mother did actually have extended family, and that they were having a funeral service for her in two days. I'm so glad I went to the county building to find this information out, as had I didn't, I would have missed my mother's funeral. After getting the information that I wanted, my next plan was to get out of the house I was staying in. I didn't care if I had to live out in the street, I wanted to be anywhere but there. I got all of my things, and did just that. I started to sleep in an abandoned bus terminal in Los Angeles.

It wasn't an ideal place for home, but I made it comfortable. I didn't have to be bothered, and yes I was homeless on the street, but I would keep to myself. Days later, I attended my mother's funeral service. There were several people in attendance, but I didn't recognize any of them. I didn't want them to know I was her son, and to reunite with my extended family. They were never there for me before, so why would they be here for me now? So I kept this fact a secret. Once her funeral was over, I was happy that I got to see my mother buried, and I can move on with my life.

I didn't have a mother now, and I was on my own. I didn't have anyone to turn to for support. I would attend school, and return to the bus terminal, where I would try to make it my own home. I rarely ran into issues being homeless. I didn't have anyone come up to me and bother me. I stayed at the bus terminal for about a month. Yes it was scary sleeping outside and being homeless, but it was my only option at the time. But I couldn't live my life like this. I couldn't continue to sleep outside in the cold, and I had enough. This wasn't my plan in life, and I had to do something.

I thought about the times when I was younger, and was interested in being creative with my skills. I knew I was far too talented to throw my life away like this. I had much to be thankful and grateful for, and I need help. I didn't know how to get it, but I knew I needed help, and I needed someone to help me escape from this trap I'm under.

I decided to go speak with a social worker one day. I had enough of this, and I just needed someone to put their hand out and help me. I was only fifteen years old, and my life couldn't end up this way. Had I stayed in the streets, my life would not have been as successful as it is now. I would have maybe turned down to a path of no return. I had hobbies, and I had skills, and I had a dream that I wanted to make possible.

I met with the social worker, and my social worker Janet, became someone who helped reform my life. Janet was a young African American woman, and she had dreadlocks. I really liked the energy she had, and I knew she was going to be someone that was going to take me out of the slump I was in.

"Jerald, we know about your situation, and we are going to help you. There is a youth LGBT shelter that you can stay at, and they will offer you all the help you need."

I was so happy to hear this news. I was going to be saved finally. This was going to be my second chance at trying to live a productive life to myself. Growing up black and gay, and not having anyone there to support me. I was looking forward to moving to the shelter, and also meeting other kids that have gone through similar events that I have. Trying to see how each of our stories relate to one another, even though they are completely different. My mother was gone, and I didn't have my family members for support, but I knew that I could make a second family. I could change the whole definition of family.

A family isn't always a group of people that have raised you, and a mother and father situation. A family can consist of people that support you, and understand where you are coming from as a person. Getting the help I need from the LGBT shelter, I can finish school, and possibly continue to aim for my dream, which is to study fashion. The first day that I arrived at the LGBT shelter, I saw all types of young people there. Whether they were gay, or flamboyant or were simply disowned by their family for being themselves. I knew this was my home, and that this is where I belonged. At the shelter, I would have my own bed, and everyone at the shelter was fed. It was a comfortable place.

The head coordinator at the shelter, was an obese Caucasian man named Bruce. Bruce was in his late 20s, and he had long blonde hair, and dressed very colorful. He was an interesting character, but he was very friendly and nice. He was the owner of the shelter, and he was a gay man himself. The first interaction I had with Bruce I'll never forget, and he was very friendly.

"Hello Jerald, welcome to our shelter. You're going to have a great time here. If there is anything you need, let me know."

There was a request that I wanted, but was unsure if it was going to be noted. As I was trying to rebuild my life at this shelter, I figured I would return to my sewing. I was going to ask them if I could be given a sewing machine. I didn't have the money to get one myself, but it was at least worth asking. I then ask Bruce for a request.

"There is one thing. I am, well at least I was in the past, very passionate about sewing. I had a sewing machine, but some bullies broke it. I was wondering if I could have a sewing machine. It's mostly for educational purposes, and I want to design clothes for my career."

Bruce let me know that he cannot make me any promises as far as the sewing machine goes, but he will see what he can do. My request was rather strange, and also expensive. Sewing machines are not cheap, so I could understand why the shelter would be hesitant to admire my request. Although, they did say they would try their best to get me a sewing machine. In the meantime, I began to adapt myself to the shelter. I made friends with everyone that went to the shelter, and we shared our stories on being queer youth, and how we felt different form everyone else. The shelter would give us rides to school every day, and they would also pick us up from school.

At the shelter, we had a curfew of 10pm during the week, and we had a curfew of midnight during the weekend. I liked the amount of freedom we had. There would also be talent shows, and other activities the shelter would have. On certain occasions, the shelter would give us field trips. They would take us to amusement parks, or to arcades or to water parks and other stuff like that. So I was very happy to be in the shelter. The only thing, is that I really wish I had a sewing machine.

On my sixteenth birthday, and having been with the LGBT shelter for a year, I was given a very special gift. Bruce gave me the best birthday present, a brand new sewing machine. I was speechless upon given the gift, and was very thankful. Bruce speaks to me, as I was still stunned over receiving this gift.

"Jerald, I found out about your story, and it wasn't easy, but I managed to save enough to buy you a new state of the art sewing machine. Enjoy."

I give Bruce a hug, and thank him. I finally had a sewing machine, and not only that, this was an advanced sewing machine. Latest and greatest, and I was most happy about it. I knew I had to show my talents off with this machine. I was gifted the machine, so I had to take advantage of it. The shelter would give us an allowance each month.

Most of the other people would use their money for candy and stuff like that, but I would mostly use my money to buy fabric, thread, and anything else I needed so I could do my sewing. It has been a while since I last used a sewing machine, so I was basically doing everything over again. My talent was still there regardless, and I was creating projects at a higher level. After a month, I had my mojo back, and I knew being a designer was what I was meant to do. Being in the environment at the shelter, was also good. For the first time, I was surrounded by people that were appreciative of my hobby. If anyone else in the shelter wanted for me to design something for them, I would. I wouldn't even charge them for it. I just asked that they show off my creation and wear it. Being in this inclusive environment being LGBT, was wonderful. The sky was the limit relating to my sewing. Every project I would do, I would make the next one even better than that. I would start sketching my outfits together, and would piece something out that was even more extravagant than the project and piece I had worked on before.

As far as secondary education, I knew that I wanted to study fashion. My only setback, was that I knew it was a competitive industry to get involved in. Being a world famous fashion designer wasn't guaranteed. So few actually become successful. I would dream of having some of work featured at fashion week in New York. Having gorgeous models wear the dresses and outfits I created. Having Kim Kardashian wear an outfit that I designed and created. To think that a little gay boy that came from the rough and tough hood from LA, to now being a world famous designer. Having my own boutique was a dream of mine as well.

I could travel the world, and go to Paris, Milan, Barcelona, Dubai, Rome. I was getting ahead of myself, but for good reason. It's okay to think big, and I didn't see any reason why I couldn't have any of that. If I could dream it, I could do it. Due to my talent, I was confident in myself that I could become a well-known name in the world of fashion. I was up to the challenge, and I was willing to put in all the hard work needed to make it possible. I wanted to motivate others as well, that I came from the bottom with nothing.

I was living on the street and homeless. I had to deal with my mother's death, and being on my own without any support. The agenda I had for my designs were bigger than I had envisioned. I wanted to reach a larger audience with my work. I needed to put together a portfolio of my work, if I wanted to create an impact with my designs. I was no longer doing this as a hobby. I was doing this because I want to be the best fashion designer in the world. I had to step my game up.

I was approaching my senior year of High School, and was researching as much as I could on fashion schools, and opportunities for me. My best course of action was to get a scholarship for school. There was no way that I could afford to go to fashion school on my own. The costs were too high, and even if I qualified for financial aid, I wasn't sure if I would be accepted into the school. After speaking with several counselors at my school, I did happen to find one fashion design scholarship. The school would be at the "Fashion Institute of Los Angeles". It was nearby, and the school has a good success record. I wanted to go to this school very much, and was going to do all I could so I could attend.

The only thing, was that it was quite complex to get into. The scholarship would consist of me designing three specific outfits, that a well-known fashion designer would judge. I would have to create a casual dress, an evening gown, and nightwear. Due to how well I designed these pieces, would determine as to whether I would be accepted into the school or not. Another issue, is that I would need to have someone to sign as a reference for me to enter into the scholarship program. This is so the school knows the participant is serious about signing up. The only person that I knew would approve me going along with the scholarship program would be Bruce. I wasn't afraid of asking him to sign. I just didn't know if he thought I was ready for this. I approached Bruce with the scholarship application form. Bruce spoke to me very deeply about it.

"Are you sure you want to do this? Do you know how many other people are competing for a scholarship? I imagine hundreds. I'll sign if this is what you truly want to do."

What Bruce said was exactly right. I never thought of it that way, and I had to be more idealistic about it. There are many people that want to get into this school, due to how prestigious it is. I then thought that maybe I should forget about this, and go to a community college instead. Even though this school had more benefits, going to a city college was nice as well. I would also be very devastated if I wasn't picked for a scholarship. I didn't like rejection, and I didn't know how I would handle myself if I were rejected from getting the scholarship. I knew I was talented enough to attend the school, so I didn't see why they wouldn't pick me based on how well I sew. I was willing to take the risk anyways. If it didn't work out, I could always go onto another plan. I end up responding to Bruce, letting him know I am certain of entering the scholarship program.

"Yes I'm very sure. Ever since I was young I wanted to do fashion. I know they are going to pick me, I just know. I really want this, and I feel I'm ready for this."

Bruce ends up singing the application to the scholarship program, acting as a reference in my behalf. The next part of the scholarship requires the entrant to write an essay, explaining why they feel they should be picked for the program. Following that, they want to see some of your sketches, and pictures of past projects and pieces that you have worked on. Hundreds and hundreds of people will send in an application, but only forty or so will then go onto the talent portion of the scholarship, to where their pieces will be judged by a prolific designer. Of those forty, only three will be given a scholarship to the school. I would have to go through many steps to get my reward, but I knew I had to get it, and I was going to get it.

In my essay, I tried to explain all the troubles in my life. I basically reversed my entire life around. Being a gay black boy in a bad environment, and doing all I could to make things better for myself. I also explained the lack of motivation I had, and trying to prove people wrong. People were shocked to see I was a young black boy that was into sewing, and I had to strive to be different and go on my own direct path. I tried to explain to them that fashion is all I have. It's what rescued me from my own confusion, and gave me a new lease on life.

After I was finished with the essay portion, I put together several sketches I had of my work. I made sure I picked different types of outfits. So they can see that I just don't have one particular style. I can do something fancy, I can do vintage, I can do swimwear, I can do urban wear. Even though the scholarship was going to judge me on female outfits, I also presented them with sketches of male outfits and sketches. I have sewn together a couple suits as well, and I'm multi-faceted.

I mailed in my application, and all I can do is wait now. This was the longest wait I ever had to experience. Even though it was only a couple weeks, the wait seemed to be extremely longer than that. Every single day, I went to the mailbox with anticipation, hoping that I would hear something from the school. Wondering if I made it to the next stage or not, of if they would send me a rejection letter. During this time, I began to have second thoughts about the whole thing. The self-doubt also came with that as well. Maybe I wasn't good enough as I thought I was. Considering the amount of people who are trying to get the scholarship, maybe they were better than I was? Every single day that passed without receiving a letter from the school, I began to feel more and more scared that I wasn't going to advance to the next round.

But one day, I finally received a letter in the mail. It was from the fashion school, saying that I was one of the forty that was picked to go onto the next round. Upon reading this letter, I jumped up and down with excitement. I mean, I knew I was going to get picked, but I couldn't be sure until it was official in writing that I had made it. I didn't waste any time to start working on the designs they wanted me to do. In the letter informing me that I had made it to the following round, they gave specific instructions as to how each piece had to be designed. If I didn't follow the rules accordingly, that would result in me automatically being disqualified for the scholarship. The type of fabric and material they wanted me to use was also complex. It was hard for me to find some of the supplies, but I managed to do it in the end.

Quickly getting to work on my pieces, I underestimated myself on how difficult this would be. The instructions the school gave were very exact, and one mistake, or one stitch that wasn't applied property will lead to me not being considered for the school. I didn't want that to happen. As I made it this far in the game, being eliminated would break me completely down. The school also wanted you to have a female model wear the clothes that you make. One of the girls at the LGBT center named Lindsay, offered to be my model. Lindsay was a bisexual girl with blonde hair, and she was kinda of a rocker chick. So it took quite some convincing for her to model fancy clothes. But she knew this scholarship was a big deal, so she was being a good sport about it. Her family never accepted her sexuality, so she came to the shelter. I'm still close friends with Lindsay today. As I'm fitting Lindsay for the outfits she will wear when I'm judged, she speaks to me.

"You're going to get this scholarship Jerald, I know it. You're talented and you have nothing to worry about."

I appreciated the moral support that Lindsay was giving me. I'm going to need a lot of it, because I was starting to feel anxious about being judged. What if the judges don't like my designs? What if I didn't get my measurements right? Whatever I put out, was going to reflect on myself and my own talent. I couldn't put out something mediocre. Not at this level, I have to be very serious about this. With the help and cooperation of Lindsay, I manage to complete my first outfit fine. There was no way the judges weren't going to appreciate this.

This outfit, I could defiantly see a leading actress wear to the Academy Awards. It was that well put together. I had two outfits to go, so I quickly got prepared to make those. The good thing about using Lindsay as my model, was that she was very tall and thin. So this was perfect. Whatever idea I had, it worked out for me, due to her size. Going onto my following pieces, I kept my same routine. Making sure the product I gave, was something that was worthy of the scholarship that I was trying to seek. Once I finished my second and third pieces, I was so confident. I was certain that the judges were going to be shocked at my talent.

Myself, and several of the other participants that were trying to get the scholarship, met at a concert hall in Downtown Los Angeles. We would be judged publicly in front of the other participants. There were nine other designers here that were trying to get a scholarship. My nerves were acting up however, I had the support of Lindsay there to calm me down. We were all standing on the stage of the concert hall, waiting for the judging to begin. I was starting to wonder who the judge actually was going to be. We were told that the judge was a well-known designer, so I was curious as to who it actually was. Several minutes later, the secret special judge then revealed themselves. I couldn't believe who it was. The judge was Christian Siriano. He was famous for being on "Project Runway", and I loved his work so much. I would watch "Project Runway" quite a bit on television at the LGBT center, so he was a major role model for me. Christian then stands in front of all of us, and speaks.

"I want to wish all of you luck. I really wish we could give the scholarship to all of you, but we cannot. We only accept the best, so good luck to you all."

Christian and his assistant then in a random order then call each participant to come up and explain their piece that their model is wearing. I was just happy that I didn't go first, as I feel that's much pressure to be the first one to present your piece. As I'm looking at the other people on stage, there is only one other person I'm intimidated and scared by. The rest I wasn't that worried and concerned about. I knew my designs were what they were looking for, and I knew exactly where the other people messed up on.

I can really pay attention to detail and pattern and instructions, and in my head I already start to see the weak points in each piece that the others have made. But I knew all of my pieces were perfect. Maybe there was one small tiny centimeter of a mistake, but I knew everything I was going to present was perfect. It was then my turn to present my first outfit.

"Hello, my name is Jerald. This is my model Lindsay. As you see Lindsay is wearing a navy blue evening gown, with a satin trim.."

As I'm explaining my piece, I knew they loved it. Why would they not, it was simply the best, and there was nothing bad you could say about it. As Christian and his assistant continue to gaze at my piece, it was then I felt truly safe with myself. I was going to get this scholarship, and I had nothing to be fearful of. As the judging continued, we were now going to present our second outfit. As I saw Lindsay model my second piece, I notice about a half an inch hole under the side of the outfit. My heart shattered into a million pieces once I noticed this. I had to tell Lindsay there was a hole in the piece, so she wouldn't feel shocked about it.

"Lindsay, there is a small rip in the dress, but it's okay. We're just going to play it off like it's not there. Maybe they won't even notice it, because I barely did."

Lindsay understands the situation, and she is very respectful about it. I'm hoping that this doesn't become an issue with the judges and they do not mind the rip. As it's getting closer and closer to my turn for the judges to see the dress, I become more scared. I'm praying that rip isn't what costs me the scholarship. I don't know how that tear happened, but it was there. It's going to haunt me forever if that's the thing that ruins it for me. The judges then approach me, and I start to present my outfit to them.

"So I have a silver lace evening party dress. I decided to go with a silver, titanium look. I wanted a more regal and royal statement, yet it still says leisure and lounge.."

As I'm explaining my piece, and as they are judging the outfit, from the way Lindsay is standing, you can barely notice the tear. The judges then thank me for presenting the piece to them, and they walk away. I think I may have gotten away with it. If they did notice the tear, they didn't mention it. So it's possible they didn't even notice it. Soon after that, I presented my third and final piece, which was the nightwear portion. I check my outfit making sure there aren't any rips or tears, and everything is fine. Lindsay models my final piece, and the judges approach me, and I explain my final piece. They thank me, and walk away. After we have all presented our outfits, Christian speaks to us for the final time.

"Thank you all. Each of you are talented, and I really wish that we could give this scholarship to you all, but we just can't. But you should hear from us by next week. Good luck."

The judging was over, and I wait once again. Either they felt the same way about my pieces that I did, or they didn't. I feel if I were not to get the scholarship, it would be because of the rip in my second piece. As much as I was hoping to really get this scholarship, I had to also prepare myself in the event that I was not chosen. Although, I was confident that I had this, and there wasn't any chance at all that they would not accept me. I waited a week to hear the results as to whether I was accepted into the school. One afternoon I was at the LGBT shelter and I received a phone call from one of the administrators at the school. Another person at the shelter answered the phone, they alerted me that I had phone call. I pick up the phone and say hello. I then hear a female's voice on the other end.

"Hello, is this Jerald Williams?"

I respond back to them on the phone.

"Yes, this is Jerald speaking."

The woman on the other end of the phone, continues to speak.

"Hi Jerald, my name is Cindy, I'm calling form the LA Fashion Institute. As you know we received a lot of applicants this time, and unfortunately we can only pick a few people to give a scholarship to. But I'm pleased to say that congratulations, we ended up choosing you."

I immediately put the phone down, and danced across the room. I mean I knew I had this 100 percent, but once I heard that I was officially going to the school, I was ecstatic. I end up thanking Cindy over the phone.

"Thank you so much Cindy. This is wonderful news. I'm so thankful. Oh my god."

I hang up the phone, and I tell Lindsay the news. I am thankful that she was my model, and she helped me get the scholarship. I tell Bruce about the news as well, and of course he is proud of me. My life started over from here, and I was going to proceed onto my dreams. I was going to Fashion School, and I had a bright future. As I continue my story, several more events happen to me. Which includes me meeting my future boyfriend Carl, and the strange occurrence as to how we first met. Going into fashion school was just only a start of a wave of activities that would soon take charge of my life.

CHAPTER 13:

MAN OF BROWN (PART 2)

Now that I was accepted into the school, I looked forward to how my agenda on life was going to change. I was going for my career and my dreams, and I was very blessed. To think there was a time to where I was at total rock bottom, and there wasn't any light at the end of the tunnel. I can now reach for the stars with my dreams, and I'm glad. I was going to meet so many new people, and explore an array of options with my career. Yes, I was excited, and I had every reason to be. I didn't want to get too overconfident in my abilities, and I was thankful for the gift and for the talent that I had. Going to the LA Fashion Institute was merely the beginning of my journey. From the time I was accepted into the school, I was now eighteen years old, and trying to fit myself into adulthood. Growing up, I didn't have the most glamorous lifestyle, but that didn't matter. I can change now, and anything and everything that happened in the past, is in the past. It doesn't make any sense to walk backwards, you always walk forward. Before going to the fashion school, I had to graduate from High School, and I accomplished that just fine. So the next step was going onto the LA Fashion Institute.

My first day at the school was challenging. I didn't realize the courses at the school were going to be this difficult. It was a major wake up call. This was the school that I wanted to go to, so I got my wish. It wasn't called a prestigious school for nothing, and so if the courses are hard, that comes with the territory I suppose. Throughout my first year at the school, I was finally around people that shared my talent, and I have to say I was intimidated by a few people. I had to accept the fact that there are going to be people just as determined as myself.

I wasn't jealous no, but it was slightly intimidating to see people come up with designs that I would have never thought of. Thinking that my style and my vision was good enough; that wasn't completely true. The students at this school were putting their game faces on, and were taking their fashion career seriously. The study work that the instructors would give us were annoying at times. Some of it I was confused on, and I didn't know how I was going to complete these courses. Luckily, I managed to find other students to compare notes with, and it made the process much easier. The school didn't have on campus dorms, but if you were at student at the school, you automatically were able to get cheap housing nearby the school.

I had a studio apartment that was about a half an hour walk away from the school. I didn't have a car, so I would pretty much walk everywhere. I would take the subway or the bus if I wanted to go somewhere outside the area the school was in. But when I would go to class, I would just walk. Having my own place was very nice, as I did have to deal with roommates or any of the drama surrounding sharing a place with people. I could have my own privacy, and I could do what I want. My studio apartment wasn't that big, but I had enough space to do my designs, and I was able to sew without being disturbed by other people. I would have some trouble when I had to carry my designs from my apartment, and to the school; and vice versa. I found a system that worked for me though, so I got used to it. I did make friends at the school, but my primary purpose there was not to socialize.

My plan was to use the school as a tool to further my design career. Which is what I did. I rarely went out to any parties that the other students would throw, and I kept completely to myself usually. My first year at the school was the most pleasant. I feel they were throwing me a bone on my first year, and were going easy on me. The instructors didn't have any issues with my designs, and they liked them rather well. I believe this was mainly because I was new, and they wanted to test me

I guess. As I continued on in the school, this would not continue at all, and they would be extremely more critical on my designs, giving me honest harsh truths about them. It wasn't because I was a bad designer. I'm in a school with the best of the best realistically, and my portfolio and my performance needs to match that.

As the years went on with me being in design school, I was now approaching my final year, and was really trying to get an internship. With this internship, I could work for Hollywood productions, and do top profile fashions. The benefits would be great, the pay would be great, it looks good on my resume and my cover sheet, so I really wanted this. However, several thousand people were hoping to get this internship. Even though the company didn't say the exact number of people that were going to be hired as interns, I could imagine the number was low.

I didn't want to let that discourage me, and I really wanted to go for this internship. If I were to get the internship, immediately after graduating from school, I could move straight onto the internship company, and I can finally say that I'm a professional fashion designer. The application for the internship was rather strange, and some of the questions I was stumped on. They wanted to test your knowledge on patterns and fabrics, and they also wanted to test your knowledge on whether or not you could tell what piece of clothing or outfit is from a particular period in time.

The questions for example were like, "Is this fashion from the colonial times?" "Is it from the Victorian era?" I thought I studied well enough about this, but I guess not. Some of the answers I gave I wasn't completely sure of. I knew that if I wanted to have a snowball chance in hell of getting this internship, I had to know what all these questions were about. I went to the library, and started to study more about fashion. The courses at the school were more related to fashion skill and technique, and they didn't touch that much on the history of fashion.

I had to research all of this myself. Once I was confident from what I researched, I went back to the application and the questions seemed much easier to answer. I was still slightly confused over some of the questions, but I wasn't completely in the dark like I was previously. I completed the application and I mailed in it. The following step was that they were going to contact me for a phone interview. The phone interview didn't guarantee that I was getting the internship. From what I heard, it meant that you passed the application test, and they wanted to speak to you more.

A few weeks later I received a call, and it was from the fashion company that I was hoping to get an internship for. The woman on the other end of the phone spoke to me.

"Hello Jerald. I'm calling to inform you that we received your application. I must say that you are a very talented designer, and we enjoy your work. However, we decided not to give you an internship position. I'm so sorry, and we wish you the best of luck towards your career."

I was polite about the news, and I thanked the woman on the other end anyways. But as soon as I hung the phone up, I was completely devastated and depressed. I couldn't understand why they didn't offer me an internship. My designs were very nice, and I thought it was exactly what they were looking for. In a way, I was happy that I was rejected, as it gave me validity. Being humble about it was the only way to go. Sometimes, you don't always get what you want, and you don't always win either. I would have liked to have gotten that internship, but it simply wasn't meant to be. So now what do I do? I didn't have a second plan, as I assumed that it was going to be for certain that I was going to get the internship. I don't have any plans after I graduate. Once I leave the school, I would have to move out of the apartment they gave me. I was hoping for job placement once I graduated, but it doesn't seem like that is going to be possible.

I was glad that I attended the school, but my main ambition was for the school to lead me on to higher possibilities. At this point right now, I don't see it. My final year at the school was coming to a close, and there was a fashion show being held for all the graduates of the school to participate in. The fashion show was mostly for fun, and a tradition that most of the graduate students would do at the end of the year. However, the winner of the fashion show would be given an internship at a high end fashion company. Only one student was going to get the internship, and there were about fifty students that were graduating in the same class that I was. So I had a one in fifty chance of obtaining the internship.

This was my last chance of trying to get an internship from this school. If I didn't win this fashion show event, I would have graduated without placing a job. For this fashion show, you could only pick out one outfit to design. The theme of the show was simple. They wanted you to create a futuristic evening gown. I can do evening gowns quite well, and this was not going to be a problem, and was confident I was going to win. Although this wasn't up to me, this was up to the judges as to whether or not I was going to win the fashion show. We were each given a model at complete random for the show. The model I had, I wasn't happy with. I felt she was too short, and I would have liked a taller model to compliment my piece. I'm not attacking her for being short, I'm just saying I would have preferred a taller model. The model was still beautiful though. Once I completed my piece, and it fit the model well, I was ready for the fashion show.

At the show, my competitors were displaying amazing pieces, but my piece was much better. When my outfit went out on the stage, I knew the judges were fascinated by it. I was sure they thought it was the best in the entire show. When it came time to announce the winner, I received third place. I didn't win the fashion show, and I missed yet another opportunity to get an internship. The guy that did end up winning, my designs were way better than his. I didn't know what the hell the judges were thinking, but they decided to go with him instead of me. That's the way it was. Being a poor sport about it, wasn't going to help.

With my degree, I'm sure I could still land a fashion job, but many of the other students are graduating with internships, and I'm not. During the graduation ceremony, I was slightly bitter at the other students who were going to work for big name companies, and I was not given the same opportunity.

For several months after graduating from the fashion school, I was still left without a job in fashion. I ended up getting a part time job as a waiter, and I did happen to find an apartment for myself still in the city. On the weekends, and when I wasn't working, I would do random sewing projects. But my dream of touring the world with my fashions wasn't coming true. I don't know what I did wrong, but it didn't happen. My goal was to work in fashion, and to be a big name designer. I was given so many chances, and I blew them all.

So what was I going to do now? I'm not particularly a very spiritual person, but I started to pray to god that I would be given one more chance. I know I was given plenty of chances to make it big into fashion, but if I could have just one more, that would be nice. If I end up destroying this chance, then that settles it. I will no longer pursue fashion, and it wasn't meant to be for me.

One night as I was browsing the internet, I came across a hiring event that Universal Studios was having. They needed designers to design costumes and other wardrobe for their company. Both professional and for theatrical purposes. I didn't want to waste any time with this opportunity. This may be the last one I'm presented with, so I didn't want to ruin this one either. When I arrived to speak with them, I had my portfolio, and they also wanted to see a piece that you recently designed. There were several other people that were also present for this event, and I began to feel scared.

Feeling nervous, I had second thoughts that I was going to miss out on this chance as well. I waited for an hour and a half to speak with them. As I was waiting, I knew I had to keep my nerves down, and be calm about it. My name was finally called, and I had an interview with a woman named Allison.

"Hello, you must be Jerald. My name is Allison, and I'm going to interview you for our wardrobe designer position. May I see your portfolio please?"

I hand Allison my portfolio, and she skims through the sketches I have, and also the past designs that I have worked on. I then respond back to her, handing her a piece of paper.

"I hope my designs are up to your standard. I also graduated from the 'Los Angeles Fashion Institute'. They had a fashion show, and I received third place."

I then let Allison see the dress I worked on. She asked me a few more questions so she could be sure that I knew different fashion terms. She then let me know if I got the job or not.

"Well Jerald, after looking at your portfolio, and seeing your qualifications, we are going to offer you a position to work for our company. Congratulations."

I finally caught a break, and it was a wonderful feeling. I thank Allison and shake her hand. I walked out of that building feeling like I really accomplished something. No I wasn't working for a high end fashion chain, and I wasn't jet setting around the world with my fashions. It was a job designing costumes at Universal Studios. Not exactly what I envisioned, but at this point, I'll take it. I'm still doing something that's my passion and my calling, and it's nice. After accepting the job offer, I quickly started to work at Universal.

I had to quit my serving job, as I didn't have time for that anymore. I was now working as a fashion designer, and that's what I was put here on this earth to do. As I didn't have a car still, in order to get to work, I had to take the subway, and I also had to walk quite a bit from my house. The hours that they would give me were quite late. I would work until nighttime hours. I assume this was because Universal Studios has many night productions, and that's when they need designers. My duties were to simply put together costumes and outfits that the performers would wear. I would also design full body suits.

Whenever you go to the amusement park and you see a cartoon character walking around, I was one of those people that would design those. Although during certain times, I would get to design more professional things. I would be in charge of set wardrobe. I was lucky on one specific occasion, that I got to work wardrobe for the "Screen Actors Guild awards". It was fun, and I enjoyed going to work. I enjoyed it so much, that I actually still continue to work for Universal.

My life was going great, until I experienced a night I won't forget. It was a night that is painful to explain again, but had I not experienced what I experienced that night, my life would not be the way it is today. It started off as an ordinary day. I had a great day at work, and nothing seemed out of the ordinary. Things started to get bad when I was on my way home. I had been swamped recently at work, so I had a large case with wheels on it that had designs that I needed to work on. They had to be completed very soon. I rode the subway home like I always do, and I got off the subway and started to walk to my apartment. It was about 10 p.m. at night, so it was rather late.

As I'm walking, I had a feeling that something wasn't right. I didn't feel safe, and it was that creepy feeling you sometimes get when you are not feeling safe. I was about a few blocks away from my house, when catastrophe struck. I'm immediately grabbed and tackled by several Caucasian men. My mind was in shock, and I was getting robbed. One of them aims a gun at me. I'm still holding onto the case that has my designs in it. As one of the robbers points his gun at me, another robber then starts to yell out to me.

"What's in the case? Give it to us now. Give us the case!"

I immediately hand the case over to the robbers, and they start to go through the case. I don't know what they thought was in it, but nothing that would concern them was in it. After the robbers realize that the only thing in the case is clothes and fabrics, they become irate.

"What the fuck is this? This is nothing but a bunch of faggoty shit in here. You're nothing but a black fag, and we have no use for you."

A robber kicks me in the abdomen, and I fall down onto the sidewalk. I feel this is unfair how I'm being ganged up on by these guys, and I can't do anything to help myself. It seemed like I was not going to leave out of this scene alive, and I didn't know if this was how I was going to die. Being robbed and bashed in the street. I couldn't imagine dying like this. Seconds later however, I hear a man's voice scream out.

"This is your final warning, you leave him the fuck alone!"

I'm still weak to get up off the ground, so I don't know how close the man is to where I am, or even what he looks like. I'm happy that someone is coming to my rescue, and is willing to help me. I was feeling lucky that someone cared about me. The robbers focused their attention on this man, and started to leave me alone on the ground. The robbers then shout to the man.

"Who the fuck are you? You don't want to mess with us, we will kill you!"

I finally manage to recover and I stand myself up. The man and the robbers are standing about fifteen feet away from me. The man that came to my defense is a Caucasian man with slightly long hair. He has a five o clock shadow, and he's quite pudgy looking. When I first glanced at him, I really liked his charm. He was ordinarily not the type of guy I would hang out with or be friends with, but I found him very charming anyways.

The man then pulls out a large knife, waving it in front of all the robbers. At this same time, a police car turns the corner, flaring its sirens. The robbers then act cowardly, and immediately begin to run away from the scene. The policeman in the car doesn't even see the robbers run, or the other man and I in the street, and keeps on driving. Now that the robbers have gone, the man begins to speak to me.

"Are you okay? Did they hurt you? You want me to take you to the hospital?"

It took me a while to speak back. I was amazed and surprised that there are still nice people in the world. This man who I don't even know, came to my defense and wanted to help me. I don't know what would have happened had he not arrived. A few seconds later, I manage to be strong enough to respond to the man.

"I'm fine. They threw me down on the ground, but I'll be okay. Thank you so much sir. I don't know what to say, I'm just really glad that you came to help me."

The man smiles back at me. He then kindly responds back to me.

"Oh, you don't have to thank me. Those guys are assholes, picking on weak people. I'm the kind of guy that doesn't like it when people are picked on or messed with."

I start to pick up my designs that the robbers threw all across the sidewalk, so I can put them back in my case. The man then helps me pick up the things on the ground. The man looks at my pieces. He then speaks to me in polite way, as he helps me put them back in the case.

"Are you a designer? Did you make all of these clothes? Wow, you're really good man, this is a good skill. I guess they thought you were a DJ and had like electronics in here."

The man was being very friendly, and I knew it was safe enough for me to open up to him. We both continue to put the items back in my case, and I respond back to him.

"Thank you. Yes I am a designer. I work at Universal. I design clothes yes. These particular items aren't finished, and I was going to take them home and work on them."

Once all my designs are back in the case, the man helps close up and lock my case, and we both stare at each other silently for a few seconds. The man then introduces himself to me, and sticks out his hand for me to shake it.

"My name is Carl. I live right around the corner, and I was coming home from an art show with some friends. I saw you getting attacked in the street, I had to do something."

I could finally put a name next to this man. His name was Carl. I was thankful that Carl took the time to come to my defense, and he is a very kind hearted man. It's very rare that you find or come across people that are nice like that, and do good deeds. I end up shaking Carl's hand, and in the process, I also introduce myself to him as well.

"Nice to meet you Carl. My name is Jerald. I live in this neighborhood as well. I was coming home from work, and those idiots started to rob me."

Carl and I remain standing in the street for a short while. It was an awkward time of silence, and we both quietly stared at each other. I then grab my case, and figure that I should start to get home. I end up thanking Carl once again.

"Thank you very much. I mean it. I am really lucky that you came along. It was nice meeting you, but I have to get going. Goodbye."

I start to walk away from the scene, and Carl grabs me by the wrist. I immediately stop, as I was shocked that he did that. Carl then silently responds back to me.

"Why don't you come over to my place? We're both artists. You're a designer, and I do art. I paint. You can't say no because I saved your life. Now come on."

This was the least that I could do for Carl saving me. I shouldn't be going with strangers though. I only met him ten minutes ago, and ordinarily I shouldn't feel comfortable going with him. However, Carl seems like a safe and friendly enough guy, that it's okay. I don't mind that he wants to invite me over. Finding out that he does art, and he's a painter was exciting. I have always found artists to be wonderful people. As a fashion designer, I work with art quite a bit, but Carl takes it to a whole another level really.

Walking with Carl to his house, I feel nervous but excited as well. Getting closer to his house, I know that it's too late to back away now. This guy could be a psycho killer, and I agreed to walk with him. I feel he is an all-around nice guy, and I don't feel any type of bad way about him. We finally reach Carl's residence, and from the outside, it's just an ordinary commercial building. Carl opens one of the outside doors, and then speaks to me.

"I have a loft that's on the top floor. Just follow me."

I continue to walk with Carl in this converted business building, which now contains residential lofts. We finally make it to the top floor where his loft is. Open entering, I notice that this is not only his home, but his art studio as well. I see several paintings hung up on the wall. I assume Carl painted those. His talent is very special, and I like that about him. Continuing to walk through his loft, I see many art supplies and paints, and different easels and blank canvases, it's like I'm in an art store. I'm continuing to look around, as Carl speaks.

"Yeah, this is my place. I like it, and I have it just the way I want it. I do all my art here, and this is where I sleep as well. It's simple, and I have everything I want all right here."

I'm not trying to be nosy, but I am curious and ask Carl a question that's on my mind.

"How did you end up getting this loft? Is this yours, do you own it? This is a very nice place you got, and it also doubles as your art studio too. Very nice."

I see that Carl is on the other side of his loft, at the kitchen area. He goes into the refrigerator and grabs two beers. He then starts to walk in my direction, handing me on the beers. Carl opens his beer up, and then responds to the question that I asked him.

"Actually, me and a friend bought this loft together. So being that we both split the cost of the unit, it wasn't that bad. However, the friend I was staying with here died, and I don't want to talk about it. But yeah. Make yourself at home I guess."

What Carl said was true. Carl had a close friend that was an artist as well, and he died rather tragically. The death of this person, almost made Carl quit being an artist for a while. But in his friends memory, he continues on with his art, for his friends legacy. I end up taking a seat on the sofa in the living area of the loft. As I'm sitting down, I continue to stare at the artwork that's hung up all across the unit, and being amazed as to how talented Carl is.

Carl then sets his backpack down on the table in front of the sofa I'm sitting in, and starts to pull out his laptop computer. As he's going through his laptop, he moves the laptop in my direction, showing me a picture of a street mural. The mural consists of several army men walking outside in a field. It's a beautifully drawn piece. Carl then explains the concept of it to me.

"This is what I worked on today. This is on the back of the warehouse that's on 4th street. The whole point of it, is to show that the soldiers are ready for battle, but how they are really feeling inside, is that they imagine being peaceful. It's complicated to explain I know."

Carl had several different talents. He was not only painted on canvas, but he also did street art. His street art was nice, and it was very lovely to see. Carl then shuts his laptop, and walks away from the sofa. He then walks over to this studio area, and begins to organize his art pallet. I continue to sit at the sofa. I can't believe that not even twenty minutes ago, I was being attacked in the street. By chance and luck, Carl came into my life. Now, I don't want to leave his loft. I was starting to be captivated by him, and I just met him. He is a perfect match to me, and he can be an amazing motivation to my own creative skills. I continue to gaze at Carl, as he puts up a blank piece of canvas on an easel. While he's doing that, I ask him a question that I'm curious about.

"Carl, I know this shouldn't be any of my business, but do you have a girlfriend?"

Carl starts to paint on the easel. He then responds to my question in the process of that.

"No, I don't have a girlfriend. Why did you ask me that for?"

The truth is, I was starting to form a crush on Carl. I only met this man, and I didn't know how he was going to react. Everything was happening rather fast, but I'm glad things were going fast. It seemed like it was meant to be, for us to meet like this. I was minding my own business walking home, and Carl comes to my rescue. It was like fate put us in that same scene together and I couldn't believe it.

I had to be honest with Carl, and tell him that I was developing feelings for him. Even if he doesn't accept the feelings, or feels the same way towards me, he still has to know that I'm thinking this way about him. I get up from the sofa, and walk over to Carl's art station. I watch him as he is painting. I then softly speak to Carl.

"Well, I have to be honest with you. I like you a lot Carl. I think you're a great guy."

Carl continues to paint, ignoring me. He doesn't respond to me, although I know he heard exactly what I told him. I wasn't angry that Carl ignored me. I didn't understand how he was feeling. I didn't know if he was feeling the same way, or if I didn't make myself clear enough. As I'm still standing next to Carl, I start to rub my hands on his shoulders. Carl still ignores me, and continues to paint. I decide to leave him alone at this point. On his art station, I see what looks like a paper cup with water into it. I wanted a drink of water, and assumed it was water, so I wanted to drink it. Because I'm stupid, I end up taking a sip from it. As soon as I did that, Carl in fear gets up and smacks the cup out of my hand. He then shouts at me.

"No, that's not water. That's paint thinner. Why did you drink that? If you wanted water, you should have said something, and I would have gotten you some."

Car then grabs me by the wrist, and takes me into the kitchen. Luckily, I didn't swallow that much of it to harm me. It tasted pretty bad, but I was going to be okay. Carl gives me a glass of water, and gives me a disappointed look. He then starts to grab his keys off the counter. After he did that, he then turns his direction over to me, and speaks.

"Jerald, I think I should walk you home now. I'm going to give you my number, and if you want to get together sometime soon, that's great. But I think you should go now."

I wanted Carl to understand that I didn't want to leave. I was having a great time at his place, and I didn't want to go home. However, I guess I should understand that if Carl wants me to leave, then I don't have a choice. But I didn't want to, and I wanted to stay. I wanted to tease Carl some more, and make it obvious that I feel a certain way about him. I end up walking back over to Carl's art station, and I grab a tube of orange paint. I then take the tube of paint, and I squeeze the paint all over Carl's shirt. Carl immediately gets angry, and yells at me.

"What the hell are you doing? That paint is very expensive, and it doesn't come off clothes. Now you really have to go Jerald. Let's go."

I then take the paint and I squeeze it over my shirt as well. I then burst out laughing, but Carl doesn't find this funny. While I'm laughing, I then start to tease Carl.

"I apologize. See, I put the paint on my shirt too, so we're both even."

I then walk back over the sofa area, and I look back at Carl. He gives me a wide smile, and he puts his keys down on the counter. He then softly responds to me.

"Sit down, and don't touch any of my stuff. You can stay, but don't touch my paints, and don't touch anything. There is stuff in this studio that could hurt you very bad."

Carl then walks back over to his art station, and continues to paint. I managed to trick Carl into letting me stay at his place longer, and it was good. I remain on the sofa, as Carl continues to paint. A half an hour later, I then decide to walk back over to Carl's art station. He is really involved with his project, and doesn't look like he wants to be bothered. I then start to massage the back of Carl's neck, and he starts to smile. Once I noticed that he was smiling, I knew that he was enjoying this. He didn't mind at all that I was showing him affection, and I was winning him over.

I knew I had to go all in at this point, and I had nothing to lose. I then lean my head over, and kiss Carl on the lips. It gets better, as I continue to kiss him, awe both land on the floor. A short time after that, Carl and I stop kissing, and he returns back to his art station. The kiss I had with Carl was nice, and I was very much in love with him. I wanted to stay with him this night as much as I could. I was having a lot of fun, and Carl was also feeling the same way. I returned back to the sofa, continuing to watch Carl paint. I am curious as to what he's actually painting, and I get up one final time to see what it is.

Carl then shows me the completed piece that he's painting, and it's a portrait of me. I was so flattered, that Carl decided to paint a portrait of myself. As Carl is sitting down at his artist station, I lean up from behind him and give him another kiss. Carl then takes out another canvas, and begins to paint another piece. I go back to the sofa area, quietly watching him work on another piece.

An hour and half later, I proceed over to Carl's bed, and I lay down on it. I was feeling tired at this time, as it was getting late into the night. Carl notices that I'm lying down on the bed, and stops painting, and walks over to his bed area. He gives me one more kiss on the lips. He then rubs my hair, and softly speaks to me.

"Good night Jerald. If you need anything, just come and get me."

Carl then walks back over to his art station, and I drift off to sleep. The next morning, I wake up with the morning sun blaring through the unit. I get out of bed, and I see that Carl is painting at his station. I get up and walk over to him, giving him a hug. Carl then smiles at me, and returns to painting. While he is painting, he begins to speak with me.

"Did you sleep good? I was thinking that today I take you on a surprise. It's going to be a mystery. I'm not going to tell you where I'm going to take you, and you can't say no."

I didn't mind at all that Carl was being sneaky. In a way, I found it very endearing. Carl had a special field trip that he wanted to take me on, and I wasn't allowed to be aware of where it was. Soon after this, I leave the loft and get into Carl's car. He drops me off at my place, so I can change clothes. After I change clothes, I get back into Carl's car, and he begins to take me to the mystery location. I was very secure with Carl, even though he may have been taking me somewhere to murder me. I didn't feel that energy from Carl, and he wasn't that type of person. The mystery aspect of it made things more exciting and fun.

I continue to ride in Carl's car, and he proceeds onto the location he wishes to take me to. Finally, we arrive at the place. I see it's the "Los Angeles County Museum of Art". I have never been here, but I heard that it was a lovely place to visit. I did appreciate art, so I was satisfied that Carl took me here. As we are walking away from the parking lot, Carl then starts to converse with me.

"So here is the top secret place. My favorite spot in all of LA. The art museum. If you can't appreciate art, than you can't appreciate me. I'm sorry. Let's Go."

Carl and I then start to head inside the art museum. Although I did understand the importance of art, I didn't know that much about the history art. This was Carl's specialty, and everything about art, he would explain to me. Whether it was on classic art, or on modern art. Impressionism, modernism, abstract. Carl could explain everything that you needed to know about it.

I was simply educating myself in everything that Carl was trying to teach me. As long as I was having him as an art teacher, everything was fine. We continue to roam through the museum, and Carl proceeds to explain all the art displays. He was able to correctly name each artist that belonged to each piece. That was mighty impressive of him. Carl was not only wise with art paintings, but he knew much about sculptures and other art pieces as well.

There were several art exhibits that the museum featured for a limited time, and Carl and I checked this out as well. One art exhibit was on tribal African Art. I guess this really hit home for me, as it was my culture. Carl was also interested in the African Art. He knew more about the art than I did, and I'm black.

Carl is actually Austrian, but he still knew his facts on African art. Once we finished looking at the exhibit, we continued to go through the rest of the museum, and we did even more exploring. We reached an area of the museum that was quite interesting. The section was totally related to street and urban art. Which this is related more to Carl's style. We saw that the museum was featuring several pieces from Keith Haring. He was a detrimental street artist.

Staying in this particular section, I saw a lovely piece which was of Downtown Los Angeles. Form the way it was painted, it seemed like it was a sunset landscape. I was really curious as to who the artist was. When I looked at the label under the piece, it had Carl's name. I immediately turned to look at Carl, and he nods his head.

"Yeah I painted that. It's nice right? It took me a while to get everything right. It's only here temporary, but I wanted you to see it. I can finally say I have something of mine put up in a museum. It's a big accomplishment for me."

I continue to look at the piece, and I end up congratulating Carl kindly.

"I'm proud of you Carl. That is very nice that one of your paintings is being featured here. You're very talented as an artist, and you deserve it."

Carl smiles back at me, and we explore more of the museum. I'm really finding this day with Carl special. I didn't know whether at this time to refer to Carl as my boyfriend, but he was someone that I had no issues being with. I don't know what it was about Carl that was driving me crazy, but he seemed like a chill guy, and that we connected to each other well. I was simply a fashion designer, and I didn't know much about art. Fashion design and art are similar fields, but being a fashion designer, and being an artist are two different things. I knew that Carl appreciated his art, and this wasn't just a hobby for him. This was pretty much his life, and if I was going to be with Carl, I was going to have to accept and get used to this. Being in the museum was a fun outing, and I learned so much throughout the day.

The relationship I was forming with Carl was good too. So I was getting two things done at the same time. I was out of the house and having an awesome time at the museum. I also had a nice guest with me, Carl, who was being a nice guide throughout the trip. The final exhibit that we went through at the museum, was a sculpting gallery.

Carl wasn't a master sculptor, but he knew some things, and still had a bunch to say related to that. We went through the gallery, looking at several statues and other sculpted figurines. Carl later pointed out a replica "Statue of David" that someone put together.

"This one I really like. I do sculpt sometimes, but I'm not good at it. But what I do like about sculpting is stuff like this. This David statue someone tried to replicate is good."

The statue was indeed good, and I thanked Carl for pointing this one out to me. I gazed at the rest of the statues in this exhibit, and Carl and I were also finding some of the statues humorous. I guess art is subjective, and perhaps it was the artists intention for the piece to have a comedic value. Our museum trip was coming to an end, and Carl and I were preparing to leave.

It is now late in the evening and around 8 P.M. We spent virtually the entire day in the museum. I didn't care, and this didn't matter. Time flies when you are having fun with someone you deeply care about. Normally museum's aren't my thing, and I may have found going to an art museum boring and a waste of time before then.

Well, not with Carl. Being with him, brought all the fun into an otherwise ordinary occasion. Not that I'm saying art is boring, it just wouldn't normally be something up my alley at all. The time I spend with him the entire day was well worth it, and I got to experience new things, and learn and educate myself on new things as well.

As soon as we left the museum, I went back into Carl's car, and he proceed to drive to another unknown location. As he's driving Carl began to speak to me.

"The trip isn't over yet. There is still more to come. I have another place that I want to take you, and you already know it's a secret."

As Carl goes to the next secret location, I realize that I'm going to be in for another surprise. I began to wonder what Carl was going to show me next. I had a feeling it was something special, and something that you only show or reveal to someone you are close to. I also knew that it more than likely had something to do with art, and I was prepared to see what it was. It was late in the night, and Carl began to drive to a barren area away from the outskirts of Los Angeles.

This was when I was starting to slightly worry. What if Carl is actually a psycho killer, and he's taking me somewhere to murder me. That's just me thinking negative. Carl continues to drive in the outskirts of town, and is now driving close to the Los Angeles harbor. I remain confused as to where he is taking me, in a strange mix of terror and excitement. Carl then finally pulls the car over in a back area of a warehouse, located at the harbor. As Carl gets out of the car, he starts to calmly speak to me.

"It's okay, it's safe. What I want to show you is just over here. Follow me."

I obey Carl, and I get out of the car. Following him to the area that he wants me to see. We continue to walk for several minutes, until Carl starts to mess with a rickety gate that's attached to one of the warehouses. As he's messing with the gate, he grunts back to me.

"It's right through here. Don't be scared. It's fine. Please trust me Jerald."

Carl manages to slide the gate open, and the both of us walk inside of the warehouse. It is completely dark inside the warehouse, but Carl takes his phone out, and uses a flashlight app to make the room slightly illuminated. The room is still quite dark, but at least you can now at least see what's inside. As I inspect the inside of the room, I see a bunch of street art painted all across the room. I then see a bunch of graffiti as well all across the unit. I have no idea why Carl is showing me this, but this is a rather remarkable location. As I continue to look through the unit, I curiously ask Carl what is it exactly he's showing me.

"Carl, what is this place? Did you draw all of this? This is a very strange place."

Carl then starts to cry as he's walking through the dark warehouse. As he's crying deeply, I then go over and try to comfort Carl. Carl instead shoves me off him. He then screams at me.

"Get off me Jerald. Don't touch my right now. Remember I told you I had a special friend who died. Well, he was my older brother Mark. We were exactly alike, we were like twins. He sadly was doing some art one day, and got hit by a train. This was his hideout."

Carl pushed me off him very violently, and I didn't like the way he did that. This was bringing a lot of sorrow to Carl. I know that losing his brother was difficult. I lost my own mother, so I knew the feeling of losing someone close to you. I try to comfort Carl once again by resting my head on his shoulder, this time trying to be compassionate and empathetic to him.

"I'm sorry you lost your brother Carl. My mother died when I was young, and I can relate and understand completely. I'm terribly sorry for your loss."

Carl then starts to rub my hair, and softly speaks back to me.

"I'm sorry for pushing you Jerald. Yeah Mark and I were close. He was more of a graffiti artist, and I was more of a contemporary artist. But we both found a passion for art. This was where he would do most of his work. So this area is top secret."

The unit only consisted of wall art and graffiti art that Carl's brother Mark had created. Carl and I were actually prohibited by law to actually be in this area, as it's a condemned warehouse. But for the sake of his brother's memory, Carl still visits this unit, as the city has not destroyed it yet. Although most of the work that Mark has done, Carl keeps back at his loft. I continue to comfort Carl, as he remains in the unit, looking at his brother's work. Carl then kisses me on the cheek, and silently whispers to me.

"We have to get out of here Jerald. We're not supposed to be in here. I just wanted to show you this. Come on, let's go."

Carl and I walk out of the unit, and Carl struggles to close the gate back. I end up giving him a hand to jimmy the gate back into the position it was. Carl then appreciates this.

"Oh thank you Jerald, you didn't have to do that. But thanks."

Carl and I manage to get the gate shut, and we walk back to Carl's car. I wonder what the rest of the night will consist of? As I'm back in Carl's car, he speaks to me.

"Jerald, I have one final place I want to take you to tonight. It's another special secret place, and I don't want to tell you where it is. You're gonna like it though."

I didn't mind the array of surprises Carl was giving me. I was having fun, and that was the main thing. Carl continues to drive, and this time we have made it back to the main metro part of Los Angeles. Carl continues to drive, and decides to give me a hint.

"I hope you're hungry Jerald, because I am. We're almost there."

Carl was going to take me to get something to eat, which was great. Because yes I was hungry. I didn't have anything to eat the entire day, and could use a bite to eat. Carl finally approaches what looks like a hamburger dive stand. I was expecting something more fancy, but this will do. I get out of Carl's car, and we both head towards the hamburger stand. Probably because it was a Saturday night, the place was rather packed with people, and the line was long. While we are waiting in line, Carl starts to explain the significance of the hamburger stand.

"Mark and I would come here all the time. It's called 'Super Burger'. I know the name sounds simple, but this place is very good. They have the best burgers in LA."

To me, it seemed like a regular old hamburger stand, but I knew the sentimental value it had between Carl and his brother. I was hungry, so whatever food I could get, I was going to eat. Carl was treating me to a free meal in the process, so I can't complain. Carl ended up ordering a chili cheese burger with fries, and I ordered a bacon cheeseburger and fries. The food was actually very good and delicious.

The hamburger stand has an intimate outdoor seating area where you could eat your food, so that was good. When Carl and I finished our food, I once again went back into his car, and Carl proceeded to drive. I didn't know if Carl had anymore stops planned, but it was becoming very late in the night. So late that it was approaching midnight. Where else could Carl take me this late into the night? Feeling curious, I turn and spoke to Carl, wondering what he had planned next.

"So Carl, where are you going to take me now?"

Carl immediately fired back at me in a strange way.

"Well, I'm going to go '7 Eleven' and get some ice cream, then I'm going to go home. If you want to stay the night again at my place, it's okay."

I smile back at Carl, and he then heads directly to '7 Eleven' to get some ice cream. After getting the ice cream, we return back to Carl's loft. Once I'm in the loft, Carl and I eat our ice cream, and he explains more about his brother Mark to me. Carl and Mark went through a lot of adventures together, which I'm sure Carl will mention when he tells his part of the story. Carl and I finish our ice cream, and Carl then goes back to his art station to paint. He's working on a giant canvas, so the project seems quite large. I am feeling tired, but I wanted to give Carl one final kiss before I went to sleep. As he's painting his piece, I give Carl a kiss on the lips, and I then walk over to Carl's bed to fall asleep.

My relationship with Carl as time went on, improved greatly. He would give me a ride to work and pick me up, so I no longer needed to take the subway. Carl was also very interested in my fashion design as well. He would buy my fabrics and my patterns for me, and he would allow me work on my designs, in his loft. I found it romantic how Carl would work on his paintings on the other side of the loft, while I was using my sewing machine and creating dresses and outfits on the other side of the loft.

After Carl and I have been seeing each other for two months, I decided that I would move in with Carl at his loft. It was a decision that I thought about deeply, and it just made more sense. The lease at the apartment that I was saying in was ending, so instead of looking for another place, Carl suggested that I move in the loft with him, so I did.

Once moving in with Carl, I started to notice bad habits that Carl has. Carl doesn't sleep until he finishes a project. He will stay up all night if he has to, and work on very little sleep until a project is done. I also found out another secret that Carl was keeping from me. Carl, and his brother Mark were both autistic. I don't know why Carl was afraid to mention this to me earlier, but I didn't mind. I'm not going to attack Carl over something that's not even his fault, and that he can't even control. I love Carl very much, and that means I love all his quirks as well. I love seeing Carl with paint all over his clothes, and how he pays close attention to the projects he does.

About once every few weeks or so, Carl would take me to an art gallery that he's featured in. I didn't particularly care for the art galleries, but my opinion didn't matter. Carl was my partner now, and whatever he was passionate about, I had to accept and tag along with. I would just pretend to be nice and socialize with people at the galleries, knowing damn well I didn't want to be there. But I loved how Carl's artwork was featured in these galleries. It was his time showcase his work, and this was his moment.

Carl also would attend some of my fashion events as well. This wasn't something he liked, but for the sake of me, he supported me. It was clear that Carl and I were going to be life partners, and we had a strong relationship between one another. Carl later proposed to me in a strange way at one of his art gallery events, and I of course accepted it. Carl is the guy for me. Going back to the day I was robbed in the street, and he was basically my knight in shining armor coming to save me. I had no idea that from that night, Carl would later become the man for me.

I love Carl, and he makes me whole. We put up which each other's quirks. With the both of us being very creative people, we share a common lifestyle goal. Carl and I may be opposite on the outside, but that's just on the outside. We are truly meant for each other.

My story begun with me as young boy coming from a tough street life. Thinking that was going to be my destiny, and there was no possible way for me to leave from that. I grew up without a father, and

I had little support from my mother. We lived under harsh conditions in the inner city, and it was looking grim most of the time. I took up knitting, crocheting and sewing as a defense mechanism to deal with me being isolated as a young boy being alone.

When my mother passed away, I didn't know what to do, and figured that was the end of it for me. I had faith though, and I kept going. I still wanted to make my mother proud. I was living on the street for a while, until I went to the LGBT shelter. From the LGBT shelter, I got a scholarship to attend fashion design school. Upon graduating fashion school, I got a job working in fashion.

From there, I met Carl the way I did, and I am thankful for that. I now live with Carl in his loft, and he's my life partner, and I'm set for life. My story was told, and I came from the bottom to succeed to the top with my current life. My name is Jerald Williams, I am man of brown, and that was my story.

CHAPTER 14:

MAN OF PURPLE (PART 1)

My name is Carl Stovek. I am 29 years old, and I am the man of purple. My reddit username is "MetallicaGuy". I guess you can say I'm somewhat of a big Metallica fan I guess. I enjoy all types of music, but I have a special place for hard rock and metal music I suppose. I was born in Boston, Massachusetts, and I now live in Los Angeles, California. I want to mention a few things before I start my story. These things make me different from everyone else. I want to start off by saying that I am on the autistic spectrum. Being autistic was a challenge for me all throughout my life, and I still try to manage life being an autistic man. My older brother Mark, was also autistic, and I'll get back to Mark in a minute. For now, I want to stick to talking about myself. So in addition to being autistic, I'm more of an introverted person, and I don't talk to people that often. I feel they are judging me most of the time, so I don't involve myself in places to where I'm going to be around a huge group of people, and if I have to talk to a bunch of people. Considering that I have somewhat of a quirky personality, I want to save myself from being humiliated or made fun of, so I stay away from stuff like that usually.

Growing up, I was like a normal kid. I grew up with a mother and a father, and I had my brother Mark as well. We lived in a middle class family. We weren't rich, but we didn't struggle either. If there was a toy that we wanted to have, or if my brother and I wanted to go to "Hershey Park", they would allow us to go. We were not spoiled, but we had an alright childhood. My parents did work quite a bit, so that was something my brother and I had to understand. Our father worked for aerospace, and my mother was a librarian. So they spent much time away from us due to them working all the time.

Other than my brother Mark, I didn't have friends. I would play with the other boys at school, but I didn't refer to them as friends. They thought that I was too crazy for them, and so they ignored me, and didn't deal with me. I became the class clown at times I guess you could say. So the other kids at school were laughing at me, rather than with me. I didn't take this personally though, as I was being myself. I figured that if I fought back the bullies, it would only make things worse.

So if they made fun of me, and treated me like a clown. I was strong and tough about it though. It didn't take me that long to realize what my passion in life was. I knew that I wanted to be an artist. My brother Mark was into art, and I wanted to do the same thing. Mark was a year older than me, but we were exactly alike, and almost like twins; inseparable really. Whatever Mark did, I automatically followed along, and did the same thing. We were that much in tune with one another.

Mark and I looked exactly the same, and we also acted the same as well. We even spoke the same, liked the same foods, enjoyed the same music, and the same habits and quirks Mark had, I had as well. Even though we were not twins, as Mark was a year older than me, it would have made more sense to tell people that we were. I would say the only difference between Mark and I, despite it being a minor difference, was that Mark was more of a risk taker than I was.

Mark was more of my morale booster, and would try to change my spirits. I was also the one that would calm Mark down as well. If Mark knew he was going over the top at times, I would be the one to bring him back to earth. I didn't do this in a negative way at all, as Mark and I seldom fought. Mark was my best friend, and I was his best friend. Yeah there were times to where we had our disagreements, but we rarely would run into an issue that caused us to get into a rift. By the time I was twelve years old, Mark and I would do many art projects together. We would walk around the city, and collect all types of junk. It was trash and rubbish to other people, but to Mark and I, we always saw it as an experiment that we could turn it into. We would spend a lot of time doing these art experiments, and it became an obsession.

Right after school, we would usually go to abandoned lots, alleys, behind shopping centers, and add a bunch of random discarded junk to our collection. We would then at a later time create art out of it. What we would create wouldn't be just any old thing. The things we would make from the junk we collected, would be something useful.

We would make tables, counters, and other useful things like that. I remember my brother Mark made an alarm clock out of scrap pieces of metal one time. He was that resourceful and artistic, to do things such as that. I really enjoyed hanging with my brother Mark. He was way more creative than I was, and I didn't know how he would come up with the designs that he did. Every single time he would create something strange, I didn't know how he would be able to top that, and he always made something even better than before.

Our parents were not accepting of us collecting trash and making art out of it. They thought of it as dangerous, and they wanted us to have a hobby that was a little bit more safer to do. In certain ways I guess I could understand. This hobby could have a dangerous side to it. Mark and I would sometimes go to areas on the outskirts of town, trying to find stuff to make art out of. Knowing that we had no business being in these areas, and we were essentially trespassing. That didn't matter to Mark and I. We wanted to find stuff to make art out of, and that's all it was.

As a matter of fact, we did have a hobby that was more conventional I suppose. Mark and I were very skilled at drawing. I was pretty sure that it was a natural talent that we both had. Mark would usually draw cartoons and things like that, and I mostly would stick to landscape drawings. When we got into our teenage years, my brother and I would go downtown. We would sit outside the subway station, take out our sketchpads and draw. Although we still secretly enjoyed collecting junk for our art projects, drawing was a more sensible hobby.

It took quite a while for both of us to realize that we were actually talented in drawing. At first, it was something we did to expand our creative mind. I remember being fifteen years old drawing in the subway, and people would come up and ask to buy some of the drawings that we did. Being shocked at first, not knowing that I could make a career out of something so trivial as drawing.

So it became a new venture for us. We would go down to the subway station, and we would start to sell our drawings. The price we charged for our art, wasn't anything that bad. As time went on, we moved onto doing more complex artwork. If people wanted us to do a custom portrait of them, we would make an exception for that, and charge them more. As we continued to draw at the subway station, we knew that there was a way for us to go further with our art.

At our High School, the school newspaper had a section to where students can send in their own comics to be featured in the paper. I was a junior, and Mark was a senior. So I knew this being Mark's last year at High School, he should go for this. Mark and I used this as the perfect opportunity to use our artwork for the paper. We knew that the other students at the school would enjoy our comic, and it would be a nice way for us to get our work out.

We immediately began to get the comic together, and drew our own characters. We thought the comic was safe enough to be included in the school paper, and we would never put out something that we thought was inappropriate. The comic mostly touched on pop culture references, and it was a nice mix of comedy and art. Once our comic was finished, we presented our project to the students who were newspaper editors of the school for approval.

They loved our comic, and immediately started to publish it in the school paper. Every week we would publish a new comic. The students that would neglect reading the school paper prior, would now start to read it, so they could see our comic. When the school started to read our comic, the reception was mixed. Some of the students loved it, and some of the other students didn't enjoy the subject matter at all. It wasn't long before some of the staff at the school expressed much concern over our comic. Mark and I didn't understand what the problem was. The comic was fine, and instead of the school appreciating our art, they complained about it. Our comic was in danger of being removed. One day the school principal, Mr. Larry Montgomery, called Mark and I into his office. We sat behind the principal's desk as he started to reprimand us.

"Gentlemen, I'm here to talk about the comic. I understand that the both of you put a lot of work into it, but it's simply not appropriate for our school. So after discussing this with the rest of the staff, we will forbid you from using your comic in the school paper. I'm sorry."

We didn't appreciate how our artistic vision was being censored by the school. However, this was the decision that the school decided to make. We were not allowed to publish our comic in the school paper. Mark and I left the principal's office disappointed that our vision was being silenced. We were not going to let this discourage us though.

The principal said that Mark and I were not allowed to publish in the school paper. He didn't say anything about Mark and I publishing our comic outside of the school paper. This was a perfect workaround, so we quickly go to work on a new comic without hesitation. With our new comic, in an act to rebel, we made it even more entertaining. The art was also more complex. We made it a point that we were not going to be silenced. Art was our passion, and you can't destroy someone's passion or talent. We printed our comic, and arrived to school earlier than the rest of students one morning.

We taped our comic on all the lockers at the school. Once the students read our comic, the reaction once again was mixed, but the students that loved our comic stood by us in support. Mark and I were happy that we continued our comic. The school had an issue with our comic being printed in the school paper, but as we were releasing our comic independently, the school can't say anything at this point.

Or so we thought. When the school staff realized that we were still distributing our comic to students at the school, they were appalled. The staff at the school did not want us releasing our comic in any shape or form. Mark and I could understand the school not wanting their name attached to our comic, but we didn't understand how we still couldn't let the other students read our comic outside the school paper. We were once again called to the principal's office, like we were before. Mark and I went to Mr. Montgomery's office, as he attacked us once again.

"I thought I told you guys that I didn't want you putting your comic out at this school? I just got through having this conversation with you both didn't I?"

Mark immediately snapped back at Mr. Montgomery.

"No, that's not what you said. You said that you didn't want us having the comic in the school paper. We can respect that. But you didn't say anything about us doing the comic outside of the school paper. So we didn't technically break your rules."

Mr. Montgomery was extremely mad at the both of us, and fired back at us.

"You guys knew exactly what I meant. Your comic is not appropriate for this school. Now this is your final warning. If I see that comic again in this school, the both of you will be expelled immediately. I don't want to see that comic again. Do I make myself clear?"

So there was no workaround this time. It was a shame, because the comic was really trying to say something and prove a point. We weren't allowed to express ourselves with the comic at school anymore. It wasn't fair at all that we were not given the freedom to express our art. We are trying to do something artistic related to the school, and they didn't value or respect that. Mark and I felt defeated, and we left out of Mr. Montgomery's office feeling like losers, and that we accomplished nothing with the comic. We then had to make the difficult decision of quitting the comic. It really broke our spirit when the school banned us from letting the other students look at the comic. We didn't see the point of wasting our time and energy making a comic for the school, if nobody could see it.

This was also way before social media became popular. So it's not like we could have put our comic on Instagram or Facebook or YouTube or on the internet. At this point, we decided to go with a different approach with our art. Mark was doing a lot research on street art, and street graffiti. This was something I didn't really consider, but it was a perfect way for us as artists to get our message across. We would start to do urban street art on abandoned buildings, and this would be the perfect way to rebel.

From the way we were silenced at the school for our comic, we wanted to go even further with our art, and try more extreme approaches. I remember the first project that Mark and I worked on. There was an abandoned train yard on the west side of Boston. The train yard had this forty foot wide, and twenty foot tall blank white wall. It was like an open canvas that we wanted to use. Mark had this perfect idea to do a piece of Dorothy from the "Wizard of Oz", and the dog Toto, running in a field. I thought Mark was crazy when he first thought of this, but I later was totally on board. We worked on the piece before school, after school, and early morning on the weekends. Mark and I would use special adhesive paint to do the piece.

Within a month, we were finished with it entirely. What we did was very illegal, but we didn't care. Since the location of the piece was in part of town away from everything else, nobody really was going to see it. Unless you happened to be walking around in the area the trainyard was in. As the months went on, Mark and I went to other abandoned parts of down, and we would continue to do more street art pieces. It was mostly done for our technique, rather than to show off. Nobody was seeing our creations though, as we did them out in the middle of nowhere. It was still a nice activity for us to do, so we could work on our artwork. Going onto street art was a new method for us, but it became something we could add to our lists of talents.

Yes it wasn't legal for us to be applying artwork to abandoned building and places, but Mark and I saw it as art. How can you silence art, and how can you restrict someone from doing their art? Our street art was our therapy, and it the thing which saved my brother and I from giving up art completely.

Mark was starting to graduate from High School, and he had plans to go to University. My concern was that I wasn't going to have time to spend with Mark anymore. If he was going to be spending most of his time at school, I wouldn't get to interact with him as much. I discussed this with Mark, to see how I was going to continue doing art with him, if he was going to be going away to school. The conversation that I had with Mark was very direct. He made it clear to me that school was going to be his primary concern, but he would try his best to make time for me. I had to understand this. Mark and I were getting older, so there was eventually going to come a time to where we would have to go our own way at one point. One good thing, was that Mark went to school here in Boston. He didn't travel that far away to attend school.

He also would remain at home. So I would see him every night when he would come from class. We just didn't have as much time for art projects as we did previously, due to his hectic school hours. In my last year of High School, due to much influence from Mark, I then decided to take up yet another form of art. I quickly adapted myself into doing oil painting. Something that I had no experience with before. I immersed myself with this new art technique.

What I appreciated about classic oil painting, was that it took a lot of patience. I used painting to calm myself down. Whenever I was feeling anxious because Mark was at school, and I couldn't hang out with him, I would take out my easel, and begin to paint various things. It wasn't long before I became very experienced with my oil painting, and I became comfortable to admit to myself that I was talented. Mark was also proud of my oil paintings.

Even though doing oil paint wasn't Mark's specialty, he would occasionally work on oil paintings too. I was on my way to graduate High School, and go onto University just like Mark, when we were presented with some very unexpecting news. News that wasn't nice to hear, and news that nobody really wants to be told. I remember I came home from school, and Mark and my mother were in the living room. I found it weird that Mark was in the living room at this time, as usually he's at class. Mark then told me the news.

"Carl, dad suffered a heart attack at a business trip today. He's dead."

Mark and my mother then immediately began to cry. My father worked quite a bit, and I didn't get to spend as much time as I would have liked with him, and hearing that he passed away upset me tremendously. My day was going well before coming home to hear this news. I can't believe he passed away. I would have liked for my father to see me graduate from High School. He was going to take time off work to attend my graduation. So it was devastating to understand my father wasn't going to be here anymore. Now that dad passed away, I knew that Mark and I had to do all we could to comfort our mother. She was having a difficult time dealing with the death of our father, like Mark and I were as well.

Due to all the bad memories, our mother wanted to sell the house after the death of our father. Her plan was to move into either a smaller house, or an apartment. We didn't understand why our mother wanted to make this decision, but that was what she wanted to do. That's exactly what happened, as our mother did end up selling the family house. This whirlwind of effects after the death of my father was difficult to deal with. After I graduated High School, I was talking with my brother Mark as to where we were going to go with our lives from this point.

"So Carl, I was talking this out with Mom, and I was thinking that maybe the both of us should move out on our own. I mean, with the recent events of dad being gone. I think it's time that we both went out on our own. I was thinking California? What do you think?"

I was unsure of how to respond at first, and slightly confused. Things were happening fast, and I was happy with the way things were. Dad dying was unexpected yes, and I didn't want to move out of our family home. I mean, Mark and I grew up here and it held a special place for both of us. On the other hand, maybe I had to accept the fact that it was indeed time for us to move on. This was the time for Mark and I to be fully independent on ourselves. I thought about it for a while, and then I gave my response out to Mark.

"I think that's okay Mark. If you feel that this is the right time for us to move away on our own, then I agree with you. Yeah, let's go for it."

Mark was satisfied that I agreed with his plan for us to move and live on our own, but part of me wasn't thrilled with the idea. I'm someone that doesn't like big change, and life was fine for us where we were. Mark wanted to move out of state, clear across on the other side of the country really. He really wanted to move to Los Angeles, and that was a long, long way from Boston. This was not going to be a simple change for us, and would require a lot of adapting to. The culture there is completely different, the people are completely different. I really didn't know. Our mother would decide to stay in Boston, but Mark and I had our plans set to move out to Los Angeles, and that was the way it was going to go. Mark was going to transfer schools, and attend school in California. I was essentially going to do the same, and go to school there as well.

Once Mark and I finally moved out to California, we were living by ourselves for the first time. We had a nice apartment in the downtown area of Los Angeles, and things were going well. Mark would go to school, and I would go to school. We would focus on our art, and our school career. This was great, but our communication lacked. We began to grow very distant of each other, and this was not comfortable for me.

I figured the whole point of us moving to California, was that we could bond closer together as brothers. It seems that the opposite happened, and not that Mark and I began to hate each other, we just drifted as far as our interaction went. Mark was never home when I was home, and vice versa. It was only naturally for me to be alarmed over this, as Mark was my best friend. Everything we did, we did together.

So now that I barely got to see him usually, I don't know. I didn't know how to really feel about it. I remember one evening, I came home early from school, and Mark was in the living room of our apartment doing his homework. I took this time to speak to him.

"Hey Mark, I was wondering if you wanted to hang out his weekend? It's been a while since we did something together, so if you're not busy, that would be nice."

Mark was deeply involved in his homework assignment, and didn't seem to really want to give me the time of day. However, he reluctantly responded back to me.

"I would really love to Carl, but I don't have time this weekend. There is this project I'm working on for class. I'm really sorry. We'll find time to hang out though soon. I promise."

I was upset that Mark didn't have time for me anymore, and we were both starting to go down our own separate paths, and I wasn't quite ready for this at all. I guess that's the price to pay when you get older as brothers. You start to go away from each other, I don't know.

I knew that both of us were passionate about our art, and Mark had his own style of art, and I had my own agendas for my art. That didn't necessarily mean we had to detach ourselves from each other because of that. If anything, that should make things easier, as we both are striving for the same things. Over the course of several years, my relationship with Mark became scattered.

As he was focused on graduating from University, his attention was solely focused on his school career, and less on me. I was starting to be only his younger brother. I wasn't his best friend anymore, and I wasn't his art partner anymore. I wasn't angry at Mark, in fact I was never angry at Mark. I was only puzzled due to his sudden change of behavior I suppose. My main hope was that this was only temporary. I knew in the back of my mind that someday Mark and I would go back to how things were before, and things would work out fine. I had to have hope, and I had to keep that hope alive.

Mark finally graduated from University, and once Mark was done with school, I knew there was a glimmer of hope that we could go back to how it used to be. I was still in school, trying to finish my final year. So Mark was finished with school, and I was nearly done with it.

As I was nearly done with my final year of University, Mark approached me one day with some news. Before he gave me the news, I knew it was bad by the sad expression that was on his face. I knew this couldn't be good. Mark began to give me upsetting news.

"Carl, mom passed away today. She had ovarian cancer, and she was really sick. I only found out about a couple hours ago."

What? First dad passed away, now mom is gone. Why does life keep doing downhill for me. Mom was the last remaining close family member that Mark and I had. The both of us kept in touch with her greatly, so we did not want to hear the news that she died. Mark and I travelled back to Boston to attend our mothers funeral. It was not a joyous experience, but my brother and I managed to see many extended family members that we don't get to usually see.

Once my mother's funeral was finished, Mark and I took this time to grieve over her death. As we got back to our home in California, we had to take a break from what we usually do. Our emotions were running too fast to concentrate on our art. It took some time, but once Mark and I accepted our mothers death, we went on with our lives. I graduated University, and I knew my mother would be proud of me. Mark and I were both done with school, and we were trying to figure out what we wanted to do with our lives next.

We both decided that it was time for us to get back to doing art. It was also time for us to go back to how it was in the past, with us working together. One night as Mark was coming home from an art group that he belonged to, I took the time to speak with him about how I was feeling. Letting him know that I want for us to go back to how things were previously, and with us doing our art together like we used to.

"Hey Mark, I was wondering if you would like to do a project soon. Remember how we did it a long time ago? I want to do that again, if that's okay with you?"

Mark then to my surprise was optimistic about my suggestion, and he responded.

"Yes, that's okay Carl. It has been quite some time since we did an art project. You know what, there is a place that I want to show you. Come with me."

Where was Mark going to take me? I had no idea, but I knew that with Mark, he was quite unpredictable at times, so this was exciting I guess. I got into Mark's car, and he started to drive. Still not having any idea at all as to where he is taking me, I sit in the car silently. He was going directly to the port area of Los Angeles.

When we finally reach the location that Mark wanted to take me to, I noticed that it was some sort of an abandoned warehouse building. Still confused as to why Mark was taking me to this area, I enjoy being in suspense regardless. The both of us get out of the car, and start to walk to one of the warehouse buildings. Mark then says something.

"I want to show you my secret place. This is my own place, and the reason why I didn't tell you about it, because I wanted my own secret place. I guess it's now time for me to tell you about it too, because of how close we are Carl."

I wasn't offended that Mark kept the location of his hideout a secret from me. In a way I could understand that he wanted his own quiet spot for himself. It wasn't because he was tired of hanging out with me or anything like that, he wanted his own spot. Mark and I continue walking towards his secret spot, and we finally reach a gate. Mark starts to open the gate, and I notice how the gate is situated rather strangely. You really have to mess and fool with it, so it can budge open. I remain watching Mark for a few seconds, but then decide to give him some assistance to open the gate. We struggle opening the gate, and Mark speaks to me.

"I have it this way on purpose. That way nobody comes in here. I'm actually not supposed to be in this unit, so if the cops find out, we'd be in big trouble."

So this was quite literally a secret area for him. I knew I couldn't tell anyone about this, except maybe someone that is really close to me that I could trust. The location of his hideout, and how he has it operated to get in and out, I don't think he has to worry about people finding out about it. We manage to finally get the gate open, and we walk inside the warehouse unit.

Even though the inside is completely dark, I can still make out certain things, and I see several art projects all over. Mark then takes out a lighter from his pocket, and begins to light some candles that were situated close to the gate of the warehouse unit. Once the candles are lit, I'm able to see what's inside a little bit better, even though it's still dark inside. I look around, and see several pieces of art that Mark has worked on, and I see art painted and drawn on the walls of the warehouse unit. The unit is reasonably large sized, and art is all over it. I knew Mark had an imaginative spirit, but some of the things that were located in the unit, I was surprised that it actually came from him. He was truly involved in his talent, and it showed. Now that I was aware of this location, I wondered if maybe I could also work with Mark here, and we could do something together. The secret spot was away from the city, and we wouldn't be bothered at all.

The only issue was, that it wasn't legal for us to be hanging in this warehouse unit, but who was going to find out? It's not like we are doing anything bad in there. It's only a bunch of art and paintings. Mark then began to tell me how he found out about the secret location. He had a strange idea to go to the port to do some urban street art. As he was walking around the area, his curiosity sparked him. Coming across the front concealed gate of the unit by chance, he wanted to know what exactly was in inside. Once he got inside the unit, he immediately began to think of it as the perfect secret place to do his art. So long story short, it became his own personal secret domain.

Mark cherished his secret area very greatly, but it was only a secret area. Mark wanted a more secure way to do this art, and to display his art. He was in discussion of leasing a store front location in Downtown Los Angeles, so he could showcase his art. Mark was also having plans of allowing me to do my art there as well. It would be our own art collective. As I was looking through the secret area, Mark let me know about this.

"I like this area very much, but it's not really safe. So I'm currently in developments of getting a more legal place to do our art. It's for the both of us."

That made sense, as this secret area was nice, but it was not the appropriate place to do art. It was fun and exciting for Mark to have this hidden area, but we needed something more official. Over the coming weeks, Mark was able to lease the storefront that he wanted, and we began to do most of our art at that storefront. It wasn't located that far from where our apartment was, so we could get there rather quickly, and we also could transport our art there easily as well. Mark had big plans of this being our own personal art collective.

We would bring in other local artists, and we would collaborate on our work with others as well. We would also have art shows as well, and it would be very exciting. Mark and I had day jobs, to where at the time I was working for and print and copy shop, and Mark was working as a graphic designer for an electronic company; but after we were finished with our day jobs, and during the weekends, we would spend all of our time at this storefront. People in the street would walk by, confused as to whether or not we were a retail store, or an art museum. They didn't know what we were doing, but they were interested.

To be honest, Mark and I didn't know what we were doing either. Most of the time, the both of us experimented, and we loved to experiment. The fact we were trying new things was interesting for us. The storefront allowed us to experiment in any type of way we wanted, and display any type of art that we wanted. As long as we had it on display, and people walking downtown in the street payed attention to it, we did our job right.

Mark and I have now been dealing in the storefront for a few months, and already at this point, several other artists have begun to join us there. During the evening on weekdays, and on the weekends all day and all night, sometimes late into the night, we all would work in the storefront, making the best art that we could possibly make. We knew that we need to put on an art show or art exhibit for the public to enjoy. We weren't going to force people to come in, but if it was something they were interested in, they could see. It would be free admission, and there would also be snacks for people to enjoy as well.

The day of the art exhibit arrived, and several people in the city decided to show up. Having so many people enjoy our art, was amazing. The last time Mark and I had this amount of people appreciating our art, was back in High School when we had our comic. The event was so great, that Mark even planned a second one.

The second art exhibit event, was even more exorbitant than the first one was. More people were in attendance, and we also had more diverse art displays being featured. People were forming a line outside in the sidewalk to see our storefront. It was an amazing feeling having so many strange people that we didn't even know, check out our storefront. Not only for Mark and I, but for other artists that were local.

This was a part that we liked, as we were giving back to other artists in the area. This allowed them to display their art without any issues. Even though Mark and I didn't have roots in this classic and contemporary form of showing our art, we were happy that our decision to try something new and different, worked.

However, things would start to spring into disaster soon. I don't want to believe in curses, but I don't know how else to explain it really. Whenever we try to do something good, and things are going good, badness or disaster has to come out of it somehow. Everything related to the storefront was doing fine, but things were going too comfortably well. The storefront was a place Mark and I spent much time at, and it was also well liked by the community, but it seems that things would go terribly wrong soon.

Mark and I would wake up early every Saturday to go work in the storefront. Saturday would be the day we would spend the most time there. Passerby's in the street would also be curious about our storefront on Saturdays. It was an important day for us. However, this Saturday would not be the same. As we were walking to the storefront, we noticed a bunch of broken glass shattered all over the sidewalk. Upon further inspection, we saw that the glass window of our storefront was smashed into. Mark and I stand in shock, and can't believe this at all. I see the look of sadness on Mark's face, seeing his storefront destroyed like this. If that wasn't bad enough, several art pieces that belonged to Mark, myself and other artists were stolen, several paintings were stolen, art supplies were stolen, and Mark's iPad was also stolen that was located hidden on a bookshelf in the storefront.

We were robbed, and this was shocking for us to deal with. Who the hell would rob a place like this? Because Mark wasn't expecting anyone to rob the storefront, he didn't install any security camera's in the building. So we would not be able to have any surveillance footage at all of the people that did this. Mark immediately began to cry on the sidewalk, picking up pieces of the broken glass off the ground, devastated. I could feel Mark's hurt, as this storefront was his vision. This was his way of displaying his art in a positive way, to the people in the community. I walk inside the storefront, while Mark remains outside on the sidewalk, frozen with his depression. I look at how the degenerates who broke into the storefront trashed everything, and stole practically everything inside.

The only thing which remained, were a bunch of empty bookshelves. I pull out my cellphone, and call the police, letting them know that our storefront was robbed. When the police arrived, they couldn't care less about what happened. It was a shame that the authorities were very unhelpful with this. We were a nonprofit business, and the community enjoyed what we put out, so we assumed the police would be more interested in helping us.

This event really caused Mark to go into deep pity. So much, that he decided to sell the storefront. This was something that I thought was a big mistake. I really wish that Mark would not have taken what happened so deeply. Yes the storefront got robbed, but we should have kept on going from that. Mark was too upset, and there was nothing I could do to get him from not selling the storefront. His mind was already made up, and I had to accept this, even though I did not agree with it one bit. After we lost the storefront, Mark stopped concentrating on his art for quite some time. I also became distant with him yet again, and this wasn't good. I was just starting to recover lost time that I had with my brother, and we went back to separating again.

Mark was using his storefront being broken into, as an excuse to go deeper into a black hole. It didn't make any sense to me, and I wish Mark didn't give up like that. This wasn't his attitude at all, and he had so much fight and strength left in him than that. I noticed Mark wouldn't speak to me, and he was hiding all of his emotions. He wasn't able to keep this up for long, and I caught him in the middle of an emotional breakdown. I was coming home from work one evening, and Mark was in our living room on the sofa. He was very upset and crying, and he seemed anxious. I was anxious looking at him. I sit down next to him on the sofa, to comfort him.

"What's the matter Mark? Why are you so upset?"

Mark continued to cry, and he struggles to speak, but responds to me.

"I don't know what's wrong. All I wanted to do was my art, and I can't even do that anymore. I have no control over my life anymore, and I feel so lost."

I massage Mark's back comforting him. He was very emotional, and I could understand. His vision with the storefront was gone, and he had no idea as to where he should go from here. Although it took some time, Mark snapped out of his slump again. This time, Mark was interested in owning a rooftop loft in downtown Los Angeles. The lease in our apartment that Mark and I were staying at was ending, so we were looking for a new place. The loft would serve as our residence, and also our own art studio. Mark was having trouble finding a place to where he could focus and concentrate on his art.

The problem was, Mark couldn't afford the loft on his own, so he needed my help to go dutch on purchasing it. On the condition that the both of us would be co-owners of the loft, and live and work in it together. Mark out of the blue took me out to lunch, and he gave me the news about the loft.

"Carl, I was talking to a friend of mine, and there is a loft downtown that would be perfect for us. I feel it's our style, and it will be our home and our own art studio. I need your help to split the cost. We both would own it, and it would be ours. What do you say?"

I was very accepting of the idea, and it seemed perfect. I agreed to split the cost of the loft, and was completely on board with it. A few weeks later, Mark and I became owners of the loft, and we began to move our things inside of the loft. The loft turned out to be a grand idea, and it was the perfect place for my brother and I. Mark would work on his art, and I would work on my art was well. Things were going well for us during this time, and it seemed as if Mark and I finally settled down with each other. Yet, there was still something that wasn't right.

Despite the fact that Mark and I lived and worked in the loft, it wasn't like how it was before with us. We eventually acted independent of one another moving into the loft. Mark had his own ideas, projects and events he would attend, and I also had my own agendas. Maybe there was nothing I could do to fix this? Perhaps the fact that Mark and I were getting older, I had to accept that Mark wants to live his own life, and I should focus on my own life as well. That part I could understand. I understand that Mark wants his independence, and the doesn't want me in his life all day and every day. The part I didn't understand, is why we couldn't work together on our art at least once in a while. It seemed Mark had no intentions of this anymore, and I would feel sad and distraught over this. When we had the storefront in operation, Mark and I would do projects together.

We also had community involvement with our art as well. However upon moving into the loft, that changed. That was not why I agreed to the loft. I agreed to move in the loft, so that Mark and I could be closer with our art. That didn't happen, and this was bugging me greatly.

Discussing this with Mark would become a challenge. I would never get to see him, as he was always gone. He would travel quite a bit with his art, and would start to participate in art shows not only in Los Angeles, but in cities farther away, and out of state too. I was proud that he was doing the things he wanted to do, but I didn't think it was too much for me to ask my brother to work on a project with me every once in a while. I couldn't bring this up with Mark, as he was always busy, and I could never find the time to discuss this with him in an appropriate way. There was an art contest that I wanted for Mark and I to enter, and this would be the best opportunity to work together again, like we used to. The contest was approaching soon, and I still couldn't make time to let Mark know about the contest. I wasn't going to enter it without him, and I really needed his help as well, so we could win.

The time for me to talk to Mark came, but it came at the expense of Mark and I fighting. I was in the loft painting, when Mark came into the loft one night very intoxicated with two companions. A young male and a young female. The two companions that he came into the unit with, sat down on the sofa of the unit, and during this time I walked over to Mark and spoke to him.

"Hey Mark, if you have a couple minutes, may I speak to you please?"

Mark ignores what I said, and turns the stereo on very loudly. The music is so loud in the loft, that you cannot hear anyone speak. I walk over to the stereo to turn it down to a more appropriate level so that someone could talk and have a conversation. I had to speak to Mark, and it was very important. Mark became extremely angry over me turning the stereo down, and gives me an angry look. He walks back over to the stereo, turning the volume up. Mark then looks at me, and angrily shouts.

"Don't touch that radio again Carl. I had a really bad day, and I don't want to talk to you. I'm here with some friends, and I'm trying to party. Go over there and leave us alone."

I began to list my options. I either leave Mark alone as he's clearly irritable right now, and clearly doesn't want to talk to me. If I leave him alone though, I won't ever get to tell him about the contest, and I don't know the next time I'll see Mark when he's not busy with a project or away from the loft. If I decide to talk to Mark anyway, he'll be mad, but at least I would have said what I had to say to him. I thought about it shortly, then I knew that I had to speak to Mark. As his brother, I come before some random friends he invited over. I once again walk over to the stereo, turning the volume on it down. Mark of course did not take this well, and shouts.

"Carl, I thought I told you not to touch that fucking radio? What is your damn problem?"

I go over to the area that Mark is in, and stand in front of him. I give him the news I wanted to tell him.

"Mark, there is an art contest next week. You need to partner to enter, but it's kinda like a game show thing. You and a partner have to create an art project on the spot out of a bunch of random items. It sounds fun right? I figured that we could go do it together. What do you say?"

Mark doesn't seem pleased at all, and I start to get disappointed. I was hoping he would be happy to hear this news, and would be glad to attend. He then begins to laugh in my face hysterically, and then in a rude way, responds to me.

"I say that sounds stupid. I'm not entering that fucking contest. Why are you just now letting me know about that? My schedule is very busy, and I don't have time for that. Sorry."

Mark doesn't want to go to the contest, and that's his choice. I can't force him to go, if he doesn't want to. Mark then directs himself back to the stereo, and turns it on. I failed trying to get Mark to attend the event with me. I didn't think there was anything else I could do to convince him. So being that I didn't have a partner for the contest, I wasn't going to go. This was unfortunate, as the event seemed like it could have been interesting. After my conversation with Mark, I didn't hate my brother, but he was changing into someone completely different. I don't know what happened to the Mark I used to know, but he was gone forever.

There was no hope at all at trying to get the old Mark back, and didn't even know if it was possible. Moving on, I left Mark alone. I know that he loved me as his brother, and I loved him, but I would leave him alone. If I was in the loft working on a project, he would complement me on whatever I was working on, and that would be it. Likewise, I did the same. Although I wasn't able to attend all the events Mark would go on, I would go to some of his art shows and compliment his work.

Mark was still dedicated to his art, but it was a more fancy smancy type of art, that in my objective opinion, didn't mesh well with his style. He still gave his best in his art, even though he didn't want to have me involved with it. Mark was hanging out with a different set of people, and I guess he thought of me as too goofy and nerdy. He wanted to be around a more sophisticated crowd, and I guess I could understand.

Mark however was later rejected by the group that he was trying to impress. He was talented with his art, but he couldn't seem to fit into the more fancy art crowd. Once Mark realized that he wasn't good enough for them, he went back to his original passion. Mark returned to doing his own style. Lick clockwork, Mark approached me randomly one day to do a project with him. I never thought that this would ever happen again, but it did. One morning, I was minding my own business in the loft, and Mark approached me.

"Hey Carl, do you want to go to my secret spot and work on something today?"

Mark was back, and I was happy. My brother asked me to do a project with him, and I couldn't be any more pleased. Trying to hold my excitement back, I respond to Mark.

"Of course. I've been waiting so long for you to say that. Let's go right now."

Mark and I start to gather all of our art supplies, and we leave the loft, going directly to Mark's secret hideaway. Once we reach the secret unit, we immediately get to work on our project. This time around, we decided to do something simple, yet still elegant. It was a mural we were going to paint. The mural was a skyline of downtown Los Angeles. We have done a similar piece before, but even if we were painting stick figures on the wall, I was pleased that I was with my brother Mark again, and we were doing our art. Even though life with Mark was like riding a roller coaster. There were ups and downs, and flips and flops. I'm happy right now with Mark. We are doing our art, and it's great. We manage to finish the piece rather quickly.

It took us the entire day to complete it, but it was nice seeing the paining up on the wall of the secret unit. Mark and I leave out of the warehouse, and return home. This was a magical moment, and I'll remember it always. This was unfortunately the final time that Mark and I would work together, so it meant a lot to me. After this, Mark went back to his very busy schedule, and I would seldom see him. Because he was so involved with his art projects, I didn't bother or pester him about this.

The last time I saw Mark; he left the loft early in the morning one day. By chance, I woke up early myself to work on something in the loft, and I saw that Mark was exiting out of the loft, with a couple male friends. I didn't say anything to him, and Mark didn't even look at me. He along with the friends we was with, were on their way to the train tracks to work on a piece. It was a mix of graffiti art, and street art. I found it interesting that Mark did not invite me to go along with them, but he didn't. I'm sure he had his reasons to neglect inviting me, but I don't know. Mark and his friends arrived at the train tracks, early in the morning, and were at this location the entire day. They had no business being here, as it was a prohibited area. Once evening hit, Mark and his friends were leaving the tracks, when Mark's foot got caught on the tracks. His friends tried to free him from the tracks, but they were unsuccessful. One of his friends called the 911 for help, but they were unfortunately too late. In a flash, a train came and ran Mark over, as he was unable to free his foot off the tracks.

I was working in the loft later that night, when I received a call from the police, saying that Mark was ran over by a train. Upon hearing this, I reacted in a strange way. I wasn't immediately sad, and I actually laughed to myself. I just saw Mark leave the loft that morning. The concept of death was becoming hard for me to take into, and I didn't know how to act or react anymore. An hour or so later, the sadness finally hit, and I began sobbing heavily. I started to throw a bunch of things in the loft around, feeling a mix of anger and depression from Mark's death. Mark is not coming back, and I refused to accept this.

I later found out the entire details surrounding Mark's death, and I had so many unanswered questions. I didn't understand why Mark and his friends were doing art on the tracks, knowing how unsafe that was. There were areas that they could have worked on their art, that weren't as dangerous. I also didn't understand why Mark didn't tell me where he was going. I more than likely would have tried to explain to him that doing the art on the tracks is not a good idea. That didn't matter anymore though, as Mark is gone. My brother and my best friend isn't here anymore, and I was left empty; having a constant feeling that I'm being punished by the universe in some way.

At Mark's funeral which was held back in Boston, several family members were in attendance. Mark was being buried and laid to rest, and I would never thought I would see the day to where I would have to attend my own brother's funeral. At his funeral, several pieces of his art were on display as well. Mark's talent as an artist will forever be appreciated. It was because of Mark, I went as far as I did with my art.

I didn't know how I was going to advance in my life, with him not being here anymore. Once Mark's funeral was over, I knew that I had no one else in the world to turn to for support. I only had myself. Not my parents, and not Mark either. Everything from this point relied on me, and only me. I was still here for a purpose, and I had to find that purpose. Back in California at our loft, I start to store all of Mark's personal items away. I can't throw them away due to the memories, but I store them in the loft. I also take a few pieces Mark worked on, and I take them to the secret hideaway unit.

I struggle to open the gate, but I get it open. I place the art pieces Mark created in the secret unit. After doing that, I look at the final piece that Mark and I worked on, and I begin to cry. I have to be strong, as I know Mark would have wanted me to keep going for the both of us, I don't know how and if I can do it, but I have to.

CHAPTER 15:

MAN OF PURPLE (PART 2)

With Mark being gone, life became completcly different from me. At first, I had to adjust with him being gone, and it felt weird for me. I would be in the loft, expecting for Mark to walk in, and he never would. I would be working on a project by myself, wondering where Mark was. Thinking to myself that he is going to walk into the loft anytime now, and he wouldn't. I then had to realize that Mark was never going to come back, and that's how it was going to be. There would be times to where I would think of something funny I wanted to tell Mark, as we would relay jokes to each other on occasion, but then I had to stop myself, as Mark is not here. Situations such as this would continue for several months after Mark passed. They would happen very frequently, and it was starting to cause me mental strain and stress. I was hoping that I would take Mark's passing well, and for the most part I did. Although, I would at times think Mark was still here, and I would anticipate seeing him or talking to him. When I had to understand that this wasn't going to happen. The only way to fix this, was that I would try my best to not think about him anymore, but this would only help me for about an hour or so. After that, I would immediately return to feeling upset and depressed; thinking about Mark, and missing him greatly.

This would cause an issue when I was trying to do my art projects. I would constantly think about Mark, and I couldn't focus on my work.

It was very difficult at first for me to continue on doing art, knowing that my brother isn't here to appreciate it. Mark was my main motivation for doing art, and I would feel since Mark isn't here, my art is meaningless now. I was not able to see the point at all of continuing art without him. Several of the art pieces that Mark worked on, were all across the loft. Each and every time I would look at them, it was impossible for me not to get into a wave of sadness due to that.

As the months after Mark's passing continued, I little by little began to simmer myself down. I knew that Mark would not have wanted me to be in this deep depression over him. Mark would have wanted me to go on with my art, and to make him proud. If Mark were here now, seeing me upset, there was no way that he would stand for that and accept it. So although it was not easy for me to go on without Mark being there at first, I had to move on. Not only for the sake of Mark, but for the sake of myself as well. Mark wasn't here, and I had every right to be mad that my brother was dead. I also had every right to grieve over him being gone. But I wasn't accomplishing a damn thing by letting Mark's death get a hold of me like this. I had to grow from that.

From that point forward, I kept Mark in my memories, and I took my art to a more advanced level. All because of Mark. I had to work even better than I was previously, so that my art can reflect the both of us, as he is no longer here. My art was more serious, and it carried a bigger meaning and message. I also went back to doing street art. I would visit the secret spot that Mark would frequent, and I would so some art there. Mark would have been appreciative of this, and I know that he would have liked this very much. Mark was heavily into street art, and urban art, and he liked huge wall murals as well. I wanted to do a really big street art piece in Mark's memory.

This time around however, I went about it the proper way. Instead of sticking to doing things illegally, and trying to sneak and do wall art without the police finding out, I wanted to make sure on the legal side of things, I could do my art. There was a piece that Mark was thinking of doing, that he never got to finish during his lifetime. He wanted to paint this mural which featured a bunch of stick figures walking across a globe of planet earth in space, with the backdrop looking like the universe. At the time I found it to be an interesting vision he had, and would have liked to have seen the final product once he was done with it. Sadly, he never got around to doing it, although he did express great interest into doing it someday. He also wanted me to help him with the piece as well. Other things got in the way, and we neglected completing this project. In Mark's memory and legacy, I now want to make sure this piece gets completed.

I took myself down to the county office, to talk to someone about legally painting this mural outside of a building in the city. I was not sure if they were going to allow me to paint this or not, but I at least wanted to try to see what they would say. I spoke with an older bald gentleman in a suit, that worked for the county of Los Angeles. He worked for the city gentrification program. The only way for me to pain the mural, is that I must get the permission from this man to do so. The man began to speak to me in a friendly tone.

"Hello, my name is Richard Ridgeman. I spoke to you over the telephone Carl, and I understand that you want to paint an art mural in the downtown area. I have decided to allow you to do it, but you must provide your own paint and supplies. So here is your permit to paint."

Mr. Ridgeman hands me a piece of paper, that says that I am allowed permission to paint the mural. I immediately begin to thank Mr. Ridgeman, for giving me the paint permit.

"Thank you very much sir. I can provide my own paint, that's fine. Once the mural is finished, it's going to be very beautiful and lovely. I want it to represent the city well, so I will do an absolute perfect job. Thank you again."

I shake Mr. Ridgeman's hand, and I walk out of his office, glad that I can now paint the mural that Mark and I were supposed to do, without any legal hassles. The only problem was, this was going to be the first mural that I would paint without Mark's help. I have painted several murals before, but each and every time, Mark was there to work on the project with me. That of course is not going to happen this time. I began to feel that this job was going to be impossible to do without the help of

Mark. However, that only made the challenge more exciting, that this job had to be done without Mark. This was going to be the ultimate test to see if I can display my talents, even though Mark is no longer here. I immediately began to prepare myself for this piece. I knew that it was going to be a difficult task, especially since I was painting it by myself. I just couldn't stop thinking of how happy Mark would be if he saw what I finished. I couldn't stop thinking about how people walking in the street would be amazed as to how beautiful the piece was. Most importantly above all, I would gain the self-satisfaction that I was the artist behind the piece. That lovely artwork was my own creation, and I made it.

The first day doing the piece, I woke up very early in the morning to start working. The building that I was going to paint, was outside of an office building, in a short walking distance from the courthouse and the civic center in downtown Los Angeles. The mural was also going to be fifty feet long, and ten feet high. The piece was going to be quite large and big. So many people would see the piece once it was done, and they would also see me paint it in action. The first day doing the piece caused me the most issues. I only used black and white paints, and didn't want to use any colors quite yet. I was still outlining and mapping my specific plan for the entire piece as a whole.

After the first day was complete, I felt like I didn't accomplish that much at all, even though I actually did contribute much to the painting. I worked on the painting all day. I painted until sunrise, until sunset basically. The outline of the piece was pretty much done, and the following day I could finally begin to add color to the piece. The next morning when I returned to the piece, I was shocked as to what I found. My entire piece was vandalized and defaced. It didn't seem to be gang graffiti or anything like that to me. I'm sure it was just some ignorant person that decided to do that. I don't know what would make someone destroy a beautiful art piece like that.

I was angry about it in the beginning, but I then realized that I was very early onto the piece, and I could correct this, and work around this. I was happy that it wasn't defaced when I added color to the piece. At that time, it would have been extremely more difficult for me to rectify.

I had to first fix what the vandals did to my piece. I covered up what they did with white paint, using it as an illusion of an eraser. After I cleared that up, which only took a short amount of time, I proceeded to go back to painting the piece.

While I was painting, I would have several pedestrians in the street gaze in curiosity at my painting. It was only natural for them to do that, as it was very easy to stop and stare at what I was doing. I wasn't getting paid for painting this mural at all. I was only participating in the art gentrification program that this mural falls under. By me painting this mural, it's making the city look more beautiful, and it's bringing art to a better understanding with the citizens in the community. But as I was painting, people would come up and ask me several questions. One of the questions that they would frequently ask would be;

"Excuse me sir, what exactly are you painting?"

As an artist, this would be a difficult question to always answer. As what I see in a painting, someone else might not see. The perception of the art and how it contrasts between the artist, is different between how it would contrast from a regular person looking at it. So even though inside this question would be hard for me to answer, I would still be polite to people. My answer would be something similar along the lines of;

"Well, this is going to be a mural of a bunch of people walking across a globe of planet earth in space. The people are represented as detailed stick figures. This is done, so you can imagine the people to represent everyone. They could be black or white, young or old, it doesn't matter."

The people in the street would then nod their heads, and figure my answer was satisfactory for them, and they would continue on about their day and business. That was only one of many questions that I would get. As I continued to paint, I would constantly be bombarded with several other questions that I would have problems answering. Another question that they would pester me much about would be.

"This painting is very large. What is the meaning behind the painting?"

Again, another question that I didn't know how to explain lightly to people looking at the piece. I'm only the artist, and as the artist I can't really explain it as a spectator would. You know the old saying that a picture can tell a thousand words? That is so true. The painting could be explained in several words. Someone can look at a painting and to them it looks like a dog on a surfboard. Someone else can look at the same painting and to them, it looks like dog on a skateboard and not a surfboard. Or maybe to them it's not even a dog, it's a cat from how they looked at it, or it's a racoon, or it's a rabbit or it's a whatever. But I would always be polite to people in the street who asked me questions such as this. My response would be identical to something like;

"Well the meaning behind it is very simple. I feel that we as people to need to all unite in peace with one another. We are all here on earth as human beings, and we need to come together to show peace, love and harmony. So that's the meaning behind the piece."

The people in the street would then accept my answer, and carry on. The questions would be presented nonstop to me. I didn't want to be rude, so I would answer every question they were curious about. Another common question that they would want to know from me was;

"What inspired you to make a painting such as this?"

Now it seems that all of these questions are the same, but they are actually all quite different. They are similar yes, but they are all different questions. They were all not easy for me to answer in addition to that. With the particular question as to what my inspiration is, this one I had a more subtle answer for. It was a simple answer, but it wasn't simple for me to say out loud to other people. My inspiration was Mark basically. This whole painting was his idea and his vision. Being that he's not spiritually here to offer his talents anymore, I am doing it for him, and to make sure that his legacy lives on. Just as like I did with the other questions people asked me, I decided to be honest with my answer to this one, and would say;

"My brother Mark was an artist, and he was really good too. He sadly passed away, but he wanted to do this painting when he was alive. He never got to do it, and so here I am. He is inspiring me to do this piece, and I do it out of respect to him."

I would tell people about Mark's death, and they would offer empathy to me, and I would appreciate this greatly. They understood my passion and inspiration for the piece, and it made perfect sense at that point. I was then starting to become aggravated over people bothering with me questions. It was distracting me from completing the piece. I wish these people would respect the artist while he's at work, and not ask him a bunch of questions. They were lucky that I was a nice person, and if someone asked me a question, I would stop the piece and answer it.

Although I wish that they would have respected that I was trying to work, and left me alone. The closer I got to completing the piece, when more and more people would ask me questions about it. That's the part that frustrated me the most, as I'm nearly done with it, and I have to stop what I'm doing to answer questions from people. But aside from that, the piece was extremely fun to do. I was having a great time waking up every morning, and every day working on it.

At the end of each day, I was slightly disappointed that I had to stop painting. I was having such a great time, and I wanted to keep going. However, it would get too dark, and I would have to suspend painting for that particular day, and pick up where I left off the next day. I would wake up the following day, and start all over. My excitement would return, and I would head back to the area to work on my painting. It was becoming a routine I liked. As I was getting closer to the completion of the piece, I had a small anxious feeling.

I wish I could work on this piece every single day for the rest of my life. But I knew that once the piece was complete, that was it. I was going to have to move on to something else in my life. Yeah I would be happy I finished it, but it is a weird feeling that only an artist can relay. Wanting to keep going with your piece, even though it's complete.

I remember the evening I started doing my final brush strokes on the piece. I was trying to contain myself from sobbing, and holding back the tears. I was not able to, and I began crying. This whole piece which was to represent both Mark and I, was coming to an end. The several weeks that I that I spent working on this piece, all have a meaning now.

It wasn't necessarily the time that I spent on the piece, but the value behind it. Painting this huge mural in downtown Los Angeles, for everyone to see. The piece actually meant more than that. It was a beautiful piece on its own yes, but it represented myself. This piece was a Carl Stovek creation, and I was so happy to sign my name on the edge of that piece once I was done. It not only represented myself, but it represented Mark as well. It represented humanity and society in a whole. The piece was really trying to say something, and that brought me joy. Even though Mark would never get to physically see this piece, I know that he's happy spiritually that I finished it.

If Mark were here, he would be so happy with it. I started to pack up all my paints, but every thirty seconds or so, I couldn't help but look back at the mural, in disbelief that I created that. I painted this very beautiful artwork. It's a feeling that's wonderful to have, and it was good. I was officially done with the piece, and I can now live with the memory of Mark in a happy way.

The piece he wanted to do, is now done. I walked to the other side of the street for a better perspective of the piece, and as the sun was setting, the piece started to glow very beautifully. I began to cry some more, just stunned that I managed to paint that. I shook my head, and this felt like a dream. I then take out my phone, and snap a picture of the piece. As much as I want to visit this piece every day, I cannot. So at least when I want to take a look at it, I'll have a reference of it always in my phone. Working on this piece was quite an adventure, and doing the project held deep rooted emotions.

After I finished this piece, I was happy to call myself an artist again. I was going to continue to do art, as I am an artist. Artists go through issues in their lives like everyone else in the world does, but that doesn't mean I have to quit. I have to keep going, and I refuse to stop doing, what I love doing.

At this point, I would start to give back to my art more. I wanted to help others with my art, something that I didn't really do before this. I would ask schools if I could teach the students how to do art after school. They said it was okay, and I would then teach the kids how to paint. To my surprise, they were actually thankful for this, and they learned a lot from what I taught them. I figure if I could get youth to appreciate art, that's doing a good service. The art pieces the kids would create I also enjoyed. Art is subjective, and whatever they put on their canvas, was perfect to me. Whatever the kids created, was good enough for me. In my opinion, there are no failures in art. Whatever the artist creates is simply perfect. I then decided to go to Children's hospitals, and teach them how to paint. Even though these children are in a terrible place in their lives, I wanted to do something special for them.

Interacting with youth, teaching them art, was a pleasant experience for me. I consider myself an open minded friendly guy, so I'm always going to help other people. That's the type of guy I am, and I've always been someone to give back to others. For some time, I even though about becoming an art therapist. I knew being an autistic man myself, and also being a skilled artist, I can be an inspiration to others perhaps. I didn't know if I could be an licensed art therapist, however I wanted to do all I could to use my art as therapy for others. I was not sure how I was going to accomplish this at first though.

I discussed this with several mental health organizations, asking if I could be a volunteer art therapist. I wouldn't get paid for the art therapy I gave, and I was doing it out of the kindness and the goodness of my heart. For my art therapy, I would work in a large group, and give them a certain theme to paint or draw on. I would then work on a piece myself, so all of us were interacting in the exercise.

Then after we were done drawing or painting, if they were comfortable enough, I would ask if they wanted to describe what their piece was. When I started to do my art therapy, I was working with both kids and adults. I noticed that when I was working with kids, the kids were more creative and engaging with their art. When I was working with adults, the adults were more serious with their drawings, and their art therapy.

I would go with a different approach when I was working with kids, than I when I was working with the adults. What impressed me the most doing art therapy, was hearing stories that these people had behind their art. Some of the kids in the art therapy program, went through devastating events. Some of them had to escape abuse and really horrible things. They would look forward to doing art therapy every other week, and they couldn't wait to see me. With the adults, it was more of a social activity, and it was to get them to vent whatever personal feelings they were recently going through.

During art therapy when I was working with the kids, I would bring snacks and candy for them to eat. I would also bring pizza too. My main goal was for them to be comfortable during art therapy, and I did my job right. I didn't run into any problems, and I didn't have not one issue with any of the kids that I worked with when I was doing art therapy.

As far as the adults, I would have art gallery events sometimes, and I would offer alcohol to them. I would bring wine, and the organization said it was okay. So you can't say that I didn't make my clients comfortable, whether they were children or adults. Sadly, because I wasn't a licensed art therapist, I was sort of corralled into my art therapy being suspended. The organization told me that due to recent conduct changes, because I wasn't licensed, I had to stop giving art therapy. Once I found out about this news, I was so upset, and I felt angry as well. I wasn't sure how I was going to give this news to my clients. When it came time for me to tell the kids I couldn't give them art therapy anymore, they of course were saddened by the news.

However, I let them know that I was going to try finding a way for me to still work with them. Luckily, I was able to. The kids I worked with, I got to see again at the community center. The only thing, was that I couldn't call it art therapy. It was simply a youth art day camp center. I worked with other artists in the city, and we would teach the kids art, and do projects. Telling the adults I worked with the news I had to stop giving them art therapy, actually went remarkably well. They understood that these things happen, and I wasn't licensed to give them art therapy. But I still kept in contact with some of the adults, and some of them even attended some of my art shows that I had in the future.

My life took an immediate left turn, when I was returning from a community art project that I was doing with other artists in the city one night. We were preparing for an upcoming art show, so it was a big deal for me. I noticed when I was at the art studio, it was getting quite late, so I decided to go home to my loft. As I'm walking home, I see a bunch of guys beating up someone. As I said before, I'm the type of person that springs into acting during times like this. I didn't like seeing people being attacked in the street, and I became instantly triggered.

Ordinarily, someone would just walk away and ignore this. I think it's the 'Bystander Effect' I believe. Well I don't operate like that. If I see something, I say something, and I take action. I see that this young man is being robbed, and I couldn't live with myself if I didn't do anything to help. When I saw that the robbers were aiming a gun at him, I knew how heavy and serious this was. They were now robbing him at gunpoint, and I was not sure if they were going to kill him or not. I had to do something right now to help this issue. I didn't know who this guy was, but I had to step up and do something quick. Even if I end up being hurt in the process, I didn't want to see this man being attacked, and being helpless. I decide to do a brave thing, and shout out to the guys.

"Why don't you guys leave him the hell alone, and pick on someone your own size? Why are you picking on him? All you guys against him, that's really brave."

I said something along those lines. I didn't think it was fair that all those guys were robbing and beating him up. The men that were robbing him, then pointed their attention towards me. The men then started to charge in my direction, shouting at me.

"Who the hell are you? We are going to kill you!"

I wasn't scared of them at all. I had nothing to be scared of. I didn't sense any fear, and didn't think I was going to die. I wanted to help the guy they were picking on, and that was my agenda. Living my life in fear was no longer an option. Living my life in anxiety wasn't an option either. After losing Mark, I had a new lease on my life, and being scared and anxious wasn't in my plan at all.

Even though this was a complete stranger to me being beat up and robbed in the street, I had to come to his rescue and help him. I end up showing a large knife to them. It was the only thing I could think of in that moment. The only reason I had the knife, was because I was doing some oil painting earlier. The knife began to intimidate the men slightly, and they knew that I meant business. I was not going to allow these guys to scare me, or to hurt this young man any further. At this time, police sirens started to wail, and a police squad car was coming in our direction.

The men I believe started to become scared, and immediately ran away from the scene. The police officer sped right past where we all were at in the street. I don't even think the police officer noticed or saw us. Me and this strange young man were standing in silence for a short while. I couldn't believe that I saved somebody, and I managed to come to his defense and rescue. I notice that there are a bunch of fabrics scattered all across the sidewalk.

I then see a case that's open and thrown across the sidewalk as well. I knew the guys were trying to rob him, as they assumed he had something valuable in the case. I then start to talk to the young man, making sure that he's safe, and he's okay.

"Are you okay? Are you hurt, do you need me to take you to the hospital?"

The young man tells me that he's fine. After looking at him deeply, I can see what a kind spirit he has. I can see that the both of us have a similar attitude towards each other. As far as romance and affection, that's not my territory at all. You have to talk to someone else. But I have to admit I was really feeling for this guy, and he was causing me to feel a certain way. During this time, I started to introduce myself to him, being friendly.

"My name is Carl. I saw you in the street like that, and I couldn't leave you there."

The young man then introduces himself as Jerald. Putting a name behind him was good. I saved Jerald from being attacked in the street, and I knew he appreciated me for that. I then found out that Jerald was a fashion designer, as I was helping him pick up his designs off the sidewalk. Even though he did fashion design, that was still an artistic passion, and we already shared something common right there. His talent was good, and I didn't know much about fashion design, but I appreciated how creative he was. Jerald began to thank me for saving him, and we remained here in an awkward silence. Jerald then began to grab his things, and he said goodbye to me. I was originally going to let him go, but I was sensing something different about Jerald.

I knew he was a special human being, and that I had to get to know him much more. Was it fate that I came across him being bashed in the street? I didn't know if it was or wasn't, but I didn't want this time to end at all. Jerald was going to have a great impression on my life, and I wasn't even aware of it quite yet. Despite the fact Jerald dismissed himself, and was on his way home, I didn't want him to go just yet. I end up grabbing Jerald by the wrist, which is something in hindsight I probably shouldn't have done. I didn't know any other way to get his attention though except by doing that. As I'm grabbing his wrist, I then begin to speak with Jerald.

"Hey don't go. I want to show you my place. I saved your life, so I won't take no for an answer. I just live around the corner. Follow me please."

I then end up walking with Jerald to my loft. This was the first time that I brought anyone over to the loft. Mark would bring friends over constantly, but this was the very first time that I brought someone over. As we were getting closer to my loft, I knew that Jerald felt safe with me. You can tell when someone is enjoying being around you or not, and Jerald was liking the fact that I was with him.

He was probably thinking of me as his savior, or some type of guardian angel. That's fine if he felt like that, because in many ways I was. I finally reach my loft, and Jerald and I walk in. Due to the fact I never invited a guest over before, I was unsure of how to act. I didn't know what to do, as I never invited company over before. Jerald began to ask me questions, and one question he asked was how I ended up owning the loft. I didn't tell Jerald at the time, that Mark and I stayed here. I kept it neutral at this point, and simply said that myself and a friend owned it, and my friend is no longer here.

I go in the refrigerator, and I grab two beers, handing Jerald one of the beers. As Jerald was walking around the loft, he was very fascinated by what he saw. He was interested in my art very much, and this made me appreciate Jerald's company even more. As the night went on with Jerald in my loft, there were times that I forgot he was even there. I invited Jerald over to the loft, and I'm being a terrible host.

But give me a break, I have never invited anyone over before, so I was unsure as to how I should act. Was I infatuated with Jerald? I guess you can say I was. He seemed like a nice guy, and I don't know. I knew I was bisexual and I liked both girls and guys. Jerald was a cute guy, I'm going to admit. Maybe due to my autism, this was difficult for me to accept this, but I don't know. As Jerald was still in the loft, I begin to work on an oil painting. I take a blank canvas out, and I begin to paint.

I didn't tell Jerald at the time, but I was planning on painting a portrait of him. I thought that if I told Jerald that I was going to paint him, it would have ruined the surprise. But if I paint and leave Jerald in suspense, it would come across much better.

As I'm painting, Jerald comes over to my art station, and watches me paint. I didn't mind him watching me, but it was slightly overwhelming having him creep over me while I'm painting. It felt kinda strange, and I was feeling uncomfortable about it. I didn't tell Jerald this, as I kept it to myself. I didn't know how to react at all, so I kept my attention on my painting.

I continue to paint, even though I know Jerald is standing right beside me. There was a cup of paint thinner that was situated next to my art station. On the outside, it looks like it's water, but it's not. I knew what it was, but I guess to someone unsuspecting, they wouldn't know. However, I had no intentions of someone picking it up to drink it. Nobody ever came into my loft, so I didn't have to worry about this. I noticed that Jerald picked the cup up, and I had to immediately act fast. Jerald had already taken a small sip of the paint thinner, by the time I knocked the cup out of his hands. I scream out to him in anger.

"That's not water, that's paint thinner. If you wanted water, why didn't you tell me?"

I don't know why Jerald picked up that cup and drank it. I would have given him some water no problem. He didn't have to do that at all. Now I was scared that he swallowed the paint thinner. I grab Jerald over to my kitchen area, and give him some water to drink. Luckily,

Jerald was going to be okay, despite him drinking some of the paint thinner. I was starting to lose my patience with Jerald, and he was slightly getting on my nerves. He was not making a good first impression with me, and it wasn't easy, but I figured the best thing to do, was to ask Jerald to leave. I had no problem arranging a time later for us to hang out, but Jerald had to leave now. I was polite and kind about it, but I told Jerald that I have to take him home now.

Jerald instantly began to act defiant, and refused to listen to me. He grabbed one of my paint tubes from my art station, and then squeezed a big portion of paint right onto my shirt. I was angry at Jerald, as this paint doesn't come off. So if you stain your clothes with it, there is nothing you could do to get it off. I was also mad because Jerald was wasting my paint like that. Jerald was acting childish, and I didn't want to deal with him right now. I begin to shout at Jerald about the paint, and Jerald then decides to squeeze some of the paint on him as well. I couldn't help but find this cute. Although Jerald was causing me much stress, I did allow him to stay in the loft.

As the night went on, Jerald became more respectful. He eventually walked over to the area my art station was in, and was curious as to what I was painting. At this point as I was wrapping up the painting anyways, I show it to Jerald. It's a portrait of him, and he stood there shocked. He had no idea I was painting him, and his reaction was lovely. Sometime during this night, Jerald kissed me, and it was okay. Yeah my interactions with him were going fast, but I didn't care. Jerald was a nice guy, and I didn't mind being nice in return to him. The night continued on, and it was getting quite late.

Jerald began to feel tired, and he moved over to my bed. I go over to the area he is in, and I give Jerald a kiss goodnight. Jerald falls asleep right after that, and I return to doing more work at my art station. I would stare at Jerald several times during the night. Looking at how peaceful he was sleeping. Watching him rest, seeing how calm he was. I enjoyed it very much. I continued to do my art all night. I did manage to take a cat nap at my art station for a couple hours, but I woke right back up, and did my art. The next morning, Jerald woke up. He was still in my loft, and he was still in my life. I wanted to make this a day of surprises for Jerald. I wanted to take him to the "Los Angeles County Museum of Art", as a test. This test was going to show if the both of us were compatible, and if he could respect my passion for art. If Jerald was happy during our trip to the museum, then he would pass the test. I would allow him to remain in my life, and the possibilities of our friendship would be endless. If Jerald wasn't appreciative of me taking him to the museum, then I would have to stop interacting with him, as he has no respect for my art passion at all.

I managed to get Jerald to come with me to the art museum. I don't tell him where we are going, as that would have just ruined the surprise. Leaving him in suspense was fun, and he knew I wasn't being creepy about it. Jerald didn't feel any danger at all with me, so it was fine. Jerald and I made it to the museum, and I knew he was excited to be there. He didn't even have to tell me, I could tell. I walk through the museum with him, educating Jerald on all the art pieces located in the museum. I enjoyed museums, and it was like being in a toy store.

There were so many artists that I looked up to for inspiration, and so many different art styles as well. I also liked how classic and warm museums were. You could get lost for hours all day staring at the art, and it brought me much happiness going to museums. I walk through several different exhibits with Jerald, wanting to know his perspective on some of the pieces as well, as we continue to tread through the museum. I also knew that there was a temporary exhibit in the museum, that had a particular piece that I did featured. The art collective that I'm currently, allowed us to display our art at the museum. This was an amazing privilege, and I was blessed that we were able to have it. I can say that my art was in a museum, and I knew I was successful as an artist then.

Although it was only a temporary exhibit, it's still a nice accomplishment to have your art on display at the museum. Seeing Jerald's reaction to this was on my mind. He probably had no idea at all, that my artwork that I created is located in the museum. Jerald and I make it to the exhibit my project is in, and I let Jerald look at the piece, without telling him it's mine. Once he sees the tag on the side of the piece with my name, he looks at me totally shocked. Jerald was very proud of me, and he showed great interest in my art. Having Jerald see my art on display at the museum was a good feeling, and I knew he was a right connection for me then.

Jerald and I left the museum, and I wanted to show another place to him. If Jerald was going to be involved in my life, I had to show him the secret hiding spot that Mark had. I could trust Jerald enough by telling him this, so I wasn't worried about that. I began to drive away from the city to the secret hiding spot. Jerald was starting to feel anxious as well, as we were travelling further away from the city. He just met me the day before, and it may have been slightly freighting for him. Jerald was okay being near me though.

Jerald and I get out of the car, and we walk towards the secret area. I reach the gate, and begin to customarily struggle with it. As we get inside the unit, it's completely dark, so I take my cell phone out and turn on a flashlight app. It gives a small source of light into the room. Jerald looks through the secret hiding spot, and likes what he sees. He doesn't know what this place is, but he's thrilled nevertheless. I then begin to speak to Jerald softly, and tell him the significance of this building.

"Remember I told you that I had a friend who died. Well, he was actually my brother Mark. This was his secret hideaway, and he would always do his work here."

It was tough coming out to Jerald over Mark's death, but he had to know this information. I then start to become very emotional, and tense up under the pressure. All of the memories that I was having with Mark, were coming back. I was feeling sad being reminding of everything, that I couldn't think straight at all. During this time, Jerald walks over to me, and starts to comfort me.

Because of all the emotions that I'm currently feeling, I shove Jerald off me. It wasn't a reaction that I was proud to do, but because of the way I was feeling, that's what I did. I felt bad for pushing Jerald away, but I was going through an emotional moment at that time, thinking of my brother Mark. I didn't want for Jerald to think that I was mad or angry at him. I end up apologizing to Jerald for doing that, and he quickly understands. This was a special spot for Mark and I, and Jerald was the only other person in the world who knew about it. I was missing Mark, and being in his personal space didn't help. Jerald and I walk out of the secret spot, and end up closing back the gate.

I wanted to take Jerald to one more place before the night was over. There was a hamburger stand that Mark and I would visit quite frequently called "Super Burger", and I wanted to treat Jerald to dinner there. We arrive at the hamburger stand, and I continue having a great night with Jerald. Once we finished eating, Jerald and I get back in my car. While we are riding, Jerald being concerned, asked me a question.

"So, where are you going to take me now?"

I wasn't intending on taking Jerald anywhere else. I was going to drop him off at home, and that was going to be it. I was going to call it a day. Well actually, I was going to go and get some ice cream, after dropping Jerald off. But I knew that Jerald wanted to stay with me. He didn't want to go home, and if he didn't want to go home, I wasn't going to force him to. I then respond to Jerald in a friendly way, letting him know my agenda.

"Well, I was going to go and get some ice cream, then I was going to go home."

Jerald was happy with me, and didn't want to leave. So he stayed with me for the rest of the night. I went to the store to get some ice cream, and then Jerald returned with me back to my loft. Once back in my loft, I went back to my art, and Jerald made himself at home. He continued to make himself at home, as he was in love with me, and I was in love with him. We both wanted to stay with each other, and it made sense.

We connected well with our passions. I did art, and Jerald did fashion design. It was an unconventional match I guess you could say, but it was a match that made sense. We were happy with each other, and it was good. As time continued, I spent more and more time with Jerald. We would go on many more dates, and our connection grew even bigger than it already was. I would give Jerald a ride to work and pick him up. I spent much time with him. Jerald would also attend some of my art shows. He didn't enjoy them that much, but he would attend them for me. I would also see Jerald's fashion shows. They were not my thing at all, but as Jerald was a close friend to me, and our relationship expanded, I supported whatever he wanted to do. I loved how talented Jerald was with his fashion, and if it made him happy, it made me happy. Whatever I did which made me happy, made Jerald happy.

I allowed Jerald to move into the loft with me. The lease in his apartment was going to end, so it was time for Jerald to move in. If Jerald was the one, which I knew in my heart that he was, then him moving in wasn't going to be any issue or problem. When Jerald moved into the loft, we had our rocky moments. I quickly picked up on the habits that Jerald had that I didn't care for. Jerald also learned to understand my habits as well. Jerald had to understand that I would work on my art deep into night.

This bothered him at first, but he got used to it fast. Jerald would also have to accept that I would be gone from home sometimes, as I would have an art project that I had to work on. Jerald would work on his designs while I was gone, and it didn't bother him as much. He didn't like to see me gone, or work late into the night on my art projects, but he accepted it. As long as he accepted it, we were okay. One day, I took Jerald to see the globe mural that I created downtown. Jerald has seen that mural many times walking downtown, and had no idea I painted it.

So it was nice when I revealed that I created it. When it became clear that Jerald and I were not going to separate, I had to do something to let Jerald know that I'm always going to be here. It was something very special in every relationship, and it's the ultimate sign that the both of you are meant for each other, and the feelings are strong. What I liked about it, was that Jerald had no idea I was thinking this way. Our love was strong, and our bond was even stronger, but this would surprise Jerald greatly, and I wanted him to be surprised. I wanted to propose to Jerald, as I want him to be my partner forever. I love him so much, and he loves me very much, so this was something that had to be done. As far the proposal, I had to make it special, and I wanted it to be a surprise for him. I had thought of several different ways to propose to Jerald in the most romantic way, and I wasn't able to come up with something that didn't seem tacky. I knew it had to be something crazy and wild and different. It had to be something weird and unusual. That was the way Jerald and I were, and we didn't go for anything conventional or traditional.

After careful thinking, I knew the best way to propose to Jerald, was to propose to him at an art contest that I was going to attend. Jerald had no idea that I was going to propose to him at this event. I told him about the event prior, and he knew how big of a deal it was. This art contest was a state wide contest, to where each artist must submit one painting to be judged. The particular painting that I was going to do, involved my brother Mark and I in a very abstract piece.

You can see two figures, that are on the rooftop of a urban building. If you look very carefully at the piece, you can see that Mark and I are painting a mural on the rooftop of the building. So it's a picture of Mark and I painting, within a picture of Mark and I painting. Ha-Ha. That's just one detail of the piece. The remaining area of the piece, consists of other buildings, with Mark and I situated in a downtown area of Los Angeles. I worked on this piece every single day, and Jerald would watch me do it, and he would complement me on my art style as well. I was not sure if I was going to win the contest, but I wanted other people to see the piece.

Reason being, this was the first time that I ever did a piece that was about Mark and I. Even though we weren't fully in detail; Mark and I were represented as just shadows; that was still us on the rooftop doing our art. This was a special piece, and I don't know if I'm ever going to do another piece which features Mark in the future. Doing this piece by itself caused me a lot of mental strain, but I knew that being an artist, I have to put all my feelings into my art, and be strong. When I finished the piece, I cried, and I was proud to cry.

Jerald came over to comfort me, as I was being very emotional. I couldn't wait for the others in the art contest to see this piece, and be amazed just as I was with it. After I explain the piece to them, it will all make sense.

With this painting, everything that Mark and I went through was explained. There was no way I would have done this painting in the past. I would have been too depressed to paint it, because Mark wasn't here. Now with pride, I can make a painting that features my brother and I, and I can accept it. It's okay for me to feel upset and sad about Mark, but I have to do it in a positive way. I have to use the art to honor the both of us. I wrapped the painting up with plastic wrap, with Jerald's help, and I was more than ready for the contest to begin.

When Jerald and I arrived at the contest, I wasn't expecting to see the number of people that were in attendance. It was a high profile fancy event, and I was hoping it was going to be a more low key thing. It wasn't, and I was starting to feel anxious over the large crowd that was there. I then started to glance at the rest of the art pieces that were in the contest. Sizing up my competition; there is nothing wrong with that. I saw the different calibers of talent, and everyone in the contest had talent. I knew the judges were going to have to think very carefully of the winner, due to the fact that every artist in this contest has a piece that's worthy of winning.

Many people were mingling and chatting with each other, but Jerald and I kept to ourselves. I put my painting up, and the judges eventually started to see my picture. By their expressions, they were in awe over it, so this was good. The judges then asked me to explain it.

"This piece, which I call "The Two Artists", features my brother Mark and I painting on a rooftop of a tall building. You can see us painting here, and you can see the backdrop of the entire downtown urban area of Los Angeles. This is around sunset time, given the perspective.."

I continue to explain the piece, and the judges start to take notes down. After explaining the piece, the judges saw how significant the piece was. When I explained the piece, I let the judges know that Mark passed away. They were sad to hear this news. I didn't do this to gain any extra points, but I mentioned it to explain how I'm coping with

Mark's death. with the picture of us. It's more than just a painting. It's a tool for me to accept my brother's death, using his legacy in a positive way. I can still keep Mark alive in my heart with this piece. The judges thank me for the piece, and they move onto judging the other pieces in contest. I begin to feel anxious, as to whether or not my piece was actually going to win. Quite some time later, the judges then made an announcement as to who won the contest. The third place winner was announced, and the person who won third place had very nice piece. I was slightly more confident in winning for some reason, and I knew the judges were moved by how I explained my artwork.

However, when the second place winner was announced, my name was called. I didn't win, I got second place. This was fine though, as I'll take it. Second place is not winning no, but I still felt like a winner. I got to showcase my artwork, and the meaning of the painting came across well, and that's fine. I accept my second place trophy, feeling proud of myself. The first place winner was announced, and the guy who won, deserved it. His piece was lovely as well. No hard feelings.

After this, several of the participants in the art show started to see all the pieces in the contest, and looked at my piece. I was then asked several questions about the piece. Here we go again with asking the artist to explain himself. I didn't mind it from the judges, as that was their job to ask me about the piece. But from normal people, it was frustrating. I just wanted people to appreciate the art. But I was respectful and polite, and explained to them what the piece was about. They were moved by my story, and the elements began to make more sense to the audience who would view my picture.

As the event was coming to a close, and more and more people were leaving. I knew I had to propose to Jerald soon. I wanted to wait until it was just us in the art gallery. I want this moment to be private, and not be disturbed or distracted by anyone else. Soon, the entire building left, and it was just Jerald and I. Now was the time for me to propose. I reach into my art bag and take out a medium sized bucket of washable orange paint. This is a special kind of paint that doesn't stain. I put some blue tarp down on the ground, as what I was about to do was going to mess up the floor. Yes it was an old art gallery building, but I still wanted to be respectful. As I'm finish setting the tarp down, Jerald looks at me strange, as I start to open the paint bucket.

"Carl, what the hell are you doing?"

I ignore Jerald as I get the paint bucket open. I then hold the paint bucket in my hand, and I stop and smile at Jerald for a short white. I then softly speak to him.

"Remember that night you were in my loft, and you poured the paint on me. Well, I didn't forget about that, and this is me paying you back for that night."

I immediately douse the paint bucket over Jerald and I. Jerald is laughing uncontrollably, as the both of us are covered in the orange paint. I then get down on my knees, and pull out a diamond ring out of my pocket. Jerald stops laughing, and becomes serious. I can see how emotional he looks, and can't believe I'm proposing to him. Jerald puts his hands across his mouth, completely shocked and surprised. I then whisper to Jerald.

"Jerald Williams, will you marry me?"

Jerald then pushes me down to the ground, and kisses me passionately. We remain laying on the floor, as Jerald continues to kiss me. Jerald then whispers his answer to me.

"Yes, I will marry you Carl."

I then put the ring on Jerald's finger, and we continue to lay down, covered in paint. This was a very strange way of me proposing to him, but I don't regret it. It went exactly the way I planned, and it was so lovely.

Minutes later, I get up and begin to clean everything. I take a towel out of my art case, and I give it to Jerald so we can clean up. We both end up getting the paint off of us, and we walk out of the gallery. When we reach back to the loft, I hang the painting that I entered into the contest of Mark and I, on the wall. It will be there always, and I'll look at it always. After proposing to Jerald, I knew my life was going to be different. Jerald and I are going to get married soon, and we look forward to that. So even though the wedding isn't planned yet, I am going to stay with Jerald for the rest of my life.

I've been through a lot. Not because I'm an artist that has autism, and I have a crazy personality. That is only a small portion of my life. The big portion of my life, is that I'm a creator and a visionary. I lost my brother Mark, and life was treating me so badly. Mark was my best friend, and I did my art because of Mark. He was my older brother that I was inspired by.

Mark was an amazing artist, and it's a shame that he is gone. His art was much better than mine, and I didn't think it was fair. But Mark still lives on in spirit, and I know he's so glad that his little brother Carl is happy. Mark would have wanted for me to go on and do the best that I could. I found a new friend with my love for Jerald, and things are fine the way they are now. Mark is in my heart, and he loves me, and he has a wide grin on his face.

My passion is still strong, and my art is still strong, and my life is still strong. My name is Carl Stovek, I am man of purple, and that was my story.

CHAPTER 16:

MAN OF GREEN (PART 1)

My name is Jamal Benson, I am 28 years old. I am the "Man of Green", and this is my story. My Reddit username is "Urbanunited". I am a more open minded individual. I have many opinions, but I usually keep them to myself. I can get along with everybody, even people that are totally opposite of me. My style is my own, and I'm comfortable with the way that I carry myself. Even though I am African-American, I was not raised in a similar household or environment. My upbringing is complicated to explain, but I will describe it for you. I never knew who my parents were, and that already was a struggle. I grew up not knowing who my birth family were, and to this day, I still don't. It may seem like it's not a big deal to you, but to me it is. Someone's family life is important, and I grew up without that. I mean, I know my parents were black, but that's about it. I never knew who my mother was, and I never knew who my father was either. I also know that I was born in New York, and my parents abandoned me shortly after birth.

Supposedly they were heavily into drugs, and they gave me up. The only thing I can do, is maybe put it in the perspective that they thought the choice to leave me, was the wise one to make. Otherwise they wouldn't have given me up. Being that I was given up shortly after I was born, I was quickly put into foster care. Let me tell you, foster care was a nightmare. I was in foster care until I was nine years old, and I didn't enjoy not minute of it.

The reason I didn't care for foster care, was basically the whole system of it. You were stuck with a bunch of other kids that were given up by their families, and you spend every single day wishing that you grew up in a normal family. It was like being in jail, and I didn't care for it. It's not something that I feel any kid should go through.

The lady who ran the foster care home that I was in, she was nice when she wanted to be, however she was mostly a wicked woman. Her name was Shirley Remmings. She was an older white woman, and she smoked cigarettes quite often. She always had a cigarette in her hand. Whenever we would address her, we had to call her Ms. Shirley. Ms. Shirley was a pain to deal with, and the thing I never understood is that if she hates kids, why is she fostering them? That didn't make any sense to me at all. Her punishments were also cruel. I don't remember what I did wrong, but I got punished one time; and I do remember that it wasn't my fault and it was an honest mistake. I was punished anyways, and Ms. Shirley would always tell me;

"Jamal, I want you to write, 'I will respect Ms. Shirley' ten thousand times."

I had to been about six years old, and she was making me do this. I would have to sit down and write lines. This bitch was absolutely crazy at times for making me do this. I would sit down for hours writing lines, and it was torture. My fingers and hands were most definitely hurting after doing something such as that. So besides Ms. Shirley, the kids in the program also hated my guts as well. I was a smart kid, so that may have been the reason why. I had a very mature mind, and the other kids thought that they could say whatever to me. That would be a huge mistake for them, as I would always set them straight.

I was the last kid to get into an argument with, as they would lose. At the foster home, they did allow us to watch television. The shows I would watch were mostly things I shouldn't be watching. I was watching a lot of westerns like "Gunsmoke" and "Bonanza". Things that a little black boy growing up in the 90s had no business watching, but I watched them anyways. I was always trying to expand my mind beyond my capacities. I figured that if I could prove people wrong by the way I acted, that would be good. People always perceive things, and most perceptions could be wrong. When I was at the foster home, I tried to make the most of my experience there. Nobody wanted to be my friend there, and there was not one other kid that I could relate to. The coordinator Ms. Shirley was also a handful. My dream was that one day I could get adopted, and I could leave the foster home. A kid was adopted realistically every other month. We would have an open day at the foster home, and one, maybe two at certain times, would get the golden opportunity to have a real family.

But until then, I remained at the foster home, accepting that this is my life. I very seldom became bitter over the fact that I grew up without a regular family. If my regular family wanted me, they would have raised me. They didn't want me, so that's the way the cookie crumbles I guess. I should mention that when I was in the foster home, we didn't go to regular school. Ms. Shirley decided to home school all of us. She was not a very good teacher, and her methods didn't make any sense. So not only was I not in a regular household, I was not being educated in the regular way. I was not with my peers at school, having that experience that normal kids in the world would get to experience.

Going to school, making friends, being taught by a teacher who is certified to teach. Ms. Shirley was not a teacher, and I doubt she had the credentials to home school us, but she did it anyways. At the foster home, when we weren't being taught, we had to do our chores usually. This was the absolute worst. Now I understand that kids have to do chores to build character. But what I don't agree with, is having kids do back breaking work for no damn reason.

Ms. Shirley would basically wake us up extremely early in the morning, and we would either be assigned inside or outside chores for the day. If we had to do an indoor chore, it could include anything from washing the dishes, to scrubbing the floors and walls, and mopping all of the floors. If we had to do an outdoor chore, it was yardwork. Whatever chore that you had to do for that particular day, was going to be a challenge to do. None of the kids enjoyed doing chores, but we had to do it without complaint. Ms. Shirley would always berate us;

"If you guys do not do your chores, I will send you to another home. This is Disneyland compared to the other homes around here, so I would count your blessings. Do your chores."

In all honesty, Ms. Shirley was typically right. Most foster homes ran by the state of New York were badly ran and operated. I swear the foster care system is the worst thing that someone ever came up with. There had to have been a better system, because the way they had it set up, was not right. I could only pray that one day I would be rescued from this place, and I could be with a normal family. Anything but this, I wanted to keep hope. At the foster home, we were not allowed to leave the walls without permission from Ms. Shirley.

If any of us escaped; and several kids did, the police would be called. If we were gone for longer than 24 hours, Ms. Shirley by law would have to report us missing. All the kids, myself included out of defiance, would at least run away once. We mostly did it to spite Ms. Shirley and to make her mad. The foster home area was located in a more suburban area of New York. It was about an hour walk away from Grand Central Station in New York. So it wasn't like the foster home was located in the downtown area of New York. If we ran away from the foster home, we would just be surrounded by a bunch of houses and it was a rural suburban area pretty much. To my knowledge as I can remember, I ran away three times. The reasons I ran away, was because we were always trapped inside the foster home.

Ms. Shirley would arrange outings for us. Like she would allow a couple of us to tag along to the grocery store with her. Or maybe like once a year, she would take us to "Coney Island". This was extremely rare though. Ninety nine percent of the time, we were stuck inside the foster home, and we weren't allowed to leave. The first two times that I ran away, I didn't run that far. But the last time I ran away, I took it to the extreme.

The very last time I ran away, I really had enough. I wanted to go out and see the city, and wanted to get out of that house. I got out of bed early one morning, and told myself that I was going to run away.

Ms. Shirley always locked the front doors, and all the windows were locked as well. But one trick and loophole that we would never tell Ms. Shirley, is that there was a window in the attic that was always kept unlocked. I went up to the attic and sneaked out that way. I then would very carefully jump off the roof and run away.

Now that I was out of the house, I had my freedom. Even though I was more than likely going to get in trouble, I didn't care. I was finally away from that house.

Even though most kids that would run away, would remain within two miles from the house, that wasn't my plan. I knew it was a long walk to the city, but that didn't bother me. I never got to experience the downtown area of New York, and I wanted to see it. Mind you, I was a nine year old kid at this time. It was a very long walk, and I was tired, but I finally made it to the metro area of New York. I got to see tall buildings for the first time, I was able to see street performers. I saw storefronts, and cafes and bakeries. Ms. Shirley would never give us spending money, so I didn't have any money. I was hungry, so I tried to panhandle money so I could buy something to eat.

I managed to get some change, but it still wasn't enough for me to buy a ham sandwich from a corner café that was close to a subway station. I was only able to panhandle a dollar and fifty cents from people in the street, and the sandwich was three dollars. I went into the café and ordered the sandwich anyways. The woman who worked in the café made my sandwich, and I was at the register, and I didn't have enough to buy the sandwich. I put the money I did have on the counter, grabbed the sandwich and ran away. I did feel guilty yes, but I was very hungry.

I kept running for several minutes, until I reached central park. I sat down at central park and began to eat my sandwich. I had a book bag that I brought with me, that had books. I didn't have a Walkman or a video game player. Ms. Shirley thought that video games and electronics were bad for children's brains. Our only entertainment at the foster home were books. So I took a couple books from the library at the foster home, and put them in my book bag. I was now at Central Park eating my sandwich and reading my books. It was so nice to be away from that group home. I knew right about this time Ms. Shirley was doing a head count, and I wouldn't say she was worried sick, but I knew she was angry that I had ran away. I wasn't going to be gone forever, but I did want some time away from that place. I had to do it. I remained at Central Park until evening time. During this time I decided to head back to the foster home.

When I arrived back, I knocked on the door, and Ms. Shirley was of course angry at me.

"Jamal, where the hell have you been? We've all been worried about you. Because you ran away, you do not get dinner. Now come inside, and go straight to bed."

Having Ms. Shirley argue at me for running away was fine. I knew she was going to be upset, so this didn't come as any surprise. Her punishing me by not giving me dinner didn't bother me either. I guess that was what I deserved for running away. The days after I ran away from the group home, I really wanted to leave. The feeling I got for being a free kid for the first time, I wanted to experience again. By being with a regular normal family, I could live that dream. There was an open day that was coming up soon, and I was keeping hope that the possibility of me being adopted was possible. I knew god was watching over me, and I wanted to get the hell out of this place. The open day finally came, and several families were there.

But I don't know, I began to doubt that I was going to get adopted. I started to feel slightly depressed, so I removed myself to the backyard of the foster home. I took a book with me to read, and I sat by myself in the yard, minding my own business. A couple hours passed, and I remained in the backyard reading, being in my own universe. All of a sudden, a couple approached me, and they were curious as to why I was reading by myself outside. None of the other kids in the foster home read. So the fact I was reading a book on my own may have caused them to be interested I guess. There was a male and female apart of this couple, and the male started to speak to me.

"Why are you out here by yourself? Why are you not with the other kids?"

I look up from the book, and I see a man wearing a suit, and he had a beard. The man was also wearing a top hat. The woman he was with was blonde haired, and she was wearing a dress. I then started to speak with the man, answering his question.

"I don't get along with the other kids, so I'm comfortable being out here."

The man began to ask me another question, this time testing my personality I suppose.

"So you like to read? That's a good quality to have. So many children these days don't value books, or appreciate the significance of reading. What is your name?"

I then closed my book, and started to feel comfortable with this couple. Although they were slightly odd looking, they seemed like they were nice people. I knew I had to primp myself if I had any chance of them adopting me. This was an open day after all, and I wanted to make the best impression that I could with them. I then began to introduce myself to this couple. I really wanted to get adopted, and anything that I could do to make myself more presentable to them, I was going to make sure that I was going to do it.

"My name is Jamal, and I'm nine years old. I been at this place my entire life, and I don't really like it here. But yes I do enjoy reading, as it's my main escape to deal with the pain here."

The man smiled, and began to take off his hat. I ended up shaking his hand, and I shook the hand of the female that he was with. The man then introduced himself to me.

"Nice to meet you Jamal. My name is Jed, and this is my wife Josephine. We were browsing around, and you're the first child that we seem to connect with. I can't believe a kid like you has to be in a place like this. We would really like for you to come home with us."

I couldn't believe it, there was a high chance that I was going to be adopted today. All my dreams of finally getting out of here, might possibly come true. I knew that this day was going to come, but I wasn't sure that it was going to be today. The couple did not want to make me any promises, but the chances of them adopting me were very likely. I end up saying goodbye to this couple, and they left the building after that. For the remainder of the day, I was having a good feeling that my time was finally coming. I was going to go home to a regular family. I wouldn't have to deal with Ms. Shirley anymore. I wouldn't have to deal with the other kids at the foster home who didn't care for me. I would have the chance to have a normal life for the first time. At this point, if someone is interested in adopting a child, they have to speak to Ms. Shirley. Ms. Shirley would then speak to the county, and the county would make the final decision as to whether I could go home with them.

Jed and Josephine were interested in adopting me, but they had to go through the proper protocols and procedures in order to do that. I first of all had to sit through a conference with Ms. Shirley and the couple that wished to adopt me. This conference would be tough to sit through, as Ms. Shirley didn't particularly care for me. She didn't care for any of the kids at the foster home, but she detested me most of all. Why, I really don't know, but she was most likely intimidated by me. She thought I didn't deserve to be adopted, and she wanted to keep me there. Her main objective was to break me into ever being adopted and leaving. During this conference, her agenda was to make it so I could not get adopted. Ms. Shirley was trying her to best to persuade and coax the couple into not adopting me.

"You don't want him. He's nothing but a troublemaker. Out of all the children I've had to deal with in my many years of working, Jamal is by far the worst. He's rude, he defies me all of the time. I beg that you reconsider adopting him."

This wasn't good, and thanks to Ms. Shirley, I was probably not going to get adopted now. She just had to run her mouth and make me look bad. During the conference, I had to defend myself over Ms. Shirley. I refused to let her dictate my position at the foster home.

"That is not true, and you know it. I have been very respectful. Sure, there have been a few times I may have done something. Boys will be boys. You should let Jed and Josephine decide if they want to take me. It's their decision and not yours, thank you."

The conference ended, and anxiety was creeping all over me. To come this close to being adopted, and for them not to adopt me would send me into turmoil. If I wasn't adopted, there was no way that I was going to stay in this foster home. I would run away forever, and never come back. This was my final hope into being happy. Luckily, Jed and Josephine didn't let what Ms. Shirley said affect them. They were still more than willing to adopt to me. Jed and Josephine then went to the county building to fill out all the necessary paperwork to bring me home. It was a long process, and I had to wait several months. I was in suspense this entire time, not knowing if I was going to be adopted or not. Finally, I was told the news that Jed and Josephine adopted me.

This was going to be the start of my new life. All the time I spent at this foster home, meant not a damn thing anymore. I was going to leave, and never ever come back. I started to pack my things, and was ready to say goodbye to this place. I was going to go home with Jed and Josephine, and finally have a family. They were going to become my new parents, and I was looking forward to this. I was unaware that life with them wouldn't be that much different from the foster home though.

They say that the grass is greener on the other side. I most definitely believe that it is. But the grass on the other side may not be cut, or there may not be any shady spots in the grass. Or the grass may be greener, but the view may not be nice. Things like that. So yes the grass is greener, but it's probably more complex than that.

I remember the first time I left the foster home, Jed, my new dad, picked me up by himself. Josephine was not with him during this time. As I was riding in the passenger seat of Jed's car, be began to speak to me in a direct tone.

"Okay Jamal. Before we get to the house, there are some rules I want to tell you. We run a Christian household, and we expect you to live by the same rules. If we ask you to do something, we expect you to do it. We go to church every Wednesday and Sunday…"

As Jed was continuing, I knew that there was some type of caveat. I was adopted, but it came at some type of condition and cost. These people are straight up religious. Not the polite and respectful religious, but the more cult and strange religious. I was out of the foster home yes, but it seems the place I was going to, wasn't much better. Jed and Josephine were nice people, but I didn't like how super religious they were. I was a spiritual person, and I do consider myself a Christian, but I'm not really hardcore about it. What was making things even more difficult at this time, was that I was struggling with my own identity.

I was an African American child, that grew up without knowing his family. That already would cause identity issues, not having a family to relate to growing up. But inside I was gay. I couldn't bring this up, as I knew it wasn't an acceptable thing to mention. I was only nine years old, but I knew that I was different because of that. I wasn't even out to myself, so how could I come out to other people? There was no way that I could bring myself to do that. Especially now that I was going to a religious household. Being gay was something I had no business bringing up. Jed continued to talk as we were on our way to the house.

They lived about an hour away from the foster home. So it was a long ride. During the trip, Jed explained that he was an ordained pastor. That wasn't his regular job. Jed actually worked as a manager for a construction company. But he also preached at the church on Wednesdays and Sundays. Josephine worked as a cashier in a nearby drug store. Jed and Josephine had three other children. All of them were adopted as well.

Jed and Josephine actually didn't have any biological children. I don't know any other official reason why, other than that was the choice they made; and it's irrelevant really. So in total there were four of us. The oldest was Crystal. Crystal was fourteen when I first arrived at the house, and she was heavily involved with the church. I didn't get along with Crystal that much, but she was very religious, and devoted her life to the bible very much. Crystal had long blonde hair, and was really tall. The second oldest was Katie. Katie was actually half African American. She had long curly hair. Her skin was very fair though. Katie wasn't as religious and strict as Crystal was, so I got along with her better.

Though we would still clash from time to time. Katie was only a year older than me when I was first adopted. She was ten. Then the youngest child was the same age as I was. He was nine as well. His name was Tanner. Tanner was kinda nerdy and he wore glasses. I related to him the most not only because we were both boys, but because we had a lot of shared interests.

All of us were adopted at different times, but Crystal was adopted first, then Katie, then Tanner, and then myself. I was the last kid to be adopted into the house, and Jed and Josephine did not adopt anymore children after I came into the house. For the first week that I was into the house, I had to get myself used to how things operated.

Josephine had a chart that was located in the kitchen, and we had to always follow the chart. The chart told us what chores we had to do for each day, and it was also our daily planner. Whenever we wanted to do something for fun, we had to mark it on the chart. Everything had to be done in order at that house. This was also going to be the first time that I was going to attend a regular school. I no longer had to have Ms. Shirley teach me. However, the school I went to was a private school. So it was different, but not by a whole lot really. Tanner and I would be in the same class, and he would be my best friend at school.

We would get on the bus to school together, and we would also come home together. Jed and Josephine, just like when I was at the foster home, did not allow any of us to play video games. We were allowed to watch television, but some of the stuff we wanted to watch, they wouldn't always allow us to watch it. If something was really violent or mature, they would cut the tv off immediately. So we mostly resorted to watching educational related things.

Every Wednesday evening, we went to bible study. Unless someone was sick, or it was a holiday, we went every single week. No exceptions at all. During Wednesday service, church was more tolerable. Tanner and I would usually be in the youth classes. We were taught the entire bible, and I was forced to live by it and learn it. I didn't have any issues with this, because it was church. You respect yourself when you are in gods house, and I was respectful of this.

Sundays were essentially the same. For basically all day, we were at church. I had to attend Sunday school early in the morning, and then we would attend Sunday service directly after that. We would usually go out to eat at a restaurant following this. Then directly after that, we would attend evening service. Sundays were church day, and that's the way it was. You became used to it after a while. Yes there were many days that I didn't feel like going to church, but I had no choice at all. If I was going to live under Jed and Josephine's house, I had to go to church every single Sunday. Jed and Josephine were rarely at the house. I would mostly only see them on Wednesdays and Sundays when we had to do our religious service.

Other than that, they were seldom seen. Josephine usually had dinner ready for us by the time we got home. Jed worked during the day, and came home late into the night usually. It was an interesting dynamic to deal with, but that's how my life was with these people. I would wake up and go to school, come home, and go to church twice a week. Something that was good, was that I was allowed freedom that I wasn't given when I was at the foster home. If our homework and chores were done, we were allowed to leave the house and do whatever fun activities we wanted to do. I would mostly go to the library and read. If I wasn't at home, I would go to the library basically.

If I wasn't at the library, I would usually play with Tanner in the backyard. I didn't associate with Crystal or Katie that often, but I would spend much time with Tanner. We would usually play board games, or play badminton and things such as that. Tanner also befriended the other boys that were in the neighborhood. I didn't talk to the boys in the neighborhood that much.

Due to how strict Jed and Josephine were, we were not allowed to play video games. During this time, video games were really popular. One of the boys in the block we lived in, had the new "Mortal Kombat" game. Tanner asked me if I wanted to go come over with them and play it. I of course said yes. Video games weren't really my thing, but it doesn't hurt to circulate with my peers. I went over to the house, and they ordered pizzas, and the boys were playing the video game. I was shocked as to what I saw, and how violent the game actually was.

I have never been introduced to something like this, and it was interesting to see. I was enjoying myself and having fun. I was not able to see any of this while I was at the foster home, so this was a new beginning for me. I know that Jed and Josephine would not approve of us playing this game. Tanner confirmed this.

"Jamal, don't tell Jed that we were playing this game. If he found out about this, they would punish us, and we would not be allowed to leave the house again. Keep this secret."

Tanner and I had to keep the fact we were being devilish, a secret from them. This was definitely not a game that they would be comfortable with us playing or watching, but we were young boys. We wanted to have fun, and be out of our element. Living with Jed and Josephine taught me a lot. I became obedient with myself, and I learned very important values that I had to live by. From going to church, to not being introduced to anything negative that would destroy my mind, body or spirit. Going by a strict schedule when I was at the house. If it wasn't for that, I wouldn't be the man that I am today. So although I didn't necessarily agree with the religious aspect of the way Jed and Josephine raised us, I became more developed that way.

I was now living with Jed and Josephine for two years now. They were no longer my adoptive parents, and more like my regular parents. This was my home. I was no longer living in the foster home, and I had my own family. It was a strange family, and a strict family, but it was still a structured family. Jed and Josephine fed us, put a roof over our heads, taught us good values. They would even give us spending money from time to time. Other than the religious orders that we had to follow, and we weren't allowed to watch anything bad on TV, I didn't mind living here. Although, things were getting far too peachy. I guess life wanted to teach me lessons I had not yet learned yet, and I wasn't ready for these lessons.

It was a Friday evening, and Tanner and I were walking home from getting off the bus. I remember Jed just left the house as we got home, and he got into his car, as he had a work related function to attend.

A bunch of the boys in the neighborhood were doing a dangerous stunt on skateboards called Luge. It's basically where you lay your back and body flat down on a skateboard, and go downhill. I didn't understand the thrill of it, but several of the other boys in the neighborhood were doing it. There was a long hill located on the eastern end of our block, and most of the other boys would do the Luge game down that hill. Tanner and I were asked to participate. I immediately said no. There was no way in hell you were going to make me do some stuff like that. Tanner however was very optimistic, and wanted to do it. Part of me wishes that I could have persuaded him not to do it, but Tanner really wanted to try it out. After much convincing by the other boys, Tanner did agree to do the Luge.

I couldn't watch them do this, so I went inside the house and started to study and do my homework. I wasn't paying attention to any of the boys outside, as that wasn't my thing. Remaining in the house doing my homework, all of a sudden I hear a loud screech. I immediately run out of the house, to see exactly what that noise was. Upon further inspection, I see many of the other boys in the neighborhood running and screaming. I knew something was wrong, but I wasn't able to fully gather everything during this time. I follow everyone, and run along with the other boys down the hill.

Upon reaching the bottom of the hill, I see an elderly woman crying heavily, and I see Tanner's body laying in the street. The elderly woman then begins to cry out.

"He came out of nowhere. He was riding on the skateboard, and I was trying to move out from hitting him, but he just turned in front of my car."

The elderly woman was driving, as Tanner and some of the other boys were doing the Luge. The woman in the car accidentally hit tanner as he was turning down the hill. As I see Tanner laying down in the street, I can't think at all. Several adults run out of the house, and begin to call 911.

My guilt was starting to ferment, as I knew that the boys playing Luge was not safe, and I was scared that something like this would happen. Tanner remained lying in the street, and he wasn't moving. I didn't know if he was dead, but his body wasn't moving. Out of panic, I ran back to our house, and I told Crystal and Katie what happened. We all run back to the scene, and this time the paramedics and police have arrived. Tanner's body is put into the ambulance, and he is quickly taken to the hospital. The events were rushing by, and I was stressed out completely. I only wanted for Tanner to be alright, and I was hoping that he was safe.

Much later, all of us were at the hospital, and Jed was starting to panic over Tanner. I explained to him that the boys in the block asked Tanner and I if we wanted to play the Luge game. I said no, and Tanner decided to go along with them. I was in the house, and I heard a noise and ran out of the house, and I saw Tanner in the street. That's exactly the way things happened. We all remain in the hospital for several hours, when a doctor comes out, asking to speak to Jed and Josephine.

The doctor took them into a separate room, and they were gone for several minutes. When Jed and Josephine finally came back from the room, Josephine could not stop crying, and Jed also looked upset. Tanner unfortunately did not recover, and died. Death was something I was never approached with before. I never had to experience someone close to me die, and it was not good. Tanner and I were close, and I couldn't understand why this happened. Why did it have to be Tanner? All he wanted to do was have fun with the other boys, and then something such as this happened.

After Tanner's death, Jed became very reclusive. I think this is because he favored Tanner most of all. Crystal and Katie were girls, and Josephine connected more to them. It's not that Jed and I didn't get along, but he favored Tanner over me. So Tanner dying sent Jed into a dark depression. He started to bargain with god, not understanding why Tanner was taken away from him. I was missing Tanner as well, as he was the only other boy in the house. I no longer had a friend to play with, or to interact with.

I spent much time by myself. Things were not the same after Tanner passed away, and the house was also in shambles. Church became something we were even more involved with after Tanner's death. Jed really used his faith to deal with everything. I could understand, as turning to faith to grieve is fine. I was not sure where to go with my life during this time, and I started to emotionally break down. Through the years as I got older, being that I was the only boy, Jed wanted to teach me important values of life. I was also dealing with thoughts related to my sexuality as well. I was moving closer into adulthood, and these were all issues that I had to deal with. My studies were my top priority. I turned to studying and doing my schoolwork as a way to define myself. I continued to read quite frequently as well.

I was doing research, and educating myself on as many topics as I could. I was getting older and older, and I was no longer a boy. I was becoming a man, and I had to adapt myself into doing adult priorities. I was going to graduate High School soon, and I still had no idea what my career was going to be. I knew that Jed possibly wanted me to go onto theology. It made perfect sense, as I was raised around the bible, and I had an intensive knowledge around that.

That however didn't interest me. I was proud of my Christian faith, and I'm actually still a Christian. Although being a preacher, wasn't what I wanted. There was something else out there for me. This was my senior year of High School, and all the other students at the school knew exactly what their college or university plans were going to be. I had no clue, and this was a problem. I had to think of something fast, or I was going to end up being confused, not knowing where I want to go with my life. My only passion was reading, and researching, so that was something that I could start with. I had very little time to figure this out, so I had to hurry.

I was coming home from school one day, and I noticed that Jed was sitting on the front porch looking depressed. He was also wearing a t shirt and shorts, and he had some sandals on. This was extremely peculiar, as Jed always wore a suit or was dressed nice. He very seldom dressed like he was going to the beach. He also had a newspaper in his hand, but he wasn't reading it. He was just holding it in his hands. Something wasn't right at all. It was that feeling you get when something isn't aligned right. I decided to walk up and speak to him.

"Jed, is everything alright? You seem kinda depressed, Do you want to talk about it?"

Jed then started to open up the newspaper, as he's reading the newspaper, he then begins to speak to me, although he's speaking very quietly.

"I don't want to talk about it, but the church has a new pastor, and I don't like him. We're not going to that church anymore. That church isn't holy, and the pastor isn't holy."

This was strange, as we have been going to that church for several years. Church was also something that was important to Jed. He was a pastor himself after all, so the church was his second home. I don't know all the details as to why he believed the church was unholy, but he must have his reasons. The stress of having to leave the church is why Jed is acting this way. So now he must focus his attention on finding another church. Meanwhile, because Jed was not comfortable with us attending that church, we stopped going. We no longer went to bible study on Wednesdays, and we didn't go to Sunday service either.

Remarkably, most of Jed's Christian teachings began to stop. This was most evident when Katie wanted to get her belly button pierced. I would have assumed that Jed and Josephine would have told her hell no. But shockingly, they allowed her to. Josephine had no issue with the piercing, and Jed didn't seem to care either. I didn't understand this at all. It was like "The Twilight Zone." This strict religious family I grew up with, was little by little changing their ways. This became more evident, when I started to see Jed watch "Law and Order" on television.

This was a show in the past you would never ever catch him watching. He then started to watch it religiously. Nothing was making sense, and it was like there was some type of code or game they were playing, that I was unaware of.

The truth was, the household was becoming more open minded. Maybe it was Tanner's death that played a part, but everyone started to become more lenient on our faith. We no longer went to church, or were involved with many religious events.

Jed still read the bible, but it wasn't something that was serious. Everyone in the house participated in several things that they didn't partake in before. It was also during this time that I began to follow suit with the way everyone else was behaving. I started to involve myself in other non-religious related topics. I started to study several different things. I began to educate myself on social studies, and I even began to open myself up more, on topics related to my sexuality. On my eighteenth birthday, I wanted to see as to whether or not the family dynamic actually changed. I remember overnight, I became a big Lady Gaga fan. I don't know how it came to be, but I began to love her music.

I related to her songs very much, and being black and gay at that young age, she became a major role model for me. However, if we were playing by old rules, I would never be allowed to attend a Lady Gaga concert. But being that it seems that everyone was changing their ways, maybe things would be different. I was in the living room one evening, and Jed just came home from work. I was eager to ask him if I could go to the concert, scared of what his reaction may be. I wasn't getting my hopes up or down. I mean, I really wanted to go to the concert for my birthday, but if he said that I couldn't go, I wouldn't be surprised. I then began to talk to Jed.

"My eighteenth birthday is coming up. There is a singer called Lady Gaga. I'm sure you heard of her. Well, she's going to be in town soon, and I wanted your permission to go."

Jed began to set his briefcase down on the living room table. I was totally prepared for him to tell me that's forbidden under household rules to go to events such as that. Although, I was caught by complete surprise. Jed then gave his answer, as to whether I could attend.

"Sure Jamal. It's your birthday right? I'll give you a ride to the concert, and I'll pick you up when it's over. You have a good time, and enjoy yourself on your birthday."

Jed then smiled at me, and walked out of the room. If I would have talked to Jed last year, there wasn't any chance in hell, that he would have allowed me to go to that concert. It would have not been Christian, and it would be against the rules, values and virtues that we go by in our household. It does seem however that things have definitely changed for the better. I am allowed to go to the concert, and I like how things have changed. I still was closeted to my family, and I.

knew there had to be a time for me to come out to them. I didn't know how they were going to take this news, but I wanted to take everything one step at a time. I will get to that sometime later. When the night of the concert came, I had the time of my life. I never been to a concert before, and it was an entertaining experience. Being able to attend was special, and things were opening up for me. When the concert was over and I returned home, I was still in disbelief as to what a wonderful night I had. I didn't understand why the household rules have been changed. Things were becoming different in a good way. My main goal at this point, was to figure out what my plans for my life were. What career goals I was going to aim for.

I applied to several schools, including NYU. I knew that NYU was a top tier school, and everyone was aiming for that school, but that's where I wanted to go. I sent my application into NYU weeks before graduation. This was cutting it quite close yes, but I was confused on my college plans. After sending in my application, I didn't hear anything.

At most, I could always go to a community college and take random classes there. But NYU was what I really wanted. When I was completing my application, I mentioned that my major was going to be Journalism. It was an off the cuff thing I did, and I'm happy I chose that. I didn't know much about Journalism, but I knew that I had a passion for reading and researching. So it was a choice I came up with that made sense.

I waited for quite some time to hear a response back from the school. When I received a letter in the mail explaining that I was accepted, I was very pleased. I was going to attend NYU after graduation, and things were turning out fine. There was one thing I wanted to do before I left. It was something important, and possibly something that might make the rest of the family disown me, and never speak to me again. I had to come out them that I was gay.

I decided to come out to Crystal and Katie together at first. They took the news well, like I knew they would. They really weren't my main concern. I then came out to Josephine. She was shocked over the news at first, but after a few minutes she was proud of me. This seemed confusing, as this previously was a very heavily Christian based household. Although I guess they were making an exception for me, and they were going to love and accept me regardless. The only person that was left me to come out to was Jed. I was starting to become anxious over what his reaction would be. Jed would be very against homosexuality in the past, and considered it a terrible sin. The fact I was going to come out to him as gay was going to be interesting. I waited one evening until Jed came home from work, and I was in the living room. I spoke out to Jed as he was walking in.

"Jed, there is something important that I need to tell you right now."

Jed then set his briefcase down in the living room, and sat on the sofa beside me. He then looked me directly in the eyes and began to smile at me. He then took my hand and held it very close. Jed continued to smile at me, and then began to softly speak to me.

"I already know you're gay Jamal. It's okay. God loves you, and I know how spiritual you are. I wasn't happy with the news, but as long as you're happy and safe, and know right from wrong, I know god is watching over you and is blessing you. I love you Jamal."

Jed and I then hug very closely, and Jed kisses me on the cheek. This was not the reaction I was expecting, but it was the reaction I was hoping for. I had the approval of being gay from Jed. I know he's still going to be involved with my life. I know he had a past of strict religious doctrines, but that was the past. Things are going to be different now, and he supports me. I started to pack my things for University, and was ready to continue on with my life. At this point, Crystal had already moved in with her boyfriend, and Katie was still in school.

Once all my things were packed, Jed gave me a big surprise, by buying me my first car. I was thankful for him for the gesture. I graduated High School soon, and this part of my life was done. Jed was proud of me, and I had to keep on going from here. Once I arrived at NYU, most of it seems like a blur because I was constantly studying. The courses that I took, were not simple, and I had to devote much of my time to them. Many of the other students were going on parties, and were having fun. Not me; I had to stick to my studies always. I was taking many journalism courses, and I would do a lot of sociology studying. This was all included in my course plan. The number of friends I made while I was at university was zero. I had no time at all to do those types of things, as my main priority was to pass all my classes.

After my first couple of years of University passed, I became more comfortable with my courses. They were still tough for me at times, but I was strong and got through it. There were several guys at the University that I would crush on, but I didn't form any relationships at all. It was difficult for me to balance that, along with my classes. So I had to make sacrifices. I could either socialize and forfeit my study work, or do my study work on the account of not socializing. I decided to stick with my course work.

My senior year of University was here, and this was a pivotal time in my life. There was an internship for "CNN". That's right, "CNN", that was available. Working for a company like that, would be a great honor. I wanted to have this internship, despite the odds that were very against my favor in getting it. At this time, I was working on my journalism skills, but I knew that they were probably looking for people with experience that I didn't have. I had no experience working with television or multimedia though.

That was my downfall. This was ultimately why I was not picked to get the internship. It was fine, as I wasn't the only one that was rejected for the internship. Thousands of others didn't get it either. Although, it would have been lovely to work for "CNN". I could have been the next Don Lemon or something. Ha-Ha. It wasn't meant to be I guess.

I couldn't let the "CNN" rejection get to me. I had to keep going and try a different approach. There was an internship for the "New York Times", that I signed up for. The "New York times", like "CNN", is also a reputable company to work for. I was thankfully given the internship at the "New York Times". Once I completed University, I immediately started my internship at the "New York Times". It wasn't fun at all, and they treated the interns very horribly. Most of my work consisted off copy editing what other journalists did. I didn't get to do any field research or studying. Everything consisted of me doing file work, and bookkeeping work. It was a paid internship, so that was nice. I was able to pay my rent. That was the only positive thing about it.

I was scared that I was going to be let go soon, due to how dispensable they were treating me. But actually, they kept me on board for several years. The internship turned into a records keeper position at the company. That was basically what my job entailed. I would work on a computer keeping records of all the news outlets. Whether it was current events, politics, entertainment and sports news. That was the job that I was responsible for. Things were going great, until I got the news that I was fired from the company. I didn't do anything bad, and my performance was okay, they just didn't need my services anymore, and were going to let me go. I didn't know what to do, or how I was going to pay my rent or my bills. I didn't have a job.

I had to find another job fast. I went on the internet, and started to apply to anything I felt I was qualified for. Whether that was a data entry job, to being a file clerk. Anything that I could do that was in my pay grade, and whoever wanted to hire me I would take. I then sent my resume into "American Express". The job was to be a record keeper, and it was something I had experience with, from when I worked at the "New York Times". They enjoyed my resume so much, that they invited me for a personal interview. I made sure I dressed nice, and I had to give a flawless impression for them to hire me for the position. I arrive at the building in downtown New York. The receptionist asks me to wait, and I start to pull out my resume. I wait for several minutes, when a man in a black suit comes into the lobby. The man speaks with the receptionist, while he is pointing at me.

"Is he Jamal? Okay, thank you."

The man then walks in my direction, and sticks his hand out, introducing himself.

'Hello Jamal. I'm Ralph Maligrino. I'm the CEO in charge of bookkeeping and records here at 'American Express'. Follow me, I'll interview you in my office. Right this way."

I shake Ralph's hand, and I follow him to his office. When we reach his office, I notice how large it is, and how the window behind his desk faces downtown New York. I take a seat in front of his desk, and Ralph begins to interview me.

"I saw your resume, and it's pretty impressive. The job is mainly you keeping track of my records, double checking everything. If I need something scanned or copied, I want you to take care of that. If I want a fresh cup of coffee, I would like for you to give me one."

So basically, I'm going to become this motherfuckers bitch pretty much? I had to be professional, because I had bills and rent to pay. Also, Ralph was very easy on the eyes to me. I mean to other people he's just a regular guy, but he seemed like a gentle bear to me. Ralph continued to interview me, and I listened to all of his words.

"So based on your resume, I would like to hire you right now, and I need for you to start today actually. Are you still interested in the position?"

It didn't even take me two seconds for me to respond to Ralph with my answer.

"Oh yes sir. Thank you sir for this opportunity. I will not let you down. Thank you."

Ralph smiles back at me, and I shake his hand. It was official, I got hired for the position. Although it wasn't what I was expecting, I was happy to have a job. As soon as the interview ended, I began my first day of work. My day consisted of me doing a bunch of tasks that Ralph asked me to do. Whether he wanted papers copied or faxed, files put into the records office in the building, or if he wants me to do computer work. I had my own cubicle on the other side of the building, to where I would do all of these tasks. Ralph would annoy me at times, by the amount of tasks he would ask me to do. If I didn't do it the exact way he wanted me to do it, he would be stern about it. It was only my first day, and I wish Ralph was slightly more understanding. He wasn't, and he was a perfectionist. Everything I did with him, had to be done perfectly.

Once my first day was over, I was so tired. I couldn't wait to get home so I could rest. How the hell was I going to do this every single day? There was no way I could ever get used to this. This job was very stressful, and out of my comfort zone. I went home feeling exhausted, knowing that I'm going to do it all over the following day. I was not expecting to end up working on the day of my interview. Day one of work was over, but it would only be more wild from here.

Maybe taking on this job was a bad idea? Was doing the job really worth it? If I thought that today was tough, I didn't see anything yet. Things only were going to become harder to deal with. My story continues with my unprecedented relationship with Ralph, and how things got tremendously more thrilling from here. I didn't even see any of it coming, and that's the part I was scared of. I went to bed that night, knowing the Jamal I was before, wasn't prepared at all for what was going to come up next.

Accepting Ralph's job offer was more than just a new job I had, it was a new life that I was going to live. Every single limit was going to be pushed. The rest of my story does allow me to be confident in myself, with whatever situations I'm faced with. I went to bed that night and drifted off to sleep, anxious and scared as to what the next day is going to consist of.

CHAPTER 17:

MAN OF GREEN (PART 2)

As I suspected, the second day that I worked for Ralph was tedious. I woke up that day, and reported to work. The minute I get to the building, Ralph starts bombarding me with several tasks. I'm basically his guinea pig, and I don't have any room to whine about it. It was a job at the end of the day. I was hired to do my job, and I had to do whatever tasks I was asked to. I did wish that Ralph was a little bit more understanding, and not as strict. That was the only thing which bothered me. I didn't mind doing my job, but Ralph constantly badgering me didn't help at all really. From all the work that I was doing, I couldn't wait until lunch break. As soon as I finished one task, Ralph would immediately give me another task to complete. I would report to Ralph's office, and do whatever he asked me to do. It was extremely cut and dry throughout the entire day. Sometimes I would have to go to my cubicle, and work on my computer. Other times, I would have to go down to the print and copy room, and do a task there. I knew I had to familiarize with everything, because I would end up doing these tasks quite frequently. I didn't have any time to chit chat with any of the other employees at the building either.

I had a schedule that had to be met every single day, and stopping to talk to people would have most definitely gotten me fired and replaced. I really needed this job, so getting fired was not something I had planned. Yes, there were times I was extremely tired and wanted to quit, but I had to build character, and do my job. A lot of people end up doing things that they don't want to do. Many jobs become an obligation, and that's how it is. I knew all the tasks that I was in charge of, were very important to the company. Ralph wasn't pushing me this hard for no reason. He needed my help, and it was my job to make sure I was representing the company well. At noon, I was finally given my lunch break. I only had an hour break, so it seems like it's a long time, but it's not really. During lunch break, I would mostly stay inside of the building. I understood that there were restaurants surrounding the building that I could have went to, but I was scared that I would come back to work late. I always would make my own lunch at home, and bring it to work later. Once I was finished eating lunch, it was almost time for me to head back to work anyways.

The second half of the day was about as equally exhausting as the first half was. Ralph would continue to relay several tasks for me to do. I was also told to do many mundane and out of my job description tasks too. For example, Ralph would make me empty his trashcans, or refill the coffee in the coffee maker. He would ask me to carry things down to his car in the parking garage. Just things like that, and I was worth way more than that. My job was to be a bookkeeper and file clerk. I make sure all the files in the company are neatly organized, and I enter data into the computer as well. My job was not to be Ralph's maid.

Not only that, but I didn't feel comfortable doing all of those things. It was sort of humiliating to be honest. However, I had no room to make a fuss about it. If it was that much of a hassle, I could have simply left the building. I would have been fired though, but the choice was ultimately mine to make if I wanted to quit. I didn't quit, and I stayed despite the fact some of the tasks I had to do I felt were not appropriate. At the very end of the shift, Ralph would give me a homework assignment that needed to be completed by the following day. So there were things that I needed to do when I was at work, and there were also things that I had to do when I was at home.

I really couldn't believe this shit. The homework assignments that Ralph would give me, would basically be stuff I had to do on "Excel", such as making spreadsheets. Or he would want me to put together a "PowerPoint" presentation for him. Things related to that nature. I always did these tasks as well. Even though in hindsight I probably shouldn't have, and I quite frankly had more important stuff that I had to do. I also wasn't paid overtime for doing any of this stuff, so legally I didn't have to do any of it. But because of my soft spirit, and I was in fear of the wrath that Ralph was going to give me if I didn't do the tasks, I did them anyways.

As I have now been at this job for a month, I have become very familiar with how the entire layout of the building is, and I knew exactly where to go to complete whatever task I was given. I also did the tasks at a faster rate than I did previously. Ralph was also starting to pick up on the fact that I was completing the tasks much faster.

As a result, he then started to give me tasks that were even more difficult. The new tasks that Ralph would give me, would have me leaving the building. Ralph would make me go to the post office and mail things, he would give me several other outside errands as well. I would have to drive to places miles away, and drop something off, or pick something up, or I would have to do some type of inventory task at another building. This as you would guess was tiring and annoying for me. My job was becoming more complex to handle, and my job duties were going in a completely opposite direction. Yet, I did not quit or leave. Perhaps it was from how Jed and Josephine raised me, but it wasn't in my nature to complain out loud, or to throw in the towel that easily. This was my job, and it was my duty to do my job well.

I was paid, and I was able to pay my rent and my bills, so as long as I was supporting myself with the job, I was going to continue it. Even though I received little to no support or congratulations from Ralph. Ralph would never tell me how much a good job I was doing, or that he was proud of me, or give me any centimeter of praise at all. This aggravated me, but I kept this to myself.

Being with the company for now three months, I don't want to say I was brainwashed at all, but my lifestyle adapted to my work. I didn't have a personal life anymore. I didn't have fun, I didn't party, I didn't have much leisure time. Every single day I would wake up, go to work, do the tasks Ralph asked of me, go home and do the homework assignments that Ralph would give, and if I had any free time left, I would read or go on the computer for a couple hours. That's how my life was. This wasn't healthy at all, but this was the life that I now had.

I didn't know how I let myself get this far, but I did. There was no turning back at this point either, as I had advanced too far into my career at this building. Time continued to pass with me working here. It seems with every week that passed, the tasks Ralph would hand me, were getting more and more difficult. At first, I ignored this. This is however now becoming an issue that I wanted to address with Ralph. He was tiring me out, and I'm only one person. He's asking me to do tasks fit for an army, and there was no way that I was going to keep this up.

I remember one Friday, Ralph was on his way to a meeting outside of the building, and handed me a stack of papers that was two feet tall. Ralph didn't give me much instructions or help, other than handing me a small piece of paper that had the address of the place I was to deliver the stack of papers to. Ralph then after handing me the papers, left the scene. I thought that this shouldn't be that hard. I have done errands similar to this for Ralph in the past, so this shouldn't be any different.

However, the address that Ralph gave me, was not complete. It did not have a zip code. This would have been helpful, as the address after I looked it up online, gave me three different office buildings. I didn't know which one was the correct building that Ralph wanted me to deliver the documents to was. I called and texted Ralph, but I got no response from him. I then called all three buildings and asked if they were expecting any documents to be sent from Ralph Maligrino.

Unfortunately after speaking with them on the phone, they alerted me that they are not allowed to give that information over the telephone, and I would have to report to the office in person to find out if they are expecting something from a particular source. I was angry after hearing that. My only choice was to go to each of the buildings, until I arrived at the right one. From the way the buildings were situated, they were all equal distance away. One building was south, one building was west, and one building was north. So no matter what building I chose, even if I was right on my first choice, it was still a long distance.

The first building that I went to was the western building. It turned out to be the incorrect one. I asked them if they were expecting documents from Ralph Maligrino to be delivered, and they said no. I then decided to go to the north facing building, as it was closer than the south. The north building wasn't the right one either. I was starting to panic at this point, as I knew that Ralph was counting on me to complete this task. I have now gone to two buildings, and wasted so much time. I then head to the final location, the south location. This is of course the correct location, however to my surprise, I see Ralph and a few other men standing in the lobby. They all seem angry by the expressions on their faces. Ralph them immediately begins shout at me.

"What took you so long bringing those documents? It has now been two and a half hours, and thanks to you, I had to postpone my presentation. I gave you one simple task to do."

I could understand why Ralph was angry, but I didn't feel like this was entirely my fault. He didn't give me the full address to the building, and two other buildings shared the same address. How was I supposed to know which was the right one? I set the stack of papers down on a table in the lobby, and I then begin to display my frustrations out to Ralph.

"Hey hey, wait a minute. First of all, the address you gave me, was also the same for two other similar buildings. You didn't give me a zip code, so I ended up going to the wrong building twice. So I don't think that's my fault I got held back over your mistake. I also tried to contact you, and you didn't answer back to me."

This was the first time that I ever raised my voice at Ralph. He wasn't pleased at all, and it was at this moment that I felt I truly lost my job. Ralph was going to definitely fire me after this. I totally forgot that he was my boss, and I went off on him like that. I didn't think that there was any way for me to recover after that, and I blew it. Ralph excuses the other men that he was with, and it's just the two of us in the lobby. Ralph then leans closer to me, speaking silently.

"Jamal, I gave you a simple task. Because of your error, I had to miss my presentation, and it was a very important presentation too. This puts my position in jeopardy, because I didn't have my presentation notes. I was counting on you, but you can't even do a simple task."

It's okay for Ralph to feel angry, but why is he attacking me? This is not my fault. I could understand if I said fuck it, and decided not to deliver the documents at all. That's not what I did. I went to all three buildings to find out which was the right place. Because Ralph didn't elaborate enough on the address he gave me, I ended up wasting time by driving to the wrong locations. So none of this is my problem. I try once again to explain to Ralph that this was a honest mistake.

"Why didn't you put the zip code on the address you gave me? If you would have given me the zip code, I would not have wasted precious time. All you had to do was give..."

I stop speaking, when Ralph starts walking away from me. Ralph then throws the stack of documents I brought into the building, all across the lobby floor. I should mention if I didn't mention beforehand, that Ralph has a really bad temper. He vents his anger like this quite frequently, and I think this was the first time I witnessed him acting like this. His rage and emotions were running very high.

Ralph continues to throw the papers all across the room, and then walks closer to me. I stand confused and anxious, looking at Ralph throw a tantrum. I remain quiet, as I don't feel that there is anything for me to say. Looking at the way Ralph is behaving, is making me speechless. I also kept telling myself that none of this is my fault at all. Ralph has every right to be upset, but I'm not the reason for him being upset. Ralph gets closer to me, and starts to whisper to me.

"You know what Jamal, you're fired. I want you go back to the office, and get all of your things. You can be replaced. I'll get someone who isn't incompetent, and can follow simple directions. You can also forget about a letter of recommendation, or a reference."

I was being fired, and it didn't seem right or fair. What the hell did I do wrong? I did nothing wrong, and now I've lost my job over it. I figured that I could sulk about losing my job later, and pick up the papers off the ground that Ralph threw. Yes I was fired, and common sense would tell me that if Ralph fired me and doesn't want my services anymore, I should walk out of the building.

But I still had ethics and values in my life, and I couldn't leave those papers on the ground like that. I start to pick the papers up, and also putting them in order as I'm doing it. Ralph is standing to the side, watching me. I find it awkward at first, being that he's not saying anything. He continues to watch me as I put all the papers on the ground in order. I pick up more of the papers, and some of the papers are right by Ralph's leg. As I'm picking those papers up, Ralph bends down and grabs my wrist with force. He then whispers to me.

"I said that you were fired. Why are you still here?"

Ralph has a stern look on his face, but I don't know what came over me, but it wasn't a natural reaction at all, but I began to smile and slightly chuckle to myself. I noticed that Ralph has a small smile on his face. Ralph then helps me pick up the papers. We continue until all the papers are picked up, and put into the correct order. We then put the papers back into the cardboard box that they were all nestled in. After we finished picking the papers up, I remain in this area, staring at Ralph silently. Ralph then begins to eventually speak to me.

"Okay, I'm going to rehire you Jamal. Only on one condition. Because I missed my presentation thanks to you, me and my associates are going to this fancy restaurant later this evening, and we'll have our presentation there. I want you to take notes, and don't fuck it up."

I immediately nod my head. Ralph smiles at me, and points over at the stack of papers. Signaling me to pick them up. I pick up the papers, and leave out of the building, following Ralph. I get in my car, and follow Ralph back to the "American Express" building. It was now three in the afternoon, and the dinner arrangements weren't until later in the day at five. Upon returning back to Ralph's office, I see two other men in his office sitting behind his desk. These were the same men that were present at the building I was just at with Ralph. But I didn't really examine them before. Now that I have managed to get a better look at them, they look like they are of Italian descent. Ralph then introduces me to these men.

"Jamal, I like you to meet my best friends, Hugo and Vincent."

I shook both of their hands. Hugo was a more heavy set obese man with a mustache and curly hair. Despite his big size, he was very friendly and welcoming. Vincent was a more slender guy that had balding thinning hair and a five o clock shadow. Vincent was still friendly, but he was more introverted, and was quiet usually. Hugo was the one who did most of the talking.

Ralph has me do several tasks on his computer in his office. In this same instance, Ralph starts to have a personal conversation on the other side of his desk with Hugo and Vincent. I do end up eavesdropping on what Ralph and his friends are talking about, but I don't join in. As I did not want them to think I was listening to their conversation. As I'm eavesdropping, I find out that next Friday, Ralph has a very important meeting that he has to attend. This meeting consists of all CEO's in charge of records and bookkeeping with companies all involved in the "New York Stock Exchange". The company I work for "American Express", is included in this list. This meeting would have all the CEO's give a presentation on how their company operates.

Once all the presentations were over, an award would be given to the person who gave the best presentation. This award would be a great accolade to the person who won it. It would lead to possible career growth, and also possibilities of working in the stock exchange.

Ralph was intending on doing a test presentation, with Hugo and Vincent acting as second and third opinions. Ralph only rented the office space for so long, and the time slot they picked ran out before I arrived. So that's why Ralph was extremely mad that I was late bringing the documents over. Ralph also really wants to win this award. This would be the third year in a row he has tried to win, and the past two years, he got 3rd and 2nd place respectively. This year he would like to take the cake, and so this is very important for him. I continue to do tasks on Ralph's computer, still eavesdropping. Even though they are speaking about it inconspicuously, it seems that Ralph, Hugo and Vincent were at one time involved with some type of secret society. They weren't being clear cut in their speech about it, but I was picking up clues. It does however seem they have severed ties with this group, but they do have a history and past with being involved with it.

To me this was slightly exciting to hear. Knowing that Ralph was an ex member of a secret group was interesting. It was also at this exact time, when I began to develop a crush on Ralph. It happened instantly like that. I don't know why I was crushing on Ralph, but maybe it was because I'm always with him. I also think that Ralph was holding back thoughts of me as well. After his fit, and he fired me, he was quick to change his mind.

Maybe he was testing me possibly. He knew that if I stayed after he told me I was fired, he knew that I wasn't like everyone else. Usually people would have ran out the building after being told by their boss that they are fired. That's not what I did, I stayed, and actually still acted like I worked for Ralph still. He must have appreciated that.

I didn't know if Ralph liked other men, and I didn't know if he was attracted to me either. It was simply a crush, and a crush usually doesn't mean anything. I finish the tasks Ralph wanted me to do, and it was now a quarter until five. Ralph is continuing to talk with his friends. I knew my day wasn't over yet, as Ralph is forcing me to attend the dinner conference. I get up and start to grab my things, and ask Ralph if it's okay if I meet him at the restaurant.

"Ralph, I can meet you at the restaurant? I promise I'll be there. I just go in my own car, and I'll meet you guys down there. Is that okay?"

Ralph suspends talking with Hugo and Vincent, and turns to look at me. He doesn't seem to like my suggestion, and then starts to angrily shout back at me.

"No, it's not okay. Sit down. You're riding to the restaurant with us. I want you to remain quiet. This is an important night for me, so I don't want you fucking this up. Just stay quiet."

I did exactly what Ralph asked of me, and for the remainder of the evening, I remained quiet. Anything that was on my mind, I didn't bring up or talk about. About five minutes later, we all end up leaving Ralph's office. I end up carrying the stack of papers Ralph needs for his presentation. What happened next, was surprising for me. We were all going to arrive at the restaurant, in a stretch limousine.

The limo belonged to Hugo, as his main job was being a limo driver. I felt like I was in a mobster film. I never in my life ever rode in a limo, and this was turning into an exciting day. I get into the limo, and Ralph and Vincent sit on the other end of the limo together. I end up sitting adjacent to the both of them. At this time, I take my laptop out, as Ralph wanted me to take notes on his test presentation. While my computer is powering up, I can't help but notice the amount of liquor bottles in the limo, and how the limo had a moderately big sized television set hanging in the back. The limo also had a sunroof as well.

It was very fancy indeed. Within seconds, Ralph then starts to open up a bottle of whisky that was located in the liquor cabinet of the limo, and also takes out several shot glasses that were securely stored in another separate cabinet. I see that Ralph took out exactly three glasses.

Ralph pours himself a drink, then Vincent a drink, and they both make a toast, and they begin to drink. Ralph sets his drink down, and pours me a shot. I probably should have said no, but listen. How many times does a gay black guy get to ride in a limo with a bunch of Italian guys? That never happens, so I most definitely agreed to drinking the shot. Plus it was "Jack Daniels". I'm not saying no to a free shot of Jack. Ha-Ha.

We continue on our way to the restaurant. Hugo pulls the limo right outside of the restaurant, and drops myself, Ralph and Vincent off. Hugo then drives away, and I walk with Ralph and Vincent inside of the restaurant. Once inside the restaurant, I see how elaborate it is. To say it was a fancy restaurant was an understatement. This was a ten star restaurant, and was very high scale. I can only imagine if the decoration and environment looks nice, the menu prices are more than likely expensive. But I'm being treated to a free dinner, so I'm not complaining or fretting at all about this. We were finally seated at a big table, in a back discreet area of the restaurant. I set the presentation papers on the end of the table. Ralph then starts to open up his briefcase, and takes several things out. I then prepare myself to take notes. Even though I was slightly tipsy from the liquor I drunk back in the limo, I had to snap myself out of that, and pull myself together.

A waitress then comes to the table and begins to hand us menus. Ralph then asks the waitress for a bottle of wine for the whole table. She then walks away. This was an Italian restaurant, and I've never had Italian food before. I was unsure as to what to order. The menu seemed foreign, and the only Italian food I knew about was pizza, lasagna, and spaghetti and meatballs. Ralph was able to notice the fact that I was struggling to find something to order on the menu. He then leans close to me, and sets my menu down. He stares at me for several seconds, and I could feel his energy. It wasn't an uncomfortable energy, but a more protective and understanding energy. Ralph then starts to silently whisper out to me.

"Don't worry, I'll order for you. Trust me. Just take notes on what I say. Okay?"

Ralph then smiles at me, and I smile back at him. A few minutes later, Hugo arrives at the table, and Ralph then starts to begin his mock presentation. I'm trying my best to keep up with Ralph, and take as much notes as I can. This presentation holds a great value to him, and he's going to rely on my notes to help him, when the actual presentation happens. Fifteen minutes into giving his presentation, the waitress returns to the table. She asks for our orders, and as promised, Ralph takes my order for me, which was the same thing he ordered. Steak and stuffed ricotta pasta.

After the waitress gets our orders, she leaves the table. Ralph then continues on with his presentation. If Ralph wanted me to present him a specific document from the stack of papers, I would give it to him. Ralph was doing a fantastic job with his mock presentation. Speaking only for myself, I thought he had a good chance of winning the presentation award. Hugo and Vincent also enjoyed his mock presentation. Ralph was an excellent public speaker, and he was doing a stellar job. Ralph continued with his mock presentation, when eventually the waitress returned to our table with our food order, and the wine Ralph ordered for the table. I was so hungry at this point, so it was great that we were finally eating.

We all started to eat, and I was happy for the recommendation that Ralph gave. I never had it before, but it was very delicious. I have never been in a fancy restaurant such as this, and I've never had Italian food before either. I was experiencing so many new things. I also end up having a couple glasses of wine. So I was feeling quite loose. As the night continued and we finished our meal, Ralph started to continue where he left off in his presentation.

Thirty minutes later, Ralph finished his presentation, and we all enjoyed it. I also took several notes during the whole ordeal, which I knew would help Ralph a lot. After this, Ralph started to talk to Hugo and Vincent for a bit, and not wanting to get into their conversation, I ignored it. Ralph occasionally would turn to look at me, and smile. I guess he could tell that I was feeling slightly removed from everyone else.

The waitress eventually came to the table with the bill. Ralph took his credit card from his wallet out, and also took some dollar bills out as a tip for the waitress. After he did this, Ralph then starts to talk to all of us.

"Do you guys want to come over to my place. I know the Patriots game is on tonight, and I thought maybe you guys would want to come over and watch it?"

Hugo and Vincent both agree to this, but I remain silent. I didn't know if I was invited as well. I was simply Ralph's coworker. I wasn't necessarily his friend, so I don't know why Ralph would invite me over. But I figured I could be sneaky about this, and just follow Hugo and Vincent. That's exactly what I did. We all leave out of the restaurant, and I bring the stack of documents for Ralph's presentation with me.

Ralph, Vincent and I remain outside the restaurant waiting for Hugo to return with the limo. At this time, I forgot that my car is still at the parking garage at work. I wasn't worried though, as I knew my car was safe. Hugo arrives, and we all get into the limo. As I'm riding in the limo, it still hasn't clicked to me that I'm going to Ralph's house. I wasn't expecting to form this close of a relationship with Ralph. During this time, Vincent takes out a long cigar from his jacket pocket. He then speaks to all of us.

"Now this is marijuana. If that's not your thing, then I'm not gonna pressure you."

Vincent lights the marijuana cigar, and takes a puff from it. He then hands it to Ralph, who takes a puff from it as well. Ralph then hands me the cigar. I have smoked marijuana before. This was not the first time. But it was just weird smoking it with my boss. I take the marijuana cigar and take puffs from it. The marijuana enters my system, and I feel extremely calm. Several minutes later, we reach a suburban area.

Hugo then pulls the limo up to a rather large modern house. We all get out of the limo, and walk inside the living room. Before I continue, I found it strange how Ralph had this large house all to himself. I never saw him with a wedding ring on his finger, so I knew he wasn't married. He also had no pictures of kids on his desk, so I knew he didn't have any children either. This was confirmed as walking through his house, I didn't see any pictures of any family in the living room either.

Ralph lived in this big house all by himself and it didn't make any sense. I had to mind my business at this point. Ralph tells me to set the stack of documents next to the table in the living room, so that's what I do. I then take a seat down on the sofa, and look at the big screen television showing the football game. Ralph then takes his suit jacket off, and gets a bowl of potato chips, putting them down in the living room table. I continue to stay silent, as Hugo and Vincent continue to speak to Ralph.

Being that I haven't known Ralph as long as they have, and I feel because Ralph, Hugo, and Vincent are also much older than me, I don't know how to speak to any of them on a personal level really. All four of us are sitting in the living room watching the game. When halftime in the game approaches, Ralph goes into the kitchen. He returns back with several bottles of beer, handing each of us one. Ralph hands me a beer, and smiles at me. Again, his way of trying to make me feel comfortable. A hour and a half later, the football game ends, and Hugo and Vincent start to prepare themselves to leave.

Maybe it was because they forgot I was with them, and I had no ride home, but in a flash, Hugo and Vincent leave out of Ralph's house. I couldn't even react or tell them that I had no way of getting home. My phone died, so it wasn't like I could call an uber. From where Ralph's house was located, it was at least a two hour walk to get to where I lived. But it was too late. Hugo and Vincent then get into the limo, and leave Ralph's residence within seconds. What was I going to do now? Ralph was in the kitchen doing dishes, and I decided to reluctantly walk up to him, letting him know I don't have any method of getting home.

"Ralph, my car is back at the office building, and my phone died. I was wondering if I could use your phone to call for someone to take me home please?"

Ralph finished doing the dishes, and he turned and looked at me. Ralph once again smiled at me, and took a sip of his beer. He then silently responded back to me.

"Why do you want to go home for? It's Friday night. You don't have work tomorrow, so why are you so quick to leave? I know you want to stay with me Jamal."

Ralph hit my weak spot. How the hell did he know I had a crush on him. All my life I took risks, and I knew had I not took a risk that night, I would have forever been struggling with myself. I knew I had to kiss Ralph, so that's what I did. But I wasn't going to kiss him any type of way. I wanted to make this special. I noticed that Ralph had a swimming pool in his backyard. I start to tease Ralph by massaging his back, and I then whisper back to him.

"Follow me outside. There is a present that I want to give you."

Ralph then follows me outside to the backyard, and I catch him off guard by pushing him into the pool. I start to laugh, and Ralph is clearly angered. His clothes are soaked in water, from me pushing him into the pool. I continued to laugh at Ralph poolside and standing close to the edge of the water. Within seconds, Ralph then grabs my arm and pushes me into the water with him. He then starts to wrestle with me in the pool, dunking and pushing my head down into the water. Then it finally happened. Ralph and I stare at each other outside in the pool. The moonlight shining down on the both of us. I lean and kiss Ralph, and it was so magical. After I kiss Ralph, he returns by kissing me back. Ralph then whispers to me.

"Okay, that's enough fun for tonight. Let's go inside and dry off."

I return back into the house, and Ralph directs me to his bedroom. I then get into the shower to clean up, while Ralph takes my clothes to the washing machine. When I got out of the shower, I noticed that Ralph wasn't there. But he laid out some sleeping clothes for me to change into on his bed. Even though Ralph was bigger than me, the clothes seemed to fit fine. I then immediately drift off to sleep.

The next morning, Ralph wakes me up. He's wearing a polo shirt, and some denim jeans. Ralph then hands me back my clothes, freshly washed. I change into my clothes, and Ralph ends up making me breakfast. Ralph wasn't a good cook, but he could still put together a few things. After that, he ends up calling an uber for me to go home.

When my ride arrives, I end up giving Ralph another kiss, and I walk out of his house. In the uber ride back home, I started to realize what mess I gotten myself into. I formed a relationship with my boss, and I kissed him. My relationship with Ralph was never supposed to get to that point, but it did. I had a mix of guilt, but also a mix of pleasure. I really loved being with Ralph, and wanted to see him again. Last night was special, and I want to experience it again someday.

The following Monday at work however, Ralph for some reason tried to forget what happened Friday night. This was evident when I spoke to Ralph during lunch break. I went into his office, and I kept my conversation professional, but I was still being soft with him.

"So I was thinking, did you want to hang out soon. Maybe we can go..."

Ralph stopped me, and his tone was very angered.

"What the hell are you talking about? What happened that night never happened, okay? If you bring it up again I'm going to fire you. Get back to fucking work now."

Ralph did not want to continue our relations. I don't know the reasons why, but maybe it was the right thing to do. Having a relationship with Ralph, and being that he's my boss, maybe it's better if I didn't continue. What happened that night was probably spur of the moment. My job was to be his assistant in the company, and do work related activities. Ralph being my boyfriend, I didn't see was possible, and I had to accept this. Ralph's presentation ceremony was coming up this Friday, and I had to put my attention towards that. The days leading up to Friday, Ralph went back to his normal course of action.

He gave me tasks that I had to do, and I kept my attention on my work. Never once did I try to be cute with Ralph, or try to tease him. I did the tasks he asked of me to do, and I went home. It went back to an employee and boss relationship. I was completely fine with this, as this is what Ralph wanted. What I was struggling with, was that my crush on Ralph remained. That night I had with him, riding in the limo, meeting his friends.

Being invited to his house. Him flirting with me, and not wanting me to leave. The fact we made out in the pool. The kiss that we both shared. None of that was a dream, it actually happened. But Ralph was trying his best to erase all of that.

The day of Ralph's presentation came. I arrived at work, and directed myself to Ralph's office. I saw that Hugo and Vincent were also in Ralph's office as well. They were probably there to give him some moral support during his presentation. The big day was finally here, and so much was at stake. Ralph really wanted to finally bag this award.

For the past two consecutive years, he came awfully close to winning, but he didn't win. So this year, he wanted to finally become victorious in winning the award. It wasn't going to be easy, as everyone else giving their presentation, also had intentions of winning. As Ralph really wanted to win, we once again for the final time did a mock presentation in his office. Ralph used some of the notes that I wrote down, and also used the presentation documents he had. Ralph was ready, and we all knew it. Even if he didn't win the presentation award, his presentation was still well organized and professional, and to me that's what was really important. I know that winning the award was something Ralph was looking forward to, but to me, I was simply concerned about him not embarrassing himself. As long as his presentation was well structured, then that's okay. But based on how well he planned his presentation, there was a good chance that he would end up winning.

At two that afternoon, myself, Ralph, Hugo and Vincent all got into Hugo's limo, on our way to the concert hall, where Ralph was going to give his presentation. There were thousands of people there, and I started to feel anxious. Ralph went up on stage with the other participants who were going to give their presentations. Hugo, Vincent and I remained in the audience. Eventually, the event started, and the host began to moderate the event. Then several CEO's of companies started to give their presentations.

I found them to be quite boring, and Ralph's presentation was put together way better. There was one person that was going to give Ralph a run for his money. His name was Solomon Molteri. Solomon, like Ralph, was also Italian, and they both had the same ambition in life. Ralph actually has a strange past with Solomon, and they both do not get along. In essence, they are pretty much rivals of each other. Solomon and Ralph both have not yet won, and like Ralph, Solomon is also hoping that he could win the award. Solomon presented his presentation right before Ralph did, and I have to say that he was doing a great job with his presentation.

Solomon came prepared just like Ralph did, and he had no intentions of losing. I still felt that Ralph's presentation was slightly better, and his chances of winning were better than Solomon's. Once Solomon finished his presentation, that was when I became scared that Ralph might actually lose, due to how well Solomon presented himself. Directly after Solomon gave his presentation, it was Ralph's turn to give his presentation.

Ralph did not let Solomon get to him, and was doing even better than he was with our practice runs. Ralph was going to win this without any issues. His performance was absolutely perfect, and there wasn't one thing that I can say he did wrong. He was entertaining, engaging, and he presented all his facts correctly. He was going to be named the winner without a doubt. Although, I did see that Solomon was starting to feel bitter and jealous over Ralph doing a much better job than he did. After Ralph gave his presentation, several more people walked up to the stage to give their presentation. But they didn't have any chance at all. Ralph was taking this, and everyone in the building knew that.

It was finally time to announce the winner of the presentation. The third place winner was announced. Then the second place winner was announced. It was Solomon. Solomon was deeply upset when he realized that he got second place. I could sense much anger in his face. He then began to stare down Ralph deeply in bitter rage. When the first place winner was announced, it was no surprise to anyone that Ralph won. Ralph was so happy that he finally achieved first place, and took his first place trophy.

However, a sudden unfortunate action would happen. Ralph's special moment was totally ruined. Not even a couple seconds later, Solomon pushes Ralph down on the ground, and pours an unknown poison over his face. Ralph then starts to scream in pain, and security guards then try to restrain Solomon.

Solomon then takes out a gun, and aims it at Ralph. He begins to pull the trigger, but a security guard ends up killing Solomon, by shooting him in the chest. Ralph continues to cry out in pain from whatever Solomon threw on his face. Hugo, Vincent and I try to run up to the stage, but the security guards stop us. We are all in fear as to how Ralph is doing, and wonder about his safety.

Minutes later, paramedics come and take Ralph's body away from the scene. After this, I then immediately ride with Hugo and Vincent in Hugo's limo, and we go directly to the hospital. Upon reaching the hospital, the staff are not being cooperative with us, and refuse to give us any information at all. I am just feeling terribly nervous and scared over Ralph. What exactly is wrong with him? I knew that Solomon threw something on his face, but I didn't know how severe it was. We all waited in the hospital for several hours, until a doctor came out into the emergency room lobby, and spoke.

"Is there a Jamal Benson? Mr. Maligrino asked us to specifically speak to him."

I turn to look at Hugo and Vincent, and they nod their heads at me, saying that's it's fine that I go with the doctor without them. I follow the doctor into a private room. From what I gathered, this was never good when doctors did this. Once inside the room, the doctor then pulls out a file, and starts to compose himself, before telling me some heartbreaking news.

"I don't know the relationship you have with Mr. Maligrino. It's not any of my business. I assume you're his companion. But he wanted me to tell you this. Unfortunately we don't know exactly what poison Mr. Molteri doused him with. It may have been some type of lye substance."

The doctor then stops himself to once again compose himself, he then continues.

"Mr. Maligrino is now legally blind. We've looked at his eyes, and his retinas are completely destroyed. He cannot see anything at all. I'm so sorry to give you this news."

I immediately drop down to the floor and begin sobbing. The doctor then picks me up off the floor, and starts to comfort me. Ralph is blind, and this news was probably the worst thing you could tell me, behind him being dead. Ralph lost a major sense in his life, being able to see. I didn't know how I was going to tell this news to Hugo and Vincent. After I walk out of the room, I go back to the hospital lobby, and ask Hugo and Vincent to follow me.

They can see I'm sad, but I don't quite tell them what happened yet. We then go back into the private room, and the doctor tells Hugo and Vincent the news. They do not take it easy either, and they both start to cry. Once we all compose ourselves, we ask if it's okay if we can see Ralph. The doctor allows us to, but only one at a time. Hugo and

Vincent allow me to see Ralph first. I go inside Ralph's room, and he's resting on the bed. I immediately tell him that it's me in the room.

"Ralph, it's me Jamal. The doctors told us what happened. I want to say.."

I'm standing next to Ralph's bed, and he grabs my arm. Ralph has his head up toward the ceiling, and he starts to grip my arm tightly. Ralph then silently whispers back to me.

"Jamal, don't ever leave me. I really need your help from this point forward. I can't see anything anymore, so I'm going to need for you to be my eyes from now on."

What Ralph said was right. I was going to have to help him. He could use his other senses just fine, and despite the fact he couldn't see anymore, he was still the same Ralph. He would however have to understand that he's not going to see anymore. I didn't mind helping Ralph, and I know Ralph would do the same for me, if the roles were switched. I remained in Ralph's hospital room for ten minutes, kissing him, and comforting him.

Ralph is confused as to why Solomon did what he did. I told Ralph that one of the security guards killed Solomon after he pulled out a gun. I didn't understand how bitter and jealous Solomon could be, to do something like that. I end up kissing Ralph one final time on the forehead, and I walk out of his room. Ralph cries out for me to stay, but I tell him that the doctor ordered that only one visitor could remain in the room at a time. Hugo went into the room after I did, and comforted Ralph. Vincent did the same after Hugo left.

Ralph was happy that we were all there for him. Ralph then asked the hospital staff if I could spend the night with him, and they said yes. I stayed with Ralph all night, and I fed him, and I took care of him for the first time. Understanding that this was the first of many days that I was going to do something like this. I knew that Ralph didn't have the ability to see any more like he used to, and would need to find methods to work around all of that.

The following morning, investigators from the police department questioned us about what happened. They also talked to Hugo and Vincent, who also stayed the night in the hospital waiting room. We gave them all the information we knew. Even though it was an open and shut case. Solomon poured the poison on Ralph's eyes, and then tried to shoot him after the poison did not kill Ralph. After explaining the events, the police then left out Ralph's hospital room The next people to arrive, were people from the news media. Being that I worked in journalism myself, we had nothing to say to them at this point. Ralph was trying to recover, and the man can't see anymore. It was disrespectful to me that they were pressuring to interview us so soon. So we ignored and shunned away the media personnel that came into the hospital, that wanted information as to what happened.

Later on in the day, a woman who works for the "National Institute for the Blind", came into the hospital room. She wanted to test how well Ralph can work with his other senses. From the level Ralph was at, he was at an advance level to where he wouldn't need much assistance leaving the hospital. The woman even suggested that he could go home tomorrow given how well he was doing.

The woman also briefly taught him how to read braille. Even though Ralph was hurting and was depressed, he was being a good sport about it. He was trying to get used to being blind, and that he's not going to see. Ralph then got out of bed for the first time, and was taught how to use a blind cane. He was able to use the cane rather well. This was much for Ralph to take in at first, but I congratulated him.

The next day, Ralph was allowed to go home, which was great. He recovered well enough to leave the hospital. Ralph decided to make me his power of attorney, and to also be his licensed caretaker. Whatever decisions related to Ralph's health, I was in charge of. This was a great responsibility to have, and I was honored that Ralph wanted me to have it. Ralph left the hospital, and Hugo, Vincent and I took him home. The first day that Ralph was at home, we stayed by his side all the time.

We each took different parts of the day to devote time to Ralph's recovery. The company that Ralph and I worked for, were also understanding, and they gave us paid off time during all of this. I didn't know when Ralph was going to report back to work, but my main focus right now, was his recovery. As the weeks went on, Ralph due to how intelligent and clever he is, started to become more independent. He still needed our help from time to time, but he was beginning to do more things on his own. He very quickly mapped out his entire house, with the help of his walking stick. Ralph also was teaching himself how to dress again. This was something that Hugo, Vincent and I would help him with at first, but he quickly learned how to do it on his own eventually.

The next step, was to get Ralph to go outside. We planned a lunch for Ralph at the park, and we knew if he could do this outing without any issues, that he was advancing in his recovery. Ralph wasn't pleased once we surprised him with the fact he was going outside.

"I don't want to go outside and have people make fun of me. I don't want people to see me with my walking stick, and see me as the blind guy. I'm not ready."

After much coaxing, we finally managed to get Ralph to go outside. The outing was great, and Ralph didn't have any issues. Some people started at us, but Ralph managed to walk to the park outside just fine. We were all proud of him, and he was doing a great job, and was quickly starting to get back to the Ralph he was before. It has now been six months since Ralph has become blind. I have been teaching him braille as much as I could. As a result, Ralph can read braille perfectly.

Ralph also with my help goes out in public more, and has no issues with that. Ralph even walked downtown, and rode the train by himself. He managed to do it. Little things like that, which allow for Ralph to be independent. We start small, then we can move onto bigger things. The relationship I had with Ralph also improved. I moved in with Ralph during this time, and he doesn't want me to leave.

He enjoys the help from Hugo and Vincent, but Ralph seems to prefer my company over theirs. I was doing freelance journalism and writing during this time, and Ralph was getting paid sick leave from being blind. It was a huge change with Ralph being blind, but things were going steady. That was until one day Ralph was coming home from an outing with Hugo and Vincent. I was in the living room doing my writing, when Ralph came in and wanted to speak with me. Ralph seemed happy, and didn't seem depressed or sad. So I was interested.

"Jamal, there is something special that I've been discussing with Hugo and Vincent that I haven't told you yet. It's very important, so if I could get your attention please."

Whatever Ralph wanted to tell me was important, so I stopped what I was doing, and was all ears at this point. Ralph then reaches his hands out for me to hold, and I hold Ralph's hands. Ralph then starts to tell me the special news

"Well, I want to get back to work. I can't be stuck at home all the time. Yes I'm blind, but I can still walk and talk and eat, and do other things. I have a job offer in Los Angeles. You don't have to come, but I would love if you came with us Jamal."

Ralph wants for me to move with him to Los Angeles. I've never been to California, but I knew it was a wonderful place. I have seen California on television and movies, but I've never been there. My answer of course was yes. New York was my home, and I grew up here, but it's time for a change. I knew that Ralph was ready to move, and to start over at a new place. I knew that the job offer in California was one that didn't make any sense to pass up. I tell Ralph my answer.

"I would love to move with you to Los Angeles Ralph. I said that I will always be here for you. Whatever you want to do, I'll support you and I'll always respect you."

I lean up close to Ralph, and I kiss him passionately. Hugo and Vincent watch the both of us kiss, and are amused. Hugo and Vincent were going to move to Los Angeles with us. They didn't tell me about any of this, but they were actually looking at houses to buy in Los Angeles. They have found a place they were satisfied with, and was large enough for all of us. Ralph and I would end up sharing a room.

We all end up help Ralph prepare to move. Going to Los Angeles is a giant step, but it's something that we need to do. After we finish packing everything up, we all end up taking a flight to Los Angeles. Upon reaching our new house, we quickly get ourselves acquainted. Ralph continues doing his therapy and recovery methods. He already knows braille, and is now working doing more tasks to help his blindness. Ralph is taking a pottery classes, and he also invites myself, Hugo and Vincent to his pottery classes as well. I go to bed every night with this man, and it's not always easy.

Ralph wakes up mad sometimes being blind. Wishes that he could see again. He wants to know what the sky looks like again. Simple things like that. But he still manages to find a way to be happy. He uses electronics and computers just fine using special technology, and he listens to a lot of audiobooks as well.

Life with Ralph, Hugo and Vincent is great for me. I know when the time comes up, Ralph and I will possibly get married someday. Ralph will of course give his side of the story as well. My story was an interesting ride, but it's a ride that I will gladly go back and wait in line, and ride once again. My name is Jamal Benson, I am man of green, and that was my story.

CHAPTER 18:

MAN OF BLACK (PART 1)

My name is Ralph Maligrino. I am 40 years old. I am the "Man of Black". I am now legally blind. I can still use the computer sometimes, and my Reddit name is "WiseguyLA". I was born and raised in New York. I was born to an Italian father, and a Cuban mother. Both my maternal and my paternal family situation is complex. None of them really got along with each other, and it was tough. It was two completely different cultures trying to mesh together. My religion was also Catholic. So I was raised having to follow Catholic rules. I had to go to church often when I was young, and that was how our family operated. I was an only child. My parents wanted to have more children, but they never did. I had cousins, but I didn't get to interact with them much really. My cousins all lived hours away. The house I grew up in with my parents, was in a nuclear area. I didn't hang out with any of the neighborhood kids. My mother worked as a telephone operator, and my father worked for "American Express"; likewise where I would later work. So yes, my parents were busy most of the time.

I have issues talking about my personal family life and my childhood. Most of it isn't attractive. I will say that my father passed away from Lung Cancer when I was eight years old. His death came as a surprise to me. My father and I weren't close all the time, but when he was there, I loved hanging out with him. Not that I'm glad my father passed away, but his death sort of made me mature at a young age. Because my mother worked for the phone company, I was home alone mostly, and I had to take care of myself. Whenever I wanted something to eat, I had to fix it myself. I was not a very good cook, but I would manage. For entertainment, I would collect toys. It was a hobby that when I got older, I completely neglected and quit. However in my younger years, I enjoyed my toy collection. Whether it was action figures, or tinker toys, or gift shop souvenirs and knickknack's. I would collect them all. Many of the toys were hand me downs from my father.

He liked collecting toys as well, so his hobby rubbed onto me. When I got older, and was around twelve years old, I would then start to go into the city, and go to pawn shops, thrift shops and swap meets. All in an effort to collect as many toys as I could. The more toys I could find, and the rarer the toy, the better. It was a shame that eBay wasn't around back then, because I could have made a fortune with my toy collection. It was due to my toy collection, that I ended up meeting several of my childhood friends.

One of the pawn shops that I would frequent quite often, was run by the father of a boy, who would be my longtime best friend. The boy I would befriend was Hugo. I immediately connected to him, because Hugo was Italian like myself. Hugo was also a chubby obese boy, and he always made me laugh. I loved his personality, and it's the reason why I am still friends with him today. Hugo would hang around the outside of the pawn shop, while his dad did business inside.

Due to Hugo's exuberance, he would attract other kids that were walking around the downtown area of New York. He would trade baseball cards, and that was his vice. Baseball cards wasn't my thing at the time, but I was quite knowledgeable in all the players, and which cards had the most value. It was because of Hugo, that I stopped my toy collecting, and moved onto baseball cards. It was an interesting move, but baseball cards I felt were more sensible. I was getting older, and collecting toys was becoming more of a childish thing.

Hugo and I went to separate schools. Reason being, is that Hugo lived with his family in the city area of New York, and I lived with my mother in the more suburban part of New York. But as soon as school was done, and on the weekends, I would walk to the subway station to hang out with Hugo. I had so many fond memories with the both of us hanging out when we were young. One of the most interesting moments that I had witnessed, was when Hugo and I saw a robbery happen live at his father's pawn shop. Hugo and I were playing baseball cards outside of the pawn shop minding our own business, when a bunch of guys dressed in all black, decided to rob his dad's pawn shop. We just watched the whole thing in fear, but luckily Hugo's dad owned a gun, and was able to scare them off. This was a risky move on his part, but it seemed to work.

When I was in school, most of my teachers were amazed at how well academically I did. I was in many advanced classes, and I always got straight "A's". I took my school career very seriously, and I knew that knowledge and education was power. Growing up, I wanted to be a billionaire businessman, and owning "Sony" or "Viacom", or "Nike", or some major corporation with big money like that. It was possible, I just had to work hard to achieve that.

So few make it big, and I wanted to be one of those few. I didn't grow up with a silver spoon in my mouth at all. There were no handouts given to me. I was in a middle class upbringing. I grew up without a father basically, and with my mother raising me, it was tough for her as she worked usually. As I continued to grow up, I was now fourteen years old. I was starting to really harvest ideas in my head. I had big dreams in my life, and wanted to be the owner of my own company.

Making millions of dollars, and living a successful life. It was during this time that I met another close lifeline friend of mine. Going into High School, I came across Vincent. The reason I liked Vincent, was due to how shy, but smart he was. Vincent always kept to himself in class and he was introverted. Unlike Hugo who was a jabber box and wouldn't stop talking, Vincent was the polar opposite of that really. Vincent was also Italian, so that was another thing that we had in common. One day when class was over, I wanted to introduce myself to Vincent. He wasn't accepting at first, and would come up with excuses for me to stop talking to him. However, he later opened up to me, and was more accepting and welcoming. I invited Vincent to hang out with Hugo and I afterschool one day for pizza, and Hugo and Vincent quickly befriended each other. So I was making friends quite easily, and I was happy with myself.

Things came to a screeching halt, when my mother passed away without warning shortly after I turned fifteen. She was sick, and she never told me. Maybe she didn't want to scare me, or have me worry, but she never discussed her health issues with me. She passed away from Kidney failure, and I was not under the impression she wasn't well. With both my parents dead, with me basically still being a child, I started to become depressed, and lost with myself. I remember I was told the news of my mother's death, by extended family members that I never saw before.

They were all discussing as to what was going to happen with me. One of them had to step up and take care of me, or else I would have to go to a group home. I didn't want for that to happen. Luckily, my Uncle Ronnie, whom I seldom saw before my mother's death, offered to step up and take care of me. My Uncle Ronnie was a very obese man, with a thick mustache. He looked like Mario from Nintendo quite a bit. I was glad that my uncle decided to be my guardian, but I didn't know much about him, or what living with him was going to be like. Uncle Ronnie had three children. He had two daughters and one son.

His son, Ronnie Junior, was the same age as me. He also looked strangely identical to me. It was almost like we were brothers. So uncanny, how similar Ronnie Junior and I looked. I met him before at family functions in the past. Going to stay with Uncle Ronnie, was going to be interesting for me. I was going to be raised in an entirely new household, and I would have to get used to the rules that they follow in their house.

Uncle Ronnie was generally a nice guy, but he didn't mess around. You always did whatever he asked you to do, and as long as you were living under his roof, you always obeyed whatever he told you. Uncle Ronnie had a wife that stayed at home. She didn't work, and she usually was a housekeeper, and cleaned the house and cooked the meals. The first day I arrived at Uncle Ronnie's house, I remember Ronnie Junior was in the living room, and he had a bunch of friends over. They were playing video games, and Uncle Ronnie went off.

"Ronnie, I know your homework isn't done. What I tell you about inviting friends over without having your homework done? You're also on punishment, so turn that damn thing off."

Like I said, Uncle Ronnie was very direct, and things had to be in order with him. I didn't have any issue with this, because I was raised to be very obedient. Ronnie Junior's friends then left out of the house, and Ronnie Junior angrily cut the video game off. Uncle Ronnie then introduced me to Ronnie Junior, and the rest of the people in the house.

Uncle Ronnie then showed me where my room was. I had my own private room, which was lovely. I had my own space, and nobody could bother me at all. For the sake of the story from this point on, I'm going to refer to Ronnie Junior as Ronnie, and his father as Uncle Ronnie. I think it's much more simpler that way. But anyways, I wasn't that close with Ronnie's sisters.

They were girls, and they were also girly girls. They were into makeup, and they would have posters of boy bands and teen idols in their room. That wasn't my style at all. But Ronnie became my third best friend. He was not only my cousin, but he was my friend as well. When I moved to my Uncle Ronnie's house, I ended up switching schools. The new school I went to, wasn't as good.

I missed my old school. Because of this, I no longer went to class with Vincent anymore. The positive thing was, I now went to school with Ronnie. We shared a lot of our classes, and we got to hang out during school as well. Ronnie struggled with his academics, so I tutored him a lot. Ronnie was more of a business minded person like myself. His dream was to own his own nightclub someday. Running a nightclub was never my agenda. Too much liability with that, and so many codes you have to follow, and getting a liquor license, and all that.

I was into more simplistic ways to run a business. Like inventing or selling something that people enjoy, or selling a productive art, or creating a financial or multimedia company. Things of that nature. But Ronnie was thinking more fun and excitement and nightlife. That was fine as well. If Ronnie wanted to open a nightclub, I wasn't going to crush his dream.

I wanted to introduce Ronnie to Hugo and Vincent. There was a video arcade in downtown New York, and I figured this would be the best place for us all to meet. I was sure that Ronnie was going to hit it off well with them. We all seem to have identical personalities.

I was also looking at the bigger picture of it. The larger social circuit that I could have, the better. However, when I first introduced Ronnie to them, he seemed to be very apprehensive. I'm not going to lie, I was slightly disappointed that he didn't connect with them as much as I hoped. I mean, he was still nice and cordial, but we all could tell that it just wasn't working out. A short time after that introduction, I was hanging out with Hugo and Vincent without Ronnie being present. Hugo then started to gossip about Ronnie to me.

"Hey, that guy Ronnie is weird Ralph. I don't know. Vincent and I don't like him. I know he's your cousin, but he's just weird, and we get a bad vibe from him."

This was tough, as I got along fine with Ronnie. I liked him equally as a friend, just like I do with Hugo and Vincent. I don't know why they didn't like him. I refused to tag along with them and downplay my cousin like that. Ronnie isn't like that to me. Yeah Ronnie is a little bit out there, and he was slightly eccentric at times. But I loved my cousin. I had to let Hugo and Vincent know that I was still going to associate with Ronnie, whether they liked that or not.

"Well, he's my cousin, and he's my blood, and he's my family. You guys are going to have to deal with that. I'm sorry y'all don't get along, but I disagree with you guys. Sorry."

Hugo and Vincent had no choice but to accept this. They were angry that I was spending time with Ronnie, despite their disdain for him. I couldn't care less. I had to find a way to do damage control. Making sure that my friendship with Hugo and Vincent wasn't strained, and that my friendship with my cousin Ronnie wasn't destroyed either. I valued friendships greatly, and I saw no reason to stop talking to Ronnie. He hasn't done anything to warrant me to stop talking to him at all. He's my cousin, and I care about him.

Going onto my senior year of High School, I was looking forward to University most of all. This was my next step into going into adulthood, and making a name for myself. Hugo and Vincent were also looking forward to University. Ronnie however had no intentions of continuing his education. His goal was to work in a bar, and work his way up to being bartender, to working his way up to eventually being manager of the club. His longtime goal being an owner of his own club.

Again, I didn't want to crush Ronnie's dream, but I wish that he was thinking more realistically. His education was more important, and the dream he had, required a lot of luck. I wanted to try my best to convince Ronnie to advance his education. His grades were good enough for him to go college, and whatever he wanted to study, could help him own his own nightclub someday. We were weeks away from graduation, and I went into Ronnie's room to talk to him.

"Ronnie, I wanted to talk to you about your plans after High School. I understand that you don't want to go to college. Why is that? You're very smart Ronnie."

Ronnie was reading a car magazine on his bed, and wasn't paying me any attention. I then decide to continue to press Ronnie, trying to get him to change his mind about college.

"You just need to apply yourself that's all. I know you have your dreams, and you can still go for your dreams. But you need to understand the importance of your education Ronnie."

Ronnie shuts his magazine, and looks up at me. He then responds to what I told him.

"I don't know man, college just isn't my style at all. I don't like school, and I don't want to do something I'm not interested in doing. I have plans, and college isn't one of those plans."

In a way, Ronnie was right. Why should I force him to go to college, if he doesn't wish to. I nod my head as to what Ronnie said, and accept the fact that he doesn't wish to go to. I proceed to walk out of his bedroom, but before I leave out of the room completely. Ronnie shouts out my name. I turn back over to him, and Ronnie then speaks to me.

"Ralph, you know what, I'll go, only if I go to the same school as you. I mean, there are going to be sick ass parties right? College can't be that bad right? I'll give it a shot."

My magical powers of persuasion worked. I don't know how in the hell I managed to do it, but I convinced Ronnie to go to college. Even though I feel this should have been a choice for him to make on his own, and I didn't like how I had to pressure him into going, I was happy nevertheless. My next plan was to make sure that Ronnie, Hugo, Vincent and I, all went to the same school. We all applied to "NYU", and luckily, we were all accepted.

This was back in the day, so the acceptance rate was better. I know "NYU" nowadays is quite difficult to get into from what I heard. But we all lucked out. All four of us were going to the same school, and I couldn't believe it. After we all got our acceptance letters, we started to pack up for college. The next thing was making it possible for the four of us to be in the same dorm room. This was something I really had to pull strings to accomplish. Dorm rooms are usually not picked out of student preference. But I wanted to make an exception for my case.

I figured if we were all in the same dorm rooms, we could keep in touch with each other better. University life is quite hectic, so if we all managed to report to the same dorm after class, it would be better for all of us. I also forgot that Hugo and Vincent didn't particularly care for Ronnie. My only hope was that they could put their differences aside.

We are all adults now, and they should get along with Ronnie. I spoke with some of the coordinators at the University, and they said that it was okay for the four of us to all share a dorm room. We were all going to be in the same dorm after all. I got my wish.

I decided to keep the fact Ronnie was moving in with us a secret from Hugo and Vincent. I told them that we would be sharing a dorm room with a mystery fourth guy. I knew that if I told them straight up that Ronnie was going to be in the dorm, they wouldn't agree to it. At this point, they still have not made amends with Ronnie, and they would have not been accepting of sharing the dorm with him, had I been honest. To make things even more worse, I also didn't tell Ronnie that Hugo and Vincent are going to be rooming with us. Ronnie would not have stood for it at all, if I came out with the secret immediately. I told Ronnie that we would be sharing a dorm with two other random guys. So both sides are going to have to accept this news, even if they are going to be mad at me for keeping this a secret. I didn't have a car at this time, but Uncle Ronnie gave us carl I had to share it with Ronnie.

It was just an old Volvo station wagon. It was transportation for us at the end of the day. It wasn't a fancy car by any means, but it was something. I ended up driving myself and Ronnie to the University. We start to check ourselves in, and I don't see Hugo and Vincent. They must have not arrived yet.

After Ronnie and I finish checking ourselves in, we then head directly to our dorm room. Once inside our dorm, we start to unpack. Ronnie then says that he wants to tour around the campus. I decide to however stay in the dorm, continuing to unpack all of my things. About thirty minutes later, I notice Hugo and Vincent walk into the dorm room. I hug my friends, and we reunite with each other.

With the fact that Ronnie is out of the room, I decide to take this time to finally reveal the secret that Ronnie would be sharing the dorm with us. They need to know this information right now, and I can't keep this from them any longer.

"You guys, I really hope you don't get mad at me. But I need to tell you that Ronnie is going to be rooming with us. I know you guys don't get along with him, but please listen.."

Hugo then immediately stops me, and displays how angry he is with this news.

"Ugh, no. We're not staying with him. Hell no. I don't give a fuck if he's your cousin Ralph. He's just plain weird, and were not sleeping with him. Nope."

I didn't know that Ronnie was outside the dorm eavesdropping on us this whole entire time. After Hugo said that, I respond back to Hugo, trying to get him to understand.

"Give him a chance you guys. He's my cousin, and he's a great guy. He has a lot in common with you guys than you realize. Just give him a chance. For me please?"

Ronnie remains eavesdropping outside the dorm. Hugo and Vincent then think to themselves for a few short seconds. They then agree to let Ronnie stay in the room with us. I was aware that they were going to be upset at the news at first. It was rotten of me to keep that secret from them. But had I not kept it secret, there was no way we would end up rooming together. I am happy that they accept this news.

At this same time, Ronnie walks into the dorm room, and he has a depressed look on his face. He then walks over to his bed and begins to unpack all of his things. As Ronnie is unpacking, he under his breath, starts to speak to all of us.

"I didn't want to be in a room with you guys either. I can't believe you lied to us like that Ralph. It's too late now though, so we're all stuck here. That was fucked up to lie to us Ralph."

I did feel guilty for doing that. Not only to Hugo and Vincent, but to Ronnie as well. I was being extremely selfish, and only thinking about myself. I wanted for all of my friends to be in the same dorm together. I didn't realize that I shouldn't force people to room together, if they don't want to. So I was in the wrong for thinking like this.

I thought it wasn't that big of a deal for us all to be in the same room, but it is. It should be a joint decision and agreement if we all want to be in the same dorm. I shouldn't be dictator and make all the decisions. This was a quality of mine that I didn't care for.

I liked to boss people around, and make all the choices. Not understanding what other people's agendas and feelings are. I was now forcing Hugo and Vincent to get along with Ronnie, and Ronnie to get along with Hugo and Vincent. Even though neither party really liked each other that much. I was optimistic that this was going to be a good idea regardless. I felt that passion and vision that we all had meant something, and we could definitely make this venture work. It was only the first day, and things could get better from this point. We all started to unpack all of our things, getting situated in our dorm.

That night, I decided to make amends for the dirty rotten secret I pulled earlier. I wanted to treat all the guys out to dinner. I wanted to take them out for pizza. It was the least I could do, to let the guys know that I want for us to all be friends, and that I want for us to start fresh.

Myself, Hugo, Vincent and Ronnie all drove to a nearby pizza restaurant that was located about half an hour away from campus. It was just a plain old pizza parlor. It was not anything fancy or elaborate.

A very simple pizza place. Once we arrived at the pizza place, I could already see that Hugo and Vincent, were keeping a distance from Ronnie, and Ronnie was also keeping distance from Hugo and Vincent. They still were holding onto much hate for each other, and despite my efforts of trying to take them out to socialize, it wasn't working that well. If all of this was a wasted effort, I would feel devastated. The whole point of me taking them out for pizza, was to call truce from the way both of them were acting towards each other. I want for all of us to be friends, and to work together as buddies while we are at college. I end up ordering a pizza for the whole table, and we all remain quiet for several minutes. This was turning out to be a disaster.

How could a simple pizza outing turn into a wreck like this? I wanted to attempt to break the ice, but every time I would try to open my mouth, I couldn't due to how the rest of the guys at the table were acting. The entire energy in the room was negative, and I started to feel that this was a horrible idea. We continue to wait for our pizza to come out, and I notice that there is a baseball game playing on a big screen television in the pizza restaurant.

I keep my attention on the baseball game, and maybe by watching the game, time will pass by quickly. I want to get this outing over with, as it was stupid of me to think that this was going to work. However, Hugo then randomly speaks to Ronnie.

"So Ronnie, Ralph told us that you want to own a nightclub someday? That's awesome man. You can make a lot of money doing something like that."

Ronnie then to my surprise, responds to what Hugo told him.

"Yeah it's my dream. I don't have a name picked out for my club, but I want it to be like 1940s Italian gangster themed. It sounds kinda tacky yeah, but I like it, and it's my vision."

They were finally getting along with each other, and my plan worked. I never thought that they would accept Ronnie, and Ronnie would accept them, but it seemed to have worked after all. They continued to chat with each other, and everything was going good. We were forming a brotherhood and a collective together, and that was all that I wanted. My plan was for us to get along and to work in harmony of each other.

From this point forward, Hugo and Vincent appreciated Ronnie, and Ronnie appreciated them. The four of us became grounded with each other, and we were the best of friends. We all would go to class, and come back to the dorm and chill. Like magic, my vision of the four of us being a team was coming into light. I knew that once we were done with school, our options from this point were going to be limitless.

Ronnie especially was amazing me with how connected he was with his studies. Once our freshman year of University was over, I found it strange that none of us decided to join a fraternity. Well I guess strange isn't the right word. I don't know, but none of us joined a fraternity. In a way, we had our own unofficial fraternity. The four of us were stronger than any fraternity out there. I knew that Ronnie was expressing how disappointed he was, that he wasn't involved in a fraternity. I mean, it is a special part of going into University I suppose.

I didn't think of it as much of a big deal. Hugo and Vincent couldn't care less that they didn't join a fraternity. But for Ronnie, he was slightly disappointed over it. As a result of this, he started to mess around with a bunch of guys that we were not comfortable with him being around.

There was nothing that me, or Hugo or Vincent could do. He was an adult, so whatever Ronnie wanted to do, we had to simply just accept. I was scared as to what he was learning from these guys. Ronnie would start to become more dangerous in his behavior. He would come home to the dorm, and act very strange around us. He changed instantly, and it caught all of us by immediate surprise.

One night, out of concern, we wanted to gain more knowledge on the type of people that Ronnie seemed to surround himself with as of late. We weren't trying to get into his business, but we wanted to know all the details of these men he was with. Ronnie came to the dorm one night, and it was clear he was drunk. He had been drinking, so maybe this was not the best of times to talk with him, but it was very important that we did. We had to get to the bottom of Ronnie's behavior. It wasn't an intervention at all. Our plan was to talk to him. Hugo was the first to show concern to Ronnie, and he began to speak with him.

"Ronnie, we noticed that you been hanging out with some guys around campus. Can you tell us how you came across these guys? You guys aren't doing anything illegal right?"

Ronnie, as I would suspect, started to feel threatened about Hugo asking him about his new group of friends he was hanging out with. He didn't want us to know about that part of his life, and I could understand. Ronnie was an adult, and he should be allowed to associate with whoever he wishes. It was simply a safety thing, and we were concerned about him at the end of the day.

He is my cousin, and I hold every ounce of responsibility if something terrible were to happen to Ronnie. We didn't know what he was doing with these guys, and that was the part that worried us greatly. Ronnie could be with whoever he wanted to, but it was the fact we were scared he was around the wrong crowd. It isn't coincidence that as soon as Ronnie began to hang out with these guys, his attitude completely changed. He's never around us anymore, and we were simply concerned. Ronnie reluctantly responded to Hugo, although feeling angered.

"Oh, that's not any of your business. No were not doing anything illegal. I would appreciate if you guys wouldn't get into my business like that. When do I ever get into any of y'all's business? I don't, right? So let me hang with whoever I want to. Thank you."

I then decided to try to speak with Ronnie. With me being his cousin, he might open up to me more, rather than with Hugo. In a friendly way, I start to speak with Ronnie.

"We're not trying to get into your business Ronnie. We are curious that's all. Is it okay if we can meet these guys? Maybe we can be friends with your friends. What do you say?"

Unlike with Hugo, Ronnie has a different approach with me, and remarkably, he seems to agree with my idea of introducing his friends to us. Ronnie then replies back to me.

"I don't know if you guys would get along, but sure. If you guys want to meet them so bad. But don't complain if they aren't your style. I did warn you, that you might not get along."

So it was official. We were finally going to meet this new posse that Ronnie was messing around with. The following day, myself, Hugo and Vincent, all went to student union, waiting for Ronnie to arrive with his friends. We waited for about thirty minutes, before they finally started to arrive at the scene. Ronnie was with three other guys. They were all of Italian descent, and I guess the best way to describe them would be "Guido". "Guido", I guess would be the equivalent of the pompous frat boy "douchebag" type. That's the kind of guys they were.

I mean, I'm sure that they came in peace. We are all young, and at the University level, we are all trying to mold ourselves, and figure out exactly what our identity is. I immediately got that vibe off them, in the moment that they are walking up and approaching us. I haven't even said one word to them, and I already pegged them down completely. As Ronnie is making his way over to our direction, I continue to gaze down at all of the guys completely. Ronnie then introduced them to us.

"Guys, this is Derek, Jojo, and Nico. Derek, Jojo, Nico, these are my roommates, Hugo and Vincent, and this is my cousin Ralph. So you guys happy now that we have all met?"

To describe Ronnie's friends, I'll start with Jojo. Jojo although he was young and college aged, looked like a grown ass man. He was bald, and he had muscles. He was a tough guy, but he was really just a gentle giant. His appearance was very deceiving. Jojo, like Vincent, didn't speak that much. He kept most of his comments to himself. I guess he was like a goon in a sense. He was like a bodyguard to Ronnie, and was quiet as a mouse.

As far as describing Nico, Nico was more slender and skinny. He also had a Fonzy from Happy Days type appearance. He was really into cars and motorcycles, and had a classic 50s style to him. Nico was a nice guy, but he was sarcastic most of the time. He had no filter when he talked, and he always said what was on his mind. Even if it offended you, he would say it anyways.

Now I'm going to discuss the ringleader of the group. That would be Derek. Derek was like a mix between Jojo and Nico. Derek also had a classic vibe about him. He like Nico, was also into motorcycles and cars and street racing. He also had many traits that Jojo shared as well. Derek also had some muscle onto him. He wasn't as muscular as Jojo was, but he wasn't slender like Nico was. Derek also showed much authority out of all the guys. He was the ringleader as I said. Whatever the rest of the band did, they had to go along with what Derek did. If Derek did not approve of what was going on, he wouldn't accept it. Derek also had a vindictive personality as well.

I mean, I think deep down he was a nice guy, but his attitude was slightly strict at times. He could manipulate you very well, and get you to agree with whatever he has up his sleeve. Derek also had a mean look on his face always. I don't know why he always looked angry. Even if he was happy, he kept that stern look on his face all the time.

The group that Ronnie was in, was called the "Road Sharks". There were several different incarnations of the 'Road Sharks", in campuses all around the United States. The group that developed in "NYU", had about fifty guys in the group, including Ronnie and the guys that he's close with. Derek is actually second vice president of the group at "NYU". There are two more guys that are above him, but he's high into the ranks. The group is actually not a fraternity at all, but they are more of a clique.

The only requirement of the group is that you have to be Italian American, and you have to pass their initiation. Once in the group, you get access to special perks from being in the group. You get to attend secret parties, get connections for whatever job plans you have once you graduate High School. But one main aspect of the group was their weightlifting competitions, and their vehicle modification contests and their street racing. The group wasn't a gang, but they did participate in illegal street racing. That was I guess the only bad thing associated with the group. I guess another bad thing to mention would have to be, some of the members did hardcore illegal drugs, and also did illegal steroids. But I guess that's in a whole another category. Derek then began to speak to myself, Hugo and Vincent.

"So, Ronnie told me that you guys are interested in joining our group? Well, if you guys want to join, me and the other higher ups have to all agree to let you join, after you sign the contract. Then, all you need to do is pass the initiation after that to be in the group. You guys seem cool enough, and you guys are going to enjoy being in the group."

Wait, what? When did we even hint at the fact that we wanted to join the group? The only thing we wanted to do, was to see the type of guys that Ronnie was hanging out with. Never did we once even consider joining the group. The expression on myself, Hugo and Vincent's faces seem to reflect this. We were left speechless.

Instead of saying that we were not interested in joining the group, we remained quiet. It was some magic spell that Derek was putting onto us. We really wanted to join the group, and was excited over that. Even though we technically didn't agree to join the group, we were now in the beginning process of joining. One thing led to another, and the following day, we met up with Derek again at student union. He gave us a long sheet of paper saying all the terms and conditions if we want to join the group. Basically how we are sworn to secrecy from ever mentioning being a part of the group to anyone.

How we are only allowed to join if we are of Italian American heritage, which myself, Hugo and Vincent are. Another requirement, is that we are to treat the other members with respect. Joining the weightlifting and the street racing events are not mandatory, but they are preferred and strongly encouraged. I don't know what the hell Hugo, Vincent and I were thinking, but we signed on the dotted line, to become official members of the group. At the time, I didn't realize how much of a big mistake this was. It was all fun and games at first. I mean, we weren't apart of any fraternity, and I guess you only go through University once. What harm would joining this group actually be?

Derek said that he will talk with the other higher ups in the group, and they will return back to us with a decision, as to whether or not Hugo, Vincent and I made the group. We waited for a week and did not hear anything. We started to assume that we didn't make the group, or they thought we weren't cool enough. I continued on with my classes, not paying the group any mind. Even though part of me did want to be accepted into the group, I didn't care either way. Although the following week, Derek knocked on the door of our dorm room. Hugo opened the door and let him in. Then Derek gave us the news as to if we made the group.

"Well you guys, I talked it over with everyone else. We do have strict guidelines as to who can be accepted. But after talking it over, we feel you guys would be a perfect fit. All you guys have to do is pass the initiation, which will be tonight, and you guys are official members."

I guess we were cool enough, as they are still interested in us being in the group. I have no idea what the initiation will be, but if Ronnie is still here in one piece, then it can't be that bad or dangerous. Little did I know, the initiation wouldn't be as easy as I thought. The only thing Derek told us to do, was to meet in a back area of campus that night.

As long as it didn't involve any of us getting physically hurt, I didn't care what the initiation consisted of. Hugo, Vincent and I waited in the area that Derek told us to that night, completely nervous. Not sure what is going to happen. All of a sudden, we see Derek, and two other guys I've never seen before, each holding a giant trash can. Derek then approaches us, and explains what the initiation is.

"Every year we switch up the initiation. But this year, it's not that bad. Each of you have to strip down to your underwear and get inside one of these trash cans. The catch is, we're going to put ice cold water in these trash cans."

Is it too late to back away now? What in the holy hell is this? What kind of torture are they making us do? We continue to listen Derek explain the initiation to us.

"In order to be accepted into the group, you guys have to be ducked under the trash cans for five seconds. You do not get a second attempt. If you guys pass, you'll be in the group."

I look at Hugo and Vincent, thinking we are batshit crazy to go along with this. However, we all start to undress into our underwear.

Mind you, it's late at night, it's cold, and it's kinda humiliating that we are in our underwear. I don't know what kind of sick initiation is this, but we were too far ahead to quit. Now that we have all stripped, Derek then has one of his goons take a long garden hose, and begins to fill all the trash cans up with water.

Then another one of his goons takes a big bag of ice, and pours the ice cubes into each of the trash bins. Derek then tells us to get inside each of the bins. Hugo, Vincent and I go inside the bins, and the water is uncomfortably cold. I'm shivering, and I didn't think I was going to be able to pass this initiation. Derek then tells us that when he says "Go", he is going to start the timer. After he says "Go", we all have to dunk our entire bodies into the trash bin.

If we can stay under for more than five seconds, we would have passed the initiation. If we get out of the bin, or come up from the bin before five seconds are up, we will not be allowed into the group. Derek then said "Go", and we all dunk ourselves into the bins. I tried to count down five seconds in my head, but the water was so cold, and I felt that I was going to catch Hypothermia.

After I counted what I believed was five seconds, I bring my body out of the bin. Instantaneously, Hugo and Vincent also come up from the bins. We all wait in suspense, for Derek to tell us whether or not we passed.

"Damn, you guys actually did it. Congrats, you guys are now official members of the "Road Sharks". You guys are so crazy to have actually done that. But you're one of us now."

Even though I was so cold, and was shaking, I was happy to be a member. It felt cool being involved in an outlaw group at the school. At this point, all I wanted to do was take a warm shower, and crawl next to a fireplace, with a cup of hot chocolate. This moment of celebration would soon end though.

As soon as Hugo, Vincent and I joined that group, things started to get worse. Many of the guys in the group were not good role models. It was like a strange mafia in a sense. Some of the guys after they graduate, continue to mess around with the group. Some guys even into their forties, still remain members of the "Road Sharks". In order to keep your membership with the "Road Sharks", you had to attend a once a week meeting with them on campus. The meeting would mostly have us talking about current events, career plans, and other activities we would do in the group. But my main issue with the group, was the way some of the guys were being brainwashed by some of the teachings of the group.

I thought it was more a cool kids club, but it was something even deeper than that really. Some of the guys were becoming ruthless with being in the club, and their personalities would change. Luckily for myself, Hugo and Vincent, we were able to differentiate between our normal selves, and the way we acted when we were in the club. However with Ronnie, the longer he remained in the club, the more he changed as a person.

As a matter of fact, if it weren't for Ronnie, we would have never been introduced to the club at all. Ronnie in particular was interested in the street racing events. If you participated in the racing events, your position as a member in the group advanced.

My only thing with Ronnie participating in the street racing events, is that many guys over the years have gotten hurt and even killed doing street racing. Because the club is top secret, the news and media would report the events as "College kids doing reckless driving", when in actuality, the "Road Sharks" club was behind most of the street racing events. But Ronnie was really interested in the street racing, and I couldn't stop him.

It was really hard to get out of the club, once you were an official member. I never knew the official protocol on how to become an ex-member, and nobody ever really quit. If you graduated from school, you simply stopped associating with the club. But the club had so many perks, and you felt involved in a second family, that you never even though of quitting or leaving the club.

We were now in our senior year of school, and the club became more of an afterthought. Our loyalty to the "Road Sharks" stayed, but my main focus was more on our schoolwork. I was trying to graduate and get my business degree, and Ronnie, Hugo and Vincent were doing the same. Also studying business. I was not sure how Ronnie was doing in his studies, as I barely saw him during senior year. He was doing more activities with the "Road Sharks", and spending a majority of his time with them. I didn't know what they were exactly doing, but it caused me concern. I didn't want for Ronnie to be distracted, and put the group before his own studies.

I knew that Ronnie signed up for the street racing event. I didn't want him to participate, but that was his decision alone to make. It was senior year of University, and Ronnie realized that this was his last chance to be included in the street racing events. I don't know where Ronnie came up with the money, but he managed to get himself a modded Toyota Camry.

He worked on that car quite a bit with Derek and Jojo. I didn't feel that the whole street racing thing was safe at all, and I didn't involve myself in any of this. Ronnie was my cousin, but this was a hobby that was up his alley, and I didn't want to barge into it really. Ronnie did ask for me, Hugo and Vincent to come and see him race. I couldn't bear to watch such things under normal circumstances. But because he was my cousin, it was difficult for me to say no.

I remember the night before the race, we were all in the dorm room, drinking and having fun. We were smoking weed, and kicking back. Derek, Jojo and Niko were in our dorm as well. Even though we were all different, we were all the same. We were all members of the "Road Sharks", and we were all essentially brothers. I really did not want Ronnie to do the race. I had a sinking feeling that the race would be the death of him. I don't know why I had this feeling.

As the party was dissipating, Derek, Niko and Jojo began to leave. Hugo and Vincent decided to walk with Niko and Jojo back to their dorm room. Ronnie and I remained in the room alone. I remember we were watching a boxing match on the television set in our dorm. Ronnie then started to speak to me.

"Ralph, you were always a good cousin to me. You were the only one who understood me. My dad never understood me, nobody else understood me but you. I'm racing tomorrow for you, and I'm gonna win tomorrow for you. I love you Ralph."

I continue to speak with Ronnie, letting him know that I appreciate him greatly.

"Ronnie, you're my cousin, so of course I understand you. I still feel you doing this race is dangerous. Are you confident you want to do this? If you're okay about it, then I'm okay. I just want you to be careful. Then we'll celebrate later after you win."

Ronnie and I smile at each other, and Ronnie kisses me on the cheek. We then go back to watching the boxing match on the television. Even though that sinking feeling still remained, I was slightly more comfortable with Ronnie going along with the race. Maybe I was over reacting and thinking too much ahead about the whole thing.

I shouldn't have had anything to worry about. Thinking about the worst that could happen, is not the right approach to go about this. I have faith that my cousin will do his best in the race. Yes it's an illegal street race, but I didn't have to worry about it. I went to sleep that night, still feeling nervous. I want for Ronnie to be safe during the race, and my nerves were starting to make me feel otherwise.

The following day, I couldn't stop thinking about the dangers of the race, and how I still was unsure of Ronnie racing. I paced back in forth in the dorm, contemplating as to whether or not I wanted to attend the race. I know I promised Ronnie that I would watch him race, but I was starting to have second thoughts of going.

I did ultimately decide to attend the race. I have to support my cousin, despite it not being something I'm comfortable watching. Later that night, a bunch of other members of the "Road Sharks", met up at a top secret location where the race will be held, not far from campus.

Only members of the "Road Sharks", were allowed to be in attendance. All the guys that were going to be in the race got into their cars, ready for position. The race was going to start in a few minutes. The night was clear, and the course was simple. It was a small quarter mile looped course that the guys would race in. There would be three laps altogether. The guy who arrived at the finish line after three laps first would win. I look at all the men racing, and I then see Ronnie sitting in his car. He looked so confident that was he was going to win.

I tried to wave my hands for him to smile back at me, or give me a thumbs up, but he didn't see me. He was way too focused on the race I guess to notice me waving. Derek was also in the race, and I found it strange how despite the friendship that Derek and Ronnie had, they were going to be competing against each other in the race.

In total, there were six guys that were racing. The race was starting, and all the guys turned their engines on. Once the flag was raised, all the guys then began to speed off. They were all racing at a fast speed, and I didn't know how I composed myself well enough to watch.

Watching them race at that high of a speed, was causing me a lot of anxiety. The race in the first lap was equally matched. All the guys managed to complete the first lap close to each other. However in the second lap, it was clear that Ronnie and Derek were the frontrunners. There would be times to where Ronnie would get ahead of Derek, and Derek would get ahead of Ronnie.

I wanted Ronnie to win, but Derek was also determined as well. The second lap was soon over, and in the final lap, Ronnie and Derek continued to be neck and neck towards each other. They were both about hundred feet away from the finish line, when something devastating happened. In an instant, Ronnie and Derek crash into each other very badly. I was in immediate shock, and the worst thing to happen in a street race, happened.

Despite Ronnie and Derek crashing, the race continued, and the remaining racers finished the race. However, Ronnie and Derek remained in their cars. I didn't know if either of them survived the crash. I continue to look at both of their vehicles that are totaled. During this time, several other members of the "Road Sharks" seemed unsure as to how to react over Ronnie and Derek crashing, and this angered me. I immediately ran over to the area that they crashed in, and yelled for the rest of the guys to call 911. I'm now at the area where both of their wrecked cars are, and cry out.

"Ronnie! Derek! Can you guys hear me?! Are you guys okay?!"

I don't get an answer, and I start to panic immensely. I start to cry, with the fact that Ronnie and Derek being dead is possible. Minutes later, the police and the ambulance arrive. Several "Road Sharks" members run away from the scene. I remain at the scene, as the paramedics take Ronnie's and Derek's bodies out of their cars. At the hospital, I later found out that Ronnie and Derek did not survive the crash. They died upon impact. Being told the news, I couldn't move at all. I couldn't think either. Ronnie was about to graduate college with the rest of us, and this happened.

I tried my best to stop Ronnie from participating in the race, but there wasn't anything that I could do to get him to stop. Derek also passed away, and it was sad for him as well. Derek was about to graduate too, and his family was proud of him for that. Two lives lost, over a stupid decision to street race. This is exactly why I don't stand for things such as this. It's far too dangerous. It may be fun and exciting, but the safety risk factor is too much.

I didn't know how I was going to tell Uncle Ronnie the news, but I had to. How do you tell someone that your son died? It's impossible. I lost my cousin, but I can only imagine how Uncle Ronnie would feel knowing that he lost a son, and how Ronnie's sisters will feel, that their brother is dead.

I then felt guilty that I should have done more to protect Ronnie. I should have tried harder to get him to not race. I ended up calling Uncle Ronnie on the phone. To say that he didn't take the news well was an understatement.

"What? Ronnie is dead? He was in a street race? How could you let him do a thing like that? You watched him race, and didn't do anything? How could you do that Ralph?"

Uncle Ronnie was very disappointed in me, and I could understand why. Being involved in the group was a bad idea, and I knew it. It was being in that group which caused Ronnie's death. Doing the street races, is what caused Ronnie to die. It wasn't something he shouldn't have been doing in the first place, but he was far too convinced.

I thought the chances of Ronnie and Derek being killed in the race was so low, that I didn't let it affect me. I had a bad feeling, but I only took at as me worrying too much. Now, Uncle Ronnie has to bury his own son, and I know how horrible he's feeling about that. My cousin is also gone. He was really close to me, and I feel partly responsible for this death. By egging Ronnie on by being a member of the club. By not convincing Ronnie to neglect to participate in the race. Ronnie's death will be something I have to accept, and understand my part in it. The "Road Sharks" club was the reason for Ronnie dying as well, and that club which was supposed to feel like a support system to the students at the University, was actually something that turned out to be a dangerous situation.

Doing street racing was not safe at the end of the day, yet it was strongly encouraged between all the members. Ronnie is gone, and my final year of University is tarnished due to that. I can't look at being in the "Road Sharks' club the same way, knowing that they pressured my cousin into doing the street racing, and him ultimately being killed. Ronnie's death taught me a lot, and you have to value the type of people you surround yourself with.

As my story continues, I move on from Ronnie's death, and how I continue my involvement with the "Road Sharks". Why in the hell would I remain a member of the "Road Sharks" even though Ronnie died being involved in their group? Well it's complicated. It was beneficial for me to stay associated with the "Road Sharks." I learned a lot about myself, and learned from my mistakes.

I also talk about meeting Jamal, and how I became legally blind as well. There is still much of my story I haven't explored yet, and so many events that have forever changed my life. Stick with me, as my story continues.

CHAPTER 19:

MAN OF BLACK (PART 2)

So where exactly do I go from here? Ronnie is gone, and I have to finish University without him. I was still feeling the guilt from his death, and still battling with myself as to what I could have done differently to prevent it from happening. I guess at this point, I should say that the "Road Sharks", wasn't the exact name of the group. For the sake of privacy and all that jazz, I did decide to change the name of the group. It was a top secret group at the University, and I don't want to take any chances with breaking privacy codes. The club did have a name, but I'm not going to say what it was. So to make things easier, I'm just going to refer to the group as the "Road Sharks". After Ronnie's death, Uncle Ronnie basically disowned me, and never trusted me anymore. He totally blamed me for Ronnie's death. I understand that he's angry his son died. I can't even imagine what that feeling would be. However, I was grieving over Ronnie as well. I didn't want him to die, and what happened really was a freak accident. I was having several seconds thoughts of Ronnie participating in the race, but I thought that the chances of him getting hurt and killed were low, and I was overreacting a bit.

I have to accept the consequences now of him being gone. Ronnie was not only my cousin, but my best friend in the entire world. During Ronnie's funeral, Uncle Ronnie wouldn't even talk to me or acknowledge me. He would forever be upset with me, and I don't think he's ever going to accept me for what happened. Even to this day, he hasn't given me a second chance, and I have to accept that. I do hope that he is able to forgive me someday. Being at Ronnie's funeral wasn't happy for me either. It was a dark setting, and having to say goodbye to my cousin for the final time, made me feel extremely depressed. It was going to be tough to continue on with my life, but I had to make it through.

Once I returned back to school, Hugo Vincent and I, started to think about Ronnie more. How we joined the "Road Sharks" group in solidarity with Ronnie. Perhaps thinking that made matters worse by supporting the group that he was mingling with. The group basically was not a positive image to have. It was more like a High School clique, rather than a college brotherhood. I know we all wanted to join a fraternity, but the "Road Sharks", was not a fraternity. Fraternities stick out for one another, and they support each other. This group was nothing but a negative influence, and the logistics of the group didn't make sense at times. It was more of a party and be cool group.

When Hugo, Vincent and I graduated college, it didn't feel the same without Ronnie. It was like the whole experience was a waste, because he was not graduating with us. It seemed like none of it mattered, because Ronnie was killed. Derek was killed as well, so two people that I was close with, and two students ended up being killed from all the shenanigans. I was starting to remember the dreams and hopes Ronnie had of opening his own bar and nightclub.

Thinking how successful he would have been at that. Ronnie would have been the perfect nightclub owner, and his personality fit it well. He's not going to have that dream anymore. The rest of us at least have a chance of going for our dreams, but Ronnie and Derek do not. It's over for them, and it's horrible to think about. My main goal now, is to live my life the best way I can. I can't let things in my past take control over me. I'll always remember Ronnie, and he'll be in my thoughts all the time, but I have to keep pushing myself. After Ronnie's death, Uncle Ronnie kicked me out of the house. He let me know that as soon as I got home from University, to pack all my things, and to find another place to live. He didn't want me living under his roof anymore. Uncle Ronnie was not taking Ronnie's death well, and he was taking his sadness out an me. I didn't want to make matters worse, so I accepted it. He doesn't want me to live under his roof anymore, so fine. I'll go and live somewhere else. It's really not that big of a deal at the end of the day.

Because I was kicked out of Uncle Ronnie's house, I now had to find another place to live. Hugo, Vincent and I found a three bedroom apartment in the downtown New York area. It was not the ritz at all, and it was kinda dingy. But it was home, and it was a place for us to lay our heads down at night I guess. You wouldn't believe how we actually got the apartment. I was shocked myself once I found out.

Hugo actually talked to one of the members of the "Road Sharks", and asked them to help us find us an apartment. So thanks to the "Road Sharks", we had a place to stay. But I didn't like how we still had debt to the "Road Sharks". After Ronnie's death, I really wanted nothing to do with this group. But we were still having contact from them, and still accepting their help and quirks.

Once we were living in the apartment, I started to get my first job. I worked as a dishwasher at an Italian restaurant go figure. It wasn't a glamorous job at all. It was uncomfortable, hot, nasty and gross. Having to clean up people's dirty plates got really annoying after a while. It was a job that allowed me to pay my rent, so I went to work every single day, and cleaned those dishes. Hugo ended up getting a job at a pizza restaurant, making pizza. Vincent ended up getting a job as a plumber. I never knew that Vincent got his plumbers certification during university. So Hugo and Vincent had better jobs than I had. I had to be in a hot, sticky, gross ass kitchen washing dishes. They got to at least have fun jobs.

I thought to myself that this is only going to be temporary. I'm not going to be at this job forever, and I can move onto a better job at a later time. When I would clean the dishes, I would dream of maybe someday being owner of this restaurant. Similar to how Ronnie wanted to own his own nightclub and bar. I wouldn't have to wash these dishes at all. I can get someone else to do all of this muck. Daydreaming is what kept me sane, while I had to clean all those dishes. Otherwise, it would have been a job that was a living hell. I ended up washing dishes for almost a year. Here I was, a college educated man, doing a job such as this. It didn't help that this was post 9/11 New York, so the economy wasn't doing too good. The "dot com crash" was also in effect. So I was looking for other jobs, but I remained washing dishes in the restaurant.

I had a business degree, so I had many opportunities for work. I would apply to many jobs, and some jobs I was lucky enough to interview for. But I was never given any job offers. I would finally get my big break, when I was accepted to be manager at a "McDonalds." This was not my dream job either, but I at least got an offer. It's a fast food restaurant yes, but it's a start.

Being a manager at the McDonalds, was also an interesting job. My main duties were to make sure that all the food and health codes were being met. That the beef was cooked at the right temperature, and that the food and condiments were also being refrigerated or frozen well. I would then have to take inventory on all the food in the restaurant. See if we need to order more hamburger buns, or we need to order more soda syrup, or things like that. I was basically being quality control, rather than being a manager. I didn't really manage a whole lot.

They had shift supervisors that would evaluate how employees would do their jobs. So I didn't hire or fire anyone in the store. All I basically did was make sure everything was in proper order, and I took inventory records down. That was all that I did. It's not that I hated working at the "McDonalds" as a manager, but I wasn't really having a great time. I was only here to put it on my resume. So in the meantime, I began to apply to other jobs.

I didn't envision myself being at this "McDonalds" for the rest of my life. Sure, it beat washing dishes, but I still wasn't satisfied being here. I would report to the "McDonalds" and work, and on the side, applied to several other jobs. Around this time, Obama got elected as president, and the economy was getting slightly worse. This was a terrible time to look for a job. So I was slightly appreciative that I had the "McDonalds" job, even though it did aggravate me at times. The last few months that I worked at the "McDonalds", because we were short staffed, I was then asked to work the drive thru windows late at night. This caused me the most pain, because I had to deal with people wanting to order hamburgers at Midnight. I still made sure my customers were happy though.

After applying to many jobs, I finally got a break when I was hired by "American Express". I knew that they were a major company, and the benefits from working at a place such as that were good. My father also worked there. The position that I applied for at "American Express", was to be a customer service agent. So basically, whenever someone wanted to apply for an "American Express" card, or if they wanted to book flight tickets with us, or vacation planning, home loans, interest accounts, or if they had any other issues or concerns or questions, they would come and talk to me.

I worked at the building located in the downtown area of New York. When I first began working, I was trained quite well, and they taught me everything I needed to know. I was told how to deal with customers, and special techniques that I could do to make their experience as a customer with "American Express", a nice one. This was the first job that I had, which really made me appreciate having my business degree. I was working in a field that I thought was where I was supposed to be, and I was comfortable with that.

I would always treat my customers with respect, and I was gaining praise from several supervisors. In addition, I have only been working at the company for two months, and they were already in consideration of promoting me into a managerial position. Although, there always seems to be a caveat in whatever situation you put yourself in.

There always seems to be someone that wants to rain on your parade, and to bring you down. This particular person was Solomon Molteri. I don't know what it was about this man, but he was truly evil. He was one of my coworkers, and we both were up for the same promotion. He was jealous of me greatly, and I could understand why. Unlike him, I actually treated people with respect and dignity. Solomon never treated the customers with respect, and his personality was wicked. This man would make it a habit to get on my nerves any chance he could. I remember one lunch break I had, I was in the break room. I was eating my lunch, not bothering anyone, when Solomon decided to come in and speak to me.

"Ralph, you're being far too nice to the customers that you deal with. You don't have to act that way around them. You're not their friend. We work for a credit card company. I don't like your attitude with the customers, and I'm only trying to look out for you."

I don't know what type of advice he was trying to give me, but it was the wrong type. This is not how you talk to your coworkers. He was doing this to get me to stoop down to his level. His plan was for me to take his advice, and feel angry about it. But it wasn't going to work. It was in one ear, and out the other. I wasn't going to let him treat me like that, and ruin my position at the job. I was finally at a job I appreciated quite well, and I wasn't going to let Solomon get under my skin like that.

Solomon wanted for me to be angry at him, so that way I would be distracted with my work, and he would get the position over me. That was his whole agenda. Luckily for me, I saw right through all of that mess. I'm leaving some key details out, so please forgive me. I'm not being completely truthful with how I got the job at "American Express". I actually talked to some of my old buddies that belonged to the "Road Sharks". I know, I know. But desperate times, call for desperate measures. I really needed a job that was successful for me. Working at "McDonald's", wasn't in my future plans, so I needed a better job.

I wasn't having much luck finding a job on my own. I was speaking with some of the members of the "Road Sharks", and they pulled some strings to get me an interview at "American Express". I don't feel bad for using their help, because in the end, my talents is what got me the job. Yes they were a slight developmental help, but I still had to interview. The company still had to hire me. So yes I used the help of the "Road Sharks", but only to a small level. Dealing with the "Road Sharks" wasn't completely bad though.

I guess you say can it was a secret Mafia group in a sense, but I looked at it as something more stronger than that. I understand the past history with them, and how Ronnie died being a member of their group. That was only an exception. The group still had many strong forces.

I have been working at "American Express" for a year now. I was doing my job great, and my career was going great. Hugo, Vincent and I, still remained living in our apartment together. We were still comfortable all living together, so we didn't see a reason to move quite yet. Hugo left the pizza restaurant, and got a job being a limo driver. I don't know why he decided to be a limo driver, but it was something that he enjoyed doing. He made a lot of money doing it, so it wasn't that bad. Vincent also moved on from being a plumber, and later got a job working for the water company. So we were all advancing in our jobs.

Things were okay for a while, until Solomon decided to get into my face yet again one day. I don't know why this man couldn't leave me alone. He was far too obsessed with causing me pain I suppose. I was wrapping up work, and about to go home, when Solomon decided to give me hell, yet again.

"Don't think I don't know what you're doing. You're trying to get that supervisor position. Rest assured, you are not going to get it. So don't hold your breath."

I ignored Solomon yet again. I wasn't going to go down to his level. That would only make things significantly worse. My best bet was to ignore whatever he said. Again, he's like a snake, and trying to inject his venom and poison into me. Then once he does that, he'll sliver away just like a snake, and be sly about it. I can't let him attack or get to me like that. I refuse to, because I'm not that type of guy to hold resentment over other people. Being that I was still a member of the "Road Sharks", I would still attend sporadic meetups that they would have. The meetups would basically have us at pool halls, or we would go bowling, or go play golf, and doing things of that sort. Right after my altercation I guess you could say with Solomon, I decided to attend the "Road Sharks" meetup.

We were all at a pool hall, and we were just going to have some beers and play pool. When I arrived, I couldn't believe who I saw.

Solomon was at the "Road Sharks" meeting. So that means that he's a member. This is such a small world. Solomon then started to show his surprise at me being there.

"Ralph, what are you doing here? Don't tell me, oh god. It can't be? You can't be?"

To prove to Solomon that I was a member, I did the secret handshake with him. Solomon was really angry at this point. It is part of "Road Sharks" conduct, that we respect a fellow member. Even if we don't personally agree with them, we still support and respect them. All of the members are Italian American, so we form a second family in the group. So while we are doing anything related to the group, Solomon has to respect me, and I have to respect Solomon. Whether we get along outside of the group, or not. As much as it was tough for Solomon to do, he had no choice but to be kind to me. I played pool with the rest of the members, with Solomon still in disbelief that I am a member of the group.

He didn't talk to me during the entire outing at all. It was slightly awkward being there. I was planning on having fun playing pool with the rest of the group members. However, it turned out to be a weird outing. When we were done playing pool, Solomon rushed out of the bar and left. I think Solomon is now torn. Being that we are both "Road Sharks" members, he understands that he can't treat me any which way. He was to respect me, and this is something he didn't want to do.

Solomon didn't like me, and there was nothing in the universe that I, or anyone else could do to make us get along. I had to be respectful towards him as well, being that he's a member too. The following day at work, I had just arrived.

I was in the break room filling my coffee mug up. I took the coffee pot off the machine, and started to pour the coffee into my cup. Solomon rushed in, and purposefully knocked the coffee pot all over my pants. The scolding hot coffee started to burn my legs. I look up at Solomon with an angry and confused expression. Solomon then smirked and began to chuckle.

"Oops, my bad. Let me get some napkins and clean you off Ralph."

I can't believe this asshole threw that hot coffee all over me, on purpose. I don't know why I didn't pour some coffee on him as well, but I didn't. I was too kind of a man to do that, so I didn't. My legs were burning from the coffee, and Solomon started to get napkins to dry the coffee off me. I don't need any of his help, so I shove him off me.

"Get the fuck off me. Why don't you grow the fuck up, you asshole. Wow."

Solomon then leaves out of the break room, still chuckling to himself. I then start to dry the coffee off my pants, even though I'm still in pain from the hot coffee. I didn't know how much more I could take of this. I really felt like going to HR about Solomon's behavior. But then I remembered the values of the "Road Sharks", and how we have to respect other members. Solomon's prank I didn't care for at all, and that was technically considered assault, but I had to forget that it even happened. I know common sense would have been to report that incident to the company, but I ignored that it ever happened. I went on about the rest of my day, forgetting about the coffee prank.

As time went on with me working at the company, Solomon would continue to do silly antics to get me to leave. He also knew that I wasn't going to snitch on him, so he kept going. I remember he slashed my tires at one point, and he also put some sort of X rated virus on my work computer, to where I would get pop ups of naked women on my monitor. I didn't let this get to me, as Solomon wanted me to react by getting violent.

I didn't know if I were to get into a fight with Solomon as to who would win, but I'm pretty sure that I would. I would explain the situations with Solomon to Hugo and Vincent, and they would urge and persist me to report what he's doing, but I couldn't. First of all, I really didn't have proof that Solomon did what he did. I would have had to find a way to audio or video record him attacking me, and that idea never clicked to me. So I kept my attention to my work, and not the silly pranks.

Time seemed to pass quickly, and I have now been working in the company for five years. The company wanted to celebrate all the employees having their five year anniversary, and held a party in our honor. It was after work, so alcohol was served, and we were kicking back and having fun. I never imagined that I would be working for "American Express" for this long. I was honored to still work for this company.

Once I hit my five year anniversary at the company, I made the decision to finally buy my own house. I had saved quite a bit of my salary from working, and I figured it was the right time. I discussed this over with Hugo and Vincent, and we all agreed it was time for me to move out of the apartment. I lucked out, and purchased a very nice home with a swimming pool. The only negative thing, was that it was quite a distance away from work. No matter, I would get up earlier for work. That was a good work around for that.

At this point, I was looking forward to getting a promotion at the company. I have been working as a customer service agent for many years, and it was time for me to move ahead. I knew that Solomon would become envious of me over this, but so what. I didn't give a fuck about him, and I knew that Solomon would get what was coming to him someday for the horrible way that he treated me. Solomon was also vying for the promotion as well. Only one guy was going to get it.

This was going to be interesting indeed. It was going to be a battle to see who was the better employee. If Solomon got the promotion, well then he would win. He was the better fit for the promotion and he deserved it. Even though he's an asshole and a terrible human being, if he got the promotion, I would have to accept that.

But if I got the promotion, then that would settle everything. It would mean that Solomon is wrong, and I'm right. All the silly stunts that he would do to me, was all due to jealousy, just like I suspected. Solomon would then have to accept that he lost, and I won. I got the promotion and he didn't.

I remember the morning Solomon and I both checked the announcement board to see who got the promotion. I was overjoyed when I saw that my name was listed on the promotion, and Solomon's name wasn't. I was moving on up in the company and he wasn't. The look Solomon gave me was so priceless. It was like a look of a sad and bitter dog. I loved it. The promotion I received, gave me the job title of "Records and Bookkeeping Manager". My duties would have me be in charge of all company records and statistics and logistics. My pay would be significantly better, and I worked more behind the scenes. I had my own private office, and the benefits that I got were so much better.

The job had more responsibilities to take care of yes, but I was up to the challenge. Because I had so many responsibilities to do throughout the day, I would have assistants and workers help me. They were mostly temp workers, which I didn't care for. They knew they weren't going to be there for a long time, so their work performance would reflect that. I had so many temp workers that would serve as my assistants. I believe I had about twenty or so. It got so bad, that I spoke with management, and I asked them not to send me anymore temporary workers.

The people that I want to work with, I want on the official payroll, and to be official employees. Not temporary employees, that don't do what I ask of them, and their work performance is lacking due to that. Solomon was still bitter about me being manager. He didn't like to see me succeed over him, and I don't want to say it made him feel better to torment me, but that's all he did. He was still working lower in the company, and he was bitter and distraught over that. I would walk through the hallways, and he would call me dirty names, or flip me off.

I remember I was in the break room one time making my coffee, and I would turn my back for a second to get the sugar packets. I would go back to my coffee cup, and I would see Solomon smirking and grinning heavily. I was confused as to why he was acting like that. I knew he did something, but I didn't know exactly what. Solomon waited until I took a sip of my coffee, before he started to chuckle. He then said;

"Hey, you know I spat into that right? Enjoy your cup of coffee my friend."

Solomon the left the break room. I immediately threw the coffee cup away after that. I do believe that he spat into that cup. There is a chance he was just fucking with me, but I doubt. He has done similar stunts in the past, so it wouldn't be surprised if he actually did it. But for several weeks after that, I hated drinking coffee. I was scared that Solomon was going to spit into my drink, or poison me, or do something else.

It really caused me to feel paranoid. Every year at the company, there is a presentation event, in which all the employees in the financial department, give a presentation on how the company can improve their operations. It requires you to study quite a bit on company history, and be knowledgeable on how the company runs. You also have to have some knowledge of public speaking.

The presentation you give will be in front of several people in a concert hall. So, if you're the type of person that gets nervous speaking in front of other people, this was something that you needed to work on. The presentation event allowed for the main district CEO's to evaluate you as an employee. If you made a good impression on them, this was good for career growth. The presentation also went on an award system. The top three guys who gave the best presentations, would get 3rd, 2nd, and 1st place all respectively. The guy who won 1st place, would automatically receive a huge promotion.

So everyone strived to get 1st place. Participating in the event was voluntarily. I decided to opt of the event for many years, thinking that I wasn't ready. But after my fifth year anniversary at the company, I knew it was now time. The first year I participated in the presentation, I didn't prepare myself at all. It showed, as I didn't plan everything well.

Solomon out of spite, also entered into the event. Luckily for me, I was better at presentations than Solomon was. Remarkably, I ended up getting 3rd place the first presentation I was involved in. That was pretty impressive, even though I could have done much better.

Solomon didn't even reach the top three. I knew I could defiantly win next year, if I applied myself more. The event next year quickly came, and I was more focused, and I planned things better this time around. I ended up getting 2nd this time, and Solomon got 3rd. So close, but no cigar. I was that close from winning, and I didn't win. After getting 2nd place, I got into that competitive edge. I wasn't going to stop participating in this event, until I won. All I have to do is keep my same composure, and I'll win for sure next time.

The following year, things would be completely different. My last assistant that I enjoyed really much, and had a good rapport with, she ended up moving. So I needed a new assistant. Several people applied for the job, and I was looking at many resumes. The people that really caught my eye, I would then invite for an in person interview.

I interviewed several people, but none of them were meshing with me well. If someone is going to be my assistant, we have to click instantly. If the chemistry isn't there, I'm not going to offer them a job. I was trying to fill this position for over a month and a half. I was still not happy with those who applied, but I wasn't going to give up hope.

I finally hit gold, when I was reading over Jamal's application. I saw that he previously worked at the "New York Times", and was impressed with his work history. I wanted to see this young man in person, and interview him. The first time I met Jamal, I was pleased with the energy that he gave. I didn't care that he was a black, or gay, or any of that. To me I was impressed with his vibe, and that's the only thing that mattered.

I was bisexual myself, and this wasn't anyone's business at all. That was my personal life. I wasn't married, and I didn't have any children, and this wasn't anyone's business to know but my own. I started to interview Jamal, letting him know what his basic job duties will be.

"The job is mostly going to be you doing tasks for me. Doing records and file sorting. If I need a cup of coffee or something, I'll ask you for that. Are you still interested in the job?"

Jamal accepted the job offer, and I was so happy to finally have a new assistant. I was surprised as to how obedient Jamal was. He never once complained at the tasks that I would give him, and he was a model employee. He really would help me if I was overbooked, and I would also give him assignments that he would have to do at home. I did this to see how loyal and trustworthy he was.

Jamal always did whatever I asked of him to do. I didn't form a personal relationship with him, as I was a firm believer that work is work. I don't like to mix work with personal affairs. I did think that Jamal was a nice young man, and he was very handsome, but maybe it was due to our age gap, but I didn't get too comfortable with him. I did know that Jamal had a crush on me.

Whenever he would be in my office, he would always stare at me. I would pretend I didn't notice him staring, but I knew that he was. It's just one of those things that you can sense, when you know someone is comfortable around you. I knew that the presentation event was coming up, and Jamal has been working as my assistant for quite some time. I really needed his help, if I wanted to win this time around.

I'll always remember that particular Friday. I was going to meet up with Hugo and Vincent at an office rental space slightly nearby. My plan was to do a mock presentation. This was something I didn't do previously, and I was going to try out this time. If I practice my presentation beforehand, when it comes down to the real thing, I should have no issues. I didn't want to do my presentation in my office, as I was scared that people would eavesdrop and maybe steal ideas.

So, I wanted to go somewhere private. I had a bunch of notes that I documented, to help prepare me for the presentation. But I wanted to test Jamal's trust. I was going to give him the address that Hugo, Vincent and I were going to be at, and tell him to bring my presentation documents there. I hand Jamal the note of the address, but I make the mistake of not putting the zip code on the note.

I didn't realize this mistake at first, but it was a vital mistake. Hugo, Vincent and I arrive at the location, and we don't see Jamal there. I couldn't believe that Jamal couldn't follow a simple instruction. Not aware that I was the one who fucked up, not Jamal. Jamal actually went to two wrong addresses, because I didn't include the zip code on the note. When Jamal finally arrived at the right address, our time slot to rent the location was over. I was immediately upset and angered. I do have a temper at times, and I took all my anger out on Jamal. I felt extremely bad at the time, but that's how angry I was.

"Where have you have been? What took you so long? I was counting on you."

Jamal being helpless, took me shouting and yelling at him well. At this time, I figured this whole ordeal was his own fault. Jamal then let me know I gave him the wrong address.

"You didn't give me the zip code on the note, so I went to the wrong location. Sorry."

I should have accepted that it was my fault during this instance. But I was so angry, and I refused to take responsibility that I was the one who messed up. I then decided to fire Jamal.

"Why couldn't you follow a simple instruction? You know what, you're fired."

I then remember I took all the document notes that Jamal had with him, and I threw them all across the room. I was so fed up with Jamal, however I knew in the back of my mind that Jamal didn't deserve the way I was treating him. But it was too late, I already fired Jamal, and my temper got the best of me again.

To my surprise though, Jamal started to pick up all the documents off the floor, and put them into proper order as well. I was expecting for Jamal to run out of the building, as I fired him. He didn't, and he was humble enough to pick up all the papers I threw down. Jamal continues to pick the papers up, and some of the papers are by where I'm standing. Jamal picks more papers up, and I bend down to grab his wrist. I then speak to him.

"I thought I fired you, why are you still here?"

Jamal smiled back at me, and I then smiled back at him. I knew I couldn't get rid of Jamal. I decided to rehire him, and keep him around. He was far too kind for me to let him go. I had to understand that I was the one who messed up, and I had no business being mad at Jamal. I didn't give the correct address, so it was completely my fault. Jamal and I pick up the rest of the papers, and I tell Jamal that I want him to go to restaurant with me later this evening.

He didn't have a choice in going, and it was mandatory. I arrive back at my office and at this time, I wanted to introduce Hugo and Vincent to Jamal. I could sense that Jamal was going to be with me for quite some time, so he needs to meet my best friends. Jamal already saw Hugo and Vincent when he arrived at the location to meet me, but he wasn't introduced to them. When I got back to my office, I officially introduced them to Jamal. I tell Jamal that I really need his help with the upcoming presentation event, and I really want to win.

It's important for me to practice my presentation, so I don't run into any problems when it comes down to the actual event. I don't tell Jamal that my friends and I were in the "Road Sharks". That wasn't any of his business. When Jamal's shift was over, he begins to walk out of my office, and speaks.

"Is it okay for me to meet you guys at the restaurant later?"

I didn't want Jamal to leave us. I wanted him to stay. I'm not going to lie, I was enjoying being with Jamal, and I was being slightly protective of him. I don't want to say I was infatuating with Jamal, but it was a strange feeling I had. I told Jamal to stay, and he did. We all left my office later, and we proceeded towards Hugo's limo. Jamal was tagging along with us, so he can take notes on my mock presentation.

As I saw the expression on Jamal's face, I could see how amazed he was once we went inside the limo. I could tell that he was assuming so many things about me. That I was some type of billionaire playboy, because we're riding in a limo. It wasn't anything like that at all. My friend happens to run a limo service, and he's giving us a ride. It's nothing more, and it's nothing less either. While we are in the limo, I start to open up a bottle of whisky to loosen myself up. I then give Vincent and Jamal a drink. We are all feeling loose from the liquor. When we finally arrive at the restaurant, I see how captivated Jamal is. He more than likely has never been in a place such as this, and I know it's a brand new experience for him to handle.

We are seated in the back of restaurant, so we have enough privacy for me to practice my presentation. I end up ordering something for Jamal, as he wasn't familiar with the menu. I ordered a bottle of wine for the table I remember as well. Before our food came to the table, I began to start my mock presentation.

Jamal was taking notes for me as well. Hugo and Vincent were acting as my judges too. I was doing flawlessly with my practice presentation. Our food later came to the table and we began to eat.

Once we were done eating, I went back to practicing my presentation a bit more. When it came time for us to leave the restaurant, I paid the bill with my credit card, and left a cash tip for the waitress. From this point forward, I was enjoying hanging with my best friends, and Jamal.

I didn't want for us to separate quite yet. So I invited them all over to my house. I very rarely have guests, so if I can find an excuse to get people to come over in a dignified and proper way, I'm going to take advantage of that. I was also thinking that Jamal was curious as to what my house looked like. I then remember on the ride to my house in the limo, that Vincent began to take a marijuana cigar out his jacket pocket. We then start to take puffs from the marijuana cigar.

When we all reached my house, Jamal started to look around quite frequently. I guess this was like a field trip, seeing how elaborate my house was. There was a football game on the television, and we were all looking at that. Jamal was completely quiet though. It didn't occur to me that Jamal and I left our cars back at the office parking lot.

That wasn't even on my mind. As the night went on, and we were drinking and having fun, I lost track of time completely. Hugo and Vincent later excused themselves home, and drove off. I was hoping for Hugo and Vincent to drive Jamal home, but due to how quiet Jamal was, I totally forgot he was even in my house.

I went into my kitchen to clean up, and Jamal comes into the kitchen and speaks to me.

"Ralph, I don't know how I'm going to get home. My phone died, I can't call an uber."

Maybe it was the fact I was kinda drunk, but I decided to toy and play with Jamal.

"Well, you don't have to go home if you don't want to. Don't you want to stay?"

One thing led to another, and Jamal and I began to play around. He then followed me outside to the swimming pool area, and threw me into the water. I was wearing my suit shirt, and my nice slacks I wear for work. I was completely soaked in the water. Jamal was standing close to the edge of my pool, so I dragged his leg into the water. We start to wrestle in the water, and we eventually share our first kiss. It happened in an instant yes, but I don't know. It was quite strange, but we were in the moment. We continued to embrace in the pool for quite some time. We later left out of the pool, and I let Jamal dry off inside.

I took his clothes to my washing machine. I also gave Jamal some of my gym clothes to sleep in. I decided to give Jamal some privacy, as he slept in my bed. I found it so cute. I ended up sleeping in the couch in the living room. The next morning, Jamal was still asleep in my bed, and I woke him up. I then cooked breakfast for him, and called an uber to take him home. However, shortly after that, I felt guilty. Why the hell did I form a personal relationship with Jamal? He's one of my coworkers, and I have no business doing these types of things with him.

I knew I had to be direct come Monday, and call it off. I had to let Jamal know that I'm his boss, and he's my employee. That's exactly what happened. That Monday at work, I shoved Jamal away, and let him know what happened on Friday, didn't happen. Jamal accepted this, and understood where I was coming from completely. He quickly then started to get back on track, and helped me with my presentation.

The day of the presentation came. It was that following Friday. I was ready, and I was prepared, and I was going to win this time. I got 2nd last year, and all I had to do was take 1st this year. Hugo, Vincent, Jamal and I all went to the concert hall for my presentation. There were many people that were in attendance, including Solomon. I haven't seen his face for quite some time, and I was shocked to see him there. Just when I thought I didn't have to deal with him anymore, I see him.

I then had a bad feeling that he was going to start something. That's how it was with Solomon. He always would bully me and make me feel worse about myself. But luckily, Solomon didn't say anything to me at all. He gave me an angry look, but he kept to himself. He didn't call me any names or anything. I still however felt that Solomon was up to no good, and he was.

We all were waiting for the event to begin, standing on stage. I saw the other participants on stage, and I was a little bit intimidated. There were many people trying to get 1st place, but I was sure that I was going to win. The event finally began, and I people started to give their presentations. They were good, but I knew where each of them messed up, and how ill prepared they were as well. They didn't study enough on what they were talking about. I also saw how many of them were letting their nerves get to them. Most of the judging was seeing how comfortable you are on stage. If you look nervous, you were going to lose points off that. It finally was my turn to give my presentation. Just like how I practiced it, I gave my presentation perfectly. I didn't mess up at all, and I already considered myself the winner based off that.

I was finished with my presentation, and I couldn't wait to get my first place prize. Solomon soon after me, gave his presentation, and I must say he was good. He did prepare himself, but my presentation was better than this. When it came time to announce the winners, Solomon received 2nd place, which I thought was good. Solomon never got 2nd in this event, and I thought that was good. However, Solomon wanted to win. He also wanted to beat me, and his envy was centered over that. I was named as the winner of the event, and got 1st place. I finally won. After all the years of me doing this event, I finally won. My celebration would be short though.

Not even seconds after me accepting my trophy, Solomon would do the most horrible thing he has ever done to me. He would take my eyesight. He approached me with a small jar, and threw the contents of the jar in my face. I don't know what exactly Solomon threw on my face. I don't know if it was bleach, or lye, or whatever. But he immediately doused my face with it. The pain was unbearable, and the worst pain I've ever felt in my life. It's like if someone was wearing spiked cleats, and were stomping on my eyes with them. I felt to the ground on stage, crying and screaming out in pain.

I then noticed that I couldn't see a thing. My vision was damaged. From what I heard, Solomon was shocked that the poison he threw on me didn't kill me. Once Solomon saw that I was still alive, he took a gun from his pocket and aimed it at me. However security guards at the event, later tackled Solomon to the ground. Once Solomon tried to shoot one of the security guards, they fatally shot him. I even heard the gunshot. I remain on the stage in pain, with my eyes burning. I am eventually taken to the hospital. Throughout this entire time, I cannot see a thing, and the only thing I want, is to be able to see again. But I would never be able to see again. My vision was gone as a result of the attack. As I was in the hospital in the recovery room, I still couldn't see.

The doctors were not telling me anything, and I began to feel scared, due to not being aware of my current condition. I remain in my hospital bed, waiting to hear something. A doctor then came into my room, and eventually spoke to me.

"Mr. Maligrino. We are sorry to tell you, but whatever substance that was thrown on your face, completed destroyed your retinas. You are now legally blind. We're sorry."

I didn't say anything once I was told this news. How can you react after being told you're blind, and that you won't be able to see a thing anymore. I could get angry, but what would that prove? Will getting angry bring my eyesight back? It won't, so I have to accept it.

I simply told the doctor thank you, and he left out of the room. Looking at the bright side, I am still alive, and Solomon's man goal was to kill me. He took my vision, but he didn't take my life, so I could be thankful and blessed for that I suppose. Much time later, a doctor came into the room, and asked if there was anyone that I wanted to be my power of attorney.

Basically being that I'm now legally blind and disabled, I need someone to watch over me, and help me sign papers, and act as my helper. The only person that came to mind was Jamal. I could have asked either Hugo or Vincent, but I chose Jamal. I was talking with god, and I knew Jamal was the perfect choice. The doctor then left the room, and a short time after this, Jamal came into the room. He was already told at this time that I was blind, and I knew he was just as upset as I was over the news. Jamal stood by my bedside, and began to cry out for me. I then told Jamal something.

"Jamal, I really need your help. I'm not going to be able to see again, so I'm going to have you be my caretaker. I need you to take care of me, and help me recover."

Jamal had no issue with this, and started to hug me.

"Ralph, I'm here for you. I'm always going to be here for you."

I was happy that I had Jamal's support, even though I knew I could count on him. After this, Hugo and Vincent were told on my condition, and I got to speak with them one at a time. Even though I was the one that was blind, Jamal, Hugo and Vincent were more upset about it than I was. I guess they were worried about me that a major part of my life is gone. Being able to see is an important part of life.

Being that it was so sudden that I lost my sense of sight, I could understand why they would seek pity on me. It's fine though, as I have to keep on moving with my life. I can't see anymore, but I'm still living, and I still have my other senses. I can still walk, I can still talk, I can still eat, I can still smell, and I can still hear. All things that I can use, despite the fact I am blind. Jamal stayed with me in my hospital room that entire night. Even though I could not see Jamal, I knew that his presence was there. I could feel his energy. Also, he would come up to my bed and massage me, and kiss me on my cheek every couple hours. I knew that was him.

The following day, the police came into my hospital room. They told me that Solomon was shot dead by the security guards, and they unfortunately cannot tell me what substance Solomon used to throw on me. Other than that, their investigation was over. I told them what I knew, and explained Solomon was just jealous, and he tried to kill me. When the poison didn't work, he then tried to shoot me. That's how everything went. The police then left the room, and I was then surprised to see members of the news media enter the room. I didn't want to talk to them or tell them a damn thing. So I rejected any interviews or interaction with them. I didn't want to talk to the news at that time. They then left the room.

Later on in the day, a woman who works for the "National Institute for the Blind", came into the room. She basically wanted to test my other senses that I had. She wanted to see how mobile I was too. It turns out due to my condition, I would recover quite well. She started teaching me braille, and I learned several words within a half an hour. The specialist also taught me how to use a guide stick. I was having issues with it at first, but I got the hang of it after a while. The following day, I did more exercises with the blind specialist, and after she spoke with the doctors, they decided it was okay for me to go home the following day. I was happy that I was leaving the hospital, and was looking forward to receiving my recovery at home.

The day I went home, it was weird at first not being able to see. I couldn't see the blue skies, I couldn't see the green grass, I couldn't see people. I began to feel depressed, but being sad wasn't going to help anything. This was how my life was going to be from now on. Once I was back home, Jamal gave me some books on braille. Both educational, and entertainment books.

"Ralph, I have some braille books that I want to read with you. I'm gonna learn braille with you. I said that I would be always with you, and I mean that."

The book that Jamal was reading to me, was like an encyclopedia book. It was a braille book which taught you a bunch of important words. After we were done reading that book, Jamal then presented me with an action adventure book that was in braille. It was actually a "Tom Clancy" book which I like. The fact I could still read books in braille was nice. There was also audiobooks and podcasts as well that I would listen to. Things were going well at home, and Jamal later moved in with me, being that he was my caretaker. I was getting along just fine, until several weeks later, I went into a depressive fit.

Jamal had went to the grocery store to pick up a few things, and I was left home alone. I was in my bedroom alone, just crying. I think there was some type of motivational television program on I could hear. I think it was Tony Robbins. He was talking about not letting past trauma effect you in life. I then got triggered due, to me being blind. I was still out of work, trying to recover being blind. I was in my bed, by myself, listening to the television. Feeling sad, that me being blind, was going to be hurdle in my life. Jamal soon came into the bedroom, and asked me what was wrong. I told him how I was feeling.

"Oh, I'm just looking at this program on television, and it got me kinda upset. I wish I could see again, and I am still trying to get used to being blind. Things aren't the same as they used to be. I want to be myself again, I want to go to work again."

Jamal then gets in bed next to me and lays his head down on my chest. He then starts to rub his hands on my shoulders, and starts to comfort me.

"You're blind, but you're still the same Ralph. The Ralph that won't let being blind discourage him. You're going to be yourself again, you're going to work again. It's going to be fine."

Jamal was right, and his words of encouragement definitely helped me. As time continued to go on, I started to go outside for the first time being blind. I would have either Jamal, or Hugo or Vincent help me when walking out in the street at first. I had my guide stick, and I had to familiarize myself with walking outside in the street, not being able to see. I then started to walk without help.

Jamal would let me walk around the block and back, without assistance. I then managed to walk better as days went on. My next step, was going back to work, and I did. I went back to work, although in a different position. I mostly did over phone transactions with other employees at different "American Express" branches. I still also do computer work, with the help of special software.

Jamal also continued to be my assistant, and helps me at work as well. I liked being in New York, but it was time for a change. I was ready to move to Los Angeles. It was something I wanted to do before I became blind, and the job transfer offer I had in California, was more satisfactory to my disability needs.

Jamal had no idea that I was going to move. He also was unaware that Hugo and Vincent were going to live with us. We were going to live together, that way I always had someone to take care of me and watch over me. I spent the day out with Hugo and Vincent, and came home and told Jamal the news.

"Jamal, we're going to move to Los Angeles, and I would like for you to come with us."

Jamal was accepting of it, and had no issue with coming to California with me. We began to pack our things up, and we were all set to move. We caught a plane, and arrived in Los Angeles. Hugo, Vincent and Jamal all helped me unpack, and get me settled in my new house. The house we had in Los Angeles, was perfect. It was in Redondo Beach. I would go to the beach several times with Hugo, Vincent and Jamal.

Yes I was blind, but I could still feel the sun on my face, the birds chirp, the smell and sound of the ocean. Things such as that which make me tolerate being blind. I still have my other senses. I returned to work now in California, and I now have my own private office space that Jamal and I work in. My office space isn't that far from the house, and Jamal is my assistant. I continue my work with "American Express", despite my disability.

I still help customers, and work on my computer, with Jamal still assisting me. Jamal is my caretaker, and I love having him here with me. I can't see anymore, but there are days to where I don't care that I'm blind. It's not that being blind isn't a setback during certain times, it is. But, it's okay now, and being blind isn't my entire identity.

My life, and my story was interesting if I say so myself. Growing up Italian, and having a raging bull spirit. My father being gone at such a young age. My mother also passing away young. Meeting Hugo and Vincent. Staying with my Uncle Ronnie, and meeting my cousin Ronnie. Going onto University, and getting involved with the "Road Sharks".

Ronnie's untimely death, and still being strong to live through that. I then unfortunately became legally blind, and not having the ability to see anymore. I remain true to myself though, and I have Hugo and Vincent, my best friends.

I also have Jamal, my other half in a sense. My story has a lot of value, and it's my own personal story, and it's my life story. My name is Ralph Maligrino, I am man of black, and that was my story.

CHAPTER 20:

MAN OF BLUE (PART 1)

My name is Frank Ealing. I am 29 years old. I am the man of blue. My Reddit username is "ElectroWaved". I was born and raised in San Francisco, California. My culture is a mix between Spanish, Mexican, and European. My mother was Mexican, and my father was mixed with Dutch and Mexican. So I come from quite a mixed background. Being that I'm Latino, you would think that I had a big family, and I was close with my family. I actually wasn't, and my family wasn't very big. I was born an only child. I didn't have any brothers or sisters. This had some advantages I suppose. I got more attention from my parents, and I didn't have to deal with sibling rivalry, or getting into battles with my brothers and sisters. I didn't have any siblings, so things like that never happened. One drawback I guess, was being alone quite often. Because I was an only child, I had to be by myself usually, and deal with problems on my own. Other people growing up, would consult their siblings with any issues they had. I didn't have that luxury. My parents luckily were loving to me, and understood my life. Something important I should mention, is that even though I am male, and live as male, and I am legally male; I was actually born anatomically female. So that would make me in proper polite terms, a transman.

Ever since I was born, I knew I was a guy. Even though I was born female, it didn't make sense for me to identify myself as that. The earliest memory I have of not being happy with my gender, was I had to been about two years old. My mother Felicia was dressing me up to attend a family function, and she put me in this very beautiful and delicate party dress. It was pink, and it was lovely, and the dress was cute and petite. However, I was not comfortable in the dress. I was not going to wear the dress at the party, and there was nothing my mother could do to make me wear it. It was a gorgeous dress, it just wasn't my style. She walked out of the room for a second, and I remember I ripped that dress to shreds.

It's something I don't regret, because I was two years old, and I didn't know how to convey to my mother that I wasn't happy in the dress. When my mother arrived back into the room, she of course was shocked to see the dress ripped. I don't know what came over my mother, or if she read my mind. But she asked me if I would be happy wearing some simple overalls. I nodded my head, and she let me wear that. As she is putting the more masculine looking overalls on me, my mother begins to lament.

"Frankie, you're going to look like a boy. But if it makes you happy, you can wear this. As long as you're happy, you can wear whatever you want to wear."

I want to sidetrack for a bit. Frankie, or Francesca was my birth name. The name I go by now Frank, or a more simplistically, Frankie. Francesca was a bit feminine for me, so I don't use that name anymore. Ever since my transition, I go by either Frank or Frankie. But going back, that was the first inkling of me not being comfortable with my birth gender. I did appreciate that my mother allowed me to go with a more tomboy image, at the tender age of two. I went to the party, and people did think I was a boy. My hair was short, and I guess it was only natural for people to think I was a boy.

I was happy being mistaken for a boy, because that's what I thought I was in the inside. Yes I was born female and a girl, but that's not what my brain said. My mind was telling me different, and that I was a guy. My father at this time, was also accepting of the way I was dressing. He didn't care at all that I wanted to dress as a boy at the party. I don't want to say my parents were picking up clues, with me being this young, but

I don't know. My father's name was Fernando, and now that I'm transitioned into male, I look exactly like him. He had dirty blonde hair, and a beard, and he was a very masculine man. He spoke fluent Spanish, because he was half Mexican, but he also looked European, because he was Dutch. He had a Spanish accent, and he was a great storyteller. My mother worked as a hotel clerk at a hotel in San Francisco. My father however worked at the shipyard in San Francisco. He worked at the docks and the port. So because of that, he worked odd hours, and late hours. But my relationship with my father was strong, and I was very close with him.

As I was getting older, I hated school. The first few years of school were fine. I would always seek the approval of the way I dressed with mother, who always looked after my appearance, as mothers typically do to daughters. She shopped for my school clothes, kept my hair short, and I would never wear anything feminine or girly to school. I always wore T shirts and jeans. Always, and no exceptions to that. I never ever wore a dress, or a jumper or a blouse. My father obliged.

I guess, I was lucky I had the parents I did. I know many trans youth have parents that don't understand, but I was lucky. To my surprise, I was allowed to have my hair short in school. I would get bullied and teased because of this, which in my early years of school, I would laugh about it, and think it was funny. They would think I was a boy, and they would try to belittle me, and humiliate me. However, getting older, when the jokes and the bullying continued, I took it more personally. The first instance had to have been during the fifth grade.

At the school I went to, all of the kids in the fifth grade go to attend a camping trip at the end of the school year. We all went into the woods, and we had no electronics, and no TV. We were just out in the wilderness. It was to teach us the value of nature I suppose. Genders are segregated during the camping trip. Boys bunk with boys, and girls bunk with girls. Being that I was female at the time, I was going to be with the other girls. On the very first day of us going to camp, I had a slight issue and altercation with some of the girls. I should explain that this was when my PCOS first started to show as well. Which let me sidetrack once again. I am diagnosed with PCOS, or Polycystic Ovarian Syndrome. Basically in simple terms, it's a growth hormone disorder that makes females take on masculine body traits. Such as developing facial and body hair, and producing amounts of other unusual traits. The disease can be serious, but luckily I was treated very carefully for it, and my case wasn't that severe.

As a result of this, I had body hair at eleven years old. You can imagine how other girls would have a field day with me because of this. The fact my hair was short, and I wore boy clothes didn't help one bit. But this was the first time I was truly attacked for being who I was. As I said, we were just standing outside the bus, on our way to camp, when the other girls wanted to start some shit. I forgot her name, but she was one of those pretty blond perfect girls. Every school had one, and she thought she was little Ms. Perfect. Anyways, she bullied me;

"You know you look like a dyke right? You look so ugly, you dyke lesbo."

I ignored her insulting me, but I didn't ignore the deeper context of it. I mean after all, I did look very butch and strange from the other girls. But this was the very first time that I was attacked for the way I looked, and it really hurt me. The rest of the camping trip was ruined because of that. The other girls would continue to bully me throughout the trip.

They would say the boys cabins are on the other side of the campground, or they would say I was confused, and they would call me he/she as well. That was a very disrespectful term that people in the 90s and back in the day would say, when I was growing up. I couldn't wait for the camping trip to be over. I went on this trip to have a great time, doing something different. But this trip would change me forever. I was first introduced to how cruel and terrible people are.

I was only being myself, and being happy looking the way I want to look, only to get punished. Coming from the camping trip, I remember I was talking with my mother, and crying in her arms. While I was crying with her hugging me, I started to speak with her.

"The other girls kept on bullying me, and I don't understand why. What did I do to make them hate me like that? I'm only being myself, and they don't like that."

My mother continued to hug me and comfort me, she then spoke back to me.

"Honey, there are people in this world that like to hurt others. That's how it is. You have to not let them get to you honey. There are going to be people that will accept you. It's okay."

My mother was absolutely right, and she would always cheer me up whenever I got into moods like this. The camping trip really taught me a lot about myself. Getting older, this was mild compared to what I was in store for. Going back to school after the trip, a sex ed therapist visited the school one day. The sex ed classes were gender segregated. The boys had their own class, and the girls had their own separate class. I learned a lot during the class, but the bit which really interested me, was when she talked about being Gay or Lesbian. Maybe due to lack of education and resources, trans education wasn't mentioned.

However, she did mention Gay and Lesbian discussion. As she was lecturing us about this, I kept thinking to myself, that was me. I was a Lesbian this whole entire time, and it would explain everything perfectly. I didn't know there was a name for what I was, but I now had a nametag to put it under. Not aware that I was actually transgender, and not Lesbian at the time; it's what I went with to make me feel better.

I was also attracted to women, so it made sense to call myself a Lesbian. I was extremely butch, hated looking like a woman, and was attracted to other women. Before then, I only thought of myself as weird and different. Calling myself Lesbian at the time seemed to make sense. Once I left Elementary School and was going into Middle School, I was faced with tragedy. I was coming home from the last day of Elementary school, and my father was in the living room upset. I sit by my father on the sofa, and he starts to hug me tightly. I then ask him what's wrong.

"Dad, is there something you wanted to tell me? What's wrong?

My father then took his glasses off, and set them down on the table in front of the sofa. He then started to cry, and was having trouble saying what he had to say. But he spoke to me.

"Your mother has passed away. She was feeling sick today, so she went to the hospital. Something wrong with her heart or something. She died at the hospital today."

I was sad to hear this, and I know my father was upset to hear this. Having my mother die, really caused me to feel angry about myself. My mother was an important part of me growing up, and she would be there for me whenever I was down. She's gone, and I'm going to miss my mother. After my mother died, I became more masculine with my appearance, and my identity. I came out to myself as a Lesbian, and for a while, I was comfortable with that. Going into Junior High School, the other students at school had so much fun making my life hell. I had no choice but to ignore it, because if I got violent and fought back, that would only make things worse for me.

The name callings were also more clever. Some of the insults were so gross and disgusting, that I don't even want to mention or talk about them. They were that bad, and they were that juvenile. Focusing on my schoolwork became a struggle. Whenever I would be in class, and we would be taking a test or something, I would hear whispers. The whispers would be the other students in the class making a disrespectful remark to me. So because of this, I couldn't focus on my schoolwork, due to their behavior.

I had no friends in school as a result of this. I was too freaky and weird to associate with the other students. I was simply the girl that thought she was a guy, and nobody appreciated that. I think nowadays, people are more accepting of all identities. This wasn't the case when I was in school, and I didn't have the respect from my peers. Instead of them accepting me for who I was, they decided to bring me down, and to I guess make me feel guilty for the way I was presenting myself.

I had no one to turn to when I felt sad over things such as this. My mother ordinarily would have been the one I consulted, but she's gone. My father, I didn't think he would understand, but he was my only hope. I had the worst day of school I had in my life, and really needed someone to talk to. My father came home from work early, and he was in the living room watching television. I then started to speak to him.

"Dad, the kids at school are giving me a hard time. They keep making fun of the way I look, and they say I'm confused, and that I'm a freak. I don't know what to do."

My father cut the television off, and then started to speak back to me.

"Why are you letting them do that to you? They are a bunch of kids that don't know better. They are probably jealous of how happy you are, being different. I love you no matter what. You're my child at the end of the day, and I support you."

The response my father gave was great. I took his moral support, and I used it whenever people at school would try something with me. I ignored them, and I took it as them not understanding how special I was. They were confused and scared of the way I was comfortable, so the only way for them to react, was by tormenting me, and bullying me.

I then improved on my studies, and didn't let these kids at school bother me. I was the butch Lesbian dyke that nobody wanted to be around, and that's fine. It didn't make me a bad person, because nobody else at school wanted to hang out with me. The only thing it meant, was that they weren't quite ready for someone like me. I would only hope that maybe one day they wouldn't be so ignorant, and they would accept me, and other people like me, for the person that they are.

I continued on with school, trying to not let my identity issues bother me. However, my gender dysphoria at this time, was starting to come out. I was under the impression that if I came out as Lesbian, that would be enough to make myself comfortable. Lesbian seemed like the perfect title to give myself. In usual circumstances, it would have been. There is nothing wrong with being Lesbian at all. But the truth of the matter is, that's not who I was. I was actually a transgender man, and I had no idea that I was. I only classified myself as a Lesbian, to make things easier. I was not educated with transgender topics quite yet, and so Lesbian was the default.

The first time I actually knew what transgender was, I was fifteen years old. I was feeling sick and ill, and so I was staying home from school. I was in the living room in my house, watching the "Oprah Winfrey Show". Nothing else on the television was on, so that's what I watched. By chance, the episode that they were talking about on this particular day, had to do with individuals who identify as transgender.

Transgender was a word I may have heard once or maybe twice before, but I didn't know what it meant. I also didn't know, how much of an impact it would have on me. As I'm watching this program, it's like the television set was reading my mind, and this was exactly how I felt. I mean before watching this program, I did know of men who wore dresses that still called themselves men, but I didn't know there were people that actually were born in the wrong gender. I was educating myself so much on this. I saw segments both from transwomen and transmen. Both young and old, and hearing their stories.

Once the program was over, I then told myself that I was transgender. I am a transgender man. I'm not happy being a woman, and this is not the life I want to live. I want to live as male, and I do not enjoy being in a female body, and appearing as a female. The only issue was, how was I going to tell my father this. Sure, he would accept me being a tomboy and a more butch woman. I did doubt that he would accept me being a transman, and wanting to change my gender.

I also didn't know what steps I should take next. Do I have to talk to a therapist? Do I need to talk to a doctor? So many questions I was asking myself as to what to do. At this point, I said that I would wait until I was a little older to come out to others as transgender. I was going to continue to label myself as Lesbian, but knowing that I'm truly transgender, and I want to life my life as a man. I didn't consider it lying to myself, but waiting until I educated myself more on the transgender topic.

Going back to school, and coming out to myself as transgender was interesting at first. I didn't know any other students at the school who were transgender, but it was weird going to school, with the new realization of me being transgender. I noticed that there was a "Gay and Straight Alliance", that my school had. I decided to attend the group during lunch period one day. Going into the group, it was mostly other students in the school that were Gay and Lesbian.

However, there was one person in the group that caught my eye. They were an African American student that was dressed very colorful and flamboyant. I thought they were a boy, but after they introduced themselves, they said that they were a transgender woman. She was born a boy, but now identifies as female. Her name was Jamie. That was this persons birth name. What I liked about Jamie, is that she was similar to myself. They weren't a transman like me, but we both identified as transgender. It was nice to have another transgender person at the school to relate to. I wanted to make Jamie my friend, and for us to learn things about each other, so we can grow. During the meeting, it came time for me to introduce myself, so I did.

"My name is Frankie. I'm in my senior year. I also identify as a transgender man. I'm early into coming out as transgender, but I know this is what I am, and I'm happy with that."

Some of the other students in the group were shocked when I mentioned that I was transgender, but I knew that Jamie felt motivated once I told her that I was. At the end of the group, I went up to Jamie to try to speak with her more.

"Hey Jamie, I figured since we are both trans, we should hang out sometime. We have a lot in common based on that, and maybe we can do something tomorrow afterschool?"

Jamie was polite, although she rejected my offer to hang out. She then in a friendly polite way, explained why she declined my offer to associate with me.

"I really would love to, but my family doesn't accept me, and they wouldn't approve of me hanging out with you. I appreciate the gesture, but I'm sorry, I have to decline."

It's a shame that I couldn't befriend Jamie. She seemed like a really cool person, and I could have possibly learned a lot from forming a friendship with her. I wanted to at least gain her experience, and understand what she went through. It could help me with my journey.

I started to ask Jamie questions about the transgender identity, to get a better understanding of it all.

"Well, do you have any tips for me? I'm new to coming out as trans, and I would like anything at all that can help me. Is there anything that you can give me for advice or help?"

Jamie and I then sat down next to each other at a table, and she began to speak.

"I want to first of all say, that my transgender journey isn't going to be the same as yours. With me being a transwoman first and foremost. I appreciate you coming out as a transman, but it's two different approaches from me and you. We are both trans yes, but it's different."

I understood where Jamie was coming from, although I do feel that yes I am a transman, not a transwoman like Jamie is, but I still feel we can relate anyways beside that. Jamie then continues to educate me on transgender related issues. I listen as she continues.

"Another thing, is about gender labels. My family still refers to me as he, but I go by she/her pronouns. I don't like to be misgendered. You of course I'm sure would go by He/Him pronouns, as you are a transman. So I want to start with gender labels."

This was exactly right. Understanding gender labels are important when trying to gain a good support with transgender people. It is respectful to use the gender pronouns associated with the gender that they now identity as. It's very disrespectful to misgender a transgender person. I remained speaking with Jamie for several minutes, learning all that I could about my new identity. Jamie then continues to educate me even more.

"The next thing I want to talk about, is transitioning. Transitioning is the process of appearing as the gender you wish to identify as. This can be done in simple ways such as changing your clothes or appearance, or more complex ways such as medical procedures."

Jamie continued on for a short while, but then she told me she had to go home. As she was on her way out, she reached into her backpack, and handed me a book.

"I want you to read this. A friend of mine gave it to me. It's a book on transgender and gender identity, and it will help you. I really wish we could hang out, but please understand my situation with my family. Frankie, I wish you the best, and we can still hang out in group. Bye."

I said goodbye to Jamie and hugged her. When I got home, I read the book cover to cover. I also took down notes, and there were so many things related to being transgender, that I didn't know about. One thing in particular, was how to erase puberty for trans individuals. I was already going through female puberty at this time, so I knew I had quite a bit to go for my transition, if I wanted to pass as a male.

Another thing I studied from the book, was top surgery for men. I did develop breasts, and I wasn't happy with them. I knew eventually I would have to get them removed, as my gender dysphoria caused me not to enjoy my breasts. I typically would bind my breasts when I went to school. I didn't think twice about this before, but I now realize this was all included with my transgender identity. As I was continuing to read the book, I later found out about testosterone injections. This was something I was interested in as well. This would be a major tool to help me on my transition.

The book was quite long, but I was glad that I read it, as there were so many things I had no idea about. I was happy that I completed the first step of my transgender identity journey, which was to come out to myself as transgender. I was not a Lesbian, and I was not simply a butch female. I think had I not come out to myself as transgender, I wouldn't have been happy with myself. But that was only the first step.

There were so many things I had to do from this point forward. I figured the best thing to do would be to make a list of all the things that I want accomplished in my life.

The first thing I wrote down on the list, was to be addressed by male pronouns. I don't want to be called girl, or woman, or she or her. I am a man, and I want to be called a man. Taking Jamie's advice with the pronouns, it's very important. By simply being called he, or him, or man, I was already happy. It was a warm feeling that made me comfortable. So now that I had the pronouns figured out, I can now move onto more complex categories.

The next thing, was understanding that I am not a Lesbian. I am a transman, and alternatively, I am simply a man. Not that there is anything wrong with being Lesbian, that isn't what my identity is, or what I truly am. I can now accept being a transman, and I refuse to let people say I'm something that I am not. The following thing I put on the list, was to speak to a gender therapist.

When I read the book, they urged that anyone who is transgender, speak to a professional during their journey. Talking to someone licensed, can help them accomplish things they want done in their lives. I went on the internet, and researched several gender specialists, and I made an appointment to speak with one. The following thing I put on the list, was to possibly take testosterone injections. If my agenda is to identify as a man, and be perceived as a man, this has to be done. I noticed the amount of things I was jotting down on my transgender journey list, and was starting to feel overwhelmed.

I was planning several things out for myself rather fast. But I knew the quicker I can get these things done, the happier I will be in my life. Continuing on with my list, I then started to list top surgery down. I was not happy with my breasts, and didn't want them anymore. I was tired of having to bind my breasts every single day, and knowing that this was common for many transmen to do, made me happy.

I wanted to get this surgery done as well. I decided to put one final thing on the list, which was to come out to my father as transgender. I was totally scared as to what his reaction was going to be, or if he was going to accept me for who I was. But if my dad really loved me, which I know he did, this news wouldn't hurt him.

A week later, the appointment I made online to speak with a gender therapist arrived. As I was waiting to speak with the therapist, I took my list out. The therapist then called me into his office. I was shocked that the gender therapist was a man, and a rather masculine appearing man. I later found out that he was actually a transman life myself. He however was well into his transition, and passed 100 percent as a man.

I would have never guessed that he was transgender. As I'm sitting behind the therapists desk, he then introduces himself to me.

"Hello Frankie. My name is Drew Northam. I'm a gender specialist here. Today I basically want to hear your story, and then we'll take it from there. So, why are you here?"

I then start to open myself up to the therapist, explaining my situation in detail.

"I'm here, because I am a transman. I was born female, but I don't want to live as female. I want to live my life happy, and the way I was intended to be, which is male. I don't know where to begin, or what I should do, which is why I really need your help."

Drew then starts to take a notepad out from his desk, and begins to write several things down. When he finishes writing, he then starts to ask me several more questions.

"So, are you comfortable being called male pronouns? Are you happy with your female body parts? Do you want to be perceived as a man? Are you experiencing gender dysphoria?"

I understand that Drew wants to be certain that I'm transgender, so these questions must be asked. He is only trying to help me, which is why he's pressing me the way he is. I am truthful with the responses that I give back to him.

"I want to be called by male pronouns. I'm not happy having female body parts. I do want to be perceived a male, and I am very much experiencing gender dysphoria with my current body. I would like to take the steps to transition into male."

Drew then starts to write down several more things on his notepad. Once he finishes writing, he then directs his vision back at me, and starts to speak to me.

"You know, this is not going to be an overnight process. It will take many months for you to achieve what you're looking for, which is to pass as male. But if this is something you absolutely want to do, then I'll do what I can to help you."

Drew smiles at me. I was aware from what I read in the book that Jamie gave me, that this wasn't going to be quick thing. Transitioning was going to take quite some time; for me to fully get into the state that I'm happy with. Drew continues to write in his notepad. During this time, I respond back, letting him now that I'm willing to go forward with this.

"Yes. I'm absolutely sure that this is something that I want to do. This is how I want to live my life, and I won't be happy, if I'm not able to do this. I finally am at a place to where I'm coming out to myself as transgender, and I'm ready to live the life I'm supposed to life."

Drew continues to write on his notepad. As he's writing, he asks me another question.

"Are you out to your family? Do your parents know that you're transgender? As you're a minor, you're going to need parent or guardian permission to start transition procedures. If your parents aren't accepting, there are LGBT programs that I will refer you to."

I then realized that I haven't come out to my father being transgender yet. This was something that he had to know, and I couldn't keep this secret from him. I was going to need my father's permission to move forward in the transition process. Even though part of me knew he was going to be accepting of me, there was still a chance that he would not take the news well. I had to be honest with Drew, and let him know that my father doesn't know that I'm transgender at all. I would have to talk to my father about this, and tell him as soon as possible.

"Well my mother passed away, but I live with my dad. He's open minded, but no, he doesn't know that I'm transgender. He does realize I'm different, and I'm sure he would be accepting of me, but I don't know. So my family doesn't know about me being trans. No."

Drew then hands me a bunch of documents. He then speaks to me.

"I want you to go home and read this. It's a list of options you can take with your transition. As far as medical drugs you can take, and other information. In the meantime, if you're comfortable coming out to him, please get your fathers permission. Once you have his approval, you can report back to me. If you can't come out to him, or he doesn't approve of this, report back to me anyways. Take care."

I shake Drew's hand, and I walk out of his office. I knew that once I got home that evening, I had no choice but to come out to my father. Even if he was going to throw me out into the street, which I knew he wouldn't do, but still. He had to know about this part of my life, and how I want to transition into male.

When I arrived home, my dad was in the living room, drinking coffee and reading the newspaper. He had no idea, that I was about to approach him with news that was going to surprise him. I end up sitting by him in the sofa, and I tried to come out with the words to tell him directly that I'm trans, but I was not able to. I instead decided to give him a hint. I set the documents that Drew gave me at his office, down on the table in front of the sofa.

My dad looked at what I put on the table, but didn't pay it any mind. He went back to reading his newspaper. I was hoping that he would have gotten the hint, but he didn't. I knew I had to basically tell him directly. Trying to find an indirect way to tell him, wasn't going to work. This was also an important conversation as well, so I needed to be serious with him. I then take my dad's newspaper, and I snatch it out of his hands. I set his newspaper down on the table in front of the sofa, and I begin to speak to him.

"Dad, there is something I need to tell you. You probably already had an idea, but if you didn't, I didn't mean to shock you with this. But, I want to live as a man. I was born female, but I am a male, and I want to live my life as a male. I need your approval and support."

My dad was shocked at the news, and he had no idea that I was transgender, or wanted to be male. He took his glasses off and set them down on the table. He then grabs me, and hugs me. He kisses me on the cheek, and continues to hug me. My dad then speaks to me.

"Frankie, you know I support whatever you want to do. This is very shocking news, but if this is how you feel, then I support you. You're now my son I guess. Ha-Ha."

My dad supported me, like I knew that he would all along. All of my worrying was for nothing, and I had the pressure of coming out to him, gone. My dad was going to stick with me through this, and I was going to into my transition with his approval. My dad and I went back to Drew's office, and Drew got to meet my father. As I was seventeen at the time I officially started my transition, that would make a minor. My dad would have to sign off for me to transition.

Once my dad signed all the papers, Drew then started to put me on my transition program. I was then given my testosterone injections. I would have to take them frequently. Starting "T", was the first step into becoming the person that I wanted to be. It was a good tool in order for me to be pleased with the way I want to live my life. I also would spend more time with my dad, as he was getting used to being around his new son. We would do father and son things now, and would go fishing and doing outdoor things. He was taking my transition well, and I was lucky to have such an open minded and accepting father. I educated my dad on several things as well, and told him what my intentions with my transition are. He also didn't mind when I said that my ultimate goal was to look like him eventually.

I want to pass as male completely, and live my life, looking the way that I wanted to look. The new relationship I had with my father was good, and I was starting a new life. I was no longer Frankie his daughter; I was now Frankie his son; and he took my transition the best way possible. I loved my father for that.

Sadly, things at school weren't going so great. Even though I was taking "T", my legal gender was still female. I was still in the process of legally changing my gender. So the school still referred to me as female. I was still going into gym class with other girls, and it was strange and weird. I understood that the school has to follow rules on the legal side of things, but it was still difficult.

At this point, I already referred to myself as male, and was living as male, but I was still technically female at school. It was okay, because I hated school anyways. The school didn't need to know about my transition. I wasn't confused over this, and the school had their stupid rules, by still classifying me as female.

I didn't have to follow them though. I still continued to go to the "Gay Straight Alliance" group at the school. I also began to associate with Jamie more. I understood that she didn't want to hang outside of group for safety reasons, but I still wanted to be friends with her. Jamie's family was not at all accepting of her being transgender, and refused to help her with her transition.

Jamie's plan was to wait until she was eighteen to move out, and she would then begin her transition. I didn't realize how lucky I was to have my father, and I wish Jamie had the same luxury. She unfortunately didn't, and had to be around family that did not want her to be happy the way she wanted to be. While I was in group, I heard more of Jamie's story, and couldn't help but be empathetic. I wish that there was something that I could do to help her. Everyone at group had terrible stories, but Jamie's story in particular was really special for me, and I couldn't let her be in misery like that. Once group was over, I wanted to talk to Jamie, and see if she was doing okay.

"Hey Jamie, I wanted to ask how are you doing. Are you doing okay? Is there anything that you need for me to do? You can talk about it with me. It's okay."

Jamie started to grab her things, and then started to cry. I could tell she was terribly upset, and something was bothering her greatly. Jamie then cried out back to me.

"No, I'm not doing okay. My family hates me, and they abuse me a lot. My mom is really disappointed in me, and my dad doesn't accept me either. My family will not accept me being transgender, and I feel they will never understand. I don't know what to do."

I then decide to hug Jamie, and I comfort her. I understand where she is coming from. It's very difficult having a family not accept you being trans. You want to be happy, and live how you want, but your family simply doesn't understand how you feel at all. As I'm continuing to hug Jamie, I let her know I'm here for her, and I understand all of her sadness.

"I know how you feel. I want you to hang in there though. It's going to be fine. You're a kind person, and things are going to get better. I'm sorry that you're having issues at home, but don't let that stop you, okay? Be strong and be tough, I'm here if you need to talk."

Jamie nods her head, and starts to grab her things. Jamie and I say goodbye to each other. After our conversation, I couldn't live with myself, by seeing Jamie in this condition. Something wasn't right with this scene, and I needed to step into action and do something to fix it. I couldn't let someone who was transgender like myself, and dealing with a terrible situation, fend for themselves. I had to step up, and do something to help. My main plan, was that I was going to ask my dad if it was okay for Jamie to live with us. Jamie was constantly shunned by her family for being trans. I wanted to remove Jamie from that environment, and give her a second chance. After group that day, I went home, and told my dad the plans I have for Jamie.

"Dad, there is a girl who's transgender at school. Her life at home is really bad, and I didn't tell her, but I want for her to come stay with us. Dad, you have to help her."

My dad thought about it for a minute, but then he agreed to the plan. Jamie was finally going to be rescued from the position she was in. She had a chance to be happy, and to transition without the hurt or punishment from her family. I wanted to help another person going through similar issues as me. I couldn't leave Jamie to fend for herself like that. Because Jamie and I didn't share any classes, the only time I saw her was in group. So I had to wait until next week to tell her the news, that my dad said that she can come stay with us. I waited every single day for group to come, so that I could talk to Jamie.

When the day of the group finally came, I was shocked to see that Jamie was not in the group. Jamie usually always comes to group, so it was unusual to not see her there. This wasn't good, as I was really hoping that Jamie would be here, so that I could tell her the good news. But she wasn't present, so there was no way for me to tell her today. My only option was to wait until next week, which hopefully Jamie will be in group next week for me to talk to her.

I waited again for group to meet up on the following week. Yet again, Jamie was not in attendance. Now I was getting slightly worried and concerned. What if something bad happened to her? What if I was too late? I was trying not to think so negative, but all of these thoughts were running through my head.

I figured that I would wait one more week. Maybe Jamie was sick, or there could have been a good explanation or reason as to why Jamie didn't attend group for two weeks in a row. But I did wait one more week.

Once Jamie was not at group for the third time in a row, something was definitely not right. I sat through group, hoping Jamie would walk in, and she didn't. Group was over, and Jamie never arrived. At the end of group, I end up asking the other people in the group, have they seen Jamie. Of course, none of them have. I didn't know what to do now. I had to find out what happened to Jamie.

I decided to go to the school guidance counselor, and told them about the situation. The guidance counselor was concerned, but it seems like she didn't really understand the situation. I was trying to persuade her into giving me Jamie's address. I figured I would go to Jamie's house, and see if I can talk to her there. Remarkably, I was given Jamie's address from the guidance counselor. Jamie actually lived on the other side of San Francisco. I had to actually catch two buses to arrive at her house. When I reached her house, I knocked on the door. I didn't receive a response. I then knocked on the door again, and this time someone came to the door. It was a heavy set African American woman, who I assumed was her mother.

"What the hell do you want? Why the fuck are you standing on my porch?"

Despite the very friendly welcome this woman gave me, I decided to be polite.

"Yes, my name is Frankie. I'm a friend of Jamie's. I didn't mean to bother you, I just wanted to know if I could speak to Jamie please? It's very important."

The woman then takes a puff from her cigarette. She then angrily responds to me.

"Jamie ain't here. He went with out with his friends. He never tells me when he leaves, so I don't know where the hell he is, or when he's coming back. Now get the fuck off my porch."

At this point I decided to leave and walk away. The fact Jamie's mother misgendered her, told me all that I needed to know. I tried to go to Jamie's house and speak to her, but she wasn't there.

My only choice was to wait until I saw Jamie at school, to tell her the news. I never saw Jamie walking in the hallways at school though. I would only see her at group. So for the fourth time in a row, I was really hoping that Jamie would be there. I was praying that she would be. Even though she wasn't there the previous three times, I still had hope that she would be there. I went to group, and sadly for the fourth time, Jamie was not there. I then thought that maybe Jamie didn't like coming to group anymore. It might not have been something complicated.

But that didn't make any sense, as group was the only thing that Jamie liked at school. That was the one thing that she looked forward to, was coming to group. So it didn't make any sense not to see her there. Part of me also then went back to thinking something wasn't right. It was that feeling I had, that something fishy indeed was going on. I didn't like the way Jamie's mother talked to me when I went to her house, and I was definitely certain that something wasn't adding up right.

When group ended, I once again asked if anyone knew where Jamie was, and they all said no. I had to find out where Jamie was, as I couldn't be comfortable with my sanity, without talking to Jamie. I didn't want to go back to her house, as I didn't like the energy at that place. But how was I going to find and locate Jamie? I had to really tell her something important.

I then asked the guidance counselor, if she could tell me where Jamie's locker was. I was going to stand by Jamie's locker during lunch break and after school, and wait by Jamie's locker. If Jamie didn't show up by her locker, then something wasn't right at all. I waited every single day at Jamie's locker during break periods, lunch period, and after school.

She never arrived at her locker. I then realized that Jamie stopped coming to school. I spoke with the guidance counselor yet again, and she gave me Jamie's attendance records. Jamie hasn't been at school in weeks. I couldn't believe this. At my wits end, I then only had one option left. I was going to wait outside Jamie's house, to see when she would walk in. If Jamie was ditching school due to personal reasons, then I understand. But if Jamie wasn't coming home, then there was no excuse for that at all. I stood outside Jamie's house all evening, and she never came into the house. I did the same thing the following day. I didn't see Jamie walk into the house at all.

After the second day of me scoping out Jamie's house, I gave up. I couldn't locate Jamie anywhere, and it's like she didn't exist anymore. I was confused, upset, and aggravated. Where did Jamie go, and why can't I find her anymore? There was nothing else I could do to find Jamie. I went home, and when I arrived home, my dad was crying heavily on the sofa. He immediately called out to me.

"Frankie, come here right now. I don't know how I'm going to tell you this."

I end up sitting on the sofa with my father, and my dad then starts to show me an obituary in the newspaper. I was hoping that I didn't see Jamie's name in the obituary, but I did. Last week, Jamie killed herself by running into traffic. The fine print was there, and Jamie died. I was too late in trying to save Jamie. I immediately became angry, and started to throw things around in the living rom.

My dad understood my anger, and was trying to calm me down. I knew that Jamie wasn't doing well, and her situation at home was bad. If only I told her the news that my dad and I were going to save her, she may not have killed herself. I don't know why I didn't reach Jamie quick enough to tell her this. I don't know why she took her life, as there are people that would have accepted her the way she was. Her family didn't care about her, but there was still hope.

Jamie didn't see any hope, and that's why she did what she did. I then started to have an reverse effect on Jamie's suicide. I got depressed as well, and had second thoughts of transitioning. If being transgender was going to cause depression and suicide, I wanted nothing to do with it. I struggled with myself as to whether or not I should transition.

Jamie isn't the only trans person to kill themselves. There are several others struggling, and it wasn't fair.

The next day, one school was over, I ended up walking past Lombard St. and I then made my way to the pier of San Francisco. I sat by myself, looking at the water in the harbor. I only hope that Jamie is in a better place, and she's happy. I wish she hadn't killed herself though. I was so close to saving her. I probably should have explained the last time I spoke with her, that my dad and I were going to take her in. She most likely would have still been here. I continue to sit by myself, looking at the water, evaluating my life.

Understanding that my transgender journey isn't starting that well, with the death of someone I was close with. Jamie didn't get to live the life she wanted, and it's a shame it ended for her the way it did. I continued on with school, and I turned eighteen.

On my eighteenth birthday, I was now a legal adult. I also legally changed my gender to male. I was now crossing another thing off my transgender journey, by having my legal gender changed to male. I went to the DMV, and had them change my gender to male on their records. I was beginning to grow more facial hair, and was passing more and more as a man. I was being called sir, and nobody would think that I was a woman. I was already sporting a beard on my High School graduation.

I like how my High School graduation photo, has me with a beard, and I'm looking the way I want. My name on the yearbook was also Frankie, which I liked. After finishing High School, I had to move onto college. It would be a great way to continue my transition. However, the school I was accepted into, was "UCLA", in Los Angeles. I would be moving to Los Angeles on my own, for school in the fall. Leaving San Francisco to LA isn't that big a of leap, but it's still a move. I never been to Los Angeles, and I was connected to San Francisco, but that was the school that accepted me.

Disaster came to me yet again. I was picking out supplies for college, and I came home. I was looking forward to talking with my dad, as I was going to be leaving for school, and I wouldn't have the opportunity to talk to him as much. As I was walking into the living room, my dad was slouched over in the sofa. I thought he was sleeping, but something told me to go over and try to wake him up. After I shoved his shoulder in an effort to wake him up, he was not moving. I then realized that he was barely breathing.

Out of panic, I immediately call 911. The police and emergency personnel reach my house, and they take my dad to the hospital. However, my dad was pronounced dead at the hospital. I was told by the doctors that he had a heart attack. The way I coped with my father's death, was by putting on a stone face. I guess that it was his time to go, so I have to move on. The stages of grief vary, and I was in the denial stage somewhat. I told my other family members about dad's death, and funeral plans were made.

After my dad's funeral, I then became owner of our family house. Being that things were happening so suddenly, and my main focus was on school, I made a drastic decision to sell the house. I gave most of my things away, and I kept only a few things that were located in the house. The house had so many horrible memories attached, that I didn't want to live there anymore. My mom and dad are both gone, and I have to go on by myself. I'm still dealing with my rebirth from being transgender, and trying to understand how I'm going to live my life. My dad's death making things worse.

After I sold the house, I then started to prepare to move to California, so I can start school. I wanted to be a police officer. I can't really explain all the details as to how I decided to become a police officer, but that's what I wanted to do. It was going to be a challenge. Here I was, transitioning myself into male, and being the epitome of masculinity. At the same time, wanting to go into quite possibly one of the most masculine careers out there.

Before I moved to Los Angeles, I wanted to talk to Drew, my gender specialist one more time. I wanted to say goodbye, as once I moved to college, I wouldn't be able to speak to him every again. I'm the type of person that likes to have closure when I form interactions with people or I would like to at least attempt to. I went to Drew's office, and he began to speak to me.

"Oh, hello Frankie. Was there something that I could do for you. What brings you here?"

I sit behind Drew's desk, and I tell him everything that has recently happened in my life, and I also tell him that I'm going to be moving away for school.

"Well, a friend of me recently committed suicide. They were trans as well. It was tough to deal with. My dad also had a heart attack a couple weeks ago. I miss him a lot. I wanted to tell you goodbye, and thank you. I'm moving to Los Angeles to attend college."

Drew was devastated to hear the news that I gave. He knew that I have been through a lot recently and I am coping the best way that I can. Drew then responds back to me.

"Well, I'm sorry for the death of your friend, and I'm sorry for the death of your father. I wish you the best of luck Frankie. I know one day you'll be at the position I'm at, and fully happy with your transition. Here's my number, you can speak to me anytime."

I take a piece of paper that Drew writes his number on, and I put it in my pocket. I then get up and hug Drew. I then say goodbye to him, and I leave his office. I was now ready to leave San Francisco. It's time for me to begin the next stage of my life in California. My journey continues, and I'm not even close to done with it. As I'm driving down in my car to Los Angeles, I start to wonder how different my life is going to be. The new people I'm going to come across, how my transition journey is going to change. I was nervous, but also excited for all of this.

I still had my plans of being a police officer, and doing that as my career. I knew I had to be careful as to who I came out to, as really it's nobody's business. I was now a legal male, and I will now live my life as a male. But as I said before, my journey isn't done at all yet.. Jamie is gone, My mom is gone, and dad is gone. This is the time for me to move on by myself. I have a lot of life left to experience, and my adventure continues. Not only being transgender, but being a person. I arrive to Los Angeles, and I make it to "UCLA". I see other students standing outside the campus, trying to admit themselves. I then get out of my car, and stand in line behind them.

CHAPTER 21:

MAN OF BLUE (PART 2)

Now that I was in University, I can start my life new. I'm still Frankie, but I'm now Frank. The old person that I was is no longer here, and I have to focus on the plans I want to do now for my life. My goal was simple, very simple. I want to finish school, then I want to join the police academy right after that. I understand that being a transman, and wanting to be a police officer, may be a challenge. I know it's a very masculine orientated job field, but I don't really care. That's thinking negative, and I don't want to have a negative mindset right now. My dreams are very close within reach, and I know that I can accomplish them. I have been through a lot of hardships in my past, but I know that I don't have time to make excuses for myself. My time is now, and I have to act right now. My nerves are going crazy, arriving to "UCLA", on my first day. Even though San Francisco and Los Angeles are similar cities, the vibe is completely different. San Francisco was more industrialized, and people were more mechanical and art based. Los Angeles is more of a metropolis and a beach vibe. It is also more contemporary in my objective opinion. But I was at University, and ready to take on my new life.

As I was admitting myself, I was looking at the other students that were there. I then started to wonder if I was passing well enough. I have now been transitioning as male for eleven months, and I was happy with the way I looked. My face was becoming more masculine, even though growing up as female, I still had many masculine traits. I was forming facial hair at this point as well. My voice has been deep all my life, but since transitioning, it has gotten even deeper. If I say so myself, I was doing a pretty good job of passing as male. It wasn't really about passing. I mean, it's good if people don't assume I'm transgender.

I want to be treated just like how everyone else was treated. But it was more about being happy with myself, and no longer feeling stuck that I'm in the wrong body, or that I'm living a life I'm not supposed to be. I still have not gotten top surgery, but I was going to wait until after I graduated school to get that.

So for now, I'm still binding my chest until that happens. I'm not going to come out to anyone that I'm transgender. I do plan on making lots of friends, connections and acquaintances while I'm here, but I don't want to be labeled as transgender. When I get to a point in my life to where I'm comfortable giving out this information, I will. But right now, nobody needs to know that.

Even though my gender specialist Drew is back in San Francisco, there are people that I can see here in Los Angeles, that will help me with whatever I need regarding to my transition. Because I want to become a police officer, and join police academy, most of the classes that I'm going to be taking, involve criminal justice courses, and other civil courses.

I'm going to be taking some law courses as well. I didn't enjoy school that much, but I knew that education was something I had to not take lightly or for granted. Being transgender, I had to support myself, and make a name for myself. If I was educated, then nothing could stop me. All the oppression that I have for simply being myself, wouldn't matter; because I at least have my education. University was also different than High School. It's much more mature, and you are dealing with more mature minded people.

In High School, there were bullies and cliques, and all types of drama. College and University isn't like that at all, so I was happy in that regard. I finished registering for school, and I see that I'm listed as male in all my records. This is a good sign, as if I saw female on my sheet, I would have been agitated about that. I also noticed that I'm going to be sharing a dorm with other guys. This was the first time to where I felt slightly uneasy. Yes I now lived my life as a male, and I identify as a male, but I wasn't too thrilled on the idea of sharing a dorm with other guys. I don't know, I was scared that they would have an issue with me being a transman, and sharing a room with them.

Then I noticed, that if I don't tell them I'm transgender, then it won't be a problem. All I have to do is keep my mouth shut about it. Because really, it's none of their business that I'm transgender. Once I started to put it in that perspective, I was no longer worried or concerned about it. I wanted to see who my roommates were going to be. If I was going to be living with these people, then they had to be cool. I started to walk to my dorm room, and I noticed that I was the first guy that was there. None of my roommates have arrived quite yet.

Due to the free time that I had, I began to unpack all of my things. About thirty minutes later, my first roommate came into the dorm room. I began to examine him closely, and he was a chubby Caucasian man with curly hair. He set his things down on the other side of the room, and then walked over to my direction. I was far too anxious and nervous to say anything to the man, but he continued to come over to the area I was in. He then put his hand out, and introduced himself.

"Hey, how are you? My name is Seth, I'm going to be one of your roommates."

I could feel that Seth was a nice guy, and that I was going to enjoy living with him. I then started to shake Seth's hand, and in the same instance, I introduced myself to him.

"Hi Seth, my name is Frank, but you can also call me Frankie as well. Nice to meet you."

Seth then walked back over to the area he was at, and started to unpack his things. There were two more roommates that have not come into the room yet. As I continue to unpack, my bag of testosterone medication and injections managed to slip out of my backpack, and land in the center of the room. I was hoping that Seth didn't see this, but he did. Feeling nervous, I didn't react, and I just stood there. Seth is probably going to be curious as to what that is, and he is going to be asking a bunch of questions. However to my complete surprise, Seth walked over to the bag, picked it up, and handed it to me. I was happy that Seth didn't make a big deal about it, or was nosy. I wanted to save face for myself, so I lied about what the medication was for.

"I lift weights, and that's why I have that. It helps me out a lot. That's all that was."

Seth smiles at me and nods his head. I thought that lying about what was in the bag was enough, but it wasn't. I wasn't comfortable with myself telling a lie like that, and I wanted to reward Seth for not being nosy when he picked up the bag. I figured I should tell him the honest truth, as I could trust Seth wouldn't tell anyone else the news I was about to give him.

"Actually, I lied. That isn't for lifting weights. I'm a transgender man, and that medication helps me. I'm legally male now, so I'm happy. I wanted to tell you that."

Seth smiles at me, and doesn't seem to mind what I told him at all. He unpacks more of his things, and as he's doing that, he gives me a friendly response back.

"Oh, that's all? I don't care about that. You're still a great guy. That was real brave of you saying that. I'm a Bisexual guy, so I don't care. I won't tell anyone, I promise."

Seth then walks over to my direction, and flares his arms out for me to hug him. We both hug for a short while. I'm so happy that I made a new friend, and that I came out to Seth that I was transgender. I wasn't even planning on telling anyone that this early, but I'm glad I broke my own rule. Seth was a nice enough person for me to direct this information to, and I trust him. We both go back to unpacking our things, and an hour later, another roommate comes into the room. He's a slender Caucasian man with glasses. He was a little bit nerdy and goofy, but I knew that I wasn't going to have any issues with him. The man then walks to the center of the room, and sets his things down on the floor. He looks at the both of us for several seconds, but then he finally begins to introduce himself.

"Hey guys, my name is Melvin. I'm a quiet friendly person. Nice to meet you guys."

Seth and I shake Melvin's hand, and we each introduce ourselves to each other. Melvin was not sociable, and he was introverted. Seth and I went back and forth having small talk, but Melvin kept to himself. We weren't having a private conversation, and we were asking open ended questions. For example, we would say, "So do you guys..", which meant that everyone in the room could chime in and say what they wanted to. But Melvin remained quiet, and ignored Seth and I. I guess he was a shy person, and that wasn't his style. I could respect that I guess.

Seth and I continued to talk, and unpacked all of our belongings in the room. A short time after Melvin came into the dorm room, our final roommate arrived. This man was a bald athletic build Caucasian man, and he was wearing a suit. I found it odd that the rest of us were wearing casual clothes, and this man was wearing a formal suit. The man stepped into the center of the room, and without hesitation, he started to introduce himself.

"Hey gentlemen, my name is Ivan. It's a pleasure to meet all of you."

We all shake Ivan's hand. Unlike the rest of the men in the room, Ivan was more sophisticated than the rest of us, and way wise beyond his years. Not only from the way that Ivan was dressed, but you could feel and tell that he wasn't like anyone else. Even though I did form a special bond with Seth, I wanted to also open up to Ivan as well.

Melvin, nothing against him, but we didn't click instantly. It doesn't make him a bad guy, and he's not a bad guy at all, I didn't click with him that's all. Ivan starts to unpack his stuff, and at this time, I'm all finished packing. I then ask Seth, if he wants go to tour around the campus for a bit with me. He agrees, and we both walk out of the dorm room. I didn't realize how big the campus was, but it is quite large.

I was happy that I took the tour with Seth, so that I wouldn't be unfamiliar with where the buildings are, and be late come class time.

As we are walking, Seth then starts to speak to me, and he wants to know my opinion on our roommates.

"So what do you think about Melvin and Ivan? I think that Melvin guy is a little weird, and I don't know about him. But Ivan seems cool. Wearing a suit though was strange."

I nod my head at Seth, and we continue to walk and tour the campus. I think about what my response to Seth is going to be for a few seconds, and then I give out my response to him.

"I wouldn't say that Melvin is weird, but he is different. I don't know about him either. But Ivan I really like. Wearing a suit is strange, maybe he wanted to give a good impression?"

Seth nods his head at what I said, and we continue to walk around. When Seth and I are finished with our tour, we direct ourselves back to the dorm room. Upon returning, Melvin is fast asleep in his bed. I guess he must have been tired. Ivan changed out of his suit, and is wearing gym clothes. Ivan then takes his duffel bag, and starts to head out of the room.

"I'm going to go workout for a while. Jogging, weight training, I'll be back."

As Ivan was walking out, I stop him, and ask if I can tag along.

"Can I come with you please? I could use a workout session, and as you're already going to the gym, why don't we just go together? You don't mind if I come with you do you?"

Ivan did not mind, and he allowed me to join him in his workout session. I change into my gym clothes, and Ivan and I start to walk to the athletic building at campus. We start to jog on the track field outside as a warmup. I think we did a 2 mile jog. It was quite strenuous. Once we were done jogging, we went inside, and started doing weight training. As we were lifting the weights, I decided to ask Ivan a curious question about his college life.

"So, what are you studying? What plans do you have for after you graduate?"

Ivan and I continue to lift weights, and he then responds to my question.

"Well, I actually want to be a police officer. All the men in my family are, so I suppose I want to keep the tradition going. What plans do you have?"

It was amazing that Ivan and I had the same exact passion. He wanted to work in the police force, and so did I. We already were having a similar connection, based on that alone. We remain doing our weightlifting, and I respond to Ivan's question.

"How funny, I want to be a police officer as well. I woke up one day, and that's what I wanted to do. Help people. Maybe we can help each other, with our career goal being the same?"

Ivan nods his head, and we both continue to lift weights. Being with Ivan, I had a special feeling with him. I am able to tell when people are sincere and kind, and Ivan was definitely one of those people. As we were lifting weights, I wanted to tell Ivan something important.

I wanted to tell him that I was transgender, just the same way I told Seth that I was transgender. However, part of me was feeling that he didn't need to know this. Not only because I was scared as to what his reaction as going to be, but I felt he had no business knowing that. It was almost like I wanted to flip a coin. If it landed on heads, I was going to tell him that I was transgender. If it landed on tails, then I was going to keep it forever a secret.

We have now been in the weight room working out for nearly thirty minutes. I then couldn't keep what I said to say to myself anymore, and if Ivan really valued me as a person, this news wouldn't be an issue with him. I stop lifting weights, and I walk in front of Ivan. He stops lifting his weights, and I start to speak to him.

"I already told this to Seth in our dorm. But I wanted to let you know, that I'm a transgender man. I wanted to tell you, because I trust you with this information."

Ivan then smiles at me, and stick his hand out. I then shake his hand. Even though Ivan was a straight cisgender man, he had no issues with people that were different. He was an open minded man simply and purely. Ivan then quietly spoke back to me in a friendly way.

"I don't care, you're still an alright guy. Be careful who you tell that you though, okay? That's really nobody's business at all. But I'm here for you whenever you need me."

I smile back at Ivan, and we both end up hugging very tightly. After our hug, we return back to lifting our weights. After coming out as transgender to Ivan, I felt that quite literally a weight was lifted off my shoulders. Ha-Ha. He took the news well, and he still supports me regardless of that. The only person left in the dorm that I haven't come out to yet, was Melvin.

I then realized it was only fair that I tell Melvin, since I told the other two guys. I'm going to be living with all three of them, so being that I ran my mouth and told Seth and Ivan, I should tell Melvin so things are fair. Later that evening at the dorm, Seth and Ivan stepped out, and Melvin and I were alone. I told Melvin the news, and he didn't care. Melvin wasn't very political, and he didn't judge others.

Now that I have come out to all the guys in the dorm, nobody else on campus was going to know about me being trans. My idea was to keep this a secret completely between myself, throughout my entire University stay. However, the first day hasn't even gone by, and I ended up telling three people. Such is life I suppose, and sometimes things don't go the way that you planned them to be always.

Several days later, I started my classes, and the courses were difficult, but I applied myself. Being that Ivan and I virtually had most of the same courses and we would attend the same exact classes at the same exact time, he became my study partner. We would help each other out with the courses, even though they were not easy. Ivan and I would do a lot of research. Whatever I didn't know and was having problems with, Ivan would know, and he would help me out. The things that Ivan struggled with, I would know the answer to, and I helped him.

We became a good pair together, and studying was simple because I had Ivan there. If I didn't have Ivan, I don't know what I would have done to survive the torturous coursework that we had to do. My freshman year at University, mostly consisted of me studying. I didn't get to have fun. There wasn't any time, and I focused on my studies. The law courses that Ivan and I did were difficult at times, and the exams were even harder. If we didn't take the time to study, we would fail the course. Studying took a lot of time, and time that could have been used on fun. But I knew that we could have fun later.

Our main priority right now was on our coursework. I completed my freshman year, and sophomore year was equally as difficult. Ivan and I continued to share classes, and help each other out with our work. There was even more material that we had to pick up on, and also additional courses we had to take.

With the help of Ivan, and with Ivan also having me there as well, we completed our second year without a hitch. Junior year shockingly wasn't that tough, and most of it was a repeat of what we went through in our first couple years in University. Don't get me wrong, the courses in junior year required us to still focus and pay attention, but it wasn't as hectic from how it was in freshman and sophomore year.

I'm making it seem like my University life was boring. It wasn't, and there were times to where we would have fun. Usually on the weekends, and once our coursework and homework was all done. The rest of the guys and I in the dorm, did manage to somewhat have a social life. We didn't always get to have fun, but the little time we could spend on fun, we enjoyed ourselves.

Once classes were over, all of us in my dorm would go out, and we'd have fun. There would be house parties that other students at campus would throw. One particular house party that happened near the end of my Junior year. It was a party that I actually at first had no intentions of going. I'm not really a house party person, and it's not my thing. But I kept on being convinced to go by everyone else, so I decided to give in. When I was at the party, I saw a lot of people having fun, and that was good. I however, was not happy being at the party. I decided to stay for a little while, thinking that my mood would change, but it didn't. I wanted to leave and go home. I walked around the house for a bit, as the house that was hosting the party was quite big.

The attendance at the party was large as well. Hundreds of students that went to the campus were at this party. I was very shocked and surprised that the police didn't come and offer a noise violation or something.

As I'm roaming throughout the house, I see this girl sitting by herself in a room, reading a book. This girl had brunette hair, but she also had light red highlights. She had a bunch of tattoos on her arms of cartoons and classic movie actors from the 40s and 50s. I also liked the dress she was wearing. She had a very alternative and goth like image to her. She was reading the "Dark Tower" series from Stephen King.

I don't know why I was instantly attracted to her, but I was. This sounds creepy, because I guess it is, but I remained standing in the threshold of the room, staring at her for nearly a minute. Perhaps it was due to the loud music at the party, but she doesn't even know that I'm standing right in front of her at all. I then decide to take a seat down next to her at the sofa she's sitting at. The woman still doesn't recognize me. As you can tell, I'm terrible at flirting, but I was trying my best to get her attention. I finally decide to use the book she's reading, as a way for me to open up to her.

"So, I see that you're reading King huh? He's one of my favorite authors as well. My name is Frank, what is yours?"

She laughs at me, and closes her book. We both then make eye contact, and from staring at her eyes, I start to see how beautiful she actually is. The woman then introduces who she is.

"My name is Laura. Yes, I'm a very big Stephen King Fan. It's nice to meet you Frank."

The both of us sit at the sofa in silence after that. I didn't know what to do now, as I'm horrible at stuff such as this. I was crushing on her, and I knew I couldn't move too fast. She was going to think I was a creep then. However, I couldn't stay quiet, as that's also bad. I had to bring up another ice breaker, so that we can become more comfortable.

"Do you like to go to stage plays? There is one coming up next Friday, it's like a Shakespeare parody, and me and my friends were going to go. Do you want to come with us?"

The worst thing that could happen, is that she says no, and tells me to bug off. I had nothing to lose, by inviting her to come. I wasn't lying either. Yeah my intentions were to flirt, and to be in her good graces, but that's just an afterthought. Seth, Melvin, Ivan and I were actually going to go to the play, and I thought it would be nice if Laura came along. Laura then laughed at me after I invited her, and she then gave her response.

"Yeah, I'm free next Friday. I would love to go. Can I have your number, so that I can text you were my dorm is, and you guys can come pick me up?"

Yes, everything was going well, and it looks like I scored this time. She was such a beautiful girl, and even though this was just stage one, I was making my way closer into winning her. We exchanged numbers, and I left out of the room. I didn't want to risk staying, and saying something stupid to make a fool out of myself. I left the party, and went back to my dorm. As I was sleeping that night, I was in slight disbelief that I flirted with a girl for the first time today.

She was the most beautiful girl that I have ever seen in my life, and I knew that I had to step it up. I then started to worry slightly, and had a nervous feeling all over my body. I did not come out as transgender to Laura, and I feel that maybe if I do have romantic feelings for her, I should have been more upfront. Then I also thought, that what if it doesn't work out between us. I would hate to come out to Laura; being brave, and telling her very private information about myself, only for us to separate soon after.

I then realized that not telling Laura upon first meeting her that I was transgender, was okay. As I don't really know her, and she doesn't know me. But, if after the get together with her on Friday I still have feelings for her, I need to come out to her about this. The days leading onto my date, if you want to call it that, with Laura was tough. I couldn't stop thinking about this girl. My plan was never to fall in love, or to find someone that I would connect with, but I guess it sort of happened the way it did I suppose. I'm not complaining that I developed feelings for someone else, but I'm not used to this. I didn't sign up for this either. I caught feelings out of nowhere, and now I have to deal with it.

Friday finally came, and this was when I told Seth, Melvin and Ivan, that I invited a girl to come along with us. They were happy to hear this, as it's strange for a girl to hang out with a bunch of guys, and a bunch of dorky guys rather. We all arrive at Laura's dorm room, and Laura actually walks out with her other three roommates. I was not expecting her to bring guests as well.

The other three girls that Laura brought, were pretty and attractive as well. So I guess that all of us had a girl to ourselves to keep us company throughout the night. We end up travelling in two separate cars, to the auditorium where the play will be set. I know that for some people, going to plays is boring and it's not up their alley. Not for me, and I enjoy plays rather well. I don't find them boring at all, and in fact they are quite entertaining. They were one of the first methods of entertainment. Way before television, and movie theatres and internet. At the play, I tried my best not to make any moves on Laura.

Despite the fact, Seth was teasing and fooling around with one of Laura's roommates, while we were watching the play. I remained respectful, and I was going to play it slow at this time. Once the play was over, we all decided to go out for something to eat right after that. We didn't go anywhere fancy, but it was a simple diner that was located nearby the auditorium. From the way we were seated, I was sitting directly across from Laura. Everyone else at the table for the most part were mingling and conversing with each other. But Laura and I sat quietly. I knew this was the perfect time for me to converse with her.

"So Laura, what you are studying, and what are you going to do after you graduate?"

Laura then immediately responds to the question that I asked of her.

"Oh, well to be honest I don't know. I'm still putting all my options out. Part of my wants to be a kindergarten teacher, and the other part of me wants to join the circus. I don't know."

I knew that Laura was joking about joining the circus, and I liked her humor quite a lot. Even though she didn't ask me what I wanted to do, I decided to explain it to her.

"Well, I actually want to be a police officer. I only decided that I wanted to do that recently, but I'm happy that I did, because I'm really interested in that."

Laura seems interested in my aspiration of wanting to be a police officer. She then responds back to that, and she seems to be very curious over it as well.

"A police officer? That's kind of a risky job. I don't think I could ever do that; way too much stress. But it's nice you want to help people, doing something that you really want to do."

I knew that Laura was being respectful, and she was also being realistic. Being a police officer does come with a lot of stress, but I was up for it. This was my passion, and the job I wanted to do. Laura and I talk for several more minutes, opening up to each other more.

Once we were done eating at the restaurant, we began to walk back to our vehicles. I then asked Laura if she would like to hang out again in the future. She agreed to that, and I was feeling good. I was getting closer and closer to winning her over. I wasn't quite at the goal yet, but I was getting closer to it. The second date that Laura and I had the following week, had us going to an art gallery. I wanted to pick something polite. Rather than going to a bar or somewhere more rough, I wanted to still play it safe with her.

At the art gallery, the chemistry between Laura and I improved, and I knew that she also liked my presence as well. After leaving the art gallery, Laura and I decided to go to an ice cream shop. I liked ice cream, and so did Laura. The ice cream shop was at the Santa Monica Pier, and so Laura and I walked by the ocean eating our ice cream. We then sat down on a bench, and things happened too fast. We ended up sharing out first kiss.

The kiss felt great, and it was then that I feel completely in love with Laura. However, I needed to tell Laura the truth about myself. Especially after the fact we kissed, it was important for me to tell her. We have advanced so far into the relationship, for me to keep this secret hidden any longer. I was dreading what her reaction would be, but if she loved me, it wouldn't matter.

This is a private place, and we are all alone, with nobody bothering us. There would not be a more perfect time for me to tell this to her.

After we finish kissing, I lean in close to Laura, and tell her the secret I've been keeping from her.

"Laura, there is something about me that I haven't told you. I wanted to let you know that I'm a transgender man. I really hope that this is okay with you."

Laura smiles at me, and kisses me one more time. By her kissing me, I knew that was her way of saying that she accepts me regardless of that fact, and things were going to be fine. Now that Laura was my girlfriend, I spent more time with her, and I knew our love was here to stay.

Heading onto my final year of University, I was starting to talk to several different police academy forces. I was talking with Ivan as well, and we both decided that we wanted to go to the same academy. It would make more sense that way, due to our close friendship. We could go through the whole experience together, and it would be fun. My first choice was to end up going to the "LAPD" police academy.

Being that it was still in the Los Angeles area, and I enjoyed being in Los Angeles very much. If I had to relocate to somewhere else for academy, that would be okay too, but I preferred the Los Angeles area. Ivan also applied for the "LAPD" police academy as well. The application made no sense at all, and there were many papers to fill out. I believe in total, there were about fifty pages, and I had to cross every "T", and dot every "I". The whole application had to be completed accurately, or you were not going to be considered.

On the gender section, I put male, as I was legally considered a male. The application didn't say anything about medical history, or if you're taking any medications. They only wanted to know if you were suffering from asthma or any other breathing problems, which I wasn't. The application would strangely be the easiest and calmest part of the procedure.

The application would ask you a bunch of morality questions, and they also wanted to test your knowledge on legal issues. They would ask you to match law codes up, with their description. They would also give you a spelling test, in which you had to correctly spell a bunch of legal words. A part in the application which I was concerned about, was that they asked for a reference. The person you put down as a reference, is going to be interviewed, and would ask them, why you think this person would be a good police officer. The only person that I could think of to put down, was Drew. I figured I could trust him, and that if they were to contact him, he would be a good reference.

The steps that would come after you submitted the application, is what I feared. If they liked what you put on your application, the following stage would have you complete a physical agility test. The agility test basically wanted to see if you could run, jump, climb, and how well your endurance, stamina and strength was. I always worked out, so I knew I was fit.

I didn't know if I was fit enough up to their standards though. Another scary part that myself and others feared, was the fact they would make us climb up a huge 10 foot wall. We had to climb the wall, and get over it, in under ten seconds. I arrived at the physical and agility test location, and there were several other guys that wanted to get into the academy that were there. It was on a first come, first serve basis, as to when it was your turn to participate. I saw the other guys do the test, and the part which was a big equalizer, was the wall climb. I saw many guys fail to get across it, but I did however happen to see guys that were able to climb across.

When it was my turn to do the test, my only worry was not being able to climb that wall. I knew to all the guys that were not able to get across, that would possibly be an automatic rejection into academy. I was doing my test perfectly, until I reached the wall. I choked up a bit for a few seconds, but I snapped out of it, and managed to get across the wall quickly. I had no time to celebrate though, as the agility course was not done quite yet. I finished the rest of the exercises in the course, and I felt very proud of myself. I conquered the wall, and I knew I passed this portion.

If you successfully passed the agility test, the next part of the process, is a mental exam, that you're given by a licensed psychologist. The whole point of the exam, is to see if you are mentally fit enough to be a police officer. Basically, you sat with the psychologist for about thirty minutes, and they would ask you a bunch of questions. They wanted to see how honest you were as well. If you were giving indirect answers to questions, or contradicting yourself, that wouldn't make you look good.

What I didn't like about this section, was that the psychologist was trying her best to trip me up on a question. I didn't want to bring up I was transgender in the session, but I almost revealed that I was, from the way she was giving me the questions. When the psychological evaluation was over, I was so glad. I wouldn't want to go through something like that again, and I was certain that I passed. If you did pass the psychological evaluation, the following step would be something similar, but not quite. You would have to go through a polygraph test, which was overseen by someone qualified and licensed. A lot of people fear the polygraph test, but that's exactly how people end up failing.

When they take the lie detector test, and they feel scared about it, the results are going to reflect that, and they might fail. There is no method to get around the polygraph test. You have to remain calm, and answer all the questions truthfully. When I got to the testing location, they put a bunch of wires over your fingers, and asked you to keep your vision forward. It felt like a hellish experience, and I wanted it to end as soon as possible. I answered all the questions honestly, and I didn't feel I had anything to worry about. I was done with the polygraph test, and was ready to move on.

If you passed the polygraph test, the following step in the process is for the person that you listed as your reference, is going to be interviewed either in person, or by the telephone by one of the police academy board members. This is so they can get a second opinion from others, if you are competent enough to be a police officer. If they talk to other people, and they say that you're a horrible person, then you aren't going to be accepted into police academy.

The person I gave for them to contact as a reference, was Drew. However, what I didn't realize, is that Drew is a gender therapist, and I didn't want to come out as transgender quite yet to the police. Luckily for me, when they contacted Drew, he told a white lie, and said that he was my mentor. This wasn't completely a lie, but it was. This was good, because it didn't out me as being transgender. Drew was interviewed over the phone by one of the academy board members, and he really gave them a good impression of me, and I appreciated that.

Once they have interviewed your reference, the following step was to take the written exam. I know this seems like a long process, but they only want to allow qualified people to advance onto police academy. The written exam is not easy, and many people fail it. There are books that you can get from the library, or buy from the bookstore to help.

There are also study guides that are online which may help you to pass the test. You had to study. If you didn't study, there was no way that you were going to be accepted into academy. Ivan also made it to this stage, and the both of us studied day and night, to pass the academy written exam.

We only had a few weeks to study, as that was when the written exams were being held. It wasn't that much time, but the only other option for Ivan and I, were to wait 6 months for the next available test day. Ivan and I figured that if we didn't pass this time around, we would take the test again in six months. But despite how difficult it was to study, Ivan and I were feeling confident in ourselves. The day before the test, Ivan and I did many mock quizzes to test how good we were. Based on how well we were doing, I wasn't worried about us not passing the test. We were going to pass it, without any doubt in my mind at all.

The following morning, Ivan and I go to the test taking location. Several hundred other guys hoping to get into the academy, and have made it this far, are waiting outside with us. We are eventually let into the building, and the exam invigilator reminds us that if we are caught cheating, using the internet to look up an answer, of if we were caught looking at someone else's paper, we would immediately be disqualified, and fail the test. We may also be banned from applying for the police academy in the future. The is also another exam invigilator, that will walk down the aisles, to make sure that we aren't cheating.

We are given the test booklet, and we are also given an answer sheet. The test then begins, and I start the test. I don't know what happened, but my confidence began to slip away. This test shouldn't be this foreign to me, but it was. I thought I studied well enough. I was being stuck on many questions, and I was taking many educated guesses. I hoped that I still was doing well enough to pass.

When the test was over, I was 75 percent sure that I passed, and 25 percent sure that I failed. There were so many questions that I was stumped on, and had no idea what the answer was. Once we left the test building, Ivan and I decided to go eat at sports bar to unwind ourselves. We needed to calm down after that test, as there were so many questions, and it really fried your brain. When we were at the sports bar, I then started to talk to Ivan about the test.

"So, how do you think you did? Do you think you passed? I'm going to be honest, I actually don't know if I passed or not. Some of the questions were easy, some were hard."

Ivan then responds back to me, trying to boost my morale up.

"You did fine. You passed it no problem. Yeah there were some questions that got me as well, but I still believe, you and I both passed it with flying colors. We'll be alright."

Ivan was right, and I shouldn't be worried about the exam. As long as we studied, which Ivan and I both did, we shouldn't be worried. Most of the questions I answered well, but I also didn't know the answer to many of the others, and I guessed quite a bit. This is what worried me, was the amount of questions that I guessed on. They could have been wrong answers, as I picked a random response. In order to find out if you passed or not, you had to wait to receive a letter in the mail from the police board, explaining that you passed or failed the test. This wait was terribly long, and Ivan and I waited so many weeks to find out our results.

Finally, the day came, and out test results were in the mail. Ivan and I both passed the exam. We both jumped up and down, feeling happy once we heard the news we passed. We now only had one final step before we could go onto police academy. We had to sit in front of the chief of police, and other very important people, in a conference room. They would ask us a bunch of questions, and test our personality, and it allowed them to get to know us on a personal level. If made a good impression with them, we went onto police academy. If they didn't like us, we were rejected.

This was one of those steps in the procedure, that there was nothing that you could do to make things easier. I guess you could make sure your clothes are ironed, your shoes are polished, you are cleaned shaved, or your beard and mustache looks trimmed, and you don't have food in your teeth, and that you smell nice. Those were just common sense things. It ultimately came down to the fact that if they didn't like you, they weren't going to accept you into the academy.

I was going to be interviewed by the board first, and Ivan was going to be interviewed after me. I arrived at the building and gave everyone a firm handshake. Things began to start after that, and they asked me an array of questions, all of which were open ended, which meant that they wanted my input more, and they wanted for me to elaborate on the questions more. The question that I remember stood out to me the most, was they asked;

"Why do you want to be a police officer?"

This question will always be special for me, as the answer I gave was great, and I knew they would be impressed by it.

"I want to be a police officer, because I relate to people, and I want to protect and serve the people in my community. I'm brave and courageous enough for the job."

I feel that answer captivated them greatly, and I was winning many points. Once the interview was over, I shook all of their hands once again, and I walked out of the room. It was then Ivan's turn to have his interview. Once Ivan was done with his interview, we both walked out of the building. We now have to wait one final time, to find out if we were accepted into academy.

The wait was long, but Ivan and I finally received our acceptance letters in the mail. I couldn't believe that I was going to police academy, and that I was going to be a cop. Ivan was also going to be in the same force with me, and it was great. I remember when I told Laura about the news, she was proud and supportive of me. I called up Drew, and I thanked him for his help for getting me accepted into police academy.

Being accepted into academy, came just in time for graduation. Seth, Melvin, Ivan and I all graduated from university. Seth graduated in graphic design. Melvin graduated in computer science. I still keep in contact with Seth and Melvin sometimes. Ivan and I both graduated in criminal justice.

Now that University was over, I now had to go onto police academy. Ivan and I were both given a huge manual for us to read over, which told us everything that we needed to know about the academy. How they work on a points system, and you need to earn enough points to graduate academy. There were so many things we weren't allowed to do, and so many rules to follow. At police academy, they had an option that allowed you to either sleep and room at the academy itself, or you can sleep at your own residence. Ivan and I decided to sleep at our own residences.

I decided to move into a one bedroom apartment with Laura. She would end up working at a bookstore, and I would go to police academy. Ivan ended up staying in a place with a female companion that he met at school named Rachel. Being at the academy was interesting. It wasn't as tough as I thought it would be, but it wasn't a cake walk either.

I would have to be at academy every single day at 5 A.M., and they would dismiss us at 5 P.M. It was mostly a bunch of exercise and training rituals that we had to do. There would be certain days to where we did course work, and were in a classroom setting. After about a month of being in police academy, we finally got our uniforms. We didn't earn our badges yet, but it was nice to finally wear a police uniform.

What was fun, was that we got to do ride alongs with official police officers. They wanted to give us on the job training. I remained at police academy, being trained quite well. I knew that in a short time, I was going to be an actual police officer, and I was going to be out in the streets at this point.

As I went further in police academy, we were all taught firearm and baton training. We were taught how to use our guns, and shooting techniques. Other training exercises they made us do, had to deal with martial arts, and how to defend ourselves with ground fighting.

Something that I didn't enjoy with police academy, was that we had to be sprayed with pepper spray and mace in order to carry it. This was painful, and I don't want to live this experience over again in the future.

Another thing, in order for us to carry a taser gun, we have to be tased and shocked ourselves. We could either decide to be hooked up to wires, and they shock us, or we could be shot directly with the taser. I decided to be shot directly with the taser. If we were use the taser on suspects, we would shoot the taser at them. So I wanted the more conventional option. Being shocked by the taser hurt very much, but it's something we had to do.

Training was almost over, and we were given a written test to complete. If we didn't pass this written test, we wouldn't pass academy. This test was a breeze, and wasn't difficult at all. I of course passed the test, and I was all set to graduate police academy. Police academy lasted for nearly a year. They wanted to make sure you were absolutely ready to hit the streets as an officer. The training program has to be extensive because of that. The next thing was the commencement ceremony, and then I'll receive my badge. I'll be an official police officer.

Ivan and I both graduated from police academy, and got our badges from the chief of police. I went to the audience, and started to kiss Laura. I was an official police officer now, and all the training and hard work paid off now. The real action starts now, and I had a bunch of people that I had to protect and keep safe. Each police officer is given a partner, once they leave police academy. Ivan became my partner, and every day I would patrol with him.

We had the afternoon, evening, and night patrol shift. We would begin work 2 P.M., and then end our shift at midnight. If after midnight we were still dealing with a case, we couldn't go home. Being a cop was an exciting job, but it was also a stressful job. I guess that you can say that I was a good cop, and so was Ivan.

But there were a lot of tyrant officers in our department. I'm not going to name names, but many of them were evil. Ivan and I were always very nice cops, and on occasion, we actually had to sadly arrest people, but it wasn't done that often. Very rarely, if ever, did we draw our guns at suspects, or used force. We weren't those types of cops at all, and we respected our citizens. They count on us to protect them, and we want to be nice to the people in the city. As the years went on with me being a cop, now for three years, I have gotten all the ropes down, and so did Ivan. Even though occasionally we both would have an array of different partners, and we would also train new officers, Ivan and I would still spend many shifts being partners.

One shift in particular, would sadly be the last I would have with Ivan. It was supposed to be like any other normal day, until we received a call in our squad car from a 911 operator.

"There is a 211 in progress at the Main Street Shopping Plaza.."

The shopping mall on "Main Street" was being robbed, and Ivan and I were just around the corner. As police officers, it is our duty to protect and serve, so we went directly there. Ivan and I were the first officers to hit the scene, and the robbers were actually robbing a "Best Buy", located at the end of the mall. The robbers were dressed in all black, and they had hostages with them. This was the first time Ivan and I ever had to patrol a robbery, but from our training, we were sure that we could handle this particular situation.

The robbers remain in the building, as they are locked inside of the store. Ivan and I point our guns at the suspects, and demand they exit out of the building. More officers arrive at the scene, and several spectators on the street watch. The news media arrive, and it's very much chaos. More officers, and this holdup continues on for several hours, deep into the night.

Finally, the robbers find a way to break one of the front windows in the store, and start to dash out of the store. Several officers begin to shoot them, and the robbers return fire. One of the robbers fires his gun at several officers. Ivan and I are both shot, and Ivan falls to the ground. All three of the robbers are shot dead by the police right after this. I'm shot on the top of my left shoulder, and the injury isn't that severe. But I walk over to Ivan's body, and I start to do CPR. He was shot in the neck, and is bleeding profusely. I panic and I cry out for help.

"Officer down! Officer down! Someone please help him, we've both have been shot, but my partner isn't doing too good. Help please!"

I continue to do CPR on Ivan, and hold onto his bullet wounds, but it's too late. Ivan later passes away in my arms from being shot. Medical personnel arrive a minute later, and carry Ivan's body away, and look at the minor gunshot wound on the top of my shoulder. Ivan was killed doing his job, and that was the part I didn't like. He was only trying to protect people, and he was killed in the line of duty.

The following day, the press took hold of the event, and I was trying my best to deal with Ivan being killed in the line of duty. I was interviewed by several news stations, and at this time, I decided to be honest with my position as a cop. The fact Ivan died, I wanted to prove a message that police are people too, and we're just like everyone else.

I was told to give a press conference about the whole entire ordeal, and I took advantage of this. I was going to come out as transgender. Right here, and right now. People who are watching this press conference on CNN, millions of people, will know that I'm transgender, but I didn't care at all. The cameras were on, and I was live, and I began to speak.

"My name is Frank Ealing, I'm a police officer for the "LAPD", and I'm here to talk about the incident that happened yesterday. It was a terrible event, and it resulted in the death of my partner and my friend, Officer Ivan Duckworth. I want to say being that I am a.."

I was going to come out at this point, but I began to have several second thoughts in my head for a couple seconds. What was I thinking coming out at a press conference like this? The fact I was transgender is something that nobody else needs to know. Now I'm going to tell so many people out there who I am? But I told my thoughts to shut up.

Ivan being killed really motivated me to be honest, and to use my position as a police officer, as an advantage for others. Although I was stuck in my thoughts for a few seconds, I successfully recovered my speech.

"A transgender police officer.."

As soon as I said that, I could hear many gasps in the audience. I didn't know if those gasps were happy and proud gasps, or disappointed gasps. But I continued on speaking anyways.

"I feel we as the police can come together with the community. We are just like you, and we go through the same problems that civilians go through. In honor of Deputy Duckworth being shot, I want the police and community to all stand together. Thank you."

As I finished my speech, I was given applause, but I also heard many sighs and moans. But I came out that I was a transgender cop, and it's no longer a secret. The next day, the chief of police called me into his office, and shockingly was proud of me.

I was then interviewed by several human activist and LGBTQ groups in the Los Angeles area, and was surprised at the reception I got. Although there has been some negativity as well, and ignorant people were quick to voice their opinions, I ignore all of that. Laura was of course happy for me.

I have to sadly say that Rachel, Ivan's friend, was seven months pregnant with their son. It's going to suck that Ivan Junior is going to grow up, and not experience how wonderful his father was. But that's the way it goes, and it's completely sad and unfair. Ivan's picture was later added to the memorial of officers who were killed in the line of duty at the police station. His legacy will forever be honored.

Since coming out as a transgender cop, I received so much support from people. I've been asked to attend events and other arrangements. I've been interviewed by "GLAAD" and "Advocate" and "OUT" Magazine, and I'm so thankful and blessed for how people have been treating me.

The reception isn't always good, and a select few people have said that I shouldn't be allowed to be a cop, and I'm mentally sick. I don't give a fuck what they think though. I focus on the positives, and the people that are happy for me being who I truly am, and for being myself. My story is going to conclude here, as I have mapped out my entire life.

I only hope to be motivation to everyone out there who is struggling to be themselves. Gay, lesbian, bi, transgender, or whatever. It's okay, and I want to be their hope and motivation. My name is Frank Ealing, I am man of blue, and that was my story.

CHAPTER 22:

GUYS REFLECT

The stories have all been told, and I remain in the living room with the rest of the men. We sit in my living room for about two minutes in total silence. All the of the men have seen their tapes, and were introduced to all the stories. I even let the guys see my own personal story. Even though it took several hours, it was all done, and all the profiles were seen. At this point, all I need is for the guys to sign the consent form, allowing me to enter the profile videos into the film festival. In addition to that, I'm going to hire a videographer to film the guys even more, to give it a more cinematic feel. This whole idea is going to be a documentary. The raw profile interviews, are going to be included with candid clips of the men doing their own thing, going about their daily life. I think it will be a nice touch. I start to unplug my computer out of the television, and I close the video files. The men continue to sit around my living room silently. Some of the guys start to look around at each other; looking at each of them with a different perspective after listening to their stories. I had no idea as to how I could change the mood. My plan during this time, is for all of the guys to reflect and review their stories.

Now that I have finished unplugging my computer, I look at all the men once again, and I see all the somber faces. I am sure they are all feeling an array of emotions. Emotions that probably consist of sadness, shock, warmth, and probably above all, hope. That was the point of my "Profiles of Hope", project. All ten of the men sitting in my living room right now, all had a story to tell, and every single story had meaning towards their lives. Every story served a purpose towards their own growth. I have decided to pick these guys for a reason, as they stood out to me. Their stories had to be heard, and they will be heard my many others, if the guys decide to agree to do the film festival. I take a sip of my wine, and I notice the men are still sitting silently.

I was hoping that one of them would have said something at this point. They continue to stay quiet, and I guess I don't blame them. We all sat through several different stories, and I know that it's a lot to take in. It's like watching a really scary horror movie, and then having to compose yourself after you watch it. Or in the worst case, you go home, go to bed, and have a nightmare about it. Ha-Ha. I then decide to finally speak to the guys, to reassure them.

"Okay you guys, I know that was a lot to take in. It was probably weird seeing your story, and all of the other stories. So if you guys want to take a break outside you can, or if you just want to sit and relax for a bit, that's okay too. Whatever you guys want to do, you can."

After I said that, the guys still remained in that awkward state, but at least I tried to calm them down. I returned back to my recliner and I sat down. This went on for several more minutes. I was fed up at this point, and this was so silly. Why were we all quiet like this? It didn't make any sense, and I didn't know if it was something that I did to make them feel like this. I tried my best to edit the stories in an appropriate way. I made sure that all of the men were portrayed well, and that they were portrayed accurately and equally.

I then remembered that I neglected to tell the guys that I was going to show their tapes to everyone. I tricked them all. They were under pretenses that this was going to be a private project, and I lied very much about that. It is possible that they still hold resentment over me because of that. Now I have to convince these guys to sign the contract, which will allow me to enter their profiles into the film festival. Many more people will see their stories, and they could possibly make a greater impact. But if the guys do not wish to participate, I cannot force them to at all. This is a choice that they will have to make on their own. I know this decision isn't going to be easy. If all the men don't agree to do the project, I won't do it. All of the guys have to unanimously agree to sign the contact for the film festival, or it won't go on.

Because I didn't know what else to do, I reach into my backpack, and I start to take the contracts out. I set them all down on the table in my living room, talking to all of the men.

"Okay you guys, these are the contracts that will allow for me to put your profiles into the film festival. The contract also will allow for me to hire a videographer that will film you guys doing everyday things. I will take those clips, along with the raw profile clips and..."

Right during this time, Steven decides to speak back to me in an angry tone.

"I'm not going to sign that shit. Our stories are personal and they are private. Who the fuck do you think you are? I agreed for these other guys to look at my story, but no way am I letting the entire world possibly know about it. Aaron isn't signing it either."

I nodded my head back at Steven, and I started to grab all the contracts off the table. I then put the contracts back into my backpack, and I set my backpack down. In a way, Steven was exactly right. What was I thinking? These stories are very special to these guys, and maybe it's not my position to showcase them like this. I thought it would be interesting, as it's something I don't think has ever been done before. However, Steven and the rest of the guys have the right to be uncomfortable over this. During this time, I notice that Aaron and Steven are preparing to leave. Steven speaks again.

"We're going to go Aaron. This time for real. I hope you guys are all happy now that our private personal lives have been exposed. I want you to delete all of that shit. If I find out that you published my story, or Aaron's story, I'm going to sue you to Kingdom Come."

Aaron then gets off the sofa, and walks over to Steven's wheelchair. Aaron has a very disappointed look on his face, and he replies back to me softly.

"I'm sorry Gary, but Steven and I agreed to sit and watch all the stories. We did that, and we're going to go home now. We want nothing to do with the rest of the project. Sorry."

Aaron brings Steven's wheelchair closer to the sofa. I wanted to do one last ditch effort to convince them to stay. I really want the guys to participate in the film festival, and I would be devastated if Steven and Aaron didn't agree to it. Their stories I feel could impact and motivate many people, and I wish they could understand this. I get it, they are private stories that they may not be comfortable letting others know about. But, I really wish that Steven and Aaron would see the bigger picture, and how their stories can impact many. I start to walk over to Aaron, to persuade them to stay. However, before I am able to do this, Harry gets up and starts to speak.

"I want to sign the contract. On one condition, I want my brothers to be in the project as well, because they are also involved in my story. If that condition can be met, I'll sign."

I couldn't believe it. Out of all the people that I thought would be the first to agree to sign the contract, Harry was not one of them. I was starting to lose all hope that the guys would sign, and that this was going to be the end of it. I thought my plans of entering them into the film festival, were shot to hell, and I had no chance. The only thing was, Harry wanted for his brothers, Louie, Leif and Harvey to be filmed by the videographer. That's fine, and I would love to showcase Harry's brothers as well. Maybe things were starting to look up. I still had to have eight more guys sign, but Harry was a good start I suppose.

I go through my backpack, take the contracts out once again, and I hand one of them to Harry. Steven was not yet in his wheelchair, and he along with Aaron watch Harry in disbelief. Harry very briefly skims through the form, and takes out a pen from his pocket. He then signs the bottom of it. Harry then speaks.

"The rest of y'all know what you have to do. If I could sign, the rest of you could sign. You only live once, and I'm not happy having my story get out, but I know there is someone out there that would be touched by my story, and I don't want to prevent someone being motivated."

Harry hands me back his consent form, and smiles at me. All I had to do was get the remaining eight guys to sign, and everything was going to be fine. Not even seconds after Harry signed the contract, Troy gets up and takes one of the contracts and signs it.

"It doesn't make sense that Harry gets his story out, and mine doesn't go either. I'm slightly embarrassed having my story public, but I don't give a shit. I'm signing this for all the other boys who were in my position. Letting them know I understand how they feel."

Troy then hands me the contract, and even though only two guys have signed, I still feel happy. However, after Troy signed, the rest of the men were not entirely convinced. Harry and Troy return back to the sofa, and sit silently. Steven and Aaron who had plans of leaving, are still in my living room. If I could read their minds, I knew that they were partly thinking of signing because the other guys signed; then they were partly thinking, that their minds are made up on not signing.

After Troy signed the contract, the guys were silent for a minute, unsure of what to do. Harry then gets up and kneels down right in front of Troy, and does something unpredictable.

"I'm hoping this will get the other guys to change their mind. If it doesn't, well at least I'm doing something that I should have already done, but I'm doing now. I don't have a ring no, but when we get back home, I'll buy you one, I promise. Enough bullshit, Troy will you marry me?"

Troy immediately starts to uncontrollably laugh, and Harry smiles at him. Troy then leaps into Harry's arms, and Harry swings Troy around his back. After they get done playing around, Harry sets Troy down. Troy then gives his response to Harry.

"You know the answer is yes Harry. I love you so much. I will marry you, yes."

Harry and Troy then take a seat down on the sofa, and begin to kiss. Myself and the rest of the men, watch them both in total confusion. I didn't mind that Harry and Troy proposed to each other in my house, but it was still random. I wasn't predicting or expecting that at all. The mood went back to being silent and awkward after Harry proposed to

Troy. However, Jerald got up out the sofa, and took two of the contracts. He handed Carl one, and kept the other for himself. Jerald then started to speak to all of the guys.

"I'm going to sign this only for one reason. That reason being, is because this is some freaky shit. I figure, why the hell not? I don't know what crazy fool would be interested in hearing my story, or Carl's story; but who am I to judge? I'm going to agree to enter the festival."

Jerald then signs the contract, and hands it to me. Three down, and six to go. Jerald then walked over to Carl and started to rub his hair. Jerald then whispered out to him.

"Baby, you have to sign it because I signed it. We don't have anything to lose, and we have a lot to gain from having our stories out there. Do it for your brother Mark, please?"

Carl then grunts back at Jerald. Carl isn't eager at all to sign, despite Jerald trying his best to get him to sign. Jerald then begins to kiss Carl on his lips. Carl then signs the contract.

"I'm signing it because, well, actually I don't know why I'm signing it. Jerald signed it, so I guess that means I should. I love Jerald, and I have to side with my partner. I'm signing."

Carl then signs the contract, and hands it back to me smiling. I have now gotten four of them to sign, and I'm getting closer to having all of them do it. I wasn't feeling that confident, as only four have signed, but maybe all the guys will sign. I'm not forcing them to sign at all, and if the guys don't want to participate in the project any further, they don't have to. But it seems like some sort of butterfly effect, after each guy decided to sign, another guy agreed to sign. The next one being Frank. Frank got up, took one of the contracts, and began to sign it.

"I'm going to sign, because I understand that me being a transman is very private, and that's my own business; but I'm willing to speak for those who cannot. If I can motivate others, then I'll feel special. My story needs to be heard, so I'm going to sign."

Frank then hands me the contract. I only need to get a few more of the guys to sign. After Frank signed the contract, the guys who have not yet signed, are still indecisive as to whether they should sign or not. Jamal minutes later, then got up, and grabbed two contracts off the table. Jamal then started to sign his contract. He then handed the contract back to me, speaking.

"I decided to sign, because people like me never get to raise their voice, or have their story told usually. My story, and my situation with Ralph is private. I may not be comfortable about it like some of the other guys are, but my story needs to be heard. That's why I signed."

Ralph then immediately started to sign the bottom of the contract, with Jerald helping him sign in the right location. As Ralph is signing the paper, he begins to speak.

"I can't read this contract at all, but I think it's safe for me to sign. I feel my story deals with a lot of delicate information, but I'm willing to take that risk. I'm not ashamed or embarrassed, and if Jamal was brave enough to sign, then I'll sign the contract as well."

Jamal then takes the contract out of Ralph's hand, and gives it to me. I then noticed that I didn't really go over the contract terms with the guys. I take this time to let them know briefly what the contact entails, and the other conditions of the contract.

"Oh, the contract basically gives me permission to use your profile in the project. It also states that I'm not getting paid for this, and it also states that I'm not responsible for what the outcome or reaction of all of this is going to be. That's basically what the contract is."

After explaining the rules of the contract, most of the guys seem to understand and accept them. All of the guys have now signed, with the exception of Steven and Aaron. It should have been obvious that they both would have signed, now that the rest of the guys have.

But actually, it seems like the reverse happened. Steven whispers something into Aaron's ear, and Aaron then starts to prepare to put Steven in his chair. As Aaron is starting to get Steven up off the sofa, Steven angrily speaks to all of us.

"You guys are sick, and this whole thing is sick. I'm not signing, neither is Aaron. Not for a zillion dollars. I'm sorry. You're sick Gary, you are. Trying to make some type of reality show, or documentary out of this. Aaron and I see right through this shit. No thank you."

Immediately after this, Ralph starts to get off the sofa, and Jamal helps him up. As Ralph is now standing straight up, he starts to speak out loud to all of the guys.

"Steven, I can't imagine what it's like not being able to walk. Yes I'm blind, but at least I can walk. You have someone for you, Aaron. You're lucky to have him. Like I'm lucky to have Jamal. Which reminds me, there is something that I need to do right now."

Ralph then immediately gets down on one knee. I didn't want to believe this. I was going to have two proposals in my living room. Not that I wasn't proud of this, I was. I was kinda slightly jealous, because I was single and waiting for my own Prince Charming to arrive. But still happy for them. As Ralph is on the floor, on one knee, Jamal is looking at him shocked, covering his mouth. Ralph then starts to speak once again out loud to all of us.

"Jamal, I'm going to keep this short, sweet, and to the point. Will you marry me?"

Jamal nods his head, and kneels down to kiss Ralph. I accidentally look over to Steven and Aaron, to see what their reaction might be. Aaron seems to be happy, but Steven has a stoic look on his face. As Ralph and Jamal are continuing to kiss, I notice that Steven is starting to cry.

Aaron notices that Steven is crying, and begins to comfort him. Steven becomes agitated, and then begrudgingly slithers his way off the sofa, and falls to the floor; unable to move. As soon the rest of the guys notice he's crawling on the floor, they all react in shock, and Harry, Carl and Frank walk over to help him up. Steven then shouts out.

"Nobody help me! Nobody fucking touch me! I'll be fine, leave me alone!"

We all continue to watch Steven crawl through the floor. He continues to crawl for several seconds, as he makes his way to the counter in the living room. Steven to my surprise takes the remaining two contracts off the table. Steven continues to cry, as he picks up the contract, and takes out his pen to sign it. He begins to write his name, but he abruptly stops.

"I...I can't do it. I'm sorry. I can't. Nothing against the rest of you guys. It's me, it's not you. If you guys want to do it, fine. But I can't do it, you guys just don't understand."

Aaron gets down on the floor where Steven is, and begins to kiss him on the forehead. They continue to embrace and comfort each other for a minute, as the rest of us watch them. Aaron then takes one of the contracts out Steven's hand, and then signs it. As he's singing the paper, Aaron is whispering out to Steven very softly.

"It's okay. I know how private you are, and I understand. But you have to sign. Think of all the people that are going to be proud of you for signing. You have to do it. Come on."

Steven then looks at Aaron for a few seconds, crying heavily. Aaron then takes Steven's glasses off. Aaron starts to clean them with a napkin. Steven then responds to Aaron softly.

"I'm going to regret doing this tomorrow, I already know. People are going to gossip about us. This whole thing doesn't make any sense. But you know what, everyone else is happy, and proud of their stories. I have to be a man, and sign. Why am I doing this?"

Aaron smiles at Steven, and hands him his glasses back. Steven then finally signs the contract, laughing to himself as he's signing it. Aaron then hands me the contracts that he and Steven signed. Steven then starts to immediately cry once again, and he is also laughing at the same time. I'm unsure if he's crying out of joy, or if he's crying because he's scared as to what may happen, or maybe it's a mix of both.

Harry, Carl and Frank then help Steven off the floor, and they place him on the sofa. Steven is continuing to cry, as Aaron tries to console him. Harry then immediately gets up off the sofa, and walks to my kitchen. He takes a beer out of the refrigerator, and hands it to Steven.

"Here man, it looks like you can use one of these. It's going to be alright. Like I said, none of us are 100 percent comfortable with having out stories out, but it's going to be fine. We are all probably going to be seen as freaks, but at least we're proud of being freaks right?"

Harry smiles at Steven, and Steven smiles back at Harry. I take all the contracts, putting them together. All of the guys signed, and although it took a lot of strength, I'm glad that it all got situated. In the process, I had not one, but two proposals at my house. Now that all the men have signed, I start to tell the men what the process is going to be at this point.

"Okay, so I'm going to keep in touch with you guys for the following weeks. I have all of your contact information, and all of your addresses. There is going to be a just a single cameraman, that will come film you guys. It won't be a big film crew. Don't worry."

I continue to explain the rest of the protocol and procedure to the men.

"He basically wants to see what you guys do on a typical day. They may want to film you at work, and film you guys out having fun. Just pretend the camera guy isn't there. It's all candid, and it's to make the whole experience more realistic."

I guess in a sense, it would be like a reality show almost. It would have elements of it being a documentary; but having them all filmed, myself included, allowed for the project to be more entertaining. It would allow the viewer of the film and the project to gain a better understanding to how these guys live their daily lives. I didn't want to have a big camera crew come, it's only going to be the solitary cameraman. I continue to explain everything to the men.

"Then after you guys are filmed, I will take the footage that the cameraman took of you guys on a typical day, and I will edit in clips of your actual raw projects that you guys saw tonight. Once I put them all together, it will come out flawlessly."

Steven then decides to ask me a question that he is curious about.

"I wanted to know if we were going to be allowed to see the what the final version was going to look like, before you send it to the film festival. I don't want anything published, I'm not comfortable with. I also don't want the cameraman being nosy when he comes in our home."

I understood completely what Steven was talking about. I had to let Steven know that the whole point of the project was that I wanted the guys to showcase their stories and their lives with as little filter as possible. But I did understand where Steven was coming from. I then decided to respond to Steven, explaining that I will let him see the final version of their segment.

"Oh yes. I will let all the guys see what their story is going to look like when the audience watches the project. If there is anything you want me to edit out, I will. But I do ask that you guys be a little open minded, as the whole point of the project is to talk about the juicy details."

Steven nodded his head, and he was satisfied with the answer I gave to him. I then continued to relay everything about the project, so that the men were on the same level.

"The film festival will be held weeks from now. I know that's a short time frame, but everything is going to be fine. The cameraman should arrive to film you guys if not next week, the week after next for sure. I will then tell you when the film is ready after that."

The guys are now all updated, and aware of how the system is going to work. It was now late into the night at this point, and the guys all remained in my house. I explained everything about the film festival, and they all signed the consent contract as well. I then allowed the guys to sleepover at my house.

It was creeping up past midnight. It made more sense for them all to stay. I had a bunch of food and beverages and other refreshments for the guys. I also had enough space for them to stay. The guys were comfortable being in my house, and were all receptive into spending the night. Being that everything was all cleared up, I wanted to take this time to talk about all the stories the guys watched, and how they felt about it. This was the perfect time, as all the profiles are still fresh in our minds. I decided to go first and talk about my story to the rest of the guys.

"I wanted to discuss our stories for a bit. I'll go first I guess. I want to say that I don't wish ex gay therapy onto anyone. It was in fact a living hell, and I'm still scarred from what I had to experience. I suffered from a lot of self-hate at that time, but I'm okay now."

Harry then decided to respond back to me directly after that.

"Yeah, I know how you feel, because I felt the same way. I wasn't happy with how I was, and I thought Troy was annoying, and I feel bad about bullying him at first. I was dealing with my own issues; being mad at the world, and I took them out on Troy. He's now my fiancé, so. Ha-Ha."

Jerald then offers his own reflection of my story.

"What I liked about your story Gary, was that you were strong enough to escape. I know having your friend Connor die brought pain to you, and you blamed being gay for that. I'm happy that you escaped from what you went through, and you're still here."

Directly after Jerald offered his opinion, Jamal then had something to say.

"With religion and being gay, I know it's a tough issue to talk about, and I know you had your Mormon values, and you didn't get to experience everything you wanted to. You're still here Gary, and you are now happy with yourself. You can rebuild your life through all of that."

Troy then said what he felt about my story.

"I'm just happy that you're safe. You managed to get away from that ex gay therapy place. From what you experienced, it's something that I wouldn't go through, nor would I want anyone else to go through. It's very courageous and brave of you, to share your story of survival."

Immediately after Troy said what he said, Frank then reflected on my story.

"Being transgender, I sometimes had thoughts of denial when I was young, and I sometimes would go to bed wondering if I could convert myself from being transgender. Although I wouldn't be happy if I couldn't be myself, so I learned to accept myself completely."

Ralph then offered his own opinion on my story.

"The thing that brought me into your story, was how conservative you were growing up. You weren't immersed in many things that your peers were, and you were totally devoted to your religion. I think that may have turned you into the grounded person you are now."

Carl was the next to say what was on his mind about my story.

"Losing your friend Connor made you sad. It also made you feel bitter too I guess. You shouldn't have blamed yourself for Connor's death, but I understand why you felt the way you did. You had no other choice to make to deal with that, but conversation therapy. It's sad."

Aaron was the next person to reflect about my story.

"I don't know much about the Mormon faith, but it was something very serious for you. Trying to battle between your sexuality and that is difficult. I'm glad that you were able to find a way to balance your religion issues, along with your sexuality."

Steven was the last person to talk about my story, offering his opinion on it.

"Gary, your story touched me because we were both dorky and nerdy growing up, and we felt out of place from everyone else. The ex-gay therapy you went through was interesting, because I even contemplated it myself. I'm happy that you had the strength to tell us your story."

I then decided to thank all of the guys for reflecting on my story. They didn't have to open up to me, but I'm glad that they were honest.

"I appreciate that you guys. It was only fair me to give my story as well. Why would I make you guys reveal your stories, and I didn't reveal my own story? Thank you all very much."

I figured that we should go in the same order as we did when I showed the profile videos. So that means Troy would be the next to reflect on his story. Troy then began to speak.

"I remember the first day I met Harry, he was just an ordinary bully. I never in my life would have imagined this man would be so close to me, and that he would propose to me like he did tonight. I love Harry very much, and I'm so thankful to have him in my life."

Harry then kisses Troy on the lips, and responds to him.

"Yeah; life is strange like that. It's too bad I don't feel the same way. I wish I never met you. You're such an annoying little brat, and you get on my nerves all the time. Ha-Ha."

Troy laughs at Harry, and they both kiss. Jamal then gave his reflection.

"I find your story amazing Troy, as you ended up forming a relationship with a guy who bullied you in school. I don't know how many people can say that, but I guess you're one of the few that can. It's kinda strange and interesting, but yeah."

Jerald then offered his opinion on Troy's story.

"Troy, I relate to you in many ways. We're both flamboyant and crazy, and I don't know if I would have done the same things as you. But it seems you don't regret what you did, and it worked out for you. The issues you went through in your life, you later recovered from."

Frank talks about Troy's story after Jerald.

"What about when Harry's friends tried to possibly kill you? I know that was a thrilling experience to be in. I don't know what stunt they were trying to pull, but you could have gotten seriously hurt as a result of it. It's a good thing you weren't hurt over that."

Steven then responds to Troy's story.

"I do find it very strange how you and Harry came together. It's going to be weird explaining that you met your partner from him bullying you at school. I guess I should be the last one to talk I suppose. Your story was still interesting Troy."

Aaron then gave his opinion on Troy's story.

"I know the feeling you have with Harry. It's the same feeling that I was having with Steven. It's hard to explain to outsiders, but it's okay. I don't judge you Troy. Be happy with yourself, and be true to yourself as well. You're a kind person."

Ralph then gave his reflections on Troy's story.

"You are definitely a strange kid, but the decisions you made were all part of your story, and lessons that you had to learn for yourself. You found support in Harry, and it worked out perfect for you. Thank you for sharing your story Troy."

Carl was the next to offer his reflection on Troy's story.

"Don't let anyone get you down Troy. You are a nice guy, and what I liked about your story, was how bold you were. That will get you far in life, and despite the hard times you went through, you're still a strong individual."

I decided to go last, and I will go last with offering my reflections to all the stories.

"Troy, what I will say about you, is that you have a kind childish personality. From what I gathered from you, is that you're a risk taker, and you're more of a free spirit. You seek sort of a protective vibe from Harry, and you both make a great pair."

Going in order, Harry was the next to reflect on his story.

"Let me say first of all. Troy is a pain, and I take back that proposal. The wedding is off. Ha-Ha. Kidding aside, yeah my story was tough for me to talk about, and I'm still blushing and embarrassed over it; but I don't care anymore. I don't."

Troy then kisses Harry on the lips, and reflects on Harry's story.

"I love you so much Harry. Thank you for telling them your story. I know you care about your brothers a lot, and I know you value family very much. You're my teddy bear, and I know you're always going to be here for me. Even if I get on your nerves. I love you."

Carl then offers his reflection on Harry's story.

"I didn't like the way you bullied Troy at first, but I guess had you not bullied him, you guys would have never gotten together. So it's a catch 22 I suppose. But you love each other."

Frank then explains his reflection on Harry's story.

"When you talked about your brother Louie getting hurt, I found that interesting. That's the part of your story that impacted me, and will probably impact others as well."

Steven then reflected on Harry's story.

"Yeah, when you bullied Troy, that didn't set well with me. But I don't know. It kinda doesn't matter at this point, I don't know. I know you and Troy love each other."

Aaron reflected on Harry's story directly after that.

"Harry, I think you're a big gentle giant, and I appreciate that about you. Troy is very lucky to have a guy such as yourself to be there always."

Jamal then reflected on Harry's story.

"The part I don't get, is how love is strange is like that. I would never think you and Troy ever had a chance from the way things were originally, but I was proven wrong I guess."

Jerald then gave his opinion on Harry's story.

"You guys are really cute for each other, and I'm happy the both of you shared your stories. Yeah it's weird that the bully fell in love with the guy he bullied with, but oh well."

Ralph then gave his reflections on Harry's story.

"We all react differently to situations. What may not have worked for me, may work for someone else, and you can flip that. Harry, I give you credit for sharing your story man."

I then gave my own personal reflections to Harry.

"Harry, what I learned from you, is that looks definitely can be deceiving. I would never assume you were as nice as you truly are. Someone else mentioned, I believe it was Aaron that you were a gentle giant, that is absolutely true. You'll do well in life Harry."

Continuing on in the order, Aaron was next to reflect on his story.

"Wow, where do I begin? I want to first of all say that I love you Steven, and I don't know what I'd do in my life without you. Next, being a gay Asian man was difficult, but I am happy with my life. Steven is a handful, but I love him so much. Life is good."

Aaron then bends down and kisses Steven, and Steven responds to Aaron.

"Even though I can be angry at times, and I know I'm difficult to deal with, I know you love me Aaron, and you put up with me anyways. Thank you, and I love you too."

Troy then reflects on Aaron's story.

"Aaron, I have no idea what it's like being a minority gay man, but I have to hand it to you. You have a lot of courage and strength, and your love for Steven is wonderful."

Jamal then offers his reflections on Aaron's story.

"Very risky to have a crush on your teacher, and to actually go along with it. I know all about forbidden crushes myself. You are a great person Aaron, thank you for your story."

Jerald then reflects on Aaron's story.

"I know you care about Steven, and your story is very strange to tell. So I support you, because the love you share with Steven really means something."

Frank then discusses his opinion on Aaron's Story.

"Forming a relationship with your teacher is very risky. I don't know. I guess it worked for you, and I'm not going to complain. I am so happy for you both."

Carl then gives his reflections on the story.

"Taking care of Steven must be hard for you, and I know you don't complain Aaron. You are a good person because of that. Helping out your man, I know that's right."

Ralph then reflects on the story.

"Hmm, I'll say that Aaron you're an intelligent guy, and I appreciate your story."

Harry then offers his reflections related to Aaron's story.

"What I want to say directed to you Aaron; make sure you always take care of that man you have. He's unfortunately handicapped, and you're going to have to be there for him always. You can do it."

I then offer my own reflections to Aaron.

"Aaron, I understand being Chinese and gay comes with issues, but you're still strong. I want you to not let others dictate you, and continue to power on with your life."

Steven was the next to reflect on his story.

"I don't have much to say. That was my story. I love you Aaron. That's all."

Aaron kisses Steven passionately, and he responds back to him.

"I love you too Steve, and I'm always going to be here for you."

Frank then reflected on Steven's story.

"I don't know about the teacher student crush thing, but you guys are so sweet for each other. I can't complain or say anything bad. I wish the both of you the best. Thank you Steven."

Carl then gave his reflections on the story.

"Steven, you have a bad temper at times, but don't take Aaron for granted. You are lucky to have him, like he's lucky to have you. Both of you are cute as a couple."

Jerald then reflected on Steven's story.

"Steven, thank you for sharing your story. I know you were reluctant at first, but thank you for having a change of heart. I was so moved by your story, and it was very nice."

Jamal then gave his opinions on the story.

"Thank you Steven for talking about your story. That was brave of you."

Ralph then reflected on Steven's story.

"Steven, I'm sorry that you can no longer walk anymore. I am blind myself, so I know what it's like to have a part of you taken away. But be strong man. If you want to hang out anytime, I'll give you my number, and we can hang out. Thank you Steven."

Troy then gave his opinions on Steven's story.

"I want to say I'm proud of you. Bald is beautiful by the way. Ha-Ha. Thank you Steven for sharing your story."

Harry then gave his reflections on the story.

"Yeah to ditto what Ralph said, if you want to hang out anytime Steven, I'm game."

I was the last person to offer my reflections on Steven.

"Okay, Steven I will say that you do have temper issues. But you're a kind man. I understand you can't walk, but please mind yourself. We are all here for you, and thank you."

Going with the order still, Jerald was the next to reflect.

"I don't want to take too much of your time. I'm happy to have met Carl, and I'm glad that I made my dreams come true. I hope you all enjoyed my story, and that's it."

Carl then hugs Jerald, and speaks back at him, kissing him.

"Oh Jerald, I love you, and that's all I wanted to say. I love you so much."

Jamal then gives his reflections that he had to Jerald.

"Jerald, you and I are both black gay men, and we relate so much. I want to continue to speak with you once this is over. There are some projects I want us to work on."

Troy then gave his reflections on the story.

"Being that you're into fashion Jerald, I was wondering if you would help me, as I plan on doing drag soon, and I don't know how to sew. If you could teach me, that would be nice."

Harry then gave his reflections on the story.

"Jerald, you're a brave young man. Thank you for sharing your story with us all."

Aaron then reflected on Jerald's story.

"Yeah Jerald, I want to hang out soon. I loved your story. Thank you for sharing it."

Steven gave his opinions towards Jerald's story.

"What I liked about you Jerald, was how you took up knitting at a young age. I know how to knit as well, so that's interesting. Thank you for your story young man."

Frank then reflected on Jerald's story.

"I liked your artistry Jerald. That's a great quality you have. I loved your story."

Ralph gave his reflections to Jerald's story.

"Jerald, you remind me of Jamal in certain ways. You're very artistic. Thank you."

I then started to give my own personal reflections I had with Jerald.

"Jerald, I will say that I saw your fashion designs, and you are very talented. Please keep this talent dearly to you, and understand your self worth. You are fantastic Jerald. Thank you."

Carl was the next to give his reflections.

"I just want to say, thank you all for hearing my story. I hope it helped you all. Thanks."

Jerald then kisses Carl on the lips, and speaks to him.

"Carl, I love you very much, and I like how crazy you are at times. We've been through a lot, and I loved hearing your story. I can't get enough of you Carl, and I love you so, so much."

Jamal then gives his reflections on Carl's story.

"Carl, I saw your mural in the street, and never knew that you were the artist behind it. You're so talented man. Your story was so nice."

Aaron then gives his reflections on the story.

"Carl, I'm sorry that your brother Mark passed away. I know you're going to use him as your muse, and I don't blame you. You're a good artist, and you're a good guy as well Carl."

Steven then gave his opinion towards Carl's story.

"Uh Carl, you and I don't have much in common, but I liked your story man."

Frank then gave his opinion towards Carl's story.

"Carl, I want you to draw a tattoo for me. I want to talk to you later about this. Your art skills are very phenomenal, and that's a good talent you have. I loved your story."

Troy then reflected on Carl's story.

"I want to come to your art shows Carl. You're a good artist. I know you get tired of us telling you that, but I'm not telling a white lie. Your art is really special, and you can work magic with your art. Thanks."

Harry then gave his opinions on Carl's story.

"Carl, we should definitely kick it sometimes. I don't know if you like to hunt and fish, but I really want to hang out with you whenever you have some free time. Let's keep in touch."

Ralph then reflected on Carl's story.

"Carl, you have a vibrant and wild personality, and it's not really something that's my style. But it works for you, and your art is splendid. Thank you for sharing your story Carl."

I then gave my own reflections that I had towards Carl.

"Carl, I will say that you are one of the most talented artists I have ever come across. I know that you miss your brother Mark, but he's proud of you. I love your spirit Carl. Thank you."

Jamal was the next person in the order to reflect on his story.

"Alright, I want to thank you all for allowing me to share my story. I hope you enjoyed it. I know some parts were cheesy, but it's okay. I love Ralph, and I love all of you. Thank you."

Ralph stood up, and kissed Jamal on the lips. He then spoke to him.

"Jamal, I love you so much, and I don't know where I would be without you. You help me so much. I'm blind, and I can't see anymore, but I have you, and everything is fine."

Jerald then reflected on Jamal's story.

"Being that we are both African American gay men, we definitely need to stick together Jamal. I would love to do something with you in the future. I'm going to give you my information, and we are definitely going to connect in the future. Thank you for your story."

Frank then gave his opinions to Jamal's story.

"I really love how you stuck with Ralph, despite the fact he lost his vision. That didn't matter to you. I know the love you have with Ralph is real. Thank you."

Troy was the next to reflect on Jamal's story.

"Jamal, when you talked about growing up not knowing who your parents were, that was sad. I'm happy that you eventually found a family that adopted you. I give you a lot of credit Jamal, and you inspire me so much. I love how you take care of Ralph too. Thanks."

Aaron then gave his reflections to Jamal's story.

"Jamal. I loved hearing your story, and I would like to hang out with you in the future as well. I love your kind energy, and you're a wonderful person Jamal. Thank you for your story."

Steven then reflected on Jamal's story.

"You're an awesome young man Jamal, and you give inspiration to us all; from how kind and compassionate you are. You take care of Ralph. Thank you very much for your story."

Harry then gave his reflections to Jamal.

"Jamal, your story was nice. I want to thank you for sharing it with all of us."

Carl then gave his opinions on Jamal's story.

"Jamal, I like how kind and considerate you are. I understand how rough of a life you had when you were young, but you didn't let that break you. I appreciate you telling your story man."

I then gave the reflections I had towards Jamal.

"Alright Jamal, I will say that I do enjoy your curiosity, and I love how mature you seem. You are a young man, but have the mind of someone much older. I love how well you take care of Ralph. I appreciate you for telling your story to us, and I thank you.

Ralph was the next person to reflect on his story.

"Okay. So even though I don't enjoy being blind, I have learned to adapt and accept being blind. I hope you all enjoyed my story, and you can use it to better your lives. I love Jamal very much, and this guy has really been my savior through all of this. Thank you all again."

Jamal kisses Ralph, and responds to him.

"I love you so much Ralph, and I know you get tired of me saying how much I love you, but I really do. I'm just as lucky to have you , as you're lucky to have me. Our love is very strong, and I support you. You're a lovely man to me, and I'm completely blessed to have you."

Carl then offers his own reflections towards Ralph's story.

"I don't know what it's like to not see Ralph, but you're a strong man to still be here. Your story was interesting, and I loved it very much. What a strong man, thank you."

Harry then reflects on Ralph's story.

"I'm going to slightly copy what Carl said. I can't relate to being blind, and I know it must be difficult for you to live like that. But you still have hope and you fight through your blindness Ralph. You're a strong man because of that, and thank you for sharing your story."

Steven then offers his own opinions towards Ralph's story.

"Ralph, I'm going to hang out with you after this. We are both handicapped. I cannot walk, and you can't see, but we're going to keep in touch man. Thank you."

Jerald then gives his reflections on Ralph's story.

"I want to say your story was very nice Ralph. The bond that you have with Jamal is nice, and the both of you love each other very much.

I appreciate how strong you are Ralph, and you're going to be fine. Thank you for sharing your story with us Ralph."

Aaron then gives his reflections on the story.

"Ralph, I know it's tough not being able to see. Steven also deals with issues in his life, and I help him out. You and Steven are going to keep in touch with each other. Thank you for allowing us to hear your story Ralph."

Frank then reflected on the story.

"Whenever you want to hang out Ralph, I'm here. I was moved by your story very much, and I would love to get with you sometime after this. Thank you for sharing your story Ralph."

Troy then reflected on Ralph's story.

"What I want to say to you Ralph, is that I love how strong you are. Not being able to see anymore must have been tough for you. You didn't let that bother you, and you kept on going. I love the relationship you have with Jamal as well. I want to thank you for sharing your story."

I then gave the reflections that I had towards Ralph.

"Ralph, I like how business orientated you are. You are a man that's very intelligent, and you go for what you want. Being blind is a setback yes, but you adapted your life beside that. I really loved hearing your story, and I know it will motivate and impact many."

Frank was the last to reflect on his story.

"Being a transgender man, I have been through a lot in my life. I struggled with my own identity being born in the wrong body. But I'm comfortable with myself now, and I am no longer confused. I'm happy that I am living life, the way I was supposed to live it. Thank you."

Harry gave his reflections towards Frank's story.

"I don't know what it's like being transgender Frank, but I know what it's like being bisexual, and growing up feeling different. You're a strong man. Don't let anyone hold you back. Live life the way you want to. Laura is proud of you too. Thank you for sharing your story."

Steven then reflected on Frank's story.

"You are going to motivate a lot of people Frank. A lot of bigoted people are going to shut up once they hear your story. Being a police officer too. There is no limit with you Frank. I loved hearing your story, and I can't thank you enough for sharing it."

Ralph then gave his opinions on Frank's story.

"Frank, I liked your courage, and how you didn't let your situation in life stop you from doing what you had to do. I can't relate to being transgender, but I love how strong you are, and how you dealt with your friend Ivan, being killed in the line of duty. Thank you for your story."

Jamal then reflected on Frank's story.

"Frank, I love how much of a role model you are going to be to other transgender people. You are motivating so many other people with the way you live your life. I love how you're a police officer as well. I loved hearing your story, and you are such an inspiration. Thank you."

Jerald then gave his reflections on Frank's story.

"Frank, I love how despite being born in the wrong body, you still did all that you could to make sure that you lived life happy. I know you were struggling, but you have come a long way. We are all proud of you, and thank you for your story."

Aaron then reflected on Frank's story.

"Frank, I love how you didn't give up. You were born in a gender that wasn't the one you felt you truly were. You had to deal with your mother passing away, your father passing away, your friend Ivan's death. You're still here, and became a cop. Thank you for your story Frank."

Carl then gave his reflections on Frank's story.

"I would love to design a tattoo for you Frank. You're an amazing man, and you make so many people proud. I know being a cop is a tough job, and you are a transgender cop as well. Very good. Yeah, we'll talk later about the tattoo design. You're a very strong guy Frank."

Troy then gave his opinions on Frank's story.

"We are all proud of you Frank, and I know you have gone through so much in your life. Being born in the wrong gender. You kept on going with life, and didn't give up. You motivate and inspire us all Frank. Thank you for allowing us to listen to your story."

I then gave my reflections that I had towards Frank.

"Frank, I picked you to be in this project, because of how unique your story is. I'm not transgender, but I felt so warm hearing your story. Understanding what you had to deal with. I give you so much credit for that Frank. Thank you very much."

Now that we have all reflected our stories, it was getting really late into the night. Most of the guys then all went to sleep. They all agreed to do the film festival, and things were wrapping up. The guys that remained awake, mostly drank and ate up all of the snacks and food that I had out. I soon drifted off to sleep myself later that night.

The next morning, all the guys were up, and I told them to all come to my backyard. They had no idea what I was doing, But I brought them all to my backyard, to take a photo. I set my camera on auto snapshot, and we all posed for a picture. Ralph, Frank, Carl, Harry and myself were all standing. Jamal, Aaron, Steven, Jerald and Troy were all sitting. The camera took our photo. I later plugged my digital camera into the computer and saw the photo, and loved how beautiful it was. All ten of us were all together. I said I would make a print for all the guys later. I said goodbye to all of the guys, and they all went home.

EPILOGUE:

This project taught me quite a lot. Not only with my own personal story, but listening to the stories of the other nine guys as well. The guys all signed the consent form to participate in the film festival, and I was starting to plan for that. The videographer that I hired for the project, was going to visit my house first, and then he was going to film the guys in the order that I interviewed them. I started to clean up, making sure my house looked nice if it was going to be included in a documentary. The cameraman was going to spend the entire day with each of us. The whole point of this, was I wanted to have a more creative feel in the final version of the film I'm going to send to the festival judges. I could have just sent all the raw video files that I edited and called it a day, but that wasn't good enough for me.

I thought it would be interesting if I edited in the footage the professional cameraman took, and mixed that in with the raw interviews that I did. I also wanted to do more editing towards the interviews. When I showed the video clips to the guys, there were still some parts that I felt didn't need to be included, and I could take out. I didn't want the film to be too long, but on the other hand, I didn't want it to be short either. It had to be the exact length, so that it was not only entertaining, but it didn't drag on as well. The film festival was going to be here in several weeks. The final project had to be completed at that point, so I had to quickly get everything in proper order. I waited in my living room for the videographer to come. The outfit that I was going to wear, was a simple suit and tie. I know I may have been overdressed, but I didn't care. That was the impression that I wanted to give when he arrived. The production company did not tell me the exact time that the cameraman was going to arrive. They only asked that we are home, or at the location we said we would be at, when he does arrive; so he can quickly set up, and start filming.

The cameraman finally arrived, and knocked on my door. I let him in, and he began to set up his cameras in my living room. As I already told and explained, he was the only one present. It wasn't a big camera crew or anything like that to make me or the other guys uncomfortable. It was only one guy who was very professional in what he did. The camera guy was very handsome and kinda scruffy I guess.

He reminded me of Harry so much, he looked just like him. His name was Rhett Nickerson. He had red hair, and he was rather tall and stocky looking. The cameraman told me to be myself, and to not be nervous. He said this isn't a television show or a movie. There are no scripts or rehearsals. Be completely myself at all times. He explained for me to not try to act like someone I'm not. It is going to come across that way on camera. After he gave me the lowdown, he turned his camera on, and began to film. I then started to introduce myself while I was being filmed.

"My name is Gary Swanson. I am thirty years old. I from Utah, but I now live in Los Angeles, and this is my story of how a Mormon kid, turned into an open minded psychologist."

I then started to mention things that I didn't when I gave my story in the raw footage. I started to show family and childhood pictures of myself. I let the camera man film the bible that I kept from Connor. I still had it. I then let the camera see all the outfits and uniforms that I had to wear when I was at Mormon school. The nametag that I had, because I was trained to be an elder. That was the main purpose of this. I hope that you get the idea of the cameraman now. Soon after this, I ended up leaving my house, and the camera man rode in my car with me. I was going to allow him to film me going to the local Mormon church that was nearby my house. Even though my relationship with my Mormon faith is complicated, I still held a lot of past history from being Mormon. I arrived at the church, and to be respectful, I didn't go inside and have him film me. I didn't have permission from the church to do that. What I did do, was have him film me walking outside of the building, and I discussed my religion and things like that. I knew I would go and edit all these clips in later, so it tied in well. Being at the church was tough for me, because I instantly got reminded all of the memories that I had. I knew incorporating him filming me at the church, would make my story shine better.

After leaving the church, I still had a couple hours left for the cameraman to film me. I quickly thought of a fun segment that could be used in the final version when I edit the project. I was going to cook a Greek dish that my mother would cook. I was going to cook some Gyro's with deep fried potato meatballs. It was a complex dish, but I had it down alright. I had him film me preparing the dish, and I mentioned how significant it was to my family, and my culture. My mother was an immaculate cook, and I loved all the dishes she made. During this time I explained how my mother would cook dishes for us, and my extended family.

"On Sundays, my mother would cook dishes such as this. She always put her best into them, as she knew she was going to be judged harshly by the rest of the family, if the food wasn't good. But it was always good, and she always delivered perfection. This dish in particular."

The segment of me cooking, I thought was a good touch. This would be the final thing the camera man would capture of me, before he ended wrapping everything up. I had him film the finished dish that I created, which turned out quite well. Then he cut his cameras off. Directly after filming ended, the camera man and I ate the dish I made, and it was good. Once we finished eating, the cameraman left my house, and said he will give me the footage of all the guys he filmed, after he did his own edits to them, before I could see them. That was fine by me.

The following day, Rhett the videographer, spent the day filming Troy and Harry. The cameraman actually met up with them at

Louie's restaurant. Troy was the one who was the first to speak to the cameraman, and filmed his introduction.

"I'm Troy, and this is my partner Harry. He's like my protector and my bodyguard. We're at Harry's brother's restaurant, the food here is lovely. Here are his brothers."

Harry's brothers, Louie, Leif and Harvey then introduced themselves to the camera. Harry then took the cameraman behind the scenes of the restaurant, and began to speak with him.

"This is my brother Louie's restaurant. This was his dream, and he made it come true. I work here, and I help him out sometimes. Louie's a great chef, you have to see him action."

Rhett then filmed Louie at work, and making several different dishes, and he filmed Louie making his signature T-bone steak. After the camera man filmed Louie doing his job, he very briefly spoke with all of the men, and Rhett wrapped up this segment of filming in the restaurant.

A short time later, Harry, Troy, and Harry's brothers then went to a nearby park for a picnic, and Rhett began to film them there. They basically relayed several things that were mentioned in their interviews, and also things I didn't know. For example, I had no idea that Harry was his brothers won first place in a fishing and hunting tournament recently. Trivial things such as that. As they were at the park, they began to speak about more of their family life. How all of them were from the south, and moved to California, due to Louie's restaurant dream.

The next segment he filmed, was at the grocery store that Harry worked at. For privacy, the front of the store wasn't filmed, but Harry was mostly filmed in the back of the store, working as a butcher. This was Harry's main job, but sometimes on the weekends, he would work at his brother's restaurant. The camera man shortly after that, filmed the department store that Troy worked at. Both of them got equal time related to their jobs. The final segment that was filmed with Harry and Troy, was late into the evening. Troy, Harry and his brothers were all in the backyard of their house, playing football. Despite only having one arm, Louie was playing along with them as well. Troy nor Harry, didn't tell me they had a large St. Bernard dog, but you could see the dog frolicking in the backyard sporadically between shots. The cameraman then wrapped things up.

The day after that, the camera man then started to film Aaron and Steven. Due to privacy, and to be respectful, I asked Steven if there was anything off limits that he didn't want the camera to show, especially being delicate that he's in a wheelchair. Steven explained to me all the things he didn't want filmed, and I understood. Rhett arrived at Aaron and Steven's home early in the morning, and at this time, they were already ready for the day. Aaron was preparing breakfast. Aaron was making blueberry pancakes, and Steven was at the kitchen table, making lesson plans for his students. Aaron then began to speak to Rhett.

"This is usually how it is every morning. I make Steve breakfast, and he's always preparing his lessons and lectures for the day. I feed him, and then he's off to work."

Steven wasn't really interacting with Rhett that much, which disappointed me. I don't know if he was camera shy, or what. But Steven was really disappointing me. Maybe he wasn't feeling it that day. Steven did manage to interact a little with Rhett though.

"Yeah, Aaron takes care of me, and doesn't let me leave the house without eating. Sometimes we do go out for breakfast. But Aaron makes me a special breakfast usually."

Aaron finishes making the pancakes, and they both begin to eat breakfast. While they are eating, they begin to talk about their lives briefly, and mostly discuss things that I already knew from their interview sessions. Even though Steven was not being active, Aaron was speaking quite a lot, so I was hoping that despite the fact Steven was holding back, the fact Aaron was very engaging, it may serve as a distraction.

Aaron and Steven then left their house, and due to HIPAA laws, Aaron cannot be filmed at work, since he works in a hospital, as a nurse. But the campus Steven worked at was filmed, and the cameraman picked up several shots of himself and Aaron, in his classroom, and at his office. Once this segment was over, the following segment consisted of Aaron and Steven talking about the school shooting that they were involved in the courtyard of the University campus. It was an event they don't like bringing up or discussing, but it was something that changed Steven's life completely.

Aaron and Steven then left out the campus, and they then went back to their residence. At home, Aaron then began to tell the cameraman, how he transfers Steven in and out the wheelchair, so he can sit in a regular chair. Steven doesn't always like to be in his wheelchair if he can avoid it, and he likes to sit in normal chairs like everyone else.

Aaron then explained to the cameraman, how he gets Steven in and out of bed every single day. It's a special technique that he figured out, which at first, he had many issues with. But Aaron is able to get Steven out of bed, or onto bed, and in and out of his wheelchair from that quite easily. Aaron and Steven were then in their living room, and Aaron began to show exercises that he does to help Steven. With Aaron being a nurse, he was quite knowledgeable on the human body. He is also Steven's official caretaker, so he knows what he's doing.

Steven again was quiet, and wasn't that engaging, but Aaron was explaining how even though Steven cannot walk, he still needs to exercise and move his body around. So Aaron has figured out several floor exercises that Steven does out of his wheelchair, that helps him. After Rhett filmed Aaron giving Steven his exercises, the next footage that I saw, was of Aaron and Steven eating pizza that they must have ordered. This was the final segment that was filmed, and it was mostly Aaron talking about how he's happy with Steven, and it was a cute final thing Rhett captured. Then he wrapped filming up.

The next guys to be filmed was Jerald and Carl. The camera man first met up with them, at the mural that Carl painted, in honor of his brother Mark's passing. Carl explained how important the piece was, and how much effort he put into it.

"This was for my brother, and I had to get permission from the city to paint it. It was an adventure painting it, and a lot of people were curious about it. It came out very nice."

As for their request, I asked the cameraman not to film the secret spot that Carl's brother Mark did his art at, but he did manage to capture them going to the area that Mark was killed at. The abandoned train tracks that Mark was doing his street art at. To where he sadly got his foot caught the tracks, and was hit by a train. This area actually was not far from the area that Carl did his mural, in honor of Mark at. The cameraman picked up Jerald and Carl walking all over downtown LA, and Carl talking about different art pieces that he liked in the city.

Rhett also managed to capture the storefront that Carl and Mark had. It was now a defunct and vacant storefront, but it was the location that they had their art collective, which was vandalized one night. Most of their footage consisted of Carl educating us about art, which was okay, but I don't know. I guess I was expecting something different. It was still wonderful, but most of the focus was like it being an art education show. The next footage consisted of Jerald explaining the exact area that he was mugged and gay bashed one time, and when Carl came to rescue him.

"This was the corner. I was walking home, and these guys all of a sudden decided to rob me and beat me up. Carl was standing on the other end of the sidewalk, and rescued me. The rest is history, but I'll always remember this corner in Downtown LA, where I first met Carl."

I enjoyed this segment very well, and it added more of a visual feel to their story. I knew when I go back to edit everything together, this will flow quite well. After Jerald let Rhett capture the area that he and Carl first met, he then filmed the both of them going to the "Los Angeles County Museum of Art".

The art museum segment meant a lot, because it was the first date that they had together. But again, it kinda dragged on, as Carl lost himself when they were at the museum. Not that it was boring, but Carl can go on and on, when it comes to art. He will not stop talking about art, once he has started. The exhibit that Carl had was still being displayed at the museum, and that was picked up. Jerald and Carl left the museum, and they later went to "In-N-Out Burger" and got some food. They didn't actually go inside the restaurant, he just filmed Carl and Jerald in their car at the drive thru. Once they got their food, the final segment consisted of Rhett filming the both of them inside Carl's art studio, which was also their home.

Once inside the art studio loft, Carl and Jerald began to eat. After they finished eating, Carl began to show the cameraman several of his art pieces, and works that his brother Mark did. Carl then let the camera see some of the projects that he's currently working on. Carl also bragged that he could paint a portrait of Rhett in under two hours.

Rhett accepted the challenge, and Carl began to paint on a canvas at this art station. During this time, Jerald started to show the cameraman, several of the designs that he recently completed, and Jerald also explained his sewing process. What fabrics he decides to pick out, and how he designs a dress. What I liked about Carl's studio loft, was how it not only functioned as his work sanctuary, but where he lived as well. So it was easy for him to do all his projects. He slept where he did all of his work.

Jerald then began to talk to the cameraman more about his fashion design career, and all the fashion awards that he won. Jerald then also points out the art award Carl won; on the night Carl proposed to him. Carl was then all finished with the portrait he painted of Rhett. I couldn't believe he finished it that fast, but he did. Rhett then wrapped everything up.

The day after that, Rhett then began to film Jamal and Ralph. Rhett arrived at their home, and he also filmed Hugo and Vincent as well. Jamal was doing most of the talking, as he gave a tour of their home. Jamal and Ralph lived in a very nice house, and I really liked the pool that they had in the backyard. This was the first time I saw Vincent, as he was cleaning the pool in their residence. Ralph was also sitting in a chair by the pool, and as it was a pretty warm day in Los Angeles. They were all wearing shorts. Jamal then began to speak with Rhett.

"We like to spend a lot of time out here in the back patio. Especially on hot days such as this. I really love the pool, and I swim in it quite a bit. Yes, black people swim, to all the people that have ignorant minds. But yeah, this is my favorite area in the whole entire house."

Jamal then spoke to Rhett some more about things that were discussed in the interviews, and he also mentioned things that I was unaware of. For example, Jamal being a skilled swimmer. Rhett even captured Jamal doing laps in the pool, and he wasn't exaggerating. He was a very good swimmer.

As Jamal is in the pool, Hugo at this time joins the rest of the guys in the backyard pool area, and starts to speak to Rhett. Hugo and Vincent then talk about how they met Ralph when they were all young, and how they appreciate Ralph as a friend. I was wondering when Ralph was going to speak and say something to the camera himself, but I thought in his own time he will I suppose. Most of the footage consisted of Jamal and Ralph by their pool. If this was the area they were most comfortable being filmed at, this was fine by me. The cameraman wanted all of the guys do be themselves, and to do things just as if he wasn't there filming. If this was how Jamal and Ralph typically were, then that was fine. Ralph at this time, began to speak.

"This is how we normally are. We hang out by the pool, and we eat dinner out here quite a bit. We drink, and have parties. We invite friends over sometimes. This is very calm and peaceful for me. I sit out here, and listen to an audiobook or classical music sometimes."

The rest of the segment, included Hugo barbecuing on their grill by the pool. I then noticed that they have invited several guests over. A house party was most likely about to happen. It's not that I was angry at this, but I wanted most of the focus to be on Jamal and Ralph. Not Jamal and Ralph, and tens of other people at this house party. I suppose this is a petty thing to complain and be angry about. Hugo continued to grill on the barbecue girl. I saw some footage of Jamal inside the house, showing all the materials that Ralph uses due to his blindness.

Jamal had many books that were in braille, which he used to teach Ralph. He also explained that Ralph likes his independence quite a bit, so Jamal doesn't get in his way. He does help Ralph from time to time, but Ralph likes to be left on his own usually. I then found out something about Jamal that I didn't know about, and that he knew how to play the flute quite well. This was something that was not hinted, or mentioned in his interviews. Jamal then began to play on his flute quite accurately and I was very impressed. This was something nice to add to Jamal's personality.

Even though there were other people present at their house, Rhett was trying his best to only focus on capturing Jamal and Ralph, which I appreciated. At this time, Ralph was still in the backyard pool area, and explained how he still can see where he is going, despite being blind. He uses his walking stick, and uses his ears and other senses to hear. Ralph was walking along the edge of the swimming pool, and said the reason why he knows where he is going, because he learned to use his other senses while walking. It wasn't easy in the beginning, but he found a way to make it work.

Footage of Hugo and Vincent explaining how Ralph is self-reliant of himself were shown as well. Rhett then captured Jamal and Ralph having their dinner outside in the backyard of their home. Hugo and Vincent were there, along with their guests. This was the final footage that was captured. Jamal as talking about how most of the people here were Ralph's business associates, and they have one of these dinner parties once a month or so. Ralph likes to throw parties, because it makes him feel normal from his blindness, and he wants to live like everyone else does. Rhett then wrapped everything up.

The following day, Rhett then filmed the final guy, Frank. Frank was at his house with Laura, and he was getting ready for the day. He had to go onto patrol for that day. The police department said it was okay for Rhett to film him in his police uniform, and doing his patrol duties. Laura and Frank were in their kitchen, making breakfast. They both were contributing to the meal.

I saw a Siberian Husky in the background of their house. Frank never told me that he had a dog when I interviewed him. It was a very nice dog, and it kept wandering in the shots. Frank and Laura then sat down, and had breakfast, and Frank talked to the cameraman Rhett.

"When I have to do early afternoon patrols, I make sure I have my breakfast. I don't know how long that I'm going to be out. I may not get back home until 12 hours later, and I haven't had anything to eat. So breakfast is an important meal for me."

When Frank and Laura finish eating, Carl then goes into his bedroom, and starts to put his utility belt on. He then puts his gun in the holster. He explains all the things that are on his belt, and the different tools that he uses as a police officer. Frank then kisses Laura goodbye, and gets into his car, driving to the police station.

Rhett captures Frank on his way to the station, and Frank describes that he doesn't have a typical day as a cop. Every single shift is going to be different. His main goal is to fight crime, and to protect and serve the civilians. Once Frank arrives to the police station, Rhett films him signing in to work, and Frank is being filmed sitting through a briefing interview that all officers must partake in before they go out for patrol.

Once the meeting is over, Frank then walks to his squad car, and Rhett follows him inside. Most of the footage consisted of Frank driving across town, and talking about his life. How he grew up being transgender, and unhappy with the way he was born; feeling that he wasn't in the right body.

Frank continues to speak as he's driving around and patrolling the city. Frank then drives to the location that his partner Ivan was shot and killed at. When Frank arrives at the shopping center, he gets out of the squad car, and takes his sunglasses off, and starts to talk to Rhett.

"My best friend and my partner Ivan was killed here. It was a robbery, and we didn't think it would go as bad as it did. There were shots that went back and forth, and I don't know how, but Ivan was killed in the middle of it. He's not here, but I still honor him."

Frank then got back into his squad car, and patrolled around the city more. Frank then for his break, decided to go back to station, and several of Frank's fellow officers in his precinct were interviewed.

They talked about how proud they are of Frank being a transgender police officer, and how brave he is. They look up to him as being one of the best officers that is on the force, and nobody has an issue with him. Frank then talks about him coming out at a live police press conference, and the reaction that followed. Frank doesn't regret coming out, and says he wants to be the voice for those that cannot speak. I completely understand what he means by that. He wants to let people know that they are not alone, and wants to motivate others that are going through the same exact issues that he is going through.

The rest of the footage that Rhett captured of Frank, was at his home. Frank was still in his uniform, and was walking their dog across the block that they live in. Frank then started to talk about his life being a cop, and how stressful and risky it is. Being that his friend Ivan was killed in the line of duty. Frank then returned back to his home, and started to show a few pictures of how he looked before his transition. Explaining how different he was, and how he didn't feel right; being in the body he was born as. Frank then discussed his transition very greatly to Rhett, and how he's completely satisfied with the way he looks now.

He passes himself as a man, and lives his life as a man. What his life was before, isn't important. The way he lives his life now is important. Frank and Laura were then captured eating dinner together. This was the last thing that Rhett filmed, before he wrapped everything up.

The following day after that, Rhett gave me all the footage that he filmed of myself, and the other guys, after he gave his own technical edits. It was now my job to do even more edits of these clips, and I also had to incorporate them into the raw interviews that I took. I didn't have much time to do this as, the film festival was coming up quickly.

I sifted through everything that Rhett captured, and I was happy with what he was able to pick up. I still had to do my own edits to them, but it wasn't that heavy. Once I sat through all the video clips, I then had to begin the difficult part. Meshing all the clips together from what Rhett took, to the raw interviews. They had to piece together well. I had some video editing skills, from when I had to do some stuff for the church in the past. But I wasn't a pro at all. I could have hired someone professional to do this, but I did it myself. Because, what the hell? It was more fun that way I guess.

One technique that I did, was I used a lot of voice overs. I took voice overs from the raw interviews, and included them into the footage that Rhett took. I either muted the video Rhett had, or lowered the volume, and inserted the sound bites from the interviews into those separate clips. It was a great idea, and it worked. I also wanted to make sure all the guys had equal time. I didn't want guy one to have more time in the final film, than another did. I didn't think that was fair. Myself included. I didn't have any more screen time, than the rest of the guys did. Despite that this was my project and my idea; and I was going to be the one that was going to send it into the film festival.

It took me three days, but I was amazed as to how quickly it took me to finish editing the video. I saw my completed project, and I did a few more edits the second time. After watching my project for the second time, I was completely ready. This was going to be the version that the film festival judges were going to see, and the version all the critics and audience were going to see.

I then began to send emails and phone calls to the other nine guys, letting them know when the film festival is going to take place, and where to meet me at. The film festival, was actually held at a concert hall in downtown Los Angeles.

It was a film festival that was strictly for documentaries and anything non fictitious. So this wasn't a film festival for short films, indie films, or anything like that, which had actors and a script. This was only for projects that fell under the documentary and reality range. So that was nice my project didn't have to share the docket with things of an unrelated nature, such as an action film or something.

I was the first to arrive at the film festival. I had to get there early, as the directors of all of the films had to be there first for some reason. The film was going to be directed by me. My name was going to fall under the director credits. Even though the other nine guys also played a role in the project as well, this was going to be billed under my name in the production credits.

I was not getting paid for this, and neither were the other guys. There were no financial benefits to this film. There was an admission price to the film festival, but all the proceeds were going to charities, and to children's cancer hospitals, and other organizations such as that. Eventually, the guys started to arrive at the festival. Frank was the first person to show up, and he arrived with Laura, and his other college friends, Seth and Melvin. I introduced myself to Frank, and the rest of his group.

After Frank arrived, Troy, Harry and Harry's brothers all arrived. I mingled and introduced myself to them. Jerald and Carl soon after showed up, and I spoke with them. Not long after that, Jamal, Ralph, Hugo and Vincent all came to the festival as well. I introduced myself to them, and spoke to them for a bit. I was getting worried as the festival was going to start in fifteen minutes, and Aaron and Steven were still not in attendance.

Maybe they got caught up into traffic? But they had still not arrived. It was now ten minutes until the festival started, and Aaron and Steven were still not here yet. I started to take several nervous sips of my drink, hoping that nothing bad has happened. Finally, Aaron and Steven do arrive, with Aaron pushing Steven in his wheelchair. They were in fact just stuck up in traffic, and that explained why they arrived so late.

The film festival then started, and different films were being shown to the audience. In total, there were six films that were being shown. Each film ranged from 20 minutes to an hour. After each film, there would be an intermission.

A film had to be longer than 20 minutes, and it had to be shorter than an hour. Those were the rules and requirements. I remember the other films in the festival; one was a documentary about a dog that was hit by a car under a highway offramp. The dog was rescued, and it turned out this dog was smart, and knew how to read and do math problems. It was an interesting film.

There was another film being showcased at the festival, that was about fish and other marine life in the Pacific Ocean. Then there was another documentary, in which a guy was researching how intelligent Bonobo apes are. I noticed that every single film was about animals, and myself and the rest of the guys were surprised by that. There were two films that were not related to animals. One short film was about a firefighter who died in the line of duty, and the documentary was about his life. Another short film was about a guy who was stranded on a beach in the Caribbean, after he meandered away from his buddies that he came on vacation with. He was curious, and wanted to see what the islands were like. For two weeks, he managed to survive, by hunting his own food. He finally kept on walking through the islands, until he reached a shore full of people that could help him.

Our project was then shown after that. I didn't know what the reaction of the people watching our project would be, but I knew that they would find it interesting at least. The way I edited the film came out great. I was proud of myself, and it was at a level and caliber of professionalism. I wasn't even a professional video editor, and it came out the way it did. The film in total was a little over an hour.

Which I don't know how in the hell I managed to take hours and hours of footage, to squeeze it into one hour. Both from the raw interviews, and the footage that Rhett took as well. Our film project was the last to be shown in the festival. So once our project was done being shown, the film festival ended, and we were told that the judges would make their decision as to what film won, within the next week.

The following week, I kept on checking the website to see if our film won, and if we didn't win, what film was the one that won the top prize. The day of the results came out on the website, and our film was tied for 2nd place. The other film that we tied with, was the documentary about the monkeys. That wasn't bad; as yeah I really wanted for our project to win, but I can accept this. Two films also tied for 3rd place, which was the documentaries about the guy stranded on the island, and the documentary about the fish and marine life. The documentary about the dog, and the documentary about the firefighter, both tied for 1st place.

After finding out that we didn't win the film festival, I was slightly disappointed, but I was going to take 2nd place with pride. I was happy to find out that our film was going to be screened to several other indie theatres all across the country. Within the coming weeks, I was shocked at the reception that it got, and how well received the film was. People were discussing about it online, and the reviews were very good. The other guys in the project as well were also amazed at the reception they got. People wanted to talk to them on social media, and people were really interested in their stories. They weren't movie star famous no, and the film never had a Hollywood premiere, but it was special in the little niche group that it was involved in. The guys were happy that they were becoming minor celebrities.

I was actually interviewed myself by other production companies that were in Los Angeles area. I was on "KTLA" morning news in Los Angeles, and myself, Carl, Jerald, Jamal, Ralph and Frank were all there. Unfortunately, Aaron, Steven, Harry and Troy were all busy, and couldn't make it. But we had our first live television interview. People were that interested in the impact of our project. I remember that clips of our short film then started to make their way online, and onto YouTube. People were really talking about our project, and how they could relate to all the stories that the guys gave. They were able to say that they went through the same exact things.

I was then thinking about possibly doing this project again. I was never assuming that it would blow up the way it did, and people would appreciate it this much. But due to how well the response was, I wanted to try this project once more. Maybe in a year's time from now, we'll see how things go. However for now, I was taking in all the fame and success, that the project gave us.

Knowing that thousands and thousands of people have seen our story. It was an amazing feeling, and it made everything worthwhile. My career as a psychologist allowed me to take advantage of experiments such as this, and I was enjoying it so much.

The guys were happy as well, and they were shocked at the response, but they handled it quite well. We are all approached by several media outlets to talk about our stories more in depth. There were so many interviews I had. Whether I was interviewed with just myself, or if I was interviewed with some, or all of the guys. There was also another film festival that was coming up, and it was a slightly larger one. Although this film festival didn't have any awards. It was only to showcase films that were highly acclaimed, and films that were getting much traction.

The guys and I all attended this special film festival too, and several celebrities were in attendance as well. We kinda felt like we were big time at this point, and special people and celebrities, wanted to come and see our film. You know what, none of us were getting paid for this. I mean we would receive compensations for some interviews, but we weren't getting paid lots of money, as if it this whole project were a blockbuster film. The whole point of this, was to bring awareness with the stories that all the guys have, and to get people to really think. How all of our stories could possibly help people with their own lives.

Which brings me to present day. It has been a month and a half since all the hoopla surrounding the film, since it has been released. Things have sort of fizzled out. I guess I can now take this time to update you on everything.

I'll start with Troy. Since the film was released, Troy continues to work at the department store. Very rarely, he'll get someone who recognizes him from the project, and he'll be friendly and cordial with them. Troy's own story really helped other young gay guys who feel lost in school. Those who feel bullied, feel like they are alone, and that nobody understands where they are coming from. Troy took humility with this story being shown, and also his relationship with Harry also being put out there. The story of how his bully, became his really close friend later in life, was also a motivation to others.

Troy continues to live with Harry and his brothers, and he spends time with them as well. Troy also keeps a relationship with his mother in addition to that. Troy managed to form a relationship with the rest of the guys in the project, including myself. I hang out with Troy quite a bit, and we do several fun things together. But Troy also started to explore his drag queen career as well, with the help of Jerald who designs all of his outfits.

With the help of Jerald, Troy has really nice drag numbers, and performs well. Harry is also proud that Troy is being himself, and is exploring something he cares about. Although Harry can't relate to Troy being a drag queen that well, he still supports everything Troy does, no matter what. At this time, Troy and Harry don't have a wedding date picked out, but they do want to get married sometime soon. They are unsure if they want to have a private wedding, or something more elaborate. I guess we will have to find out what they chose later.

As far as Harry. He remains working at the grocery store as a butcher. He also works as a chef, at his brother Louie's restaurant as well. Harry remarkably doesn't like to talk about the project in depth really. I mean, he had to get used to the reaction and reception that the project gave at first, but now he's comfortable with it. It was something that he simply did, and he's happy that he did it, but he's continuing on with his life. If his story affected others, then he was happy with that. Harry also gets on quite well with Louie now.

Although they do fight from time to time, Harry still loves his brother. The past strained relationship that he had with Louie, doesn't exist anymore. They get along fine, and are now the best of friends. Louie's restaurant is also doing well, and it's quite successful. Especially on the weekends, when it gets very crowded full of guests. The promotion the restaurant got in the film, helped very much. Harry loves his brothers Leif and Harvey as well. Harry still hunts and fishes with his brothers, and does many outdoor things. He does get into small arguments with Troy, as Troy really isn't an outdoor person, but they still figure a way to make things work out, so that they are happy.

Harry has been trying to keep a low profile since the fame of the project went out. He doesn't participate in many interviews, but from the interviews that he has given from being in the project, he is very thankful and happy. Harry keeps in contact with Carl and Steven quite a bit, and they also participate in activities. Harry tries to get Steven outside more, and Harry actually arranged a camping trip that the remaining nine of us have actually been on. It was a fun experience for us all.

Aaron still works at the hospital as a nurse. He works a lot of hours, and the patients at the hospital and his rounds come first, before doing interview or press related things, following the project. Aaron has received much recognition and praise from being in the project, and he takes it rather well. There have been some slight backlash, from the relationship that he formed with Steven. It's only a rare number of people that seem to have an issue with it, but it has been complained about quite often. People think that Steven took advantage of him, when that isn't true. The feelings that Aaron and Steven had, are up to them. I have no bearing as to what to say related to that. But as a psychologist myself, and being that I'm able to read people quite well, I don't think that's the case in this particular situation. I think I would be able to know if Steven was taking advantage of Aaron, and he wasn't. But Aaron ignores all the negative press anyways, and only focuses on the positive things.

He takes care of Steven when he's not working at the hospital, and they enjoy their lives together, being married. They go outside from time to time, but because Steven teaches a lot, and Aaron is working in the hospital for many hours, they don't get to go out as often as they like, or participate in events with the rest of us. But the free time they do have, is special. There have been a couple times to where Aaron and Steven have met up with the rest of us. Such as the camping trip Harry had, and other events. Aaron maintains friendships with Troy, Jamal and Jerald. They hang out quite frequently when Aaron isn't busy working. Aaron was glad to do the project, and lives on with his life.

Once Steven found out that I was going to publicly show the raw interview that I gave of him, his reaction was less than ecstatic. Which I can understand, as Steven's story in particular was really touchy. Being that he can no longer walk, I don't blame him for keeping his story hidden for the rest of his life. But I knew that Steven's story had a purpose, and he needed to let others see.

I know Steven himself understood this, but part of him was ashamed of getting his story out. I think part of Steven is still ashamed. He very rarely gives details in interviews after the event, and not that he's upset about it, he's most likely just shy, and that's his way of dealing with it. Steven's students, and other people at the campus he works at, were also proud of him, and happy of all the accomplishments that he was able to do in his life, despite him being paralyzed. Steven took up the promise of hanging out with the rest of the guys. He has a close friendship with Ralph, and the both of them connect, being disabled. Steven also interacts with Harry, with Harry trying to get Steven to be more active, and Steven agreed to go on the camping trip that we all went on. Steven's relationship with Aaron is also quite strong, and they continue to be there for each other. They both work extensive hours, but the time they have together, they cherish greatly, and they actually are deeply in love with one another. Steven also drives on his own sometimes, and has had his car modified especially for him to drive.

Despite Steven being shy about the post reception of the project, I know he's proud that he did it. He didn't want to sign the consent form to participate in the project, out of embarrassment or fear of his story getting out, but at the end of the day, he stopped caring, and wanted for other people to understand his story.

Jerald continues to do his fashion design work. He still wants to be the best fashion designer in the world, and every piece that he creates, he gets better and better at his skill. Although he still hasn't hit the international fashion market, he still has his hopes up someday that he will. God willing with this talent, he can definitely make it happen, and I have absolute faith in him. Jerald also formed a close bond with Jamal, being that they are both gay black men. They learned from each other's hardships, and their friendship is strong. Jerald is one of the guys that has been the most active, after the project went out. He's doing way more interviews than the other guys are, and is doing a lot of promotion for the project. I've been dealing with Jerald myself with this, and I'm happy that he still wants to do all he can do, so that the project lives on. Even though it's over with, we still have a lot to do, in an effort to get people to recognize the project.

Jerald still lives with Carl in the art studio, and I can say that they both secretly got married a few days ago. They didn't have a big celebration or anything. They eloped. I'm happy that Jerald and Carl married, and I'm sure that they will have a wonderful life together.

Jerald supports Carl's art, and they seem to both be on the same level, when it comes to their lives.

Carl is still doing his art, and he's very talented at it. Since the project hit the press, more and more people are commissioning Carl to do artwork for them. He's getting so many job offers, and I am very proud of him. To think that Carl almost gave up on his art, and didn't want to do it anymore, after the death of his brother. He kept going on with his passion. The mural that Carl painted in respect to Mark, also received lots of headlines, and many people were interested in it. Due to the reception of the project, Carl decided to add some revisions to the piece, and added more details to it.

Carl was really loving the reception that he was getting from the people who watched the project. He was able to gain many new associates and acquaintances, that want to collaborate with him on future projects. Carl became close with all the other guys, including Harry, Frank, Ralph and Steven in particular. Carl even got Steven interested in doing sculpting, and I was shocked to find out that they sculpt together. Carl and Jerald secretly eloped together recently, and so Carl is really secure in his life.

Jamal started to write several blogs and articles related to the project. He does interviews quite often as well, and isn't afraid to talk about the project. Like with Jerald, Jamal does promotion for the project heavily, and hangs out with myself and Jerald quite often. Jamal has made friends with virtually all of the other guys. Being close with Troy and Aaron in particular, and being extremely close with Jerald, being that they are both gay black men.

Jamal continues to help out Ralph with his needs, and his business. Jamal's future plans from this point forward, is to create several nonprofit organizations for homeless LGBTQ youth, and other children that are stuck in foster care, without a home. Jamal doesn't want to see kids stuck without having a family, or people that love them. He also doesn't want to see people that are LGBTQ, homeless and out on the street. So he's been doing a lot of activism work, as a result of that. Taking the reception that he got from the project, to work with people to make these plans happen. Jamal wants to get married to

Ralph soon, but in their own time. They will pick a date to get married, and it will happen when it happens. Jamal doesn't wish to rush it at this particular point in time. He knows that Ralph is always going to be there, and he's an important part of Ralphs life. Jamal continues with his life in a positive way.

Ralph, similar to Steven and Harry, has kept a low profile once news of the project went out. It's not that he doesn't take the fame or reception well, he would just rather focus on his life, and not let the success of the project get to him. Ralph is aware that he has inspired many other people who deal with disabilities. Especially other gay and bisexual men who have to deal with being blind. His story taught people to never give up. Even if something devastating and catastrophic happens in your life, to just keep going. Ralph still is friends with Hugo and Vincent. He continues to live with them, and with Jerald. As far as the friendships he formed with the other guys in the project; he is really close to Steven. They both have attended activism groups for individuals with disabilities. Being that Steven is paralyzed and Ralph is blind, they find a way to reach awareness to both issues.

Ralph and Steven have become really close best friends, as a result of this project. Ralph also spends time with Frank, Carl and Harry. Ralph, Frank, Carl, Harry and Steven, all usually go out for beers every once in a while. Ralph also invites all the guys over to his house occasionally for parties too. The relationship that Ralph has with Jerald is still going on strong, and they both plan to be married at a later date. Ralph loves how caring and trustworthy Jamal is, and they take their love for each other quite seriously. Ralph may deal with the success of the project differently from the rest of the guys, but he is living his life proud.

Frank motivated so many other transgender men, and transgender people out there. He is completely done with his transition, and is satisfied with how he is. He managed to get top surgery recently, which was one major goal of his. His transition is done, and at this point, he doesn't wish to do anything else to his body. Frank has done a lot of activism work related to the project. He has worked with many transgender organizations, and has gone on many interviews. He was also interviewed by other LGBTQ police officers as well. Being that a police officer is such a masculine profession, the fact there are LGBTQ officers out there, needs to be known. Frank wanted to work with Carl, to design a tattoo for him, which Carl did design. The tattoo was in honor of Frank's deceased friend Ivan. Carl isn't a skilled tattoo artist, so he actually drew the design that the tattoo artist was going to copy. Frank continues to live with Laura, and the both of them have recently gotten married. It was a ceremony that the rest of the guys attended, and were happy to be involved in. Along with Carl, Frank also hangs out with the rest of the guys. Hanging out Harry, Ralph and Steven the most.

Frank loves bringing transgender awareness to the public, since the project went out. He was once a transgender man that kept his trans identity to himself, now he's not ashamed. He accepts if other transgender people wish to keep their identity secret, and in some cases Frank recommends it due to safety. Frank is very happy that he was able to come out as a transgender police officer. Frank is a motivation to many, and I'm so happy with the way he's living his life.

As for me, well I don't know where to begin really. I'm doing fine, and I'm still learning more about people. That's my job as a psychologist. I am taking things one day at a time. So, I guess that's about it. I'm going to begin to end things at this point. I explained what the project was, the guys, including myself, all gave their stories. The guys all reflected of their stories, and they each became the best of friends.

I also made nine close friends in the process, and I feel there is nothing left to explain at this point. I want to briefly go back to the thoughts I had of doing this project again, with nine brand new guys, and I most definitely will. I'm going to wait a year or so, before I decide to do it. I would like to do it next week, but right now is much too soon.

The guys are still being praised for this current project, so I want to wait until things are more level headed. I don't think people are ever going to forget this project, and they will remember it always. This was definitely a risk that I took for doing this, and I don't regret it for one second. I loved it so much, that I'm going to do it again real soon. Ha-Ha. But for right now, I want to take a much needed vacation.

I want to drive to Vegas. I think that's a pretty good idea. But I'm going to go just by myself. I do like the other guys company, and I will always stay in touch with them. I just want to do this on my own and by myself. I'm hoping that with this vacation, I'll finally meet my Prince Charming. Who knows? Ha-Ha. I mean, I'm not forcing love, but it would be nice if it happened. I prepare for my Vegas trip, wrapping up this project. This was a wild ride, and I want to thank you for riding it with me.

Well, I'm off to go on my trip now, and I'll catch you guys later. My name is Dr. Gary Swanson, and I'm a psychologist. I want to make a difference in the world. I want to make people feel happy. I want to help and empower people. I want to leave you by saying that we all, have a "Profile of Hope."

THE END

ABOUT THE AUTHOR

Brennen Tammons, was born in Los Angeles, California. He is an African American, gay writer. Having a unique imagination, allows him to explore diverse topics with his writing. He enjoys dancing, aerobic exercise, all types of music, (having a soft spot for jazz, soul, urban and electronic music), playing Nintendo games, and researching new topics and ideas.